PENGUIN CANADA

UTHER

JACK WHYTE is a Scots-born Canadian who has been around long enough by now to have done most of the things he ever wanted to do, and all of those seem to have been connected, in one way or another, to story-telling. His novels have been translated into a number of languages and are now sold worldwide, a fact that Mr. Whyte finds gratifying and astonishing at the same time. Having brought his Arthurian cycle to a close with *The Eagle*, he is now well launched upon a trilogy of novels on the rise and fall of the Knights Templar, the first of which, *Knights of the Black and White*, was launched in August 2006, with the second, *Standard of Honour*, set for publication in 2007. Jack Whyte lives with his wife, Beverley, in Kelowna, British Columbia.

Also by Jack Whyte

A DREAM OF EAGLES

The Skystone

The Singing Sword

The Eagles' Brood

The Saxon Shore

The Sorcerer Volume I:
The Fort at River's Bend

The Sorcerer Volume II:
Metamorphosis

∞

Uther

∞

THE GOLDEN EAGLE

Clothar the Frank

The Eagle

Uther

JACK WHYTE

PENGUIN
CANADA

PENGUIN CANADA

Published by the Penguin Group

Penguin Group (Canada), 90 Eglinton Avenue East, Suite 700, Toronto, Ontario, Canada M4P 2Y3
(a division of Pearson Canada Inc.)

Penguin Group (USA) Inc., 375 Hudson Street, New York, New York 10014, U.S.A.
Penguin Books Ltd, 80 Strand, London WC2R 0RL, England
Penguin Ireland, 25 St Stephen's Green, Dublin 2, Ireland (a division of Penguin Books Ltd)
Penguin Group (Australia), 250 Camberwell Road, Camberwell, Victoria 3124, Australia
(a division of Pearson Australia Group Pty Ltd)
Penguin Books India Pvt Ltd, 11 Community Centre, Panchsheel Park, New Delhi – 110 017, India
Penguin Group (NZ), cnr Airborne and Rosedale Roads, Albany, Auckland 1310, New Zealand
(a division of Pearson New Zealand Ltd)
Penguin Books (South Africa) (Pty) Ltd, 24 Sturdee Avenue, Rosebank, Johannesburg 2196, South Africa

Penguin Books Ltd, Registered Offices: 80 Strand, London WC2R 0RL, England

First published in Viking Canada hardcover by Penguin Group (Canada),
a division of Pearson Canada Inc., 2000
Published in Penguin Canada paperback by Penguin Group (Canada),
a division of Pearson Canada Inc., 2001
Published in this edition, 2006

5 6 7 8 9 10 (OPM)

Copyright © Jack Whyte, 2000

*Publisher's note: This book is a work of fiction. Names, characters, places and incidents
either are the product of the author's imagination or are used fictitiously, and any
resemblance to actual persons living or dead, events, or locales is entirely coincidental.*

Manufactured in the U.S.A.

NATIONAL LIBRARY OF CANADA CATALOGUING IN PUBLICATION

Whyte, Jack, 1940–
Uther

ISBN 0-14-026087-0

I. Title.

PS8595.H947U83 2001   C813'.54   C2001-930647-4
PR9199.3.W59U83 2001

Visit the Penguin Group (Canada) website at **www.penguin.ca**

Special and corporate bulk purchase rates available; please see
www.penguin.ca/corporatesales or call 1-800-810-3104, ext. 477 or 474

For my wife, Beverley,
and the Clan:
Jode, Mitch and Holly,
Jeanne and Michael,
and Phyllis

ACKNOWLEDGMENTS

I had a difficult time in the early stages of writing this book, purely because of my perspective on the story. I knew what I wanted to achieve, and Uther's story was all there in my head, intact from the outset, but I gradually allowed myself to become ensnared in the need to avoid rehashing events that had taken place in my novel *Eagles' Brood*, which I convinced myself had already covered the same ground. And then I read and was riveted by Orson Scott Card's novel *Ender's Shadow*, a "parallel novel" to his earlier masterpiece *Ender's Game*. I devoured it, and with enjoyment came enlightenment as I realized that, in agonizing over repetitiveness in *Uther*, I had painted myself into a false corner within my own mind, and that the story of Uther Pendragon's life really bears only the faintest resemblance to the story of *Eagles' Brood*, sharing common elements and time frames, but unfolding independently of the tale of Caius Merlyn Britannicus and his upbringing in Camulod. From that moment, I started all over again, from the beginning, and the storyline flowed as smoothly as fishing line off a reel when a big fish takes the hook. And so I hereby acknowledge my indebtedness to Orson Scott Card for his contribution, albeit unbeknownst to him, to the development of this book.

I also want to offer my thanks publicly to Mark Burgess in San Diego, who runs my "official" website at camulod.com. Mark is the webmaster who originally set up the Reader's Forum within the site, and in the few years that have elapsed since then, thanks to Mark's foresight, I have come to know hundreds of my readers from all over the world, corresponding with them through the Forum. Their feedback has been invaluable, and their responses to the sample chapters

I have posted on the site have helped me greatly in shaping various elements within this book.

No one, however, has been more influential in shaping the book, all the way from rough draft to completion, than my editor, Catherine Marjoribanks, whose keen eye for inconsistencies and irrelevance continues to astound me after an association of almost ten years. The author-editor bond is a strange and unique phenomenon that surpasseth understanding, in this case involving close communication and much mutual, nitty-gritty give and take between two people who seldom meet and who live half a continent apart. It is a relationship that I would hate to lose or have to change.

Jack Whyte

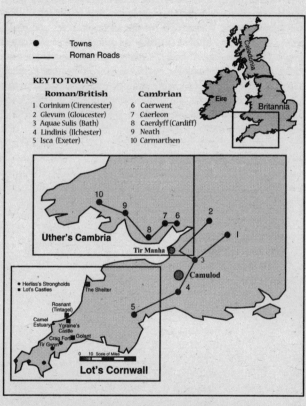

Southwest Britain

PROLOGUE

This was no spontaneous gathering to welcome her as a young bride to her new home; Veronica Varrus recognized that truth very quickly. What was happening here had nothing to do with her at all. Her arrival, mere moments earlier, accompanied by her new husband and his father, King Ullic Pendragon, was no more than a coincidence.

Veronica had no idea what was going on, or even what she was seeing ahead of her in the darkness. There were simply too many people crowded between her and the centre of all that distant activity. But whatever was happening over there on the other side of the crowd looked exciting and mysterious. She stretched up on tiptoe and craned her neck, bobbing and twisting as she tried to find a clear view between the black, jostling outlines of the people ahead of her. Close behind her and around her, most of the other members of the group who had been her travelling companions seemed to be as awed and curious as she was, muttering among themselves in tones that betrayed their uncertainty. King Ullic Pendragon, who had been moving ahead of her at the head of the group only moments earlier, seemed to have vanished suddenly, swallowed up by the swarm of people.

The source of all the excitement was fire, that much she could identify. In the distance, fifty paces or more ahead of where she stood, dense, rolling clouds of yellowish smoke belched upward from several large bonfires, the undersides of the billowing columns reflecting the light from the flames beneath them, and against that roiling, volatile background, grotesque shapes and shadows danced and cavorted, all of them obscured and ill-defined against the blackness of the surrounding night.

She could smell something strange in the air, too, some kind of thick, smoky odour that had nothing to do with the burning wood of the bonfires—a dense, heavy smell, vaguely familiar and yet alien somehow. She sniffed again, deeply, trying to identify it and failing, but knowing that recognition would come to her sooner or later; she could only assume that the strange, cloying aroma had something to do with the festivities. This was a celebration of some kind, she was convinced of that, if only because she could conceive of no other reason for such a huge concentration of people to have come together.

Perhaps everyone here at Tir Manha, the place that was to be her home from this time on, had been forewarned of their approach and had stayed awake this far into the night simply to welcome her and her new husband, Uric Pendragon. That had been her first wishful thought, but Uric's reaction had quickly banished it. One glance at his face had shown Veronica that he was as surprised as she to find this hive of activity where they had expected to find only a sleeping settlement. But his surprise contained no sign of gladness, pleasure or delight. The scowling frown that had swept over his normally open, smiling face had filled her immediately with concern and deep misgivings.

Now she looked up at her husband as he stood beside her, unusually silent and still, staring back over his right shoulder at something she could not see.

"Uric . . . ?"

He gave no sign that he had heard her, and that brought a quick frown to her face, because for the ten days since their wedding in her parents' home in Camulod, Uric Pendragon had seen and heard nothing but her, had lived only for her, anticipating her every word and wish. Now, finding herself ignored and seeing the urgency in his posture, the strained set of his neck and shoulders, she moved quickly, stepping around him to see what he was looking at.

Something important was going on between his father the King and the party of elderly men with whom he now stood in conclave. Ullic was a huge man, even though on this occasion he was not wearing the great eagle helmet that made him appear even larger than he was. Looking directly at him, Veronica could see that for the first time in weeks Ullic's face bore no semblance of a smile. His expression was grave, cast into deeply etched shadows by the flickering light of the torches held by the men surrounding him, the elders of the King's Council.

Ullic was listening attentively to what one of the oldest men was saying, and whatever he was being told, it was not pleasing to him. Finally, after he had listened intently for a long time, interrupting the speaker only twice, and briefly, Veronica saw the King turn away from the old man quickly, as though in disgust, and then glance in her direction, as if checking to see if she and Uric were watching. She saw him bring his hands up to his face and cover his eyes, cupping his hands with a squeezing motion, almost as though he were washing his face, and then pressing his fingertips hard into his temples before dragging them down his cheeks all the way to his beard. When he took his hands away, dropping them to his sides, he tilted his head back and sucked in a great breath, stretching himself hugely, spreading his fingers and rising almost to tiptoe before sinking his chin upon his breast and crossing his arms over his chest. He stood like that for long moments, frowning intensely, while Veronica counted a full score of her own heartbeats.

When at last Ullic straightened up, determination was in every line of his bearing. He nodded his head abruptly, and the elder who had been haranguing him and had been watching him closely ever since, clearly waiting for a decision, spun around and raised his arm vertically, then brought it sweeping down in what was obviously a prearranged signal. Immediately after that a whirling ball of fire went flying up into the air, describing a high arc before falling back to the ground.

Even as the fireball arced upwards, Veronica recognized it as a whirling torch, hurled into the air by someone who had been nursing it carefully for just such a purpose. Others followed it, and almost immediately the night sky was filled with flickering, whirling lights in colours that ranged from orange through yellow to bright blue. They seemed to be falling into some kind of pit on the other side of the screen of people who blocked her view, but before she could even begin to move forward to see what was happening there, she felt her husband, Uric, grasp her by the upper arm and begin to pull her back and away from the flaring, spinning torches. Surprised and slightly displeased, she twisted in protest, shrugging her arm free of his grasp and continuing to move forward, but he caught her again immediately, before she could even begin to evade him, his grasp this time quicker and stronger, clamping her right wrist. She heard his voice close above her head as he pulled her arm up behind her back, gently but firmly, and swung her around, his free hand flat against her belly.

"No, love, this is not for you. Come now, away with the two of us, you and me, and to bed."

"*What?* Uric, let go of me, that hurts! Why should . . . ? I don't *want* to go to bed!"

She dug in her heels and fought against his pull, trying to twist out of his grip again, but instead of releasing her, Uric swiftly transferred his grip, seized her by both elbows and lifted her. Then he spun her in the air as though she were weightless and threw his arms about her from behind so quickly that she was imprisoned before she could even guess his intent.

"No, woman, no!" His voice was huge, raw and angry in her ears, and the roughness of his grasp around her ribs was painful enough to make her catch her breath in the beginnings of panic. His left hand closed over his other wrist beneath her breasts, hugging her even closer against his chest. Ignoring her cries and furious kicking, he strode away with her, carrying her towards the blackest part of the night, away from the swelling noises of the crowd and the flickering glow of the fires.

Veronica suddenly found herself filled with a violent, consuming fury, fuelled by the sheer impossibility of what was happening to her. This man who was restraining her, confining her and virtually abducting her was her new husband, the guardian to whom she had been wed a mere ten days earlier and who had sworn, in the presence of her family and all their friends, to nurture, defend and protect her. Now he was acting like a man demented, treating her like some kind of domesticated beast, mauling her painfully and hauling her away into the darkness for some twisted purpose of his own.

Without warning, they came face to face with Ullic Pendragon in the darkness, his face faintly illumined by the light from the distant fires. Veronica saw his eyes widen in surprise at the sight of them, registered the quick glance down at her kicking, scissoring legs and then saw the way his eyes returned to his son's face.

"Uncullic! Help me!" It had always been her special name for the King, coined before her infant tongue could master the intricacies of "Uncle Ullic," but this time it failed to have any effect. The King nodded to his son, then stepped aside to let them pass. Only when she shrieked his name again, angry and confused and humiliated, did he look her in the eye. Then he reached out briefly and touched her cheek with the knuckle of one finger before acknowledging her.

"Daughter," he said, "I regret this, but I had no way of knowing, nor did he. Better you should not be here. Go now with your man."

"Go? Go where?" Veronica was wailing as her husband carried her on into the darkness of the night, his enormous strength making light of her frenzied struggles. But suddenly, unable to see quite where he was going, Uric placed one foot firmly on a spot where there was nothing to sustain it. His ankle twisted in the hole his foot had found, and he fell heavily sideways, grunting with the pain and releasing Veronica as he instinctively threw out his arms to try to check his fall.

In an instant, she was up and running, completely unhurt and filled with the strength of angry youth, holding her skirts high above her knees where they would not interfere with her speed as she fled back towards the flickering lights and the roiling smoke. Behind her, she heard Uric roar her name, but she ignored him, concentrating only on where she was placing her flying feet.

A tiny part of her mind knew that she had no reason to be running back towards the fires and no reason, really, to be running anywhere, but its small, sane whisper went unheeded. Veronica Varrus was too far out of her depth by then, and too suddenly terror had leaped up to overwhelm her reason. Surrounded by darkness, whirling smoke, strange faces, stranger noises and smells and

a crushing press of unfamiliar people, she found no logic in the
world that yawed around her.

Now, as she approached the frenzied celebrants, their enormous fire-flung shadows dancing before her, she looked back over
her shoulder and saw that she was not being pursued. No one was
following her, and in relief she slowed her pace until she came to
a complete stop, her heart hammering in her chest and her ribs
heaving painfully as she fought to bring her breathing under control. Her mind was filled with the way her beloved Uncullic had
ignored her, and a great ball of grief ached in her chest.

And then, finally, she became aware of the screaming. It had
been there all along, mixed in among the mad cacophony of the
crowd. But it was far louder now, and increasing in both volume
and intensity even as she listened: an insane, soul-searing screaming, a kind of screaming she had never heard before. Frantic and
appallingly indescribable, it sounded like nothing that could ever
issue from a human throat. With an overwhelming, dehumanizing
fear, a quaking awareness that the skies might split apart at any
moment and rain down death and destruction, Veronica Varrus realized that what she was hearing came not from one human throat
but from scores, perhaps hundreds of voices.

Moving now in a kind of terror-stricken dream, her footsteps
following one upon the other without volition, she walked forward
towards the light and the indescribable noise, aware of the people
around her now, looking at her and moving out of her way, until
she stood in the forefront of the crowd, gazing on the sight from
which her husband had sought to protect her. Though she had no
memory of raising them, her hands were pressed tightly over her
ears in a futile attempt to shut out the infernal noises. Yet she made
no move to cover her eyes; if this was the truth her husband had
tried to keep from her, she would *know* it.

The crowd had fallen back, away from the heat, and she could
feel the flames searing her face even from twenty paces distant.
Someone had dug an enormous pit in the centre of a vast, open
space. It measured roughly ten paces to each side and extended
four paces into the earth. As she saw it, a door to memory opened

somewhere in her mind, and so she was unsurprised to see the enormous gallows frame that had been erected over it. She had once heard someone, either Ullic or Uric, talking about such a thing, although she had paid scant attention at the time. She remembered a description of wood soaked in pitch, of everlasting fires, of Druid sacrifice.

The great gallows frame reared up six or seven long paces in height above the top of the pit, and from it, suspended by chains, hung three wooden cages. Each of these was tightly packed with men, some of them evidently dead or unconscious, but most of them still alive—and screaming. The flames from the pit beneath, fed by the tarry pitch, had reached the cages easily by this time, and the wooden frames were all alight, the middle one burning far more fiercely than the two flanking it. As she watched, stupefied, there came a loud, sharp crack, clearly audible above everything else, and the middle cage broke apart, splitting into pieces and hurling its living contents down into the inferno underneath. The unfortunates in the remaining cages, seeing the fate that awaited them and recognizing its imminence, began throwing themselves against the burning bars of their cages in despair. In another cage one side fell away, and a knot of men threw themselves immediately outward and down into the pit, disappearing from view in the incandescent heart of the fire. The thrust of their leaping and the shifting of their weight threw the entire cage out of balance and it tilted violently, dislodging even more screaming prisoners, some of whom leaped frantically outward, vainly trying to leap over the fire and land in safety on the side of the pit.

Veronica watched them fall and disappear, melted into liquescent nothingness by the white heat at the centre of the furnace, and when she raised her eyes again towards the last surviving cage, all movement there had ceased. Everyone in that cage was dead, and it only remained now for the bars or the floor to burn through and release the bodies to tumble into the fire.

Unaware that the screaming had ceased, Veronica continued to press her hands over her ears, but now she looked at the people surrounding her, seeing them leering and gibbering and gesticulating like demons in the aftermath of the horrendous slaughter. The faces that she saw with her flat, emotionless gaze were without exception vacant and ugly, empty of any humanity, devoid of any trace of sanity. These were King Ullic's Celts, she thought numbly, the people amongst whom she would now live, the people she had travelled so far to meet in this bleak place called Tir Manha. These were her husband's kinfolk and her future neighbours. Her destiny now lay in sharing their lives and their activities, living in their midst, learning their language and their customs and rearing her future children to conform to their ways and to observe their traditions: burning their enemies alive in wooden cages suspended over an enormous firepit in the dead blackness of a moonless night.

She felt hands grasping her shoulders and turning her around, and then the searing heat was gone from her face, leaving her skin feeling stretched and taut as it was pressed gently into the front of a large man's tunic. She felt a hand cradling the back of her head gently, an arm stretching across her back from shoulder to waist and the breath from a man's lips soft against the top of her head. From the smell of the man's clothing, she knew it was her husband, Uric. She could hear nothing, and after a while Uric stopped trying to pry her hands from over her ears and simply held her close, rocking her gently for the longest time.

Uther

BOOK ONE

Childhood

Greetings, my dear daughter:

I have been thinking about writing to you for weeks now, making up snippets of things to tell you and composing entire passages in my mind as I go about my household tasks, but I sit down to it only now, almost afraid that I might be too late, and unpleasantly surprised, all at once, by how quickly time has passed since I last wrote! Last night, as we sat together before going to bed, staring into the fire, your father remarked that the leaves have begun to turn yellow, and pointed out that, before we know it, it will be winter, and both you and Picus's wife, Enid, will be facing confinement and childbirth. That shocked me profoundly, and my immediate reaction was to chide him for exaggerating. It seems like only yesterday that I was writing to you, describing my excitement over the newly delivered tidings that you were with child and would be giving us a grandson or a granddaughter at the start of the New Year. And now, so soon, your term is more than half elapsed! And that, of course, means that you have been a wife, a married woman and the mistress of your own household for almost two-thirds of a year, and for that entire time I have not set eyes upon you. How must you have changed in appearance, from the merry-faced, laughing little daughter whom your father and I loved so much and in whom we took such pride, knowing how close we had come to losing you completely when you were tiny.

I was interrupted between writing those last words and these, and a full day has elapsed in the interim. Writing is a slow and sometimes painful process, for the hand is unused to clutching a stylus for so long a time. And yet Publius writes every day, for long periods each time, so I must believe that the pain wears off with practice. I do hope you are thriving and that your pregnancy is causing you no great discomfort. As you know, I had not a speck of trouble with you or any of your sisters at any time, except for the anguish (merely occasional, thanks to your father) of having failed to produce a son to carry on the name of Varrus. It is too late for that now, and so the name will die, I fear, with my dear Publius, for I know of no other males of the family Varrus now alive. Let us pray, however, that we need not think of that for many, many years. In the meantime, your father's pride and manliness, his heritage and all his nobility will live on in your children, and although their name will not be Varrus, their mother's blood will make them both Varrus and Britannicus, and they will reflect, in their natures, all the elements that made their mother's father the fine man that he is. But I was speaking of your pregnancy and wondering how you are bearing it. Most women, God be thanked, take the condition in their stride, suffering no ill from it at all. Others thrive visibly, blooming while they carry the child and achieving a beauty they seldom recapture in fallow times. And then again, there are the others, poor creatures who cannot sustain the role that has been thrust upon them and who suffer untold agonies and endless sickness through their entire term of carrying. These are the ones who, all too often, have Harpies awaiting their delivery and who too frequently die in childbirth. I know that this is not the case with you, my dear Veronica, or I should have heard of it long since, and I would be there with you now, instead of

*sitting here writing you this long and rambling letter. Your
father is calling me.*

*Well! Another day gone by. I begin to believe that,
once interrupted, it becomes impossible to resume writing
the same day. Yesterday, when I went to your father's call,
I found that one of the young stableboys had been kicked
by a horse. He must have been careless in some way, but
we will never know, because he died without regaining his
senses. He was only eight years old, and your father was
very angry that the child had been left alone to do a man's
work. We had a noisy and exciting evening of heated arguments and cold anger as he tried to discover the truth of
what happened from a number of people who really did not
know. Generally, however, your father is well, in radiant
health and strong as a man half his age. He continues to
spend the greatest portion of his time in his old forge,
banging away at white-hot metal, all the while in danger of
suffocating from smoke and noxious fumes. But he is hap-
piest when he is there, so what can I, a mere woman, do to
dissuade him? It makes me smile to recall it, but there was
a time when I thought he must regret that I had so little
interest in his forge and what he did in there. I was wrong.
I have learned to believe that your father is perfectly happy
to have me stay in my place, here in our home, and allow
him to do as he must in his place of work. And when he
comes home to me, as he always does, I never doubt his
gladness at setting eyes on me. Now that is a gift I wish I
could bestow on you, daughter. But the only person who
can grant that gift to you is your own man, Uric, and the
only means you have of influencing him to do that is to
manage his home, share in his dreams, encourage his
visions and love him.*

*It is a beautiful day here, and the sky is flushing pink
with the promise of a wondrous sunset. It is strange to think
you might not be able to see it where you are, among the
hills. It might be raining there, or be dark and foggy.*

Well, child, now that you are a child no longer, know that we love you none the less, your father and I. Carry your own child proudly and with gladness, whether it be boy or girl, and never fear about your ability to bear men-children for your husband. I produced only girls, but the women of our family have always been breeders of strong men, so perhaps I was an aberration. You, I am convinced, will bring forth boys. I will not insult you by asking you if you would come home to have your child. I know your place is there in your husband's land, as Enid's is here, in her husband's, even though Picus is away at war. I remind God every day and night, in my prayers, to keep all of you strong and healthy and safe above all. God bless you, child. You are in my mind and my heart at all times.

Your loving mother, LV

Greetings, my dear Mother:

I overheard Uncullic this morning telling Uric that he intends to ride by Camulod on his way to wherever he is going in the week ahead. Thus, mindful of the enormous pile of papyrus you sent me recently, hinting that should I ever think to write to you I should not lack the means of doing so, I thought to take this opportunity to write and let you know that I am well and having no trouble at all with the burden I am carrying. The grandchild I will bring to you is all male. His strength and his lack of delicacy and con-sideration tell me that he could be nothing else. But he has been well behaved, generally speaking, and I am quite sure he will cause me no insurmountable difficulty when it comes time to bring him out to face the world in which he must live. My dearest hope is that you and my father are both as healthy as I feel, because if you are, I should rejoice.

We are caught up in the end-of-the-year celebrations, although Samhain, the winter solstice, has already passed

*long since, and the days are beginning to lengthen. Now
that I am living among the Cambrians and have made their
way of life my own, I am often astonished to see just how
different their customs and celebrations are from ours. I
can clearly remember sitting listening to Bishop Alaric on
one bright, lovely summer's afternoon several years ago as
he told us about the various ways in which the communities in the small territories wherein we live have come to
use different ceremonies and rituals to celebrate the same
important events throughout the year. Events like the sol-
stices, when the sun reaches the limits of its flight and sets
off again upon its return course. But even our beloved
Bishop could not convey the scope of such differences.*

*I know that our own tradition in Camulod is rooted in
our Roman past. But the Celtic clans celebrate Samhain
when we celebrate Saturnalia. I had heard the name
before, and I recall that as a child I passed the Samhain
festival with you and my father in two small communities
that I remember lying to the south and west of Camulod.
Neither of those two occasions, however, bears any slight
resemblance to what goes on here in Cambria at this time
of the year. And then recently, within those regions and
among those clans where Christianity has spread, the rituals and the events we celebrate are changing every year.
But all that matters is that we celebrate. It matters not what
name we give to the celebration or how we observe it. The
people are glad of the opportunity to celebrate something,
anything, and they are ready for the pleasure. The crops
are safely in, the fields are all prepared for winter, and the
lagging year is drawing to a close amid the hope brought
on by lengthening evenings and small unseen promises of
greener, warmer days to come in a year that is entirely new.*

*Not all of us in King Ullic's household are celebrat-
ing this year, however. There is one unfortunate woman
here whose heart is sore and heavy, and where I, in similar
circumstances, would be blessed and strengthened in time*

of need by my beloved husband, she lacks that source of strength and comfort. She has a husband, but he is a very different kind of man from mine. Her name is Tamara, and her husband, whose name is Leir, is a Druid. He is also related to Uncullic, a cousin of some kind. I have been told that his grandfather and Ullic's father were first cousins, born to the brother and sister of the first Pendragon King of the Federation, another Ullic, as you know, Ullic Green Eye, who ruled almost a hundred years ago. I wonder if that means he had only one eye? Or one green eye and one of another colour? But that cannot be, since all these Cambrian kings must be physically perfect. I must find someone to ask about that.

I stopped when I had written those last words and walked away from my table, because I found myself writing nonsense. And my fingers were starting to cramp. They are blackened to the first knuckle with ink, too. Unlike you, however, I have been able to come back to the task the same day, for less than an hour has gone by since I stopped writing.

I set out to tell you about poor Tamara and her trouble. I have come to know her quite well these past few months because, like me, she was with child, her first. Alas, no longer. Tamara is very small, a tiny wisp of a woman, but her child, a boy, was enormous, so large, in fact, that there were whisperings of twins among the elderwives here, before her time arrived. Twin births are not looked upon with favour among the Celtic peoples, I have learned, and this is particularly so among King Ullic's clans here in Cambria.

As it turned out, however, and despite what the elderwives might mutter during their shadowy gatherings, Tamara was unfortunate in that she bore no twins. Instead, she bore one single, monstrous lump of a boy who tore her cruelly while forcing his way, a month and more before his time, out of her small body. That was four days ago, and poor Tamara remains abed, too weak even to sit upright. I am astounded that she has survived this long. Mother, she

*lost so much blood! I knew it was going badly with her.
Anyone with ears knew that. And I wanted to do something
to assist her in her terrible pain and loneliness, although I
know not what that something might have been, but the
elderwives kept me from the chamber, so that I could only
listen to her screams and moans growing more piteous as
she herself grew weaker. It lasted more than an entire day
before the child was finally born, deformed, his head completely flattened on one side by some hideous mischance. In
the normal way of things in this land, which can be frighteningly savage, the child would have been stifled at birth
because of his deformity, but for some reason, concerning
which it seems to me everyone is being very secretive, the
elderwives were loath to kill him before consulting with his
father, the Druid Leir.*

*Leir came, eventually, although he had not cared to
show his face during poor Tamara's travail, and he spent a
long time alone with the child, who was his firstborn son.
Everyone assumed that, being a Druid, he must be praying
for the infant, but then when he emerged from the room, he
refused to let them kill the boy. I know, because I have been
told, that the elderwives were much surprised by this and
greatly at a loss. It would appear, however, that Leir has
great power, sufficiently great, in fact, to flout established
custom, although I know not upon what it is based. I do
know that no one dared gainsay the man. Uncullic might
have, and many here expected him to do so, but for some
reason, as King, Ullic chose to ignore the matter, and so
the child still lives.*

*Leir, unsurprisingly to me, has laid all the blame
upon the unfortunate woman, Tamara. It is no fault of his,
apparently, that there were problems with the birthing of
his child; no deficiency could possibly apply where he and
his are concerned. It is the woman and her evil, vicious
ways that brought the child to grief. The obnoxious creature has ignored Tamara completely since the confinement*

began. And, if the truth be known, I think it possible that he has ignored her much longer than that. She is disconsolate, of course, but fortunately she is also far too weak to really be aware of what goes on about her.

There is something loathsome about the Druid, and my flesh chills whenever he approaches me. He has a slight cast in one eye and a formless vacancy in his expression. Uncle Caius likes to use the word vacuous to convey this notion of utter emptiness. He told me it means filled with empty nothingness. It is the perfect word for what I sometimes see in this Leir. There are times when, looking at his face, I would swear he is demented. There are very few who will talk about him at all, however, and that really surprises me, for Uric's people are a talkative clan, much given to minding other people's ways. Those few who will do so with caution and then have nothing really substantial to say.

After four days, it now appears that the child, who has been named Carthac, will live, despite the wishes of all who hoped that he would die. Equally, it appears that his mother, Tamara, will die, despite the best wishes of her many friends.

I am not at all afraid that the tragedy of what has happened to her might have any effect upon, or any similarity to, what will happen to me when my time comes within the next few weeks. Tamara's case was awful, but it was bred of her own tiny stature and the leviathan girth, weight and sheer size of the monstrous child she bore. I am much larger than she was, and my child is that much smaller. Besides, I have a husband in whose love I float like rose petals upon water, and he has a father who has known and loved me all my life. No harm will come to me here, and my child will emerge into the love and warmth of all his father's relatives. And he will thrive therein until he has the additional good fortune to encounter, at a very early age, the love of his mother's family, too. We have decided that his name will be Uther.

Kiss my father for me. I will write to you again as soon as I may after your grandson is born. I hope all is as well with Enid as it is with me.

Your loving daughter, Veronica

ONE

Even when he was a small boy, no more than four or five years old, Uther Pendragon knew that everyone around him believed that his mother, Veronica, was different from everyone else. They even had a special name for her: *the away one*. It didn't make sense at first. After all, his mother had never been *away* from him. Veronica was and had always been a constant in his young life, along with his nurse, Rebecca. Those two women, between them, had made their presence absolute in everything young Uther did during his earliest years, while he was yet too young for his presence to be noteworthy to others. In the beginning, there were only those two.

One of the very first newcomers to join this tiny group was a woman called Henna, who had been assigned by Uther's grandfather, King Ullic Pendragon, to cook for the newcomers at the very outset of Veronica's life in Ullic's stronghold, eight months and more before Uther was born. Henna had quickly warmed to the King's new daughter-in-law, despite the younger woman's alien upbringing and Outlandish behaviour, so that, for one reason and another, she had never stopped cooking for her new charges and had been completely absorbed into their new life as a married couple. By the time Uther grew old enough to look about him and observe his surroundings, Henna the cook was a fixture of the household in which he lived. And after he had learned to run and to talk, he quickly learned that if he ran and talked to Henna, she would give him wondrous things to eat.

Henna was the first person Uther ever heard using the term *the away one* to describe his mother, and although he did not know then who the cook was talking about, he knew that there was no slight or disparagement intended in the strange-sounding name. He understood right away that *the away one* was a woman, unfortunate or afflicted in some way. And as he grew older, and he heard the name repeated more and more often by people who thought he was too young to be listening, he soon came to understand that this mysterious woman was different in some important respect from "normal" people. He knew that all of the women who gathered in Henna's kitchen liked *the away one* and held her in high regard—that was plain in the tone of their voices when they spoke of her—and he knew, too, that they all felt sorry for her in some way. But for a very long time he was unable to discover the woman's identity.

On one occasion, frustrated by something particular that he had overheard, he even asked his mother who *the away one* was, but Veronica merely looked strangely at him, her face blank with incomprehension. When he repeated the question, articulating it very slowly and precisely, she frowned in exasperation, and he quickly began to talk about something else, as though he had never asked that question in the first place.

Despite having broached the question with his mother, however, he had never been even slightly tempted to ask Henna or any of her friends, because he knew that would have warned them that he was listening when they talked, and they would have been more careful from then on, depriving him of his richest source of information and gossip. And so for long months he merely listened very carefully and tried to work out the secret of *the away one*'s identity by himself, looking more and more analytically, as time went by, at each of the women with whom he came into contact in the course of a day. He knew that there would have to be something about this particular woman that set her noticeably apart and gave others the impression that she was never quite fully among them; that her interests held no commonality with theirs; that she was someone who was not wholly *there*.

He floundered in ignorance until the day when, in the middle of talking about the mysterious woman, Henna suddenly hissed, "Shush! Here she comes"—and his mother walked into the kitchen. Uther was stunned by the swiftness with which the truth dawned upon him then, because it was immediately obvious that Veronica met all of his carefully defined criteria. His mother did not associate with Henna and her people in any capacity other than that of the mistress of the household, aloof and set apart, issuing commands, expressing her wishes and expectations and occasionally complaining and insisting upon higher standards in one thing or another. And yet it was plain that they all liked her and that they respected her integrity and her natural sense of justice.

Uther had developed the ability to reason by the time he was five and now, having discovered at six years of age who *the away one* was, he felt immensely proud of himself for having solved the mystery all on his own. His pride, however, was short-lived, because within the month he overheard another conversation in which a newcomer to Ullic's settlement, a weaver woman called Gyndrel, asked Henna why they called the mistress *the away one*. Henna, a woman who loved to answer a question with a question, promptly asked Gyndrel why *she* thought they would call her that. Gyndrel's first response was that the name must have come from Veronica's obviously foreign background, from the fact that she came from someplace away from Cambria, but Henna snorted with disgust almost before the words were fully out of Gyndrel's mouth. Veronica, she pointed out, might have begun her life as an Outlander, but she was now the wife of the King's eldest son, and no one in the entire Pendragon Federation would dare to insult or defame her nowadays by hinting that she might be anything less than acceptable. Henna then told the woman, her words dripping with disdain, to stop drivelling and use her mind for once.

Sitting on the far side of the fire from the women, concealed from their direct view by a pile of firewood, Uther nodded smugly to himself as Gyndrel eventually answered with all the plausible reasons he would have given in her place. But his head jerked up in shock when Henna dismissed all of them with a scornful laugh.

Nah, she scoffed, pulling her shawl tightly about her shoulders and shifting her large buttocks in search of comfort. When Gyndrel grew more familiar with this family and what went on under this roof, she would soon learn that *the away one* meant simply what it said: the mistress was all too often away in a place of her own within her own head, far from Cambria.

That dose of information gave young Uther much more to think about than he had ever had before, and he began to watch his mother closely, examining her behaviour for any sign of these "absences." But of course it was useless to attempt anything of the kind, because his mother's behaviour was no whit different than it had ever been, and he had never seen anything strange about it before. Nevertheless, he remained alert after that for signs of *awayness* in her.

After that day, he took special pains to safeguard and protect his virtual invisibility in the kitchen while the women were gossiping, removing himself from view whenever the conversation promised to be especially enlightening, and he never failed to keep one ear cocked for any mention of his mother's "other" name. He learned much over the course of the ensuing four years, and he began to recognize the "away" intervals in his mother's behaviour. But he never did learn anything in the kitchens about the underlying cause of Veronica's supposedly strange behaviour, and he eventually became convinced that Henna herself did not know the truth, no matter how hard she tried to appear all-knowing.

The first plausible explanation that Uther ever heard came years later, in a conversation between his father and his mother's father, Publius Varrus. It took place in Camulod in the early spring of one year. Uric had brought his wife to visit her parents, Publius and Luceiia Varrus, and to collect his son, who had spent the entire winter in his grandparents' home with his "twin" cousin, Caius Merlyn Britannicus. The two boys had been born within hours of each other on the same day, albeit miles apart, one of them in Cambria and the other in Camulod. They were very close—in blood if not in temperament—and they had been the best of friends ever since they had grown old enough to recognize each other. Caius's father, Picus Britannicus, had once been a cavalry commander—a full legate—in the Roman legions under the great Flavius Stilicho,

Imperial Regent and Commander-in-Chief of the boy emperor
Honorius. When his wife was killed by a madman, shortly after
giving birth to their only son, Picus's Aunt Luceiia, Uther's grandmother, adopted the infant Caius as her own charge in the enforced
absence of his father.

When the two boys were very small, barely able to walk and
run, Uther's mother Veronica had insisted that they spend as much
time as possible in each other's company, for both their sakes and
for the good of the family, and so it had become normal for Uther
to spend much of each winter down in Camulod, and then for
Caius—or Cay, as he had come to be known by his friends—to
return with him to Cambria for much of the summer.

On this particular afternoon, Uther was once again playing the
role of invisible listener, his eavesdropping skills long practised and
honed by his years of hiding in Henna's kitchen. It was a dismal,
rainy day, and the boys had been playing indoors in the old Villa
Britannicus, once the ancestral home of Caius Britannicus, Caius
Merlyn's grandfather, but now used as quarters for visiting guests,
since the family had moved up to live in the new fort at the top of
the hill less than a mile away.

Uther had been hiding from Cay and his other friends, well
concealed behind a curtain in his grandfather's favourite room.
When he heard the sound of approaching footsteps, he remained
utterly still, believing it was his companions come looking for him.
It wasn't until he heard his grandfather Publius begin to speak that
he realized his error, and he began to emerge from his hiding place,
but almost immediately, perhaps by force of habit, he hesitated.

Uther's father had followed Publius into the room, and his
grandfather asked his first question without preamble. It was suddenly too late, and so Uther remained where he was and listened.

"You can tell me to mind my own business if you wish, but
there's something wrong between you and Veronica, isn't there?"

Uther stood motionless, holding his breath as he waited to hear
his father's response. The silence that followed seemed to last for
an age. Then Uther heard the sound of slow footsteps and the
scraping of wood on stone as someone moved a chair.

"Has she said anything to you?" his father asked.

"No, she has not . . . not to me or to her mother . . . but neither one of us is stupid, Uric, and Veronica is not a facile liar, even when she keeps silent. The trouble's not ours, for all that we love our daughter . . . it's yours and hers. A daughter and a wife are two distinct and very different creatures, coexisting in a single woman. But, as I said, if you don't wish to talk about it, I'll respect that."

Another long silence stretched out and was shattered by the brazen clash of a gong, making Uther jump, so that for a moment he was afraid he might have betrayed himself. Nothing happened, however, and as his heartbeat began to slow again, he heard another voice, this one from the far side of the room.

"Master Varrus, what may I bring you?"

"Ah, Gallo, bring us something to drink, please. Something cold."

Gallo must have retired immediately, because the silence resumed, and then his father spoke again.

"I don't really know what to tell you, Publius. Something definitely *is* wrong, and it has been wrong for a long, long time. There's a part of me that thinks it understands, but even so, it doesn't really make sense even to me, so how can I explain it to you?"

It was some time before his father spoke again.

"Not that we are unhappy, you know . . . It's simply that . . . well, we sleep together and behave as man and wife, but I know—" Uric Pendragon broke off and then continued in a rush. "She won't have any more children. None, Publius. And I don't mean she is incapable of having any more. I mean she *will not* have them. Doesn't want them, won't hear talk of them. She takes . . . she takes medicaments and nostrums to guard against becoming pregnant. Gets them from some of the old women who live in the countryside beyond our settlement, the ones who are supposed to be the priestesses of the Old Goddess."

"The Old Goddess? You mean the Moon Goddess?"

"Aye, the greatest of all our gods and goddesses, Rhiannon. She is very real and very present out there among the people of the mountains and the forests."

"Why on earth would she go to such lengths to avoid having children? That does not sound like the Veronica I know. All she ever dreamed of as a girl was having a brood of children of her own. You must have—" Varrus broke off and cleared his throat. "Damnation, it's difficult to say some things without sounding wrong. I'm not blaming you for anything, yet . . . Have you any idea what happened?"

Uther heard his father sigh, a great, gusting breath.

"It has to be connected with that first night we arrived in Cambria, newly wed, and the debacle that took place there, the deaths. By the time I discovered what was going on, it was already too late to prevent it. I tried to hide it from her, to take her away and protect her from it, but I couldn't, and I know it frightened her badly . . .

"But then, over time, once all the excitement had died away, she seemed to settle down and gradually grew more calm. I tried to explain it to her—all the whys and wherefores of how it happened. But she merely listened, and finally I stopped talking about it altogether. We never spoke of it again. I thought she had forgotten it at last."

They were interrupted at that point by the return of Gallo, evidently accompanied by another man bearing a tray of drinks. Uther felt his bladder stirring faintly and resolutely ignored it, concentrating instead upon the muttered, indecipherable mumbles of small talk and the clinking of dishes. Moments later, he heard the sound of liquid pouring from one container into others. He translated an inarticulate grunt from his father as a wordless acknowledgment of gratitude, and then someone—he assumed it was his grandfather because it was he who spoke next—replaced his cup audibly on a surface of some kind.

"So, you were saying she recovered from her horror, eventually . . ."

"Aye, I thought she had. She was terrified at first. I think she believed that the things she had seen were common—probably thought we burned all our enemies alive. There was a time afterwards when she was so . . . I don't know . . . so *gone* from me that I was afraid I had lost her and her love forever. Then Uther was born, and we were lost in the wonder of watching him grow stronger and more beautiful each day.

"Months went by, then years, and I began to fret over her failure to have another child. It was not for the lack of trying, and so I began to worry and to question myself. She'd had no trouble conceiving when we were first wed . . . in fact, I believe she caught with child on our wedding night. But then when I began to harp on that to her, wondering why it should be so, Veronica reacted strangely. She grew hostile and refused to speak of it, turning away from me each time I raised the subject. And that was when I began to be aware that something was badly wrong between us . . . That would have been . . . what? Four years ago? No, closer to five. I knew I had done nothing to cause any such wrongness . . . nothing harmful . . .

"I've never doubted that she loves me, but there is a deep, deep sadness in her all the time, Publius, a well of grief. And I feel powerless to help her. As I said, she won't even consider having any more children. Not at all."

"And you don't know why?"

"No, I do, it goes back to that first night, the night of the fires. The last time we fought, she said she would *never* bring another child into this world to be betrayed and blackened by the Druids."

It took his grandfather some time to respond to that.

"I think, Uric, I would like to hear what really happened on that occasion. By the time we learned anything about it in Camulod, it had all been over for months, and everyone was trying to forget it, stepping over and around it and saying as little as possible. I know there was an uprising of some kind among the Druids and that many of them were killed, and I know that several other people died in a fire. But what did Veronica actually see that night?"

Another long silence ensued, and Uther stood motionless, trying not to breathe too loudly lest the sound of it be noticeable to the men on the other side of the curtain. Every time they paused, as each man thought deeply before saying what he had to say next, it left a silence into which he was afraid the sound of his breathing or his heartbeat might easily intrude.

Finally his father spoke.

"She witnessed a burning."

"A burning . . . What does that mean? Are you telling me it was deliberate, that she saw someone being deliberately burned to death?"

"Aye . . . more than one."

"How many more, in God's name?"

"Thirty-two."

"By the Christian Christus! Thirty-two men? She was barely sixteen years old! You allowed her to watch thirty-two men being burned alive?"

"No, of course not! I allowed nothing. But there was nothing I could have done. Even my father was powerless to stop it. We arrived in the middle of things, with no warning."

Another long silence and then the sound of footsteps pacing up and down. When his grandfather's voice came again, Uther could imagine him looking out and away, with his back to Uric. "And what *was* going on, Uric? Tell me about it now."

"There's not much to tell. It all came to a head while we were here in Camulod for the wedding feast, but it had begun a long time before that—a plot born and nurtured in secrecy, protected by blood oaths and the fear of visitation by demons. What forced it into prominence, however, was sheer circumstance and coincidence. While the King and his strongest supporters were away in Camulod making merry, a force of Ersemen raided our southern coast. Four boatloads of them. By the merest chance, we had a force of our own down there at the time, under the command of Powys, one of my father's best captains. By the time Powys learned of the enemy presence and caught up to them, however, the raiders had burned four settlements along the coastline. Powys fought them as soon as he found them. Caught them away from their boats and cut them off, then slaughtered them—or most of them. Not enough of them, as it turned out. We found out later that Powys had been spending time in the company of certain of our Druids, and because of that, instead of simply killing the raiders out of hand as he ought to have, he brought them back as prisoners."

"Why would he do that? Your people don't take slaves, do they? And you've no place and no time for prisoners. In any case,

I thought your Chief Druid was with us in Camulod at that time. Was he not the one in the red robes, officiating at the nuptials along with Bishop Alaric?"

"Aye, he was. Llew was his name. He's dead now and was replaced by a man called Daris five years ago. The trouble had begun elsewhere among the Druids, long before my marriage to Veronica, with a group of disaffected malcontents known as the Black Brethren. These people thought they could break away from what they saw as weaknesses in the faith and re-establish the ancient ways—or *their* ideas of the ancient ways. They revived the traditions whispered of in the tales of the great human burnings, when captured enemies were offered to the gods in sacrifice and Cambria was strong and proud. Such tales as those you have probably never heard, for nothing of the kind has happened in more than half a thousand years. But the stories persist among our people, and the tradition has never been forgotten.

"These mad priests used their power and their place within our lives to instill deep fear of the ancient gods in those people who would listen to them. And many people did, many people from all levels of our folk. Powys was not the only Chief or lesser chieftain they seduced. And they moved quickly, once they had decided to go forward with their plans. They enforced their viewpoints and their commands in secrecy, using blood oaths and dreadful threats of punishment for betrayal, exercising fear as the potent force that it is. Their movement, if you could even call it that, was a kind of insurrection against Llew the Chief Druid and his ways. It came to naught, as it turned out, because that single incident of the Tir Manha burning brought about their end.

"When we arrived from Camulod that night, sunset had caught us within several miles of home, but since we anticipated no danger there in our own lands, we decided to press on in the darkness and sleep in our own beds in Tir Manha . . . You can have no idea how much, or how often, I have regretted that decision."

"No, I believe you. But wait you . . ." There came another silence, and then Uther heard the sound of more footsteps approaching from a distance.

"Caius?" he heard his grandfather ask, his voice tight with irritation. "What are you doing in here? You know you're not supposed to bring your friends clattering through the house like raiding Outlanders."

"We're looking for Uther, Uncle."

"That matters not to me, lad. If you have eyes in your head and the sense with which to use them, you will see that Uther is not here. Now, off with you and seek him somewhere else. Your Uncle Uric and I are trying to talk, so away you go and leave us to our affairs. But go quietly, because if your Aunt Luceiia finds you charging through the house like that, you'll all be in trouble. And close those doors as you go out, if you please."

Moments later, after the footsteps had retreated more quietly than they had approached, Varrus spoke again.

"So, I gather that you arrived home to find this sacrifice already underway. But you must have known what was happening, from all the light and the activity. Surely you could have spirited your wife away from all of it? The glow from thirty-two fires must have been bright indeed."

"Thirty-two—? No, there was but one fire, Publius, in the burning pit. The prisoners were all confined in cages, suspended above it." In the space of a few stark moments, Uric outlined the sight that had awaited the returning party on their arrival, and Uther listened, fascinated, as his mind tried to recreate what the scene must have looked and sounded like.

When Uric had finished speaking, Publius Varrus remained quiet for a while, absorbing what he had been told.

"By the Christ," he said eventually in a flat, stunned voice. "I remember your father describing this pit to me, years ago. But he made no mention of that kind of thing. This is barbarism beyond anything I have ever known or heard of. And Ullic did nothing to stop it?"

"He was as confused as all the rest of us. Nothing like that had ever happened in living memory, and none of us really knew what to expect."

"Your Druids must have known!"

"Aye, the dark ones did—the Black Brethren—but they were the only ones. And they had had time to work on those of us who had stayed home by invoking the three-day law. The prisoners had been captive for three days by then, you see. And our ancient laws decree that if a prisoner is to die, he should be killed within three days of being taken. Failing that, he should be kept as a working slave or else set free. If he is killed after three days, however, his spirit remains to haunt and terrify his murderers."

"That is nonsense."

"No, Publius, that is our ancient law . . . Druidic law."

"Based upon fear and superstition."

"Based upon our beliefs. Cambria isn't Camulod, Publius." Uther heard his father pacing anxiously and the exasperation in his voice when he spoke again. "You have open spaces, high walls and Roman comforts. You have warmth and light in abundance—fine, pure tapers and candles of beeswax, with bright, coal-burning braziers and blazing torches fuelled by carefully rendered tallow and clear oils. Not so with us. We are ruled by the night and the darkness, and our people fear the beings that infest the night. You, with your Roman-bred beliefs, you can smile at us for being superstitious, but we must live with who we are and what we know. We believe that the spirits of the dead walk freely among us in the dark of night, and that only the goodwill of our gods keeps them from terrorizing us. When the gods are not pleased, we are at the mercy of the night. We are Celts, Publius, not Romans. That is not superstition to us . . . it is the very stuff of life and truth, and believe me when I tell you it is difficult to feel that you are being foolish and superstitious when your blood has turned to water and your bones to jelly because of the blind terror that has eaten you whole."

"Aye, I suppose . . . and your Druids encourage you in all of that."

"Of course they do. They are our priests."

"So what of this Llew, what did he do that night?"

"Nothing. He was overpowered and knocked unconscious by the rebel priests as soon as he arrived, captured out of our sight and carried off before any of us knew what was going on. Then my father's councillors came to us, suborned as they had been by the black priests, and convinced him that it was the will of all the gods— and all the Druids—that the sacrifice proceed and that the spirits of the prisoners be freed, since plainly we could not turn them all loose or keep them all penned up as slaves and prisoners. My father saw the truth of that and thus permitted them to proceed, albeit with great reluctance, and the sacrifice began. Only then did I begin to realize what was really happening.

"The burning pit had always been there, since before I was born, and I had seen it used on several occasions to burn the remains of high-born men, chiefs and Druids. But I had never known of its being used to burn the living. I tried to take Veronica out of there then, finally aware of what might happen, but in seek-ing to protect her, I made the mistake of not telling her what was really taking place, and so she balked and ran away from me towards the fires and the smoke and the sacrifice, not knowing what was there . . ."

"And . . . ?"

"It was a full month and more before she spoke another word, to me or anyone. It was as though she lay in a trance, even though she ate and drank when meat and drink were offered her. I almost lost my wits before the end of that."

"Why did we hear nothing of this?"

"Because that was how Veronica wished it to be. As she recov-ered, she decided that it could serve no useful purpose to upset you and her mother with word of what she had endured. And by that time, she was well swollen with little Uther and no one wanted to talk much of anything other than that."

"Aye. And your own people, how did they react to what was done that night by these Black Brethren?"

"Well, talking about offering a human sacrifice and actually performing a human sacrifice are not at all the same thing. Once our people saw the smoke and heard the screams and smelled the stink of charring flesh, they quickly lost all their lust for the old days. Tir Manha was a quiet, shame-filled place for long, long weeks after that night."

"And what about the priests, these so-called rebels who dreamed up this thing?"

"Well, we found out by the following morning what had been happening, and we found them on the point of killing Llew just in time to stop them. Then we killed them all."

"How? You burned them, didn't you? Threw them into their own pit?"

"No, Publius, we did not burn them. That thing, that burning was . . . there is a Roman word for it I've heard you use . . . an *aberration*. It was an evil thing, born of a few evil men who made it happen through fear. We Pendragons are not a wicked people, Publius, and we are certainly not evil. You know that. We have never burned another person since that night, and we never will. We simply cut the rebel priests down wherever we found them. No ceremony involved. That would have made them seem important. We simply killed them out of hand. And then we filled in the burning pit completely and used it for their common grave, leaving it unmarked. There were forty-four of them in all in our lands. More than a few, but not enough, in the long run, to generate any significant threat to Llew, his brethren and their teachings. There might have been others of their kind elsewhere, beyond our territories, but if there were we heard nothing of them once the word had spread of how the Black Brethren in King Ullic's land had died."

"Aye, well . . ." Publius Varrus sighed deeply. "Uric, I know you are not evil, nor is your father. But I tell you honestly, I cannot conceive of such a thing happening ever, under any circumstances, among our people in Camulod or elsewhere in any other place that I know of. There is something fundamentally, intrinsically wrong with people who could do such things, no matter what the provocation."

Uther listened, his chest tight, waiting for his father to digest those words and then respond to them. And for the longest time, it sounded as though no answer would be made. But then his father spoke again, his voice little more than a whisper.

"You're right, Publius, you're right. There is a darkness within our Cambrian spirits that permits us, as a folk, to do such things. We did them in the dim and far-off past, in the smoky shadows of

black night and at the urging of our priests, and we have shown that
we could do them still today, given the proper drive. It is cause for
deep shame."

"No, son, it is cause for awareness and great care in future time,
but not for further shame. As you have said, you've never burned a
man, and you never will. Be sure to remind your people, though,
that they did once, and that they regretted it. But Veronica—tell me
truly, what has this to do with her wanting no more children?"

When Uther heard his father's voice again, it was filled with
certainty and conviction. "I believe she is determined that no child
of hers will ever grow to live in Cambria among the Pendragon and
offer human sacrifice. I think she blames all of my people for what
happened that night. She has made friends among us I have no
doubt of that, but she will never fully trust any of us ever . . . I
believe, too, that something has gone wrong within her mind, and
because of that, she fears now that any other children she might
have with me will be infected with the darkness that lies in our past
and in our blood. That, I truly believe, is the root and cause of her
refusal to have more."

Another pause as his grandfather pondered, Uther supposed,
and then a sigh. "I think the same, Uric. And I believe it rests with
you and me to help her forget all about this." Uther could imagine
the two men sipping thoughtfully from the cups they held. Then,
"One more thing. What about the boy?"

"Uther? What about him?"

"How does she feel about him?"

Listening breathlessly, Uther knew the time that elapsed then
must have been short, but to him it seemed endless as he waited for
his father to reply.

"What do you mean?"

He had a mental image of his father's face creased in
puzzlement.

"Well, if she is so upset over the thought of having more children to be corrupted by your Druids, or whomever else she sees as
being responsible, then it seems to me that it might be because of
something she has seen, or thinks to have seen, in young Uther.

You did say that for several years she gave no indication of her fears. Something, then, must have triggered them, and it occurred to me it might have been the boy."

Uther could barely understand what his father was being asked. Was he being accused of hurting his own mother? Apparently his father was equally confused, because it was some time before he answered, and then he said simply, "Publius, he's your grandson."

"I know he is, and I could not love him more were he twins. But Uther possesses all the attributes that any other, future child of yours might have . . . and that means he has all the failings and the flaws, as well as the strengths. It is those flaws and failings—how did you refer to them earlier, as a darkness that lies within your past and in your blood?—that Veronica claims to fear. How, then, does she perceive her son? Is she afraid of him or for him?"

"No, of course not! Neither one nor the other. She loves him. I swear it, Publius. Veronica loves Uther."

To Uther's ear, however, his father's words rang unconvincingly. There had been a pause, a hesitation, that lasted a tiny moment too long. His grandfather thought so too.

"I think you're wrong there, Uric, and I think you know it, down in the depths of you. Oh, not in the part about her loving him, for I believe wholeheartedly that my daughter loves her son—it shines out of her like a pure light whenever she sees him. But I believe in my gut that Veronica fears deeply for the boy and always has, ever since his birth, and probably for months before that. I believe that is why she has always insisted, ever since the boy was old enough to walk, that he spend as much time as he does in Camulod with young Caius. I'm beginning to suspect that Uther would be sent to Camulod each year even if Caius were *not* there."

When next he spoke, Uric sounded unsure of himself. "If what you say is true, there is no logic in it. I had never thought of it before now, but Uther himself ought to be a shining reason for Veronica to want more children. There's nothing wrong with him."

"But we are not discussing logic here, Uric. We are discussing women, their ideas and their instinctual fears. It is not her unborn children that threaten poor Veronica, it is the dread of what evil men might do to them, and therein lies her folly and her sickness, for if all women were to shut themselves up as she has, refusing to bear children for fear the world might damage or corrupt them, then our whole race of men would soon die out and leave this world to the beasts . . .

"Our task, as I see it, is to work from now on to convince your wife that her own teachings will be stronger than the urgings of evil men. She is the one who, as a mother, will show her sons and daughters the light of hope and goodness that burns in the deepest darkness. You agree?"

"Yes . . . yes, of course I do."

"Good, then let's go and make a beginning."

When the two men had gone, Uther emerged, holding the edge of the curtain carefully and lowering it gently as he left his hiding place. He moved slowly across the room towards a large padded and upholstered armchair facing the stone hearth in the end wall, stopped when his hip bumped against it but made no move to sit. Instead, he stood staring sightlessly into the empty fireplace, his eyes unfocused as he grappled with the strange and troubling new thought that had been implanted in his mind: *his mother feared him.* His mind had accepted what it heard, because there was no logical reason to do otherwise . . . the two men speaking had not known that he was there, so they'd had no reason to speak other than truthfully. But his young mind, overwhelmed by that sudden realization, had also failed to establish any distinction between his mother being afraid *of* him and afraid *for* him.

Uther Pendragon was now a very different person from the carefree boy who had dashed into the room a half-hour earlier. Then the biggest and most immediate problem in his mind had been the need to find a perfect hiding place. Now he had been changed forever and had aged immeasurably. Now he was fighting to accept, and to adjust to, the awareness that his own beloved mother was afraid of him, afraid of some dark side of him, some elemental *thing* that lay imbedded in his very nature, some aspect of his being that she had learned to fear and distrust long before he was born, when she herself was a young girl, not many years older than he was now. Whatever it was, that thing had terrified her thoroughly, enough to alter her lifelong determination to mother an entire brood of children.

Uther discovered that he had no wish to know what that thing was, for if it had the power to terrify his mother, he knew it would frighten him beyond bearing. He hated the thought that his mother might be afraid of him, but he hated even more the suspicion that she might distrust him in some basic, formless way. He knew she loved him. He had heard his grandfather say that her smile lit up the room whenever she set eyes on him, and he knew that was true because he had seen it with his own eyes. How, then, could she be afraid of him? What was there in him, in his very nature, that could make even his mother fear him?

That was a question Uther Pendragon would never be able to answer, for he could never know that what his Roman-bred mother feared lay not within him, but in the very nature of his Celtic people.

TWO

Garreth Whistler might never have heard the sound had he not been in love. As it was, his mind was so full of thoughts of the woman called Laminda—and the risk he was taking, meeting her in broad daylight with her husband close by—that he was temporarily incapable of whistling, and he strode quietly across the meadow surrounding the King's House, hearing only the sound of his own feet swishing through the long grass that awaited the scythe. As he neared the ancient stone-built cattle byre beneath the large oak tree on the southeast corner of the King's Holding, the portion of land allocated to the King by his people for his living, he hesitated, wondering which of two possible routes might offer him the best chance of reaching his assignation unseen. And in that moment of utter stillness he heard a stifled whimper coming from the ruined building.

When he stuck his head around the corner and saw the tear-streaked, dirt-smeared face of a small boy who huddled against the wall there, wrapped as nearly into a ball as he could achieve, his arms clasped around his upraised knees and his shins oozing blood, Garreth experienced a lucid moment of decision that would surprise him later when he considered what it might have cost him. He recognized the child, saw his misery, in the same instant had a vision of Laminda amorously awaiting him—and he chose immediately to comfort the boy.

"Uther? Is that you? What's wrong, lad?"

Uther's eyes flew wide, and his seven-year-old heart quailed as he saw the hero who towered over him. Garreth Whistler was his grandfather Ullic's greatest champion, a mighty warrior whom no one could best with sword or battle-axe, and who could wrestle and beat any other two of King Ullic's Pendragon warriors at any time. Uther was appalled to think that this man, of all men, should be the one to find him cringing and cowering, bawling like a baby and girlishly nursing his hurts. But Garreth Whistler had already propped his shield and his two-headed iron axe in a corner and was now down on one knee in front of him, gently pulling his arms away to uncover the lacerated shin bone that still oozed blood. As he looked at the swollen bruise and the blood that trickled from its centre, the big warrior's frown deepened and his long white moustaches seemed to bristle.

"What did this, a stone?" The child shook his head, gulping. "What then? A stick?" Another shake of the head. "Did you fall? Let's have a look." He raised the boy's leg and peered at the abrasion closely. "It's a cut, a straight edge. Looks like a blow. You didn't hit anything, something hit you." He paused and glanced up at the boy's face. "Something like a leather-soled boot?"

Uther nodded miserably.

"Who?"

"Ivor."

"Ivor? Cross-Eyed Ivor?" Again the child nodded. "But he must be, what, three years older than you? He's twice your size." Uther said nothing.

Garreth sighed and braced himself with one hand, then twisted down and around to sit beside the boy, adjusting his short, wide-bladed sword so that it lay comfortably on the ground alongside his thigh before settling his back against the rough stone wall.

"Well," he said, "I've always got time for a good story, and I suspect you have one to tell. So let's start right at the beginning— tell me why a great lump like Cross-Eyed Ivor would want to kick a bright little fellow like you."

The boy sat silent for a while, staring down at the ground, and Garreth made no effort to speak, allowing the silence to stretch until it became clear that the boy would not break it. When he felt it had been long enough, he moved to rise again, speaking as though to himself.

"Well, if you don't want to talk, I'll be on my way, then, and leave you to your sorrows—"

"No!" The boy was evidently so shocked at his own vehemence that he sat blinking at his temerity in using such a tone when addressing the King's Champion.

Garreth ignored the look. "No? Does that mean you want me to stay?"

"Yes."

"Fine, then I'll stay a little longer, but what good will that do if you won't talk to me?"

"I'll talk to you." The words were barely more than a whisper.

"Then why don't you start by telling me why Cross-Eyed Ivor kicked you." Before the boy could even begin to respond, Garreth held up his hand, palm outward, to silence him. "Wait, I want you to listen to me carefully first, and take note of what I have to say. Will you do that?"

The boy nodded, mute.

"Good. Now you are probably thinking that I won't believe what you tell me and thinking, too, that you will be shaming yourself by even talking about it . . . and you might even be thinking that I'll think you are making everything up. Are you? Is that what you're thinking?"

"N-no."

"Are you sure about that? You don't sound very sure."

"No, I'm sure." The boy's voice was growing stronger and more confident.

"Well, I'm very glad to know that, because here is what is really in my mind. You are cut and bleeding, and I can see plainly that someone has been beating you . . . beating you fairly thoroughly. Even before you told me who it was, I knew it must have been someone older and bigger than you are, because I know you are your father's son and your grandfather's pride and joy, and I know you would never stand still and allow anyone to do that to you unless he was much bigger and older than you are. Am I correct?"

Uther nodded hesitantly, his eyes wide with amazement at hearing praise and encouragement where he had expected scorn.

"I knew it. And it was only one boy, wasn't it? It was only Cross-Eyed Ivor who hit you?" The boy nodded again, but this time his eyes remained cast down, and Garreth went after the information he suspected would be there. "Am I correct? Or were there others there? Were there others with him?"

This time the nod of Uther's head was very small.

"Aha! And did any of the others hit you?"

"No, only Ivor. But they watched, and laughed."

"Why? Why were they tormenting you?"

"They don't like me."

"Well, I don't know about that . . . For all we know, they might be afraid to show Ivor what they really think of him, in case he turns on them. He's a big strong clod, isn't he?" The boy nodded, and Garreth tilted his head in agreement. "Yes, well, it wouldn't be the first time people have ganged up on someone else, someone smaller than they are, to protect themselves from being tormented by a big strong clod of a bully." Garreth Whistler let that sink home for a few moments and then continued. "Why were they tormenting you, anyway, do you know? Did they tell you?"

The boy mumbled something.

"What? I didn't hear what you said."

Uther cleared his throat and then spoke again, more loudly. "They called me an Outlander."

"An Outlander? Hah! They must be mad. You're no Outlander, you're the King's own grandson, born and bred right here in Tir Manha. Of course, your mother might be called an Outlander . . . Hey, hold on there! Do you intend to fight me, too? I only said she *might* be called one . . ."

The boy had blanched and started to struggle to gain his feet, his full lips pulled into a grimace and white with rage.

"She is not! My mother is *not* an Outlander."

"I know that, lad, I know! Listen to me!" Garreth had gripped the boy by the wrists, imprisoning his hands and restraining them effortlessly. As the man's words penetrated his rage, Uther slumped back and relaxed, and as soon as he did, Garreth released him.

"That's better. I thought for a moment there that you were going to injure me. Are you going to be quiet now? Am I safe?" He examined Uther's expression closely and then nodded, apparently satisfied with what he saw. "Good lad. Now look here, let's be truthful about this, you and me. Your father, Uric Pendragon, is the King's firstborn son, isn't that so? What that means, then, is that had your mother been an Outlander of any kind, then your father, as the King's son, could never have wed her. You know that's true, don't you?" Uther nodded. "Good. We are agreed on that, and therefore we can agree, too, that it doesn't matter what any other fool might have to say on the matter. So now you can settle down and chew on some of these."

He reached into the leather scrip that hung from his waist and produced a bag of shelled hazelnuts. The boy took it hesitantly, shook out a small portion of nuts into his palm and began to pop them into his mouth one by one. Garreth did the same, crunching the nuts audibly and with relish between strong, white, even teeth as he continued speaking.

"Now me, I'm a real Outlander, you know, because of my father—my real father, I mean. I was born here, too, but the man who raised me was not my real father. Nobody here ever saw him or knew who he was or where he came from. But with just one look at me, they can tell he was an Outlander from *far* away." He laughed, disparaging himself, and Uther did not know how he should react. Garreth Whistler looked very different from everyone else, but Uther had never heard anyone mention the fact aloud. Then, incredulous, he heard the big man say, "You and I have many things to tell each other, Master Pendragon."

They sat in a more companionable silence for a time until they had eaten all their nuts, and then Garreth ventured a little further.

"That was it, wasn't it? Ivor was saying things about your mother and you fought him."

"Yes." The voice was soft again, almost too quiet to be heard.

"That's what I thought . . ." He reached into his open mouth with his right pinkie and delicately picked a piece of nut from between two teeth. "It's a necessary thing for a man to defend his mother's name and honour. But a clever man ought to stop and think before throwing himself into a fight he can't win. You didn't think about that, did you?"

"Yes, I did. I didn't want to fight. But they made me. They found me and made me fight."

"You mean they made you fight by laughing at your mother and saying bad things about her?"

"Yes."

"Where were you when they found you?"

"Hiding."

"Hiding from them? Why would you do that?"

"Because . . . because I was afraid. They always beat me." The boy hung his head, peering down at himself, the very picture of shame and dejection.

Garreth Whistler kept his voice pitched low when he spoke again. "Hmm. I know what you mean. Being alone and surrounded by enemies makes you really afraid. I know the feeling well."

At the edge of his vision, Garreth saw the boy's head come up and swivel towards him, the eyes wide with disbelief, and he swung his own head to return the look.

"What? You don't believe me? You think I'm lying, is that what you think? You think that because I'm the King's Champion I've never been afraid?" He sat up straight, bent his knees, reached down with one hand and pushed himself up easily from the ground. Then he reached down again and helped young Uther to his feet.

"Come on, let's take a walk, you and me. I have to meet someone, but you can come with me. It won't take long, and on the way back we'll get you cleaned up so that the sight of you won't frighten your mother." He paused and squinted down at Uther's bleeding shins. "How are the legs? Can you walk on them, or should I carry you on my back like a baby?" His tone was jocular, teasing, and the boy rewarded him with a shy smile.

"I can walk."

"Magnificent!" Garreth Whistler busied himself for a moment adjusting the hang of his sword and collecting his axe and shield, and then he stood upright again, looming over the boy who now stood gazing up at him. "There, that's better! Now, young Uther, let us walk together, the two of us, and share ideas."

Uther Pendragon thought his heart would burst with pride as he walked solemnly towards the village in the company of his new and unexpected ally. Garreth Whistler was the most highly regarded warrior in King Ullic's entire domain, a naturally gifted fighter of exceptional speed, grace, strength and stamina. His skills were admired by everyone, envied by most and equalled in no one. He was not yet twenty years old, but he had been recognized as a paragon of military prowess since long before his formal coming-of-age four years earlier. He was too young yet to lead armies, people said; he lacked experience in dealing with large numbers of men. But even Uther, who was seven years old, knew that when it came to single-handed feats of arms, Garreth Whistler of the Pendragon had no peer and would bow the knee to no man except his lawful king, Ullic Pendragon.

Garreth was also beautiful, Uther knew, at least in the eyes of women, for he had heard Henna and her friends in the kitchens discussing the King's Champion in great and lurid detail, praising his hair and his perfectly muscled body. Uther found himself almost walking sideways, peering up at the very tall man who strode beside him. As Garreth himself had observed a short time earlier, he was startlingly different-looking. And he was mysterious because of that, for no one could point a finger towards his origins and say that was where he came from. Henna had said that his mother, whose name was Bronwyn, had been born and raised in Tir Manha, but she had been abducted in a raid just prior to being married to a man called Dunvallo, one of the clan's most prominent warriors. Dunvallo had been severely wounded in the same raid. Many years later, without explanation of any kind, Bronwyn had returned to her homeland, unable to speak because her tongue had been cut out during her captivity. She had been far advanced in pregnancy when she arrived, and Dunvallo, her former husband-to-be, who had never married because of the wounds he had received in the raid that snatched her away, took her into his home without hesitation and looked after her until she gave birth to her son. Bronwyn did not survive the birthing, and she had never been able to communicate the secret of her child's paternity, and so it fell upon Dunvallo to name the babe and care for him during his infancy, in ignorance of whether the child had been the fruit of a loving relationship or a casual, brutal rape. Dunvallo did all that needed to be done for the child whom he named Garreth, and did it very well, until a lethal, lingering fever drained the life from him when the boy was eight years old. Orphaned then for the second time in his short life, Garreth managed to survive on his own.

Local lore, however, remembered that Garreth had been born a mystery and remained that way. There was no doubt that he was an anomaly among this race of thick-set, dark-skinned, raven-haired mountain dwellers. Garreth's tangle of long blond curls, almost snow-white in colour, and the pale blue eyes that blazed prominently beneath a high forehead and white eyebrows, seemed to heighten and intensify the golden colour of his tanned skin. Where most of his compatriots were long-lipped, flat-faced and snubnosed, Garreth Whistler's nose was long and straight and narrow, his cheekbones were high and prominent, and his jaw was almost square, sloping down to a strong, deeply cleft chin. Uther's Grandmother Luceiia Britannicus had once told his Grandfather Ullic that Garreth Whistler looked like a Hellene, with his long limbs, golden looks, white hair and Grecian features. Uther asked what a Hellene was, and Ullic told him that it was an Attic Greek. That was the end of that conversation, and although Uther clearly remembered the description, he had not the slightest knowledge of what an Attic Greek was or what it meant.

And now this golden man Garreth Whistler, the King's Champion, was walking slowly by Uther's side, talking to him as though Uther Pendragon were his equal. He had even slowed his pace unobtrusively so that Uther could keep up with him without having to run or even trot.

They made one foray into the dense woods together. Garreth bade Uther wait for him, and then went forward to meet a woman whose face Uther could not see and whose voice was too low for him to recognize. As Garreth had promised earlier, the meeting did not take long, and the King's Champion soon returned, shaking his head ruefully.

"I hope that by the time you grow up, young Uther, and arrive at the knowledge of women, you will have arrived also at an *understanding* of women. I never did, and I suppose I never will. Women are utterly unfathomable creatures. I thank all the gods, though, that they exist! Now let's head back and clean up your combat wounds, for that's what they are: wounds acquired in defending your mother's honour. But first I have to pee."

When he had finished, the tall man turned back to his small companion and they resumed walking.

"You do know that everyone in the world has to pee every day, don't you?"

"Yes, and cack."

"Exactly. Everyone does . . ." They walked on in silence for a while, then, "Have you ever had to pee really badly and not been able to because you were in a place where you couldn't just untie your flaps and do it?" Uther nodded gravely, ignoring the fact that until his seventh birthday he had gone uncovered much of the time. "Hmm. Where was that, d'you recall?"

"In the King's Hall, when the Druids were offering sacrifice."

"That was just last month."

Another grave nod. "I know."

"How long did you have to hold it, a long time?" The boy nodded. "That can be very painful, having to hold it in for too long. Did it hurt much, that day?" Another nod. "Aye, I'll wager it did. It always does, you see, and it doesn't get any easier as you grow older. When you are an old man, even older than your Grandfather Ullic, there will still be times when you have to pee really badly and for one reason or another you won't be able to. So you'll hang on to it and hold it in until you think you have to burst, and it really, really hurts . . . Fear is like that, too."

"What?" The boy stopped dead in his tracks and stood staring up at the tall golden man.

"I said fear's like that, like having to pee. Everyone in the world has to pee—even women—and sooner or later, everyone in the world has to put up with the pain of not being able to do it when they want to. Same thing with fear, young Uther. Come on, keep walking.

"Everyone in the world suffers from fear, sometimes every day. And fear hurts; don't you let anyone tell you otherwise. It doesn't stop hurting as you get older, either. It still hurts me as much as it did when I was your age. Sometimes it even gets worse. You just have to learn to deal with it."

"How?"

"Ah, how . . . now there's a question difficult to answer. You see that piece of rope there, lying on the ground?"

They were passing by one of the stables on the outskirts of the village now, and Uther looked to where Garreth pointed.

"Yes."

"Then tell me quickly, how long is it?"

"How—? I don't know."

"What d'you mean, you don't know? It's a piece of rope, isn't it? You've seen pieces of rope before, haven't you?"

"Yes." Uther was frowning slightly, wondering what Garreth was talking about.

"Well, then, my question was simple enough: How long is it?"

Uther was now completely mystified, but he drew a deep breath and answered firmly, "I don't know. No one could tell, until they had measured it. They're all different. Every piece of rope is different."

"Good lad, you are absolutely correct! Every piece of rope is different. And so is every piece of fear. That's why the question you just asked me is so difficult to answer. How does a person learn to deal with fear? There could be a thousand different answers to that, because one man can have a thousand different fears, all of them biting him at the same time. He might be afraid of falling from high places, and he might be afraid, too, of drowning in deep water. Can you see how that might work? Good. But at the same time on the same day he might also be afraid of being punished by the King for something he did, and of being punished differently by one of the King's advisers for something else that he forgot to do. He might be afraid, too, of going home to face an angry wife that night because of something he did earlier that day or the night before, and afraid, at the same time, of his neighbour's dog because it always growls at him when he passes by. He might be afraid of thunderstorms and lightning, and afraid of being made to look foolish in front of his friends. You see what I mean? Being afraid can be really complicated. Here, let's stop by the trough there and clean some of the blood off you."

As Garreth carefully cleaned the cuts and scrapes on his legs, Uther thought about all he had learned that day. Most of his attention, of course, was taken up with what was happening right there, with people stopping and staring and whispering among themselves, some of them speaking to Garreth Whistler, although none of them had the courage to come right out and ask Garreth plainly what he was about.

Finally Garreth straightened up again and dried his hands by rubbing them against his leggings.

"There," he said, his eyes still on the job he had done, "that's better. Now, I've thought about a way to answer your question." He turned and began walking again, this time slinging his light, circular shield so that it hung down his back from his left shoulder, and Uther fell proudly in step beside him. They walked again until the crowded village square with its staring busybodies, as Garreth called them, had fallen far behind them. Then Garreth led Uther over to the base of a large old elm tree, where he lowered himself to the ground between two moss-covered roots and rested his back against the trunk.

"Suppose there was a place—a very special place—where you went to do the same thing every day. What do you do every single day without fail? Can you think of something, something you always do—other than peeing?"

Uther thought hard for a few moments, then slowly nodded his head. "I always look each morning to see if I can see the top of the Dragon's Head."

The Dragon's Head was the highest headland to the northwest, closest to Tir Manha, and local lore had it that if the peak were visible in the morning, free of clouds, the day would remain fair.

Garreth nodded. "Where do you look from?"

"In front of our house."

"Is that the best place to see it from?"

"No. I like to see it from the top of Denny's Hill; it's clearer from up there."

"That's good. Now suppose you were in the habit of going there every single morning, up to the top of Denny's Hill to look at the Dragon's Head, and then one morning you found a big dog up there, a very unfriendly dog who had decided to live there and did not like you intruding. Suppose you tried to win him over and befriend him, but he wouldn't have it, and he attacked you every single morning without fail and eventually started biting you. What would you do? Remember, he's a very *big* dog."

"I . . ." Uther bit down on what he had begun to say, and instead thought quietly for a long time. Garreth waited patiently, and eventually the boy nodded to himself. "I . . . I would find some other place where I could see the mountain."

"Aye, and so would most other people. But there's something wrong with that solution. Can you tell me what it is?"

Uther sat staring, his eyes troubled and his brow slightly furrowed, and Garreth tried a different tack.

"Would you be happy with your new viewpoint, think you?"

The boy sat mum, considering that, then shook his head. When he spoke, he sounded unsure of his answer. "No . . . I don't think so . . ."

"Of course you wouldn't, because what you did was run away from a brute beast! You are more clever than all the dogs that were ever whelped, so how could you possibly be happy about having let one beat you at anything? Now, suppose that, instead of running away, you had gone looking for a good solid stick, like a club, and carried it with you, so that every time the dog attacked you, you whacked it, just once, really hard across the snout. What do you think would happen then? I'll tell you what would happen: that dog would soon stop attacking you, because it would learn, very quickly, that attacking you earned it a sore snout every time. Dogs can be stupid, just like people, but unlike a lot of people, they do learn lessons.

"So here is what we are going to do, you and I. We are going to teach you to how fight against big dogs. We are going to see to it that no matter who attacks you in the future, he'll go running off with a bleeding snout and his tail between his legs. You wait and see; it won't take long. But, first, we have to ask your grandfather the King to permit us to work together. I am his personal champion, after all, so I can't really teach you unless he approves. Shall we go and find him?"

From that day forward a great part of Uther's life, and perhaps the most important part, was spent in the company of Garreth Whistler, who taught the boy not only how to fight, but also how to live his life, first and foremost as the grandson of King Ullic, but then as a future warrior, approaching the world with decency, honour and a sense of responsibility for himself and his own actions.

King Ullic, seeing the advantage to be gained from the bond between his champion and his young grandson, soon appointed Garreth to be responsible for Uther's overall moral and military development, transforming him from teacher and trainer to body-guard and mentor.

With Garreth's help, by the time Uther turned eight, he had earned the opportunity to begin a formal cavalry-training program during the summer months he spent each year in Camulod with his cousin Cay, starting out at the very beginning as a stableboy and groom. And so when Uther's burning desire to become a Camulo-dian trooper overcame all else in the boy's awareness, Garreth Whistler decided, with a strong degree of reluctance, that, as an extension of his duties, he too should learn the elements of horse-manship and cavalry warfare in order to maintain his authority over his young charge. To his surprise, however, he discovered that the discipline of horsemanship brought him new and demanding chal-lenges and a fierce enjoyment the like of which he had never known. Consequently, he threw himself into it with more enthusiasm than anything he had ever undertaken before, so that in less than half the time normally required to train a trooper, Garreth Whistler had sur-passed his training mates and gained the right to seek promotion.

He held back from that, however, because he was a Cambrian warrior first and foremost, and he knew he could never be a Camulodian. Garreth Whistler knew exactly where his loyalties lay.

Uther, unfortunately, did not. But then, Garreth was twenty-two when he first learned to ride a cavalry horse, whereas Uther, achieving the same feat, was barely nine, his entire world filled to the exclusion of all else with the pressing need to learn and to master skills that intrigued and excited him. Uther had no consciousness of arcane things like loyalties.

Uther lived—or so he had always implicitly believed—in the best of all possible worlds. Ever since he had been five years old and able to think for himself, he had lived in parallel states of euphoria. Each year he would be shipped off from his home in Tir Manha to spend the late autumn, winter and early spring months with his maternal grandparents in Camulod, along with his first cousin, Caius Merlyn Britannicus. Then, in the full flush of late springtime, when the Cambrian mountains were finally free of snow and the rugged countryside around his parents' home was decked in its brightest, most promising greenery, Cay would accompany him back to Tir Manha to spend the remainder of the spring, the seemingly endless summer and the early autumn months in the Cambrian mountains among Uther's father's folk. Over the space of three long boyhood years, this was how his life had been lived, and as far as Uther and Cay were concerned, so it would continue forever.

To Uther's mind, each of the two places had its own delights. Camulod, in his eyes, was more of a temple than a fortress, a place dedicated to the military virtues defined and epitomized by men like his uncle, Picus Britannicus, the Legate Commander of the Forces of Camulod, and the heroic officers and troopers who served in his command. It was a light-filled world of superb horses, fine armour and disciplined, military training—a paradise for a boy like Uther. There everything existed in a carefully prescribed manner and for a set, clearly defined purpose. Even the buildings, beginning with the magnificent Villa Britannicus, contributed to the nobility of the place. They were spacious, elegant and luxurious, with central heating and sophisticated bathing facilities. Each time Uther went to

Camulod, he embraced it with a delight that was sustained by the excitement of the place until the very day he departed. And each time he left, he marvelled again at the paradox that governed his leaving, his grief offset by the gut-level excitement he felt to be escaping its stringent disciplines and returning to the freedom of a carefree boy's life in his father's home in Cambria, with ghostly stories at night around the fire and wild, unsupervised adventures among the mountains and forests where his father's people lived.

Camulod and Cambria were both home to the boy, and he was equally welcome in each of them, but he had always been aware of the significant differences between the two places, for they were poles apart in almost everything, including the way the people dressed. Each time he made the transition from one place to the other, he would find it jarring for the first few days. He wondered, from time to time, if Cay felt the same way, but he had never discussed it with his cousin, feeling, somehow, that by speaking of it he would be demeaning himself in some strange fashion. Every time that thought popped into his mind, he ignored it until it went away. But it persisted, and it always made him feel guilty and somehow disloyal. Cambria suffered, in many ways, by comparison with Camulod, and Uther was afraid that if he once gave in to the folly of examining the differences too closely, they would overwhelm him.

Strangely enough, however, all the differences that concerned him were physical. He had never believed that the actual *people* of Camulod and Cambria were different from each other in any major respect until he heard some of his Cambrian elders, clearly disgruntled, muttering darkly about "them *others*, in that damned Camulod place . . ." and he came to wonder how and why some people seemed to delight in making an insult of the word.

He asked Garreth about it one day. The King's Champion looked up from the sword he was sharpening and stood thinking for a long moment before nodding his head and returning to his task. Watching the big man and thinking that he was going to say nothing more, Uther rephrased his question, offering it this time as a comment rather than a direct inquiry. Garreth, however, had merely been considering how to answer, and now he nodded towards a high-legged stool, indicating that Uther should perch on it. When the boy was seated, Garreth inspected the sword blade closely, then laid it carefully on the bench at which he had been standing, and he pulled another stool over close to Uther.

He had been expecting this kind of question for some time now, he told the boy, surprising him greatly.

"*Otherness* . . ." Garreth began. "Well, people like to be sur-rounded with things they know." They were most comfortable, he explained, with familiar situations, and they felt best when they were dealing with people and circumstances they knew and understood from past experience. So anything unknown . . . anything unfamiliar was unwelcome and untrusted. Strangers to any group were always regarded initially with fear, suspicion and hostility. Even among ani-mals, a single, differently coloured whelp among an entire litter would be singled out by its litter mates and killed. People who were noticeably different from their neighbours usually suffered because of it. It might be the occupants of a single house or it might be a gang of boys or even an entire clan, and occasionally it might expand to include an entire people, like Cambrians as opposed to Ersemen or Caledonians. And then the result would be war.

In most instances, though, Garreth said, things never got quite so serious. Small numbers brought small outcomes. It might take time to resolve those differences and settle all the fears attached to them, but usually the differences came to be first accepted, then ignored and then forgotten altogether.

After that conversation, thinking about what Garreth had said, Uther began to see things in a different light, and he did not like what he saw. He found his memory teeming, all at once, with remembered insults—freely offered by unsmiling men—that he had absorbed and ignored at various times over the previous few years, failing to recognize the barbs for what they were. And all of them, he saw quite suddenly, had had to do with Camulod and with his yearly journeys there to visit his mother's childhood home and live among her people. Each time he returned from Camulod, and for a period each year before he left Cambria to go there, he had been forced to swallow and ignore more than a few sneering comments and cruel jibes that cast slurs upon himself and upon his mother's people.

That recognition hit him hard and unexpectedly, and it left him with absolutely no understanding of how he had incurred such ill feelings. He had never knowingly done anything that would give offence to any grown-up person, and he could not see how his annual stay in Camulod could be harmful to anyone. But the truth was that the men of Cambria, and most particularly the older men, strongly disapproved of the time Uther Pendragon spent in Camulod. And, naturally, that gave rise to the question of why this should be so . . . a question that Uther, a small boy, was unqualified to answer.

With a few more years behind him, however, Uther became utterly convinced that the Cambrians' scorn of Camulod and all things Camulodian was built upon envy and plain jealousy. In terms of all the finer things of life, Camulod had everything that Cambria lacked. As he grew older and used more and more of the facilities that Camulod had to offer, Uther came to appreciate his annual half-year there more and more, and to look forward to his return to his own home less and less. Each year, he was more and more hard-pressed to guard his tongue every time some smug clansman cast a slur upon his absence, or his friends, or where he spent his time away from Cambria. These slurs were usually couched in the kind of question that asked, "What have they got there that we don't have?" and, "Why would you want to waste so much time with them?"

In response, Uther would have given anything to be able to shout out the list of truths that would answer such smug questions: that Camulod had baths and hot water and steam, and that the people there looked clean, were clean and smelled clean, so that he didn't have to hold his breath when he first met them in order to give his stomach time to settle at their stench; that Camulod had large and spacious buildings and houses filled with clean, warm air, centrally supplied by furnaces that burned all year long; that the cattle in Camulod were kept in barns, in stalls and stables, and did not live in the houses with their human owners; and that Camulod had smart, uniformly armoured soldiers—disciplined garrison troops and cavalry, mounted troopers trained to work and fight together as invincible military units.

None of these things did he ever say to any of his father's people, but all of them remained in his mind every day while he was at home in Tir Manha, because he pined for Camulod, with its baths and horses and troopers, its rolling grasslands and lush forests, and perhaps most of all for its carefree laughter and light-hearted camaraderie, so dyed-in-the-wool different from the scowling dourness that was normal among the dark-skinned people of his own mountainous homeland. He pined for those things, and as he grew older month by month, he writhed with guilt because of that, but he kept the guilt well hidden, and not even Garreth Whistler suspected its existence.

One day, when he had been feeling particularly disgusted with himself for what he had come to perceive as chronic and shameful disloyalty to all that was his own, Uther asked Garreth Whistler to tell him what he had been thinking of on that first day years earlier when he had decided to look out for the small boy he had found in the cattle byre.

Garreth's tuneless whistle died immediately, and he stopped what he was doing. Caught off guard by the sudden, unexpected question, he gazed speculatively at his young charge.

"What's making you itchy, then? You've never asked me that before." Uther shrugged but made no attempt to respond, and Whistler's eyes narrowed. "Are you feeling all right? You look . . . different. Are you coming down with something?"

Uther shook his head. "I don't think so. I feel the same as I always do. What did you think that day?"

"How d'you expect me to remember that after all this time? Can you remember what you were thinking on any particular day that long ago?"

"Yes, I remember thinking that you would laugh at me when I saw you coming into the byre."

"Do you, then?" Garreth's pause was less than a heartbeat in length. "Well, you were wrong, weren't you? I didn't laugh at you."

"No, you didn't. But what did you think?"

Garreth had been scaling rust from an iron breastplate that someone had unearthed from a patch of ground outside the walls, close by the main gateway to Tir Manha. It was the front half of a Roman cuirass and it had been buried for a long time, so that Garreth was not sure he could salvage it. But well-made iron armour was invaluable, and so he was trying, rubbing the pitted, scaling metal industriously with an abrasive mixture of sand, wood ash and tallow. Now he placed his tools carefully on the ground beside him and wiped his tallow-slick fingers on a rag tucked into his belt.

"Well, let me think . . . I saw another small boy crying close by here last week some time. Are you sure you wouldn't like me to try to recall what I thought then, too? I've seen a lot of small boys crying over the years."

Uther nodded, his face serious. "I believe you. But what did you think of me that day?"

"Well, it might be easier if I start slowly, remembering what I saw before I get to what I might have thought." He paused, frowning deeply and staring into nothingness, and Uther waited, intent on his answer. "I think . . . I think I remember being absolutely astounded to see a small, grubby boy with a squished-up, dirty face encrusted with snot and large, bleeding cuts and bruises on his skinny little shins. I looked at him, and now I remember thinking, *What an ugly, ill-featured, misshapen little brat!* And that was but my first thought . . . Are you sure you want to hear more?"

Finally Uther broke into a grin. "No," he said, "I want to hear no more of that rubbish."

"Very well, then." Garreth Whistler nodded his head with finality. "You tell me why you want to know, and I'll tell you."

Uther looked away, unwilling to meet Garreth's eyes. "I . . . I don't really know why I want to know."

"No, of course you don't . . . not any more than you know why you would expect me to believe such an obvious lie. Well, when you do know, come back, and I'll think about telling you."

The boy threw up his hands. "Very well, I'll tell you." He paused to collect his thoughts. "I was . . . I was feeling lonely, I suppose, and sorry for myself. I've been feeling that way quite a lot recently. And

I suppose, too, that made me think of that day you found me, which had been among the very worst days of my life until then. I could remember how I felt, and I could guess how I must have looked to you, the King's Champion, and so I wondered what you could possibly have thought to make you behave towards me as you did."

Garreth Whistler shrugged his broad shoulders, then picked up the rusty breastplate again, although he made no move to start work on it. "Have you considered the obvious answer to that?" he asked. "I was the King's Champion, as you say, and you were the King's small grandson. Perhaps I saw immediately that I could do myself some good in my patron's eyes by doing some small good for you."

"No," Uther replied. "I don't believe that. Do you want to know what I think? I think you simply chose to help me because you wanted to. What I am curious about is why you would have wanted to."

Garreth dropped the cuirass to the ground again and stood up quickly, inhaling deeply through his nostrils and placing his hands on his hips as he gazed off, head high, into the distance, his broad back to Uther. The boy said nothing, having learned long since to wait until Garreth was prepared to end a silence on his own, and eventually the tall, golden warrior turned back to face him.

"Do you recall my telling you that I am an Outlander?"

"Aye."

"And did I mention that I was orphaned twice, once at my birth and then again when my adopted father, Dunvallo, died?"

"Aye, you did."

"Well, I was eight, not quite nine, when that happened, and I was left to fend for myself. I did it successfully, too. But I know now that I could not have done it without the goodwill of the villagers. It was they who sustained me and kept me fed . . .

"Not all the villagers were supportive of me, though, and their sons were definitely not. I was an Outlander, and I looked different from anyone else, and that meant I was fair game for anyone who cared to hunt me. And they hunted me, Uther. Not a day went by without my being thrashed by someone, and usually it was a group of someones. But that is where, and how, I first learned to fight. I was fortunate in being tall and strong for my age, but that only brought me into conflict with bigger boys, who would not have bothered with me had they not been provoked by my size, my height. And then I was befriended by a man who saw something in me that no one else had seen. He took me into his household and placed me under his own protection, and my days of being persecuted were at an end. Can you guess who he was?"

"My father, Uric?"

Garreth smiled. "No, for he himself was barely beyond boyhood then. It was your grandfather, King Ullic, and I have been grateful to him ever since." His smile died away. "Thanks to his good regard, I was able to train properly and become the warrior I am today, and my duty is total loyalty to the king. But I never forgot how it felt to be as unloved as I felt before your grandfather found me. I never forgot the misery of being hated and abused for no good reason. I never forgot the pain of being rejected or the other pain, far worse, of being scorned and ridiculed. So when I saw you there that day, hiding in the byre, it seemed but natural to do the things I did and to offer you some comfort and understanding, because believe me, Uther, I knew exactly what you were feeling and thinking. So how can you ever repay me for such kindness? Well, you'll know when the opportunity comes along, and when it does, you won't have to tell me what you did, because I will know. Now, you tell me . . . why have you been feeling so low for the past week?"

Uther shook his head. He wanted to confess his feelings to Garreth about Camulod and Cambria and his disloyalty, but the time was not right, not yet, and so he shrugged away from any satisfying explanation and felt yet more guilt for knowing that Garreth knew he was being evasive.

THREE

Nemo did not often feel the need for solitude, for she never thought very deeply about anything. She had never felt a need to avoid the company of others in order to debate within herself on anything, and she had no training of any kind in structured logic or formal analysis.

On those very few occasions when she did have things to think about, however, Nemo had discovered a place where she could go to be alone and undisturbed. She thought of it as the "Place of the Bows," a name given to it by her alone and known to no one else. It bothered her not at all that it was one of the most sacred places in all of Pendragon Cambria, access to it forbidden to all but the King and the Druids. She had no interest in harming or changing or defacing anything there, no interest in the normal purposes for which the place was used and no interest in making anyone aware that she might venture there from time to time. The Place of the Bows was Nemo's private spot, and she worked hard to ensure than no one ever saw her there or saw her approaching or leaving the area.

It had originally been a grove of three ancient oak trees, the only trio of such trees in a region that was generally too rocky to support anything other than hawthorns, scrub willows and stunted birch, which was why it was a hallowed spot, sacred to the Druids. But one of the venerable trees had been sundered by lightning ages earlier, and little remained of it now but a blackened, shrunken stump. A second tree had died much later of natural but undetermined causes, and most of that one remained in place, its mighty branches dried and cracked, stripped of all traces of bark and weathered by long, withering decades of rain and snow, frost and blistering sunshine. Only the third of the trio remained intact and alive, and its upper branches were choked with clumps of mistletoe so thick and luxuriant that they could conceal all signs of human presence were anyone to crouch up there among them. Nemo frequently did exactly that, having found a high crotch among the clumps where she could rest unseen and in great comfort, reclining on a couch of springy, strongly anchored mistletoe and looking down on the neighbouring area. And it was there that King Ullic's bowmen practised daily, all day long, firing their long, carefully fletched arrows at the targets they had made from bundles of tightly packed straw, bound together with leather thongs and draped with cloth coverings marked in concentric rings.

Between this practice area and the tree from which Nemo watched them, a stand of bushy young evergreens served as an extra screen, separating the practice area from the sacred grove. The saplings, she had discovered, were yew trees, and they were tended jealously by the Druids, watched over and carefully nurtured, trimmed and pruned. Each one of these young trees would some day grow to reach the size at which its limbs could be cut, then individually dried, shaped and carved to form one of the mighty, man-high bows of which King Ullic's people were so proud. Pendragon longbows, they called them, and never had the world seen such weapons. An arrow fired from one of those bows, even at a distance of two hundred paces, could pierce a tree—or an armoured man—with ease, and transfix either, protruding front and rear. Nemo knew this was true; perched high up in her oak tree, she had seen the evidence with her own eyes.

Uther loved the Pendragon longbow; while he was in Cambria he spent hours each day practising with the huge weapon, and Nemo spent those same hours watching him. Nemo was not interested in the bows, however. She would rather have spent her time among the men and the horses of Camulod, the cavalry, as she had heard Uther name them. Those she could have watched all day and all night, too, for everything about them excited her: the size and sheer brute strength of the great animals and the beautiful leather-and-metal harness that they wore; the height and bearing of the riders; the splendour of the weapons they carried; and even the glittering armour they wore, burnished and blazing, blinding in the sunlight and twinkling with reflections in the light of the moon. But wherever Uther Pendragon went, Nemo followed. Uther was her single, all-consuming interest. She thought of him all the time, believing, ever since she had first met him, that he was the biggest part of her destiny—the only person who had ever looked beyond her startling ugliness and seen a person worth tolerating hiding underneath.

Jonet the Toad, they had called her in the days before she met Uther, and she had answered to the name, believing it to be apt and no more than she deserved. Her raw, unleavened ugliness had always weighed upon her like a yoke carved from stone, blighting her with the guilt of her appearance. She had always been aware of it, always felt its presence, always acknowledged her duty to grovel to the world because of it.

One of the very first truths that she had been conscious of was that she was different, in some unknown but unpleasant way, from other children. Her earliest lessons, overwhelmingly repeated and reinforced, informed her that she was an unlovely and unlovable creature, unacceptable, unfit and undesirable. It never crossed her mind that those surrounding her in her first days were all male, since she had no mother and no female intimates, or that they were much older than she was. It never occurred to her to doubt them, or to question their views of her, or to challenge their dictates. They were her judges, her accusers and her condemners, and that was made obvious by the way they acted and by the fact that no one ever contradicted anything they said or did. Many of them were her half-brothers and many more were cousins of varying degrees of consanguinity, but all of them were united from the first in decrying and condemning her unique unloveliness.

It had been hammered home to her ever since she was old enough to walk and listen and understand that her appearance and her looks were offensive. The girls of her own age were all prettier than she, even the plainest of them, and they all liked to make themselves feel prettier by laughing and jeering at her lack of anything that might be called attractive.

So one of the first things she ever learned was that she must never cry, because whenever she did, whenever she allowed her tears to flow and to be seen, it brought her more grief and more trouble. She might be beaten or more cruelly used, or her tormentors might laugh at her and throw things at her, or they might take away from her whatever she was holding or clutching at the time. Once they had killed a wounded crow that she had found and nursed almost back to health. When they saw how deeply she grieved for the dead bird, they laughed and took note and waited for her to betray a fondness or a liking for some other creature, and then they killed that, too—a rabbit she had raised from babyhood, and then a goat she had been set to guard one summer's afternoon.

The boys, some of them her brothers, had beaten and abused her that day, tying her up and jeering at her as they killed the goat out of sheer, pleasurable malice, and after it was all over and they had all run away, the uncle who had set Jonet to the task beat her with a heavy stick for having lost his goat. It was plainly her fault the goat was dead, and everyone agreed. No point in seeking to place blame on any of the boys; no one expected anything better of them. But Jonet the Toad was neither boy nor girl. Jonet was simply there, available and unsightly, blameworthy by her very appearance.

After that day, Jonet had refused to be a victim any longer. Thereafter she had shown no kindness to anyone, shown no concern for any creature, nor had she ever permitted herself to weep openly again. By the time she was seven, she had not shed a tear for anyone to see for almost two whole years.

Of course, she wept sometimes, but only when she was alone. At such times, although she herself could not have said why the tears flowed from her, she wept for herself and for the creatures for whom she dared show no affection. She wept, unknowingly, out of loneliness and heartache, out of friendlessness and despair, and out of a cruel awareness of her own unsightliness and ugliness, but always she wept in the privacy of some deep nook she had created for herself, far from prying and unfriendly human eyes. She trusted no human being to deal with her without causing grief or pain.

Even her father had called her a foul toad and kicked her away from him one day when she had been beaten by one of her brothers and had vomited from a punch to her gut, fouling the front of her rough smock. So for a long time after that, Jonet had thought of herself as a real toad, a cold and slimy nasty thing beloved by no one, and she had examined herself carefully for similarities to the creature she believed she resembled.

She took note that her whole body was stocky and thick-set. Her limbs were short and burly, her legs bowed and muscular, and her arms, hands and fingers as stubby, thick and strong as any boy's. Her hair, too, was thick and coarse, wiry and ungovernable even when it was clean, which it seldom was. In fact, her body was compact and strong and dense with muscle, but she would have found no pleasure in those attributes, even had she been aware of them or paused to consider them. Compactness and strength were not what she required of her body, and those elements she longed for and would have given anything to have—long legs and silky hair, blue eyes and white, even teeth—were simply not hers. Jonet was a toad.

And then one day she heard someone, some old woman in the village, say that toads had wondrously beautiful, liquid brown eyes—the most beautiful eyes in all the world of animals, and she grew excited with the hope that she might own something, one physical attribute, that others might admire and envy. But of course, she had to find some way of seeing her eyes for herself.

Jonet had never seen a mirror, but she knew that such things existed, and that you could see your entire face in one of them. In a village as poor as hers, however, no one was wealthy enough to own one. And even had there been several, the very thought of how people would ridicule and torture her if they even suspected her of wishing to look at her own face was enough to frighten her into immobility. And so she learned to be content to close her eyes and simply dream that she possessed the most beautiful eyes in the world.

Leir the Druid, the man who had fathered her, was one of the most powerful members of the Druid confraternity in southern

Cambria, which meant that he spent much of his life conferring with his priestly colleagues, travelling between and among the various communities for which he held a shared responsibility. While doing that, of course, he spent little time in his own home—a fact that provided his daughter with one of the few pleasures in her bleak life.

One day he returned home from one of his long journeys, however, accompanied by a new wife, and Jonet chose to disappear for a while, as she often did, in the hope that her father's travels had merely been interrupted by this marriage and that he might still depart again, with or without his bride.

Even at the age of nine, Jonet was well aware that Leir's wives were generally short-lived. Her own mother, whose name had been Naomi, had apparently lasted little more than two years, dying quite suddenly shortly after Jonet was born and leaving the baby to be cared for by an adolescent servant girl called Tamara. Barely two years after that, Tamara herself—whom Leir had taken to wife within months of Naomi's death, and who would be the closest thing to a mother the infant girl ever knew—also died in childbirth, sacrificing her own life to give life to Jonet's loathsome half-brother Carthac. Leir, Jonet knew from the village gossip she had listened to so avidly, had not even bothered to visit Tamara during the final months of her pregnancy, and it was common knowledge that he had shown no grief at all when she died.

Since then, Leir had taken five more wives, and all of the five were dead, as were the three who had preceded them. There had been a first wife, before Jonet's mother, but Jonet had never known her name. Then had come Naomi, then Tamara, then the following five, which made the new wife number nine. Three of those latter five had borne children to the Druid, and one of those three had died in childbirth. The other two had simply died, somehow, once Leir had begun to tire of them. Of the remaining two, who had not borne children, one had died of a broken neck after falling from a low wall on a dark night, and the other by drowning in a flooded stream bed during a sudden mountain storm. Jonet could not even recall their names. She had neither known nor cared for any of them. She believed implicitly, though, that her father, the Druid, had killed all of them.

He was a frightening man, Leir the Druid, with empty, loveless, even lifeless eyes. Jonet would watch him closely as he sat alone, staring into the distance, even in a tiny, lightless room, muttering to himself in strange and meaningless words. At such times, she knew, he was oblivious to who and where he was. And even though she had no proof that such a thing was true, she knew beyond doubt that he would kill anyone who disturbed him then. He would snuff out their lives without remorse and without pity, simply for having brought themselves to his attention when he wished to be alone. That, she was convinced, was what had happened to his wives.

Of course, Jonet knew, too, that no one would ever dream of voicing aloud any thought that Leir might be a murderer. He was far too powerful for anyone to take the risk of thus offending him. Jonet seldom thought about such things, but she had not the slightest doubt that he would kill her, too, if she were ever foolish enough to bring herself again to his attention.

So, on that day of the advent of the ninth wife, Jonet moved quickly away from her home into the forest before she could be noticed. She went almost without forethought, unaware that day that she would never return to her home village. With her she carried, as she always did, her small travelling pack containing the fine sharp knife she had stolen the year before from a neighbour's house, together with a length of strong, stout twine she had pilfered months earlier from a visiting peddler and three barbed iron fish hooks she had found stuck into the clothing of a long-drowned man whose corpse had washed up on the bank of the river close to the southern end of the village when Jonet was eight and long since inured to the sight of violent death. The fish hooks had been rusted, but she had known their usefulness and had salvaged them carefully from where they had been securely fastened into the left foreshoulder of the dead man's tunic. She had then cleaned them patiently and carefully, rubbing them delicately with a fragment of a broken, fine-toothed file that she had found outside their local smithy's two years before.

Once safely away from the Druid's house that day, she walked less quickly, but still covered the ground at a good pace, trying not to think of the Druid or what his return entailed, forcing herself to dwell on enjoying the peaceful warmth of the day and listening to the singing of the birds until she gauged that she had walked ten miles, perhaps more. She was truly beginning to believe herself alone and safe when she heard and instantly recognized the discordant, squabbling voices of the boys who goaded her constantly, and so she ran from the path to hide from them, cursing her own stupidity. She had thought herself far enough from home to be safe from her tormentors, but they were ranging as far afield as she was this day, and the realization of that made her think about how everything in her life was tied to the starting point that was the village into which she had been born. Wherever she could go, anyone else from the village could go too—if she could travel as far as she had this day in the space of a single forenoon, why should she be surprised to find the village boys in the same place? The boys reached her hiding place, though they did not discover her, and there they settled down to rest and while away the afternoon, playing their noisy games and boasting and squabbling among themselves while Jonet crouched above them, high in a huge old elm tree.

By the time the boys eventually left, evening was approaching rapidly, dusky blue shadows were beginning to gather among the trees, and Jonet had made several important discoveries. The first of those was that it was already too late for her to return home that day, unless she wanted to run and catch up with the boys from whom she had been hiding all afternoon. The second was that it was almost too late for her to find a suitable stream and a spot where she could fish for something to eat that night. But the third discovery was momentous, and it involved the new awareness that if she failed to return home she would be able to start the next day's journey from wherever she had spent the night—far, far ahead of anyone else starting out that morning from her village. Her heart swelled and pounded with excitement as she made the next mental step towards acknowledgment that if she were to do the same the following day and the day following that, she would soon be so far from her village that no one, not even the Druid, would be able to find her.

Jonet travelled for several days—she soon lost count—and gradually, as she put more and more distance between her and the village, she became suffused with an easy, unaccustomed sense of well-being. Then one day while she was creeping through deep woods to check a snare she had set for rabbits, she came face to face with herself in a woodland pool.

Jonet had never thought to see herself so perfectly reflected anywhere, but the stark, bare, incontrovertible reality of what she saw struck her to the very soul, so that she could say or do nothing other than stare, immobilized and helpless, at her own face, noting and memorizing every flaw and imperfection.

Her eyes were small, and they were dull, lacking any spark or twinkle of originality or verve, and even she could see that they were set too close together on either side of the bridge of her nose. She bent her face closer to the pool, searching for a demarcation line between the blackness of her eyes' centres and the muddy brown darkness of their irises, but the two areas blended together so that each eye seemed to be no more than a deep, black hole set in a muddy, brownish expanse of white. Above the eyes, her brows grew together in a thick, heavy bar, with no visible line of separation. Her entire face seemed to hang slack and heavy, and her full lips appeared to dangle pendulously as she leaned forward on stiffened arms, staring down at herself.

Slowly, as she hung there looking at herself, a great ball of grief and sorrow welled up inside her, weighty and palpable as a physical growth, threatening to cut off her breath. And then she was on her feet, running headlong through the thick woodland, completely blinded by tears so that she ran with her eyes closed, her face whipped and lacerated by twigs as she increased her speed, miraculously avoiding trees and boulders until she reached the precipitous edge of a deep, rain-scoured ditch and plunged out and down, head first, stunning herself and driving every vestige of wind from her lungs with the jarring impact of her fall.

For some time after that, she was utterly confused, fluttering between consciousness and oblivion. She had landed face down, and the pain in her chest, born of the inability to breathe, was an agony the like of which she had never known. After a time her breathing began to return to normal, so that she was able to release the cross-grip of her arms on her own chest and to straighten her back and shoulders without increasing the pain that racked her. All of those ills were physical, however, and she could cope with and adjust to them. What caused her real concern and confusion was what seemed to be happening outside and beyond the cocoon of sudden, crippling pain that had enveloped her. There she saw, through eyes swimming with outraged tears, a boy looming over her, a strange face intent with . . . what? Something. Anger?

When next she opened her eyes, briefly, the face was gone and she was apparently alone, squirming in solitary agony. But then someone turned her over, and she felt strange hands—large, male hands—on her legs, pulling them straight and spreading them. She kicked out wildly, spitting and screaming because she knew what that portended, having seen it happen many times to others. But her flailing kicks were smothered effortlessly by stronger arms. And then there was another pair of arms about her shoulders, crushing her and pinning her arms to her sides as someone, some third person, knelt over her. Cold water splashed against her face and a cool, moist cloth wiped her eyelids free of whatever had been blinding them so that she could see.

For a moment she lay motionless, blinking up at the three shapes that towered above her. Three men—no, two men and a boy, all kneeling over her. The man behind her held her clutched against his lower body, her shoulders pressed against his thighs, her neck bent forward by the push of his chest against the back of her head. The man by her feet sat back on his legs, holding her more gently now, and he was smiling. Between these two, the boy knelt at her left side, holding the cloth with which he had wiped her face. All three were staring at her, but she had no thought of reading their expressions. Instead she began to fight again, kicking out strongly with more aim than before and squirming like one possessed to escape.

She almost succeeded, too, for the savagery of her attempt caught them unawares just as they had begun to relax, thinking her calmed down. The man holding her legs lost his grip on them and Jonet swung her right foot strongly upwards, aiming at his mouth, hoping to kick his teeth out. Briefly she saw blood on her own leg, much blood, and then the man reacted, blocking her scything kick with his forearm and clamping his great hand on her leg again, this time above the knee, digging deep and agonizingly with hard fingers so that her leg straightened involuntarily. As it did so, he caught her with his other hand, this time seizing her by the ankle and forcing her leg back down until he held it flat against the ground. Raging, she tried to kick out at him with her other leg, her left, but for some reason she could not make it move at all, and a sudden fear welled up in her. The man above her released the grip of his right hand above her knee and grasped her other ankle effortlessly, pulling it down and out until he held her still. She felt it move, but otherwise felt nothing.

"Talk to her," the man grunted, forcing the words out between gritted teeth.

"Listen to me!" It was the boy who spoke, the urgency of his tone cutting through the rage in her so that her eyes went without volition to meet his gaze. His face was tight with strain.

"Stop fighting us. We don't want to hurt you. You need help."

Jonet spat at him, her saliva spraying up and then falling back onto her face. The boy gazed back at her, looking right into her eyes and shaking his head.

"Spit all you want," he said then, "but listen to me. I don't know you. I don't know your name, and I don't care what it is, but we don't want to harm you. You've hurt yourself badly enough. I saw you running, just before you fell, and then you ran right off the edge of the ditch there, and fell down here. You landed on a fallen tree . . . smashed your head and gashed your leg on a broken branch. I tried to help you, but when I saw the depth of the hole in your leg and how much blood you were losing, I ran to fetch Garreth, and Glenn came back with us. Garreth will stop the bleeding and bind your wound, if you'll let him, but you have to stop fighting. Nobody's going to hurt you. I am King Ullic's grandson, Uther

Pendragon, and Garreth is Garreth Whistler, the King's Champion. I swear you will not be harmed. But that wound is bad. You could die of it. Look at it. *Look at it!*"

The arms holding her about the chest relaxed so that she could move, and she looked down to where the boy was pointing. Both her legs were drenched in blood, but it was the left one, the one she had been unable to move, that looked so gory. There was a great hole torn high up on her thigh, and deep inside it she could see the gleam of pinkish white bone, but below the point where the bone was visible, bright red blood welled profusely. The sight shook her from head to foot, and every vestige of fight went out of her. The man behind her caught her as she sagged back against him, and then her head began to spin and she lost consciousness, the last thing in her awareness being the boy's face frowning down at her, his huge eyes bright and troubled.

For a time after that, Jonet seemed to hover between sleep and wakefulness, and sometimes she dreamed long dreams. Amid all of that, she knew she was in a hut, and in a bed, sheltered from the weather, which she also knew was foul, because every time she awoke she could hear the howling of the wind and the incessant pounding of driving, torrential rain. Two men were looking after her, one or the other of them always present when she woke up. The larger of the two men, she learned, was the one named Garreth . . . Garreth Whistler. The other man, smaller and quieter, was called Glenn. Neither of them spoke much to her, but neither of them showed her any cruelty, either. Whichever one of them was there when she awoke—and sometimes they had to waken her solely for this purpose—would change her bandages, removing the soiled dressing and setting it aside for later disposal, then washing her wounded leg in hot, stinging water before poulticing the wound anew and binding the whole in fresh, clean dressings.

In time, she seemed to sleep less often and for shorter periods, and in that same time the frightful hole in her thigh, its edges sewn together somehow by Garreth Whistler, scabbed over and began to heal, so that eventually the pain of it was replaced by an incessant itch that Garreth told her was a sure sign of healing.

She could not have said how long she remained there in that bed, in that small hut, but she knew that the boy did not come back to see her again. For a very long time she said nothing, telling herself she didn't care whether he ever came or not, but as time went by and he continued to stay away, she found herself growing angry again, and beginning to believe that he was just like all the other males in her life, hard and cold and uncaring. But then Garreth and Glenn were men, and they too had once been boys. And they had done nothing to hurt her or torment her. They did not say much to her, but they spent all their time looking after her.

And then one morning Garreth came early and proceeded to remove her bandages as usual, but when the poulticed dressing peeled away this time, it took the thick, black, shrunken mass of the scab with it, leaving her thigh clean and new-looking, the length and width of the newly healed wound showing as a bright, broad patch of shiny skin.

Garreth sat back and smiled at her. "There you are, good as ever. Now all you have to do is learn to walk again, and you'll be free of this place."

Jonet scowled at him, not because she was angry but because her face knew no other expression. "Learn to walk again? That's daft. I can walk."

His grin didn't falter. "*I* know you can. And *you* know you can. But your *legs* don't know. They're weak now, no strength in them, because you've been in bed for more than a month, and in all that time you haven't used them. You don't believe me? Very well, let's see."

He stood up and walked away from the bed, turning back to face her when he had gone three paces. Then he held out his hands to her.

"Come then, Nemo, walk to me."

"What?"

His head tilted to one side, unsure of what she meant.

"What did you call me? You called me something."

"Oh, Nemo." He laughed. "It's a Roman name, and it means 'No One,' or 'No Name.' We didn't know your name and we needed to call you something, so Nemo seemed right. Don't you like it?"

She swung her legs clear of the bed and sat there motionless, facing him, saying nothing.

"Nemo it is, then. Come on, stand up and walk to me. It's not far, see, and I'll hold out my hands. Don't be afraid. If you fall, I'll catch you."

Still she made no move.

"Come on, what are you waiting for? You can't be afraid, because I know you aren't afraid of anything. How old are you, ten or twelve? Big, strong legs. Come on, up you get, only three steps to me."

Jonet stood up—and promptly sat down again when she felt the floor buckling beneath her feet. Thoroughly frightened by the sensation, which was unlike anything she had ever experienced, she sat there for a time, clutching the bedclothes tightly and staring down at the floor. It was of hard-packed earth, swept clean, and in all the time she stared at it, it didn't move. Finally she drew a deep breath and tried again, this time managing to remain erect for three or four heartbeats while the entire hut swayed about her. On her third attempt, she managed to remain standing, although her legs refused to move when she told them to. She had a brief, flashing vision of the way her wounded leg had refused to respond to her attempts to kick Garreth on their first meeting, and her belly heaved in panic. Her right foot left the floor and moved to complete her first step, and then her entire leg folded beneath her as it met the floor again, and she pitched forward face first.

Garreth caught her almost before she could begin to fall and picked her up easily, spinning with her to lay her back upon the bed.

"Now do you believe me? Don't worry, it won't last. We'll try a few more steps again later today, and then tomorrow morning and afternoon, and by the following day you should be moving about quite normally. Uther will be back by then, too. He'll be glad to see you well again."

"Who?"

"Who what?"

"Who will . . . be back?"

"Uther. You remember Uther. He's King Ullic's grandson."

"The boy."

"That's the one."

"Where is he?"

"He's in Camulod. Has been since the day after you fell. But now he's coming back. He's due home tomorrow or the day after that, depending on the weather. No one would want to ride in weather like this if he didn't have to, and Uther doesn't have to. So they may wait until the weather breaks and then come up when it's finer."

She lay silent for a few moments, digesting that before asking, "Camel . . . What was that place you said?"

"Camulod."

"Where is it?"

"It's where Uther's cousin Cay lives, and his grandparents on his mother's side. Uther spends much time there with his cousin, living with the Lord and Lady Varrus, and then the two boys come back here and spend an equal period here in Cambria with King Ullic, who is also Uther's grandfather, but on his father's side."

And listening to his lulling tones, exhausted from her exertions, she fell helplessly asleep.

When Jonet awoke, alone now, she lay wondering at all Garreth had told her. The boy had not been to see her, but it was not because he did not want to come. He had been far away since then with his grandparents on his mother's side. She frowned at that, wondering what it meant. She had never had a mother, so she did not know what a mother's side was, let alone a father's side . . . Her own father, even had she felt like asking him, could have provided her with little insight, she felt. He had never given her anything that she could remember, other than the two things that had led jointly to her being here in this hut: confirmation that she deserved the name by which they called her—the Toad—and a final incentive to escape, to run far from her miserable home in the silent, unformulated hope of finding a better life.

She was beginning to realize that these men would not hurt her, and she wondered whether she ought to tell them her real name, but one night she had a vivid and frightening dream in which the Druid, searching for her, found her by her name, which she had casually given to a stranger. So, for now at least, she would be Nemo, and her real name would remain unknown. She, on the other hand, knew the names of one boy and two grown men who had done nothing to cause her any hurt or pain, and one of those, the boy called Uther, would be coming back the following day or the day after that. She decided that she would not learn to walk properly again until the boy came back, because if she could walk before he came back, she would have to walk away.

Despite her wishes and her best resolve, however, she was thwarted simply because Garreth Whistler had been right. No one was keen to travel in the kind of foul weather that covered all of southern Britain at that time, and those fortunate enough to be able to postpone their travels did so. Among those was the party travelling from Camulod to Ullic's Cambria. They remained in the warmth and comfort of their home base for ten days before the weather broke, far longer than they had originally intended, and by the time they arrived in Ullic's territories, she had regained her full strength and moved out of Garreth's care, since she no longer had reason to stay. She did not stray far, however, for she had no desire to live alone in the woodland again, and since she had no intention of returning to her former home, the woodland would have been the only option available to her. Instead, filled with single-minded resolution, she set about making herself useful to the villagers, beginning with those who lived closest to Garreth's hut. These were the only people she had been able to observe—and she had watched them closely—during the final days of her recuperation. One of them, an old, bent woman, lived alone with no man to look after her, and Nemo had seen that Garreth treated the old woman with courtesy and kindness, carrying burdens for her and stopping to speak with her almost every time he passed her door.

On the first day of her new life, she approached the old woman and offered to work for her in return for a place to sleep. The old woman accepted her offer, but wanted to know her name, and Jonet, with barely a pause for thought, told her that her name was Nemo. The old woman then provided her with a pallet in one corner of her single-room dwelling, close by the fire. She was grateful, and even more so when the old woman spoke well of her to her neighbours. Within a matter of days, thanks to this kindness, she had managed to ingratiate herself with several other people, establishing that she was a hard and willing worker, providing real value for the pittance in food she consumed and the space she occupied at night. She was feeling better about herself, too, by that time, for the name Nemo had reminded her of her own mother's name, Naomi. She had never known her mother, but she liked the sound of the name, and it was close enough to Nemo to be remarkable to the girl, so that, in the quiet safety of her own thoughts, she began to call herself Naomi and to think of herself by that name—very tentatively at first, and then with increasing pleasure and confidence as she grew used to it. Naomi was a beautiful name, and she simply knew that no person with such a name could ever bear any resemblance to anyone known as Jonet the Toad.

Thus she was at hand, known to all the villagers as Nemo, when Uther Pendragon returned and came seeking Garreth Whistler, and she watched the boy, wide-eyed with surprise over how young he was. She had remembered him as being her own age or older, but in fact he was considerably younger than she was . . . almost as young as her disgusting half-brother Carthac, although bigger and far better-looking. Carthac had been damaged at birth, in the act of being born, and his entire skull was deformed, flattened on one side so that the features of his face were all askew. While she would freely admit that she herself was unsightly, there could be no question that Carthac's ugliness went beyond that: he was grotesque. Nine children out of ten would not have survived such a birthing, but Carthac seemed more cruelly strong and healthy because of the disadvantage with which he had to contend.

She sidled closer so she could see Uther more clearly. He waved a greeting of acknowledgment and recognition, smiling briefly at her before turning his attention back to his hero, Garreth, and she felt her face flush and prickle with a rush of blood that confused her sufficiently to make her hide herself again.

Nemo made her home in Tir Manha after that, and was accepted as a useful presence, willing to do the work that others thought unpleasant and tiresome. She was still, from time to time, an object of ridicule because of her appearance, but she was long accustomed to keeping her head down, and as time passed, these instances of cruelty and mockery grew less and less common. In any case, the only person whose opinion truly mattered to her was Uther, and his acceptance of her, even when it manifested itself as benign indifference, was like a balm to her soul. She was by now completely besotted and obsessed with him, and within the narrow confines of the world in which she lived and dreamed, she believed, without conscious thought, that Uther was just as aware of her.

Nemo was ever determined to be of service to Uther in return for the kindness he had shown to her. Sitting one day in her high perch in the Place of the Bows, she had heard Garreth telling King Ullic that one of the local boys, a hulking bully called Cross-Eyed Ivor, whose father was one of King Ullic's warriors and councillors, had taken it upon himself to make young Uther's life a misery since his return from Camulod, knowing his own father's rank would protect him from any grave consequences of his bullying. This Ivor, who was of an age with Nemo, almost two full years older than Uther and therefore much bigger, had gathered a large following of younger boys, most of whom were terrified of him and hoped that by toadying to him they might escape having his nastiness focused upon them.

Uther, seven at the time but big for his age, had ignored Ivor for as long as he could, according to Garreth's account of what had happened, but ignoring the lout had been the worst possible course of action. Uther had ended up with a bruised and bleeding leg.

Nemo was outraged to learn that Garreth had not immediately gone looking for the boy called Cross-Eyed Ivor and punished him. But it was not and could never be his place, Garreth said to King Ullic, to intervene physically in this affair between boys. That was something Uther must resolve alone and in public view. Garreth could not be seen to be involved, because he believed that any intervention by him, the King's Champion, would surely destroy any chance young Uther had of escaping from the older boy's tyranny through his own efforts. If Uther were to gain the respect of his peers in this, he could do it only by standing alone against the bully. And so, Garreth informed the King, he had advised Uther to cut the bully down to size by approaching him again directly and tackling him immediately when he, Uther, was ready to fight, instead of waiting for Ivor to come to him when Ivor was ready.

Nemo listened carefully as Garreth Whistler reported to his patron how he had spoken to Uther of honour and duty, of commitment and dedication, and of the urgency of knowing how to distinguish friends from enemies. He had talked to the boy, he said, about degrees of enmity and friendship, defining them clearly and using, in some instances, words that Nemo had never heard. A friend he defined as anyone who reacted benignly to a leader's presence, plans, actions, results and ultimate objectives. An enemy was anyone who did not. And, Garreth had insisted, the only way to deal with an implacable enemy was to convert him to a friend—or kill him, if that was the only way of gaining his compliance. Nemo took clear and careful note of that. He should do all in his power to endear himself to friends, Garreth had explained. And if he did it well enough, he would have no living enemies.

No sensible man ever likes or chooses to fight when there is no need, Garreth had told the boy, for fighting always entails the risk of serious injury and death. But once a man decides that he *must* fight, then his commitment should be total, and his attention to the outcome—his eventual victory—should be tightly focused upon that end alone. Any man who fought without that kind of dedication was a fool, Garreth said, and deserved to die.

A few days after she overheard that conversation, the seven-year-old Uther, this time armed with a heavy stick and accompanied only by his cousin Cay, once again went looking for the bully Cross-Eyed Ivor and found him in the market square, surrounded by his entire crew of sycophants. Wasting no time, Uther shouted a challenge at Ivor across the intervening space and then ran directly to the attack. Cay moved aside, interposing himself between Uther and the onlookers, keeping one eye on the fight and the other, more warily, on Ivor's cronies, lest any of them be tempted to take Ivor's side. His presence was unnecessary. Those who witnessed the fight reported that Uther's ferocity made him seem like a madman, heedless of danger. His face distorted with rage, he ignored the blows being directed at him, using his stick two-handed, as a club at times, to keep the larger boy beyond arm's reach. At other times he also used his stick as a lever, with which he eventually tripped his opponent. He brought him crashing down on the cobblestones of the market square and then thrashed him until he howled for mercy. But as soon as he, and all the others watching, could be sure that Ivor was beaten, Uther stopped the punishment and stepped back, calmly lowering his weapon to his side. Ivor rolled over, sobbing and blubbering at first, but gaining more control of himself as he pushed himself upward to his hands and knees, where he remained for a while, head downward, drooling blood and spit onto the cobblestones.

Uther watched him for a space of heartbeats, then stepped forward again, placing the thicker end of his stick on the other's back, between the shoulder blades.

"Ivor," he said quietly but clearly. "You and I should be friends, for the time will come when I will have no living enemies. Think on it." Uther Pendragon then turned slowly, eyeing each of the watching boys individually. Many of them had never harmed him, but some among them had been quick to torment him in the past at Ivor's urging. Few of either kind would meet his eye, however, and so he nodded to Cay and then turned and walked away, swinging his stick. Cay, grinning with delight, followed him in silence.

To celebrate Uther's victory, which in his eyes marked a momentous step forward in the boy's life and training, Garreth Whistler decided that he and his new student, accompanied by some of Uther's friends, should go fishing. They left that very afternoon and were gone for seven days.

Ivor the bully might have thought afterwards on what Uther Pendragon said to him concerning friendship, but no one would ever know, for in the course of that same night someone, or some supernatural agency, introduced a deadly adder, Britain's only venomous serpent, into young Ivor's bedding, and in his thrashing to escape from the embrace of the sleeping skins in which he had wrapped himself, the boy was bitten many times. He died before the sun rose, and Uther Pendragon, ranging the forest riverbanks that morning fishing for silver trout, had no idea that his lifelong reputation had been initiated.

Nemo would smile, thinking of that, hugging her secret to her bosom, exultant in the knowledge that no one, not even Uther himself, knew that it was she who had exacted revenge for him and started building the name that would keep all men in awe of him and his prowess. From then on, they would say of him that he was one who had no enemies—alive.

Nemo followed Uther around closely whenever he was in his Cambrian grandfather's lands, arranging her itinerary from day to day so that she could always be somewhere near to him if possible. And during those dreadful occasions when he would disappear for long months, detained by his relatives on his mother's side in far-off Camulod, Nemo would hold herself tightly in control throughout his seemingly interminable absences, swallowing and ignoring her frustrations with great difficulty, thanks only to her certain knowledge that King Ullic would never permit his grandson to stay away from Cambria for too long.

Nemo knew in her heart that Uther would always be her champion, no matter where he went, and he never failed her. Not even on the day, years later, that she had thought would be the end of the world.

She had left the hut early on a bright morning in early summer, the year she turned twelve, making her daily journey to the well, carrying a brace of water pails mounted on a yoke across her shoulders. She had passed the corner of the barrel-maker's shed and was angling to her left, towards the well, when a man came into view on her right, cutting diagonally across her path from the gates leading into the village. She glanced at him incuriously, attracted more

by his movement than anything else, and then she froze in mid-
step, her mouth falling open and her heart leaping up into her
throat in fear. The man was Leir the Druid, her father, and slightly
behind his tall, stooped figure, she saw the smaller, shambling
shape of her half-brother Carthac, his gross cranial deformity visible even from a distance.

Certain that she had been seen, and overwhelmed by panic, she
hid behind the barrel-maker's wall and stood motionless for a long
time, her heart hammering at her rib cage. There was not the slightest doubt in her mind that they had discovered her whereabouts by
some gross mischance and had come to take her home with them.
There was also not the slightest doubt in her mind that she would
die here in Tir Manha rather than go with them.

She let the heavy wooden yoke fall from her shoulders, its pails
clattering in the morning stillness, and fumbled for the short knife
she carried at her belt. It was scarcely a dagger, but it was all she
had, and she ran the ball of her thumb nervously over its sharp
edge, looking around her to see who else was watching. Not
another person moved anywhere in sight. She strained her ears for
the sound of approaching footsteps but heard nothing, and eventually, in spite of her terror, she approached the blind corner of the
barrel-maker's shed and slowly poked her head around the corner.

The streets lay empty on both sides, and for a moment she was
tempted to believe that she might have dreamed it all. But she knew
she had not. Leir the Druid was in Tir Manha somewhere. He had
found her, and soon the entire village would be turning out to look
for her, to send her home with him. Fresh terror flared up inside
her. He could be anywhere now, from the King's Hall to a neighbour's hut or even inside the shed she was leaning against. The sole
place she could rely on his *not* being was behind her.

Slowly, taking one step at a time and leaving her pails and her
wooden yoke abandoned where they lay, Nemo began to back
away, feeling her entire body vibrating with tension, expecting at
every moment to hear her name shouted with a command to stop
where she was and give herself up to her father's care. But the
shout never came, and no one came close to where she walked, so

that she made her way unnoticed across the entire space of the rear half of Tir Manha until she could turn and run, fast and far.

The previous month, she and Uther had found a bear's winter den on a heavily treed hillside in the forest, less than a mile from the walls of Tir Manha. They had stumbled upon the place by accident while trying to locate Uther's best hunting arrow, which had brushed a sapling branch and been deflected high and to their right to disappear among a jumble of broken slabs of rock on the side of a steep, moss-covered cliff that was literally held in place, slabs and all, by the massed and massive roots of ancient oak and elm trees. Nemo had climbed higher than Uther at one point, attracted by a faint pathway descending from the upper edge of the cliff and disappearing behind one ledge of the green, moss-encrusted rock face. The path had been beaten by a large bear whose tracks, made months before, were still visible, set in dried mud in front of the hole that led into a small but deep, dark cave. Since then, the two of them had used the spot as a private meeting place, telling no one else about it. She knew that Uther would know where to find her once it had become clear that she had disappeared.

Nemo reached the bottom of the cliff and within moments had reached the entrance to the cave. It was summer, but nonetheless she threw a large stone through the entrance and waited, listening closely, before she moved to enter the den. She heard nothing, and nothing came charging out at her, but even that did not mean the cave was empty. She knew that the proper thing to do would be to light a fire and then to throw a lighted brand into the blackness. That would bring out any frightened animal that might be crouching in there. But Nemo had neither the time nor the patience to go looking for the materials to build a fire. She drew her small knife and sucked in a huge breath, then stepped inside. For the space of a heartbeat she held her breath, her face a rictus of anticipation, but then she relaxed. The cave was empty.

She turned and looked for signs of her passage, but none could be seen. Because it was still early summer and the heat had not yet had a chance to penetrate the depths of this ancient stretch of forest, everything visible, the entire enclosure of the sylvan world stretching in front of her, was still painted in shades of green. High above Nemo's head, the towering treetops were crowned with a thick canopy of leaves, and even the great, thigh-thick ropes of root looping the cliff face all around her were covered with a greenish, mossy growth.

Uther would be coming sooner or later.

Nemo looked down at the ledge she was standing on and then lowered herself to sit with her legs dangling over the edge, her back comfortably lodged against the cliff face by the cave's entrance. The air was warm; the sun filtered through the leaves. She finally closed her eyes and allowed herself to think, without panic now, about her narrow escape from the Druid.

Uther did arrive in the middle of the afternoon, and she watched him as he climbed silently and swiftly up to where she sat. When he reached her perch, he stood looking down at her for a while, his face expressionless, and then he dipped his hand into his scrip and pulled out a wedge of cold fowl, leg and thigh, wrapped in a clean piece of cloth, handing it to her silently. Nemo took it with a nod of thanks and attacked it. She had eaten nothing since the previous night, and she was ravenous. When she had finished, Uther stood waiting, leaning indolently against the rock face with his left shoulder, his weight braced on his right foot, his head cocked to one side. He had learned long before that day that words were a commodity she used but sparingly, and sometimes heeded even less, and so he was content to wait, knowing that she had something to tell him.

She finally tilted her head back and looked up at him, wiping her lips with the sleeve of her tunic.

"They came for me."

Uther frowned. "Who came for you?"

"The Druid and the boy."

Uther was plainly perplexed. "The Druid? You mean the new fellow? The one who came this morning? Why would he come for you? Why would you even think such a thing? He came to see Daris. All the Druids come to see Daris. He is the Chief Druid."

"The boy."

"What about him? He's the Druid's apprentice."

Nemo shook her head. "No, no, he's not."

"Come on, Nemo, of course he is. He's an ugly whoreson, but an apprentice is probably the best thing he could be, with that face of his."

Nemo frowned. "He's my brother, Carthac. My brother. And the Druid's name is Leir. He is my father."

Uther sat down beside her rather suddenly, as though his legs might have given way, and sat staring at her for what seemed a very long time, while Nemo kept her eyes fixed on the emptiness ahead of her in the middle distance. Finally she heard him snort, and from the corner of her eye she watched him draw up his knees and wrap his arms around them.

"The Druid is your father . . . What did you say his name is? Leir? Your father?" Nemo made no response, and he continued as though talking to himself. "Very well, then. And the boy is your brother." There was another long pause, and then he moved again, turning himself sideways so that his legs hung out over the cliff like hers. He slipped his hands flat, palms downward, between the backs of his thighs and the hard stone of the ledge.

"Why did you run away?"

Nemo thought about that for a moment. "Because I was afraid of him. He came home with a new wife, and—"

"No, I don't mean then, I mean today. Why did you run away from him today, from Tir Manha?"

Nemo sniffed and turned to look at Uther. "Because he had found me. He—"

"He had not found you, Nemo. He had no idea you were there. He still has no idea."

"He would have asked for me."

"What would he have asked about, then? A runaway daughter? A child? A slave? If he had wanted to find you he could have done so easily, long before now. He is a Druid, after all . . ."

They sat silently for a time, and then Uther asked, "You hate him, don't you?"

She nodded, and he nodded back. "Aye, I can see that. But why? What did he do to you? Did he beat you?"

She shrugged her shoulders. "Sometimes. Mostly he frightened me. I knew he was going to kill me one day. He killed my mother, and he killed all his other wives, too. Nobody ever spoke of it, but I knew . . ."

Uther sat staring at her again, and then he reached out and squeezed her shoulder. "Well, look, Nemo, here's what we'll do. We'll wait him out and tell no one where you are. You stay here, and I'll go back to Tir Manha and fetch you enough food to last you for a day or two. This Druid won't stay long, you'll see, and he won't be looking for you. He probably thinks you died in the forest somewhere. I'd wager he has even forgotten that you ever lived."

"Someone will tell him my name."

"But what did he call you when you lived at home? He didn't call you Nemo, did he?" She shook her head, on the point of telling him that her real name was Jonet, but he was charging ahead. "Of course he didn't. I know that's not your real name. So how could this Druid ask about you? D'you see what I'm saying?"

Responding to the tone of his voice, Nemo looked at him, then sniffed loudly and even managed to smile, tremulously, wiping her nose with her sleeve.

"Good, then bear this in mind from this moment forward. The Druid might be your father. There's not much you can do about that. But he is not your keeper, so stop worrying about him coming back and claiming you as some kind of slave. I won't allow it. And if I have to I'll complain to my father about him, and to Daris, the High Priest." He broke off, grinning at her. "On the other hand, there's nothing much I can do about your brother. You're stuck with him, I'm afraid." The grin faded from his eyes. "He's a nasty little brute, though. He had a dead rat in his scrip. I saw him take it out when he thought no one was looking, while his father was talking with another Druid, waiting to see Daris. He took this thing out of his scrip, then cut one of its legs off and dropped the rest of the carcass back into his scrip. Then he started playing with the severed leg, trying to skin it with his fingers. Filthy little toad."

Uther was completely oblivious to the shudder that shook

Nemo when she heard him use that expression. His mind was still busy with thoughts of young Carthac.

"What happened to him, anyway? What happened to his head?"

"He was born that way. It happened during the birthing. Everybody thought he would die. But he didn't." Even as she said the words, Nemo recalled seeing Carthac earlier that day and thinking immediately that he looked far worse than she remembered.

Uther was rising to his feet. "Well, he's an unsightly little monster, and not so little either. How old would he be?"

Nemo shrugged. "Younger than me. Younger than you, too. I think I was three when he was born . . . that's what I remember being told."

"So, if I'm two years younger than you are, and he's a year younger than me, he's nine . . . He's *huge* for a nine-year-old."

Nemo shrugged. "Yes," she said, "he's big."

No more was ever said, but Uther's stature as her guardian, protector and benefactor was forever fused into Nemo's consciousness that day. He had soothed her and relieved her of her fears without either scorn or ridicule, and he had personally guaranteed her safety, offering to enlist his father the King, and even the Chief Druid, on her behalf. Nemo thanked him simply and accepted the truth of everything he had told her, and eventually her life resumed its normal round.

Leir left again shortly afterwards, following a stay of mere days, leaving Carthac in Tir Manha with Daris, the High Priest. Before he could return at summer's end, word came back that he had fallen prey to a sudden, raging fever and had expired within a matter of days, frightening everyone with fears of plague and pestilence. Carthac was left an orphan, and no one was quick to offer to take on the responsibility of looking after the misshapen boy. But word passed among the people, subtly reinforced by the authority of the High Priest, that as the son of a Druid, the boy was entitled to a measure of support from the clan at large, and lodgings were eventually found for him until he could be apprenticed to another Druid. The waiting period was short and unhappy, but Carthac was placed with another Druid from the north and soon moved on.

FOUR

In her entire life prior to arriving in Tir Manha, no one had ever taken the time to speak civilly to Nemo, so it had quickly become one of her greatest joys that the boy Uther would often talk to her, sometimes for hours on end, looking her directly in the eye from time to time and speaking urgently and for her ears alone, without a hint of cruelty or derision. No one observing the two of them at such times would ever have thought to call what passed between them conversations, for Nemo never said a word, never made any attempt to respond to anything Uther said. She was content to listen and to enjoy the recognition in being spoken to, and it would never even have occurred to her that Uther spoke to her thus out of any feeling of fraternity or equality. She simply accepted the situation and enjoyed it, knowing that the boy spoke to her only because she remained silent, listened avidly and made no effort ever to interrupt him. Whenever he felt the need to hear himself think aloud, she was there, willing and available to serve as his audience.

Uther had been born into a family wherein the men were accustomed to thinking aloud and did so all the time. His grandfather and his father were both celebrated, among a people who placed great value upon such things, for their oratory and the soaring music of their voices. In matters of debate and dialogue, in argument, arbitration and level-headed negotiation, they were renowned talkers, powerful persuaders and manipulators of multitudes.

Young Uther had known, however, from the earliest days of his childhood, a truth that most people did not: that the liquid flow of

persuasive urgings that spilled from the mouths of the male elders
of his family was anything but spontaneous. The sweeping, seemingly fluid exhortations to their clansmen and kinsfolk were carefully and painstakingly structured, then rehearsed and polished for
days prior to being delivered. Uther's childhood had been filled with
instances of seeing his grandfather, especially, pacing the floor for
hours, shoulders hunched in concentration as he muttered for his
own ears the words and arguments he would later pour out for the
attention of his assembled people. It had taken Uther a long time to
realize and accept that the passionate flow of eloquence spilling
from King Ullic's lips was made up of the same words to which he
himself had been listening for the previous few days or sometimes
weeks, whispered or muttered almost inaudibly as the King moved
from room to room, or from corner to corner, deep in concentration.

When the time came for the words to be said in public, however, all of the repetitive work of stringing them together in the first
place came to fruition, so that the speaker, knowing the words fluently, could concentrate upon delivering them to maximum effect,
using tone, pitch, rhythm and cadence to sway his listeners. Once
he had learned that lesson—and he had shivered with an overwhelming rash of gooseflesh when it finally sank home to him—
Uther had been stricken with awe at the combined powers of words
and forethought. From that moment forward he would never lose
sight of the importance of knowing in advance exactly what he
would say when presenting an argument or defending his opinions
on a particular topic.

Uther came to seek Nemo out more and more often, until what
had begun as a whimsy had become a habit. The habit bred a strange
form of dependency upon her presence, so that after a relatively brief
period of time, Nemo, in a strange and uncritical way, had become
Uther's Witness. She became a part of his audience, openly or in
concealment, every time he had important things to say to anyone,
and since in those youthful days that usually meant to his family—
particularly to his father and his grandfather—it also meant that
Nemo had to listen from some hiding place. Neither of those two
august beings, Ullic and Uric, would have been likely to accept the

presence of a common urchin like Nemo. And so it came to pass that Nemo became an expert at concealment, hiding herself securely far ahead of time whenever she had to witness Uther speaking out on anything important. Uther, in turn, had come close to the point of losing conscious awareness of her presence, even when they were alone together, and he frequently spoke to her as though he were musing aloud to himself.

Never again would Nemo be open to such a profusion of lessons to learn and profit from. Every day she spent watching Garreth Whistler and his friends or listening to Uther, either in private or in public, brought her new awareness and important knowledge of the world in which she now lived. Thus it was that she learned of Uther's insecurity over the regard in which he was held by his Grandfather Ullic. Uther walked in absolute awe of the King, and for a long time Nemo found that puzzling, since she could see nothing awe-inspiring about the old man. Ullic was big, certainly—bigger than any other man Nemo had ever seen—and even among a proud and warlike people whose facial hair could be intimidating, his great, wild beard made him look ferocious enough to frighten anyone. But she had never heard anyone complain about the King's ill temper, and she had never seen him beat anyone. Indeed, she could remember no single instance of complaint about his behaviour. Ullic Pendragon merely looked ferocious; he did not behave ferociously. And he was old, his beard shot through with streaks of grizzled, wiry grey hair.

Through Uther's commentaries, however, Nemo soon came to see the Pendragon King in a different light. The boy loved his grandfather deeply, to such an extent that he was almost afraid to approach the old King too closely, lest he do something boyish and ill-considered—and Nemo quickly discovered that Uther believed he had a natural talent for such things—that might displease the great man. Uther always strove to keep himself close enough to be able to watch and see, hear and admire the King's feats, his opinions and judgments, formal and informal, and yet he remained far enough removed from the proceedings most of the time to be able to slip away whenever he wished, without having been noticed.

It took her a longer time, however, to realize that Uther had a deep-rooted and very real fear that his grandfather, his beloved and revered Tata, disapproved of him. This confounded Nemo, for even she could see, as unobservant and incurious as she was, that Ullic Pendragon, not the kind of man to dote on anyone, was fiercely proud of Uther. Uther himself, however, was absolutely incapable of seeing or believing anything of the kind. In his own eyes and for his own reasons, he judged himself unworthy of his grandfather's respect and admiration, and so he condemned himself to a life without either. He believed his grandfather disliked him, and he hurt himself so badly with this misguided conviction that he found himself driven constantly to attempt impossible things in order to win recognition and approval from the old man.

Because he was yet very young, however, Uther invariably failed to see the vainglorious aspect of all the wild things he tried to do, and because he never liked to talk about anything he found even slightly discomfiting, let alone embarrassing, he seldom spoke to anyone about what he was trying to achieve at such times. As a result, what his father called "Uther's escapades" usually ended in failure and dejection, the pain of them amplified because invariably King Ullic saw only what he believed to be the harebrained results of his grandson's mercurial nature.

One such incident occurred in the early autumn of the year Uther was ten. He had returned from Camulod sooner than was usual that year, and for some reason, unknown and unimportant to Nemo, Cay had not come with him. Uther had been different when he came home that year: he had grown considerably during the summer months and was far bigger than he had been when he left, but Nemo also noticed that he was more confident, and that was not quite so readily apparent to others.

He came home that year enthralled by several things he had learned from the craftsmen in the Colony, and one of these was the phenomenon of lines of cleavage, the almost magical divisions known only to jewellers that exist between the planes and structural elements of natural crystals, enabling a knowledgeable man to split a precious stone into smooth-faced, multi-faceted portions with one sharp, well-placed tooled edge and a few gentle taps.

Uther, who had always been a creature of great burning, but short-lived, enthusiasms, had seen this feat performed by a veteran craftsman called Murdo, a native from some far northern clan who made silver jewellery and decorated it with bright yellow and purple stones, clear as glass, that he brought from his homeland. Before seeing the man himself, Uther had seen a sample of Murdo's work, a large, circular and splendidly imposing brooch with a huge yellow jewel at its centre, and he had dismissed the jewel as a pretty but worthless piece of coloured glass. One of his companions had corrected him, however, insisting that the decoration was, in fact, a real jewel that the craftsman had cut from an ordinary stone and faceted with his own tools.

Uther's rejection of such an outrageous claim was instant and raucous. Any fool, he said, could see that the jewel was made of glass, the same kind of glass that had been used to make the yellow drinking cups owned by his Grandmother Luceiia Varrus in Camulod, and he had seen for himself how those were made when his grandfather took him to the glassmaker's foundry. The glass was beautiful, but it was made in a furnace and then rolled and shaped while it was soft and *ductile*—he had used that word impressively, taught its meaning by his Grandfather Varrus, the smith, although none of his friends had paid it any attention—but at no point in its production did anyone cut it or split it with a blade. His friend was adamant, however, and totally unimpressed by Uther's vehemence, refusing to be shouted down and insisting that he had heard his father tell how Murdo the Bauble-maker had learned his craft as a boy, at the Emperor's court in Constantinople, and had then come home to Britain to practise his craft for more than twenty years in Londinium, prior to the departure of the legions.

Such a spirited defence of Murdo, with its absolute defiance of Uther, constituted a serious challenge and called for an absolute resolution one way or another. And so the entire troupe of boys, nine in all, went directly to Murdo's hut and demanded that he show them one of his rough, unpolished stones, and then show them how he split and shaped and polished it to make such a jewel as the one in the brooch.

Watching as Murdo did what they asked—he was only too happy to reward their interest in his skills—Uther found himself totally engrossed in the procedure that unfolded before his eyes. From the moment the dour-faced Murdo first produced an ordinary-looking, rough-textured pebble the size of his fist and held it up beside a much smaller, many-faceted jewel of what appeared to be blazing yellow glass, claiming the two were one and the same substance, a material called topaz, Uther's imagination was in thrall to what he was being told and shown. He watched, spellbound, as Murdo cleaned the rough stone of surface impurities, immersing it time and again in a bath of some bubbling, caustic fluid, then withdrawing it, using long, tapering pincers, and vigorously rinsing it clean in water. In the intervals when nothing particular seemed to be happening and waiting was all there was to do, he asked Murdo, insistently sometimes, about the sources of his skills and knowledge. The man sought to avoid and deflect the boy's questioning at first, but Uther Pendragon's was not the kind of personality that accepted dismissal easily, and the craftsman's reluctance, once overcome, soon gave way to the pride every artisan takes in explaining and demonstrating his abilities to people who are both less gifted and genuinely intrigued.

Uther's friends were not interested, beyond the first novel and introductory stages of the cleansing process, and they soon drifted off to amuse themselves elsewhere. Even Cay went away with the others, unimpressed by what he had seen to that point, but Uther remained behind, his attention focused entirely on what Murdo was doing, and under the boy's watchful gaze, the jewel-maker eventually buckled down to doing real work, rather than simply seeking to amuse the lad. As Uther watched, frequently holding his breath with the intensity of his concentration, Murdo unveiled some of the true secrets of his craft, gripping the rough, uncut stone securely in the jaws of a jeweller's vise and then cutting the stone to expose the glowing treasure at its heart, working roughly at first in the initial, shaping cuts, and then refining his approach and the size and temper of his cutting tools as he approached the finer elements of his task.

Uther remained with Murdo for the entire day, and at the end of it he went away unable to think about anything other than the amazing transformation he had witnessed. He returned the following day to pester the craftsman into showing him the process time after time and explaining the logical processes and techniques involved. And when he wanted to try it himself, Murdo allowed him to do so, knowing what the result would be. But then, in a natural act of kindness after Uther's stone had been smashed to dust by an over-enthusiastic hammer blow and the boy's chagrin knew no bounds, the veteran craftsman took Uther aside and showed him the lines of cleavage in a large piece of the soft coal they used in Camulod to feed the central heating furnaces. The coal was extremely soft and quick-burning, but because of its very softness, Murdo was able to split it with his hands along the natural lines of cleavage formed in its beginnings, millions of years earlier. He showed Uther how the black stone split into layers and how, with a modicum of care, anyone who knew what he was doing could split the fuel into impressive-looking flakes.

On his return to his grandfather's territories, Uther told Nemo what he intended to do and what he hoped to achieve. His primary objective, as always, was to impress his grandfather the King, this time by demonstrating how, with the edge of a sword blade, he could split a stone—represented by the large piece of coal he had chosen—by striking it once, cleanly and without great effort. Nemo listened closely to Uther's long and rambling explanation and understood almost nothing of what he was saying. Uther had been home from Camulod for more than ten days by that time and had been separated from Murdo for almost twice that long, so that his memories of what the old craftsman had told him and taught him were beginning to grow hazy around the edges. He knew beyond dispute, however, that Murdo called his jewels "stones," and since Murdo's stones all contained invisible lines of cleavage, it seemed to Uther that all stones must contain them. His stone for the demonstration would be a large piece of coal. He was familiar with the attributes and qualities of coal, and it would suit his purposes perfectly.

Nemo was determined that she would be present in the Great Hall to witness the proceedings when Uther demonstrated his feat to the King's Council. Though most of the dwellings in Tir Manha were round-houses with thick walls of mud mixed with willow laths and low roofs thatched with straw, there were other, larger structures too, most of them the rectangular buildings known as post houses because of the way they were constructed around and upon strong sunken pillars. The Great Hall was by far the largest and the most impressive of these, an enormous, rectangular structure with timber rafters mounted upon gigantic tree trunk pillars, its walls constructed of shaped and layered logs, sealed and weatherproofed with mud and Roman mortar. Nemo knew that women were forbidden by ancient custom to attend Council gatherings and that not even Uther would dare to flout that law. She had spent days, however, searching for the perfect hiding place, and because she had no fear of heights, she had finally located the ideal spot, high among the rafters that spanned the enormous interior, in a deeply shadowed corner beneath the roof.

The interior walls were lined with woven screens of reeds covered with dried, smoothly plastered mud, and they were impossible to climb, but not so the exterior walls. Nemo quickly identified an easy route, using the roofs of several outbuildings abutting the Great Hall that would take her up within reach of the high ventilation windows under the thatched eaves of the main building. The massive hall stood in the middle of Tir Manha, and because it had never been intended as a fortification, no attempt had been made to secure it from penetration from outside. She made her way unseen up to the window she had chosen as offering the easiest access, and slipped inside, delighted to discover there that she could make her way with ease into a corner that was fortified with angled beams and was far safer than the ample crotch of the great oak tree she frequented in the Place of the Bows. Satisfied then, she made her way out, content to wait in silence until it was time for her to climb up there again.

At dusk, on the night before the meeting of the King's Council, Nemo made her way up into the rafters, this time carrying a leather satchel that contained some food and water, a woollen blanket and a covered earthen pot to hold her own bodily wastes, should she become sore set. She slept well, high in the roof, and climbed out of the window again before the dawn broke to relieve herself in safety on the crest of a rooftop in the darkness. Then she climbed back into the building and made herself comfortable again, dozing intermittently until the Council began to assemble below her, the sound of their assembly and the swelling volume of their voices forcing her to lean forward and concentrate hard on one small group at a time, trying to overhear what they were saying. The noises of voices and movement blended together into a chaotic meld that rose directly upwards to where she watched and listened, and it was impossible to hear anything clearly, let alone understand what was being said.

By the time King Ullic entered the Hall and called the Council to order, Nemo had begun to regret having wasted so much time and effort in climbing up to her high perch, but then Uther entered the Great Hall a very short time later, and she suddenly found herself perfectly situated to observe what happened and able to hear every word perfectly.

Two of Uther's companions entered behind him. They were carrying a flat board between them on which lay a very large, obviously heavy piece of coal from which every trace of dust had been carefully removed; the entire surface had been burnished to the semblance of a gloss. They placed the coal in the middle of the floor and then withdrew. Painfully aware of all the eyes focused on him and the intense curiosity—some of it hostile—that was being directed his way, Uther stepped forward and asked his grandfather's permission to bring a borrowed sword into the room in order to make his demonstration. It was the law that no weapons were ever permitted in the Council chamber, and Uther's request was therefore received, after an initial concerted hiss of indrawn breath, in a scandalized silence. King Ullic nodded in acquiescence, however, humouring his grandson and saying nothing to dissuade him. Another of Uther's companions who had been waiting outside the doors brought in the sword and handed it to Uther, then left hurriedly.

Uther drew a deep breath and then looked about him at his grandfather's assembled Councillors. Among them he saw his father, but he looked away quickly, refusing to meet Uric's eye and forcing himself to review instead what he was to do in the following few moments. Before coming here, he had thought about a number of things he might say to King Ullic to explain what he was doing and what he had discovered, but then he had dismissed all of them, convinced that actions would speak more clearly than any words. Now, trying not to acknowledge the fluttering hope that he had been right, since it would indicate that he might possibly be wrong instead, he made no attempt to speak before stepping forward to stand in front of the large lump of coal. He gripped the sword tightly in both hands and bent close to the coal, narrowing his eyes as he carefully laid the edge of his blade along one of the thin, almost invisible lines that marked the outer surface. Every eye in the gathering was on him, and he felt the scrutiny of each of them. No one spoke and no sound marred the perfect silence in the Hall.

Sucking in a deep, silent breath, Uther drew himself erect slowly and raised the sword carefully above his head, keeping his arms stiffly extended and his eyes fixed on the target lines he envisioned. Then his blade slashed swiftly, sibilantly downwards, a strong, clean, accurate blow that produced a dull, clanging sound. But instead of falling apart in neatly severed sections, the large piece of coal remained stonily intact, save for a number of flint-like splinters that broke off and whizzed away in all directions, clattering and sliding across the floor.

Uther gazed, stricken with horror at what had happened. The blade of the borrowed sword had twisted and bent with the impact of his deliberate blow, the dubious quality of its temper mercilessly exposed in this sudden, violent encounter with obdurate stone. And despite the numerous washings that the piece of coal had undergone, the impact had generated a small cloud of fine black dust that hung in the air, almost motionless, hovering as though to draw attention to the fact that Uther had just failed at something else, although no one could have guessed what that might have been.

Uther stood there, unable to move, his head lowered, his mind filled with dull, sluggish echoes of the sickening sound the sword had made against the coal. He would tell Nemo later that a hundred different thoughts swirled through his mind in the few moments after the sword landed, and most of them were questions: What happened? What went wrong? What had he been trying to demonstrate? What had he hoped to achieve? How could he have gone ahead with it without letting anyone know what was involved? How could he have been such a fool as to attempt this thing in public—not merely in public, but in full view of his grandfather's scowling Council of Elders, all of whom disapproved of him? Why didn't the coal split as it ought to have? Why hadn't he tested both it and the flawed sword earlier? Why, why, why, why?

As he stood there, frozen, Uther heard a swell of sound as his audience began to stir and to talk among themselves, quietly and with decorum because they were in Council. It would have been a grievous insult to the King had anyone permitted himself to laugh aloud or to voice his scorn of something that the King himself had authorized. And so they kept their voices low, their disapproval muted.

Uther's eyes moved to meet his grandfather's, and he saw the old man's hand come up, finger pointing, ordering him to leave the Council chamber. He nodded and began to turn away, but Ullic's voice stopped him.

"Take the weapon."

Uther stooped and retrieved the useless sword, seeing only now the rust that pocked it and the tawdry workmanship of the warped and twisted blade. Then, carrying the thing in both hands, he trudged from the Hall dejectedly, crushingly aware that his humiliation was not yet complete. He would have to face his grandfather later in the day, and probably his father, too, and attempt to explain what it was that he had been trying to do. Had he really tried to split stone with a sword? What practical purpose had he thought to achieve in doing such a thing? Uther writhed inside himself with shame and humiliation that he could ever have been so scatter-brained and so irresponsibly precipitate. He had failed again, utterly, to govern his compulsive enthusiasms, and he had failed to do an advance investigation of possibility and probability, when even a cursory investigation could have shown him that their hard, local Cambrian coal, dug from the exposed seam that surfaced close to their village, would not split as readily or cleanly as the softer coal used in Camulod. Uther knew he could blame no one but himself. He had walked—no, he had almost forced his way—into his grandfather's presence while the King was in Council, and he had used his status as a family member to gain his grandfather's attention. And then he had proceeded to humiliate himself, begging everyone there to witness his apparently mindless destruction of what must have seemed to them to be a perfectly good sword. It must have looked to everyone like a ceremonial sacrilege, some kind of inane, insane rite devised simply to outrage all of them.

His friends were waiting for him when Uther reached the doors and closed them behind him, but after one look at his face, none of them sought to join him as he strode past them and away. For his part, he did not even notice them. His mind was filled with the vision of his Grandfather Ullic's face and the stern disapproval that had filled it as he had glowered down from his dais.

As Uther was striding away, fleeing to hide his shame and humiliation, Nemo was witnessing an altogether different aspect of what his demonstration had evoked, one that would have confounded the boy had he known of it. She had been leaning forward, peering between two rafters in order to watch him as he walked away, carrying the sadly twisted weapon he had used in his "demonstration," and as the high doors closed behind him, she became aware of the deep silence that now held sway in the room below, one that no one seemed eager to break. She shifted her position, moving her head from one side to the other of the rafter she was straddling. Below her and to her right, the King still stood in front of his ceremonial seat, a thoughtful expression on his face as he gazed at the doors through which his grandson had made his exit. Every other eye in the room was fixed upon him, and Nemo had the feeling that everyone down there on the floor was holding his breath expectantly. The silence stretched and grew, and no one made a sound or moved to take a seat. Eventually, however, Ullic Pendragon turned his head back towards his expectant advisers and waggled his fingers in their direction.

"Sit," he said. "Sit down."

As they did so, the King moved slowly down from his dais to where Uther's lump of coal lay on the floor. He stood gazing at the coal for the space of several heartbeats, and then he slowly backed away from it until he was close to the main doors of the Hall. He turned and pulled them open, and as the doors swung wide, Nemo saw one of the guards outside twist in surprise. Then the King said something and held out his hand.

Ullic approached the coal again, this time carrying a sword he had taken from the guard. While everyone gazed silently, he stood for some time looking down at the black mass. Then he sank to one knee, shifting the sword to his left hand and reaching out with his right to touch the tip of his middle finger to the deep score that Uther's blade had made on the black surface. His gaze sharpened, and he leaned closer to the lump of coal, spreading the fingers of his hand wide over the surface for a moment and peering closely at something. Then gently, tentatively, he drew his thumbnail straight down along one of the fine lines he had detected.

Nemo heard him mutter something to himself at that point, but his voice was pitched too low for her to hear. It was obvious, however, that something had occurred to him. He straightened his back, still on one knee, and took the sword back into his right hand. He held it point down, like a dagger, and braced his fist against his shoulder as he used his left hand to position the point of the blade very carefully against the coal. When he was satisfied that it was properly in place and would not slip, he brought his left hand up and cupped it over his right fist, and then he thrust downward, hard, using the strength and weight of his arms, shoulders and torso to drive the sword point into the coal. A sharp crack, and the lump split cleanly into two flat-sided parts, almost throwing the King off balance with the suddenness of its division. Ullic threw out one hand to retain his balance, and then tested the smoothness of the split sides with his open hand. He nodded his head wordlessly, and then rose to his feet again with a loud sigh, brushing his left hand against his tunic to wipe the coal dust from his palm. He turned next towards the open doors where the guards stood gaping and held out the hand with the sword. Its owner immediately came forward to retrieve it.

"My thanks," the King told him. "Close the doors again when you go out." He watched the doors as they closed behind the departing guard, then made his way back up onto his dais, where he faced his Councillors again.

"If I have learned nothing else about my grandson Uther," he said to them, "I have learned this: the boy, young as he is, is no fool. What you saw him do today might have looked foolish to you, but that is only because none of you knows what he was attempting to do.

"No more do I. But I know that he had a purpose in coming here today, and I know that he would never set out to make himself look foolish before me or before any of you. Think hard upon that before you give voice to scorn when you leave here. You are the King's Council, and when you gather here to advise me, as you do from time to time, your dignity is guarded carefully, and the respect shown to you is unique. How many grown warriors do you know who would dare to walk into your gathering and demand your attention?

"The boy had something in mind with this . . . this thing that he attempted. Clearly, it had something to do with what I did a moment ago, splitting that coal with a blade. I want no sneering stories of what happened here to make their way beyond this Hall. Is that clear? I will not tolerate being crossed in this. We will not punish the boy, even by silence, for one error, no matter if it be of judgment or execution or of simple nervousness. If our young people show self-reliance in any way, we must encourage them, not laugh at them or scorn them." Ullic broke off and looked around at the faces watching him. "I've no doubt, either, that there are some of you sitting here listening to me now and thinking me a fool for saying the like. Well, if you are thinking that, keep the thought to yourself. It would not please me to hear it said aloud or even whispered, and I doubt I would even like to see it showing in your eyes . . . Think me foolish if you will, but keep your thoughts inside you and your faces schooled. And know I believe that we would be the fools to punish any of our bright young lads for trying something new or different.

"Now, we have important matters to discuss, so let's be about them."

FIVE

Uther paused in the empty vestibule that lay inside the massive outer doors of the Great Hall, wiping his sweaty palms as he gazed up at the tall interior doors to his grandfather's Council chamber for the second time in one day. He swallowed hard and drew a deep breath, willing himself not to shudder with dread. He was alone in the vestibule, the guards having been dismissed when the Council gathering ended more than an hour before. Desperate for an excuse, any excuse, to postpone opening those doors and entering the Hall to face his grandfather, he allowed himself to think for a moment about the Guards of the Great Hall, as they were called. They were proud and independent Pendragon warriors, not soldiers like the garrison guards in Camulod, who were allocated guard duties in strict rotation by their officers. Those who stood on guard for the King's Council in Tir Manha did so voluntarily, and the rotation by which they took their turns to serve was an informal one, an honour shared among equals in recognition of time-hallowed custom.

One of the two who had stood guard earlier in the day had been sent by Ullic Pendragon to find the King's grandson afterwards and bid him return to the Hall, and Uther had followed him with leaden footsteps. The time had come for him to explain himself and accept responsibility for his behaviour, which he knew his grandfather and his father must be considering inexcusable. He drew one more deep breath, squeezed his eyes shut and then reached out for the iron handle on the right door, twisting it firmly.

"Uther!" The cry, urgent and muted, came from behind him and he hesitated on the point of pushing the door wide open. He knew it was Nemo; he had recognized her voice immediately. He paused, wavering, as she called his name again, then turned to see her running hard towards him across the cobblestoned yard outside the massive doors of squared oak beams that always stood open on the days of Council gatherings. Frowning and shaking his head, he waved her away. She had no right to approach the King's Hall—as a woman, she would be trespassing.

Nemo saw the anguished look on his face and the peremptory way his hand came up to stop her, and she slid to a halt, leaning against the edge of one of the huge, grey wooden doors, her heart pounding and her breath catching in her throat from running all the way around the buildings to reach the only entrance to this courtyard. She had taken the risk of being seen and caught only when she had heard King Ullic say to the Chief Druid, who had been the last man to leave the Council chamber, that he expected his grandson at any moment.

Moving as quickly and silently as she could, she had then climbed back through the window under the eaves and made her way to the ground, although much more slowly than she would have wished. It had rained only a short time before and the surfaces she had to cross were slippery and treacherous. Then, as she had dropped cautiously down the last, dangerous slope of the lowest outhouse in her "ladder" of roofs, she had seen Uther pass by in the distance, evidently headed to meet his grandfather.

Now he stood glaring wildly at her, his face a grimacing mask, waving her away with one hand. Pitching her voice so that he alone might hear her, she called to him, "He's not angry, Uther! The King's not angry." But before she could finish, he stepped inside, and the door closed behind him.

Uther had heard what Nemo said, however, and he found himself instantly angry at what he saw as her presumption in daring to tell him something that he knew to be untrue. But then he saw his grandfather, and all thoughts of Nemo were dashed from his mind.

Ullic stood with his back to the doors, so that Uther saw only the imposing height of the old man and the enormous breadth of his back and shoulders. He suspected his grandfather knew he was there, but he could not be certain.

"Tata?"

"Come over here. What were you trying to do?"

Uther's heart sank at the directness of the question. This was going to be even more difficult than he had feared. He moved forward, speaking to the back of Ullic's head.

"I don't know."

The King swung around to look at him. "What's that supposed to mean? Of course you know. I know, so you must. Look here."

Uther stepped to the old man's side and looked at the piece of coal that lay in front of him, cleanly split into two pieces. His jaw dropped open in astonishment.

"I didn't do that."

"No, I did it. But it's what you were trying to do, isn't it?"

Uther nodded, unable to take his eyes off the split coal. "Yes."

"Good, then we both know what you were trying to do, so perhaps I asked you the wrong question. Let's try again. If you had succeeded in splitting this the first time, what else would you have done, afterwards?"

"I don't know . . . I'm not sure."

Ullic Pendragon said nothing for a long time, standing with pursed lips, gazing down at the sundered stone, and then he looked again at his grandson. "But you did think it was important . . . that you could split this thing?"

"Yes . . ."

"Why? And *don't* tell me you don't know again."

The boy bit back the words that had been rising to his lips and stood quietly for a moment. Then he frowned in puzzlement and looked up at the old man who towered above him.

"You're not angry."

"No, I'm not angry. Should I be? Or do you intend to make me angry, insisting that you know nothing about why you interrupted my Council this morning?"

"No, I'll try not to . . . But I might not have the right words."

"Well, you won't be the first man I've listened to who suffered from that complaint. Why did you attack the thing the way you did? And where did you get that awful weapon?"

"The sword? I borrowed it from my friend Lucius. His uncle gave it to him. It was not a very good blade."

"It wasn't a blade at all. The thing split and broke like a dried-out branch. If that's the best you can do on your own behalf, I'll have to make sure you get a decent blade. But why did you swing the thing over your head like that? Why not simply split the coal the way I did? Come and sit down with me. I'm getting too old to stand all day on a stony floor."

He led the way up onto the dais that held the King's heavy seat of ornately carved oak and sat down, thrusting a footstool towards Uther with one foot as he did so. Uther caught the stool, hooking it with his foot, and pulled it over to him to sit, avoiding his grandfather's eyes while his head spun with wonder over so much ease and friendliness where he had expected bluntness and pain.

"So," his grandfather continued, "why the overhead swing?"

"Forgive me, Grandfather, but this time I truly don't know, save that it seemed to be the right thing to do at the time. But of course, it wasn't. How did *you* split the coal?"

"With a blade, the way you tried to do it. But I used the point of mine like a wedge and forced it into the crack with the weight of my body." Ullic leaned back until his shoulders found the comfort of his deep chair, then crossed his arms, lowering his chin onto his chest as he stared at his grandson. "I'll admit, you had me wondering for a moment or two if you had taken leave of your senses . . . especially when I saw what happened to the blade of the sword. I just about had you thrown into a cell then to teach you a lesson about good manners. Only one thing stopped me. Can you guess what it was?"

"No, Tata."

"The coal. Had you merely wanted to look like a fool and humiliate me and your father, you could have chosen any old stone on which to break that sword, but instead you chose a piece of coal—black, dirty, hard to find. And soft—softer than any other kind of stone. Once I began to think about the coal, I couldn't stop. So I went and looked at it. Your blade hacked a big chip out of it, destroying itself in the doing of it. But I could not make myself believe that you would go to such pigheaded lengths simply to destroy even such a poor weapon. It seemed beyond belief that you would be so stupid and vicious. So I told myself that you must have had a reason for doing what you did, even if I could not imagine what it was . . .

"And then I saw the lines running along the coal from one end to the other, and I remembered the care with which you took aim, the way you bent down and laid the blade so carefully against the stone before bringing it up to strike. You did all that slowly and with great concentration. And so I guessed that what you were trying to do must have had something to do with those lines. They looked strangely familiar, even though I had never noticed anything like them before, and the only thing I could think of doing with them was to split them, to force them apart, and so I did that. I drove the point of a sword blade hard into one of the lines, and the entire block fell apart in two pieces."

Ullic stopped and looked appraisingly at his grandson. "I was impressed that you would have known that would happen, even if you did not know quite how to achieve it. But tell me, if you will, man to man, *why* you did it. What do you think is so important about being able to split coal?"

"Nothing, Tata . . . I mean, there's nothing important about doing it with coal. Coal is easy, or it should be easy. What I didn't know until this morning is that there are different kinds of coal. I know now."

"What d'you mean?"

The boy shrugged. "The coal they use in Camulod is very different from ours. It is shinier and cleaner-looking, almost polished, if you know what I mean. And it's lighter, too . . . easier to carry and easier to break apart. I never thought to ask about that, and I never thought to question the weight of the piece I brought here today. I knew it was heavier, and I knew it was duller, and I knew it was dirtier . . . dustier . . . but it never occurred to me that it could be a completely different kind of coal."

Ullic sat staring at his grandson for a moment and then shrugged, frowning slightly. "I know what you are saying must make sense to you, but I have no idea what you are talking about. You began by telling me that coal is unimportant, but since then all you have talked about is coal."

"Oh . . . well, yes, I know it must sound strange. But you see, it's the stone and cleaving it that matters . . ."

King Ullic Pendragon stood up and raised his arms high in a mighty stretch, yawning and rising to his tiptoes as he did so. "I'm hungry," he said. "You must be, too. Come with me and we'll pass by the kitchens and find something to eat, then you and I will walk for a while and talk, and perhaps by then you'll be able to tell me sensibly about what's in your mind."

Within the space of the hour that followed—thanks to the pleasant distractions afforded by visiting his grandfather's kitchens and procuring an entire feast, comprising a hot, freshly spit-roasted hare and a cloth-twist bag of salt, a loaf of fresh bread, a damp cloth full of soft, new-made cheese, a small raw turnip cut into wedges and a jug of cold beer—Uther went from being angry and afraid to feeling completely at his ease. He and his grandfather shared the load as they carried their meal with them, sauntering at their leisure through the King's Holding and into the woods outside Tir Manha. Only three men attempted to approach King Ullic in that time, and he waved all of them away, growling an explanation that he was spending time with his grandson and did not wish to be interrupted. Uther said nothing about that, but he was highly conscious of the honour being accorded to him and, in consequence, even more appreciative than his boyish appetite would normally have made him when the two of them finally sat down side by side on a fallen tree trunk and shared the delicious meal.

By that time, he had also come to accept that his grandfather, far from being angry at him, was honestly interested in what Uther had to say. As a result, when the time came to start from the beginning and explain all that had been going through his mind in recent weeks, he found that every trace of complexity had vanished, and he was able to tell the story fluently and without pause, going from his first encounter with the old craftsman Murdo in Camulod through all that he had learned from the old man and almost successfully through the ensuing labyrinth of thoughts, many of them contradictory, that had brought him to this day's doings.

When he had finished talking, his grandfather sat staring at him for some time, then sniffed and made a low throat-clearing sound somewhere deep in his chest.

"Very well," he said. "I think I follow you . . . At least I know what lines of cleavage are now. Here I am, more than five times your age, and I never knew that before. So. You hoped to split the coal—or the stone, if you prefer—with your sword. Why? What would that have proved?"

"That it could be done."

"What d'you mean?"

The boy shrugged. "It would have amazed you, Tata, don't you see? Because you didn't know it could be done. Do you think any of your Councillors would have known, when you didn't? What would you have said, or thought, if I had been able to do it . . . if the stone had split clean in two?"

Ullic Pendragon nodded and actually chuckled. "You're right, I would have been amazed. And I might even have been amused, too. But what makes you think I would not then have thrown you out for interrupting my Council?"

"Because I did it with a sword."

"A sword . . . I don't follow you. You're ten years old, and you've lost me. What are you saying?"

"I don't know, Tata—I know you told me not to say that but it's the truth. It's a—I had a vision, I think."

"A vision. I see. What kind of a vision was it?"

"It happened one afternoon last week when I was thinking about Murdo's chisel striking one of his big, yellow topaz stones. He always does it—splitting a stone, I mean—with great care, and he spends ages studying each stone before he can decide where to place the chisel blade. If he selects the wrong spot, or if he strikes too hard or not hard enough, he can destroy the stone, smashing it into powder. He let me try it once, and I ended up with a small pile of yellow dust and splinters. But when Murdo does it right, Tata, he splits the stone cleanly, and each side of the split is smooth, as though polished, like the glass in Grandma Luceiia's window in her family room in Camulod. And then I thought of something that I hadn't thought about before . . . and I saw it again today when I came back into the Council chamber and saw how you had split the coal . . ." His voice died away and he looked up into Ullic's eyes.

"And what's that?" the King asked. "What did you think?"

"I thought—no, I *knew*—that a stone struck properly like that is split forever. It can never be put back together again."

"I see. That was your vision?"

"No, in my vision I saw a sword splitting a stone. And then the stone became an army, divided by a sword stroke. And then, instead of a sword, I saw a force of Camulod's cavalry, a wedge squadron formation, striking an army and splitting it apart."

"So it could never be rejoined . . ." The King's voice was quiet, and he had a far-away expression in his eyes. "Hmm!" Ullic sat up straight and wiped his hands on the bottom of his tunic. "So you brought your idea to me. Good. But you should have brought it sooner."

"Why?" Uther now sounded depressed. "My idea didn't work, and I broke the sword. And besides, we don't have any cavalry like Camulod's, so it won't do us any good."

"Aha, so that's what you're thinking, is it? Well, lad, you're wrong. What's important here, it seems to me—although, mind you, I'm naught but an old man—what's important here is that *I* broke the coal. Don't you agree?"

"Yes, I know you did, Tata."

"Aye, but did you hear what I said? I said that was the important thing."

"I know, Tata, I heard you."

"Good, then you can tell me why it was important."

"I . . ." Uther sat silent, blinking, and his grandfather took pity on him.

"It was important, Uther, because what you had done, or tried to do, set me thinking about it . . . And so I was able to do it, after

I had thought about it for a bit. But I would never have thought about it at all if it hadn't been for what you did. It would never have occurred to me to try such a thing, even if I lived to be twice the age I am now, if you had not provided the original idea. Do you hear what I am saying to you, Uther?"

Ullic waited, peering into his grandson's face, but then, seeing that the boy had not understood, he kept talking. "The *idea*, Uther, the idea was yours, and that is more important than the success or failure of what you tried to do with it. Once the idea has been put forward, someone will always come along to make it real, to make it happen, but it need not be the person who first had the idea. There are very few people in this world who can do what you did in this—who can conceive ideas, lad—who can come up with the original thought required for progress, and the knowledge that you, my own grandson, could be one of those few people makes me very proud." Again Ullic waited, and again the boy did not respond the way the King wanted.

"But I failed, Grandfather. I didn't do it."

"*Dia!* Very well, let me think about this for a moment . . . Here, try this. You admire your Grandfather Varrus, no?" Uther nodded. "Of course you do, and so you should. And the reason you had that thought of cavalry splitting an army is because you admire the cavalry at Camulod almost as much as you admire Publius Varrus, am I right?" Again the boy nodded. "Good then. So you must be really proud of your grandfather's prowess as a cavalry leader, and of the way he looks on horseback, all decked out in his fine armour on his huge cavalry horse, right?"

Uther was shaking his head, frowning. "No, Tata, Grandfather Varrus does not ride. I've never seen him in armour on horseback. He is not a cavalryman."

"What? But he commands all Camulod's cavalry, does he not?"

"No, he does not. He used to be the Commander, but he gave that up to Uncle Picus when Uncle Picus came home to Britain."

"But why?"

"You know why! Uncle Picus used to be an Imperial Legate, the supreme cavalry commander in Britain, before I was born."

"I see. So you are saying your Grandfather Varrus is a failure." The boy's eyes went wide with shock and outrage, but before he could respond in any way, Ullic held up his hand to forestall him. "No? That's not what you are saying? Then what am I to believe? Why would Varrus relinquish his own power to another man—any man?"

"He did not, Tata! Uncle Picus is not just any other man! He is Tana Luceiia's nephew, and he is a great commander of cavalry, better than Tata Varrus could ever be. Tata Varrus would have been stupid not to allow Uncle Picus to take over the command, because Uncle Picus does that best, and Tata Varrus had other things to do."

"Aha! Other things, you mean, that he could do better and more profitably, making better use of his time."

"Yes. That's what I mean."

"Excellent, then let us move on. No, stay where you are," Uther had moved to stand up. "I meant let us move on in our discussion. We can do that here.

"I want you to think upon these things. You swung your blade; I used the point of mine. You picked a point to hit among the lines on the coal, then took your blade away, allowing it to waver as you moved it. I inserted my point firmly and kept it there. You risked everything on a wild swing with an inferior blade. I concentrated all my force and weight behind a single, firmly held point. You assumed, wrongly, that you were dealing with the same kind of coal you had used in Camulod and that it was soft and would break apart easily, whereas I, knowing nothing about coal, only looked for what I could find within the coal that lay in front of me.

"So you failed on every count, and I succeeded. But look at the reasons for your failure, Uther. You used a different kind of coal, because you didn't take the trouble to make sure it was what you thought it was. That is an error you probably will never make again. You learned through bitter experience that you can never afford to assume anything, and from now on, I would dare to say you'll always check to make sure that things that might be important to you are, in fact, what they appear to be. Am I correct?" The boy nodded. "Good. Next, you took careful aim, and then you swung your blade up over your head, and that cost you everything you had gained in taking careful aim. Lesson: you may do that when you are swinging at something large, impossible to miss and undefended, but when your target is as tiny and difficult to hit as a thin line drawn on a stone, why, then you must use your head and find a different way to hit it. Then, too, the poorness of your blade was self-defeating. Nothing ever will be more important to you in a struggle than the quality of your weapons. In almost every instance of hand-to-hand fighting, your life will depend, almost absolutely, upon your having the best blade. Never keep or use an inferior weapon. You might as well chop off your own hands.

"So, those were the points that governed your failure in Council today, would you not agree? I thought so. Well, were you faced with doing exactly the same thing tomorrow, and if you look to those same points, remembering what happened today, you would surely succeed. And you could do it time and time again thereafter and succeed every time, because you have learned your lessons. Do you understand me?"

Uther nodded his head wordlessly and Ullic repeated the gesture. "Good. Now let's look at my successes in the same light. I succeeded in splitting your stone, but I didn't know what I was doing, and I did not know what was going to happen. I did all of the right things, but I did them all because I came to them with curiosity and time to study them. I had no pre-formed notions of what I was about or of what I thought to achieve. I was merely inquisitive and curious. But I would never have done anything at all, boy, had you not brought that piece of coal, together with a blade, to my attention. So, hear me on this, Uther, and hear me clearly.

"Your Grandfather Varrus is a very clever and admirable man, and he has no fear of assigning work to other people who are suited for it. That is a Roman idea, called *delegation*—I'm sure you must have heard the word in Camulod. It means work allocated to someone by the direct order of his legate, his commander, along with the authority and responsibility to complete it properly. Delegation, through what the Romans refer to as the chain of command—from legate to tribune, to junior tribune, to centurion, all the way down to

the common soldier—enabled men like your Uncle Picus and his
father, Caius Britannicus, both of whom were Roman legates, to
build an empire. You spend almost half of your time in Camulod, and
you're a clever and observant lad, so you already know much of what
I am telling you, but from now on, keep that word in your mind . . .
delegation. It's something we here in Cambria are not good at. In
fact, it does not exist here. We Cambrians have too much foolish
pride to let ourselves be seen to delegate tasks, because it might
appear that we are shirking doing them ourselves; and we have too
much pride, as well, to submit ourselves to being selected to perform
them, lest we appear to be inferior and too easily led. We suffer
greatly by such stupidities, and you'll see that as you grow older.

"But there are other words I'll wager you'll hear Publius Varrus use in much the same way as he speaks of delegation. *Strategy*
and *tactics* are two of them. Do you know those?"

"I think so, Tata. They're war words, are they not?"

"Aye, and very important war words, too. *Strategy* is the art of
planning, of drawing up a series of ideas for waging a campaign of
war, moving large groups of men around, in theory, as though they
were pieces in a table game. Strategy is the working out of battles
in an army commander's mind. *Tactics*, on the other hand, is the art
of putting strategy to work, making it reality. A legate like your
Uncle Picus might dream up a strategy for fighting a war or a campaign, and he might even visualize the kind of tactics necessary to
achieve his ends. But when the die is cast and the blood begins to
spill onto the ground, he is forced to rely heavily on his battle commanders, that collection of individual group leaders that the
Romans called staff officers, to make up their own tactics in the heat
of the fighting and to make decisions, sometimes at a moment's
notice, on how to use their forces to best advantage in order to
achieve victory along the lines their legate planned at the beginning.

"It's the field officers who define the fighting tactics, boy, and
don't ever lose sight of that truth: the battle commanders decide the
tactics when the war turns real. They're the decision-makers in the
middle of a battle, because they are the men who can best see
what's happening around them, when the enemy is hammering at

them with everything he has. They're the men at the centre of spur-of-the-moment urgency, and it's their responsibility to move their troops as needed and to be flexible enough to be able to adjust to instantaneous demands. Strategy and tactics, Uther. Neither one can succeed, or perhaps even exist, without the other. And I know, too, that only very seldom can the same man put both into action."

Ullic fell silent for a while, and his grandson sat staring at him, wondering what would come next. Eventually the King nodded his head and spoke again. "Your idea today was pure strategy. Where you fell down was in your tactics, because you had not thought them through. But tactics can be taught, Uther, and you have the finest teachers that any boy could have . . . Garreth Whistler, here in Cambria, and all your tutors down in Camulod. They'll teach you tactics, and you'll learn them easily. Strategy, however . . . Well, that's another matter.

"Strategy can be taught, but only by using examples of what has been done already. Every time a Roman legate won a great victory, the details of his plans were written down and widely discussed afterwards. The Romans are great keepers of written records. We, on the other hand, write nothing down because it is forbidden by our ancient laws. And yet we still keep records, carefully guarded in the lays of all our Druids. Great tales and records of history's great fighters, just like those the Romans have.

"Now anyone with a memory can learn and memorize the battle plans of history's great generals . . . not all of whom were Roman, by the way. But the true greatness of the very finest strategists who ever lived, men like Julius Caesar and Alexander of Macedon, lay in the fact that every one of them was an original thinker. Men like those don't use other people's ideas. They dream up their own . . . ideas that have never been heard of before. And that is what you did today. That's a great ability, boy, and it is one that should be close-guarded. I learned about Caesar and Alexander from Caius Britannicus before you were born. Caius is dead now, of course, but his sister, your grandmother, knows as much about these things as he did. I will have her spend time with you, talking of things like that . . . Roman things.

"In the meantime, from this moment forward, I want you to start thinking of yourself as a commander of men, because you will be one some day. It might not be soon enough to please you, and you might not ever take my place as King, because it is not hereditary and therefore not within my power to bestow, but you will sit, as my first-born grandson, in my Chief's chair some day, when your own father dies. And as a Chief of Pendragon, you will have scope for all the strategy, all the ideas you can devise. You will need fresh notions of how to make things better for your people, but even more you will need to surround yourself with men you can trust, men of ability and men of strong personal honour to carry out your ideas and to improve on them with tactics. So I want you to remember what I told you about delegation. As I said, our people distrust it today, but who knows, if you work at it hard enough you might be able to change that, to everyone's benefit, by the time you achieve the Chief's chair."

The King stopped and looked his grandson straight in the eye, reaching out to grasp the boy by the upper arm. "You are ten now, are you not? Well, that's much more than halfway towards manhood, so you've spent more than half your time learning to be a boy. Now you have less than that amount of time to learn to be a man. One of these days—and it won't take long, believe me—you will be a warrior. And you will be a good one, I have not the smallest doubt. Your father and your mother have done a fine job of making you what you are today, and I find myself looking forward to the enjoyment of watching you grow older.

"You will find no shortage of people in this place, however, who will disapprove of everything you do . . . they do that already. Let them. All you have to do to rise above whatever they might say to you or about you is to keep what I tell you now in your heart: much of their disapproval—all of it, in fact—is born of envy. You are my grandson, Uther Pendragon. You are born to be a Chief and to enjoy privileges they will never know, so they will demand that you be perfect, without flaw or blemish . . . and that, of course, no man can be. So they will continue to be disapproving, but they will accept you, and they will respect you grudgingly, so be it you remain true to yourself and them. And for all of their complaining, they will obey you nonetheless. That is the way we Cambrians are, Uther. It is a thing inborn in all of us, whether we be Griffyd, Llewellyn, Pendragon . . . we are a race who do not smile easily, and we have no great admiration for the attribute of tolerance. We distrust everything we do not know and do not understand, and there is very little that we do know and understand. But we are an old people, Uther, ancient and strong, and we have reason to be proud of who and what we are. I believe it will be important for you to know that in the future and for you to understand it fully, although I don't think I understand it fully myself, even after a lifetime.

"So be it. I think the gods are telling me to pay more attention to you than I did to your father . . .

"More than twenty years ago, closer to thirty if truth be told, Caius Britannicus and Publius Varrus told me that the Empire would collapse one day soon and that the Romans would be gone from Britain then, leaving us to go our way alone. I remember I laughed aloud the first time I heard that. Thought they were mad, I did. They were the Romans, not I, and yet I was the one who believed that Rome was eternal and rock-steady.

"Well, I stopped laughing over that long ago, because I began to see the signs of what they had described becoming plain in the months and years that followed hard on the heels of our early talks . . . and now it has been three years since the last Roman army units patrolled Britain. Everything is changing, Uther, all the things I knew and believed when I was your age, all the things in which I had trust. Your father is a man now, and there's nothing more that I or anyone else can teach him. All that remains for him to learn is what every man must learn for himself. But you, boyo . . . there are many things I know I can teach you, so you and I are going to spend a good deal more time together after today. I am going to teach you how to be a Chief."

Seeing the expression on his grandson's face, he shook his head and wagged one finger in the air, drawing his features into a serious mask.

"It is not as straightforward as it sounds, despite what people may tell you. A man may hold the name and status of Chief but be a nothing all his life, doing no one good, including himself. It happens all the time . . . far from unusual. But for a man to be a Chief in reality and not in name alone is another thing altogether. To achieve that, a man must have worked hard to learn a few choice and specific things. And a good Chief will make a good King, because a King is simply a Chief with greater powers. I will teach you about honour and integrity. I'll teach you how to look at your people, man and woman, and at the problems that they have among themselves from time to time, the squabbles and the differences that soon call for judgment, and I will show you how to assess, in your own mind, the rights and wrongs and strengths and weaknesses of each case, so that you may judge wisely and without bias. There's more involved than simply being a judge, of course, much more, just as there is much more to life, but that's the kind of thing I *can* teach you. Would that please you?"

The boy nodded, wide-eyed, and his grandfather grinned and stood up.

"Good. Then let's return to those that love us—and to those who drive us wild with impatience."

SIX

Ullic was true to his word, and in the weeks that followed his talk with Uther, the two were often seen wandering together or fishing in a stream, up to their knees in icy water, talking earnestly together. At such times the King would brook no interruption, and his fierce gaze was enough to frighten off anyone who came close enough to claim his attention.

Less than a month after the day on which he made the promise, however, the King died of an apoplexy that suffused his face with blood, turned his eyes blood red and killed him instantly. He had been sitting, thinking, in his favourite spot atop an immense, round-topped boulder that lay on a hillside close by Tir Manha and from which Ullic, who had sat there almost every day of his life, had been known to swear that he could see into every part of his holdings when the light was right.

On the afternoon of his death, he had been shouting down to one of his advisers, who had approached him against all custom, defying the unwritten law that no one might disturb the King when he was on his Thinking Stone. An envoy had arrived, this man reported, bringing information that demanded an immediate response and therefore had to reach the King's attention instantly. Ullic had risen from his seat and was in the act of moving to climb down from the stone in his normal way and by his normal route when, according to those who saw it, he suddenly reared up to his full height, stiffened into rigidity and fell over backwards, crashing to the ground at the rear of the stone, out of sight of the watchers.

By the time they reached him, Ullic Pendragon was already dead. Several witnesses swore that he appeared to have caught his heel on some projection of the stone's surface, but nothing that might have caused the King to trip, stagger or lose his balance could be found, despite a most careful search. The stone was as smooth as an egg, and the Druids declared that Ullic died of an apoplexy—a flux of blood to the brain.

Uther would never forget the day that it happened, because he had been hunting alone with his father for the first time ever, accompanied only by an escort of Pendragon bowmen. Uther was revelling in the unaccustomed pleasure of sharing practically unlimited time and close intimacy with his father, and he knew that he owed thanks for this privilege to his grandfather. Ullic had been talking with him about Uric, about the amount of time the two of them spent together, father and son. And it had been less than three days later that Uric had called the boy to him and told him to be ready to ride out hunting with him the following morning.

Uther loved his father deeply and enjoyed his company greatly, but he had always known, because it was a fact of life, that his father was his own father's son, and therefore a Chief in training. The King's rank and title lay in the gift of the seven ruling Chiefs of the Pendragon Federation, but the Chief's rank and title were hereditary, so Uric would inherit the Pendragon Chief's chair one day in the future when his father Ullic died, and by the same token, Uther would one day inherit the Chief's chair from his own father. Uric might never be King Uric, but so long as he outlived his father, he would most certainly become Chief Uric. Ullic was more than happy for his son to begin taking on some of his responsibilities, but that left Uric little time to enjoy his own son's companionship.

It was late afternoon, and they were returning, father and son and a few bowmen, to the camp they had set up the day before in a grassy meadow where two shallow but respectably wide rivers met and joined together. The hunting had not been good that day, but they were far from discouraged, and they were talking about trying to catch some trout for dinner as they rode their mountain ponies through the belly-deep grass of the meadow surrounding the low knoll on which they had built their camp. Only moments after reaching the height of the knoll, however, they saw a runner coming directly towards them, moving at great speed, and something about the way the man held himself alerted them, long before he reached them, that he bore important tidings. Neither of them, however, could have anticipated the news that he brought. The King had fallen from his Thinking Stone, the fellow said, injuring himself gravely, and the Lord Uric was summoned home immediately.

Uther could see his father's frustration begin to build from the moment they first heard the news, because they were many miles and hours of travel away from Tir Manha, and the runner could tell them nothing more. He himself had not been anywhere near the scene of the "accident." He was merely the last link in one of the four teams of runners that stood ready at all times to carry important tidings at high speed from one end of the Federation territories to the other, radiating north, south, east and west from Tir Manha. The information given to such men was always as short and simple as possible, as a guard against both forgetfulness and confusion. But Uric's concern and fears for his father's welfare demanded more information, and so within moments, Uric had begun the tasks of breaking camp and setting out immediately for home. He and Uther were the only two mounted members in the party. All the others were on foot—some thirty men in total—since this was a genuine meat-hunting party and not merely a sporting foray. Unless the two riders struck off immediately on their own to make their best speed homeward to Tir Manha, leaving everyone else to follow at their own pace, they would be tied to the pace of the slowest members of the party, the butchers, whose responsibility it was to dress, cut and transport the meat killed by the hunters.

As Uther expected, his father wasted no time in deciding to abandon the rest of the party and strike out for Tir Manha, but he was genuinely concerned that Uric might decide to go without him, thinking him too young for such a rugged and dangerous ride. There were at least four hours of daylight remaining, Uther knew, and mounted as well as they were on their sturdy, mountain-bred garrons, the two of them should easily be able to ride upwards of sixteen miles in that time, which would take them halfway home. But Uric would not allow mere darkness to stop his progress. He would keep riding into the night until he could go no farther, and if the night was clear and no accidents befell him, he would be close to home by dawn. It was that thought, that consideration, that made Uther fear his father's decision, for it seemed highly likely to the boy that Uric would not wish to endanger his only son on a long, perilous journey in the darkness through unknown territory.

He need not have worried, for if Uric had even thought of the journey from that viewpoint, he must have dismissed the thought immediately as irrelevant. He had far more important matters on his mind. His only words to Uther were instructions to go at once to the head cook and ask him to fill Uther's saddlebags with enough provisions to keep the two of them, father and son, well fed for the next forty-eight hours. And as soon as he had the supplies, including a plentiful quantity of drinking water in skin bags that they could hang about their ponies' necks, Uther was to arm himself with a full quiver of arrows for his bow—a boy-sized version of the huge Pendragon longbow made especially for him by his grandfather's own bow-maker—and rejoin Uric at his tent as quickly as he could. Uric wanted to be away and headed for home within the quarter hour, he said, and Uther needed no further urging.

Once on the way, they rode hard, pushing their mounts for maximum speed but taking great care at the same time not to overtax the beasts, as they had but one animal each. Since the actual hunting was done on foot, they had taken one horse each along with them purely as a measure of luxury and self-indulgence. Now they rode in a way calculated to cover distance most economically without exhausting their ponies, riding at a walking pace for a mile or two, then increasing their gait to a canter for a similar distance and then to a loping run for an equal space, avoiding any flat-out gallop that would tire the animals unduly. And for one quarter of every hour, they would dismount and allow the animals to graze and refresh themselves.

Uther had hoped to be able to talk to his father at greater length and more intimately once they were on their own, away from the others, but he could see that his father's attention and concerns were focused elsewhere. Most of the questions he asked Uric in the first hour of their journey were met with grunts or with utter silence, and the few responses that he did receive were distracted and practically incoherent. Uther soon accepted his father's preoccupation and fell silent, riding thereafter with his own thoughts for company.

It was plain to him that his father was very deeply troubled by the tidings that had come from Tir Manha, although Uther himself could see nothing dire in the message he had heard. Grandfather Ullic had fallen from his Thinking Stone and injured himself, but there seemed to Uther to be no reason for great concern in that. Uther had seen the Thinking Stone a thousand times and had clambered all over it when he was no more than an infant, and the thought of anyone, and most particularly his Grandfather Ullic, hurting himself badly through a fall from its edge to the ground seemed ludicrous to the boy. No more than five days earlier, Ullic himself had sat on the very edge of the Thinking Stone with his buttocks on the stone itself and his feet on the ground, resting his hands on his bent knees while he talked with Uther. At its centre the stone was probably the height of one tall man sitting on the shoulders of another, but its top surface was enormous, easily ten long strides across and almost twice that in length, and gently rounded like a huge, smooth egg. It would be impossible, Uther knew, to fall directly to the ground from the boulder's highest point. And yet, Ullic's advisers would not have sent the runners looking for his father without good cause. Ullic himself would have chewed holes in their hides if they had.

Uther could see worry stamping itself more visibly into Uric's face. His grief and his concern for the King gradually became so evident, and his impatience and frustration with the slowness of their progress so pronounced, that Uther eventually found himself anticipating the worst and beginning to come to terms with the formerly inconceivable notion that King Ullic Pendragon might actually be in danger of dying as a result of unimaginable injuries.

In Uther's short lifetime he had known three invincible, unmovable, impermeable personalities: Ullic Pendragon, Uric Pendragon

and Garreth Whistler. All three of these men were his heroes, and
their indestructible permanence anchored his own identity. He had
never ever considered any of them to be capable of dying.

When they reached home, they found their worst fear confirmed: the King was dead.

As was the custom in such cases, and hard on the heels of Uric's
formal confirmation that the dead man was his father, Uric was
taken to attend a gathering of his clansmen and was formally named
the new Chief, assuming his father's duties and the Chief's chair left
empty on Ullic's death. He was distraught, his mind overwhelmed
by his loss, and he showed little appetite for the tasks to which he
was being appointed and no interest at all in the ceremony surrounding the event. The Druids were prepared for that, however,
and moved around and about him as though he were functioning as
normally as they were so that the rites and legalities of succession
were quickly observed and ratified by Druidic custom. King Ullic
Pendragon had been dead for three days, and Uric was now Chief
of Pendragon, the rightful occupant of the Chief's chair.

All of these thoughts passed through Uther's mind now as he
sat staring at the bier and the armoured corpse displayed upon it,
laid out for the burial rites. Ullic Pendragon—if this were really
he—lay flat on his back, his eyes held shut by two small, flat pebbles and his hands crossed on his abdomen, loosely clasping the
hilt of his sword, a Roman short-sword made for him personally by
his close friend Publius Varrus of Camulod, Uther's other grandfather. Publius Varrus himself was there too, seated across the bier
from Uther with his wife Luceiia Britannicus Varrus by his side,
both of them gazing at the corpse on the bier and thinking their
own thoughts, paying their respects in silence.

Finding himself in the intimate presence of death for the first
time and looking at the corpse of his beloved grandfather, Uther discovered that he seemed to be incapable of the kind of grief he could
see overwhelming everyone around him. He had no time for grief, it
seemed to him, and no capacity for grieving. The body, laid out in all
its finery upon the bier in the Great Hall, surrounded by heaps of
fresh-cut blossoms and aromatic herbs and pine boughs, looked

quite like someone else's notion of King Ullic. Uther could hardly believe that it was really his Tata. The nose was too sharp-edged and bony, for one thing, and the cheeks too grey and sunken, creating hollows in the face of this fellow that were never visible in the laughing face of Ullic Pendragon. And this man, whoever he might have been, was visibly smaller, over all, than Ullic Pendragon. His arms, despite their familiar, silver-chased leather armbands, were far slighter, much slenderer than Ullic's massive forearms, and his hands looked skeletal, bony and thin-skinned, with brownish blotches on the backs of them. Ullic's hands were enormous and filled with life, strong and deft in everything they did. Even the dead man's beard looked different from Ullic's. Ullic's beard was iron-grey and rich, a dense and bristling bush concealing his mouth, chin and neck from the wind and other people's eyes. The beard on the dead man was a wispy, sad thing, unkempt and unimposing.

Uther was far from convinced that the dead man was King Ullic Pendragon.

He could see, nonetheless, that everyone else believed it. His mother's eyes were swollen and red from constant weeping. She had been weeping when he and his father arrived home from their journey, and she had not ceased since. His father had been weeping too, and although Uther found that hard to credit, there was no doubting the evidence of his own eyes. Uric's eyes were as red and as swollen as his wife's, and his cheeks were grimy with smeared soot from the fire, where he had sat huddled for hours, shrouded in whirling smoke and staring into the coals, occasionally wiping tears from his cheeks with the back of his hand.

Uther's grandparents had also brought Cay with them from Camulod to honour the dead King, who had been Cay's uncle—eldest brother to Enid, the mother Cay had never known. Cay now sat behind Uther, slightly to his left. A quick backwards glance over his shoulder revealed that his cousin was sitting with his eyes closed, and the thought occurred instantly to Uther that he might be asleep, tired out by the swift and unexpected journey from Camulod. That thought then led to a ludicrous vision of Cay snoring aloud and startling himself awake, outraging everyone, family and Druids, and for a long time after that Uther had a hard time fighting an insane compulsion to laugh out loud. He had no wish to laugh, but the urge to bray out guffaws of mirth was almost insuperable, and he was terrified that he might give in to it and disgrace himself.

Desperately then, in a frantic effort to divert his thoughts, Uther stared at the bier and tried to think of all the ways he had heard of to dispose of a dead body. Everyone died, he knew, but it had somehow failed to register in his mind prior to this episode that "everyone" included all the members of his own family. Ullic Pendragon had been but the first to go in Uther's lifetime, but now, looking at his grandfather's bier, Uther realized for the first time that within Ullic Pendragon's lifetime he, too, had had to stand and bid this kind of farewell to beloved family members . . . his own grandparents, born more than a hundred years before King Ullic's death, and his own parents after that. He accepted, too, for the first time, that just as surely as Uric Pendragon was now mourning the passing of his father, Ullic, he, Uther, would one day have to mourn Uric and his mother, Veronica, and the kindly couple from Camulod who were his mother's parents. All of them were bound to die.

His mind reeling with the anticipation of so much loss and sorrow, Uther scrabbled frantically inside his mind for something to distract him from such thoughts and remembered that he had been counting ways to dispose of bodies that had ceased to live and breathe. He forced himself to focus upon that again, willing himself to empty his head of everything but the logistical problems caused by death.

The fact that everyone died entailed the logical conclusion that everyone's body had therefore to be disposed of. This was a novel and astounding thought for Uther. He looked around the gathering assembled to say goodbye to King Ullic and made a cursory attempt to estimate the number of people there. It was well over a hundred, all of whom must die eventually. From there, he visualized the population of Tir Manha, as he had seen it at official festivals and functions. *So many people*, he thought. *So much death. How could I have reached the age I have without falling over corpses everywhere?*

Everybody died, and astounding as it might seem, those left alive were able to absorb the deaths and deal with the remains of those who died. And everyone, all of the peoples in the places he had known in his short lifetime, appeared to do so differently. He knew, because he and Cay had discussed it once a few years earlier, that in Camulod most people were buried according to the Roman military system. Individuals were usually buried standing upright, in the case of men, or sitting upright if the corpse was female. None of the adults he had asked, including his Grandfather Varrus, had been able to tell Uther why this should be so, but some of them, after discussing it among themselves for a time, had suggested that the custom of upright burial had come into being in the early days of the Roman Republic's foreign expansion and conquests, when the need to dig postholes for temporary fortifications, and sometimes in search of fresh water, had still been commonplace. For those purposes, army units had carried wide iron augers the breadth of a man's shoulders in their supply trains. These devices could drill a vertical hole into soft ground as quickly as two-man teams could twist the handles in a circle. And once the cylindrical hole was dug, a corpse could be dropped into it feet first, then quickly and completely covered, leaving a narrow, vertical grave that was less likely to be seen by enemy searchers than a horizontal one. That had apparently been important in early, pre-Christian times, when vengeful enemies would seek out and disinter dead soldiers, knowing that a desecrated grave would deny its soldier occupant access to the Underworld.

For burials involving larger numbers of people, Uther had learned, the Romans had used mass graves, and the bodies laid in those were covered in quicklime to aid the process of dissolution and to burn away the stink of rotting flesh.

In Cambria, he knew from experience and observation, most of the common people were not buried at all but were instead closely wrapped in cloth or leather bindings and hoisted up to lie on burial platforms among the branches of the sacred trees until their flesh had been consumed by the creatures and spirits of the air, and their bones polished by wind and weather. The noble families and the Druids, on the other hand, were usually burned after death, although exceptions to that rule were common, and the smoke and essence of their burning was offered up as a sacrifice to all the ancient gods of the Cambrian pantheon.

Great Chiefs and Kings, however, were treated differently upon their deaths. From time immemorial, Celtic Kings and Chiefs had been laid to rest in longhouses. These were dwelling places built entirely beneath the surface of the ground, then stocked with everything the occupant might require during his passage to another life and finally sealed protectively against the curiosity of living men before being buried under a high-piled mound of earth. Ullic Pendragon would be buried thus today, on the third day following his death, and the presence of his earthly remains, secure in his longhouse, would bring blessings on his people. He would be entombed in his finest clothing and armour, but he would be entombed alone, and his weapons would go into the longhouse with him. In the very ancient past, Uther knew, slaves and servants would have been killed and sealed into the longhouse with the King, to serve and protect him on his journeys through the Land of the Dead. Ullic's great war helmet, the Eagle Crown made for him as War Chief—a rank that could only be won by physical prowess in battle and had nothing to do with the hereditary rank of clan Chief—would go into the grave with him too, to signify his rank and status to the spirits he would meet on his long voyages. No one else could ever wear it after Ullic's death, and the next War Chief of the Pendragon Federation would have his own Eagle Crown fashioned and built to fit his head alone, and that was as it should be.

The Druids were singing a mournful, undulating dirge, and the pungent smell of burning pine needles and green mistletoe made Uther catch his breath, drawing him out of his reverie. Across from him, on the other side of the King's bier, something flashed in the dim light and attracted his eyes. It was a golden pendant, resting on his grandmother's breast. Now he focused on the golden trinket and stared at it, until his gaze drifted up towards her shoulder and the shawl she wore to cover her long hair. The shawl was a strong, dark, vibrant blue, and the dress beneath it was a lighter, even brighter hue, so that each brought out the warmth and texture of the other and emphasized the brightness of Luceiia Varrus's blue eyes. Uther had no idea of his grandmother's age, but he was suddenly struck with the awareness that, old as she was, Luceiia Varrus was the most beautiful woman present at the King's funeral. Publius Varrus sat beside her, and as Uther looked at him, a quick thought enlightened his mind. Publius Varrus was dressed as he always was on formal or festive occasions, in one of the military-looking suits of soft and supple multicoloured leathers that were made for him by his own wife. This suit, sombre and sober, befitting the occasion, was made of pliant, dark brown leather, trimmed with a black key design, with a short, waist-length outer garment of thicker, highly polished plates of hide loosely and decoratively sewn together to resemble an armoured cuirass. Publius Varrus looked magnificent. Both he and his wife stood out sharply because of the clothes they wore and the way they wore them, and that realization stung Uther into remembering the guilt that consumed him every time he returned to Tir Manha from Camulod. It always felt to him at those times that he was returning from light into darkness, from laughter into grimness, from carefree happiness into careworn anxiety and apprehension. Publius and Luceiia Varrus were like magpies among daws. They burned like beacons against the drabness of those surrounding them, including Uther's own parents, who were among the best-dressed Cambrians in the gathering. Uther allowed his eyes to move critically now across the spectrum of the gathering. He felt the tugging of old guilt again, but this time he was able to ignore it. Tata Ullic was dead, and he would never see him again, but it had not been as dreadful as Uther had feared it would be. It hardly hurt at all inside. And after today his grandfather would be buried underground, and everybody would go home again to their own homes, wherever they were. And best of all, he himself would return to Camulod with Cay.

The Druids' chanting rose to a crescendo and died quickly away. Uther crossed his arms on his chest and bowed towards the bier with the Chief Druid and everyone else, whispering goodbye to Ullic the King as he did so.

Within the month, in response to the urgent summons of the Chief Druid, the seven Chiefs of the Pendragon Federation assembled to select a new King from among their own number to fill the place left empty by Ullic's death. Their unanimous choice, to no one's surprise other than his own, was Uther's father, Uric.

BOOK TWO

*Greetings, Daughter, from your father and myself. Both of us
are well, our health better than it might be, considering how
ancient we are grown, and for that we give thanks to God.*

*My grandson came to visit me this morning, to say his
farewells and tell us that he is to leave for home tomorrow.
It was the size of him, and the speed of his growth from
infant to man, that made your father and me face up to the
fact that we are, too rapidly, growing old. His visit
reminded me, too, that the seasons have flown by again and
that if I am to write to you this year, it must be done today.*

*I hope that all is well with you in Tir Manha. Uther
says the mountains are very lovely there at this time of the
year, but I felt, when he said it, that he was merely making
conversation, being polite to his elders. Your father agreed
with me, too, and we have both formed the distinct impression that our grandson is reluctant to leave us this year.*

*The explanation for that is easy to provide, and it has
little to do with a reluctance to return to Cambria. This
year, for the first time, I believe, Uther is loath to leave the
girls of Camulod, and one girl in particular. Her name is
Jessica, and she has been visiting here with her father, an
old friend to Picus, who now lives in Gaul. She is a pretty
little thing, sufficiently so to have turned the heads of Uther
and Cay both, stirring a form of rivalry between them that
is new. I suspect that my dear grandson fears he is leaving*

the field to his beloved cousin uncontested, and he seems completely unaware that his fears are groundless. Jessica will be returning to her home in Gaul within the week, and I doubt that she will ever return here, since her father is in failing health. Alas, love appears immortal to the young.

I wanted to tell you about that so that you will not be too concerned should you notice any listlessness or unease in your beloved son on his return. He may simply be pining, and if he is, it will pass. He has had no physical knowledge of love yet, to the extent of my knowledge. The child, Jessica, is an innocent, and I know she is at least as well guarded by her parents in such matters as Uther and Cay have been guarded recently by each other in that respect.

Both boys have grown this year, nevertheless, as I said, from infancy to young manhood almost overnight. It is hard to believe that fifteen years have passed since they were newborn babes.

Farewell, my dear Veronica, and I hope we will be able to see each other again soon. Know that you are in our minds and in our prayers every day, and that your father and I are proud of the grandson with whom you have blessed us.

LV

SEVEN

Mairidh was dreaming of the boy when the horse woke her with its snorting and stamping, and the moment reality began forcing itself upon her, she moaned and fought against it, refusing to open her eyes. The weight and warmth and smell of the man lying against her side, the feel of his heavy arm across her waist, gave her no pleasure, and she refused to open her eyes to look at him, knowing that when she did she would start an entire new day filled with pain and fear and brutality. He was snoring slightly, his face thrust into her armpit, his breath fluttering against her breast, and the rancid stink of his body made her want to vomit. The *Pig*. The name had sprung into her mind when she first saw him, and she had heard no other name to gainsay it. She had lost count of the number of times he and his companion had taken her the previous day and night, both of them seemingly insatiable. Now the thrust of his morning hardness pressing against her flank warned her that as soon as he awoke he would be back at her again.

Mairidh was no maiden. She had known her share of men—some said far more than her share—and she exulted in her body and the pleasures it gave her. These two, however, had abducted her after killing the boy. They had brutalized her and dragged her off with them, forcing her to run at the back of her own horse while they both rode the poor beast. They had tethered her by a too-short length of rope, so that as she ran she was in constant danger of being kicked by a flying hoof. Time and again she had fallen and been dragged, but even the beatings she endured for slowing them down had become preferable to the agony of stumbling and staggering behind the horse, hands bound in front of her. Eventually she had fallen into a stupor of exhaustion in which her body ran mechanically while her mind lost all awareness of what was happening.

They had killed the boy, and she had made it possible. Her reward—abduction and violation—had been immediate and inevitable. And even though her complicity in the killing had been unwitting, for a time she had felt that there must be some kind of arcane justice in what was happening to her. Such a beautiful boy, and she had lured him to his death.

Eventually, when they had decided they were far enough removed from the scene of the murder, they had made a rough camp and built a tiny fire, tying Mairidh to a nearby tree while the taller one went off to look around and check that they were where they ought to be and that they were in no danger. He had returned quickly, grinning and nodding to his companion that all was as it should be, and then the two of them had finally let down their guard and relaxed. They had relieved themselves, squatting within sight of her, and then they had eaten, giving her nothing. After that, the evening's entertainment had begun.

They had thrown dice to see which one would have her first, and the shorter of the two, the Pig, who lay beside her now on her right side, had won. The other had held her down, kneeling on her arms. She had fought them at first, but they had beaten her bloody, splitting her nose and lips, and eventually she had submitted and lain still, emptying her mind of everything but her husband's compassionate face while they took her, one after the other, time and again, arousing each other by example long after she would have believed they could sustain such lust.

On countless occasions over the past ten years, Mairidh and her husband Balin had discussed the ramifications of what she was now enduring, facing it as a distinct possibility because of the great amount of travelling they did together. The roads were unsafe everywhere in Britain nowadays, the entire countryside swarming with wandering bands of homeless and desperate men and women, and anyone faced with the prospect of travelling any distance from home had to give serious consideration to the possibility of robbery, abduction and violation in the course of their journey. In consequence, few people travelled nowadays in small groups, preferring to wait for company upon the road in order to enjoy the relative safety offered by larger numbers. Women, as always, were especially vulnerable.

Balin had been endlessly, and at times tediously, insistent upon the need for Mairidh to consider, realistically and ahead of the fact, all that might be and could be involved and entailed in such a misadventure. Her life was the first and most obviously endangered thing: she could be killed attempting to defend herself, or she could be killed from sheer brutality or by accident in the commission of a robbery. Whichever way the death occurred, it would end everything. Next came her health: they might break her bones and rupture her internal organs; they might scar her or mutilate her beyond recognition; or, even less pleasant to consider, they might infect her with some dreadful, incurable disease. Once, when she was a mere child, Mairidh had come face to face unexpectedly with a leper whose facial deterioration was far advanced and horrible to see. She had thought the incident forgotten, but for a term of months following Balin's initiation of these discussions, Mairidh had had terrifying dreams about being ravished by a progression of lepers, all of them as disfigured as the poor creature with whom she had come face to face.

She had railed at her husband then for what she saw as his obsession with her eventual defilement, but she knew now why he had been so concerned, and she blessed him for it.

Balin had known one young woman years before he met Mairidh who had been a clean-living and devoutly religious Christian. This young woman had fallen into the hands of brigands and been repeatedly beaten and violated before being abandoned, naked and alone, by the side of a road far from her home. Her dubious good fortune at being left alive by her abductors was set at naught, however, by the fact that the next group of travellers to come her way was a squad of Roman legionaries who had deserted their post and were fleeing into the mountains—this had been in the north country, almost twenty years earlier, during the final days of Rome's occupation of Britain. These ruffians used the woman even more brutally than had her original captors, but they, too, left her alive when they went on their way.

She was eventually found, close to death, by Balin himself, who was passing that way with his usual large armed escort. He took her into his care, directing his people to make camp right away and then see to the young woman's needs and nurse her back to health. For more than a week—an insignificant amount of time to Balin, who was in no hurry to arrive anywhere by any particular date—they remained in the same spot while the woman recovered her health and faculties, and when she was sufficiently recovered, Balin went to her tent to visit her and asked her to tell him about what had happened to her. She told him all he needed to know, including the details of who she was and where she lived, but he was most concerned by the fact that she seemed to be consumed with guilt, as though all the misfortunes that had happened to her had somehow been her own doing.

Balin tried to comfort her then, to put her mind at ease, for he could see that it was her mind that had been most affected—far more than her body—by what had happened to her. Her body was already beginning to heal, her bruises showing the colours that meant they were fading and improving. Her mind, however, in Balin's judgment, was making no such progress. He talked to her for long hours on each of the three nights she stayed in his camp during her recovery, and on each of those occasions he took the greatest care to stay far removed from her, well beyond the range of any accidental touch, because he had seen the terror that overtook her face whenever he approached her too closely. On each of those three nights, he talked to her quietly, purposely keeping his tone soft and soothing. None of the fault for what had transpired was hers, he told her time and again, but he never began to believe that she paid any heed to his assurances.

On the morning of the fourth day, he awakened to find that she had killed herself during the night, evidently unable to bear the feelings of guilt and uncleanliness that had filled her with despair.

Balin never recovered from the shock of that incident, Mairidh knew. And when he found himself, years later, all unexpectedly blessed with a brilliant and beautiful wife decades younger than him-self, he became increasingly concerned about taking steps to ensure that she would never be infected with that kind of crippling, despair-filled guilt, a concern that eventually matured into a mild obsession.

Travel is the function of ambassadors and messengers: they carry tidings over long distances. Balin had to travel, and Mairidh insisted upon going with him. And so Balin had turned his mind towards the instruction of his wife, teaching her to believe that she should feel no guilt if she should ever be forced or violated sexu-ally by anyone.

Her body, Balin had convinced her, was merely the vessel that contained what the Romans called the *animus*, her soul. As such, her body might be destroyed or mutilated, but her soul, being immortal and immutable, could not be affected by anything earthly. Mairidh now knew, and her mind accepted, that nothing these two men could do to her would change the truth of who she was. They might kill her, and they probably would, but at the moment of her death all power to harm her would be lost to them. Alternatively, they might leave her nurturing a fertile seed. If that were so, she had a score of ways to deal with it, the last of which would be to have the child and pass it on to someone else to rear. They could injure her physically, too, but the pain would heal. What they could not do was hurt her mentally, unless she herself permitted them to do so, and that she never would. The indignity of suffering their animal lusts and brutality was an inconvenience, no more. The filth of their unwashed bodies could be laved away. The marks of their beatings would diminish, and the memory of their foulness would fade.

Her only lasting regret over this incident, she realized, would be for the beautiful boy.

Now Mairidh lay naked on the ground, her arms stretched above her head because they had tied her wrists again and attached the rope to the tree behind her, leaving no slack. It was difficult to breathe lying there, and more difficult still to move at all. The sparse grass on which she lay did nothing to soften the stony ground beneath her, and Mairidh had never known such pain. Her arms were the least troublesome—they soon grew numb, and her awareness of them dwindled to a constant, throbbing ache in her shoulders that flared into white-hot pain only when she attempted to move. The rest of her body was a mass of individual aches and agonies—rope burns on her wrists and a seemingly endless progression of bruises, abrasions and contusions, lumps and welts, and cuts and scratches. There were whole areas where the skin had been torn from knees, ankles, hips, thighs and buttocks when she had fallen and been dragged behind the trotting horse. Her cheeks and brows throbbed dully from the fists that had battered her when she tried to fight them, and her ribs and flanks were sore from the kicks they had used to urge her to her feet whenever she had fallen behind the horse.

For a long time she had thought she might die of cold during the night, but the shorter man had risen to piss and to throw more wood on the fire, and had noticed her lying shivering on the grass. He had stood gaping at her for a while, scratching himself, before dragging his smelly blanket over to where she lay and throwing himself on her again. He had then fallen asleep on top of her, and eventually he slid off to lie huddled against her side, one leg and one arm across her, holding her down. She had not dared to move for fear of wakening him again, and eventually she had slept.

Now she could sleep no more, and the pain in her arms made her want to whimper. Her bladder was full, too, and had been for hours. She knew she could not hold it much longer; the agony was too intense. But if she moved, she would waken the Pig, and then she would have to squat in front of him, naked, and the thrust of his manhood against her hip left her no doubt what that would bring. And that would waken the other one, the big one, who if anything, had been worse than his companion.

The Pig stirred and snuffled, hitching closer, thrusting himself against her and then sliding one heavy leg up along her thigh and onto her belly so that the full weight of it bore down on her swollen bladder. She could no longer fight against the pain or the pressure, and so she gave in and voided where she lay, feeling the scalding heat flooding her thighs, the relief of it almost approaching sexual pleasure. She made no sound, and as the warm reek of her urine rose to her nostrils, it seemed sweeter to her than the goatish stink of her abductor. The heat went quickly from the wetness, however, and she felt it turn icy against her skin. *Don't let him feel it!* she prayed. *Don't let it wake him up!*

She knew there were others close by. She had learned that much the previous day, listening to the two of them. They had not talked much, and when they had it was in a dialect she had never heard before, but she had been able to decipher enough to gather that they belonged to a party of twelve who had landed their boat here on the coast and then split up and travelled inland in twos and threes in search of whatever plunder they might find. They were to meet again and disembark for home this morning, and anyone who failed to reach the meeting place by then would be abandoned, presumed dead. These two could have joined their friends the previous night—the short foray made by the tall one on their arrival here had verified that—but they had been unwilling to share her with the others and so had stayed here to keep her for themselves.

Mairidh had no illusions. She knew these two would leave her dead behind them. *Her body*, she thought. That they could take and destroy, but not her mind, not her spirit—not the *animus* that was her self.

The man beside her stirred again and grunted, and she froze. For several heartbeats nothing happened, and then she felt his hand move to her hip and push her away, rolling her over onto her side. The hand moved then to her belly, grasping her and pulling her backward, hard, against his loins. But as she tensed against the thrust of him she heard a scuffling noise, and then the sound of a meaty, concussive, crunching blow directly behind her head. The man convulsed, flinging her away from him and filling her ears with a gasping, gurgling, outraged noise that sent her scrabbling, legs scissoring in panic, all thoughts of her philosophy forgotten as she rolled wildly in search of survival, her eyes wide-stretched in terror, her tethered arms preventing her from making any attempt to gather or protect herself.

It was still dark, just before dawn, and she saw the blackness of a hunched figure stooping over the body of the Pig, then straightening, wrenching something free. Whatever he was pulling broke away suddenly, with a grating, sucking sound, springing high and stopping at the level of the crouching figure's head. Mairidh recognized it as a small axe and rolled away again, face down this time, waiting for death. But the noises moved away, leaving her, and she rolled back, fighting for leverage to sit up, knowing it to be impossible. She twisted sideways instead, struggling to see, and in the murky half-light she saw one leaping figure with an upraised arm confront another surging up from the ground. The axe swung down, and again she heard an awful bone-splintering impact, altered by distance this time and followed immediately by a scuffle of falling bodies. She felt vomit surge in her throat, and then she remembered what these animals had done the day before, and the nausea was gone. She looked to where the Pig lay, stiff-legged, his head a featureless black mass.

Her rescuer—could he be that?—was back now, looming over her, and she closed her eyes again, afraid to look. She felt his hand touch her right breast, and some part of her mind was acute enough to register the contact immediately as being a touch—an accidental touch, not a caress or a squeeze—and she began to hope. The hand—both hands now—moved swiftly upward, following the line of her stretched arms to the wrists. She heard an intake of breath and then a fumbling, followed by a grunt of effort and the sound of the axehead biting into the tree behind her, twice, and then a third time. The pressure on her arms lessened, and she knew he had chopped through the rope. He was already pulling and tugging at her, forcing her to rise.

Her arms were on fire, as though they had been torn from their sockets, and she floundered uselessly, unable to use them either to push or to support herself. She felt the smoothness of bare skin as both of his arms slipped about her waist, encircling her and attempting to lift her. He hissed in her ear.

"Move!"

She was too weak. She knew this man would save her, and the knowledge robbed her of any strength she had left. Yet somehow, supported by his arms around her middle, she managed to pull her legs beneath her and then hobble forward like an ancient crone, exhausted and incapable of straightening her back. He took her through a screen of leaves between two trees, and the ground fell away in front of them into a shallow depression. She lost what remained of her balance on the slope and fell forward heavily, so that only the restraint of his arms stopped her from crashing face down. She heard him grunt with the effort of holding her, and then he was turning her, lowering her to the ground, shifting his grip to pull and haul at her until her back was against the sloping bank. Mairidh's mind was spinning, incapable of fully understanding what was happening. She became aware of a sharp, intrusive pain in her left leg, and then she felt a hand behind her knee, lifting and pulling, and another on the inside of her right thigh, doing the same. Stuporous, knowing what he wanted, she spread her legs wide, but he grunted and pulled her knees together again, so that she sat straight-legged. Her head sagged and then snapped up again as he slapped her lightly on the cheek, but her eyes refused to open.

"Mairidh! Mairidh, it's me! Come on now! We have to be away from here."

The voice was coming from very far away, but it sounded like the boy, and that could not be. The boy was dead. Mairidh knew he was dead, because she had watched him go spinning off the cliff. She knew she must be dreaming again. Then she felt someone hauling at her hands, pulling them forward, and the pressure on the ropes that bound them increased. She opened her eyes, feeling the puffiness of them, and peered down to where a knife blade sawed at the knots between her wrists. The ropes fell away, and then two hands began chafing at her wrists, the thumbs digging deeply. The pain overwhelmed her, and she heard herself moaning in protest. A blackness arose within her own mind then, and she felt herself falling into a whirlwind of chaos where she was battered and assaulted by wildly spinning impressions and images.

A short time later, when her eyes snapped open again, she found herself alone. The sky was still grey—lighter than it had been, but the sun still had not risen. Her wrists burned—she raised them and

looked down, feeling, but unable to see, the angry rawness where
the skin had been lacerated and rubbed away completely. She was
filthy, her naked body covered with dirt, some of it dried mud and
crusted with scabbed scrapes and cuts. Remembering then, she
struggled to sit up, grunting with pain from the effort, and as she did
so, she saw a shape running towards her, stooped over as though to
avoid being seen. It was the boy. The boy she had believed dead.

He came to a stop in front of her, kneeling and holding out a
double handful of clothes—the single filthy, tunic-like garment in
which she had been abducted and the long, saffron-coloured gown
she had worn at the start of the previous afternoon before the attackers had found them. Mairidh ignored the offering. She merely
blinked at him, devouring every detail of his appearance. He was as
naked as she was and almost as dirty, but she was mainly aware of
his face, remembering how it had looked gazing down on her from
above in the sunlight the previous day, the way the thick, black curls
had fallen onto his forehead above startling, bright blue eyes and the
solid, tanned column of the strong young neck. A beautiful boy.

"You died."

The boy shook his head, smiling quickly. "No, I didn't. I'm
here."

"They killed you."

"No, but they will if they find us here now. There's more of them
close by. Can you stand up? I'll help you. Here, put these on." He
thrust the clothing at her again, but she still frowned at him, ignoring the clothes, dimly aware of how stupid she must seem, sitting
there, naked and filthy, gazing up at him. But her last sight of him
filled her mind again, his face screwed up in agony as the larger of
her two abductors swung him by one leg and the hair of his head and
hurled him, screaming, from the edge of a high cliff.

"I saw you die. They killed you."

He shook his head again, his face now betraying impatience.
"No, you saw me fly, not die. They threw me off the cliff, and you
thought I must be dead. So did they. But the fool threw me too
well—too hard and too far. I flew out and missed hitting the stones
of the riverbank. Instead, I fell into deep water and landed on my

belly. It drove all the wind out of me, but I swim like a fish, and I made it to shallow water. When I finally was able to walk again, I climbed back up, but you were gone. Here, take my hand, and put these clothes on."

Mairidh took his hand and forced herself to rise, leaning heavily on his supporting arm and weaving gently backwards and forwards until she felt confident enough to release her grip. He was staring at her, his eyes wide and concerned, and she forced herself to look away, back to the clothes he held.

"You brought my robe."

"I knew you'd need it."

She held up the other garment and saw that it was ruined, torn and stained with earth and blood, and she looked down again at her battered body.

"Why did you follow us? You didn't have to . . . You didn't even have a weapon, did you? I know, because the Pig took your dagger."

The boy shrugged. "No, no weapon. But I knew I could steal one from them if they gave me the chance."

She shook her head slightly, as though dismissing some minor confusion, then looked back at the torn tunic and began pulling it over her head. The boy straightened up while she did so and stood gazing back the way he had come, his entire body radiating tension. She spent a moment trying to get the torn shoulder of the tunic to hang properly, then dismissed it and wrapped the long robe about her. It was clean, and it was soft, and it covered her completely.

When she looked up from tying the sash about her waist, he had vanished again. For a flashing moment, filled with fear, she thought she must have imagined his being there, but she was free and alone, and the clothes she had put on were real—her own clothing. Weaving on her feet again, she looked around, but there was no sign of him, and she sat back down against the bank to wait, convinced that he would return for her. Moments later, he did, reappearing silently from the fringe of bushes on her left.

"Can you walk?"

Mairidh nodded meekly. "I think so, but I don't know how far I can go."

"Far enough to stay alive?" He smiled again, a small, very tentative smile, but she was amazed that he could. "We need to put some space between us and the shore over there, and between us and those two dead men."

She looked at him and nodded her head again, still uncertainly. He was wearing his own clothes again—the rich, white woollen tunic and the leather overshirt that had first caught her eye and which the Pig had stuffed into a sack before fleeing the scene of what she had thought to be the boy's murder. The sack itself now lay at his feet, stuffed with whatever contents the Pig had found to cram into it. The boy had also cleaned the axe and thrust it into his belt, and he had recovered his own long dagger from the Pig's belongings and his bow and arrows from where they had lain beside the other dead man. The dagger now hung at the boy's left hip, opposite the axe, and he had slipped the strung bow and the full quiver of arrows over his shoulders with the taut bowstring and the strap of the quiver crossing in the centre of his breast. The right side of his tunic was thick with blood, and he glanced down as he saw her notice it, touching the clotting mass with the pad of one fingertip.

"It's not mine," he said. "I'm not hurt at all. Ready?"

She drew a deep breath and nodded firmly, and he reached out to take her hand and pull her to her feet before leading her away from the clearing, deep into the undergrowth. There they found a wide and well-used game path that led them through the densest thickets of the forest. They made good time then, and the urgency of their progress diminished as the sea coast fell steadily behind them, so that the boy eventually stopped pulling her along and fell back to walk behind her, allowing Mairidh to choose her own pace.

Mairidh's exhaustion waxed and waned as she moved forward, sometimes threatening to overwhelm her completely and at other times fading into the background of her awareness. As long as their route was level and straightforward, she could function with an appearance of ease, but whenever the going became heavy, when they had to force their way uphill or through brush looking for another trail, the weight of her legs and feet seemed to increase dramatically, and the sound of her heartbeat grew loud in her ears.

At those times, she wanted merely to fall down on the grass and sleep, and invariably, when she was close to yielding to the temptation, she found herself wanting to weep. Yet it was that very awareness of her own weakness that forced her to keep forging ahead each time she had determined to give up.

At one point, on the summit of a low hill that had seemed far higher when they were climbing it, she stopped and turned to the boy.

"How long have we been walking?"

He glanced around him and shrugged. "Three hours . . . something like that. It's mid-morning."

"Then we must be almost there."

"Almost where?" He was gazing at her quizzically.

"Back. Where they found us. I gauged we had travelled for about four hours yesterday before they made camp."

He shrugged his shoulders and nodded. "Hmm, but we're on a different route, and we've been moving at about half the speed they maintained yesterday. Remember, they had a horse."

"Remember? I had to run behind the thing. But why are we not riding it now? Why did you leave it behind?"

"Think about that for a moment, and you'll know the answer. If we had taken the horse, we would be tied to the road or to pathways that the horse could use. Once those raiders find their dead companions, they'll turn the place upside down looking to discover who killed them. We have left no tracks behind us, but had we taken the horse, we would have, and they would have come running after us."

He stopped talking and stood squinting at her. Mairidh could barely keep her eyes open. He nodded. "Hmm. You need rest."

"No, rest is not enough. I have to sleep, even if it be for no more than an hour. I barely slept at all last night and had no real rest. Now my body is screaming for sleep. Please?"

Again he looked around him, as though checking for signs of pursuit, and then he grunted and nodded, looking down into the valley ahead of them, then up to the sky, where the rain clouds that had threatened them all morning were beginning to scatter, showing broad tracts of blue.

"Aye. We'll be safe enough now. I know where we are, but we're still half a score of miles and probably more from where we want to be. There's a pool down in the valley there that you will love, I promise you, and you can sleep there for a few hours. While you are doing that, I'll find us something to eat."

EIGHT

It was the smell of food that finally awakened her. Mairidh lay for
a long time, watching the boy as he crouched over the fire he had
built. Above it, on a framework of green twigs, he had skewered a
hare. As she watched, he reached out and carefully turned the spitted meat above the flames, and she heard the hissing sound of fat
dripping into the coals. Her mouth filled with saliva, and she swallowed, but she took care to make no move that would alert him to
the fact that she had finally awakened.

The boy had stayed with her while she bathed in the miraculous
pool of naturally hot water that he had promised, which welled from
an underground spring like the famous one she had visited in Aquae
Sulis many years earlier. She had been incredulous, at first, watching the wisps of steam that rose from the gently roiling surface of
the water, and the boy had told her then how he had sat in it one day,
warm and wonder-struck as snowflakes drifted down from above
and chilled his skin with tiny icy pinpricks.

Later, reclining in the hot water, beginning to feel clean again,
Mairidh had wept silently, tears of thanksgiving for her rescuer and
for the fact that his life, too, had been spared. By the time she had
climbed out of the pool, he had built up a roaring fire in a sheltered
angle between two large, flat stones that someone had set on end in
the past. She had dried herself in front of it using a large, soft
woollen cloak from the Pig's sack as a towel. Then, with a solici-
tude that had seemed more suitable to a father or an older brother
than a young lover, he had helped her tend to the worst of her cuts

and bruises, gently wiping those she could not reach herself. Afterwards he had lowered her gently down onto a thick bed of newly gathered moss, wrapped her in her saffron robe and covered her with his leather overshirt, and over that with the woollen cloak. She had fallen asleep almost immediately, overcome with feelings of peace and well-being and the release from danger.

Now, judging by the westering sun, she knew it must be late in the afternoon. Knowing that he thought her still asleep, Mairidh allowed herself the luxury of simply looking at the boy and wondering.

He was tall and strongly built—as big as any full-grown man, in fact—and yet she judged him to be no more than fifteen years old, perhaps sixteen. More than that, however, he was beautiful, in a time and a place where male beauty, in the classic Roman sense of the word, was something seldom seen. It was his . . . what was it? She sought the word . . . his wholesomeness, the cleanly proportioned, hairless *Roman* look of him. Of course, she knew he was no Roman. There had been no Romans left in Britain for more than a decade and a half since the legions left. Moreover, this boy was clearly a local Celt, with his black hair, fair skin and bright blue eyes. But he was tall for his people and strong, with wide shoulders, long arms and a narrow waist. He was also clean in the fastidious way of the Romans, with a glowing, healthy, well-scrubbed look to him. The combination of that cleanliness with the clearly muscled shape of his lithe young body had caught her eye and her fancy in a way that seldom happened to her nowadays.

She had first seen him swimming in the river with several friends of his own age, and he had glittered among them like a jewel among broken glass. So she had watched him from afar, perched high on a cliff and concealed from their view by a screen of low-growing shrubbery. She remembered her surprise when he had finally emerged from the water and dried himself with a thick towel produced from a leather satchel, then dressed in what she could see was rich and well-made clothing. The knowledge that he was thus obviously the son of a wealthy and powerful man had intrigued her and enabled her to pretend she had another reason altogether for returning the following day to watch the boy again, this time without the young woman who, acting as her companion, had first led her that way.

She could not have given a coherent reason, even to herself, to explain why she might be content to crouch alone for the better part of a day, spying on a boy who must have been at least ten years her junior, but she had felt no desire to justify anything she did, least of all to herself. The watching gave her intense pleasure, and she had long since learned never to spurn such gifts.

Her husband, Balin, was no longer a young man, and his interest in sex for its own sake had begun to wane. A few years earlier, when he and Mairidh first wed, he had been more than able to acquit himself handsomely and had taken lustful and glorious pleasure in the voluptuous blandishments of his lovely young wife. He no longer had the potency with which to express his feelings, but his wife had, and he would never have denied her the right to express and enjoy her sexuality. Balin's beliefs were his own, gathered and assimilated throughout a lifetime of travel, observation and discussion of various religions, including Druidism and Christianity. Sex, he believed, was an elemental part of religion and religious fervour. Men and women were born of sex, he maintained, and therefore owed the gods their gratitude, which they could express through sex, irrespective of age or gender. He believed implicitly that Mairidh's love for him would be unaffected by her enjoyment of casual, normal sex with others. Love was ineffable, Balin believed, and sex was nothing more than private prayer.

Bolstered by that knowledge and having come to share her husband's beliefs over the years, Mairidh now felt no fears at all about the way Balin perceived her. She knew that his love for her was secure.

Even when she returned the third day and the boy had not appeared, Mairidh had smiled wryly to herself before admitting that she was more disappointed than she might have thought possible mere days before. But she had had nothing better to do, and the boy was beautiful enough to justify her efforts, so she had resolved to return on the fourth day.

The boy came swimming once again, accompanied this time by only a few companions. Once again she watched from the concealment of her high ledge, this time hoping against all logic that his friends would go away and leave him alone, since it was inconceivable that she might make any approach to him while they were present. They were mere boys, younger-looking and far less mature than he appeared to be, loud, boisterous and irreverent, with the bruising noisiness that all boys of their age possessed. Mairidh had no difficulty imagining their prurient reactions should they discover her spying on them, and she smiled grimly to herself and remained in hiding.

And then, quite suddenly, between one moment and the next, they vanished without warning, their presence and their noise dwindling until finally engulfed by the surrounding forest. For whatever reason, the boy had remained behind, alone, floating tranquilly on his back in their waist-deep swimming hole. She waited for a long time, her heart pounding, before she was able to accept that the others had really gone away and were not sneaking about through the undergrowth, playing some boyish game of raiders. Once she did accept it, however, she moved quickly, wasting no more time.

She descended quickly to the riverbank, careful to move quietly lest she betray her presence, and then she paused to collect herself, drawing several deep breaths in an attempt to calm her suddenly racing heart. When she was sure that no sign of any kind could betray her appearance of unsuspecting innocence, she began humming to herself very quietly and stepped forward, allowing her long-skirted clothing to brush audibly against the bushes lining the narrow riverside path.

The boy was taken completely by surprise, a picture of wide-eyed confusion as he realized that he was floating on his back, utterly naked and exposed to the eyes of a beautiful woman smiling at him from the waterside. He almost drowned himself with the sudden violence of his reaction, spinning in the water and attempting to dive out of sight, yet trying to cover his nakedness with both hands as he did so. Of course, he failed to disappear and instead merely exposed his white, vulnerable buttocks while inhaling vast quantities of water.

Watching him sputtering and flailing around with his eyes closed against the indignity of what was happening to him, Mairidh stood with her hand across her mouth, her eyes alight with laughter that she knew she must put down completely. By the time he regained his composure, she had mastered herself, and her eyes showed only concern for his welfare. He stood facing her eventually, his eyes wide and his whole body trembling slightly with tension and perhaps embarrassment, both hands held low in front of him under the water, covering his maleness.

Mairidh stepped closer to the bank, looking directly down at him.

"Are you . . . ?" She stopped herself, aware that the question would seem either foolish or patronizing. The boy simply stared, and she paused for the length of three heartbeats before continuing. "I startled you, forgive me. It was inconsiderate of me to approach so close without giving some kind of warning . . ."

"You knew I was here?" His voice, this close, was conversational and deeper, huskier than she had expected from the few shouts she had heard from a distance.

"No, of course not. How could I know that?"

His frown pressed a tiny crease between his brows. "Then why would you think to give warning of your coming?"

Mairidh smiled. "You are right, that was silly of me. I will leave you. Forgive me."

"Wait!"

She had drawn a deep breath and turned to go, moving slowly and giving him time to note the depth and shape of her bosom. Now she paused, half-turned and looked back over her shoulder towards him.

"Yes? What is it?"

He glanced about him frantically, looking for she knew not what, and then he looked at her again, perplexed. "Are you alone, Lady?"

"I am."

"But—" He stopped short, and she waited for three more beats before responding.

"But? It seemed to me you had much more to say than that,

when you began to speak." She smiled to take any edge of criticism from her words.

"You . . . you should not be alone out here. It is dangerous."

"Dangerous?" Still smiling, she looked about her. "How so, dangerous? I sense no danger here, and my senses are acute."

There was a log lying close by, its upper surface smoothed by years of long use by the boys who came to this spot to swim. Mairidh moved casually to it and sat down, gathering her skirts about her, and from that moment on, inexplicably, the tension departed, and the two of them began to converse easily. The boy began an attempt to explain the dangers that could lie in wait for an attractive woman travelling the woods with no one nearby to protect her, but since he himself was utterly innocent, he had no real idea of what those dangers might be, and he was soon floundering. Seeing his dilemma, Mairidh immediately and gently put him at his ease, provoking his embarrassment by appointing him her extempore guardian.

Thereafter, matters progressed smoothly, from Mairidh's viewpoint. She enjoyed his uncomplicated, admiring reaction to the sight of her every time she moved and took even greater pleasure from his blushes whenever she smiled at him or teased him gently. She had decided that she would have this boy, convinced that he was virginal. That conviction excited her almost unbearably, and now, knowing that she had his complete attention, she set about her seduction of the lad with great care, feeling the excitement flare and flicker in her in a way she had not known in years. She flirted with him blatantly there on the riverbank, taunting him gently and subtly, knowing intuitively that his modesty would not permit him to come out of the water, naked as he was. Drawn like a moth to a flame, however, and emboldened by her warmth despite his evident nervousness, the boy finally waded closer to where she sat, moving on his knees when he found it necessary to protect his modesty, and seated himself precariously on a stone in the river bottom where the silt-laden water was deep enough to cover his nakedness. He sat staring at her, his eyes fixed on her face, his arms floating on the surface of the water, which came up almost to his chin.

She told him much of the truth about who she was and why she was there. She had come to the region accompanying her husband, who was elderly—she had made that sound like *ancient*—and had weighty affairs to conduct in this part of the country. Those affairs, involving much talk and protracted dealings with local dignitaries and leaders, left his young wife with much free time by herself. She could have accompanied him in all things that he did, but she admitted that she found the endless talking and discussions of his errands wearisome and boring. And so she spent much time alone and in need of pleasant and amusing company.

By the time Mairidh rose to leave that afternoon, she knew that the boy's name was Merlyn—he pronounced it the old way, *Myrrdin*, in his lilting, lisping Cambrian tongue—and she knew he would be there the following day. For the entire length of that first afternoon she had exulted in the unguarded, wide-eyed way he looked at her; she had revelled in the awe with which he watched her every move and expression. And she had smiled at him often with her wide mouth and mobile lips, loving the knowledge that he was utterly unaware of his own beauty.

She rode out the following day in a light cart pulled by a single horse and found him awaiting her alone by the swimming hole, his face radiant with longing as he reached out his hand to help her down. His obvious delight and undisguised excitement at her arrival made it clear that he had not really expected her to come, and she had to breathe deeply at first to maintain her own composure. Her heart beat even faster as he gripped her hand tightly and then released it with great and evident reluctance. She looked about her then, pretending surprise that he had brought no friends with him, and he flushed with embarrassment, too unsure of himself to be confident that she had come to see him alone.

Some time later she pointed upward to the place from where she had first seen him and asked him what was up there. When he told her it was no more than a flat, grassy spot high above the river, she asked if it was accessible, and then suggested that they climb up there to eat the food she had brought with her in the cart. He was quite startled to discover that she might actually want to make the effort to climb all the way up there, but when she insisted, he was happy to assist her in making the climb, holding her hand tightly every step of the way and bracing her manfully whenever she had to lean on him for support. Only once did she slip on the way up to the heights, and it was close to the top. She went ahead of him on the last stretch, lost her balance, teetered precariously and then began to fall, twisting towards him and throwing her arms about him, clutching the back of his head in apparent terror as she pressed her face into the sweet-scented softness of his neck.

Once she had assured herself that she was safe again, she showered him with gratitude for his rescue, flattering him outrageously and squeezing his arm, pulling him close to her as they made their way up onto the thick, mossy carpet that covered the flat ground at the top of the cliff. And there, three full hours later, on the lush green grass overlooking the river far below, she took him to herself after a long drawn-out seduction, savouring the delicious first fruits of his young manhood, glorying in her power to shape him, all unknowing, to her desires, rendering him speechless and awkward, and thrilling to the hard, clean strength of him and the growing confidence with which he rose over her eventually, once the first gushing outpourings of his initial fear and tension had abated.

And then, in the midst of their idyll, while they were lost in the exploration of each other, the brutal savagery of the attack had come—the succession of kicks and heavy blows raining on the boy from every direction and his helpless efforts to avoid them and protect himself; the bestial panting and the mindless, grunting, gleeful violence of their two assailants; and the sickening sight of the boy being whirled around by one of them, free of the ground, and then hurled off the cliff top down into the river far below . . .

Now, in her safe haven, as she watched the boy preparing their food, she flinched, recalling the horrible scene. The boy noticed the sudden movement and looked over. He stiffened, and a small frown appeared between his brows.

"What? What's wrong? What is it?"

Mairidh shook her head. "Nothing. I was remembering what

happened." She sat up, holding her robe tightly at the throat so that it covered her completely. "You killed both of them."

An expression of surprise made his face go tight, and then he shrugged. "Aye. But you sound disappointed. Should I have let them live and left you with them?"

"No, of course not. That's not what I meant."

He half turned towards her, squatting back on his haunches, watching her eyes. "What did you mean, then?"

"I don't know, Merlyn. It's simply that until I saw you there, until you did it . . . I would never have considered that you might . . ." Her voice tailed away.

"Might what? Might have been capable?"

"I suppose so, yes. You seemed too young . . ."

He lifted the spitted hare away from the fire, and his muttered response drifted back to her over his shoulder. "Well you were wrong. I'm not too young. I'm almost sixteen."

She knew, intuitively, that he had misconstrued her words. "I meant too young to kill—not too young to be a man . . ." she explained.

"Is there a difference?"

Now she knew she had offended him, but she had no idea how to undo the damage, and her voice was uncertain. "Merlyn?"

"That's not my name."

"What?"

"I said that's not my name!" He looked back at her, his face flushed and guilty-looking. "When I said my name was Merlyn, I lied. Merlyn is my cousin. My name is Uther."

Mairidh merely blinked at him, uncomprehending. "Why? Why would you lie about a thing like that?"

"Because I knew who you were, and I thought you might recognize my real name."

"You knew who I was? How could you? And how would I know you as—what is it? Uther? I have never heard that name before. Why should I recognize it?"

"It's Uther Pendragon. My father is Uric, King of our people." As understanding began to come to her, he pressed on. "You told me about your husband, and I knew his business was with my father. His name is Balin. You told me that, too, but I already knew it. I have seen him, although I have never met him, and I felt . . . strange learning who you were. I knew even then, the first time I saw you, that I loved you . . . and although I would not have dared to think that I might ever touch you, I feared that if you knew I was my father's son, you might not wish to talk with me."

Now Mairidh smiled at him, savouring that admission of love—the all-consuming first love of adolescence. "Well, now you know it was a foolish fear, don't you?" she said.

"Do I? Would you have lain like that with me had you known who I truly was at the outset?"

"Of course I would! I *did* know who you truly were, Uther, and in the most important way of all for any woman: you were the one person in the world I most wanted to lie with me and take me as you did. Your *name* was the least significant thing in my mind."

He stood staring at her now, his hand lowering the peeled stick that spitted the hare so that the cooked carcass was in danger of sliding off the end of it. She nodded towards it.

"You're going to drop that into the fire, you know. Much better if you simply set it down, and we'll eat it. I'm starved."

The boy glanced towards the roasted hare, then moved it away from the flames, lowering the end of the spit to the grass as he looked back at her, his eyes searching hers for any sign of mockery.

"Do you mean that? You enjoyed . . . what we did?"

"Well, of course I enjoyed it! Come here, closer, over here . . ." She waited until he approached close enough for her to be able to reach out and touch his cheek. "Now look at me, look close into my eyes! I want you to read the truth there. Look at me and hear me . . . I loved every moment of it, and I have no regrets . . . none at all. Do you?"

His denial was immediate and emphatic, a wordless, negative head shake.

She smiled again and spoke more softly, caressing him with her tone. "Well, in truth, I do have one regret . . . I regret that we were interrupted so brutally, but that is the only regret I have. No, that's untrue, too . . . I also regret not knowing you would follow me and save me from those creatures. It would have been far easier had I known you would come for me." She paused, eyeing the hare again. "Are we going to eat that?"

He raised the stick again and withdrew it from the carcass, bracing the hot, smoking meat with a smaller stick until the main skewer came free and then laying the cooked meat on a large burdock leaf beside the fire. "I've no salt, though."

Mairidh laughed and allowed the robe to slip from her shoulders. "Let's eat it then, because I'm famished. If I need salt, I'll lick some sweat from your chest."

Later, when they lay temporarily sated with eating before the sun went down, Uther wanted to make love to her, but Mairidh demurred gently, pleading soreness and exhaustion and reminding him of all she had gone through the night before. Instantly abashed and embarrassed by his own thoughtlessness, he was profuse in his apologies, but she soothed him then and made him lie down beside her, and for a space they were quiet. But soon his awareness of her closeness stirred him afresh, and she took pity on him, relieving him with her hand in the space of a few heartbeats.

After that he slept for a short time, for he had had even less sleep than she the night before.

Later still, when his breathing changed sufficiently to tell her he was no longer asleep, she smoothed her hand up his flank as far as his hip bone, and felt him grow tense, anticipating more intimacy.

"How long will we stay here, Uther?"

"Hmm?" He was almost asleep, but he roused himself and looked around at the willow trees that stood silhouetted against the late-evening sky and screened their refuge from the rest of the world. "Tonight. We'll sleep here and head homeward in the morning. We'll be there by noon. They'll be looking for us by now, though. My father will be angry . . . Your husband will be too, I should think."

"Worried, certainly, and fretful. But not angry. He knows I would not simply run off. Had I wished to do that, I would have done it long since, and had I not wished to be here with him, I would not have come to Cambria. So he will be afraid I've come to harm, and hence he will be happy to see me returned safely by my rescuer. He will be very grateful . . . particularly when I have told him how heroic you were following me, alone and unarmed." She felt him go tense beside her. "What? Did I say something wrong?"

"What will you tell him? He'll know we were—"

She silenced him by laying her hand flat against his chest, gentling him with its steady pressure.

"Hush you! He will know only what I tell him. You were swimming and came running when you heard me scream. My attackers turned on you and beat you, then threw you into the river and stole all your possessions. But instead of drowning, you climbed back and followed them, killed them both and set me free. And then you brought me back with you. Most of that is true, save for the opening . . ."

He said nothing, and she lay silent for a spell. Then, "Was that the first time you ever killed someone?"

He turned his head away, and for a long time she thought he would not respond, but then he drew a deep breath. "It won't be the last." He kept his face averted, and she stroked the soft hairs at the nape of his neck.

"You sound very sure of that."

"I am. I am the King's son, and I'm of age. I'll be a warrior soon, and I must be a champion." His voice was very quiet.

"What do you mean by that, a champion?"

He turned back to her, wordlessly, his right hand moving in utter confidence now to her breast, the thumb brushing her nipple, stirring the smouldering fires in the depth of her so that her breath caught in her throat and she shuddered, reaching for him, yet turning her body so that his maleness thrust against her hip.

"Wait! Wait, not yet—"

He stopped, raising himself over her to peer down into her eyes, and she could see no sign of the callow, hesitant boy of the day before.

"Forgive me," he said. "I forgot, again. It shouldn't be possible for me to forget, I know, but when I am near to you like this, beside you—"

She silenced him by placing her fingertips against his lips. "Hush," she whispered, "you have done nothing wrong, and what you feel is only natural. I am the one who should feel regrets, and believe me, I do, for I want you as much as you want me . . . In fact . . . wait . . ." She moved her lower body, twisting sinuously yet carefully against him. "There now, see what you can achieve. But gently, gently . . ."

He moved delicately and with great gentleness, fitting himself to the contours of her body and lifting her cautiously with one supporting arm until he could sheathe himself, and they made love in silence, slowly and almost without moving.

When it was over, and they lay entwined, she turned her head and smiled at him. "That will improve," she whispered, "now that we have discovered how to do it without hurting any of my bruises." She moved her bottom, pushing it into the hollow of his lap. "Now, tell me what you meant earlier when you talked of being a champion rather than a warrior."

He pushed himself up on one elbow, looking down at her. "You don't know the difference?" She shook her head, gazing back at him, and he reached down beneath the coverings and hooked his other elbow gently beneath her knee, raising it and pulling it towards him, then insinuating himself into the space he had formed. For a long moment he remained there, staring into her eyes, and then, his voice thick with desire, he whispered, "Later . . . I'll tell you afterwards."

She shuddered and smiled, closing her eyes.

"Being a warrior means fighting at any time . . . But being a champion means winning all the time. It means defeating every enemy who challenges your championship, and doing it so thoroughly and so completely that he will never think to challenge you again . . . Being a warrior means fighting on command and fighting to survive. Being a champion means killing constantly in response to challenge and being challenged constantly."

Mairidh had no idea how much time had passed since Uther had last spoken. She had had other things to occupy her since then.

Listening to the sound of his voice now, however, and feeling the
sweat cooling between her breasts, she became aware that he was
repeating something learned by rote, not expressing his own opinion. She twisted her body in order to squint at him where he lay so
close beside her.

"Being challenged constantly by whom?"

"What?" He sounded now as though he had been on the verge
of sleep when she spoke.

"You said something about killing in response to challenge and
being challenged constantly. Who are these challengers?"

He made a sound that might have been a laugh or a sob. "Anyone who wishes to challenge you," he muttered sleepily. "When
you are champion, everyone wants to best you."

"So every man is your enemy, is that what you are saying?"
She waited, but he did not respond. "Uther!"

"What?"

"Don't go to sleep now. I'm talking to you. Are you saying that
all men are your enemies?"

He grunted again, then sat up, stretching his arms above his
head and then bending over her to brush his fingertips through her
pubic hair, setting her skin tingling.

"No," he said quietly, his eyes intent upon her body. "Not enemies, but rivals . . . challengers. You're all shivery . . . A champion
has no enemies . . . not living ones, at least."

She reached down and caught his hand in hers, holding it gently but firmly to rid herself of the distractions it was causing. "Who
taught you that?"

He glanced up at her and smiled, tugging gently to free his
hand. She held it fast.

"Garreth."

"And who is Garreth?"

"Garreth Whistler. He's my . . . teacher. Cay . . . Merlyn . . .
calls him my mentor, but he's really my personal guard, appointed
by my father and grandfather for my protection when I was a child.
I grew up, but Garreth remained with me. Now he teaches me to
fight the Pendragon way."

"Why do you call him Garreth Whistler?"

"Because he whistles all the time, and better than anyone else."

"Of course, why else such a name?" She was smiling gently now. "But if he is your personal guard, where is he now? Should he not be with you, protecting you at all times? Or is he merely lazy, guarding you only when he feels like it?"

The boy was outraged. "Garreth is not lazy! He is not here in Cambria, that's all. My father sent him away on the King's business three weeks ago, and he is not expected back until next month."

"Ah, I see. Forgive me, for I had no way of knowing that, and so I must ask you to convey my apologies to Garreth Whistler for the slight. Tell me about this Merlyn . . . or is his name *really* Merlyn? Did you not call him Cay a moment ago? Where does he live?"

Seeing her smile, his own smile grew wider, the pull of his hand increasing slightly. She closed her other hand about his wrist. He pressed downward, one wiggling fingertip brushing her belly.

"Aye," he said. "Both names are right. He is Caius Merlyn Britannicus. The family and his close friends all call him Cay. He's in Camulod."

"Camulod? I've heard of Camulod, but I've never been there." Mairidh paused, thinking. "Nor have I ever met anyone who has, now that I come to think of it. It's somewhere to the east of here, is it not, inland?"

The boy nodded. "Aye, southeast."

"And is it far from here to there?"

He shrugged his shoulders. "Far enough, depending upon how quickly you want to travel."

"Is it a Roman town with walls?"

"No, it is not a town at all . . ." His hand went limp, and he fell back to lie beside her. She did not release his hand, in case his surrender might be no more than a ruse, but he was looking up again now to where the sun was disappearing behind a cloud. "It's going to rain," he said, then looked at her again.

"Camulod is a place built by my grandfather and my great-uncle, about four days' travel from here. I've lived there half my life, half of all my time. The other half of the time I'm here with my father's people. Cay and I are usually together all the time."

"You like him, this Caius Merlyn, don't you?"

"Of course. He is my cousin and my closest friend. We were born on the same day, four hours and four days' travel apart. Him in Camulod, me here in Cambria. But Cay loves to read and write and learn things out of books. I don't. I prefer to learn things otherwise, by training and example, as Cay says. He thinks I'm mad not to love books."

Now it was Mairidh who smiled. "And you disagree?"

"Well, I think *he's* mad to waste so much time reading. I prefer to spend my time with Garreth. That's why I'm here this summer while Cay stays in Camulod. Garreth is training me to use the longbow properly and to fight with an axe and shield. The truth of the champion was the first thing he ever taught me, and I've never forgotten it. He taught me about fear."

"Tell me," she said.

His arm tightened very gently around her shoulders.

"You have to understand about Garreth if you're to understand what I'm going to tell you next. And you're a woman, so you might not be able to understand it. Garreth was my father's greatest warrior, the King's Champion. He would fight any and every man who sought or thought to undermine the King's authority. He was, and he still is, unconquered and unbeatable. But that day, he told me that he had always been afraid of going into battle—of fighting and of being hurt or killed."

His voice died away, and for a long time Mairidh wondered if he had forgotten that she was listening and would say no more. Finally she stirred against him, prompting him to continue.

"The only time you need be ashamed of fear, he told me, the *only* time, is when you allow your fear to rule you, for then it changes and becomes cowardice. So what you have to do is recognize your fear and then ride over it. It sounds easy enough, but it's really very difficult at first, because most men don't know what's involved. They know only that they're afraid and that they don't want to be hurt. No one has ever told them that they can face fear and overcome it simply by not allowing it to beat them. I've overcome it many times now, and it grows easier every time . . . not because your fear grows smaller, but only because you become more aware of the need to do it and get it over with. And if you do it well enough, knowing that everyone else is just as fearful as you are, then you can reach a state of mind where you can out-think your enemies and beat them by doing what they least expect. You seize the moment and make it yours. You hit first with all the strength you have and with the biggest, heaviest, sharpest weapon you possess, when he is least expecting it."

It was a long speech, the longest she had heard him make, and when he reached the end of it, she sat silent, waiting, unsure how to respond, doubting that there was anything to say that would not sound foolish or patronizing. But then he spoke again, almost inaudibly, as if he were speaking to his own inner ear.

"The rules for being a champion are simple. Conquer your own fear first."

"Really? Is it that easy?"

He turned his face towards her, half smiling, half frowning. "There's not much more than that, whether your name is Hercules, Julius Caesar or Uther Pendragon. You have to identify your enemy, face him as soon as you can and cut him down before he can fell you. No half measures, no compromises. You hit him as hard as you can, as soon as you can, and while he's reeling, you hit him again until he goes down and doesn't get back up. Do that once, and men begin to respect you; do it often enough, and they begin to fear you; do it ruthlessly enough, and eventually no others will challenge you."

"And what about you now? Have you begun to change, to become a champion, by killing those men this morning? Is that what you are trying to tell me?"

"No, it's not. I killed those men this morning because there was nothing else I could do, other than run away and leave you with them. That's part of overcoming your fear, you see . . . knowing what you have to do and then doing it before the fear of it can undo you."

"I see. But those *were* the first men you have ever killed . . . am I correct in that?"

"Aye, although I tried as hard as I could to kill another boy when I was twelve."

Mairidh had no adequate response to that, and so she subsided into silence and squirmed closer to his lean, hard body. She lay still for a time, cradled in the crook of his arm, feeling the warmth of his breath and the rise and fall of his chest until something—perhaps the depth and regularity of his breathing—told her he was asleep. She moved one hand along his forearm, feeling the solid bulk of muscle there, and she smiled to herself, enjoying the thought of how the man in him was so often usurped by the earnest, innocent boy. For now, the boy was hers to enjoy, and she was grateful. She was not tempted to consider that the man in him might some day be hers too; Mairidh was too wise for that. She smiled again and turned her face to smell the scent of him, and some time later she, too, drifted off to sleep.

When they woke up again, the first hints of dawn were beginning to lighten the sky, and they busied themselves in cleaning up, bathing in the hot pool and ransacking the Pig's sack for useful items. They found some cloths that they could use to dry themselves, but nothing else really useful, and so Uther ended up dressing himself in a loincloth made from Mairidh's sadly damaged shift and insisting that Mairidh cover her nakedness with his quilted tunic, over which she wore her own long, loose robe, effectively concealing herself from neck to knees. Then, their toilet completed to the best of their resources, they struck out for Tir Manha again.

NINE

Their homecoming occasioned a celebration even greater than they could have anticipated, for no one had connected their absences prior to the moment they reappeared together. Uther's friends had simply returned home without him on the day of his disappearance, and even when he failed to follow them by nightfall, no one was alarmed, for he was within a month of undergoing the manhood rituals, after which he would be a warrior, beholden to no man for permission to do whatever he might wish to do. Uther had been in intensive training for two years now, living in accordance with a strict regimen under the close and critical scrutiny of his tutors, studying the rituals and their forms, and preparing himself for the rigorous initiation rites and ceremonies that would mark his graduation from boy to warrior. As a natural part of that training discipline, he had long since established a pattern of spending days and weeks alone in the forest in all kinds of weather, surviving by his wits only, sometimes armed with nothing more than a knife or a sling, killing his own food and finding his own shelter. Some minor concerns began to be voiced, however, when one night became two. There were procedures and responsibilities involved in preparing for absences of two days or more—especially for the King's son—and had the young man not returned by noon the following day, his continuing absence might have caused greater excitement even than Mairidh's.

The case of the woman Mairidh was sufficiently different, however, to cause something of an uproar. This was a married woman, the wife of one of the King's honoured guests, and her disappearance was a matter that could not be taken lightly. A search had been launched by sunset on the first day of her disappearance when she had failed to return for the evening meal, and everyone who might have guessed at her whereabouts had been closely questioned. But neither search nor questioning had yielded any positive result. Even Brenna, the young woman who had accompanied Mairidh on the day of her first visit to Uther's swimming hole, had shaken her head in wide-eyed innocence when asked if she knew where the Lady Mairidh might have gone.

When the two missing persons appeared together, then, late in the morning of the third day following their "separate" disappearances, the effect on the entire populace of Tir Manha was joyous. They were seen from the walls the moment they emerged from the forest to approach the settlement surrounding the main gates of the stronghold, and by the time they had crossed the cleared fighting space, two hundred paces wide, to reach the first huts, the entire community, including Uther's parents, Uric and Veronica, had come pouring out to see and welcome them. And they were worth beholding. Both of them looked severely abused, barefoot and covered from head to foot with dried mud and dirt, bruises, cuts and abrasions. But it was Uther who drew the most attention at first, because he walked almost naked, holding himself rigidly upright, his loins covered by a length of material that very few there could have been expected to recognize: the last tattered remnants of the clothing Mairidh had worn beneath her long, loose robe on leaving the King's encampment.

Veronica Varrus stood still, slightly behind her husband and one of his advisers, frowning slightly as she looked closely at the pair. She assessed the appearance of each of them separately, noting and setting aside her observations on the small, unobtrusive ways in which they reflected an awareness of each other. When she was satisfied that she could learn no more from looking, her face cleared, and she stepped forward, smiling, to embrace her son and to welcome back her errant guest.

As Veronica embraced her son, Mairidh's husband, Balin, moved forward from the crowd surrounding the King, holding out his hands, and Mairidh moved quickly to him, bowing her head slightly as though in submission. He grasped her lightly by the upper arms and then laid one hand on the crown of her head before drawing her gently into his arms and hugging her to his chest. At length her husband pushed her back from his embrace, still holding her gently by the arms and gazing at her questioningly, his glance flicking from time to time towards Uther, who stood with his mother's arm about his shoulders, watching them, his chin held high.

Uther kept his gaze fastened on Balin and watched as he examined his wife, taking her chin softly in his right hand and tilting her face up until her eyes met his. Uther could see no trace of anger or resentment or concern in the man's face, other than that of a fond parent regarding a beloved child.

"Are you well, Mairidh? Have you been hurt?"

The woman nodded her head in a tiny gesture of acknowledgment. "Both, Husband, yes and yes. I have been hurt, but I am well. I was abducted close by here while I was walking alone by the river. The men who captured me were strangers, speaking an alien tongue. They must have landed on the coast some way from here in a boat from only the gods know where. But I was rescued by this young man here, whom I have found to be the son of King Uric, and who risked his life in saving mine."

Mairidh turned her head and smiled at Veronica before addressing the King. "Your son does you and your lady wife great credit, King Uric. If he should follow you in years to come, he will be a mighty king. He is already a great warrior. Unaided, he slew the men who took me captive, even after I thought they had killed him." She stopped and swayed slightly, speaking now to Balin. "Husband, I am sore, and I am soiled, and I am hungry beyond belief. Will you welcome me back and wait until later to hear my tale?"

Hours later, washed and bathed and dressed again in rich, soft clothing, having eaten and drunk her fill, Mairidh regaled her husband and Uther's parents, together with the King's entire retinue, with the tale of Uther's heroism. Uther himself was not present, since his father had expressly banned him from the gathering, confining the young man to his own quarters until Uric himself was satisfied that no harm had been done to his regal reputation and that his son had, in fact, behaved appropriately throughout this strange episode. So, while Mairidh told her tale of his exploits, Uther waited in suspense elsewhere, fretting over what she might let slip to his father.

He worried needlessly, for Mairidh's tale was as she had promised it would be: no more than the truth, save for a minor alteration of the opening details of the events and the omission of the personal intimacies that occurred between them afterward.

She had been taken unawares, she told them all, surprised completely while resting on a high cliff, a moss-covered promontory in the woods above the riverside, where she had chosen to rest for a time, daydreaming, with never a thought of danger in such a lovely spot so close to the King's stronghold. Her attackers had leaped out at her from nowhere, it seemed to her, giving her no opportunity to resist or to defend herself as they bundled her up in her own robe and dragged her away. One single scream was all she had time to voice, and that was cut short by a clenched fist that knocked her half senseless.

That single cry had been heard, however, by young Uther Pendragon, who came quickly to her rescue. Unfortunately, he had been swimming in the river below when he heard her cry, and so he came running and scrambling precipitately and unprepared, climbing the cliff naked and weaponless.

Uther was then swiftly and brutally dealt with by the larger of her two assailants. The fellow had waited for the boy to reach the top and then pounced on him and beat him savagely, after which he hoisted the senseless youth into the air, holding him by one ankle and the hair of his head, spun him around several times and threw the boy high into the air from the cliff down into death on the river stones beneath.

From that point onward, aware of her wide-eyed audience and satisfied that she had convinced every one of them that what she had said at the outset was the literal truth, Mairidh kept herself strictly to accuracy in her tale, merely omitting any mention of how she and Uther had kept themselves warm during the long, chilly nights and cool during the long, warm days. And when she had finished, no one, including the boy's mother, thought to doubt a word of what she had said.

Uther knew things had gone well with Mairidh's reporting when the door to his chambers swung open later that afternoon and his father, King Uric, entered smiling. Drawing himself up to his full height, Uther masked his relief and fought to keep his nervousness from showing, for he had been more than mildly apprehensive of being discovered as the Lady Mairidh's lover. The glaring fact of her status as the spouse of one of his father's most exalted guests meant that in coupling with her, irrespective of her willingness and eager participation or even of her initiation of the process, Uther had broken one of the King's most sacred rules of hospitality. It mattered not that it was a personal and unique rule, designed and implemented by the monogamous king in deference to his Christian wife, Veronica. Nor did it matter that the rule caused outrage and sniggering among Uric's own chiefs and chieftains, who considered their King to be too soft by half in such matters. What was important was that the rule was enforced with a grim lack of magnanimity that was unusual coming from his otherwise tolerant father.

From that perspective, Uther was grossly at fault, both culpable and vulnerable, and his greatest fear had been that Mairidh might betray him inadvertently, thereby exposing him to the King's anger, which was legendary in both its rarity and its ferocity. Now, seeing the King's demeanour, the boy knew immediately that his secret had been kept safe. He moved to meet his father, extending his hand while carefully keeping his face empty of expression, but Uric came straight to him and threw his arms about his son's shoulders, hugging him tightly, saying nothing. Then, after a short time, he spoke over Uther's shoulder, as though he were addressing the wall behind them.

"There was a time there, you know, when you first arrived this morning, when I had the thought—but only for a moment—that you might have failed me and done something . . . regrettable . . ." He let that hover in the air briefly. "Then I recalled who you were and what you are, and my own reason told me I was being stupid and unworthily suspicious. And yet, you had been gone, and the Lady Mairidh had been gone, and so the thought occurred to me—and to more than just me, I'll wager—that it might . . . that you might have been together, man and woman, I mean, on an assignation."

Uther tried not to stiffen in his father's grasp, but the King had not finished saying what he wished to say.

"As soon as the Lady Mairidh began to speak, of course, she gave the lie to that," he went on. "Then again, I thought, beautiful women have been known to lie with great fluency when putting horns upon their husbands." He stepped back then and grasped his son by the shoulders, looking him straight in the eye. "And now we have all heard it, and I am proud of you, my son. You have done well. But I would like to hear *your* version of the tale. I'll wager it will be more bloody than the Lady Mairidh's."

Uther shook his head and tried to smile, hoping that his father might think the flush that stained his face was caused by modesty and not by shame at having to pretend heroic nobility when all he had achieved was deceit. He tried to demur and avoid the telling, but his father would have none of it, and so the tale was told again, mindful of Mairidh's changes to the start of it, but faithful thereafter to chronology and details, ending with the killing of the two raiders, the escape from their encampment and the decision to leave the horse and make their way on foot back to where they had set out.

The King nodded slowly, visualizing the situation and agreeing with the logic of his son's choices. "Good. Good for you, lad. You've a sensible head on your shoulders. And that reminds me, the lady's husband, Balin, wishes to receive you as soon as you may go to him. He is extremely grateful, and I believe you will find him more than generous in rewarding you for saving his wife's life." The King smiled again, this time at the new flush that swept over his son's face. "Come, now," he said. "You have earned the praise and the rewards, now accept them as your right. But if the thought appalls your modesty, you should go and get it over with now, as soon as you can."

On the point of dismissing that suggestion out of hand, Uther bethought himself and stood silent for several moments longer, musing on the pros and contras of an immediate meeting with the man with whose wife he had lain with so recently. Postponed, the meeting would grow no easier, he knew. Better perhaps to get it over and done with quickly, before the aggrieved husband would have time to dwell upon what might have taken place while his wife was absent—before she had been covered with her rescuer's tunic . . . Besides, Uther knew that his father would soon come to wonder why his son should be so reluctant to meet with a man who must be deeply in his debt. The King of the Pendragon was no man's fool and had not achieved his high station because he was short-sighted or stupid. Finally he nodded his head.

"You are right, Father. Best get it over with, although I did nothing heroic, so I would rather not be thanked. There is nothing commendable about sneaking up on two sleeping men and braining them in the darkness. All I had to do afterwards was cut the woman loose and bring her home . . . So I suppose I'll go and meet her husband now. Will you come with me?"

His father smiled and shook his head. "No, Uther, and if you think about it, you'll see why: the man will wish to show his gratitude and obligation to you. I am the King, and I'm your father. That alone obliges him to show impressive gratitude. My presence would place an intolerable burden upon him, adding to that obligation. I cannot do that to him."

Uther nodded, then looked about him, sucking in a great breath. "Well, I ought to go and see him now, d'you think?"

"Yes. He'll be waiting for you."

"Very well, then . . . I'll go . . ."

Thinking back on it years later, Uther would remark to his friend Huw Strongarm that he came very close to leaving his father's stronghold that afternoon and fleeing to Camulod to avoid the confrontation that his guilty conscience had assured him must take place between him and his father's honoured guest. It was only the awareness that in so doing he would be acknowledging a guilt of which no one had yet accused him that kept him from going. And had he left that day, he mused to Huw, then the entire development and course of the wars with Cornwall and its self-styled King, Gulrhys Lot, might have turned out very differently.

As it was, he approached the quarters that housed Balin and his wife with great reluctance and trepidation, and when he saw a smiling Mairidh waiting in the doorway to greet him, his guilt and fear grew to confusion and near-panic. Nothing in Uther's experience had prepared him for the sight of a carefree, smiling Mairidh, and although he knew with one part of his mind that he should be glad, he was not yet mentally spry enough, or perhaps not yet cynical enough, to adapt instantly to the unexpected sight of her unworried smile.

Unaware of his confusion, Mairidh grasped him gently by the wrist and turned away, pulling him with her as she moved directly to the closed door at her back, and Uther, his heart hammering in his chest, the softness of her hand burning the skin where she touched him, thought for one mad moment that she was abducting him somehow, pulling him into a private room to make love to him beneath her husband's very nose. In a complete panic, he began to pull back, tugging against her, but she had already knocked on the door and turned to face him, still smiling widely.

"Balin?" she called. "My rescuer is here. Shall I send him in?"

The door opened almost before she had finished saying the words, and Balin, a tall, elderly man with long, silver hair, stepped forward into the light of the doorway and inclined his upper torso in something approaching a bow, a courteous gesture conveying respect that included both Mairidh and Uther. "No need for that, my love," he said in a deep, quiet voice. "I am here to welcome our benefactor myself."

He extended a hand, waving it gently to usher Uther into his sanctum. "If it pleases you, Uther Pendragon, come into my world. You have already entered into it, and into my life, with your rescue of my beloved consort, so now it will please me greatly if you will accept my gratitude and my freely granted access to the remainder, which is but little when compared to all I might have lost. Come in, come in, and sit with me, talk with me."

Disarmed, flattered and thrown decidedly off balance by the charming manner and the unmistakable sincerity of the man who greeted him so amiably, Uther allowed himself to be ushered forward into Balin's chamber, and presently he found himself seated in front of a glowing brazier, holding a cup which his host was busy filling with yellow sparkling wine.

Mairidh had vanished silently into another part of the square-built house, which, though small in area, was rich in its amenities as befitted the dwelling reserved for the King's most important guests, and so bemused was Uther by the attention lavished upon him by her husband that he had not even been aware that she had not followed him into the room. What he could not have known, however, was that she now sat close by, on the other side of the wall closest to him and within two paces of where he sat facing her husband. There, secure in her own privacy, she sat in comfort in a thickly padded armchair, sipping a cup of the same wine the men were drinking and listening to the voices that came directly to her over the top of the wall-like partition that divided the large room into two equal halves. She heard every word of the conversation taking place in Balin's room as clearly as though she were sitting there herself.

Rapt now, Uther sat watching as the bubbling liquid reached the rim of his cup, and his host pulled the ewer away without allowing a single drop to spill. Balin's face was tense with delight as he peered at Uther, waiting for him to taste the wine, but Uther made no move to do so. He had tasted wine before, but never yellow wine, just *vinum*, the rank, sour red wine mixed with water of the Camulodian cavalry troopers. In his father's mountainous country of south Cambria, wine was seldom drunk, simply because it was seldom, if ever, available.

"Drink, taste the nectar of the gods." Balin filled his own cup and hoisted it to his lips, holding the ewer high in his other hand as he drank. Watching him, Uther drank too, but cautiously, sipping carefully and apprehensive of what he would find in his mouth, mindful of the gut-wrenching sourness that had almost sickened him on first tasting *vinum*. Instead of bitterness, however, he found his mouth filled with liquid sunshine, with a delicious, almost syrupy-sweet explosion of rich flavours that set his entire mouth tingling and his mind reeling as he sought to identify the tastes that blended and melded together on his tongue.

"Is it not wonderful? Have you ever tasted its like?"

Uther could only shake his head in wonder as he took another mouthful.

"It is from the very central regions of the lands of the wild Germanic tribes the Romans could never conquer, and the grapes from which it is made are grown on the slopes along the shores of the vast river they called the Rhenus, which marked the northeastern borders of Rome's Empire. This nectar that we drink is the greatest contradiction in the world, for the people who perfected the making of it are so savage, so ferocious, that they stopped Rome's legions and defied them entry to the farthest regions of their lands—the only people in all the world who ever did so, save only for the northernmost Caledonians, whose land is so unwholesome and infertile that the Romans felt no desire for it. And yet, in all their fury, these untamable Germanic tribes have the ability to make this magnificent wine. The grapes they grow on their hillside terraces are pale green, I am told, and very sweet, rich in sugars and perfect for the making of this nectar, which is found nowhere else." He stopped speaking and sipped delicately at the liquid in his cup, rolling it on his tongue and savouring it lingeringly before taking a second taste.

"It is difficult to come by this, as you might imagine, now that there is little commerce between Britain and Gaul. I have a . . . a supplier, however, whose connections extend far and wide and who relies upon the truth that people everywhere have need of his trading skills. The last time I saw him, thanks be to all the gods, when I revisited my home in Cornwall, he had a good amount, but even he cannot guarantee a constant supply—" Balin stopped short, startled by the way Uther had suddenly scowled and sat up straight and stiff-backed. "What is wrong? Do you not like the wine?"

Uther's scowl deepened. "I did not know you are from Cornwall."

Balin held his head slightly higher, his face reflecting surprise and amusement. "Of course I am from Cornwall! Where did you think I hailed from, and why should it seem so unpleasant to you?"

Uther realized belatedly that his reaction had been truculent and ill-mannered. "I . . . I knew only that you were here on some kind of diplomatic business with my father. I assumed you were from . . . it shames me that I was not interested enough to find out."

Balin now offered a small half-smile. "No need for shame, but you do sound disappointed."

"I am, sir. Disappointed at myself. I am the King's son, after all."

Balin inclined his head in a gesture that signified both agreement and respect. "It is true you are the King's son, but you are not yet a warrior in the formal sense. You face the Manhood Rites within the month, is that not so?"

"Yes, that is true."

"Well, then, since you are legally a boy and not yet a warrior with a warrior's responsibilities and duties, why should you feel shame over not having identified my origins? Even had you been curious about me, your curiosity would have gone unsatisfied. Forgive my mentioning it, but you are yet too young to participate in men's affairs."

"But not too young to ask questions. Not being a warrior is no excuse for being unready, Lord Balin. Had I been unready a few days ago, your wife might not be here now."

Balin inclined his head in acknowledgment of that truth. "But why would you even think to ask where I was from? You make it sound highly important that you should know such a thing."

Uther stood up and placed his cup carefully on a small table near his chair. "It is, sir, when the answer to the question is Cornwall. Now I must leave you. Thank you for the wine."

"Great Dagda!" Balin subsided into a chair as quickly as Uther had sprung to his feet, but he was smiling in disbelief. "You intend to leave me, just like that, for being from Cornwall? Are we then mortal enemies, and have you found yourself in here with me by misadventure? Do you fear, then—tell me quickly—for your life?"

Uther felt a flush steal over his face. "Well . . . no."

"Aha! Then sit, if it please you, and finish your wine, and while you are doing so, inform me, if you will, why it should surprise you so unpleasantly to discover where I make my home. Have you enemies in Cornwall?"

"Yes, I have. A mortal enemy." Uther sat down again, but made no move to pick up the wine cup.

Balin, whose question had been facetious, now sat staring blankly at him for a space of moments before he spoke again. When he did, the entire tone of his voice was different, cautious and faintly speculative.

"Your father made no mention of this." .

"My father knows nothing about it."

"But how can that be? You have a mortal enemy, but unknown to your father? Not that I doubt you, of course, but it seems . . . strange. You have never visited Cornwall, have you? So whence comes this enmity? Is it recent"

"No, it began three years ago."

"Three *years* ago? Then you were but a boy indeed, a child! What happened, and with whom were you at odds?"

"Do you know Duke Emrys?"

"Of course I know Duke Emrys. He is my lord."

"And his son, Gulrhys Lot?"

"Lot? Great gods! Were you the one, then, the boy who attacked Lot in Camulod and almost killed him?"

Uther shrugged. "I suppose I was. But he attacked me, too . . . Look, see where he chopped me." He extended his right leg and pulled up the hem of his tunic to expose a long, deep scar on the outside of his thigh, a hand's breadth above the knee.

"Indeed! That is a man's wound, a battle wound. But you were mere children, boys."

"No, Lord Balin, I was twelve years old, and Gulrhys Lot was as old as I am now, and he insulted my mother beyond credence or bearing. Had my uncle, Picus Britannicus, not stopped us, Gulrhys Lot would not be alive today. I would have killed him."

Balin sat silent for a spell digesting that, then nodded, his face blank. "I see this struck far deeper and was of greater moment than I was given to believe. You say Lot insulted your mother . . . sufficiently to provoke you to the point of killing? I find it hard to believe that Duke Emrys would have permitted such gross behaviour from his son."

Uther merely blinked, his own face betraying nothing of his thoughts. "Duke Emrys was not there at the time. There were but the three of us—Lot, my cousin Cay and me. The Duke knew nothing of what happened until it was all over. And Uncle Picus found us only by accident. He was passing by and heard the sound of our swords."

"May I ask what you were doing in Camulod? I have never been there, and I am curious about the place. Some of the tales I hear of it seem too wondrous to be true. This uncle of yours is an important man there, is he not?"

Uther hesitated, then picked up his wine again and sipped at it. It was clear that the anger he had expected to inspire with his revelation about Gulrhys Lot would not be forthcoming. Either this Balin was indeed a more skilful diplomat than he betrayed, or he was genuinely uncaring of what might have befallen his lord's son. Uther rolled the delicious wine around on his tongue and then took a larger gulp, filling his mouth and holding the beverage captive, feeling the tiny prickles of the sparkling bubbles. Then finally he swallowed, conscious that his father would be displeased to see him drinking unwatered wine of any kind and would be even less pleased by the overt pleasure he was showing in the drinking of it. He replaced the cup carefully on the small table, then smiled at Balin, who sat watching him.

"My uncle, Picus Britannicus, is Legate and Supreme Commander of the Forces of Camulod."

"A very grand title."

Uther nodded soberly. "Aye, sir, and a powerful one. He assumed command from my grandfather, Gaius Publius Varrus, who had inherited the title from his friend and brother by marriage, Caius Cornelius Britannicus, who was Uncle Picus's father. Great-uncle Caius and Grandfather Varrus were the founders of Camulod, which was originally a collection of large and prosperous farms."

Balin sat blinking, fingering his beard abstractedly and frowning slightly in perplexity. "Farms? Explain that, please. I don't quite understand. Camulod is a fortress, from what I have heard. No one has ever spoken of the place in terms of farms or farming."

Uther fought to keep his face expressionless, because he was surprised and fascinated by how much he was learning here. Before his discovery of Balin's Cornish identity, he had assumed that this man, as an honoured guest of his father and an ambassador from some distant king or chief, would know everything there was to know about Camulod, Pendragon's closest and strongest ally. It now appeared, however, that the man knew almost nothing, and that made it instantly obvious to the boy that his father had been unresponsive to the questions Balin must have asked him.

Uther's mind was churning, his thoughts chaotic. Why should his father have been so secretive? It must have stemmed from distrust, he decided—if not of Balin himself, then certainly of his master, the Cornish Duke Emrys. Although he had often been glad in the past that he was not expected or permitted to sit in on the frequent and all too often tedious gatherings of his father's Council, Uther now found himself wishing heartily that he knew more about these things. Then, remembering Garreth Whistler's warning that it was most often better to say little and listen closely, he shook his head and smiled, allowing himself to look slightly perplexed.

"Have you never been in that part of the world at all, Lord Balin, the lands around Aquae Sulis to the east of here?"

"Yes, I have, but not for many years, and I never gained any great knowledge of the region. I understand that Camulod itself is not far from there, a matter of a few days' ride . . ." Balin paused for a long time, evidently musing on other things, before continuing. "It is a strange thing, because I have travelled widely over the years in my role as adviser to Chief Emrys, long before he took upon himself the Roman title of *dux*, or Duke. I began as his *factotum*, to use the Roman word for it, standing in his place to assist and mediate in his early trading ventures, and my responsibilities in the service of the Duke have gradually increased as time has passed. In each of my several capacities I have seen the entire length of this island—along the coastlines of both Britain *and* Caledonia, on both sides, east and west—on several occasions, and I have even crossed the western sea to Eire three times.

"Before the Romans left, in the first great exodus when Stilicho recalled the British legions, I wandered over the entire country, looking after the commercial interests of my master—" He broke off suddenly, and his face lit up in a smile. "Strange, is it not, how all things change, even our ways of thinking of ourselves? You are too young now to see the truth of that, but some day you will. I spoke about myself and Emrys. Now he is Duke Emrys, and I refer to him as my lord. Formerly, however, he was Chief Emrys, and before that merely Emrys, an able and gifted trader and a formidable fighter." Balin paused again, staring into his cup, and then resumed, still gazing pensively into his wine.

"Beyond Britain, I am also familiar with most parts of Gaul, and I would have trouble, I suspect, deciding with any accuracy on how many times I have been to that land, both north and south. That is where I formed my taste for fine wines like this one we are drinking now. I have friends and acquaintances and contacts and go-betweens among the Burgundian peoples and the Frankish clans who are settling into those territories where the Burgundians have not yet gone. So it seems strange that, with all that travelling spread over all too many years, I should have missed some areas so close to home. Nevertheless, I suspect that much of life is like that. We seldom see what is closest to our eyes. So, if it please you, tell me about Camulod and how it came to be."

Uther smiled and shrugged and shook his head in self-deprecation. "Well, as you yourself have said, I am not a warrior yet, so there is much I don't know . . . much to which I am not privy. I cannot tell you much about Camulod today, Lord Balin—about its strengths or weaknesses or how it is organized or governed. But I can tell you about how it came to be what it is today. I have been well taught regarding that story."

Balin inclined his head. "Do so, if you would. You mentioned it was founded by two men, relatives of yours."

"Aye, that's right. The story of Camulod began when my grandfather, Publius Varrus, first came to this region to visit my great-uncle,

Caius Britannicus, then remained here to marry my grandmother, Luceiia Britannicus. Before that, there was no Camulod. Publius Varrus married my grandmother Luceiia almost fifty years ago, and it was after their marriage that the territories of the place they called the Colony were assembled and drawn together, in preparation to defend themselves after the Romans left Britain.

"They chose the old hill fort we now call Camulod as being the best place from which to organize the defence of all their farms. It was centrally located among their Colony's holdings, and it had served as a defensive fort in ancient times, long before the Romans ever came to Britain. Publius Varrus's only use for it in the beginning was as a rallying point, a base from which to launch his forces, who were all infantry in those days.

"Somewhere around that same time, my other grandfather, Ullic Pendragon, befriended Varrus and Britannicus, and they made alliance between them, Pendragon Cambria and what Caius Britannicus called the Britannic Colony, each to defend the other's back in time of war and peril. The towers of Camulod began to grow then, too, first as wooden palisades and then as walls of stone, and they began to breed and rear horses, because of the speed they offered—the best and fastest means of moving men to defend the Colony's borders.

"Then when the Romans left Britain for good, about the time I was born, my Uncle Picus, who rode with the Roman Regent Stilicho, arranged for his father, my Great-uncle Caius, to take possession of more than six hundred head of prime Roman cavalry stock, and since that time the place has thrived."

"Hmm." Balin sat relaxed, enjoying his young guest and making no attempt to hide his amusement. "So, given that Camulod was founded by your family, will you rule there one day?"

"Gods, no, that's not for me! My cousin Cay will undertake the governing of Camulod, and he will be magnificent at doing it. My rightful place is here in Cambria, among my father's mountains and his warriors. But I am grateful to my friends and kin in Camulod for the gift of horsemanship. Because horses are weapons, the greatest and most powerful weapons this world has ever seen."

"Horses?" Balin's smile had vanished, and it was evident that he was now quite bewildered. "But . . . but horses have been here for as long as men have . . ."

"Of course, Lord Balin. What is new is the *use* that Camulod makes of horses. Cavalry such as theirs is in—" Uther broke off in mid-word, aware that he had been on the point of saying "invincible," and something, some unexpected prompting, had forbidden him to say the word. He snorted, as though choking back a self-deprecating laugh, aware that Balin was still waiting for him to finish what he had started to say, then shrugged his shoulders, shaking his head slightly, as though in dismissal of his own silliness.

"Anyway," he resumed, "weapon or no, I am grateful that I have a horse of my own and can roam free where and when it pleases me."

"Aye, there's nothing finer than being free and untrammelled, but few of us after we reach manhood are able to enjoy that feeling. Had it not been for this drive of yours to go wherever you wish, whenever you wish, I would have lost my wife. She has told me in great detail about all that you did for her, and I am in your debt forever. I will not insult you by offering you gold or jewels, although I have both in plenty and they are yours for the asking, should you so desire, but I feel that my debt to you involves a price far higher than any that can be paid in jewels or specie. I do not know, at this time, how I will repay you, but a means will come to me. Or it might come to you—some form of recompense that you would value greatly but which I might never consider. Bend your mind to that, young man. Think of me as a friend, and do not let yourself be bound by any other considerations in this. Who knows what you might require? And who knows what I might be able to do for you?"

Unable to think of anything to say in response to that, Uther rose to his feet and looked around the room. Normally this chamber, and the others that served with it as guest quarters, sat vacant, but always clean and well aired, ready to be used at a moment's notice. And while it was true that the room generally reflected very little of the people who passed through and used it, there were visitors from time

to time who imprinted their personalities and moods visibly upon the
room and its furnishings during their stay.

There was a stringed instrument of some kind leaning against
a chair by the room's main table, and Uther placed his wine cup
down gently and crossed to examine it more closely. Although he
knew the instrument was a harp, it was unlike any harp he had seen
before—larger and more solid-looking in the main pillar of the
frame. Careful not to upset it, for it looked carefully balanced, he
stretched out a questing hand to touch the strings and run the pad
of one finger up and down one of them, feeling its rough texture.

"Gut," Balin said. "Dried animal gut. Swine, I believe, or perhaps
it is sheep gut. It is an Erse harp. I found it last time I was over in Eire
and bought it from the man who owned it. The fellow couldn't play
it at all. He kept it because it had belonged to his first wife, who had
died while yet young enough to be lovable. And you are barely listening to what I am saying. What is it that distracts you?"

Uther looked up and smiled. "I was thinking about how surprised I am that you are not angry. I thought you would be."

"Angry? And why should I be angry?"

"Because of what I told you . . . about Lot."

Balin shook his head and flapped his hand in dismissal of that.
"What happened between you and Gulrhys Lot was personal, and
it happened long ago. I see no reason in that for me to grow angry
thinking about it . . . do you, really?"

"No, Lord Balin, I do not, now that I think about it in that light.
It—"

"But I *could* grow angry, I believe, were I to allow myself to
dwell upon the ideas you formed and the conclusions you drew
from that long-ago confrontation."

Frowning, Uther started to say something else, but Balin cut
him off again, raising one hand swiftly, palm outward. "No, it is
true. You emerged from that encounter with Gulrhys Lot fully convinced that everyone from Cornwall is as he is and behaves as he
behaves, and you have not changed your thinking on that in—how
long ago was it, three years? For three years you have walked
around with poisonous nonsense flowing through your mind, and it

sprang out of you the moment I mentioned that I am from Cornwall. You looked at me as though I had become a writhing serpent. Do you deny that?"

Uther shrugged his shoulders, feeling his face flush with discomfort. "No, I cannot."

"But why would you even think such a thing? Lot may be as evil and pernicious as you think him to be. But why should I and every other person from Cornwall be so vilely tainted by your memories of that one man?"

"Because my memories of him *are* vile and bitter."

"I have no doubt of that, Uther Pendragon, and you are not alone in feeling as you do. My loyalty is to his father, the Duke Emrys, and there it ends. I bear no allegiance at all, of any kind, to Gulrhys Lot, and I swear there have been times when I would have happily wagered that Emrys himself cannot stomach the boy he fathered . . ." He paused, gazing at the boy who stood watching him, his face troubled. "I think I am going to have to teach you a little about Cornwall, Master Uther. Sit down now and drink your wine while I tell you about my nephew, who is older than you— three years older, in fact, since he is of an age with Gulrhys Lot. His given name is Lagan, and Mairidh tells me that in recent months he has won the name Longhead, by virtue of his intellect and his far-sightedness. By some strange coincidence that I have never quite understood, he and I ended up married to sisters. His wife, Lydda, a beautiful young creature no more than a year or so older than you are, is Mairidh's youngest sister, so Lagan is not only my nephew by blood, the son of my elder brother, but he is also a relative of some other kind by marriage."

In the course of the half hour that followed, Uther learned much about the young man known as Lagan Longhead, and in listening learned much, too, about the customs and rituals that governed the passing of boys into manhood in Cornwall.

On the other side of the wall, Mairidh smiled and closed her eyes, listening with pleasure as her husband spoke of home and family.

TEN

Nemo saw Uther as her personal champion, and so she was unsurprised when, in the time of her greatest need, he appeared. She would have expected nothing less.

It happened early in the autumn of the year she passed seventeen, when she walked blithely into peril in a way that her younger self would never have permitted. Three men, travellers passing through Tir Manha, had noticed her shortly after the midday meal when she walked by them heedlessly, daydreaming of Uther, who was due to return home from Camulod that day or the next. Nemo had long since learned to keep herself clean, acutely aware that Uther set great store by cleanliness, thanks to his long Roman-influenced periods in Camulod, but she had never come to realize that her cleanliness now gave her a distinctive scent that could be alluring and arousing to rough men passing by in a condition of enforced abstinence. Watching her, the three paid no attention to her heavy facial features or the rough texture of her hair. Instead, they smelled sexual challenge in the clean, alluring scent of her and saw it in the firm young strength of her limbs and buttocks and in the thrust of her seventeen-year-old breasts.

Having noticed her, they followed, watching her closely, waiting for a suitable time and place. Then, when circumstances seemed right, they attacked her like wolves, leaping from behind and bundling her into the long grass by the roadside, pulling her quickly and quietly down out of sight into concealment among rank growth and thick shrubs.

It was not the first time Nemo had been waylaid by sexual predators, however, and her ferocious, silent and deadly response took her three attackers unawares. Extremely strong and implacably savage by nature, Nemo was a burly badger of an opponent, and she fought them as any wild thing fights confinement, single-mindedly seeking to save her own life and to inflict maximum damage on her tormentors in the process. Hunched over and battling grimly, making the most of her solid bulk and her low centre of gravity, she refused to yield or submit in any degree, so that even outnumbering her, her opponents had great difficulty in subduing her. So great was their difficulty, in fact, and so total their concentration upon immobilizing and holding her down for their gratification that all of them failed to notice the approach of the fast-moving horseman who came charging down at them from the hillside above.

Nemo was on her back, fighting for her life, hemmed in and confined, it seemed to her, by an entire forest of men's legs. She kicked and chopped and gouged fiercely, catching one man in the groin with a hard-swung but glancing blow and dropping him to his knees. One of his two companions who had stepped back from the fray, pulling at his breeches to free himself in preparation for claiming the first fruits of her, saw the man drop and looked towards him, grunting and starting to laugh barely a moment before Nemo lunged at him and snatched at his rigid phallus with rending, long-nailed fingers. His laughter turned to a scream as those fingernails dug deep, drawing blood, and Nemo's thick, muscular fist closed around his hardness, wrenching violently, twisting downward and inward hard, pulling him towards her as her other fist smashed brutally upward into his exposed and unprotected scrotum. His knees, too, gave way, and he collapsed on top of her, barely conscious, just as young Uther Pendragon, screaming a war cry of some kind, threw himself from his horse's back directly into the middle of the struggling knot of bodies.

He landed on the shoulders of the only one of the trio who had been able to grasp a firm hold of Nemo. With his arms around her waist from behind and his crashing weight, Uther took the hunched figure of the man and the woman beneath him face downward into the grassy bottom of the ditch. Then, before anyone else had a chance to react or move, the long, single-edged dirk in Uther's hand rose up and plunged down again to bury itself between the fellow's shoulders. The stabbed man reared up violently, almost throwing Uther completely off his back, and then he stiffened and gave out a wet, gurgling sound before falling forward, dead, covering Nemo completely so that she had to fight to crawl out from beneath the weight of him.

Before the corpse had even toppled, however, Uther was moving, ripping his dagger free and stabbing out hard again, sideways this time and to his right, at the man Nemo had savaged. This fellow was hunched over in agony, his spindly, bare thighs ludicrously pale and hairless above the trousers that were pushed down about his knees, and his entire attention was concentrated upon finding respite from the excruciating pain of his damaged testicles. He had not seen his companion die, and he did not see the blow that took his own life. The point of Uther's blade penetrated the unprotected base of his throat and then sliced down and across as Uther slashed deep.

The remaining attacker, the one whom Nemo had kicked first, had seen all of this, and now he leaped to his feet and began to run. He had barely taken two strides, however, when he found his way blocked by another horseman, and before he could even think to dodge, the rider's armoured boot, lodged in its heavy, wooden stirrup, rose up and smashed down again, hitting him full in the face and sending him reeling and falling backwards to where young Uther Pendragon was already lurching forward, bloodied dirk raised high.

"Uther, *no!*"

The call from the armoured rider came too late. Uther's arm was already encircling the other man's neck, and the long-bladed dirk was digging deep, probing upwards between the ribs for his heart. Uther Pendragon, grim-faced, held the dying man close against his chest, straining against the convulsions of the body until they ceased, and then he released his grip and allowed the man to fall, retaining his tight grasp on the dagger's hilt so that the dead weight of the corpse pulled it free of the blade. When the body lay at his feet, he stood gazing down at it for long moments. Then he bent slowly and pulled the head covering, a length of plain brown cloth, from the corpse.

His mounted companion watched closely as Uther cleaned his blade with the cloth, his face expressionless and calm, his eyes unfocused. Then, when the blade was clean, fastidiously wiped free of any lingering trace of blood, Uther Pendragon replaced it carefully in the sheath that hung from his belt and turned his head to look at the young woman who sat on the grass, staring up at him in silent worship with her bent knees spread, her skirts somewhere up around her waist, her entire lower body uncaringly exposed. Gazing at her, narrow-eyed, he shook his head. Nemo had no idea why he did that or what he was thinking. Before she could think any further about it, however, he stepped towards her, holding out his hand, and she reached out and took it, using it as an anchor as she pulled herself smoothly up from the ground. Neither she nor he spared as much as a glance for the three dead men at their feet.

"Are you hurt at all?"

Nemo shook her head, overcome with shyness as she always was when he spoke directly to her. She was forever unable to trust her voice around him, afraid that it would tremble and break. Uther, however, paid no attention to her silence, reacting instead as if she had spoken and nodding now towards the three dead men.

"What happened here? Do you know these people?"

She shook her head again, and he sniffed, looking down at the closest corpse.

"Well, even if you did, it would make no difference now. Good thing we came along, though. Have you had a man before?" Nemo's eyes widened slightly, but she took no offence, and he assumed from her expression that the answer to his question was negative. He pursed his lips. "Best think about it, then, and get the painful part over with. Find yourself a decent fellow and pleasure both of you. Once you've done it once or twice, there's no pain to it thereafter, no matter how they violate you. First time, though, against your will, can be brutal, I'm told. Go home now. There's no danger left here."

She nodded her head and bobbed in what might have been a subservient bow, and then she turned and was gone, disappearing quickly into the bushes that lined the road.

The two men watched her go, then Uther sucked pensively at his teeth, producing a speculative, squeaking noise. The man on the horse cleared his throat.

"Are you going to puke?"

Uther looked up at Garreth Whistler. "No, I am not. Why should I puke?"

"I thought you might. Most people do when they kill a man, it being an unusual event. You just slaughtered three men with your bare hands, so I thought you might want at least one heave."

"I used my blade, not my bare hands. But no, I don't feel sick."

"You should, boy. Sick over your own stupidity, if nothing else."

The younger man's head jerked up as though he had been slapped. "What is that supposed to mean?"

"It means what it said. That was stupid . . . needless."

"Needless? They were about to violate her—and then they'd probably have killed her."

"But they were already *caught*, Uther. We arrived, and that would have been the end of it then and there, if you hadn't gone insane."

"I didn't go insane!"

"Oh, is that so? If your father had seen you, he would account himself justified in having me hanged or disembowelled for having permitted you to reach such a degenerate condition."

Uther's eyes narrowed, so that he was almost squinting up at his friend and guardian. "You permitted nothing. I did what had to be done."

"Oh, please! Come now. 'Had to be done?' *Had* to be? How so? Those fellows should have been taken and hanged, Uther. I'm not disputing they deserved to die for what they were attempting almost within sight of the King's own Hall. But to tackle them the way you did was nothing short of plain, black-faced stupidity. You're what, fifteen now? Fifteen. Ten years ago, you had barely learned to talk! And now you think you're a man."

Garreth Whistler swung himself down from his tall Camulodian horse and kept his back to the younger man, ignoring him. His physical demeanour radiated disgust as he began dragging the bodies of the three dead men to where he could lay them side by side. But as he worked, even though refusing to look at his companion, Garreth talked, betraying not the slightest sign or sound of effort as he manhandled the dead weight of the corpses.

"You're big for your age, I'll grant that. Could be seventeen easily. And you're stronger than most other fifteen-year-olds." He laid the last body in line with the others and straightened up, wiping his palms against his hips where the material of his tunic was not covered by armour and finally turned to look at his pupil.

"But by all the gods you're unutterably stupid sometimes, and that comes of being fifteen. Y'see, a seventeen-year-old is *legally* a man, and a *man* would have stopped these animals, just as surely as you did. But he'd have done it from horseback, sitting up high and mighty and looking down at them, threatening them with a drawn sword. And then when they were properly chastened, he'd have had them chained up and taken into custody by other armed people on foot. He would never have dismounted. That's all you need, you see . . . to be on horseback. Scares the dung out of people on foot to see a big man on a horse, towering over them, especially if he's wearing armour and carrying a sword, and even more especially when they're in the wrong.

"But you're fifteen, too young to know any better . . . too young to show any sense, I suppose . . . You're still a bit of a baby, really, and so you go leaping off the horse and throw yourself right down there to roll in the cow dung with the commoners."

The boy was bridling, clearly resentful of the way he was being treated, and yet equally clearly aware that he had been foolish. He glowered at his teacher.

"Very well, so I'm young. You're always telling me that. But that doesn't make me stupid."

"Yes it does, boy! Oh yes it does. You know better than to do what you did there! I've taught you better than that. You had a dirk in your hand going in, and you dived off your horse without taking

a heartbeat's space to check for danger. What if one or two of those
three had had knives of their own? You could have been dead from
the moment you hit the first man. And where would I be now if that
had happened? I'll tell you where I'd be. I'd be on my way to my
own death, facing your father. Uric Pendragon wouldn't believe his
own son could be stupid enough to do what you have just done, so
he would blame *me* for endangering you. And he would be right.
Then I'd be dead as well as you. And for what? Because you
needed to satisfy an urge to impress an ugly girl? Grow up, Uther.
Men don't behave that way."

For a long space of moments those words hung in the air, unanswered, unchallenged and undisputed. Then the younger man
grunted, nodding in agreement.

"She is ugly, isn't she?"

Garreth Whistler nodded, his face solemn and judicious. "Well,
she's not beautiful, your Nemo . . . no more so than vomit frozen
to a cold road."

They both broke into giggles, but Uther sobered quickly, waving his laughter away with a sharp pass of his hand. "We shouldn't
laugh at her. She can't help the way she was born. You're the one
who told me to be considerate of young unfortunates. I like her,
Garreth, though I don't know why."

"Well, why not? You've known her long enough by now. No
reason at all for not liking the girl simply because she's not
comely." Garreth Whistler's face broke into a grin again, and
Uther's own smile reappeared as his friend and mentor continued.
"Just so long as you don't rut with her . . . or if you do, don't look
at her in the middle of it. I saw you looking at her hairy belly there,
but her face—a face like that could turn you to stone if you looked
at it close up."

Uther shook his head, his smile fading. "I don't know, Garreth."
He nodded his head in the direction of the three bodies at their feet.
"Something attracted these three to her, despite what you may say."

"Aye, desperation probably. Aided by the fact that at least she
doesn't stink like a sour sow, the way most of her neighbours do."
Garreth Whistler, too, had been seduced by the Roman ways of

cleanliness and hygiene, and taught thus, through his nose, he had learned to be fastidious in his womanizing, which meant that he went virtually celibate during the six months that he spent each year among Ullic's people, few of whom were even familiar with the concept of bathing. Now he glanced again casually at the three corpses, then swung himself up into the saddle.

"Come on, let's get going. We'll send a wagon out for these later."

"Why? Why bother? This is human refuse. Let it lie here and stink."

Garreth Whistler tilted his head to one side and eyed his young charge quizzically. "My word, we are ill disposed today, aren't we? Stop for a moment and think about what you are saying. If we leave these characters to rot here, we'll be doing no kindness to our own people who pass this way every day. You may have killed more than your share of men already, but it's clear you still have to sniff your first rotting corpse up close, for if you had ever smelled one, you'd never think of leaving one unburied. Three dead men will make an unholy amount of stink and breed a heaving mountain of maggots. By rights, I ought to make you dig a grave for them all by yourself. Now mount up, and let's get out of here."

He sat watching sternly as Uther walked to his own mount and pulled himself up into the saddle, but then his gaze sharpened as the boy sat stiffly, staring down at the ground to his left. Garreth looked in the direction of his gaze, but there was nothing there that he could see.

"What are you staring at?"

"Nothing." Uther kept his eyes fixed on the ground.

"And what colour of nothing might that be? Look at me, boy! Don't just sit there scowling and pouting like a spoiled little girl. If there's something in your nose, hawk it out of there, get it out in the open. Tell me what's wrong with you—and *don't* say it's nothing."

The boy's eyes flickered towards the three dead men. "I didn't do anything wrong killing those men. If my father had found them doing what they were doing, they would be just as dead. But you're angry at me. Why are you angry at me?"

"By the Christian Christ . . . You still don't know, do you?"

Garreth Whistler pulled his horse up on its hind legs into a rearing turn, then spurred it into movement. Behind him he heard the thumping of hooves as Uther's mount followed him, moving up gradually until the lad was less than half a length behind. Then, knowing that Uther would stay with him, Whistler kicked his mount to a canter and turned his head to shout back over his shoulder, pitching his voice to overcome the thudding of heavy hooves.

"Hear me now, boy, and this time pay heed, for I'll only say this one more time. You fought well enough . . . proved that I have taught you well how to fight with a dirk."

Uther kicked his horse harder, edging it forward until the two men were riding side by side, but Garreth Whistler did not moderate his tone.

"But you are too damn hotheaded—far too *impetuous*. Isn't that the word your Grandfather Varrus used? He told me it means impulsive, ungovernable, lacking in control. And I thought, *Yes, that's the word for our boy Uther . . . lacking in control.*"

Their horses swung apart, one right and the other left, to pass on either side of a huge elm tree that had somehow been permitted to grow up right in the centre of the ancient causeway, and Garreth waited until they came together again before he continued.

"Control . . . it's very important, Uther. Crucial, in fact. It's all-important in a leader of men, whether he be a soldier, a king or the leader of a gang of cattle thieves. If he can't control himself—his emotions, his temper, his rages—then he'll never be able to control others, because he'll never be able to hold their respect. No man will willingly follow someone he doesn't trust implicitly, someone he doesn't believe he can rely upon to stay in control at all times . . . in control of himself and in control of all the conditions he might encounter. Doesn't matter that his control might send his followers to their deaths in battle. That's why he's in command, and they'll forgive him that and anything else as long as they believe he's in control. Do you hear me? Do you understand what I am saying? Shout out, lad, so I can hear."

"Yes, I hear you."

"Aye, and you've heard me before, and yet still you wallow in your boneheaded stupidity. Stop! Stop your horse and listen to me, one more time." As he said the words he hauled back on his own reins, bringing his big horse to a plunging halt, and Uther's mount stopped in the same distance, so that the two remained side by side, almost touching. Before he spoke, Garreth sat staring, wild-eyed, into the face of his student.

"You could have been *killed* back there, boy! Stupidly, pointlessly, needlessly. Now I know you think you're immortal, but you are not. If you think about it, you might remember that you bleed when you cut yourself, and you break bones when you fall badly. D'you remember doing that last year? Well, spilled blood and broken bones are indications that you are mortal like the rest of us. You leaped off your horse back there, and you sacrificed control. Not merely your self-control, although the gods know how important that is, but control of the situation and the circumstances governing it. Any one of those three fools could have had a weapon and used it against you while you were grappling with the others. A small knife can cut your throat as easily as a dirk. Even a small club, hard swung, can crack a skull. You might have been dead, Uther, before you ever had a chance to know about it."

"But none of them *had* weapons, Garreth!"

"No, none of them did, but that was sheer good fortune. You leaped in there with no thought of anything other than your anger. You looked, you saw, and you reacted without thought, overwhelmed by anger and outrage."

"There's nothing wrong with anger and outrage. I've heard you—"

"*Dia!* Will you stop interrupting me, telling me what you think I'm saying! Just be quiet and listen! You've heard me say so, isn't that what you were going to say? Well, your main trouble is that you hear only what you want to hear, Uther. Yes, you have heard me say that there's nothing wrong with anger and outrage, but you have also heard me say a hundred times that anger and outrage call for clear thinking and sober analysis before you make any move that might endanger you or any of your people. Isn't that so? Isn't it?"

"Yes."

"Yes, and if you sigh like that again when I ask you a question, I'll knock you arse over head out of that saddle. Big for your age you might be, but you're not big enough yet to challenge me, and don't you lose sight of that. Now, let's get moving, because there are people waiting for us, and one of them at least, your father, likes not to be kept waiting by any man."

After Uther had saved her life that day and sent her back to the village, Nemo wanted to slip away to the Place of the Bows immediately to relive in her own mind what had happened. But more work than usual seemed to fall to her lot that day, with most of her regular dependants calling upon her services, and it was late in the afternoon by the time she managed to get away and slip unseen into the sacred grove. There she quickly climbed up into the branches and settled herself in her favourite cradle of limbs. She lay back against her springy cushion of mistletoe, closed her eyes and allowed her mind to drift, recalling what it would.

The attack itself, the attempted violation by the three unknown men, had been in the forefront of her mind all afternoon, filling her awareness and shaking her, from time to time, with strange, unfamiliar and unwelcome sensations. She had felt hard, invading fingers probing into the centre of her, thrusting up hungrily into her body, digging for her innermost parts, seeking her very soul, it seemed to her, and violating her inner sense of wholeness. And each time that image came flashing into her mind—and it was always unexpected—it jarred her and brought anger flooding up into her throat in hot, salty waves of fury. The memory of the grasping violence of brutal, calloused hands and the scraping of thick, hard nails on the soft flesh of her inner thighs made her shudder and squirm with loathing, and rippling wavelets of disgust and horror writhed up the muscles of her back like human fingertips.

Nemo had known about such things for years before that day. She had seen many of her female companions taken and used thus by single boys, by entire groups and sometimes by fully grown men. Some of the girls had been taken against their will, but many others had complied gleefully and diligently, evidently gaining and enjoying great pleasure in the exercises. Nemo had seen girls struggling and fighting uselessly on the muddy, dung-strewn floors of stables and byres, screaming and weeping in the vain hope of attracting help, but she had seen others, too, who smiled and pulled up their skirts before lying down or bending forward or backwards over fences, tables or sacks of grain to welcome their invaders.

At all such times, however, Nemo had been but an observer, unnoticed or ignored, and she had remarked that none of the girls, even the most ill-used, had died of such abuse or had wept for more than an hour or two. Occasionally, one would swell up with child as the result, but no one paid much attention, and the child would be duly born and absorbed into the life of the community.

It had never occurred to Nemo that she herself might be treated as the other females were, and the truth had caught her unawares. The only male she had ever thought of as a rutting mate—for Nemo had no notion of romantic, spousal love—was Uther himself.

She thought now of Uther, pausing to dwell on his strength, his long, hard limbs and his kind face. The recollections rapidly grew warmer and more enjoyable as she remembered, so that flickering lines of light pulsed and seemed to swell and grow within her. As so often happened when she thought of Uther in this mood, she soon found herself breathless and physically awash in surges of sheer pleasure, so that her hand sought their source, involuntarily, increasing the pleasure of the surging, purging waves until she could absorb no more and had to stop, shivering and convulsed.

On this occasion, however, as the waves retreated, leaving her exhausted and gasping for air, thighs quivering with the intensity of her release, Nemo's reverie was broken by the deep sound of distant male voices raised in argument. Uncaring at first, and indolent in the aftermath of what she had just achieved, she dismissed the noise initially as a quarrel among the bowmen at the distant butts, but as the sounds continued to grow closer, she realized that the men were approaching the oak in which she lay concealed. Whoever they were—and there seemed to be no more than two voices—they suddenly became a threat, and a very real one, reminding her that she was in a forbidden place, profaning a sacred oak tree with her presence. If she were found there, the consequences would be unpleasant, and they would certainly involve Druids.

Her immediate reaction was to draw into herself, seeking to make herself smaller, catching her breath and willing her pounding heart to be still while she thrust her skirts down and tucked them about her to cover her nakedness from her own eyes and all others. Then, once she had made herself as small and inconspicuous as she could, she sat huddled and motionless, scarcely daring to breathe, waiting to be discovered.

The two men below were speaking very quickly and were keeping their voices low, but Nemo recognized one of them, and soon her curiosity overcame her fear completely. Slowly, being careful to make no noise, she sat up straight and leaned cautiously outward, bracing herself against one of the limbs that formed her seat as she scanned the space below. Sure enough, directly beneath her so that she could see him but not his companion, King Uric Pendragon stood, silent now, supporting his jaw with the ball of one thumb as he smoothed the tip of his right index finger down the length of his thick moustache to his chin.

Uric jerked his head and released a tightly suppressed sigh, expelling it so loudly that the sound carried to Nemo's perch far above him, and when he spoke, his voice held that indescribable tightness that betrayed reluctant acceptance of the inevitable.

"Very well, then, I'll grant that you're right. What's done is done, and there's nothing we can do to undo it. He might have been killed, but he wasn't. He came to no harm, and for that we should be grateful. Well, I am, and may the gods take note of it. But I would still like to take my boot to his arse and to Whistler's, too—" He held up his hand, palm outward, to forestall his companion's response.

"I know, I know, I've heard your arguments on Whistler's side of it. But if I've learned one thing as a King, it's this: responsibility defines itself and always rests most heavily on those who earn and hold it. You know that too, because it's part and parcel of your priestly code, hammered into you since you were old enough to understand what you were hearing. And if you believe in that, then you must also believe that in every man's life there must come a time when he is seen and acknowledged to accept responsibility for those things, those duties, that are his alone. Garreth Whistler has failed me, at least in this. I had thought better of him."

"Uric, that is untrue and unjust, and you know it."

Nemo guessed that the other speaker must be the Chief Druid, Daris, one of the King's most trusted Councillors. Now she leaned forward even farther, risking her balance in the attempt to see. As she did so, however, Daris saved her from further danger and discomfort by stepping out towards Uric, into the light. Uther's father, in the meantime, had folded his arms upon his breast, cocking his head at the priest's protest.

"Garreth Whistler has no control over Uther, Uric. He cannot jerk him to heel like a half-trained dog, and you would not have it otherwise. What would you? How could he control him? How could anyone? The boy is your son and Ullic's grandson! He's a Pendragon, and since when has a Pendragon firstborn been answerable to anyone in Cambria? By the gods, Uric, be honest! If Uther were weak enough to permit anyone to control him, you would have been casting about long before now to father a replacement for him. Look me in the eye and deny it."

Uric Pendragon made no attempt to deny it. He merely turned his head and gazed into the distance.

"Whistler has done wonders for the boy, Uric, and I know it better than anyone. Uther will be Chief one day, perhaps even King, and so I watch him closely. Garreth was charged—your own father charged him personally—with teaching the boy to be a warrior worthy of his name, and by the blood of every Druid ever killed in Britain, I say he has done that superlatively well. Your son, at fifteen, is a warrior, superb in all respects, and now he can boast three more dead men to adorn his name even before he assumes his formal manhood."

"Unarmed men." King Uric's voice was a growl.

"Unarmed or not, the men are dead, and that's done with. Besides, I was talking of Garreth Whistler, not of Uther's escapade.

"It was no part of Garreth's duty that he himself should become a horse warrior. He is the King's Champion, the flower of his people—our people. But Uther spends much time in Camulod and so, therefore, does Garreth Whistler. Uther is besotted with the Camulodian cavalry and must, perforce, become a mounted Camulodian trooper. Whistler, much as he might dislike that thought, sees nonetheless that the young Uther can never be a mere trooper. As your son he must command, and so he must be taught to be a commander of cavalry. It follows, therefore, to Garreth Whistler's logic and loyalty, that he, himself, must become a mounted trooper in order to learn those things that he must teach, in turn, to the boy who is his charge."

Daris paused again, and the King stood silent, waiting for him to resume. Far above their heads, Nemo sat back down again and made herself more comfortable.

"So—" Daris's voice was quiet now, but every syllable carried clearly up to Nemo "—we may not speak ill, or even think ill, of Garreth Whistler, you and I. He has given up more than either of us in the service of our young heir, for in relinquishing the honour of being King's Champion he has forfeited much. He has almost become a foreigner, mounted upon a foreign horse and carrying foreign weapons. He has learned to speak a foreign tongue. He is still greatly loved, and rightly so, but there are some, envious and disgruntled, who yet whisper that he has become an alien among his own family and people . . . and all for his selfless and total dedication to the duty we have put upon him."

"What are you saying, priest?"

"I am saying that Garreth Whistler deserves your full gratitude and no trace of anger or dissatisfaction. And I am saying that he could no more control young Uther's impulsiveness in the grip of angry emotions than you could. Uther is a hothead, sudden and volatile and violent—always has been—and you and I have quarrelled over that before, when it was you who said it and I who disagreed with you out of too much fondness for the boy. Uther has always had that tendency to be headstrong and sudden. I believe that there is simply a well of violence simmering in the boy and likely to break surface at any moment when he is crossed severely enough to stir up his passions."

"Hmm." The King was silent for a time, and then he grunted again and nodded his head. "I agree with you. The boy is far too hot-tempered for his own good. But would you agree with me if I told you that I have noticed—and Garreth Whistler backs me in this—that he seems to respond well to responsibility that extends beyond himself?"

"I don't know if I would or not. What are you saying?"

"The boy does well when he is put in command of a situation. Set him to a task and explain to him what's involved and what depends on the outcome, and he'll do it conscientiously and well, without allowing himself to be distracted until the job is completed. Would you agree?"

There was a long pause, and then Daris responded, nodding his head. "You're right. He sticks with his task until he has acquitted himself completely of all responsibilities, and only then will he allow himself to be lured into other, more pleasurable things. At times like that he never allows himself to be distracted or seduced away from what he has to do and never allows his emotions to take control of him."

"Good. Then I think I might have the answer to his hotheadedness. An ongoing task, a large responsibility. One that only he can handle."

"At fifteen?" There was heavy skepticism in the Druid's tone, but the King ignored it completely.

"There could be no better age. Do you remember the story Publius Varrus told you the last time you and he were here at the same time of how it fell to Uther and Cay to teach the troops of Camulod how to sit in a saddle and control a horse with stirrups? And the boys were, what, eight years old at the time?"

"Yes, but they—"

"But nothing, Daris! They did it because they were the only two in the entire place who could use the single saddle that Camulod possessed. The thing had been sitting there in plain view for years before the boys were born, and no one had even suspected what it was. Varrus had captured it from some Franks taken in a raid years earlier and kept it as a keepsake, thinking it to be some kind of chair fashioned for a crippled boy. But it was a new form of weapon, a saddle with stirrups, made to fit a boy's legs. They never thought to see it as a thing a full-grown man might use, and so they saw nothing until young Cay grew into it and showed them how it should be used."

The High Priest nodded. "I remember that. I was impressed, but I fail to see—"

"Cay taught Uther how to ride in that saddle, Daris, immediately after he himself had learned to, because the two of them were of a size. And they became, in very fact, the first of Camulod's cavalry troopers. But they achieved it simply because their youth, their size, gave them the ability to do so. They had the equipment, while the others, fully grown men, had to wait until their saddles could be developed and manufactured. That was less than eight years ago, Daris, but Camulod is strong with cavalry today. So here is my idea. And hear me out, if you will, before you seek to undermine my logic with any argument . . .

"Camulod is hungry for our new Pendragon longbows. We now have more than a hundred, with several hundred more in various stages of completion. Camulod has uses for our bows, and to give our friends their due, they have never tried to buy the bows alone. They know the value of the weapons to us and the difficulties involved in not only producing them—growing the wood and then curing and shaping it before each weapon can be made—but also in the training of men to use them. So they are prepared to use our people and their bows, and to reward us handsomely for the use of our superior weaponry. Do you agree with what I have said so far?"

"Of course."

"Good. Now I propose that it is time for what the Romans called a *quid pro quo*, a giving in return for a gift."

"And what might that be?" Daris was smiling.

"A benefit to us in Cambria from *their* superior weaponry."

"Their—you mean their cavalry?"

"No . . . ours."

The Chief Druid pushed back his high cowl and scratched his head. "Forgive me, Uric, I must be misunderstanding something very simple. What do you mean?"

Uric let out a single, booming grunt of laughter. "I mean the answer to our problem with young Uther's hotheadedness: responsibility. Look, he travels every year between here and Camulod, there and back, no? Always with Garreth Whistler, but sometimes they travel with young Cay in tow, too, and when that happens there is usually an escort of some kind to ride with them from Camulod. Sometimes—most times, in fact—the escort is not really an escort but a military expedition of one kind or another, perhaps a patrol that would be travelling this way even if the boys were not.

"But now we find ourselves approaching a new kind of difficulty. In the past, the boys were merely boys, and they were travelling through our own lands, so they were in little danger—certainly no danger that Garreth Whistler could not handle with or without a military escort. Today, however, everything has changed. My son rides over a rise, finds an assault in progress and reacts predictably. He flies out of control and leaps into the middle of what might have been a disaster. I believe, nevertheless, that had he been in command of a body of troops, *responsible for them*, he would have reacted differently. I believe he would not have risked his life under those circumstances."

Daris said nothing and Uric continued. "Besides, the men he attacked today were vermin, but they were our own vermin and harmless enough, overall. It might not always be so. We no longer have the control that we used to have over our territories. There are invaders everywhere nowadays, and the risks of travel, any kind of travel, are far higher than they were even a few years ago."

The silence that followed this statement was so prolonged that Uric himself was forced to break it.

"Well? You disagree?"

"No, not at all." Daris's response came from a deep well of thought. "No, I'm merely trying to think through and beyond what you said. Are you suggesting that we approach Camulod to give Uther command of a cavalry troop?"

"No, I am saying that Uther should have a guard of his own."

"Of Camulodians?"

"No, Daris. Of Cambrians—Pendragon volunteers, trained and fully equipped with arms and horses—in Camulod. A King's Guard, my Guard, commanded by Uther as my appointee, with Garreth Whistler as his right arm. Camulod will be happy to accede to our wishes, for it will be to their ultimate advantage to have allied cavalry in place here, and besides, in return we'll increase our commitment to them in terms of men and bows."

Daris gazed at the King, and his entire face lit up slowly with admiration and approval as the various benefits of such a move occurred to him one after the other.

"Uric," he murmured eventually, "I have always been a dutiful and admiring Councillor . . . most of the time, anyway . . . and I have always marvelled, since I grew old enough to see and appreciate such subtleties, at the foresight and capacity for long-range planning that you and your father share, but this . . . this is incomparable! This is magnificent! We have no need for heavy horses in our mountains, but their presence—disciplined cavalry here in the lowlands—would be a great asset. It would make a massive difference to everything we do. No invader is insane enough, I think, to attack us in our hills, but anyone thinking of attacking us down here would have to think twice, knowing that we have fast-moving cavalry. Were I not a priest, I would be prepared to split a skin of wine with you in simple admiration and celebration of the brilliance of this sole idea."

Uric the King stood back and looked at him, then nodded. "Excellent. That's as it should be . . . but we'll be drinking mead, for you know damned well we have had no wine to speak of since the Romans left, other than what we've scrounged from Camulod."

Nemo sat silent in her perch, watching the two men as they left the confines of the sacred grove. She had not understood everything they said, but she had understood enough to know that they would soon begin recruiting volunteers for Uther's new Guard of Camulodian-style troopers. And she knew enough, too, to understand that if she moved quickly, presenting her case carefully and clearly to Garreth Whistler, she might win access to this new corps. She was a woman, certainly, but women had always borne weapons in Celtic society, and no woman had ever been denied the right to fight beside her friends and loved ones. No competent woman, indeed, had ever been denied the rank of warrior.

The following morning, shortly after sunrise, Nemo was waiting on Garreth Whistler's doorstep to catch him as he emerged. When he did, she faced him squarely, knowing that he was unlikely to have heard already about Uric's plan. She was blunt and straightforward as always, incapable of making any attempt to be obscure or to appear mysterious. She simply told Garreth Whistler that she wanted to ride with Uther as a mounted trooper. If ever there should be a call to arms for volunteers among the warriors of Cambria, she said, to form a corps of cavalry about the King under the command of the Prince Uther, Garreth Whistler should remember that her name had been presented first and foremost.

Whistler listened to her, his eyebrows raised in good-humoured puzzlement, but then he smiled and promised her that he would bear her request in mind from that day forth. Satisfied, she grunted her thanks and then disappeared into one of the narrow lanes that surrounded Whistler's residence.

By that afternoon, Whistler had received direct instructions from King Uric to call for a muster of volunteers to ride with Uther Pendragon and form a King's Guard of cavalry. Uric had no doubt that Camulod would concur with his wishes in this—he knew how badly they wanted access to his bowmen and their weaponry—and he already considered his new cavalry force to be a reality.

Whistler nodded and accepted his instructions with a slightly bemused look on his face, but Nemo's was the first name he inscribed on his mental list of personnel. It never occurred to him to question the young woman's fitness for the task, for he had long since come to admire her solid strength and her unquestioning loyalty to Uther in all the young man did, and he knew he would find many others among the volunteers, all of them men, who would pose him far greater problems than Nemo ever would. He merely

wondered in passing how Nemo had gained her foreknowledge of
what was happening.

The new Guard was formed quickly, with more volunteers than
there were posts available, and shortly thereafter Nemo and her
new companions were plunged into a period of frantic and intensive training that culminated six long weeks later in a series of tests
involving both disciplined drills and skills, as well as hard demonstrations of physical achievement and prowess.

Nemo was unsurprised that she won her place among the men,
but she held it jealously, competing chin to chin with males of her
own age and older, defying all of them and drilling, training,
working overtime to deny them the opportunity and the pleasure
of besting her in anything she tried. She graduated from training
ahead of all of them, winning from Uther's own hand the Roman
rank of decurion, or squadron leader, before they ever left to travel
to Camulod.

By the end of the first month of harsh competition, Nemo's
squadron mates had stopped resenting the fact that she was female.
Around the same time, after several bruising fights in which Nemo
had inflicted much pain and grief in sudden, violent shows of disin-
clination, they had also stopped trying to bed her. By the time they
left for Camulod to begin their real training, however, Nemo had
achieved her greatest triumph over her messmates: they had come to
regard her as an absolute equal and had forgotten, by and large, that
she was a woman. They called her Hard-Nose, saying it with respect,
and Nemo found it infinitely preferable to the Toad. She marched out
of camp proudly, her mind filled with the vision of King Uric himself saluting her and her mates. Ahead of her, filling her vision with
the splendour of his gold-embroidered military cloak and his great
Roman helmet with its high, crimson crest, Uther Pendragon rode
proudly on his enormous chestnut horse, accompanied by Garreth
Whistler. Behind him marched all his new King's Guard.

When they returned from Camulod, Nemo knew, they would
not be marching as they were now. By then the Guard would all be
mounted on horses as fine as those their commanders rode, and people would automatically accord them the respect and admiration

they had earned and deserved, awed and impressed by their equipment and their magnificence, their training and their discipline. By then, too, she knew with certainty, everyone seeing them would recognize and know the squadron leader, Nemo Hard-Nose, riding at their head. "Everyone," however, was unimportant to her. The only one who mattered in her eyes, the only man in all her world, was her Commander, Uther Pendragon. She knew, beyond any vestige of doubt, that her reason for existence was to protect him against any and all threats to his destiny, whatsoever those threats might be and whomsoever they might involve.

BOOK THREE

Mother:

*I trust that this will find you and all the other mem-
bers of my beloved family safe, well and in good health.
God grant that this be, and remain so.*

*I am writing to you in some haste on this occasion,
primarily because I have the opportunity, presented suddenly and quite without warning, but also because I feel the
need to share my thoughts with another woman, and there
is none closer to my heart than you. I have friends among
the women here, of course, several of them very dear to me,
but there is no one of them with whom I could find any satisfaction in sharing what is on my mind at this moment.*

*All my life I have known and respected you as a lov-
ing, dutiful and obedient wife to Publius Varrus, my father.
But I have also always known and understood that your
obedience was born of my father's natural honesty, honour
and good nature. Had he been a different kind of man, you
would, I know, have withheld your willing obedience.*

*I know and understand that there are many times when
every woman will nod judiciously and agree with a man
until he has passed from her sight, after which she will proceed to do what she intended to do before he came along, but
in matters that are truly important, matters that have real
significance or may have lasting effects upon our lives and
the lives of our families and children, we, as mere women,*

are utterly dominated by and subservient to the men among whom we live. In Cambria, however, that situation is more real and more noticeable than elsewhere. All the women here, it seems to me, from the highest born to the meanest serving maid, are completely dominated by the men and the men's way of thinking and behaving. Since I arrived to live here in what was then King Ullic's domain sixteen years ago, I have seen no single instance of a Pendragon woman actually standing up to and defying a male or a male viewpoint on something she considered to be worth fighting for. The women of Pendragon appear to have no strong opinions on anything that is important. Their daily lives are trivial and immutable, and they do as they are told in meek obedience. They must think what they are told to think and behave at all times as their men expect them to behave. And they appear to be content to have things thus.

I made some futile attempts to speak of it with a few of my closer friends here, but invariably they would laugh, always awkwardly, and change the subject quickly. When I pressed them further, they became visibly uncomfortable and ill-at-ease, and on several occasions it became abundantly clear to me that they simply did not, and do not, know how to deal with the thoughts I was trying to introduce to them. When I became aware some time ago that two of my friends now refuse to speak with me or be alone in my company, I knew I could no longer keep speaking of such things, lest I appear to be actively undermining my husband and his authority. And so you, dear Mother, are become the sole source to which I may turn for recourse.

We have had a visiting dignitary from Cornwall living with us here in Cambria for the better part of a year now, a high-born man called Balin, who travels with his wife, much younger than he, whose name is Mairidh. Balin is a gentle and learned man, highly placed in the Council of Duke Emrys, but he has also been for many years a close friend of Uric's family, beginning when Uncullic was a youth himself.

They have been welcome and worthwhile guests, despite the length of their stay, and I for one will be sad to see them depart. Mairidh has been perhaps the one woman with whom I might have been able to discuss the things I have been describing to you but for her status as an Outlander.

As Uther will already have told you, a special messenger arrived here some days ago, having travelled at breakneck speed, apparently, all the way from Cornwall, and Balin and Mairidh have been summoned back immediately by Emrys, for what purpose we know not, although none can doubt its urgency.

We have been increasingly troubled with seaborne raiders in recent months, and the roads, as I am sure you know, are becoming increasingly unsafe for any but the strongest armed parties. With that in mind, and being at pains to make his Cornish guests' departure smoother and more efficient, Uric and his advisers have decided that Uther's Camulod-bound party will escort the pair and their own escort, which is no longer deemed large enough to protect them, until they reach the safety of the sea coast, where one of the Duke's galleys awaits them. Having seen Balin and Mairidh safely aboard, Uther's party will then strike back inland and make their way directly to Camulod, where, as I am sure you know by now, they will begin a new and different regime of training, teaching Uther's Cambrian volunteers to ride and fight as cavalry. The idea was Uric's, and I know he has been exchanging messages with Daddy on the subject for months past.

Uric thinks that, as usual, I am being too protective of the boy, for in his eyes his son can do no wrong, and at that point our recent spousal discussions have entered the territory of which I spoke earlier. I have now begun to approach the daunting point at which I find myself preparing to dig in my heels and defy my husband, although God knows I have no desire to do so. In the cause of justice, however, and in defence of Uric's point of view, I know that

I do tend to be protective, and perhaps too much so from time to time. But then, on the other hand, I frequently feel that Uric inclines too far in the opposing direction and allows the boy too much freedom from supervision and accountability. And that is what has now been sticking in my craw for several months.

Uther is wild sometimes. He has a dark side to him, and as his mother, I find it upsetting. It concerns me greatly, and I am even more concerned that I seem to be the only person in Uther's entire world who feels any concern at all. It is expected of a Cambrian warrior that he be savage, fearless in war and in peace and forever prepared to confront and kill his people's foes. That is what all warriors do.

Even so, Uther can never be a simple warrior. He is destined, I fear, always to be perceived as much more than a "simple" anything. He is the grandson of King Ullic, the son of King Uric and a potential future King in his own right. It is therefore deemed right and fitting that Uther Pendragon should be a fell and fearsome warrior.

Uther has already killed several men, and everyone is proud of him for that. Everyone, that is, but me. It appalls me that at the age of fifteen years he has already killed five men. I wake up in the night sometimes from seeing him in dreams, his innocent young face running red with blood that coats his skin and fills his mouth, staining his teeth. That terrifies me.

I find myself growing jealous of poor Enid, who has been dead since Uther was born. How proud she would have been of her son, Caius Merlyn. In him, golden-haired and fair of skin, I see everything that I would wish to see in my own son. Cay is to Uther as day is to night, not just in colouring but also in moods and temperament. They love each other dearly, the two of them, and I have never known any two boys who were not brothers to be closer. When they are together, they are inseparable, riding like centaurs, side by side, vying with each other constantly for friendly dominance. And yet they are so different, each from the other. Cay is sunny, open and generous, affectionate and amiable, always smiling and ever trustworthy and reliable. Uther is more sombre, concealing his feelings more closely, masking his thoughts much of the time. He is no less amiable than Cay and no less affectionate, and he is perhaps even more generous than his cousin, and were I not his mother I would swear he is more handsome than his cousin when he smiles. And yet he is more distant somehow. His inner workings, if one can speak in such a way of a mere boy, are less clearly discernible. Uther is my son, and when all is said and done, he is wonderful, constant and utterly trustworthy, but there is something dark in him that chafes at me, and I know not how to speak of it. I find myself wondering if there ever could be a word for what I am trying to describe. How would any other mother react to the knowledge that her only son, her beloved firstborn, not only possesses but has exercised the capacity to kill others prior to undergoing the Manhood Rites? Five men left dead by my sweet son, all discovered while engaged in brutality and ravishment of women. Most boys his age would see such things occurring, and they would be afraid for their own lives and run for help, but not Uther. He has this well of reckless violence inside him that enables him to pit himself against grown men and kill them.

His father seems to think that this is admirable, and so, in fact, do all the other men around us here. They praise the boy's courage, his ferocity, his single-mindedness. I find myself unable to see beyond their wrongness. How can they even think such nonsense, let alone voice the thoughts? They are applauding the emergence of murderous traits in a mere boy—my boy!—and I am finding it more and more difficult within my own heart to forgive Uric for what I now see as his callousness towards his son.

Although what I am about to say might seem strange to you, and you might perhaps even think me disloyal to my

husband in thinking such a thing, let alone setting it down
in writing, I have no intent here to voice either plaint or
grievance. I have no wish to complain at all about anything, Mother, but I find myself under a compulsion to say
this to someone, to anyone who will listen without condemnation. I have learned to appreciate that I really came
into a different world when I left your home to live with my
husband's people. I never knew how sheltered our lives
were in our Colony or how hard you and Daddy worked to
keep us safe and protected as children from the realities of
the life most other people know. Growing up, we, or I at
least, had no awareness of how privileged and fortunate we
were to be living as we lived. Even so, I can remember that
we had many instances of violence in our Colony, incidents
caused by raiding parties of various kinds from Outlanders
to bandits and even domestic battles and upheavals. I knew
that people died in such incidents, and I also knew that
many others were savagely wounded, but that awareness
was far less than real. And, in truth, nothing that I had ever
seen or experienced could have prepared me for the
extremes of violence I have found here in Cambria.

   In this land, even here in Tir Manha, life itself is considered to be of little value, and most particularly so if the
life being squandered or lost or taken belongs to a stranger
or someone who does not belong to one's own family or
one's own village.

   In our beloved Camulod, men consider themselves to
be either farmers, artisans or soldiers. All three ranks and
standings are equal, and no man feels any shame in being
what he is. In Cambria, on the other hand, every man is a
warrior first, and then perhaps something else afterwards.
And if that something else involves manual labour of any
kind, there is always the taint of shamefulness about it.

   Until I came here I did not know that there is a difference between the terms "warrior" and "soldier." Now I
fully realize just how great that difference is. Soldiers are

disciplined, and warriors need not be. Even more impor-
tant, however, is the fact that soldiers, operating to a plan
as a single organized force, are accountable for their
actions, and warriors are not. When a soldier behaves
badly, breaking a law or otherwise behaving in a criminal
manner, he can be brought to answer for it by the system
that governs or employs him. Not so with warriors. There
is no system for warriors. The only source of rebuke and
discipline for a warrior is another, stronger warrior, and
the rebuke takes the form of violent death.

My Uric is King over seven clans of warriors, all of
whom are every bit as savage and unpredictable as those
Saxons whose very name fills people elsewhere in Britain
with fright and fear. That savagery permeates our entire life
here. And now I fear very greatly that it has affected my son
and that I failed to see it happening. So much so, in fact, that
I now find myself resenting things, circumstances and tradi-
tions and customs that have caused me no concern at all
these past fifteen years.

The last time young Cay was here, I found myself
looking at him, not simply once but frequently, and com-
paring him to Uther, may God forgive me, searching for the
finer elements in him that were not present in my own son.
Cay is a gentle and wonderful young man, and all of us,
Uther perhaps most of all, love him dearly. So there is, in
his pleasant, sunny nature, much that any mother would
enjoy seeing in her own son. He calls me Auntie Vron, his
own personal name for me, and it makes me feel warm and
content each time he does so. I know he calls you Aunt
Luceiia, but I wonder if you are aware that he refers to you
very lovingly as Auntie Looch whenever he talks of you to
others. Cay is more circumspect than Uther in dealing with
the feelings and sensitivities of others. He will seek to
pacify and to soothe ruffled feathers and hurt feelings, and
will strive to find a peaceful way to settle altercations and
differences of opinions. Not so my darling Uther. He

abhors nothing more than dishonesty, admires nothing more than forthright truth proclaimed in all its shameless purity. And he believes, and always has believed, that anyone who cannot stand to hear the truth laid out openly should stay away from those who stand behind it. It is a hard, uncompromising attitude he takes for one so young and one that sometimes fails to make friends for him, but his father the King admires him for it and so do his Councillors. So, too, do I, I suppose, although I sometimes wish he were not quite so forceful in his beliefs.

Please watch him closely, Mother, when he is with you in Camulod this time. I know you always do, since he is your firstborn grandson, but this time I would ask you to look upon him with a more discerning eye now that you have read some of my concerns and reservations. I know you will speak of them, too, with Daddy, so please tell him that his Magpie might be losing her sight, or at least her insight, since she is having difficulty nowadays seeing the sparkle in what has always been her dearest possession.

Ask Daddy, too, if you would, to find some reason to speak with one of Uther's companions, the one they call Nemo Hard-Nose, and warn him that, even though he might have trouble discerning it at first, Nemo Hard-Nose is a woman, She is aptly named. Hard, unyielding, more male and more warrior than the toughest of her companions in training, she betrays nothing female in her behaviour or comportment, and judging by the way Uther and the others speak of her, none of them has any awareness of her as a woman. I find her strange and unsettling to be around, although I have been in close proximity to her on only two occasions. I have asked Uther about her, but all he would tell me is that he has known her since she was a child and that she has earned her place among his troopers. When I pressed him further, he grew uncomfortable and told me that he could not discuss any of "his men" with Outsiders. He is their Commander, and he has a duty *to them to respect their privacy as long as they do what they are supposed to do. I asked no more after that, not wishing him to think of me as being over-inquisitive. But the girl does not like me. I felt hostility emanating from her as I passed by her. She never looked at me or spoke to me, but I could sense her dislike so strongly that I felt cold, and I knew she was jealous of me. Of what could she be jealous? Of my being my son's mother? That makes no sense. Tell Daddy his opinion on this matter, on this man-woman, is important to me.*

I know you will write back to me eventually, and until you do, I will be waiting and wondering what your response will be. Give my dearest love, please, to Daddy, but keep half of it for yourself.

Veronica

ELEVEN

Because Uther led his raw recruits into Camulod beneath the ancient banner of his clan—a red dragon outlined in white on a field of green—the Camulodian troopers coined an instantaneous jibe about the rabble who were sent with the fifteen-year-old Uther: they called them the "dragon guards." Uther, acutely aware of how closely he was being watched by the governors of Camulod—his Grandfather Varrus, his Uncle Picus and all of the Council of the Colony—bit down on his anger and decided, against all his urgings and with the able assistance of Garreth Whistler, to do and say nothing in response to the goading. Garreth, at twenty-seven, was by far the eldest of the contingent Uther had brought with him, and if anything, he had more to contend with than any of his companions, for his Cambrian status as King's Champion earned him nothing in the way of respect from the Camulodians, who had heroes and traditions of their own and regarded anyone and everyone from Cambria as upstart savages. In their eyes, Garreth Whistler was simply another bumpkin recruit from the mountains, and an elderly one at that, compared to the youthful know-nothings with whom he rode.

Later, looking back on that time, Uther would be both proud of and grateful for the restraint he had exercised during their first few weeks in Camulod, but he would also acknowledge, forever afterwards, the support and assistance provided to him by the example set by his stoic friend and mentor. Without Garreth Whistler's patience, fortitude and good sense, Uther knew, he would never have been able to control the rage that flared in him daily in the face of the disdain and derision he and his people had to suffer in the condescending sneers of the Camulodian troopers. It had been Garreth who reminded Uther constantly of the objectives he had set himself and who kept him pointed in the right direction.

Much of the baiting the new recruits endured was good-natured, but they had to suffer a good deal of abuse that was malicious and deliberate. Nevertheless, they bore it all stoically in silence and absorbed everything that was thrown at them. Within a month, the abuse began to taper off, and the tenor of the baiting became less punitive as the newcomers continued to drill doggedly and to learn quickly, and began thereby to win a modicum of acceptance and respect.

And then, when their basic training had been completed, they were finally issued the uniform armour and saddlery of regular Camulodian troopers.

They passed their final inspection flawlessly at a dawn parade the following day, resplendent in their new uniforms, and were granted a day-long furlough to celebrate their success. Uther remained with them that morning until they were dismissed, and then, thinking it might be the right thing to do, he left them to their celebrations and went to join Cay and his Uncle Picus Britannicus, where he sat in on the discussions of how the new troop was to be split up among the veteran squadrons for the next stage of their training. Later in the day, however, Garreth came looking for him and took Uther back to where the celebration was being held, and the young man was touched and delighted by the welcome the Cambrians gave him. He stayed with them then long into the night, enjoying himself thoroughly but drinking only sparingly as he watched the free-flowing ale take hold of the young celebrants.

When Garreth eventually called curfew and supervised the bedding down of the new troopers, most of whom were by then too drunk to protest, Uther went to his own bed, where he lay awake for a long time, thinking about the celebration and the strange, moving and contradictory thoughts that had occurred to him while he watched his companions.

The following morning, immediately after the dawn parade, in which the haggard looks and woebegone expressions of the

Cambrian troopers had gone conspicuously unmentioned, Uther presented himself at the garrison headquarters and asked to speak with the Legate Picus Britannicus. He was shown directly into the Legate's day room, where Picus sat gazing at him quizzically, one eyebrow raised high as Uther saluted him formally. Picus nodded casually, acknowledging the punctilious greeting.

"How are you feeling?"

Uther, still standing at attention, blinked at his uncle, surprised by the question, and then realized that Picus thought he might have drunk too much the previous day. He shook his head. "I feel fine, Uncle, perfectly normal."

"Good. What may I do for you?"

"Ahh . . ." Faced with the need to speak, Uther found that he did not know where to begin, but while he was searching for the words, Picus forestalled him by taking a sheet of papyrus from a small pile by his right hand and pushing it across to where Uther could reach it. Even upside down, Uther could see that it was a list of some kind.

"Sit down, Nephew, there's no need to be formal when there's just the two of us. You can save me some time here if you would not mind taking that to your man Garreth when you leave."

Uther nodded and sat in the chair in front of the Legate's work table before picking the paper up and turning it towards him. "Of course, Uncle. What is it?" Noting the fact that it had not been rolled up or folded, he had no hesitation in showing his curiosity.

"It's the new roster, the one we discussed yesterday. The allocation of your Cambrians to the regular squadrons they'll be working with from now on."

"Ah, yes." Uther cleared his throat nervously, suddenly uncomfortable and wishing he had not sat down. "Yes, well . . . that's what I've come to speak to you about, Uncle."

Picus sat waiting for a few moments until he realized that his nephew was at a loss for words.

"And . . . ? What is it that you want to say?"

"Well . . ." Another long, painful pause, and then, "It's about the roster. Is there . . . Is it . . . Is there any other way to do this?"

Picus wrinkled his brow, not understanding. Uther interpreted the look as a frown, and his nervousness increased.

"I don't understand," Picus said, his voice mild. "Any other way to do what?"

"This . . . to avoid splitting up my men."

"*Your* men?" The Legate's lips twisted in a tiny smile. "You mean the Cambrian troopers? Perhaps we should clarify their status, you and I. As long as they are billeted here, training under my command, they are most emphatically *my* men, Camulod's men. Your father understands that, I believe. Do you disagree?"

"Well, no, sir, they are, sir, but . . ."

"But? But what, Uther?" His question went unanswered as a flush stained Uther's cheeks, and Picus continued. "Where has this sudden 'but' sprung from? You sat here yesterday while we discussed this, and you gave me no indication that you had doubts about any of it."

Uther nodded, his expression miserable. "I know, sir. And I didn't. It was only last night that—" He cut his own words off before they could be uttered, and before Picus could make any response they were interrupted by the arrival of one of his clerks. Picus had obviously expected him, for he stood up and passed another pile of papers on his desk to the man, who nodded, clicked his heels and left immediately.

Picus glanced back at Uther's still red-face, and then he rose and went to the door, where he leaned out and told the other clerk outside that he did not wish to be disturbed. He closed the door and came back to his table, where he perched casually on one corner and gazed down at his nephew.

"I think," he said, "that you have something weighty on your mind, and I know you would not come here simply to waste my time, so I'm prepared to listen. Now take your time and get your thoughts in order, and then try to explain to me why you suddenly believe I should keep your troopers together as a body, instead of splitting them up among our veterans, as we traditionally do, for the next, highly important stage of their training."

Uther nodded and thought for a few moments.

"It was last night, sir. I couldn't sleep, and I didn't know why. But my thoughts were full of what happened yesterday . . . the muster in the morning and the men's graduation to full troopers. They were full of it, and very proud of themselves, and I was surprised and . . . I don't know if I can describe what I mean."

Picus hitched himself further onto the top of the table, bracing himself with his straight arms as both feet left the floor. "Well, you've made a start, anyway. You were surprised, you say, and . . . what?"

"I was surprised and perhaps, I think . . . excited. About what I was seeing . . . what they were showing me. I'd never seen it before, and I suddenly knew it was important that I . . . that we keep it. Very important."

"Important enough to break with a tradition that we have built up here in Camulod since our beginnings for reasons of sound, tested common sense? That must be monumentally important." He held up a hand towards his nephew. "Wait you, I am not belittling you or casting slurs on your judgment. I am merely making a point." He thrust himself forward off the table and moved back to his own chair, settling himself comfortably.

"When I was your age, I left home to join the legions, and I did my earliest service in Gaul before the Romans had even begun to develop heavy cavalry. I spent several years there as an ordinary infantry grunt, engaged in some heavy fighting, and then I met Flavius Stilicho and fell in love with horse warfare. But even then, by which time I was close to twenty, I faced opposition whenever I tried to convince the older officers that cavalry warfare was to be the way of the future. They thought me—and Stilicho as well—no more than a jumped-up, overweening boy, out to change a thousand-year tradition to suit his own ends." He paused and eyed his nephew questioningly. "Do you see what I mean? Their experience, impressive as it was, told them that someone of my experience could know nothing. That's your situation at this moment. You see something you believe to be important. I, as your legate rather than your uncle, see an inexperienced, fifteen-year-old boy who appears to want me to change the way things are done around here, although I have no idea why. But I am granting you the benefit of all my doubts, so convince me. Tell me what it was that your men were showing you yesterday. Take your time."

Uther felt relief flowing through him, closely followed by a rush of admiration for his uncle's patience and understanding. Instead of plunging into his argument, he remained still, grappling with his thoughts and feelings, until finally he began to see it taking shape in his mind.

"It was unity, I think, sir . . . Yes, that's what it was. It was unity. They had achieved something together. Something difficult. Something to be proud of."

"Of course they had. They'd achieved the status of Camulodian troopers. They're unique now."

"Aye, but that's just it, sir, they're Cambrians, not Camulodians. They're Pendragons."

There was a silence, and then Picus nodded. "Aye, they are, but they are still troopers in the cavalry of Camulod. And their differentness simply presents another excellent reason to split them up as I normally would and dilute the distinctions between them and our regular troopers."

Uther felt frustration swelling in his chest, but he knew that to show any of it would be the worst thing he could do. Unconscious of the disrespect he might be showing, he held up his own hand as he sought to balance his thoughts.

"Sir, have you ever been to Cambria, to Tir Manha, I mean? Have you spent any time there?"

"I've been there several times, but I've never stayed there. I know little of your people and their ways, if that's what you are asking me."

"It is, Uncle, it is . . . You see . . ." He took a great breath and plunged ahead. "We Pendragons *never* act in unison on anything, except in emergencies—when there's a King to be chosen or when an enemy invades us. Even then, in war, we will turn out in masses but we fight as solitary warriors, every man for himself. We don't have the kind of discipline or organized training you take for granted here in Camulod. Even our bowmen with the new longbows, they're

incredibly powerful together, but each one is his own man . . . aims
and shoots his own arrows. I'm not making sense, am I?"

Picus shrugged. "Yes you are. I think I'm beginning to see
what you mean. Carry on."

"Well, that's what surprised me . . . I think. I had never seen
my own people behaving the way they behaved yesterday, and I
couldn't get it out of my mind. I've never seen Pendragons work
together as these have . . . not with so much discipline and in a common cause. It's against everything Cambrian, absolutely everything."

Picus was silent, making no attempt to interrupt, and Uther sat
frowning, thinking deeply, then burst out talking again.

"These men came here with me because my father urged them
and encouraged them to come. He wants to forge a closer alliance
with you here in Camulod, and to have some cavalry available to
him in Cambria—Camulod's cavalry, with Camulodian officers,
but made up of Cambrian volunteers under my command. He
believed there might be young men in Tir Manha who would leap
at the chance to get away, to try something different. But he never
thought—none of us did, including me—about what might happen
in the doing of that. And that's why I think it important to keep the
men together. If we split them up, as you propose to do, we risk
losing this . . . thing that has them all united in this new way."

His uncle smiled, shaking his head slightly. "But that makes no
sense, Uther. Their confidence will *grow* with further training as
regular troopers."

Uther nodded, but he was not about to back down now. "That
is true, sir, their confidence will increase, but their sense of . . . the
only word I can find is unity . . . *that* will melt away. They'll be
good Camulodian troopers, as you say . . ."

"But?"

"But that's all they'll be." The words came out in a rush.

Picus leaned his head back and laughed aloud. "Is that supposed to win me over to your viewpoint? That's *all* they'll be?"

Uther was appalled by his gaffe. "No, Uncle, I didn't mean it
like that. I meant no disrespect. What I meant to say is that they
could be much *more*, in a different sense. They could be . . . will

be . . . a Cambrian corps of Camulodian troopers, who will return proudly to Cambria and cause envy in the hearts of others like them. They will be the King's Guard from Camulod, but their comradeship, their pride and their discipline will raise other volunteers who can then be trained normally in the traditional manner."

"Hmm . . ." Picus sat silent for a long time, mulling over what Uther had said, and then he nodded. "Well, you've given me much to think about. I think you should leave me now. You have not convinced me, but you have captured my attention, and if you have half the brains I think you have, you will leave me to convince myself. I'll send for you before the day is out and give you my answer. In the meantime, say nothing to anyone of what we have discussed, and leave that roster here with me."

Uther pushed the list back across the table and Picus picked it up, gazing at it with unfocused eyes. Uther rose, saluted and left his uncle to his thoughts.

Then late that evening, only an hour before curfew, a trooper came looking for Uther to summon him to the Legate's quarters, where he was surprised to find Picus in conference with Garreth Whistler, the two of them sitting companionably beside a glowing brazier. They stopped talking as he approached the open door, and Picus beckoned him inside. Wondering what was happening, Uther entered and nodded to Garreth before taking the seat between them. He made no attempt to salute Picus, as all of them were out of uniform. His uncle wasted no time in coming to the point.

"Well, Nephew," he said, "I have thought of nothing but your strange request all day long, and I tell you openly I had almost made up my mind to deny it. But then I decided to consult with Garreth here, since the outcome of my decision would affect him, too, and I knew that he would not hesitate to speak the truth of what he felt about your suggestion. I was very surprised to discover that he knew nothing about it."

Uther glanced at Garreth and felt the hot colour sweeping up into his face. Before he could say anything, however, Picus continued.

"I outlined your proposal to Garreth then and tried to state your reasons for it as truthfully and accurately as I could, and afterwards he and I talked about the matter at some length . . . longer than I had anticipated. You will be delighted to know that, despite your failure to confide in him, Garreth agreed with you. More important, however, he convinced me to agree with you, too.

"So, here is my decision. You will have this year to keep your Cambrian contingent intact so that they may return to Tir Manha with you as a fully integrated unit. Thus, you will have your opportunity to build upon this new fellowship you speak of and to impress your fellow clansmen with their discipline and pride, and we will hope for additional volunteers in time to come, inspired by the example of your first levy." He held up a peremptory hand to forestall Uther's gratitude. "Wait you, you might not like what I say next. You are fifteen, a mere recruit, and hence unfit to command a unit in Camulod at this time, no matter what your father's wishes might be. And so Garreth Whistler will assume command of your contingent for the time being, until you have earned the right to lead them on your own. Garreth will command while you remain in Camulod, and you will be a trooper, no more than that. And to aid Garreth in his task, I will second a cadre of my best officers as guardians to your guards. When you return to Tir Manha, you may do as you wish, to suit your father's designs and conditions, but here in Camulod, you will conform to mine. Do you object to that?"

Uther merely shook his head, and Picus nodded. "Good. So be it. But next year, when your troopers return to Camulod, they will be dispersed among the regular troops as they should have been this year. And at that time, you yourself will enter a program of intense officer training under my best teachers. Cay will join you. Is that clear? I hope it is, because I must tell you that, in breaking with tradition in this way, I fear I may be loosing a deal of resentment on your people that you yourself might not have thought of. They will be perceived, rightfully but for the wrong reasons, as receiving preferential treatment. I can post clear orders defining at least some of my reasons for this action, and those should take care of the surface difficulties, but I doubt very much if it will stifle the resentment of our ordinary troopers. Your Cambrians might be in for a difficult time in the months ahead, but you have your wish and your opportunity to make what you can of it. And now it's almost curfew. Sleep well, and don't try to thank me, please, because I am not at all sure that I have done you any service."

Picus's assessment proved to be correct. The reaction of the veteran troopers in the other squadrons was less than friendly. The "dragon guards" found themselves treated as pariahs again, but a new spirit had been born in them with the knowledge that they were not to be split up, and they decided spontaneously, with the perverse obstinacy that frequently governs such developments, to adopt the name that had been so insultingly bestowed on them in the beginning, loudly proclaiming it as their own and taking a defiant pride in referring to themselves as the "Dragon Guards."

Then some time after that, as all things change and settle, the name was eventually accepted and shortened by everyone to become simply the "Dragons," and the new Cambrian troopers demonstrated that they were as good and as proficient at their tasks as any other troop in Camulod. It took long hours and killing work to establish that beyond dispute, but they thrived on it and grew stronger every day. By the time they eventually set out again, beneath the red and green Pendragon standard, to return to their home in Tir Manha, no one even remembered that they had initially been scorned.

It quickly became evident, however, that there was little useful purpose to be gained in taking the newly formed Dragons back to Cambria during the summer months. Summer was when the Camulodian cavalry worked hardest, not only in training and manoeuvres, but in the practical realities of patrolling their territories and defending the Colony's borders. Uther's Dragons, stuck in the far-off mountains of Cambria, thought often and enviously of the Camulodian troopers with whom they had trained all winter long and knew what they were missing.

They also felt, correctly, that their strength as a fighting force was being ignored in Cambria and therefore wasted. Uther agreed with his troopers for the most part, but he did his very best, assisted by the Camulodian training officers who had accompanied the

Dragons home, to keep them busy and occupied with drills and patrols of their own territories.

Their morale suffered badly when the only two raids of that entire summer took place along the mountainous coastline, far beyond the terminus of the Roman coastal road at the legionary fort of Moridunum. The local tribes had taken over the old fort when the Romans abandoned it and called it by its ancient name, Carmarthen. It was now home base to Chief Cativelaunus, head of the powerful Griffyd clan and one of the seven Chiefs of the Pendragon Federation. Passage beyond the end of the Roman roads at Carmarthen was difficult at best for Uther's cavalry, since their heavy, lowland-bred horses could not make the transit of the harsh and dangerous mountain terrain quickly enough to enable the Dragons to take any part in the fighting that was taking place farther along the rugged coastline. Their compatriots, on the other hand, riding their sturdy but ludicrously small-looking mountain garrons, traversed the high mountain passes directly on their surefooted little beasts, making twice the speed of the vaunted cavalry from Camulod. By the time the Dragons reached the scene of the battle that had stopped the raiders, everything was over, and most of the Pendragon warriors had already left again to return home.

That such a thing should happen was infuriating; that it should happen twice was unbearable. Although Garreth Whistler said nothing in criticism, Uther nevertheless learned a valuable lesson in fieldcraft from the repetition of failure. Never again would he lead his cavalry into a situation that was unsuitable for their tactical skills. Fighting on their own terms, in their own element, his Dragons were invincible, but fighting on terrain unsuited to their strength, versatility and purpose, their usefulness as a cohesive force would always be severely limited and the outcome potentially disastrous. Twice his Dragons had ridden out and achieved nothing. Twice they had arrived too late and been constrained to turn around and retrace their steps without striking a single blow at any enemy. Twice they had endured the scornful laughter of those warriors who had used their shaggy, short-legged little ponies to reach the scene first and had then employed their huge bows and merciless long arrows individually to slaughter the invaders. Twice they had known the humiliation of having to grit their teeth and swallow the sneers of their clansmen, who laughed at their fanciful name and dismissed them, along with their eye-catching uniforms and their disciplined formations, as the pampered, useless residue of the corrupt and vanished Romans. After much thought, however, Uther was convinced that he was the only person in his whole command who could add a more positive element to that humiliating litany: twice they had ridden out at his insistence and despite the cautionary urgings of his officers, and twice they had come home without a man or a horse lost through accident or circumstance or catastrophic ambush, and that was truly fortunate, for he had blundered into both situations without sufficient forethought, in blind ignorance of the odds stacked high against him. He would not soon expose his forces to such dangers again.

As soon as he had thought the matter through, Uther sought out his father, in company with Garreth Whistler, and laid the entire structure of his thoughts and findings before the King with characteristic bluntness and uncompromising honesty. He and his troopers were wasted in Tir Manha, he told Uric. They had no role to play in the kind of hit-and-run warfare waged against incoming raiders along the shores of the mountainous coastline in the summer months. Raiders landed one boatload at a time, usually in places that were inaccessible to heavy cavalry, and then they might scatter to burn and pillage, returning only at some prearranged time to sail away again and strike elsewhere. In that kind of situation, Uther swore, his Dragons were worse than useless. Better, he said, that he and his troopers should spend useful time in Camulod the following summer, learning to sharpen and tighten their fighting skills, than lie around in Tir Manha being laughed at by their own clansmen.

In time, he insisted to his father, his Dragons would be strong enough and confident enough to take their proper place among their own people, and should there ever come a day when the Pendragon Federation entered into an invasive war, then each of his troopers would be worth ten of the horseless, unarmoured and undisciplined warriors. Under those circumstances, he pointed out to the King, with entire armies of hostile troops flowing through the mountain valleys and lowlands, his Dragons would be a maul with which the enemy, whoever he might be, could be utterly smashed each time he ventured into open spaces. Using the network of fine Roman roads throughout their lands, his Dragons could and would dictate, determine and dominate all troop movements and supply routes in the eastern two-thirds of the low-lying areas in the country's interior. In the higher lands, into which the enemy would then be forced to withdraw, the Pendragon bowmen and their fearsome, unequalled long-range weapons could be relied upon to deal with any resistance that remained.

Uric listened to his son's harangue and then sent for those of his Councillors most suited for the hearing of such things, telling Uther at the same time to call in his own senior officers. When the entire group had assembled, Uric instructed them, without any preamble, to listen carefully, and then he turned back to his son and told him to repeat what he had said before.

When Uther had done so, the King looked around the circle of listeners until he met the eye of Uther's most senior Camulodian officer, a youngish man called Phillip, who was of an age with Garreth Whistler, a good twelve years older than Uther.

"What think you? Do you agree with my son?"

Phillip shrugged, then smiled. "I do, in this instance, King Uric."

"Why? Because he is your Commander?"

"No, sir, because his assessment seems to me to be accurate and correct."

"Hmm." Uric turned and looked at his own senior Councillors, who stood beside Daris, the High Priest. "Gethel, what say you?"

The old warrior called Gethel had stood listening with his right elbow resting on his left forearm, curling one of his long, white moustaches between his thumb and forefinger. Now he sucked in his lips and sniffed and nodded his head tersely. "Aye," he said. "It makes sense. The gods all know his people are doing no good here now, the way things stand. Better, then, that they should learn more of what it is they are supposed to do so well. And if we ever are invaded, then we will have a force that should be valuable. I say let them go."

"Daris? Have you anything to say?"

The Druid shook his head, his face sober. "Nothing more, King Uric. I agree with Gethel."

"Very well, does anyone else have anything to add? Anything negative? No? So be it." Uric turned back to his son. "We will miss having you here next summer, but perhaps your mother may travel down to Camulod to visit her own family then as well. Make arrangements, please, with Publius Varrus, to house you and your . . . Dragons . . . for the whole year. There should be no difficulty involved, but inform them for the sake of courtesy, will you?"

Everyone there, with the single exception of Daris, would have been surprised to know that Uric had decided to allow his son's request while he was listening to it for the first time and that this gathering he had called had been purely for the sake of policy and appearances. In fact, the King's decision had been made for what some might have seen as the wrong reasons, but at that level, deep inside himself, Uric did not care about what others might have thought. He had decided to accept his son's contentions and his recommendation based purely upon his own reaction to the dedication and responsibility he had seen shining in Uther's eyes, for there he had recognized the absolute vindication of his decision to send the boy to Camulod to form and train his novice cavalry using Camulodian discipline and Cambrian volunteers. Already, both he and his troops had changed beyond recognition. The wide-eyed volunteers who had departed but a few months previously as an undisciplined rabble were now proudly calling themselves the Dragons, and Uther had become their true Commander, strong and confident in the role, committed and dedicated to the prosperity and the responsibilities of his men. Uric was happy with the transformation and with the boy. The boy truly was his, and the father was more than pleased.

By the time they were both seventeen, Uther Pendragon and Caius Merlyn Britannicus had learned many lessons, seen many changes and crossed many bridges, not the least of which was the bridge between boyhood and manhood. That one they had crossed twice: once together in the Manhood Rites that symbolized a youth's transition from boyhood to warrior status; and then once more, this time separately, in the nameless rites that signified the transition from boyhood daydreams to the physical knowledge of women.

That second bridge crossing had been far more profoundly significant than the first for both young men, in that they had spent years training in the disciplines that were required for the Manhood Rites, and thus knew what was required of them at the testing time, whereas they had spent just as long talking and dreaming about the other manhood rites—and failing utterly to learn anything at all about the skills and disciplines they would need to learn in dealing with women. Each of them entered that arena alone, as all men must, and thereafter each progressed according to the dictates of his nature. And while both felt inclined from time to time to trumpet some particular success or triumph, each carried his personal failures and doubts in that most personal of all arenas securely concealed inside himself—or so he hoped. And to compensate for the sometimes overwhelming feelings of doubt and insecurity that would inevitably arise, each allowed himself to be perhaps a little more flamboyant than he might otherwise have been in those areas in which he felt most confident: outward appearances, military efficiency and disciplined precision in every endeavour.

The dispersal of the Dragons on their return to Camulod signalled the beginning of the next stage in Uther's training, as the Legate Picus had promised. Summoning Uther and Merlyn before him, Picus introduced them to their future: further advanced training in the art of command under the tutelage of one of his own imperial cavalry veterans, a senior centurion called Dedalus. Garreth Whistler would have no involvement in this part of Uther's training and would be lodged, like the rest of the Dragons, with a veteran company until such time as Uther's training should be completed for this year. In the meantime, Uther and Cay were to present themselves to Dedalus immediately following the noon meal, and Dedalus would give them his own instructions from that point.

Neither Uther nor Cay knew Dedalus personally, for the centurion was a field officer and therefore not as much in evidence around the fort as were the Legates Titus and Flavius, the members of Picus's retinue best known to the two boys. Dedalus was one of those who had returned home to Britain with Picus after the Emperor's assassination of Flavius Stilicho, when Picus and a small band of his most faithful officers and associates, warned in advance by sources close to Honorius, had escaped mere hours ahead of the heavily armed, five-hundred-man cohort of imperial Household Guards sent out to arrest and imprison Picus.

Uther's first thought on coming face to face with Dedalus that afternoon was that the man should have looked older if he had indeed been a veteran with Picus Britannicus in Stilicho's cavalry. It had been nine years since Picus Britannicus had come home to Camulod, when Uther and Cay were eight, and the former imperial legate and his group of friends had been travelling for almost a year by that time, crossing the continent in stealth, fleeing the wrath of a vindictive Emperor. According to Uther's mental arithmetic, Dedalus, a surviving centurion of Stilicho's campaign in Thrace against the Ostrogoths under their War Chief, Alaric, should have been no younger than thirty-five, and yet he looked no more than twenty-five, and that, Uther thought, could not be possible. Dedalus looked in every respect to be the epitome of a burnished, gleaming and polished Roman centurion, up to and including the large transverse crest on his helmet and the nine thick, decorative rings that were fastened to his breastplate in three rows. Each one of those decorative rings, Uther knew, had been awarded to its bearer for valorous and distinguished behaviour on an imperial campaign or in a specific battle or engagement.

Dedalus eyed his two new charges with disdain and something else that Uther thought, for no particular reason, might be regret. For a moment or two, the boy felt an indistinct but intuitive stirring of sympathy for the man, beginning to discern, if only vaguely, the difficulties that he must be facing in this situation. No one enjoys having unwanted responsibilities thrust upon him, and no man worth his salt can easily enjoy being exposed to nepotism from the exploited end of the arrangement. He had had two unknowns thrown into his care and could have no idea what to expect of them. The only thing of which he could be sure was that his superior required him to pass these two idiots along, irrespective of how good or bad they might be.

Neither of them would fail in this, Uther knew, and both of them would be not merely senior, but superior, officers.

"Tomorrow, we will go out on our first patrol." Dedalus's voice was deep and flat, his tone betraying nothing about what or how he was thinking or feeling. "It will be what we call here a patrol in strength: two squadrons, each of forty troopers, plus decurion officers and you. Each of you will ride with one of the decurion squadron leaders. You will watch him at all times and learn from him, observing how he works and obeying any commands he might issue to you. At all times, however, you will be directly answerable to me. You will do nothing without my prior approval, and that includes obeying a command from the squadron leader or taking a piss. Am I clear?"

Both boys nodded. Cay mumbled, "Yes."

Dedalus clamped his lips tightly together and inhaled deeply through his nostrils.

"Let me make myself clearer. That means that I am your Commander. It also means that each decurion is your superior, but that I am superior to all of you. It means I have the power of a living god—*the* Living God—over your miserable days and nights, all of them, all the time, from this moment forward.

"I have asked about you. And I have learned that you are a pair of dunghill cocks, the two of you, accustomed to crowing whenever you feel like it, uncaring that you disturb and annoy everyone about you. Well, cocks, those days are ended. You are mine now, both of you. Your daddy and your uncle—and whichever one of you is which could not concern me less—have abandoned you to me. He trusts me to make men out of you. Commanders, he suggests. I am flattered by his trust, but from what I know of you, I seriously doubt that I can do it.

"However, above and apart from all else, he has given me the power and the authority to decide whether or not you will ever be given command of troops in years to come. Therefore, I am your God, and you will treat me with the greatest of respect. You will treat me with even more respect than you extend to the Legate Britannicus. Whenever you address me, you will do so only because I have invited you or ordered you to speak, and when you speak you will address me as Centurion. You will say *Yes, Centurion*. You will say *No, Centurion*. You will say nothing more. Ever. Unless it be that I instruct you on what to say and when to say it. Do I make myself clear?"

There was half a heartbeat's space of silence, and then Uther and Cay snapped out, "Yes, Centurion!" together.

"So be it. Be outside my tent in full gear before dawn. Do *not* be late. Dismiss!"

Bewildered, the two young men snapped to attention, saluted as crisply as any newly trained recruits, spun on their heels and marched away in lock step, neither one of them daring to relax or slow down until they had turned a corner and put a building between them and the spot where Centurion Dedalus might still be standing glaring at them.

As soon as they rounded the corner, both boys slowed down and looked at each other wide-eyed. Nothing in their combined experiences prepared them in any way for what they had just undergone. Cay was the first to put their amazement and shock into words.

"Did I hear that man correctly? We are to be his indefinitely?"

Uther grinned, but shakily. "Aye, Cousin, that's what he said. He owns us, and your daddy has abandoned us."

Cay drew a deep breath and held it for a long count of seven before expelling it. "Well, then, we had better think carefully about that. What do you think we ought to do?"

Uther glanced around them, his gaze taking in everything. "I think . . ." he began, and then he paused, looking around him again before turning back to face his cousin. "I think we ought to spend the remaining hours of daylight looking about us at everything we can see, so that we'll be able to remember what life used to be like before we fell into this fellow's grasp . . . and then I think we should take extra-special care not to sleep late tomorrow morning."

As it transpired, the patrol might have been worse. As Cay pointed out, they might have died, somehow, in the course of it. Uther, for his part, refused to allow his cousin to shrug the experience off so easily. Death, he pointed out, would have been an improvement over what they had actually undergone.

The expedition lasted for eight days, during which the patrol rode completely around the perimeter of the Colony's landholdings, checking for signs of organized incursions by large groups of hostile interlopers, visiting each outlying farm and inspecting each peripheral guard outpost. These guard outposts were the Colony's first line of defence against infiltration and invasion, and each was garrisoned by a small force of infantry, a double-squad, twenty-man unit, which rotated twice each month, spending half the time in barracks at Camulod and the other half on outpost guard duty.

During the time that they spent in garrison, they had the companionship of others when off duty, and they could make use of the facilities of the fort and its surrounding settlement. On outpost duty, on the other hand, they were stuck with their own squad mates and left to their own devices. They were unable to leave their posts at any time during the half month of their tour of duty, since the importance of their task demanded a four-hours-on, four-hours-off system of shifts around the clock for the ten-man squad on guard each day, with the other ten on constant standby.

Sticking on post like stones in mud was how they described it. No forays into the wild woods for them, they muttered. That was reserved for the cavalry, the clean-faced, do-no-wrong boys who had everything served up to them in luxury. The poor old infantry was expected to stay close to home, to stand guard duty night and day in all kinds of weather, then do the chores, maintain the buildings and fortifications and keep the stables clean for the cavalry horses.

The garrison troops had no love for the pampered cavalry. That much quickly became clear even to Uther and Cay, and each of them made a mental note to talk about it with the other as soon as they were allowed the time to relax.

Dedalus, however, gave them no rest. The man was everywhere, indefatigable in his all-embracing mistrust of his two charges. He assigned them duties every morning and inspected them closely as they worked, sniffing and poking and carping and prying to ensure that all was done as it should be, according to his criteria of excellence. And when he saw them approaching completion of the projects he had set them, he would have replacement duties ready, announced in advance, instructions readied and presented in sufficient time to disallow the possibility of either boy stealing any rest between assignments. He kept them in the saddle all day long, ceaselessly moving in a never-ending spiral of motion that lasted throughout the normal marching breaks enjoyed by their companions, so that, to the disgust of both boys, who had believed themselves to be expert riders, when the order came to dismount at the end of each day's patrol, they both went reeling, barely able to walk upright. Only when they were in the final stages of discomfort over their natural functions each day did he allow them to dismount for long enough to relieve themselves, but even then he stayed beside them, affording them no privacy, denying them any opportunity to calm themselves or stretch their limbs. Within the space of the first four days of the patrol, both boys had learned to loathe the sight of him and to detest the sound of his carping, hectoring voice.

Eventually, however, as all things must, the patrol came to an end. Their first ordeal was over and neither of them had disgraced himself. They had taken every piece of spiteful pettiness that Dedalus could throw at them and they had chewed it up and swallowed it without overt complaint or covert whining—the latter only because Dedalus had given them no private opportunity for it. They arrived back in sight of the hill of Camulod before noon on the ninth day following their departure. As the towers of the fort came into view, Dedalus wheeled his horse around and trotted back to where they rode in formation, and then, signalling to each of them to follow him, he wheeled about again and rode to the head of the column. Uther and Cay followed him, but hung back from overtaking him, unsure of what was expected of them, until Dedalus, without looking back, raised one hand and waved them up to join him, then used both hands to indicate that they should come one on either side of him.

When they were side by side with him, he rode for a while in silence, then glanced from one to the other of them. "You smell, cocks. A few hours in the baths will do neither of you any harm. Ride half a pace behind me now, as you are, and spare my sensibilities." They fell back half a length, glancing mutely at each other, wondering what this new position signified, but Dedalus gave them no indication of anything, either by word or gesture.

As they crossed the training ground on the plain below the hill of Camulod, approaching the start of the road up to the hilltop fort, Uther began to take notice of the off-duty troopers, who seemed to be swarming everywhere. It seemed to him that he had never before seen so many of the garrison troops out of uniform, but the most amazing thing he could see was that most of them were bareheaded, and every man who was bareheaded was also completely bald, their skulls shaved clean of any hair. Uther gaped at Cay in amazement, although he dared not speak riding so close to Dedalus, and Cay nodded back to him, although he did not look in the least surprised. Dedalus turned his head slightly and saw the wonder and lack of understanding on Uther's face.

"Delousing," he said, his face hidden behind the large cheek-flaps of his helmet. "Head lice. Every once in a while we have an infestation, and when we do, we have to delouse everyone. It's not enough to simply bathe the men and make them wash their hair; that doesn't help. They have to be shaved clean bald, as well, to get rid of the nits—the louse eggs in their hair. There was talk of this for a while before we left. Be glad we missed it." He turned away again, leaving Uther agape over the civility he had been shown, and twisted around in his saddle to look over his other shoulder at Cay, noting the equanimity on the other boy's face. "You've seen this before, haven't you?" Cay made no move to reply, and Dedalus added. "You can speak now, the patrol's over. I asked you a question."

"Yes, Centurion."

"Hmm." Dedalus looked forward again, and Cay turned to look at Uther, who was gazing back at him, mystified and round-eyed. Cay simply shook his head, warning Uther not to be gulled into speaking out of turn, but the warning was needless. The impression Dedalus had made on both boys in eight days would prove to be indelible.

The noise from the mass of soldiers milling about them was indescribable, but from the lack of attention paid to it by Dedalus, Uther could only surmise that at such times of mass delousing, the normally stringent rules governing soldierly deportment and behaviour were relaxed to the point of non-existence. Suddenly, off to their left and no more than ten paces from where they were riding by, a scuffle broke out, and the disruption it caused spread quickly, as such things always do. Uther drew rein, turning in his saddle to see what was happening, but it was only the usual soldiers' brawl, with some men holding others back, restraining them from throwing themselves into the fray, and others wrestling violently, some on the ground, some yet on their feet. In the act of turning his eyes away again, however, Uther recognized Nemo Hard-Nose in the middle of everything, wrestling with a fellow twice her size. As his startled gaze settled on her, Nemo reared back, pushing herself with both arms, then grasped her opponent by the shoulders and snapped her head forward, butting him brutally on the bridge of the nose, the contact so solid that the meaty sound of the impact came clearly to Uther's ears across the intervening space and noise. The man dropped immediately, his knees instantly giving way beneath the hammer blow, and the weight of him dragged Nemo off balance and down with him before she could let go.

Not wishing to see any more, Uther turned his head quickly and made to kick his horse into motion again, only to find Dedalus right in front of him, watching his face. Beside them, the eighty members of their double-squadron patrol had almost passed them by.

"Wasn't that one of yours? The Hard-Nose?"

"Yes, Centurion."

"I thought so. Well named, it seems, unlike the other fellow." He tugged at his reins and swung his horse about again, then kicked it into a trot to regain the head of the column. Uther followed him, idly aware of the dexterity of the foot soldiers around them, who seemed to melt out of their way by magic. Once again, he was thinking, Nemo had managed to appall him and repel him with her mannishness, and he would have sworn that Dedalus had no idea she was a woman.

When they finally reached the main courtyard of the fortress, Dedalus reported their return formally to his fellow centurion Nellis, the guard officer of the day, and then dismissed the troopers, still under the command of their decurions, on a well-earned one-day furlough, although ordering them first to attend the bathhouse on the plain below the hill for scrubbing, delousing and shaving with all their fellows as soon as they had finished tending to their mounts and gear.

No one hearing the dismissal was under any illusion that they had really been dismissed. The last few items of which Dedalus had reminded them would amount to several further hours of work and would take the majority of the troopers well towards the end of this working day, since every man had to see to the cleaning, grooming, feeding and watering of his own horse before doing anything for himself, and then undertake whatever might be necessary for the care and maintenance of his saddlery and armour, removing the evidence of all the miles and all the wear and tear accumulated since the last thorough in-camp inspection they had undergone. Although it was yet barely noon, for some of the troopers, the unfortunate minority who had suffered some kind of damage to their equipment or trappings, it would be after dark by the time they finished all they had to do. The day that followed would be one of rest for all of them, absolutely free of responsibilities, but on the morning after that at first light, they would be on parade, going through a complete and painstaking inspection of their individual mounts and their gear.

Dedalus remained mounted, facing forward until everyone except Cay and Uther had gone, and then he turned finally to them. "As officers, you two are permitted to use the baths here in the fort or to avail yourselves of the facilities down in the Villa Britannicus. That's where I'll be headed after I've made my patrol report to the Legate. By that time, of course, you two should be long departed and asleep. Use your day of rest well, cocks. Day after tomorrow, be outside my tent at dawn. Dismiss."

The two cousins saluted, then swung down from their mounts and led them away towards the stables, holding themselves rigidly upright until they were completely sure they were out of Dedalus's sight. As soon as they knew they were safe, Uther threw his arm around Cay's neck, pulling him down into a headlock, and swung him around in circles until both of them fell down at their horses' feet. The animals merely stood and blinked at them, offering no criticism, and for some reason both boys thought that was extremely humorous, so they laughed until their sides ached. Then when they had sobered slightly, they threw their arms around each other's shoulders and made their way to the stables, where contrary to all the rules of Camulod, they bribed one of the stableboys to feed and groom their mounts while they sneaked off to the bathhouse.

TWELVE

Exactly one year later, two days before the *kalends*, the first day of August in what Christians would call 419 *Anno Domini*, Uther Pendragon and Caius Merlyn Britannicus had almost completed their first and last jointly commanded patrol. By that stage of their training, they had successfully completed several perimeter patrols of the Colony lands and had then gone on to complete three far more extensive and demanding territorial patrols, which were expeditions undertaken by an entire cavalry division, a two-hundred-man grouping of five squadrons acting as one army unit. These territorial patrols swept out from Camulod every second month, alternating to cover all the lands to the north on one occasion in a twenty-mile-wide area extending as far as Aquae Sulis and Glevum, and all the territories to the south on the next, covering the same width of land and descending as far as the old legionary fortress of Isca. Uther and Cay had been twice to Isca in the south and once to Aquae Sulis and Glevum in the north within the previous eight months, on each occasion under the command of Dedalus, who had turned out—to their immense surprise—to be an excellent and supportive commander, an inspiring tutor with a keen sense of humour and a good friend, once they had convinced him that they were worth knowing. The two cousins were now on the last probationary phase of their training, in joint command this time of their fourth patrol in division strength, and only nominally under the supervision of Centurion Dedalus, who rode with them purely as an observer on this final occasion.

The patrol arrived at the northern end of their excursion in the town of Glevum. This was a river port built only a few miles upriver from the throat of the estuary that separated Cambria to the north from Cornwall to the south, spilling out into the western sea between Britain and the island of Eire, which the Romans had called Hibernia, the Winter Place, because of its seemingly permanent cloud cover and its rainy, blustery, damp-cold climate.

Glevum was greatly favoured by coastal traders because of its sheltered inland harbour and its close proximity to the sea. Because of that popularity, the town had grown immensely wealthy over the previous decades and centuries of Roman occupation, so that it boasted numerous public and civic buildings with fine marble pillars, ornate pediments and entire walls clad in sheets of the finest marble imported from across the seas. The town had also been the regional administrative centre with a permanently assigned garrison to reinforce the edicts of the governing bureaucrats, and for many years its population had flourished and expanded, been nurtured and nourished by the wealth of trading activities and been protected by the military strength of the resident garrison and the nearby military base at Corinium.

Since the departure of the Roman garrisons, however, less than two decades earlier, Glevum had degenerated rapidly, and its dissolution was plain to see in the dilapidated condition of the streets, where weeds grew between the cobblestones on the main thoroughfares and entire sections of the sophisticated system of stone-carved water conduits that had once served the residential needs of the citizens had been broken and left unrepaired.

The civic government established by the Romans continued for some time after the military withdrawals. But when the army left Glevum and every other town in Britain, the power to enforce the law went with it, and the entire country began to fall, *ipso facto*, into a condition of anarchy. It took some time after that, however, for the truth of the situation to be fully understood, because although the force behind the law had departed, the reputation of the law remained. For hundreds of years in Britain, the ordinary people had been conditioned to behave lawfully, respecting the traditions and the proscriptions set in place by the legal, military-backed authorities, and so they continued to do so for months, and in some instances for years, after the fact of law had broken down and ceased to exist. Only very gradually did it become clear that the government had become a toothless guard dog and that people could now behave with abandon and break long-standing laws with impunity because there was no organized force in existence to stop them or to punish them for their actions.

Many of the former Roman towns took steps to safeguard their own welfare by organizing their citizens into quasi-military defensive units, while those that had the wherewithal undertook to hire mercenaries, who then functioned as private armies, policing the towns that paid their way and nominally protecting them against incursions by organized bands of brigands and raiders. Inevitably, however, even in the most successful of those arrangements, the seeds of failure and dissolution had already been sown. Hiring mercenaries to protect wealthy communities was akin to hiring wolves to protect sheep, and so within the space of ten or fifteen years, the towns of Britain, with very few exceptions, began to be abandoned by their citizenry, even though most of those citizens had nowhere better to go. It would be less hazardous, most of them thought, to take their chances of survival in the open countryside or in the forests than to remain, like sacrificial cattle, in once-wealthy towns that were natural targets for thieves and raiders.

Somehow, against great odds, Glevum had contrived to be one of the few towns in the west to retain a few shreds of its original dignity and stability, and Dedalus had told Uther and Cay on their first visit that he suspected its continuing survival had much to do with the ongoing need for its port, docking facilities and warehouses. As long as there were trading ships still plying the sea routes and merchants waiting in places such as Glevum and elsewhere for those ships' cargoes, then an incentive would exist for men of wealth and strength to fortify and defend the ports that served their needs, even if that entailed supporting them from afar and at great cost. That belief was reinforced by the presence of a strong force of mercenaries in Glevum, a force that Dedalus said had been in residence there for more than eight years. These people worked most of the time as stevedores, loading and unloading the ships and barges that came into the harbour. They guarded the docks and warehouses and otherwise kept to themselves, by and large, living a self-contained existence with their own women and everything else they needed in a few of the large dockside warehouses that they had converted into living spaces. They seldom mixed with the citizens of Glevum, but they allowed the town's populace to go on about its business without interference from them.

Whenever a force of any size approached the town, however, the stevedores put down their burdens, took up their weapons and were transformed into mercenaries until they had either discounted the threat or thrown the would-be raiders back to limp away with their tails between their legs. The Camulodians had been challenged thus on their first patrol through Glevum, and although no hostilities took place at any time between the two forces, the Camulodian commander, the Legate Picus himself, negotiated the terms of an ongoing accommodation with the town's defenders. The Camulodian patrols could find safe refuge in Glevum but were to leave the governance of the town and its affairs to the occupying mercenaries. Picus had ascertained that these people were not the common run of mercenaries, little advanced from bandits, but were well-disciplined Germanic troops of exceptionally high quality, all of them veterans of the legions and transported here to Glevum from beyond the sea for the specific purpose of guarding the dock facilities and keeping the harbour open and safe for shipping. Because of the tight-lipped discipline of the individual mercenaries, however, and the infallible discretion of their leaders, Picus had been unable to find out anything about the men's employers. Because of the enormous expense represented by their presence, he suspected that they were being kept in place in Britain by one of the surviving great trading houses of the Empire and that the investment in their presence, whoever was supporting it, was still proving to be worthwhile. To date, Dedalus had told the boys the year before, all potential disruptions of the town's trading routines had been prevented, and the thrice-yearly arrival of the cavalry

column from Camulod had become a commonplace occurrence,
causing no concern.

The patrol reached the town just before mid-morning to discover a regular market gathering in full swing. They set up their
route camp close by the town gates in the same large meadow they
had been using for that purpose for several years. By noon everything was in place: the horses had been groomed and set to grazing; the guard of the day had been installed; and those troopers due
for off-duty time had been released to enjoy the market, under
strict orders to be back in their places by sunset. The weather was
warm and pleasant, sunny with only a few clouds to throw an occasional shadow, and Uther, finding himself briefly free of duties, left
the camp in the care of Cay while he went off on a leisurely walk
through the Glevum marketplace. When he returned, he would
attend to his official duties for the day, and then, beginning on the
following day, he would have three days of official rest, relieved of
all duty and responsibility for a full seventy-two hours. For the
time being, however, he was prepared to settle for a short, enjoyable stroll through the centre of the town.

His stroll, however, soon became little more than a shuffle. It
seemed that every single person from the countryside for miles
around had come into town for the market day. The place was
jammed with people of all sizes and ages, completely overwhelming the presence of his own off-duty men, one hundred strong.

Even away from the marketplace, the streets were so crowded
that he found it impossible to walk for more than two or three
paces without having to step aside for someone carrying a load of
merchandise or to avoid tripping over some slower person in front
of him or simply to get around a knot of people who had met and
stopped to talk where they stood, exchanging greetings and information, not having seen one another since their last journey to the
market.

Impatient at first with his lack of progress through the dense
crowd, Uther soon gave up and laughed to himself. The people who
hemmed him in and blocked his way on every side were all there for
the pleasures to be gained from simply being here. There was an air

of festivity everywhere, and it was obvious that nothing else in their lives could give the ordinary citizens of Glevum so much delight as enjoying their own marketplace on a pleasant summer day, meeting their neighbours, trading goods and talk, and eating and drinking the appetizing wares of the stall holders—pie-makers, bakers, spit-roasters and brewers—who appeared to be selling food everywhere and were being paid in the small Roman-minted copper coins called *ases*, which were obviously still considered valuable currency in Glevum.

Uther stopped and looked around at their faces, searching for ill humour, and none of them, not a single face, was frowning. Laughter and smiles were widespread that day, and he shook his head and went on his way, grinning gently to himself and feeling oddly, formlessly content.

At one point he found himself gazing in admiration at one of three young women behind a stall that sold pottery and a selection of splendid pieces of barbaric, colourful jewellery. She was an exotic-looking creature of an age with him, he suspected, and he was captivated by the way her eyes flashed and sparkled as she talked and laughed with the people around her. She was wearing a tunic of bright blue material and over that a vibrant yellow shawl of some soft, delicate-looking fabric, and the brilliant colours set off her dark hair and skin to perfection. He could not see much of her body from the shoulders down, because of the pottery piled high on the table in front of her, but what he could see was alluring enough to make him work his way to the front of the stall to catch her attention.

She came and leaned towards him, head cocked to hear what he might say to her, so he asked her to show him some of the silver jewellery she had on display and to tell him where she had obtained it. Her name was Anna, he quickly discovered, and she had made the pieces herself. He admired them all quite honestly, for they were beautiful, and then, claiming to be unable to decide among them, he asked her which was her favourite. She picked out one of the two pieces he had already decided he liked best: a wide, circular brooch engraved with the thorn and leaf pattern of the north Cambrian clans. He had already visualized it gleaming on his mother's shoulder, and he knew Veronica would be delighted with it. Saying he had no goods to trade, he asked her what she would take for the piece were he to pay in coin. She gazed at him with enormous dark eyes for several moments, assessing him for a potential purchasing limit, then smiled widely, showing off perfect teeth, and named a price. It was not low, but Uther reached into one of the compartments of the scrip that hung by his side and produced a shiny, polished silver *denarius*, holding it up to her gaze between the tips of two fingers. The young woman's eyes went round with surprise, for the coin was certainly the brightest of its kind, and possibly the only one of its kind that she had ever seen.

Now it was Uther's turn to lean towards her, holding the gleaming coin up for her inspection, and she bent forward to allow him to speak into her ear. Her long hair tickled his nose as he spoke, and the clean smell of her set the short hairs on the nape of his neck bristling. A moment later, the young woman straightened up, a peculiar expression on her face. Then she smiled again, less widely this time, and shook her head in the negative, turning slightly as she did so to indicate an enormous and attractive-looking young man standing off to the right side of the stall. Her message was unmistakable. She was not available.

Uther looked straight at the young giant opposite, who stared back at him, straight-faced, and then he dipped his head slightly in acknowledgment, annoyed to discover that his face had flushed with discomfiture. He turned back then to the girl, smiling again, and pointed to the second piece of jewellery, which he had chosen as being almost the peer of the circular brooch, and indicated to Anna that he would exchange his *denarius* for both pieces. She accepted immediately, aware that she would never find a bargain of the like again, and wrapped both pieces of jewellery quickly in a square of soft blue cloth. Uther carefully placed the package in his scrip, thanked the young woman politely, smiled at her again, nodded in farewell, cast one more glance and a nod of tacit acknowledgment to her suitor—or perhaps it was her husband—and moved away into the crowd.

Far from being upset by his failure, Uther felt exhilarated by the challenge and the response he had generated from the girl

Anna. She had refused him, but the reason for her refusal had been standing right there, glaring at him, and Uther had felt with absolute certainty the reluctance underlying her refusal. At another time, under different circumstances, his request might have been smiled upon. He moved on, casting his eyes around now in search of someone new to test himself against, and he thrust one hand idly into his scrip, stirring the coins there with his fingertips, aware of the smooth, almost oily texture of the shiny metal discs. All of Uther's silver coins were highly polished, ever since he had noticed one of his Grandmother Varrus's household staff using a strange-smelling mixture to clean the tarnish from silver tableware. Intrigued, Uther had asked the man to show him what he was doing and how it was done, and had then acquired a small amount of the polishing material for his own use, so that now when he went on patrol, the silver coins he carried in his scrip all gleamed, catching the eye and stirring the cupidity of all to whom he showed them.

It had taken Uther some time to grasp the concept of coins as specie when he first became conscious of it. In Cambria, no one used money, although uniformly sized bars and ingots of gold and silver, copper, tin and lead were commonly used in trade, and each had a relative value ascribed to it, depending upon availability and ease of procurement. One copper ingot, for example, was equal to five of tin, and one silver bar to five of copper, whereas one bar of tin might sometimes be valued at six bars of lead, and sometimes at fifteen or even twenty bars. The most valuable of all, of course, was gold, and one bar of gold was the equivalent of twenty-five bars of silver.

The Romans, however, had taken that concept much further than anyone in Cambria had ever thought or sought to take it. They had issued coins of differing kinds and sizes, in gold, silver and copper, and had ascribed fixed values to each one. Uther would never forget his astonishment on learning that those values had persisted for hundreds of years until a shortage of gold had developed. From that point onward, the value of gold had escalated and had been followed some time thereafter by the value of silver, so that the ten or twenty copper coins that had once been deemed equal to one silver coin had lost their value, and now it might take as many as a hundred copper coins or more to purchase one silver one. That made no sense to Uther when he learned of it, and he still had not come to terms with the theories behind such things.

In Camulod, however, and in the countryside surrounding it, as in his home in Tir Manha, no coins were used at all. All trading was conducted by barter. And yet the Colony was rich in coinage, gold and silver both. In the economy of Camulod, which depended upon the sustained manufacture of iron tools and weapons for its farmers and soldiers, an ingot of iron was worth a hundred ingots of raw gold, for nothing useful could be made with gold. Only when Camulodians went out into the urban Roman world, where some people still revered the idea of money, did they carry coinage, mainly gold and silver, to purchase the things they needed, and those were mostly raw iron ores and ingots of smelted metal.

When Uther first ventured out on territorial patrol, Cay had been the one to take coins with him, but Uther watched carefully and was greatly impressed as Cay used them, exchanging several of them in a marketplace in Aquae Sulis for various commodities he might not otherwise have been able to acquire—a unique clasp knife with a curved blade and a hilt plated with horn was one thing Uther remembered clearly.

It had been on his return to Camulod after that incident that Uther saw the silver being polished, and he worked diligently throughout one entire afternoon polishing a pile of fifty silver coins for his own use. Since then, he had only ever used five of these, but he noticed that his brightly polished silver coins invariably attracted more attention and gained him more bargains, than the dull, ordinary silver *denarii* used by his cousin.

Uther had not gone very far when he heard a noise beginning to swell behind him, and he knew that some kind of disturbance was underway. Voices were growing louder, and as he turned to look back, he could see that people were starting to shout and mill about, attempting to get out of the way of whatever was going on. He felt a distinct surge of pressure as the dense crowd at his back swayed against him, and he heard the first screams of terror and panic rising from women who found themselves trapped helplessly in the heaving crowd.

Cursing the loss of his good humour and telling himself that the upheaval, whatever it was, had nothing to do with him or his people, Uther nonetheless began to make his way back towards the source of the sounds, elbowing his way through the press and looking around him constantly for any sign of his own troopers among the crowd. He caught sight of three familiar helmet crests to his right. Climbing up onto the low wall of a fountain that he had passed moments earlier, he attracted the attention of the three decurions by whistling loudly and waving. They began making their way towards him as soon as they saw him, and by the time they reached him, they had been joined by three more of his men who had been close by and curious. Now that they were seven, they formed a wedge and began to make more rapid progress as they approached the scene of the disturbance. Uther was issuing orders as they went, preparing his men for anything they might encounter, but when they did emerge from the crowd, without warning, into the marketplace, they were unprepared for what met their eyes.

The crowded marketplace had been transformed into a scene of chaos, with people running in every direction, screaming and shouting to escape the vicious brawl that was seething among the stalls and in the open space that fronted them. Men struggled everywhere, hand to hand in pairs and in groups, butting heads and flailing at one another with clenched fists. Some of them even used cudgels and other blunt weapons, drawing blood and breaking teeth and bones. Occasionally one or another of the grappling men would knock or pull an opponent off balance, reeling and toppling over to sprawl and roll among the debris on the ground. The scene bore no resemblance to the orderly marketplace Uther had left mere moments earlier, and at least one brawler in every group bore the red dragon of Pendragon on his left shoulder. The heart of the marketplace was already in utter ruin, with stalls and tables overthrown and upended and all their goods scattered and smashed and trodden underfoot. Several still forms lay scattered here and there, and one of them Uther recognized instantly as the young giant who had so silently laid claim to the young woman, Anna. Close by the huge man, almost at his feet, lay one of Uther's own men, face down and utterly motionless.

Stunned and taken completely aback, Uther nonetheless waved his decurions forward with a terse order to stop this and arrest everyone. The noise of the conflict had attracted other Camulodian troopers by this time, and the three decurions began hauling all of them into action, setting them to rounding up the miscreants who had caused the damage. The fighting was abating by that stage anyway, it seemed, the energies of the contestants bleeding away rapidly as exhaustion set in, and they began to realize that they had gone too far and might now have to pay for the excesses they had committed.

Uther remained on the outskirts of the action, breathing deeply and trying to control his anger. He felt betrayed and confounded by the fact that most of the damage seemed to have been done by his Dragons. Someone would have to do penance for this, he knew, but for the time being he was unsure of what his next steps should be. He forced himself to look once more at the group of prisoners being herded together and admitted that it was not as bad as he had feared, nor were they as numerous as they first appeared to be. He counted eight of them, and one more lying in the gutter close to Anna's big suitor. Once again he looked towards the body of the giant Celt, and as he did so he saw the man's head twitch and then his shoulders heave as he stirred and tried to sit up, only to collapse back onto the ground. Then came a hurried explosion of bright blue, and Anna dashed out from among the watchers to the big man's side, carrying a steaming bowl containing a moistened cloth with which she began to wash away the blood clotted over her lover's left eye.

Ignoring both of the young people, Uther looked back to where the prisoners stood huddled together, dejected and deflated now that their killing rage had died away. They were his men, one and all; he named them individually in his head and realized that one particular member of the group was missing. Feeling sick now, he moved to where the fallen trooper lay face down and stooped over, reaching beneath the jaw to search for a pulse. He found one instantly, strong and steady, and in his relief he gripped the shoulder strap of the trooper's cuirass strongly and heaved hard, flipping the unconscious body completely over onto its back with no pretence of gentleness.

As he had suspected, it was Nemo. Dim-witted, stubborn, savage, wilful Nemo of the too-close-together eyes, the sullen surliness, the scowling temperament and the strangely moving, endless loyalty. Rage and frustration filled him, and he pushed himself to his feet to find himself face to face with Anna. Her face was cold and distant, containing no trace of the smiles she had shown him earlier. Now she looked disdainfully at the embroidered dragon emblem that adorned his shoulder, and then dropped her eyes to look at its less ornate image on the shoulder of Nemo's uniform. As she did so, he saw that she, too, was bleeding, a sullen trickle of blood that emerged from the hairline above her left temple and flowed down into her ear before continuing downward to the point of her jaw and on into the collar of her blue tunic. Slowly, moving carefully, the young woman bent her knees and reached down to free her bright yellow shawl from Nemo's nerveless fingers. As soon as she had it, she straightened up and walked away to her man without a backwards glance.

Uther stood blinking after her, utterly bemused, seeing the stiff, unyielding posture of her back and the brilliant yellow blaze of her shawl. And then suddenly he knew, without any need of words, that Nemo must have snatched the shawl from Anna as soon as his back was turned, or at least as soon as he had left the marketplace, and that had precipitated the brawl as Anna's friends moved to defend her. He had no idea why Nemo would have done such a thing, but he could only assume it was motivated by some kind of jealousy, and the rage in his belly flickered higher.

Close to where he stood on the ground near the ruins of a fishmonger's stall were two rope-bound wooden water pails, and as one of his decurions approached him to report, Uther picked one up and emptied it over Nemo's head, bringing her back to consciousness quickly and effectively. She came up from the ground snarling and spitting, looking murderous, completely unaware of where she was or who had assaulted her but bent on revenge, her outstretched hands clawing for his neck. He remembered the head butt with which he had seen her fell one of her mates and immediately moved in towards her, lowering his head and tucking his chin into his shoulder so that as she butted him viciously, the rim of her helmet smashed into the crown of his with a concussive clang. Uther had been waiting for it, but Nemo was unprepared. Expecting to hear her assailant's nose being crushed, she had driven her own head into what might as well have been an anvil. The violence of the impact blinded her and sent her reeling off balance. As she staggered backwards, Uther leaped after her and straightarmed her in the chin with the heel of his right hand, knocking her sprawling again. He knew that everything around him had gone still, and a part of him knew he should not be brawling with one of his own, especially a rebellious ranker, but Uther was beyond caring. He felt violated and betrayed by Nemo's behaviour, and he wanted to punish her with his own hands.

Nemo lay sprawling in the welter of overturned stalls and their contents, her legs moving spasmodically until she could pull them beneath her. She knelt for a few moments, shaking her head to clear it, and as she did so, Uther launched a sweeping kick that caught her beneath the edge of the cuirass and sent her flying again. She was checked by an overturned table, then came to her feet roaring with blood lust, drawing her short-sword as she rose. Uther's own dagger slithered out with a ring of keen metal, and they began the first formal steps of the killing dance, crouched in the fighting stance, sword against dagger, each of them circling slowly to the right, focusing more and more tightly on their opponent's weight and balance. A part of Uther was appalled that Nemo would ever draw her blade on him. He had always thought her loyalty would be too great for that. But here she was, intent on gutting him, and he knew he would kill her as soon as she came close enough to cut.

And then Nemo's eyes cleared and she saw who crouched across from her on the other side of the blades. She made a strange, breathless kind of grunting noise and jerked upright as though she had been pulled up by a rope, holding her sword out at arm's length and spreading her fingers wide so that the weapon fell loudly to the ground. Staring and plainly shocked, she straightened her shoulders and snapped to attention, bringing her clenched right fist to a salute on her chest. Seeing her do so, Uther knew that she had not known until that moment who he was, and most of his anger fell away from him instantly. As Nemo stood, appalled, he allowed himself to straighten slowly, sheathing his dagger carefully and deliberately and then looking around for the decurion who had been closest to him when this happened.

The man was still standing where Uther had last seen him, ashen-faced, as were his companions. No one spoke, and it was apparent to Uther that no one even wanted to move. He looked back to Nemo, who stood there motionless, blinking to clear the fishy water from her eyes. He turned again and spoke to the decurion, his voice expressionless.

"Everyone involved here—theirs and ours, including this one—whoever was captured is to be taken back to our camp immediately, then gagged and tethered to a horse line on the outskirts under close guard. Once that has been done, you can hand over responsibility for them to Commander Britannicus, and then be on your way as you were before this happened. But be sure the gags are properly placed and the tethers are tightly tied and the prisoners closely guarded before you go anywhere. If I hear any noise from any of these people, you will be in trouble, and if any one of them escapes, I'll have your hide. Do you understand your orders?"

The decurion indicated very softly that he did, and Uther sent him on his way, after which he stood alone and watched until no sign of any Camulodian except himself was to be seen anywhere.

The crowds had settled down now that the tempest was over, and people were already setting up the damaged stalls again, salvaging all that they could from among the debris. Uther turned back towards where he had last seen Anna and her giant consort and was just in time to see them vanishing around a corner. Moving quickly, he followed them and caught them just as they were about to enter a low doorway. Not knowing the big fellow's name, he called out to Anna, and both young people swung back to face him, neither of them betraying a single sign of welcome. He spoke before either of them had a chance to start to turn away again.

"Forgive my approaching you after that out there. I have no knowledge of what happened. I promise you, however, that I will find out. Those men are mine, as you surmised, Anna. If they are guilty, I will punish them, I promise you. In the meantime, hear this." He spoke now to the big man. "I do not know your name, but you appear to have some presence here in Glevum, so I will address myself to you officially as a stall holder in the marketplace, if nothing else.

"Once I have discovered what went on here, there will be a reckoning. In the meantime, however, I want you, if you will, to tell all those who lost goods due to the damage done or caused by my men that they will be recompensed in silver coin. That I pledge you on my word as a Commander of Camulod."

The big fellow nodded. "I am Mark, a sawyer. I will tell the people of your offer."

"Good." Uther looked now from one to the other of them. "What happened? Can either of you tell me how it started?"

Mark grunted. "Aye. Someone threw a jug that missed my head and felled the man beside me. As I bent to see how badly he was injured, someone kicked me in the ribs and in the shoulder, and before I knew anything, I had three of your people hammering on me." He stopped, eyeing Uther with one eyebrow raised high. "There was no provocation, no argument involved, no angry words with anyone. You had been there mere moments earlier, yourself. You know how calm it was."

"Aye, I do. But this makes no sense. No one ever starts a brawl like this without reason."

The big man shrugged his shoulders. "Until today I would have agreed with you."

"Hmm." Uther turned back towards the girl. "Your shawl. How came my . . . man . . . to have it in his hand?"

The girl raised her head high. "He snatched it from me, but by accident. He was grasping at my hair. His fingernails did this." She pulled her hair back at the temple to expose twin scratches, deeply gouged into the skin of her scalp.

Uther winced and shook his head. "Then who knocked—who knocked him down?"

"I did," said Mark.

Uther blinked at him. "But you said you had three men all over you."

"I had, for a moment or two, but I soon lost those. And then I saw that creature of yours attacking Anna. All I had was a broomstick, but had it been a blade, that whoreson would be dead. I caught him across the back of the neck and dropped him like an ox. And then someone hit me with something. I have no idea who or what. You know the rest."

"Aye, I do indeed. Thank you for this. I shall return again tomorrow. How will I find you?"

"Let us find you. We know where your camp is."

"Very well, then. I am Uther Pendragon. Ask the guards for Commander Uther. I'll leave word that you are to be expected, and they will bring you directly to me."

"Commander Uther . . ." Uther stopped in the act of turning and swung back to face them as the young man continued. "Know that the estimated costs of the damages will be accurate," said the man called Mark. "You will not be cheated. That I can pledge to you."

Uther inclined his head, conscious of the courtesy extended to him. "My thanks to you. So be it. Until tomorrow then."

THIRTEEN

"You say there are nine of them?"

Cay sat sprawled in the command tent in front of the ancient but magnificent folding campaign desk that had been a gift from his father just prior to leaving Camulod on this, his final patrol as a trainee commander. Despite its great age, it was made from richly polished wood, although it was nicked and scarred with the blemishes of a hundred years of use, for it had travelled on campaigns across the world, serving generations of his ancestors before ending up in his first command tent. He was relaxed, his legs indolently spread, one heel resting on the edge of the box in which he carried books, maps and documents that could not be stowed inside the desk for travel.

"What do you intend to do with them?" Cay continued. "And how will you justify arresting eight townspeople?"

Uther shrugged with disgust. "I don't know, Cay, and that answers both your questions. I undertook to pay silver in restitution for the damage done, but if all of this happened because some bad-tempered stall holder took a dislike to a trooper's face and decided to rearrange his features, then that will affect the apportioning of costs, not merely of blame. Who started it all? That is the major question here, and the way we handle it once we discover the truth will greatly affect the way we are greeted next time we come to Glevum.

"No matter what we decide to do, it will have to be something draconian. My guts are telling me my people started it. I was right there moments before it happened, and there was not a whiff of tension anywhere in that marketplace. Whatever those troopers did, they did instantaneously and for reasons of their own. I would give anything to know what those reasons were and which of them was the instigator." He turned his head to where Dedalus lounged in a folding chair in one corner of the command tent, leaning back against a supporting pole. "Dedalus, do you have any suggestions?"

"About what? Punishment?" Dedalus had been peering at his fingernails, biting a ragged edge on one of them, and he continued to worry it as he considered Uther's question. Finally he sniffed and spread his fingers, holding them up to the light. "Execute all of them. They probably deserve it for half a score of other reasons quite apart from this one, and they won't be missed."

Uther made a wry face, completely forgetting that he had been terrified of this man a mere twelvemonth before. "That is very helpful, Dedalus. I can just imagine the Legate's reaction on learning that we've started executing our own troopers."

"Well, you asked for suggestions. You didn't specify that they had to be practical. Put the idiots on chain duty, then, and suspend all privileges for the next three months. No furloughs, no liberty, constant latrine duty, stable cleaning and nightly guard shifts." Chain duty referred to the direst barrack-room punishment detail, an unbroken chain of misery and sewage.

"But how do I establish their guilt?"

"You don't have to, lad. They established their own guilt when they were arrested in the middle of the mess they made. Besides, you are their commanding officer. You rule by decree, and if your decree is chain duty, then that's what they do."

"Aye, perhaps. But how will I find out who was the ringleader?"

Dedalus snorted and pointed his finger straight at Uther. "I'll wager five to one, right now, that your pet creature Hard-Nose was at the bottom of it all. From what I know of her—"

"Dedalus, you didn't even know she was a *woman* until I told you, and you'd been living in her company for nigh on a year by that time, so please don't advise me about Nemo based on what *you* know of her . . ."

"Oh, well, if you're going to be that particular over niceties, I'll shut up."

Uther paced the length and breadth of the large tent for a while, deep in thought, and his companions made no effort to interrupt his reverie. He had returned from Glevum half an hour earlier, hard on the heels of the three decurions and their party of prisoners. After waiting for Cay to return to his tent after taking delivery of the prisoners and seeing them disposed of according to his instructions, he had launched into the story of what happened in the marketplace. Uther himself had not yet been anywhere close to the prisoners since his return.

He stopped pacing after a while and drew himself up to his full height.

"Very well then, there's no point in putting this off. Here's my decision. You and I hold joint command, Cay, so we both have to be involved in this. There's no choice there. We will hold a court of inquiry right here in the command tent. We'll have the entire troop of them, including the townspeople, paraded in here one at a time, and we'll question all of them about what happened. They've all been gagged and tethered since they were arrested, so they've had no opportunity to confer together or cook up any false stories. We'll listen to all sides, we'll discuss our own conclusions and opinions, and then we will reach a judgment among the three of us."

"Oh, no, not among the three of us!" Dedalus lowered the front legs of his chair to the ground and stood up. "You two are in command here, not me, not this time. I am an observer on this outing, and that is all."

"Centurion Dedalus, sit down, if you please. A few moments ago you were telling me I am expected to rule by decree."

Dedalus sat down again slowly, looking pained, his face twisted up as though his mouth were full of a bad taste.

Uther nodded at him. "Well, then, I am decreeing that you, as the most experienced officer present, will sit on this tribunal for the purposes of advising us in assessing responsibilities and rendering judgment. No more discussion on the topic. Now, who's the captain of the guard today? We'd better speak to him now, and tell him what we intend to do, because we are going to need both his help and his people."

The inquiry lasted for more than three hours, but by the end of it the inquisitors knew what had happened, even if they had not discovered the underlying motivation. The prisoners were paraded one by one before the three-man tribunal, marched in under escort and treated as though they were on defaulters' disciplinary parade, which in fact they were, troopers and civilians alike. The eight townspeople were brought in first, their wrists in iron shackles and their mouths gagged so that they were unable to utter a single word of protest. Before the gag was removed, each of them was informed by Dedalus, as senior magistrate, that the tribunal was being held in order to discover the truth about the events leading up to the brawl in the marketplace, and for that purpose alone. No one among the three judges, they were told, had the slightest interest in listening to any prisoner's complaints about his treatment. The prisoners were here in this predicament and under martial law as the result of their own actions, because they had been committing mayhem in a public marketplace, endangering other law-abiding citizens.

Each prisoner testified that he had become involved in the brawl either in self-defence or to protect a friend, neighbour or spouse. In every instance, the men told of a sudden outbreak of brutal violence unleashed without provocation by Camulodian troopers.

Listening to all they had to say and knowing that none of these men had spoken with any of the others since their arrest, the judges had no reason to doubt what they were hearing. Before the first of the troopers was brought in, therefore, the judges had agreed that the blame lay firmly with the Dragons, and that their priority now was to identify the ringleader. After that, if the questioning of the prisoners went well, they might have some hope of being able to identify the cause. Dedalus was still insistent that the instigator must have been Nemo, the natural leader of this particular group. The hard men in her squad, the Boneheads as they were known, revered her for her insane courage under stress. Despite all that, however, Uther was unwilling to believe that Nemo might be at fault in this instance—not without provocation.

Within the hour, however, it quickly became apparent from the evidence of her squad mates that Nemo had been the one to initiate the fighting, hurling a heavy pot at the head of Mark, the giant sawyer. Her Bonehead mates had all been around her at the time, and always ready for a fight, they had joined gleefully in an indiscriminate assault on the townspeople. It became painfully clear as the inquiry progressed that the Boneheads were aptly named. None of them showed the slightest sign of guilt or remorse or even regret at appearing in front of the tribunal, and all of them seemed to take great delight in incriminating themselves and each other in the activities that were being investigated.

Nemo, brought in last of all, was not even questioned about her role in the events. She was simply accused of having started the debacle, and she made no attempt to deny her guilt. She provided no reason for her attack when invited to speak in her own defence. She had nothing to say, and she said nothing. She simply stood and glowered at a spot somewhere above the heads of the tribunal, as though defying them to do their worst with her. And so they did.

All nine of the accused were summoned together to face judgment, and when they were assembled, Centurion Dedalus informed them of the tribunal's findings and sentence. They had disgraced their own unit and the name of Camulod, he told them, and their behaviour had cost the Colony not only the goodwill of the citizens of Glevum, but also a substantial measure of the dwindling reserves of the coinage the Council of Camulod kept for emergency use. Because of that, and since they themselves had nothing of any value to offer in restitution other than toil and sweat expended in the common good, they would spend four months on chain duty, all privileges suspended for the duration of that time. They would participate in no training exercises or patrols during those four months, but would spend the entire time confined to garrison cells when they were not working punishment duties. Their confinement was to begin immediately. They were placed under open arrest, disarmed and guarded until they could be incarcerated on their return to Camulod.

It was a savage sentence, and four months was an unheard-of commitment to chain duty, lacking the commission of some extraordinary military crime such as attacking an officer or killing a comrade in a fight. But all three judges had concurred in adding an additional month to the sentence they originally considered, as a response to the utter absence of any sign of fear, shame or remorse among the offenders. The nine miscreants stood side by side and accepted the judgment solemnly, and none of them offered so much as a grunt of protest. Dedalus finally waved a hand in disgusted dismissal and they were marched away, leaving the members of the tribunal to look at each other in silence. None of them felt like discussing the matter any longer, and soon they split up and went their separate ways.

On the morning following the tribunal, Uther, in a foul frame of mind, disappeared on a three-day furlough. Later that same day, however, urgent word arrived from Camulod that Uther's grandfather, Publius Varrus, lay dying, and Caius Merlyn went galloping off in search of his cousin, leading two extra horses and claiming that he knew where Uther might have gone. Cay found him under attack in a roadhouse in the company of several sluttishly attractive serving maids more than willing to fulfill a soldier's needs. Together the two of them fought off Uther's attackers, thieves who had hoped to catch him off guard while he took his pleasure with the women. Afterwards, Uther, in recompense for the villainous proprietor's participation in the murderous attack on him, burned the roadhouse to the ground. Then the two cousins made their way as quickly as they could towards Camulod.

Publius Varrus was great-uncle to Caius Merlyn, but he was also Uther's maternal grandfather, and both young men loved the old smith deeply. Before he died—and his grief-stricken wife Luceiia would swear that he hung on to life for that sole purpose—Varrus spoke privately, first to his grandson and then to his great-nephew, of his hopes for them and for the union between Cambria and Camulod, and both had listened carefully and taken his dying testament to heart.

From the day of his death, two changes were noticeable in the young men: Cay, who had always been known formally as Caius Britannicus, insisted that everyone call him by his Celtic name, Merlyn, from that time on. Uther, for his part, sobered somehow

upon the death of his grandfather, becoming different, more dignified and perhaps in some elusive, indeterminable way even more
manly in his bearing. Uther had grown up, matured within the space
of the few days that had elapsed from the first word of his grandfather's illness to the completion of the old man's funeral services
and his burial in the main courtyard of Camulod beside the grave of
his best friend, Caius Britannicus, Proconsul and Senator of Rome.

Not once in the entire four months of her sentence did Nemo Hard-
Nose set eyes on Uther. In the close confinement of chain duty, she
was utterly incapable of tending to her self-appointed duty to
protect and serve Uther, and she found that intolerable.

Nemo harboured few illusions about Uther or about herself, but
she and Uther saw what happened in the marketplace that day in
Glevum very differently. Uther suspected that Nemo had seen him
flirting with the woman, Anna, and had been jealous. He was wrong.
Uther was her god, and Nemo knew that mere mortals cannot hope
to rut with gods. What Nemo had seen and noted was the threatening demeanour of the giant Mark, who had stood glaring at Uther
while Uther spoke to Anna. Nemo, standing among her squad
mates, had defined a threat in the big man's attitude and had immediately decided to bring him down simply for his overt disapproval
of Uther. She had launched her attack without warning the moment
Uther walked out of sight. The woman, Anna, had been included in
her ire solely because she had been the catalyst that had precipitated
the threat against Uther. In the course of chastising Anna's giant
lover, Nemo had sought to punish the woman almost casually, in
passing, as an incidental indication of her disapproval.

As soon as she and her companions were released from custody
at the end of their four-month sentence, Nemo spruced herself up
and appeared in her best uniform outside Uther's quarters, where
she requested and received permission to report to him for duty.
Escorted into his presence, she stood at attention until he turned to
look at her, his face devoid of expression.

"So," he said, "Trooper Nemo. You've been released to duty.
Did you enjoy your stay with the provost martial?"

Keeping her stance perfectly rigid, she assured him that she had not enjoyed it and did not intend ever to repeat it again. He nodded then and reiterated formally what he had already intimated in his opening words to her: that she would be starting out again from the beginning, demoted to the lowly rank of trooper. That did not concern her; she had lost her ranking as troop leader more times than any other trooper in her intake, but she had always managed to win it back through sheer guts and determination. Uther then dismissed her so that she could meet with her decurion commander.

Nemo was troop leader again within the month, and she worked hard after that at keeping her nose clean and her performance as close to perfect as was achievable, so that within the year, she had won promotion to decurion, the highest rank she had ever attained. No one really expected her to keep it for long, but this time, she swore to herself, things would be different. She was determined to remain a decurion, and months eventually passed into seasons without her earning a single demerit, let alone a demotion.

During the years that followed, Uther and Merlyn became men in fact as well as in name, passing from eighteen years old to twenty-two, and their professional abilities as soldiers matured and became finely honed and unimpeachable. They became known behind their backs by their admiring and sometimes resentful men as the Princes of Camulod, and the life they led was a full and rewarding cycle of duty, achievement and enjoyment. Nemo Hard-Nose soon became inured to the sight of the processions of beautiful young women that came and went with unfailing regularity through the private quarters that Uther and Merlyn called their "games rooms." The numbers of women and the degrees of hilarity and high living fluctuated only in response to the presence or absence of Merlyn's father, the Legate Picus Britannicus, who was still the Legate Commander of the Forces of Camulod, and whose disapproval was the only thing that could really keep the two young men in line. Uther's grandmother, the widowed Luceiia Britannicus Varrus, also exercised great power over the behaviour of her grandson and great-nephew, but she was seldom seen around the fort; she preferred to spend her time alone in her home with the women of her household.

Towards the end of the fourth year, however, in the autumn, Uther and Merlyn found a young woman in the forest at the far end of one of their regular perimeter patrol sweeps when they had been riding apart from each other. Nemo's squad was there with Uther at the time, and it was Nemo who first saw the young woman kneeling on the ground among the saplings in a clearing away from the road as she rode by. Investigation would show that the young woman, who seemed to be unable to speak, was mourning the deaths of two elderly people who were lying beside her and who everyone supposed were her parents. There were no signs of violence on either of the bodies and no obvious signs of sickness. Nemo sent one of her men riding to fetch Uther, and after a cursory examination of the scene, Uther ordered two of his men to dig a grave and bury the dead. Then he swung the young woman up to ride behind him, where she remained until they arrived back in Camulod. By the time they got there, it had been established that the young woman was mute, and in the need to call her something, one of the young commanders gave her the name Cassandra, after the tragic prophetess of Troy.

On the night they returned from the patrol, in the privacy of Merlyn's games room, something happened between the two cousins that would permanently damage their relationship.

Uther disappeared in the middle of the night, taking only a few of his Dragons and riding away without informing anyone where he was going or why he was leaving so suddenly. That same night, the young woman called Cassandra was savaged and beaten to the point of death. She survived, however, and was confined under heavy guard in the surgeon Lucanus's infirmary. Then the following night, she disappeared from a guarded room in a building ringed with guards, and people started whispering that Merlyn had used sorcery to spirit her away. The woman Cassandra vanished completely from Camulod.

Shortly after that, Nemo began to pick up disturbing snippets and fragments and mutterings—nothing that made complete sense and nothing more definite than vague rumour, but the cumulative effect was that whatever might be wrong between the two commanders, Uther and Merlyn, the woman Cassandra was at the root of it all.

Merlyn, it appeared, suspected Uther of something nameless but reprehensible. It could not have been the attack on Cassandra, Nemo reasoned, because she knew that Uther had left the fort during the midnight watch, shortly after storming out of the games room. One of the Dragons from her own squad had been on guard duty outside the tower that night and saw him stride away, and still others had been posted at the main gate of the fort and checked Uther and a half score of their fellows through there shortly thereafter. They had told her, too, that Uther was in no sweet frame of mind.

Uther returned directly to Tir Manha upon leaving Camulod on the night of his quarrel with Merlyn, and many months would pass before he returned. He sent word of his whereabouts to Picus Britannicus immediately upon his arrival home in Cambria and requested that his Dragons be dispatched to join him there. He had need of them, he said, for the next stage of their training, which would be in the lowland valleys of the southeastern part of the country. Picus sent the Dragons home immediately, under the command of their own Cambrian officers, of whom Nemo was one. But it was not to be her fate to remain in Tir Manha, for Uther immediately sent her back to Picus in Camulod bearing important messages, and after that time she lived neither in one place nor the other, the majority of her time being spent on the road between them.

Uther could not stay away from Camulod permanently, however, no matter how disagreeable the circumstances of his departure had been. He had duties and responsibilities to attend to, and his conscience would not permit him to ignore them for long. On his eventual return, he and his cousin Merlyn, despite the unresolved tension between them, were jointly honoured by Picus Britannicus, who presented his two youngest commanders with sumptuous new armour and identifying standards. Uther received a magnificent new cloak, banner and shield, all bearing the device of a great golden dragon woven in thin gold wire on a deep red background. The blazon was similar to the ages-old red dragon emblem of his Cambrian Pendragon people, but it was subtly different so that it would be personal to Uther. To top off the gift and render it perfect, Picus included a new high-plumed bronze helmet in the Roman officers' style, complete with ornate, hinged cheek-flaps to guard and conceal his face in battle. Merlyn, at the same time, received a black war cloak lined with soft white wool and bearing the blazon, woven in fine silver wire, of Merlyn's own insignia: a mighty, rearing bear with spread arms and enormous claws, commemorating his killing the largest bear anyone in Camulod had ever seen while armed with nothing more than a large spear. Like Uther, Merlyn also received a new war helmet, this one made, like his personal armour, of black enamelled iron and crested in alternating tufts of black and white horsehair. With it also came a new standard and shield, each bearing his device, the silver bear on black.

The following day, however, word arrived that Camulod was under attack from two directions. One of the outlying farms, a stock-breeding operation in the south of the Colony, had been robbed, its entire two-hundred-man garrison wiped out. And simultaneously, an invading fleet of Erse galleys had landed in the north, their presence reported by King Uric's people, who had seen the galleys passing upriver. Lot of Cornwall had engineered his first double assault on Camulod, and from that day onward, Camulod would be almost constantly at war with Britain's southwesternmost region.

After the initial outbreak, with that successful raid against the Colony's southernmost farm, the war progressed swiftly. Under the overall command of Picus Britannicus, Uther and Merlyn split their forces, Uther riding south and west against Lot and Cornwall with seven hundred highly mobile cavalry, while Merlyn headed north with four hundred cavalry and three thousand foot soldiers to stop the invading Ersemen. Merlyn's campaign was completely successful, ending in the capture of a high-born Eirish hostage, but Uther's cavalry was ambushed and decimated along the northern coast of Cornwall by an enemy force using poisoned arrows, which killed every one of Uther's men who sustained even a scratch from their envenomed tips.

Uther was not completely convinced, however, that his attackers were Lot's people, for there was sufficient evidence to the contrary to raise genuine doubts. A short time before the attack, his scouts had found the remnants of a massacre in which some sixty people had been stripped, then bound and slaughtered. Lot himself, speaking through a Christian bishop sent out to Uther as an intermediary, claimed that those were his own people, captured unawares and slaughtered by a strong force of seaborne raiders of unknown origin. That unexpected claim was sufficient to give Uther pause and make him doubt himself. The murderous group who attacked his force had overshot themselves foolishly, expending all their poisoned arrows far too quickly, so that the survivors of Uther's army, still more than six hundred strong, were able to rally and pursue their erstwhile attackers. But the attackers had galleys waiting for them right below the cliffs where the attack had occurred, and they were afloat and at sea before Uther's men could close with them. Uther had to wonder if Lot might be telling him the truth. His gut feelings told him otherwise, that the sixty dead might well have been the sweepings of Lot's jails expediently disposed of simply to hide Lot's guilt in the ambush; but his training in logic, acquired in Camulod under his Uncle Picus, suggested the contrary. And so he gave Lot the benefit of the doubt and released the bishop to return to Cornwall, despite his strong conviction that the man of God would rather have remained a captive in the custody of Camulod.

The bishop's visit was followed rapidly by the arrival of two strange-looking, foreign-born envoys called Caspar and Memnon, who claimed to have been sent as ambassadors from Lot, King of Cornwall, to Picus Britannicus, the Legate Commander of Camulod. Uther arranged to accompany them safely to Camulod, but beyond that he paid them little notice, and his failure to question their motives or to examine them more closely would cost him and Camulod dearly.

Within a day of Uther's bringing the strangers home to Camulod, the men were recognized, and Merlyn was able to identify them as spies and sorcerers, the men responsible for Lot's poisoned arrows. He threw them into jail in full expectation that their master, Lot, would be following hard on their heels, knowing that he had his two loyal creatures on the inside and expecting to find Camulod lulled into a false sense of security. Merlyn was correct, and Lot's treachery almost captured Camulod, but forewarned, Merlyn's and Uther's combined armies were able to defeat Lot's forces and rout them.

While the defeat of the forces from Cornwall was taking place down on the plain below the hill of Camulod, however, Lot's sorcerers managed inexplicably to escape from their cells, and thus they were able to open the rear gate of the fortress to a party of their own people sent to burn the place down.

That attack was discovered and fought off before it could develop fully, but still the fighting inside the fort was fierce and bloody. The back alleys of Camulod, close to the rear wall, were choked with corpses before the rear gate could be securely shut again. Many of the buildings within the walls had been set alight and were already uncontrollably ablaze.

When Uther and his cavalry abandoned their pursuit of Lot's fleeing forces and came riding back to Camulod a few days later, a thick column of black smoke brought them spurring from its first sighting, and only as they approached the fort did they notice that there were no signs of ongoing battle. Great open pits had been dug on the plain below the hill of Camulod, and the corpses of the slain were being interred there beneath layers of quicklime. The smoke that they had seen was from a funeral pyre. Only then did they learn that Picus Britannicus, their leader and Legate, had been murdered in his bed during the sorcerers' escape and before the night attack. Uther found his cousin Merlyn standing by the pyre, one of the chief mourners. Battle weary and still in their armour, Uther and his men stood silently at the back of the crowd to observe the rites and honour the dead.

Within a matter of mere weeks, more tragic tidings arrived in Camulod, brought personally to Uther's attention this time by Garreth Whistler. Another army raised by Gulrhys Lot, this one a compact, deadly effective striking force built mainly of foreign mercenaries, had invaded Cambria near the time when Lot's main army was attacking Camulod. This small, hard-hitting force, barely large enough to deserve the name *army*, had created havoc, having caught the Pendragon Federation totally unprepared for invasion from the south and ill-equipped to adapt with any kind of speed to counter a sustained attack from that direction. Uric's people and the concentration of his forces had always been primarily attuned to threats emerging from the northern boundaries of their lands, both coastal and landward.

Despite their unpreparedness, the Federation had nonetheless managed to respond with admirable speed to this new threat, Garreth reported, and the Pendragon forces had rallied well under great pressure. Meradoc, the dominant Chief of the Llewellyn clans, had distinguished himself in the campaign, as had young Huw Strongarm, Chief of the northern Pendragon, who at sixteen was the youngest Chief of a Pendragon clan in living memory. At the peak of the short, bloody campaign that followed the invasion, however, the insurgents were brought to battle, and in the course of the fighting, Uther's father, King Uric Pendragon, had been killed, felled by what had turned out to be a poisoned arrow.

Uther met the news with blank incomprehension. He heard the words and accepted them, but his mind failed utterly to accept or to even consider their import. Nemo was standing by, awaiting his instructions on some matter that would now never be mentioned again, and she watched him closely, prepared to jump forward and catch him if he fell. His eyes had gone strangely dead as though he had lost all ability to focus on anything, and he began to nod his head as though agreeing with some voice inside him that spoke to him alone. He reached behind him with one groping hand and found the chair on which he had been sitting. Pulling it towards him automatically, he lowered himself very slowly to its seat and then asked Garreth for word of his mother. Where was she now? Did he need to go to her immediately, or would she come to Camulod to her own mother, Luceiia Varrus? And when would his father be buried and where?

Garreth Whistler looked uncomfortable, and his gaze went from Uther to Merlyn Britannicus and then to the other senior officers of Camulod's garrison. The report he would now deliver, he told them, had come directly from Meradoc, the ruling Chief of the strongest of the three Llewellyn clans in the Federation. King Uric was already buried, he reported. He had been dead for ten days now and was buried within hours of his death in the place where he had fallen. The enemy had been all around the Llewellyn position, and Chief

Meradoc's overriding priority was to rescue his own people from the trap in which they found themselves. The formalized, royal burial of what was by then essentially no more than one more corpse among hundreds had had to be set aside. There would be opportunity later, Meradoc had decided, to mourn and honour the dead King once the living were secure and safe again and the enemy was put to flight.

Uther showed no reaction to any of this, and so it was Merlyn who asked Garreth what King Uric had been doing among the western Llewellyns when he should have been with his own forces in south Cambria. Garreth turned his head towards Merlyn and sniffed before glancing towards Uther, who sat staring vacantly back at him. After a moment, evidently having decided that Uther's attention was engaged elsewhere, Garreth turned back to Merlyn and the others.

From the moment word of the invasion of Cambria first arrived in Tir Manha, he explained, King Uric had delegated command of his own Pendragon clansmen to him, Garreth Whistler, as the King's Champion. From then on Uric had spent most of his time touring the territories of the Pendragon Federation, accompanied by a small escort of hand-picked warriors, rallying and encouraging the fighting men of the other federated clans and demonstrating his support for each of his Chiefs in turn.

At the time of his death, Uric was visiting Chief Meradoc's host of Llewellyn warriors, the largest and strongest armed force in his overall command, and prior to that he had spent time among the warriors of the Griffyd clans with their Chiefs Cativelaunus of Carmarthen and Brynn of Y Gaer. When his visit to Llewellyn was complete, Uric intended to move on to visit the army of Huw Strongarm, Chief of the northern Pendragon.

Enemy activity had been thick and heavy around the Llewellyn territories just prior to Uric's arrival, Garreth told them, and the fighting was heavy enough that Meradoc sent word to the King warning him of the extreme danger and suggesting that Uric postpone his visit. Uric, however, would have none of that and insisted on holding to his original schedule, and so he and his escort had ridden into Llewellyn's lands and died there.

At that point Uther spoke again in a flat, emotionless voice, demanding news of his mother, and Garreth turned back towards the younger man.

The Lady Veronica, Uther's mother, he reported, had been devastated by her husband's death but had recovered quickly, showing great strength and resilience. It had been her original intent, he said, immediately after her recovery from the shock of the news of her husband's death and burial, to return to Camulod in order to be with her mother. But she had changed her mind, for reasons known only to herself, and decided to remain in Tir Manha, at least for the time being. She wrote a letter to her mother, Luceiia Varrus, explaining her thoughts and her decision to remain in Cambria. Garreth had delivered that earlier.

Uther nodded his head slightly and then made no more effort to communicate with anyone. For a time no one moved or spoke, everyone apparently grappling with the complexities of the changes that had occurred within the past short space of weeks. Garreth Whistler, however, had not yet completed his purpose in coming to Camulod in person, and in order to emphasize the importance of what he had yet to communicate, he dropped to one knee in front of Uther's chair and grasped Uther's wrist tightly, forcing the younger man to look up into his eyes.

"You're Chief now, boy. And you can be more than that, if you so wish, if you move quickly enough. Daris the High Priest has sent me to bring you home for the Choosing. In truth, he has grave doubts about your suitability, but give him his due, he wishes you to have the opportunity that is yours by right as a Pendragon Federation Chief. It will happen soon, the Choosing—this is no time for our people to be without a King. And if you harbour any hope or wish at all of following your father and grandfather to the King's seat, you have to come with me, and soon. You have to take your place among the other Chiefs for the judgment and the vote. If you come late, you'll lose your chance, for choose they must, and quickly. Do you hear me, Uther? Do you understand what I am telling you?"

Uther had listened in silence, his staring eyes fixed on Garreth Whistler's face. Now he sat for a while longer, empty-eyed. Then he sucked in his cheeks and nodded to the Champion, speaking in a voice barely above a whisper.

"I hear you, Garreth. I understand. But I must think. I need time to think."

He stood up and walked from the gathering without another word, not to be seen by another living soul for two days. Garreth's tidings had been grim enough, but no one had expected Uther to be so badly shaken by them or that he would shut himself off from all contact with anyone while he came to terms with his own grief.

He emerged from his seclusion on the morning of the third day and sought out Garreth Whistler immediately. Uther was stern-faced and showed none of the eager enthusiasm that had always marked him in military matters.

"We will go," he told the Champion tersely. "But we will need a week beforehand—no more than that—to drill the Dragons. See to that for me, if you would, starting immediately. Drill them until they drop, cursing you and me. They've been getting fat and lazy for the past few months. I want them to be at their peak when we ride into Tir Manha. If I am to be King, and I intend to be, they'll be the central core of my new armies, and I need them to be magnificent, to stir envy and admiration among our young Pendragon men and generate new troopers. See to it, if it pleases you. I'll join you later today and work with you from then on, but I have matters to attend to first."

Garreth Whistler only nodded, offering no comment, and watched the young Chief stride away.

Uther went straight to Nemo and summoned her to ride with him. She followed him to the stables and then rode close behind him as he left through the main gates of the fortress, merely waving in response when Merlyn called to him from afar and spurring his mount out onto the downhill road to the plain beneath.

They rode hard and far, and neither of them spoke a word for more than an hour when Uther finally drew rein and turned his horse around, ignoring Nemo's mount as it sidled and stamped beside him. He led them back and around by a circuitous route to a slight rise overlooking the broad drill plain below the fortress from the northeast, the same spot from which he and Merlyn had watched

Camulod burning luridly against the night sky a mere two months earlier. Now from this distance, even in the bright morning sunlight, no sign could be seen of any damage to the fortress, and there was nothing visible to indicate that anything had changed here in years. Even the three huge mass graves that had been dug on the plain were no longer visible, for the earth that covered them had been levelled and compacted by thousands upon thousands of hooves since normal cavalry training resumed following the cleanup after the battle that was waged there. They sat together in silence for a while, looking at the fortress so seemingly secure upon its distant hilltop, and then Uther spoke over his shoulder.

"We have lived through the end of an era, Nemo, you and I." Nemo made no response, and after a few moments Uther continued: "Do you know what an era is?" He turned to glance at her as she shook her head, and then he looked away again, gazing at the distant towers of Camulod's walls.

"An era is a period of time, Nemo—a long period of years or even decades, sometimes centuries—that can be measured from a clear starting point to an ending. They tell us the Roman general Julius Caesar came to these shores decades before the birth of the Christians' Christus among the Hebrews, and that the last of the true Romans, the Emperor Constantine the Third, left Britain in the year I was six. That means the Romans remained here in Britain without leaving for more than four hundred years. That was an era." He glanced at Nemo again and smiled, shaking his head gently. "You don't know what I'm talking about, but what I am saying is true. That fortress over there on its hill belongs to another era, a more recent one . . . an era that overlapped the Roman one, beginning before I was born, before my father had even met my mother."

He waved his hand towards the distant buildings. "Before my grandfather, Publius Varrus, came here, there was no fortress on that hilltop. There was no Colony, no Camulod. There was no cavalry here, no garrison and no alliance between Pendragon and these people. And there were no longbows among the Pendragon. Did you know it was Publius Varrus who was responsible for bringing the longbow to Pendragon? Well, it was. He brought a giant bow with him from Africa, and our people admired it greatly. They sought to make others like it, and our long yew bows were born. All of those things have come to pass since Publius Varrus married my Grandmother Luceiia almost fifty years ago. Their marriage, in many ways, marked the beginning of the era."

Uther's voice faded into silence, and Nemo sat staring at him, waiting for him to continue. He did not even glance in her direction, keeping his gaze fixed on the hilltop fort, and she sat on his right, less than half a pace to his rear, her close-set eyes fixed unblinkingly on the point of his jaw, watching for the tiny initial flexing that would herald his next words. She was, as always, content to wait upon his pleasure.

"It began with Caius Britannicus and Publius Varrus; it grew with Ullic Pendragon and Picus Britannicus; and it ended with the deaths of the last of them, my Uncle Picus's short months ago and my father Uric's weeks ago." Uther hawked and spat. "Camulod will continue to exist, and it will grow and prosper, I've no doubt of that. Merlyn Britannicus will keep it safe and hale. But it will never be the same again, because the treachery and greed of Gulrhys Lot of Cornwall have brought about changes that were never foreseen. He has destroyed the calm of Camulod as surely as the serpent destroyed innocence in the garden the Christian priests talk about. And such changes can never be unmade. And that means that Camulod—my own Camulod that has fed and nourished me since I was a boy—is ended."

He kicked his horse into motion, keeping its head directly towards Camulod, and Nemo's fell properly into step beside him, maintaining a half-length space behind him so precisely that Nemo had need of neither reins nor bit.

"And so now we must return to Tir Manha," he continued, speaking to her without looking at her. "And this time, I think, we will stay there. It is my home, after all—everyone delights in telling me so—and it has been yours, too, for so long that I'll wager you can't even recall where you came from in the first place. But I will tell you a secret, Nemo, that no one else in Camulod would ever suspect: I do not want to go back there, not to live, and especially not now that my father is dead. I have no wish to go back to what everyone else insists on calling my home . . . grim old Cambria with its harsh-faced people. I have no need of their ill-mannered glowering, and I cringe at the very thought of living with their foul-tempered and humourless dislike day after day, year after year. My father's death, far, far too soon, has taught me that a man is a fool to live in hopes of a better tomorrow. I have a thousand better ways today to spend what time remains ahead of me, and I have brighter, lighter and more pleasant places in which to spend it . . ."

Nemo glanced sharply at him then, her curiosity piqued as he made a noise in his chest that almost sounded like a smothered laugh. "You know, Nemo, I sometimes thank the gods that you exist, for if you did not—" He left that thought unfinished and then resumed again immediately. "There is not another person in the entire world to whom I could confess this openly in the absolute knowledge that it will never be passed on. So here is my dark and dire secret: I would prefer to spend my entire life here in Camulod, without ever having to return to Cambria and Tir Manha. That does not sound like such a massy secret, does it? And yet it is, for if that word got out among my friends, I wonder just how many of them would remain my friends . . . I could not tell that truth even to Merlyn, because I fear he might take it amiss and see it as a threat to his designs for Camulod, thinking that I might seek to undermine him here. And I would not, Nemo, believe me. I would not.

"But this is my life's centre, Nemo, this—" He stood up in his stirrups and waved his hand broadly, indicating the entire country-side that surrounded them and the looming towers of the fortress on the hill ahead of them. "Tir Manha has a beauty that I can't dismiss and can't deny—the sight and smells of the land move me and stir up my blood in a way I can't describe. But Camulod has become my home, far more than Tir Manha has ever been. My father and my mother lived in Tir Manha, and so did Grandfather Ullic, and because of that I returned there every year . . . But it was my mother who insisted, first and most strongly and ever afterward, that I should spend as much time as I could in Camulod. And I have always, ever since my earliest boyhood, been eager to return to Camulod when the summer waned and the weather began to change.

"And why would I not? Even you, Nemo, must resent returning home each year. Think of all we relinquish when we do . . . Think of all the things we have in Camulod that people lack in Cambria! Baths, for one thing—and bathing is one mighty, all-eclipsing thing! Hand in hand with bathing, Nemo, in a scented, wondrous silence, walks a more than pleasant absence of revolting people smells.

"And then there are hypocausts—furnace-fed hot-air ducts—and heated buildings. Floors that are warm in winter and rooms that are high and bright because the warmth coming through the hypocausts allows you to live in them without having to block all the exits and shut out all the light. And space, Nemo! Think about space—high-ceilinged vaults and room to walk about upright and at ease. You can't do that in the gloomy, low-roofed huts of Cambria."

Nemo listened in wonder. She was used to hearing him speak, but she had never heard him go on like this before, not at such speed. His voice was far more forceful, it seemed to her, than she had ever noticed before, his words appearing to rattle one against the other as they spilled from his mouth. And then, quite suddenly, he was silent again, and the only sounds to be heard were the thudding of their horses' hooves and the creaks and jingling of saddlery. She waited, and just when she was beginning to think he really would say no more, he spoke again, his voice more normal now.

"Of course, you might be tempted to ask me, if you cared at all, why it should be that my mother, who had every intention, according to Garreth Whistler, of returning to Camulod after my father's death, should have changed her mind at the last moment and decided to stay in Tir Manha. If it is really such a dreary place as I believe it to be . . ." He turned to look at Nemo.

"Are you tempted to ask that, Nemo? No, I can see you are not. Well, I'll answer it anyway. I believe my mother has decided to remain in Cambria because she fears that if she does not stay there . . . if she comes home to Camulod while I am here . . . then I might not return to Tir Manha at all and might forfeit my blood rights, my birthright and my Chief's rank and title. And there are numerous people, myself not least among them, who would say she had good reason for such fear . . . But they would all be wrong, Nemo, all of them. Because I will go back. I am going back. It may be that I am going back for all the wrong reasons a man could conjure up. But I am going back."

He stopped for a moment and then snorted again with the same smothered, ironic mirth that he had used against himself earlier. "Strange, is it not? After years of listening to Cousin Merlyn going on and on about duty and how sacred it is, often boring me to tears with his righteousness, I am now the one who is incapable of doing what I want to do because my duty forbids it. Well . . . it does, and none of it is Merlyn's fault. I must go to Tir Manha and release my mother to return to her mother, knowing that I will stay and do what I must do. I am my father's son, Nemo, and I am Ullic Pendragon's grandson and Publius Varrus's grandson, and no man among the three of those was ever known to shirk a duty or be irresponsible. I am clan Chief, and there is no escaping that, for I promised my father to take up the task and do it properly . . .

"I might not be chosen King, but by the gods, if I am not, it will not be because I was not there when the Chiefs took up their chairs. Not all the people are grim miseries, and they will need the strongest King that they can have. And I believe that means I must be King . . . at least for the duration of this war with Cornwall. After that, when we are all at peace again, who knows? I might give up the King's seat. It could be done, no reason why it could not be . . .

"Anyway, if I am to be King, we must go soon, Whistler says, and I believe him. I have a few things I need to do before we leave, nevertheless. The Dragons need a week's training, and I need to spend some time with Commander Merlyn planning strategy and future tactics for any joint campaign we might have to fight against Lot. I have a strong feeling that it will be a case not of *if* but of *when*. So, Nemo, as I see it, we will be leaving very soon for Tir Manha. If you have anything that you must do in Camulod before we leave, then see to it."

Nemo nodded her head deeply but said nothing. In her mind, however, she reviewed everything she might need to do before departing, and her list was very brief.

BOOK FOUR

The Choosing

Dear Mother,

Two weeks have gone by since they brought me word of Uric's death. Two blank, empty weeks spent in nothingness. I remember seeing Daris, the Chief Druid, approaching me that day, and I remember being frightened by the look on his face. After that, I can remember nothing until yesterday, when I saw Daris again. He had come this time to ask me when I wished to leave for Camulod, and I did not know why he would ask me such a thing.

It was then that I discovered that I have been living in some kind of waking dream. According to Daris, I have been acting normally and showing commendable strength throughout my ordeal, but the truth is that I have been aware of none of it. I know only that my husband, my beloved Uric, is dead.

Daris tells me that I have been calmly and rationally discussing leaving Tir Manha to come and live with you in Camulod. It seems strange to me that I would not remember saying such things. But yet another part of me, after a sleepless night last night, now knows that it is true.

When I first heard Daris speak of this yesterday, I had no doubt, despite my shock, that it was a fine idea and the sensible thing to do. My husband is gone, I told myself, and my son is already in Camulod. No need, I thought, for me to remain in Tir Manha—Uric's home but never really mine.

But at that moment, in making that admission to myself, all the pain of my loss came home to me and overwhelmed me. For the first time that I know of since my husband's death, I wept. And then I lay awake all night long, surprised to know that my mind was filled with unfamiliar yet familiar thoughts and even decisions.

Daris spoke to me at great length about the ceremony of picking a new King for the Pendragon people, an event known as the Choosing.

This Choosing will now take place as close to Midsummer as may be possible due to the upheavals of this war. There are two traditional Choosing times each year: Midsummer and Midwinter, with Midsummer being the more potent. My Uric will be replaced then by a new King selected from among the current Chiefs.

I have been through it once before, when dear Uncullic died and Uric was selected as the Chosen One by his fellow Chiefs, all seven of them, including Uric, voting in conclave. At that time I thought little of it. It seemed inevitable to me that Uric would assume his father's position, becoming the fifth in his direct line to serve as King of the Pendragon. It was plain for all to see that Uric was the best man.

By the same token, the new King should be Uther as Chief of Pendragon in his own right. I know his father dreamed of that and wished it might be so, for we talked of it, he and I, not long ago, when it seemed like an event destined for some distant, future day.

Now, cruelly, that day is here, and Uther is not merely unprepared, he is almost unknown by the Chiefs who will select the new King. He has been too long gone from Tir Manha and from Cambria itself, spending most of his time in Camulod, mainly at my insistence. The fault is mine.

I have always been afraid, since my earliest days here, of what too much exposure to the Cambrians and their savage ways might do to my son. And I have always

*insisted that he spend at least half of his young life with
you and father and my family in civilized surroundings. I
regret that bitterly today, because I now know, too late, that
I was wrong. We are at war with Cornwall, as are you in
Camulod, but Uther is seen here as being one of yours and
not as one of ours, and the wars have thrown up another
warrior Chief, a man called Meradoc, Chief of the largest
of the three Llewellyn clans, who means to claim the King's
Seat. I detest the man, and I know Uric had little time for
him, but my personal distaste counts for nothing in the
reality of things. The man is an able Chief, it seems.*

*And so I must remain in Tir Manha in the hope that
others, including you and Garreth Whistler, with whom I will
send this, will be able to convince Uther that his duty lies
here, and that he owes his primary loyalty to his Pendragon
heritage and to the memory of his father and his ancestors.*

*I know my son, and I know his failings and how head-
strong and proud he can be. I know, too, that should he
choose not to contest his birthright in the Choosing, he will
regret it forever afterwards. This Choosing is his destiny. I
know that now beyond dispute or foolish maternal selfish-
ness. And if my presence in Tir Manha will urge his return,
then my place must be here.*

*So, dear Mother, my request of you is to send my son
home, however unwilling he might be. I pray that you will
use every persuasive power at your command to convince
him that he must be here by Midsummer to represent his
family, his people and himself.*

With all my love, your grieving daughter, Veronica

FOURTEEN

"Come on, lads! You'll be a King's escort on the way back, so let's start to look like one now."

The disordered column of armoured, mounted men making their way up the steep slope reacted to the jibe in their individual ways. Some groaned in mock protest, others muttered good-humouredly and a small number scowled, but most had a grin or a smile for the man haranguing them from the knoll by the side of the path they were climbing. Only a few kept their eyes downcast, too concerned with the treacherous ground beneath their horses' hooves to spare any attention for their leader's high spirits. The climb had been long and hard, their path a dried-out stream bed choked with water-smoothed pebbles and boulders. On either side, the flanks of the deep gully towered over them, coated with impenetrable brush and gnarled, stunted ancient trees, cutting the struggling horsemen off from the world. Now, as they approached the crest, the percep-tible lessening of the heights above was the only sign they had that they were nearing the summit.

"Almost there now, lads. We'll rest at the top."

At that moment, one of the rocks littering the stream bed rolled under a misplaced hoof, and a horse went lurching sideways, skitter-ing for a foothold and somehow managing to remain upright, although it almost unseated its rider, whose skill was the only thing that saved him from a dangerous fall. In the moment of feeling his mount lurch off balance, the trooper transferred all his weight, jamming his left foot hard into its stirrup and shifting his upper body forward to his right, dropping the reins to grasp the horn of his saddle with his right hand while he threw his left arm out as a counterweight. So close was he to the side of the stream bed that his outstretched hand touched solid ground and he used it to brace himself, leaning on it for a moment before thrusting himself back, straight-armed, into the saddle.

"Well done, Marc!" the leader shouted, but the rider, busy gathering his reins again and soothing his startled horse, paid him no heed. He moved on, his eyes now scanning the ground ahead of him, and the few remaining horsemen followed him, equally careful. The watcher on the knoll waited until the last of them had passed, and then he turned his head to look at his companion, who was staring back down the hill the way they had come.

"You see something down there?"

Garreth Whistler shrugged his broad, green-clad shoulders and pulled his horse around. "No, Uther, I see nothing," he said, sighing but smiling. "I was thinking, that's all."

Uther Pendragon grinned, shaking his head ruefully. "Garreth, Garreth, Garreth, there's little hope for you at all, with all this thinking! How many times have I told you it's dangerous to think?"

The Whistler sat silent in his saddle, gazing at the younger man and making no response other than a slow puckering of his lips as he nibbled at the skin of his inner cheek.

Uther raised one eyebrow. "So what were you thinking about this time?"

"Several things. One was that I've been spending too much time in Camulod."

"How so?"

"I'm being Romanized, that's how! Here we are out of sight of that damned road for barely an hour, and I'm mourning the loss of it. I've grown too soft."

Uther Pendragon glanced down to where Garreth had been staring and his smile gave way to a pensive, speculative look. The road Garreth spoke of lay miles behind them, utterly lost in dense forest. The narrow wedge of sky filled with broken clouds that stretched above their present resting place was the only thing in sight that was not forest.

"Roads are good," Uther muttered. "No better, faster way of crossing country. The Romans were remarkable for that, if nothing else."

"Aye, but why didn't they build a road across these hills when they were building everywhere else?"

Another smile tugged at the corners of Uther's mouth. "Roman roads had but a single purpose, Garreth: to transport Roman armies from place to place in the shortest possible time in order to confront Rome's enemies and stamp them out. We of the Pendragon were too few then, and too distant, to attract their ire."

"Hmm! So now we have to struggle overland. Someone should have told the Romans we were here."

Garreth was now in his early forties, and he had been Uther's mentor, friend and self-appointed bodyguard for ten years. That alone would have entitled him to keep himself apart from the ruck of Uther's troops, even without the rank of Second in Command that the Chief had bestowed upon him. Garreth knew that, too. Although he rode saddled and stirrupped like the others, Garreth alone wore none of the uniform armour and trappings that marked them all as troopers of Camulod, despite the fact that most of them were Pendragon warriors. Instead, and to set himself apart, Garreth proudly wore the garb of his own people, Uther's people, the Pendragon Celts from southern Cambria.

A bright green, knee-length tunic of heavy cloth, bordered in a deep, dark, brownish red and pulled up to accommodate his saddle, was belted at Garreth's waist, and beneath it his legs were trousered in the same green cloth, the bottoms tucked into a pair of high, thick-soled, spurred boots that were his pride and joy, and the only Camulodian things the Whistler owned. A long, plain cloak of darker green was fastened at his breast by an intricately carved clasp of silver, and the sides of it were thrown back from his shoulders to hang down his back, spilling over his horse's rump and leaving his arms free. His head was bare on top of his long, curling white-blond hair. His arms, wrists and legs were heavy and strong, thickly roped with muscle, and the short, broad, sheathed sword that hung by his left side seemed slender because of their bulk.

"I was thinking, too," Garreth continued eventually, "that you were being very free with your expectations of kingship. You're not the King yet, and you might never be."

Uther blinked, and when he spoke his voice was quiet, all trace of raillery gone. "I know that, Garreth."

"I know you do, but the men don't know it—or if they do, they don't care. But what happens if the Chiefs should choose someone else? That's going to leave you looking foolish."

"And why would they choose someone else? They—"

"They might see you as too much the Outlander, that's why. You spend too much time away in Camulod, they'll say. They've been saying it for years. Too much time in Camulod and not enough in your own land. They'll disregard the fact that all the men who ride with you are their own men from Cambria. And if anyone brings it up, they'll be shouted down, and your men will be categorized as you are, strangers and no longer to be trusted. They've learned too many alien ways to be pure Cambrian warriors. And you, you're too much the Roman nowadays for some of their proud stomachs, despite your birth and boyhood. You're never here where you should be, always too far away and for far too long."

"But that's—"

"That's true, Uther, as far as they are concerned. They believe, and rightly so, that a King must tend his people all the time. Remember that these are not merely disgruntled malcontents who have nothing better to do than complain. Like you, these men are Chiefs of the Pendragon Federation—Pendragon, Llewellyn and Griffyd. They will decide upon the kingship, and you have but one vote. They have a weight upon their minds and hearts, Uther. They have a binding duty to pick the best man from those available among their own number. There are seven from whom to choose, and six of those are always more available year-round than you have been these several years."

"They will pick me, Garreth. They need a warrior."

"Balls! They *are* warriors, even the oldest of them—tried and tested leaders."

"Aye, but four of them are too old to take the kingship."

"Right! And that leaves three to pick among. And two of those are better known and may be better liked than you. Huw Strongarm is the youngest Chief ever to rule the northern Pendragon clans, and he's beloved by everyone—a warrior and a champion, a bard and a lover. A fine, upright young man. He'll be a great King some day."

"But not this time."

Garreth nodded, a terse jerk of his head that conveyed his reluctance to agree. "No, not this time. He's still too young, little more than a boy. That leaves only Meradoc, but he would be your biggest threat even were Huw old enough. Meradoc has the love and trust of all his own folk—" Garreth broke off, twisting his face wryly at the disbelief that had sprung into Uther's face. "Well, I may be overstating that a bit—he is Meradoc, and that in itself makes him hard to love—but nonetheless it is undeniable that he has strength enough among his own people to win. He has support, and that means he has the numbers, and it matters not whether he holds them through love or fear."

"Numbers mean nothing in this. There are but seven votes. Seven single voices."

"Numbers mean everything, Uther. Think you that the Chiefs will be unmoved by the opinion of their people? Would *you* vote in defiance of your own people, flouting them simply because you wish it? You could, because you are their Chief. But how would that affect the way your people think of you? Do you think after that they'll follow you willingly, or any other Chief who disregards their wishes, into battle, into death?" Garreth paused to let that sink in. "Meradoc will vote for himself, and you will vote for yourself, so those two votes are gone. That leaves but five, and of those five you will need three. You'll have no time available for courting anyone, because the Choosing will begin the moment you arrive. Everyone else will have shown up already, and you can be sure that Meradoc was the first to get there, to lay his claim for support among the others."

"He'd serve himself better by keeping quiet. Meradoc has no skill in bending men to like him."

"Perhaps not, but he is an able man, you can't deny him that, and that will speak loudly for him. He leads his people well, and the only real victories we have won so far in this war with Cornwall have been his—his planning, his force and his leadership. There's more than one minor chieftain who thinks that Meradoc would make a strong King."

"Aye, and the people would weep beneath his feet forever after. Meradoc is a bully, Garreth, and he's greedy."

Garreth shrugged. "*Ambitious*, isn't that the Roman word? He wouldn't be where he is now if he were not ambitious, and neither would any of the others, including you."

Uther Pendragon drew a deep breath and looked about him before responding to that. The last of his men had long since vanished up the steep stream bed, and even the sound of hooves had faded into silence. Finally he returned his gaze to Garreth Whistler, and his voice was as expressionless as his face.

"You think him stronger than me? The better man?"

Garreth curled his lip and kicked his horse into motion. "I should knock you off your horse for even asking that, boy. Come, we ought to keep up with the others."

As Uther swung his horse around to follow, Garreth set his mount to the rocky slope, half turning in his saddle to talk back over his shoulder.

"All I meant was that you should be careful of how you behave— to your own men and to the men who must judge you before choosing you. Don't look too confident, and don't look arrogant. But above all, don't look too Roman! If you ride into the gathering wearing that armour, you'll destroy any chance you have of being chosen. You know the Chiefs. You know how they think, how they disapprove of anything they see as *differentness*. Don't hand them the power to thwart you. Old they may be—several of them too old, perhaps, to remember how it feels to be young—but none of them has lost the taste for exercising power when he can. This conclave gives them that opportunity . . . the power to kill younger men's dreams."

Uther was very quiet thinking about that as their horses scrambled up the last portion of the steep climb to the crest. He knew Garreth was right, that something as insignificant as his appearance could cost him the King's Chair. How much better it would be if he could spring into prominence and into the kingship as his grand-father had.

Within the Pendragon Federation, Ullic, as Uther knew, had been the first man in living memory to serve as both King and War Chief. He had been elected King by the unanimous choice of his fellow Chiefs when he was only twenty-one, directly following the death of his own father, Udall. But Ullic Pendragon had already been wearing the huge Eagle Crown of the War Chief of Pendragon at the time of his election to the kingship.

A natural warrior, bred of generations of fierce fighters who led their clan with honour and distinction, Ullic had come early to recognition upon the unforeseen death, in a brilliantly executed ambush, of Ullic's Uncle Daffyd, War Chief of the Federation, and his entire staff of close subordinates. Their leaderless army found itself outflanked and outmanoeuvred by an enemy far more numerous than they had expected, led by a brilliant general, rather than by the simple seagoing brigand that they had all expected to find in command, and disaster loomed over all of them.

Within moments of the death of his commanding general, a lacklustre nonentity called Dennys ap Corfyl found himself promoted, *ipso facto*, to the rank of senior surviving chieftain in a trapped army. The hapless fellow, caught flat-footed, was overwhelmed by circumstances beyond his control or understanding. To young Ullic Pendragon, who had only recently celebrated his seventeenth birthday, it was evident that the man was totally at a loss. What few wits the fellow possessed were by that time thoroughly addled, and the faces of the men around him, who looked to him for leadership and salvation, were beginning to show strain and signs of panic.

Ullic reacted immediately and without thought, springing forward from where he stood and using a nearby boulder to help him jump up to a rocky ledge where all could see him and know who he was. For the first time ever, he raised his great voice to draw all eyes to him, and then he began to issue orders, crisp and terse and succinct. It never crossed his mind, after that first step, that anyone would seek or wish to gainsay him, and the men he harangued accepted his command immediately and instinctively, moving to obey his fast-flying instructions without the slightest hesitation.

He called on all of them to form up in their clan groups behind him and to follow the moves of his uncle's own personal guard of clansmen, over which he then assumed undisputed control. As he took his place at their head, they cheered him once, loudly and deeply, as their kinsman and commander, and then he led them forward, directly towards the left centre of the enemy army that had outflanked them. Inspired by his fiery enthusiasm, they smashed through the extended enemy formation facing them and then wheeled back to left and right, the sheer mass of their numbers and the fury of their determination rolling the enemy up in confusion, battering at them and pressing them back upon themselves so that they hampered each other in their dense-packed closeness.

There was nothing Roman about the way Pendragon warriors fought. They fought as their ancestors had, in small, tight-knit groups of individuals who knew and trusted each other completely. Capable of combining with other groups to form heavy and dense formations, they preferred to preserve the integrity of their small units, guarding one another's back and generally combining their weight and initiative to achieve the ultimate in ferocity and, with that, victory. Ullic, they quickly learned, could lead them with the sureness of a master, inspiring all of them with his flamboyant leadership, his courage, his immense strength and his great roaring voice. Within a very short space of time on that first day, the Pendragon forces went from being outflanked and close to defeat to being utterly dominant, sending their attackers reeling and finally routing them completely.

That afternoon when the battle was over and the last of the fleeing enemy survivors had disappeared, one of his father's senior veterans brought Ullic the dead War Chief's great helmet, and backed by the cheers and applause of the army, he insisted that the young man put it on. It was against tradition, for no one ever presumed to wear the Eagle Crown of a dead War Chief, but the day had been special, and Ullic felt he had acquitted himself well and given honour to his uncle and his kinsmen, and so he held the helmet above his head, straight-armed, and then lowered it gently over his brows, shouting his father's name.

At that moment, as the weight of the heavy helmet settled on his brows, young Ullic felt the truth at last: his uncle was dead. The knowledge must have overwhelmed him. Unable to speak, he removed the helmet at once and held it up in front of him, blinking his eyes rapidly until they grew clear enough for him to see and appreciate what he was looking at. The Eagle Crown was the personal symbol of the War Chief of the Pendragon Federation. Each one was different, just as each man who held the post was different, and for the making of each crown a golden eagle, the greatest and most majestic of all birds of prey, had to die.

The body of each Eagle Crown was a curved, conical helmet of fine iron, larger and more massive-looking, although actually less thick than a regular war helmet. Specially crafted to be an exact fit for the head of the new War Chief, its interior was padded and filled, then lined with a wide, thick, comfortable leather headband. High on the front of this huge helmet, the eagle's head was affixed, cunningly worked and furnished with gleaming, wicked eyes of glass above the polished, viciously curving beak. Beneath that the feathers of the neck and breast swept down to cover all sign of the helmet's iron forehead. The wings, folded but partially open, their pinions not quite at rest, were then fitted carefully on each side, and the magnificent tail feathers were attached behind, meticulously set, arranged and spread so that they swept outwards and down to cover the shoulders of the wearer. It was as though the wearer carried a living eagle on his head, poised to take flight. Each Eagle Crown was a superb work of art, a tribute to the man who wore it and to the skills and energy of the craftsmen who fashioned it, and this one had belonged to Daffyd Pendragon. He would never wear it again, nor would Ullic ever see him again. He turned away, holding the crown out to the man who had brought it to him. The other took it in silence, and Ullic walked away; the onlookers watched him leave in utter silence.

Ullic Pendragon became the most admired War Chief the Federation had ever produced. His armies never suffered a defeat in all the years of his command, and his fame was widespread, his name known and respected far beyond the boundaries of his own lands. Even the Roman Overlords, as they used to call themselves, admired and respected Ullic for what he was.

Now Ullic's grandson, Uther, could feel the weight of the legacy of his forefathers lying heavily on his soul. Five generations of his direct ancestors, one after the other, had borne the title King of the Federation. Would his be the hands to lose their grip on the title?

Uther kicked his horse into motion and hurried to join his men, who were taking a well-deserved rest at the top of the hill.

Once the troops had fed and watered their mounts and enjoyed a brief respite from their saddles, Nemo Hard-Nose, the decurion in charge, barked the order to remount. Uther stirred himself, brushing away the crumbs of dried nuts and grain that had fallen on his breast as he ate from the small bag of food in his scrip. He pulled the drawstring tight, slipped the leather bag back into his pouch and rose to his feet, making his way to his horse without having said a word to anyone since he dismounted. For once he was completely unaware of the looks on the faces of the men as they filed past him, until one wag barked out, "King's escort, Commander!"

Uther's head jerked at that, and then he barked a solitary note of laughter before swinging up into his saddle, kicking his horse into motion and riding forward alone, passing the forty men of his squadron and delivering an occasional offhand remark to one or another of them until he rode at their head again.

The ground over which they now rode was utterly different from the thickly forested land at the bottom of the steep ascent they had just climbed, and they made swift, easy progress riding across a treeless, gently sloping plateau that fell away to the west and southwest, covered with long, tasselled grasses that reached as high as their horses' bellies. The terrain was studded in places with high, solitary granite tors that reminded Uther of menhirs, the ancient upright monoliths that his people believed were the dwelling places or the resting places of their gods. A movement caught his eye in the distance below, and for a time he watched the moving dot that he knew to be a returning scout making his way

towards them. When less than a hundred paces separated him from
the man, Uther held up his arm to halt his column and rode forward
alone to greet the newcomer.

The scout had nothing to report. He and his companions had seen
no signs of life within a clear hour's ride, ahead or on their flanks.
About a mile below, he reported, the meadow Uther and his men were
crossing ended suddenly at the edge of a ridge, concealed from view
now by a fringe of scrub. Beyond that the ground fell more precipi-
tously, and from the bottom of the scree slope there was a narrow path
to follow, little more than an animal track winding among and
between low hills. Here and there it was almost choked with bush and
thorn, and so might present difficulty for the horses. Apart from that,
the scout reported, there was nothing: no human presence, no danger,
no signs of life.

Uther thanked the man and raised his hand in the signal that the
decurion behind him had been waiting for, and he heard, without
looking, the sound of the relief troop of ten scouts separating from
the remainder of the group. They would ride back now with the man
who had brought the report and would relieve the men who had been
scouting the land ahead since before daybreak, leaving the weary
scouts either to return to the following troop or to rest for a while
until the troop came up to them. Uther waved the remainder of his
squadron back into motion before the departing group had ridden a
hundred paces, and he beckoned to Garreth to ride with him.

As they paused at the crest of the ridge that fell away beneath
them, Uther became conscious of the heat of the early-afternoon sun
against his armour, and he hitched his shoulders uselessly against
the itchy trickle of a bead of sweat that suddenly broke free and
made its way down between his shoulder blades. He reached up and
loosened his chin strap, pulling his heavy helmet off and blotting
sweat from his face with the sleeves of his tunic. Uther kicked his
horse's flanks, and he and Garreth began to ride down the treacherous slope, leaning backwards so that at several points their animals'
rumps almost touched the earth.

By the time they reached level ground, the two men found
themselves alone again, because the first bend in the narrow path

before them had already taken the others out of sight and hearing. They loosened their reins and spurred their mounts to a canter to catch up, but they were surprised at how long it took to overtake them, for the tightly twisting path on which they now rode was narrow and constrictive, offering no room for the horses to extend themselves, and frequently doubled back upon itself so that at times they seemed to be riding back the way they had already come. When they did catch up, they were constrained to ride behind the others for what Uther estimated to be a mile, breathing in the dust stirred up by everyone who had preceded them along the stone-strewn, dusty trail that led them, in some places, between high walls of solid rock. It was slow going, but eventually they passed through the last of these rocky defiles, and the pathway opened up sufficiently for them to pass on up to the head of the column, and thereafter they rode in relative comfort.

It was Garreth who detected the noise first, and he called, "Uther! Did you hear that?"

Uther pulled his horse to a halt and turned back. "No. What was it?"

Garreth cocked his head, listening intently. Behind him, the men following came to a halt, suddenly tense, aware of Garreth's attitude.

"Bear," Garreth said then, and Uther realized that he had been watching the other man's mouth, waiting to read his lips, because his own hearing was muffled by the protective earflaps of his heavy helmet. He tugged it off as quickly as he could and heard the sound immediately, far off and muffled by distance, yet unmistakably the enraged roaring of the largest animal in the forests and mountains of Britain.

"Sounds like a big one."

"Aye, big and very unhappy. I wonder what has him so stirred up?"

"It's probably a sow with cubs. Something must have threatened her."

Garreth looked sideways at him. "You think so? What kind of something?"

Uther shrugged. "Another bear?"

"Then why can we hear only one? If there were two of them, they'd both be roaring, trying to frighten each other off."

Uther glanced at the men behind Garreth, all of whom sat listening intently, staring off in the direction of the distant noise. "What, then?" he asked. "It's lasting a long time."

"Only one thing other than another bear could cause a bear that much fury, and that's a wound."

"Inflicted by a man, you mean—but there's no one around here, according to our scouts."

"It could be one of them, one of our scouts. Do you want to come and look?"

Come, not *go*, Uther noted. He nodded, not even pausing to think. "I think we'd better, although whoever wounded it will be dead by the time we get there."

"I think not. The roaring would have died down. He may be up in a tree. I think the thing can see him, but it can't reach him, and that's why it's making so much noise."

Uther nodded and glanced to where the decurion sat watching them. "Nemo, keep the others here. Garreth and I are going to see what that's all about."

Nemo Hard-Nose nodded, raising her right hand to her cuirass in an acknowledging salute, but Uther and Garreth were already moving off the trail. Both men pulled their long Pendragon bow staves from the leather sheaths that kept them close to hand hanging on the left front of their saddles. They paused before entering the trees to string the weapons, and then they moved forward again, and the leafy boughs quickly screened them from view.

They rode several hundred paces into the forest before abandoning their mounts among bushes too dense to penetrate on horseback. Now they were moving forward on foot, covering perhaps the same distance again.

"Can you see anything? The whoreson sounds as though he's right in front of us."

The bellowing of the bear was deafening. The growth here, as it had been all the way downward from the path, was almost solid:

rioting thickets of bramble, elder and hawthorn and chest-high grasses among which sapling beech, elm and birch struggled for survival. Uther held up a hand to forestall any more questions as he peered all around. They were in the beast's element. It lived here among this choking growth where they were blind and hampered, their ability to use their weapons critically impaired.

"Can't see a damned thing and I don't like the feeling," he said eventually, turning back to Garreth. As he spoke, his eyes were moving, looking upwards for a tall tree nearby, and he saw one immediately, perhaps forty or fifty paces from where they stood. It was a large oak, the closest of several he could see now. "Over there," Uther said, indicating the direction with a nod of his head. "If we can get up there into one of those, we'll be able to see more than we're going to see from here."

"Aye, and we'll be safer, too. This is madness. Let's go."

They moved as quickly as the undergrowth would permit, leaving the enraged roaring behind them on their right, and even before they reached the first tree, they saw that they would be able to scale it, although Garreth grunted that it looked easy enough for the bear to climb it, too. Uther made for the lowest limb, but Garreth caught at his cloak.

"Wait, let me go up first. I'm not wearing armour. You stay here until I see what's to be seen."

Moments later, he was leaning forward, shouting to Uther below his perch to tell him that there was a clearing ahead of them and that he could see the bear. Uther reached for a low branch and hauled himself upward until he was standing beside Garreth, only slightly out of breath from the effort of climbing in full armour.

"Ancient gods! Will you *look* at that thing!"

Uther ignored the comment. He had taken in the giant beast in one glance. What he needed to see most was the reason for its rage.

"There, Garreth! There's a man trapped up there on the cliff just above the beast, beyond its reach. Whoever he is, he's finished if we don't help him. It looks like he's hanging on to the sheer cliff face, and he can't move up or sideways. Look! The damn thing's within a handspan of his feet. If it backs up and runs at the cliff, it'll reach him."

At that point the bear did exactly what Uther had predicted, backing away and then hurling itself towards the cliff face, where it launched itself upward in a mighty leap. The man trapped there braced himself somehow on his arms and drew up his knees, and the mighty paw that swept towards his legs rushed on by, seeming to miss him by little more than a finger's width.

"He won't last much longer," Garreth growled. "He's hanging on like a spider, but his weight's almost all on his arms. I'd hate to be up there in his place, wondering whose strength will give out first. At least he's not one of ours, as you said, so it's no loss to— Are you mad, man? You'll never hit that thing from here. You don't have a clear shot!"

Uther had positioned himself carefully on the huge oak branch beneath his feet, leaning into his own weight and pulling his bowstring back almost to his cheekbone. He sighted deliberately, his nostrils flaring, and then released the tension and lowered the bow, drawing a deep breath.

"I don't expect to hit it, although it's within range. You're right, there are too many branches between me and it. But if I can send one close enough to distract the thing, the fellow up on the cliff might be able to escape. It's better than doing nothing. We can't just leave the poor whoreson there to die, no matter who he is." He inhaled deeply again and held his breath, then leaned slightly forward, bracing himself with his left foot as he flowed into the motions of pull and release. The arrow arced high and fell, as far as they could gauge, close by the ravening bear. Neither of the distant antagonists noticed it.

"Damnation! We have to get closer. The growth opens up over there, closer to them. That should give us a clearer shot at it."

"Aye." Garreth was already bending to climb down. "And it'll give that big black whoreson a clearer run at us, too." He leaped nimbly down to the ground, leaving Uther, hampered by his armour, to descend more slowly, but once both were on the ground, they struck out directly towards the sounds of the deafening commotion ahead of them.

The going was difficult, and despite the fact that they knew the bear was directly ahead of them, there were moments when the vagaries of sound made it seem as though the noise had passed them by and lay behind them. They pushed forward, ignoring the apparent evidence of their ears and aware that they had no dire need to be silent; the bear's own bellowing would mask the sounds of their progress. And then, quite suddenly, they were at the edge of the dense vegetation, and a clearing lay in front of them, formed by a spreading mound of scree that had fallen from the cliff that now faced them. The bear's back was to them, at the very top of the scree mound less than thirty paces from where they stood, and it stood upright on its hind legs, vainly, frantically attempting to reach the cringing figure that clung to the cliff face just beyond its reach. Uther tried to see the man's face, but a rough outcropping of rock kept most of the man's head hidden.

Uther gripped Garreth's arm. "Do you know him?"

"I don't know. Can't see his face from here, but he's one of us, Pendragon. Must be. Look, his bow's over there beyond the bear. He had time to fire one arrow, at least. It's sticking in the thing's left side. Deep. See it? No wonder it's so angry."

Uther paid no attention. His mind was racing. "Go you to your right, cautiously," he said quietly. "Keep moving until you have a clear shot and we can take him in a crossfire. He'll be confused to see two of us, but he'll move quickly enough once he decides which of us to charge. At that point, the other must rain arrows on him, all well aimed, for the chosen man will have but a short time to live lacking help."

Garreth nodded and began moving quickly but cautiously away to his right. As he did so, the man on the cliff face saw him and called out. Perhaps he was startled or in his relief he might have tried to free one hand to wave. In any case, he lost his hold on the cliff face and tumbled forward, head first and screaming, to land directly on top of the bear. The beast, which dropped to all fours again, did not see the hurtling figure falling towards him until the man's full weight landed on its back. The huge animal leaped away in fright and reared up, roaring in protest, sweeping its head around to see its unknown attacker and failing to notice that its former tormentor was now sprawled at its feet. Instead, it saw Uther, alone by the forest's edge.

He had been in the act of nocking an arrow to his bowstring, and he froze as the beast's small, furious eyes found him and focused upon him, so that for a moment it seemed as if the whole world had stopped moving. The enormous animal hung motionless, and Uther had time to see the pig-like eyes take note of him; then the creature dropped to all fours and charged, bellowing, its terrifying jaws stretched wide, lined with huge, glistening teeth. It seemed to move slowly at first, and its lumbering motion broke the initial shock of terror that had held Uther spellbound so that he raised his weapon immediately and leaned forward into his shot. Even as he did that, however, his mind acknowledged the chilling speed with which the creature was now approaching, flashing across the broken ground, its great maw gaping, slavering for his blood. One shot, he knew, was all he could hope for against such speed—one tiny arrow against the onrushing mass.

Now the space between him and the terrifying creature had shrunk to less than half and he had not yet decided where to aim. There was no need to choose, however; the creature's wide-stretched maw was all he could see, and he sensed the soft palate and the moist, vulnerable flesh of its throat behind the lolling tongue and flashing teeth. His bow was fully bent, and he released his arrow, leaning into it and watching the speed of its flight as it snapped across the inter-vening distance and smashed fully against one of the enormous, curving canines, snapping it off and driving it back into the open mouth even as the tooth's ivory deflected the point and sent the arrow flashing outward. It missed the open throat and ripped through the creature's cheek instead before vanishing beyond its left shoulder.

The beast was checked by the violent impact of the hard-shot arrow, knocked off balance by the shocking force of it and stunned by the agonizing intensity of the pain it caused. It lurched and reeled sideways, then swayed and fell over backwards like a drunken man, but it rolled even as it fell and rose immediately to its feet again, and now there was a new note to its screaming.

Uther was surprised to find a second arrow in his hand, the notched end of its shaft already hugging the bowstring. Now he swung the bow up again and fired in one smooth motion, seeing the missile's flight end this time in the great animal's throat, burying itself almost to the flights and jolting the mighty creature again as Uther pulled a third arrow into place. He could see blood—old blood—on the beast's coat, some of it already clotted, and the arrow Garreth had noticed earlier, a short, broken, blood-covered shaft protruding from the beast's left side below the ribs. Obviously it was the shot that infuriated the bear in the beginning. It must have been aimed badly or carelessly by the man on the cliff, who having failed to kill his quarry, had become the hunted one.

The enraged behemoth rose to its full height, its arms extended and its enormous claws clearly visible, and Uther suddenly had a vision of the great silver bear emblazoned on his cousin Merlyn's black cloak. That emblem represented the monstrous bear that Merlyn had attacked and killed single-handedly from the back of a horse, and in his terror Uther wondered at his cousin's courage on that occasion. Merlyn had killed his bear; Uther had no confidence that he would kill this one.

He raised his bow for his third shot as the bear rallied to charge him again, but even as it began to move, another arrow struck it from the side, smacking into its body with a solid, meaty sound and piercing deep beneath its shoulder. The great beast reared up and swung about with an outraged bellow, and Uther felt a stirring of pity, suddenly sure that they would kill the animal now and that this was a wretched fate for such a magnificent creature. Another arrow struck and then immediately after that another, which Uther guessed must have been fired by the man who had fallen from the cliff. His bow had been lying on the ground close to where he fell.

The bear swung around again to face this new attack, and as it did so, Garreth Whistler's third arrow seemed to sprout from its eye, snapping the giant head backwards. For long moments the bear seemed to hang immobile, its entire body somehow hunched, as though straining away from the agony of the outrageous pain being thrust upon it, and then it turned once again and staggered a few steps towards Uther, who held his bow steady now, inexplicably unwilling to loose his third arrow, which was still nocked and drawn. The massive creature slowed almost to a halt as it approached, and its roaring dwindled quickly into silence. Watching it, Uther was reminded of a scene from his boyhood when a wild and deranged man in Camulod, after wreaking havoc among his neighbours and emerging victorious from fighting with half a score of opponents, some of them members of the Camulodian guard, had suddenly stopped and keeled over in the street, regaining consciousness later with no recollection of anything that had happened.

Even as that thought occurred to him, the bear straightened up completely to stand erect on its hind legs, pawing at the arrow protruding from its head and mewling softly and incongruously in pain. Then it swayed and fell slowly sideways, toppling to the ground so close to Uther's feet that he had to skip away to keep clear of it, lowering his weapon yet keeping it at full draw. He knew the bear was dead as it fell, but even so, he watched it closely, staying warily out of reach of its fearsome claws. Only when it lay motionless did he release his pent-up breath and the tension in his bow.

It was some time before any of the three men spoke or stirred, and Uther realized that he was trembling violently. He swallowed hard and forced himself to move, fighting to appear casual and relaxed although all three of them knew that was impossible. He stepped to the carcass and looked down on it. Even dead and supine, the creature's bulk reached to above his knee. The huge head was shattered, the point of Garreth's last arrow having passed completely through the eye, transfixing the brain and then emerging through the back of the skull.

Uther glanced from the wound to Garreth. "Did you aim that shot?"

Garreth shrugged. "Aye, I tried for the eye, but it was fortune that led it home, not judgment. I thought the whoreson had you."

"So did I." Uther subsided onto a rotten, moss-crusted log alongside the dead bear and wiped his free hand over his face before laying his bow carefully on the ground along with the arrow it still held. Then he looked at the stranger who stood silent, his gaze moving from Garreth to Uther and back while he held one hand pressed to his face. A sullen stream of blood flowed over the man's wrist and trickled downward towards the cuff of his sleeve.

"Are you all right? How badly are you hurt?"

The man looked at his hand covered in blood and shrugged. "I'll live. Slashed my hand and banged my face when I fell. It's not as bad as it looks." He covered his bleeding left hand with his right, squeezing together the edges of the wound on the side of his palm. Uther could see now that the cut on his face was no more than a gash on his left cheek below the cheekbone.

"Who are you?"

It was Garreth who answered, before the other had a chance. "Owain's his name. They call him Owain of the Caves."

Surprised at the tone he heard in his friend's voice, Uther turned to look at Garreth, then switched his gaze back immediately to the stranger, who drew himself up until he was standing stiffly erect. Garreth spoke again, this time directly to the stranger. "That is your name, is it not?" The fellow nodded. "I thought so. I've seen you several times, although you never seem to come to our part of the world. You're one of Meradoc's men, one of his . . . captains, no? The newest of them all, if what I heard is true. You are . . . a Northerner, not even a Pendragon, am I right?"

Owain of the Caves inclined his head slightly for a second time in what might have been dismissal or agreement, but Garreth paid no attention.

"Came south with Meradoc last year, when he met last time with King Uric, but you kept yourself well removed from all that was going on. I noticed you, though, and wondered why you would be so unwilling to be seen. So I asked about you. Huw Strongarm said you were a newcomer, but already one of Meradoc's most trusted men . . . and he thought you might prefer to keep your face hidden, to keep you free for Meradoc's most important work, which demands faces that are not known . . ."

"What was this all about?" Uther nodded towards the dead animal close by his feet, choosing, for the moment, to ignore what Garreth was saying.

Owain of the Caves gazed back at him steadily for the space of several heartbeats and then shifted his gaze to the bear, shrugging slightly.

"I don't know. I only know it happened too quickly for me to do anything except what I did. I must have surprised it. It might have been asleep. I don't even know where it came from. One moment I was alone, crossing this clearing, and the next, this thing came roaring at me. I managed to get an arrow out, but it was too close for me to get a clear shot—it was coming at me too quickly." He looked about him, examining the ground. "I was right about here, I think. Yes, right by that tree there." He indicated a large, solitary conifer about five paces from where he stood. "I ran behind the tree, trying to break the line of the thing's charge, and it swerved to catch me as I went around, but I doubled back and gained about ten paces on it. Then I turned to take my shot, and my foot must have landed on something unsteady. I almost fell, and I loosed too soon and hit the whoreson in the ribs. That was the only chance I got, and I didn't know how much damage I had done, but I couldn't wait to see. I might have had time to get off another shot before it recovered from the first—it was up on its hind legs, screaming and smashing at the arrow—but I didn't want to have to wager on that. So I ran for the cliff face and managed to haul myself up out of reach just before it hit the wall beneath me. One pace slower, and I'd have been its dinner then and there." He looked up now at the sky, glancing at the afternoon sun. "That was about an hour ago."

"At least that long," Uther answered, mildly. "It's been an hour since we heard the roaring. We were about half a mile from here, I'd guess, up on the trail from the ridge behind us. Lucky for you Garreth doesn't wear a helmet."

"What?" It was clear Owain had not understood the comment.

Uther tapped his finger against the heavy metal helmet he wore. "I would never have heard the noise through this. Garreth was the only one among us riding bareheaded."

"Oh." Owain of the Caves looked at Garreth. "I owe you my hide then."

"No," Garreth Whistler responded, shaking his head slightly, his face empty of expression. "You don't. Up to me, I'd have left you here to die the moment I saw you were a stranger. Had I known who you were, in fact, I would have done the same, because I would have judged you no friend of ours." He reached into his scrip and pulled out a ragged piece of clean white cloth. "Here, wrap that around the cut on your hand." As he did so, Garreth continued. "Why risk my arse against a crazed beast like that for someone I don't know? Only a fool would do anything that stupid." He nodded towards Uther. "He's the fool, although I'd not say that to his face normally. He decided he wouldn't leave you here to die, and so we came running, and he almost ended up dead. You owe *him* your hide. Here, hold your hand still. I'll tie that."

Uther watched in silence as Garreth used the cloth to bind up Owain's injured hand, ripping off narrow strips from the edges with his teeth to use as bindings for the makeshift bandage. As the final knots were being tied, Owain looked over Garreth's shoulder to his rescuer and nodded a wordless acknowledgment.

Uther stood up, picking up his bow as he did so, and slipped the unused arrow back into his quiver. "What were you doing here in the first place?"

Owain drew a deep breath, pursing his lips tightly. He looked once more at the dead bear and then up towards the spot where he had been trapped on the cliff face. When he spoke, his words were more of a question than an answer.

"Uther Pendragon."

Uther kept his face expressionless. "What about him?"

"That's you. You're him."

"What makes you think that?"

Something that might have been the barest hint of a smile flickered briefly at one corner of the stranger's wide-lipped mouth. "Garreth Whistler went away more than a month ago to bring Uther Pendragon back for the Chiefs' Gathering. Garreth Whistler has come back. You came with him."

Garreth spoke before Uther could respond. "Pity it would be to have saved your life only to discover a need to spill your blood myself, Cave Man."

The other man nodded, unperturbed. "Aye, I can see that, but you'll find no need. Owain of the Caves is a man who pays his debts." His eyes flicked back to Uther. "This time, the debt is a life. It is paid."

Uther tilted his head to one side, a tiny smile of incredulity appearing on his face. "What? I'm not sure I understood you there. Are you saying you are now saving my life in return for your own?"

"Aye." A plain, bald statement of fact.

Uther's smile grew to a broad grin, and he looked to Garreth for a reaction. Garreth Whistler, however, was staring hard at Owain of the Caves.

"You were sent here to kill him?"

"I was sent here to make sure that Uther Pendragon would come late, if he came at all, to the Chiefs' Gathering. I'd have done it, too, if it hadn't been for the bear."

"How? You're a long way from where we crossed the ridge."

"Aye, but I was there when you approached it, and I watched you coming. Your scouts missed me completely, because they were looking for people and movement. I was one man, hiding until they passed me by. I picked out the one who must be Uther Pendragon and then fell back towards the place I had picked for my attack. The bear interrupted me. Had it not done so, you would have reached the spot by now, and I would have completed my task."

"And you yourself would be dead."

The tall man shrugged. "Mayhap, but I doubt it. I chose the place with care—and not for its beauty. It was a trap for you, not for me. Four ways out for me, all of them safe." Owain looked at Uther now for the first time since he had started speaking. "But you would have been dead with my first arrow."

"No, Garreth!"

Whistler's sword had slithered from its sheath with a quick, sibilant hiss as he dropped into a fighter's crouch. Now he hovered, glaring at the tall Northerner who stared back at him unconcernedly, making no attempt to defend himself. Slowly, visibly, the tension seeped away from Garreth and he straightened up, still holding his sword ready, to look at Uther. Uther, in turn, was gazing at Owain of the Caves, a peculiar expression on his face.

"So, you give me back my life." He nodded slowly. "I accept it, and I am grateful. What will you do now? Meradoc won't thank you for your scruples. He is the one who sent you, isn't he?"

The other shrugged. "Aye, so I'll move on. Meradoc has no patience when it comes to failure, and he'll take this as a failure. If I go back to him, he'll have me killed. He's a great one for rewarding treachery with death, is Meradoc."

"So am I . . . but you did nothing treacherous here."

Owain's mouth twisted in a wry smile. "Leaving you alive to cross him? He might see that otherwise."

Uther looked about him, coming to a decision. "Sheathe your sword, Garreth. Owain, will you ride with us for a way? I want to talk more with you, but we have a party of men up there on the path, as you know, and they will start fretting if we don't soon return."

Owain of the Caves shrugged his wide shoulders. "I don't ride, but I'll walk with you awhile if you'll feed me at the end of it. The devil there destroyed my pack, and with it all my food. After that, we can talk if you like, and then come morning I'll be on my way to wherever I end up."

Uther glanced down one last time at the carcass of the bear. The blood-filled eye socket was already filled with a heaving, crawling mass of metallic-looking flies, and the buzzing of hundreds more was growing stronger as he looked. He counted quickly, estimating that six of the arrows that had killed the animal were salvageable. He nodded his head.

"Good. Then let's retrieve these arrows and get started."

FIFTEEN

It was late in the afternoon before they found a suitable spot in which to build a camp for the night. Uther had had no opportunity to talk further with Owain of the Caves since rejoining the main party that afternoon, but he had really not sought one. After introducing him briefly on their return to the curious troopers, he left the stranger to his own devices.

Owain had walked silently ever since, keeping close to Garreth's side. Garreth, for his part, showed no hostility to the man walking beside him, but neither did he go out of his way to make him feel welcome.

Some time after that, Uther's scouts reported finding some strange tracks, and he decided to ride out himself to look at them. Rather than risk wasting time, however, he checked first with Owain to determine whether the tracks might have been made by others in his party, but Owain assured him that he had travelled alone.

Less than two hours later when Uther returned, he smelled the appetizing aroma of roasting pork even before he reached the camp. Early in the afternoon, while Uther and Garreth had been dealing with the bear, one of the troopers had found and killed a young wild pig, a yearling, and now the entire squadron was hovering close to the fire, salivating over the sight of it turning on the spit. Bear meat was all very well, and few of the men doubted that some people might think it a delicacy, but for sheer delight in the mouth, nothing could compete with young pig.

After he unsaddled his horse and rubbed it down for the night, Uther shouldered his bedroll and made his way to where Garreth and Owain sat together beside a fire of their own, their backs against a long, mossy log. They shifted to make room for him between them, and Owain grunted a question.

"Did you find out who made the tracks?"

Uther straightened up in the act of stooping to lay his bedroll down. He could not decide whether Owain was interested or merely making conversation. He nodded.

"Aye. They were all made by one man, coming and going."

Owain's eyebrows went up. "One man? And your scouts had to take you out there to tell them that? Could they not work it out for themselves?"

"They had by the time I arrived, but they had to find a soft spot in the earth in order to do it. Mountainous terrain shows tracks, but not in great detail. They had to look for more than a mile in both directions before they found a watercourse with soft ground. Must have been some hermit or anchorite or madman living up here alone and walking each day to water. He wore a track eventually, and that's what my scouts found. They're not trackers, you understand, but they are the best at what they do."

"And what is that?"

"Fighting on horseback with disciplined tactics."

"Ah!" Owain nodded and returned his gaze to the fire.

Garreth met Uther's gaze and rolled his eyes, saying nothing.

Uther grinned and lowered himself to sit between them, stretching out his hands to the fire and thankful that in summer there was no need to pitch a tent. He had barely settled, it seemed, when a shout went up from the cooking fires, and it was time to eat.

Afterwards, sated with the delicious, fatty meat of the young pig, Uther sat gazing at Owain of the Caves, who in turn sat staring into the fire. Nemo Hard-Nose had shared their fire for the duration of the meal but was now gone, seeing to the first guard watch of the night. Garreth sat with his head back against the log behind him, eyes closed, enjoying the warmth of the fire, breathing deeply, perhaps asleep.

Owain turned from the fire and looked away into the darkness beyond. "Fire blind," he said without looking at Uther. "You can see wondrous things in the depths of a fire, but nothing at all when you move your eyes away. You said you wanted to talk to me. Ask your questions, then. But know I might not answer them."

Garreth opened his eyes at that and sat up, stretching hugely. "Well," he said, "I might sit here all night listening to the two of you exchanging thoughts, and I might even learn something from it . . . But one thing I already know, learned long since: if I have no part to play in two men's talk, it's a waste of time, and I might as well be warm and snug abed. I'll bid you a good night and pleasant dreams, if e'er you get to rest."

Smiling, Uther watched him depart and then turned back to Owain of the Caves. "He is a good friend, Garreth Whistler."

"Mayhap. I'd be no judge of that. Ask me your questions."

Uther stirred and shifted his backside, searching for more comfort. "I have a few, but I think I know the answers to most of them already. Do you really believe that Meradoc would have you killed for not killing me? If I am any judge of men, and I believe I am, your loyalty is faultless."

That drew him a wry, sidewise look that condemned him as a fool. "You are still alive, and not even delayed in your journey. Therein lies an end to both my usefulness and my loyalty in Meradoc's eyes."

Uther shook his head. "Am I that big a threat to him?"

"Ask yourself that, not me. My only care now is staying alive. The gods served me a bitter dish today, but I learned long ago never to question what the gods offer."

Owain turned his gaze towards the fire again so that the leaping flames picked out the details of his long, clean-shaven face with its wide mouth and deep-graven jawline. Uther searched that face for signs of bitterness or anger, but he saw only a strange, almost melancholy sadness in the man's eyes.

"Meradoc demands perfection in his . . . followers," Owain said. And then, disconcertingly, he smiled—the first real smile Uther had seen from him—and reached down to pull a burning twig from the fire. He held it up to his mouth and blew at the flames before he continued, crinkling his eyes against the sting of the smoke as the tiny flames died out. "We are but few, we who do Meradoc's bidding, and for our services we are well rewarded. But as the payment for success is great, beyond a poor man's dreams, so, too, is the penalty for failure.

"Loyalty, obedience and success. Those are Meradoc's demands. He sent me out to perform a task, and I have failed to do it. I am a walking corpse until my former allies find me."

"That is insanity. Where will you go? I mean, I know you've said you don't know, but surely your friends—"

"Friends are for ordinary folk who live and behave in ordinary ways. I kill men to please those who employ me. Men such as I never have friends."

"You are a warrior. All warriors are killers, Owain. That's what the word means."

Owain of the Caves turned and looked directly at Uther, and the younger man was astonished to see what he took to be pity in the other's gaze.

"I know that, Uther Pendragon. But you are wrong in this . . . I am no warrior. *You* are a warrior. Warriors make war. They stand and fight or run away, according to the rules of war—if such things truly exist. The way I see it, those rules are made by those who win, or want to win, and have the strength to try. Warriors fight, and they take pride in being seen to fight. People like me, on the other hand . . . we never fight unless we must. Fighting involves the risk of being killed, so I avoid it. I am a killer, bought and sometimes, though seldom, sold. I often kill in stealth, and sometimes I kill openly, but I never, ever kill in the heat of the moment. My killing is deliberate; it is *planned*. Few of my victims ever see me coming or recognize the moment of their death."

Uther kept his face straight, despite his profound shock. He had known many men throughout his life who were little more than brutes—vicious and violent and lawless—but he had never before met a man who could speak calmly as this man did of casual, dispassionate killings carried out on behalf of others in cold blood and for personal gain.

Uther cleared his throat. "What do you mean by 'bought and sometimes sold'?"

Owain flicked the twig back into the fire. "Meradoc has sometimes sold my services to others."

"*He* sold them? Not you?"

The barest shrug of his wide shoulders was the only indication that Owain had heard the question, and for a long time Uther thought he was not going to answer. Then the words emerged in a flat monotone. "My services were his, for him to . . . bestow. I did what he instructed me to do."

"How long have you been doing this, this—killing?" Uther resisted using the word that was in his mind, *murdering*.

"I have never *not* done it. It's what I do."

"What, you were born a killer, even as a babe?" Uther, irritated by the man's disinterested monotone, recognized the pettiness of the question even as it left his lips, but he was incapable of biting it back.

"I must have been. I have no other memories. There was a woman once who cared for me, I think, but she was killed one night when I was very young. I tried to rescue her, to help her, I suppose, but I was a helpless brat of seven, mayhap less. They beat me and broke my legs and threw me in the fire. That's why I limp."

Uther glanced down at the long, trousered legs stretching towards the fire. "I saw no limp."

"I limp."

"Who were 'they'?"

He watched the profiled face break into a wolfish, bitter grin. "My father? Brothers? Let's say my family. They were a small clan, and I have seen enough since then to know they were not . . . not as others are. At the time, though, I knew no other people, no other way of being. I thought they were all there was."

Uther felt a rush of gooseflesh, and the short hairs on his neck stirred in sheer horror at the vision of the seven-year-old boy squirming in the middle of a roaring fire.

"Who pulled you out, from the fire? You said your legs were broken."

"Aye, they were. It was another woman, Jess, I think her name was. Couldn't stand the noise or the stink, she said, so she dragged me away and threw me into a corner in another cave, and I lay there till I healed."

"What caves? Would I know them?"

"No, you would not know them, nor would you wish to. It has been more than twenty years since I last saw them, and I have no wish to go back. Anyone who passed that way became our means of living from the one day to the next. We killed whoever came along . . . robbed them, then killed them. Kept the women alive, for a while at least, until we found others, but we always ended up killing them. Sometimes we ate them, parts of them, if the winter had been long. Eventually, after too many travellers had been lost, people stopped coming that way, so we went out to hunt them.

"One day, some of our people were pursued and followed home. When the fighting was over, I was the only one left alive, and that was because I had been thrashed and thrown into a hole again the day before. The men who had come found me there, half dead, and took me out and made a slave of me until I grew too big to beat. Then one night I killed my keeper and left."

Uther had never heard anything to equal this, although he knew there were terrifying tales told of such things in the distant regions of the land, far from the holdings and customs of the major clans.

"Who were these people, the ones you grew up among?"

"The Cave People. They had no other name that I, or they, knew of. They lived barely, and to live, they killed."

"And that is how you grew up. No wonder you do what you do. But—if that's the way you live, why would you scruple to kill me? Especially when you knew it would cost you your own life?"

Owain drew a long, single-edged dirk from his belt and fingered the edge of the blade, and watching him, Uther experienced no more than a momentary, fleeting surge of alarm. After inspecting the weapon closely for several moments, Owain turned it in his fist, bent forward at the waist and drove its point into the ground, right at the fire's edge.

"I am sitting here wondering why I am telling you all this," he said mildly. "I kill because I have always killed, and life—my own included—has never seemed to be an important thing to me. We were all born to die. The killing provides enough wealth for me to live in comfort. But I do not steal, Uther Pendragon, nor do I lie. I do not harm women casually. I do not eat the dead. I pay my debts, I keep myself away from simple folk who would be frightened by my shadow, I live according to a way of life, by rules I made myself, and I respect the gods.

"Not long after I killed my keeper and ran off—I must have been fourteen years old, or something close to that—I fell sick and almost died. I lay unconscious in a wood somewhere, close by a spring, and I was found there by an old man and his wife who lived nearby. They took me home and into their lives, and by the time I had grown healthy again and fit to walk, a process that took months, they had . . ." Owain's voice faded away for a moment as he sought a word. "They had *tamed* me . . . I suppose that would be the proper word. I was a wild creature when they found me, feral and unnatural and utterly devoid of any trace of civilization or humanity, trusting no one and nothing. They tamed me. They taught me, by their example, by treating me with decency, tolerance and great patience, that there is kindness in the world. And then, with them, for a time, the only time I can remember, I was . . . free of care.

"Their names were Gerrix and Martha, and they wove baskets and sold them. Gerrix had lost a leg as a young man. He had been a cleric then, in the home of some high-ranking Roman magistrate. He taught me to read and to write during the first winter I spent in their home. He had a store of books that was his greatest and only treasure, and I read all of them several times. Gerrix and I would discuss them, because he had no one else with whom to speak of such things. He taught me much, including how to speak, because the truth is that before he and Martha came into my life, I had never really *spoken* to anyone. The thought of speaking to another person for pleasure—of discussing something logically and without passion—could never have occurred to me."

"Evidently." Uther nodded his head. "How long did you remain with them?"

"For four years." The glow that had animated Owain's face was gone. "They were killed. In the fourth winter after I joined them, I went hunting. Game was not plentiful that year, and I was gone for nigh on two days. While I was gone, marauders found them and killed them. They took what they wanted, which could not have been much, and then burned the house . . ."

The silence that followed these words was so long that Uther thought again that Owain had finished, but as he began to say something that would express his condolences, the other sniffed and cleared his throat noisily.

"I found them . . . the killers, I mean. No great task. They had not expected to be followed. Four of them. I captured them all alive, and then I killed them, very slowly, very thoroughly and very painfully, one at a time, taking care to remind them each day of why they were dying. By the time the last of them died, having watched his friends precede him, his regret at having led them in doing what they did was very real.

"Somehow, I don't know how, someone found out what I had done and told others. Soon afterward, another man, a wealthy man, came to me and offered to feed and clothe me and provide a roof over my head in return for what he called my 'protective services.' From that day until this, I have made my living by selling those services. But thanks to the gifts I received from Gerrix, I have been able to do it on my own terms and according to my own beliefs."

Uther had listened carefully, wondering at the incomprehensible logic of this man. He could see that honour played a large part in the tall Northerner's behaviour, but he was at a loss to understand the workings and the dictates of that honour, since the man's professed way of life was in violation of all that Uther held to be honourable. He decided that he wanted to understand more.

"Tell me, Owain, why did you admit to me so quickly that you were sent to kill me? Had you no fear of our reprisals? We could have killed you then, before your words had died away."

"And if the gods had wished that, you would have. I but spoke the truth."

"I know that, but why? You could have waited and kept silent and then done what you were required to do afterward. You could have killed me when I least expected it and then returned to Meradoc as a hero. I don't understand why you made that decision . . . Or do you still intend to do it later?"

Owain of the Caves pulled his dirk from the ground and rubbed the point clean with the ball of his thumb, then turned his face towards Uther and smiled again. Uther was amazed at how the man's whole face lit up when he did so.

"Impossibility. You don't see that, though, do you?" He twisted his body, reaching behind him to replace the dirk in his belt. "Do you know anything of honour down there in that place called Camulod?"

"Of course we do."

"Well, then, you should have no difficulty understanding. You saved my life at risk of your own. That laid a heavy claim on me. How then could I kill you and be a man of honour?"

"Because it was an accidental thing, my saving you. Had I known you were there to kill me, I might not have been so quick to expose myself to that bear."

"You did what you were driven to do, Uther Pendragon. So did I. That's what a man—any real man—does."

"Hmm." Uther frowned slightly and shook his head in annoyance. "And so this with Meradoc. You claim he'll have you killed if he can find you, simply for behaving, as you see this thing, with honour. And yet I detect no anger in you towards him."

"What good is anger? It's a pointless thing, most of the time destructive."

"Very well, then. So you were to kill me, but the gods forestalled you. Why were you sent to look for me at all?"

"I was sent to make sure you came late to the Gathering. I told you that earlier. The decision to kill you was my choice, since I could think of no surer means of making you late."

"Meradoc did not order my death, then?"

"No, not in words, but his choice of messenger did not lack meaning."

"Because you tend to do things thoroughly."

Owain inclined his head slightly.

"So Meradoc sees me as an enemy."

"That seems obvious."

"Well, at least it's clear enough. I do not like Meradoc, but that hardly sets me apart from the mass. But I have never given him the slightest cause to see me as an enemy."

"Meradoc needs no cause for things like that. He *is* the cause. Think about that. You are not a stupid man, though I begin to wonder if you are not naive. It is not unheard of for an ambitious man to take matters into his own hands with power as important as a King's at stake. And yet for Meradoc there is more." The big man sat up straighter and sniffed, then wiped at his nose with the back of his hand. "Guilt, man! *There's* cause enough for hatred and for fear . . ." His voice died away, and then resumed. "Look you, you saved my life and fed me well, and you have made no move to hinder me or hold me, so tomorrow I will be gone, and we may never set eyes each upon the other again. Your life for my life I gave, so accept this for the meal and the freedom. Think upon your father, Uric the King. Upon his death."

"I have thought much on it. He died by a poisoned arrow, shot by one of Lot of Cornwall's men."

"Aye, but where?"

Uther had grown tense. "What do you mean, 'where?' In battle, where else?"

"No!" Owain shook his head. "I don't know where you heard that tale, but Uric was in his camp, at night, in the middle of his army when he was killed. Now ask yourself this . . . how came the Cornish there in Uric's own camp? Who was in charge of the King's safety? There were guards who died for their carelessness that night, but who was responsible for assigning all those guards?"

"Meradoc?"

"Aye, Meradoc. Someone arranged things so the Cornishman could pass through ranks of guards. And Meradoc was in charge. He had the guards all killed at once, so great was his rage, for failing in their duty to the King. They were all dead almost before the word was spread."

"And dead men can't speak out, is that what you are saying?"

"You said it, not me."

"That is . . ." Uther's voice was choked with loathing. "You *know* this? You are convinced this happened?"

"No, I was far away that night, up in the north, so I don't know it. But I know Meradoc and I know his greed, and what his wishes were and are. Meradoc sees himself as High King of the Pendragon Federation, but Uric was already there in place. So, to a man hungry enough and peering through a shuttered door at food on a table, the problem would have seemed simple: remove the obstacle between you and the table, then eat your fill." He moved his legs and rose to his feet. "Is that cause enough for enmity? Ask him yourself, when next you meet him. Now I'm going to sleep. Is there anything else you wanted to ask me?"

Uther simply shook his head, incapable of speech, and watched Owain walk into the blackness beyond the fire's range.

"I had doubts of my own, but didn't want to voice them to you until I knew more. His words have the ring of truth to them." Garreth's voice came from the darkness of the trees behind Uther's back. Uther sat silent, then spoke without turning.

"How long have you been listening there? I thought you went to bed."

"I did. I couldn't sleep."

"You suspected this treachery of Meradoc's? You should have told me, Garreth."

"Told you what, that I smelled a stink of fish? We live beside the sea, Uther. Anyway, now you know more than I knew. What will you do?"

Uther rose to his feet and picked up his bedroll, then walked away into the darkness without answering. When he came to where Owain of the Caves was stooping to lie down, having spread his blanket beneath the boughs of an evergreen, he stopped and spoke.

"Owain!"

He heard a stirring in the blackness beneath the tree. "Aye?"

"You have a place with me if you want one. Meradoc might yet kill you, but before he does, he'll have to kill me and mine as well, and I intend to give him no chance at that before he dies."

There was silence for a spell, and then the voice spoke from the darkness. "I'll think on that."

"Good." Turning to leave, Uther stopped once again. "Think on this, too, while you're about it. I prefer to do my own killing, with my own weapons. Should you choose to stay with us, you will live in new ways and in new days. And if I ever call upon your *services*, you will deliver them openly, by my side and shoulder to shoulder with my friends, my companions and my warriors."

There was no response, and he walked away through the long grass, swinging his bedroll up over his shoulder and thinking deeply.

SIXTEEN

Daris ap Griffyd, son of Darin and grandson of the revered and long-dead Druid Derwent, stood high above the temple gazing down from the eastern heights of the earthen wall that sheltered the sacred place, vainly trying to empty his mind of distractions. Behind him and far below, the tide of movement and noise that had driven him away in a vain search for peace and quiet showed no sign of abating. It was, he knew, the inevitable accompaniment to a great gathering of people, but, coupled with the discord of his seething thoughts, it made it impossible for him to concentrate on what he should be doing. Grimly, conscientiously, he squeezed his eyelids shut and forced himself to focus upon what must be.

He would stand here again tomorrow, in this precise spot, but on that occasion he would be dressed in the spare but splendid regalia of Chief Druid, his bright red robes brilliant in the sunlight, his beard and his long white hair brushed and carefully combed beneath the leafy corona of mistletoe that would crown his head. The same great staff he bore today, the symbol of his rank as High Priest, would be in his right hand as always. It was a solid shaft of dried and polished oak, its upper length chased in spiralling whorls of beaten silver that swept up to enfold a sun disk of solid gold, a hand's span in diameter. He would stand alone then, too, isolated by his rank. But twelve paces beyond him, on either side, the people of the clans, awed into quietude for once by the solemnity of the occasion, would crowd along the circumference of the wall, waiting for the day's ceremonies to begin. Their presence in the temple itself would profane the sacred rites to be observed there that day, so the top of the protecting wall, where he stood now, was the closest they would come to the ceremonies below.

Daris willed away the vision of the crowd and concentrated only upon the place where they would gather. The triune symbolism of the site pleased him—a circle within a circle within a circle—and he breathed deeply in a pattern of long, regular breaths designed to permit him to immerse himself in its peaceful symmetry and to ignore the debilitating tension in his guts.

The outer circle on which he stood was a massive earthen wall erected by his people when the first rapacious Roman legions came to Britain, hundreds of years before. It had been built for one sole purpose: to protect and defend the hallowed ring of sixteen uniformly quarried and dressed menhirs—standing stones each twice the height of a man—that formed the second circle. This was the original temple created untold ages earlier by craftsmen who might have been Daris's own ancestors, although the ancient legends spoke of another, older race of smaller people who had lived here in the long-forgotten past. Fortunately, the wall had never been required, because although the Romans felt driven to eradicate the Druids of Britain, they never felt a need to invade or own the ancient temples that the Druids had built. In consequence, the original circle of ancient stones remained as it had been since time immemorial.

Twenty long paces, each interval exact, separated each of the standing stones from the baseline of the surrounding defensive wall, and the circle of stones itself was thirty great strides in diameter, the precision of the whole demonstrating that, no matter who the ancient architects and builders were, they possessed quarrying and construction skills the like of which were quite unknown in the land today.

The third circle, carefully laid out within the ring of the menhirs, was temporary, purely ceremonial: Daris himself had supervised its arrangement that very morning. This was a ring of eight large, solid, wooden chairs, each placed with great care five paces in front of a specific stone, so that the chair's occupant sat with his back to that stone, flanked by two others. Each chair was separated from the one directly facing it across the circle by twenty paces, and the chairs were as uniform as the menhirs, save for one. The one designated for the King was larger than all the others, though carved from the same ancient, blackened oak. It sat in front of the menhir at the westernmost point of the ring's circumference and faced directly east, towards the rising sun.

Tomorrow, Daris hoped and prayed, only the King's chair would sit vacant, for the King was dead. Tomorrow, all the seven Chiefs of the Pendragon Federation—given the blessing of the gods—would convene here to choose another King from their own ranks. And when the King was chosen and duly set in place upon the great King's seat, then one of the Chiefs' chairs would remain empty until the King died. Because the Chief ruled by right of heredity, the rank passing from father to son, that succession was usually a formality, with an appointee from the King's family sometimes filling the post during a boy's minority. Only very seldom, when a king died with no son to claim the Chief's chair, was the succession resolved by the elders of the clan council.

But would all seven Chiefs be present come the following day? That question was the reason for Daris's tension and ill temper. The Choosing must proceed regardless, and that, Daris suspected, might be disastrous for the people. There was already much ill feeling in the matter of this Choosing, for the choices were severely limited and none of the options was pleasing to everyone, or even to a clear majority. Three of the seven ruling Chiefs were too old to occupy the King's seat, another was too young, and a fifth was too infirm. All five were thus disqualified from kingship by ancient law, save for the possibility of ruling for a brief period in time of dire need—that gap the Romans called an *interregnum*—between the death of one King and the legal Choosing of the next. There would be no interregnum here, on this occasion. Two Chiefs were qualified to assume the King's place and sacred seat, and one of those was already in attendance at the Gathering.

Daris snorted and gripped his staff tightly in both hands until his knuckles whitened. His gaze flicked from one side of the inner circle to the other, singling out the chairs of the two men eligible to be chosen. The laws determining who might serve as a reigning King among the Celtic peoples were clear and specific. The King must be physically unblemished, in the prime of manhood and sound in limb and wind; he must be a warrior of high repute, renowned in battle and in hunting; and he must have wealth enough to provide his people with relief in times of great hardship. Both of these men were qualified in all the main respects, but Daris knew that each of them had serious shortcomings, flaws which, while they did not contravene the ancient laws, were yet strong enough to cast doubt on either one's ability to serve the people as he ought. Although Daris himself would have no vote in the Choosing of the King, as High Priest he must look to the welfare of the people. His opinions on the candidates were expected, and would be duly considered and heeded by most of the seven Chiefs. Daris had not yet raised his voice on behalf of either man, and that fact had not gone unnoticed. His silence, if it continued much longer, would be considered irresponsible by those who looked to him for guidance and support.

Daris turned away from the temple and looked outward and down to his left towards the distant encampments—one large and the other much smaller and set apart—that had sprung into being within the week that had passed. The wide, pleasant meadow in which they had been built had already been obliterated and turned into an arid wasteland by the comings and goings of thousands of people and livestock, and Daris knew from past experience that it would take a year and more for the pasturage to return to its normal lushness. But then, he reflected, these Gatherings—happening once in five, ten or a score of years—were the reason the meadow had been carved from the surrounding forest in the first place.

For as long as Daris could remember—and that remembrance included all the memories also held and passed down to him by those elders who had died during his lifetime—the ordinary people of the clans in this part of south Cambria had called themselves the Pendragon Federation. This term was not strictly accurate, however, and there were ambitious people in the crowd down there for this Gathering who would do anything in their power to substitute their own name for that of Pendragon. An attempt to do precisely that would be made at this coming Choosing.

Three clans made up the Federation: Llewellyn, Pendragon and Griffyd. The Romans, when they first arrived, had issued their own names to the clans, misunderstanding everything about them, from their makeup to their ancient holdings. *Durotriges*, they had called the southernmost, and *Belgae* the people directly to the north of those, not realizing, in their foreign ignorance, that these were people of the same ancestral blood, and that they were Pendragon, possessors of the land flanking the great estuary to the north of the peninsula that the Romans had called *Cornua*, the Horn, now known as Cornwall. The other two great clans, the Llewellyns and the Griffyds, from the southern half of Cambria on the western side of the estuary, the Romans had named the *Silures* and the *Demetae*, foolish names thrust by an invader on an unconquered people. In the aftermath of their adjustment to the Roman "conquest," the three clans mingled peacefully, melding their holdings so that they could coexist in peace and relative strength without attracting the ire of the conquerors, and over the hundreds of years that then elapsed, that mingling evolved into a federation, dedicated to preserving their joint holdings.

Three clans, Daris reflected now, but seven distinct groups among them: three Llewellyn, two Griffyd and two Pendragon, each ruled by a Chief. The attraction that had bonded them one to the other in the beginning had been self-serving—each of the three clans had hoped to preserve and enhance its own status through alliance with the others—but all three had prospered equally, sharing the benefits of their closeness. And so it had come about that for more than twenty generations now, the seven Chiefs had chosen from among their own ranks a King whose voice would speak for all the people and whose primary duty was to safeguard all of them from Rome's displeasure. From those earliest days, no clan-directed rule had governed the Choosing of the King; no sequence of clan names had been applied; no precedence or preference had been permitted. Each new King had been selected by his peers, acknowledged as the most suitable among them for the task and chosen according to the ancient law.

As Rome's presence and rule settled into peaceful occupation and civil administration, and its soldiers and citizens learned to live in the comfort and security of their wall-girt towns, the people in the remote mountain regions, among them the clans of the Federation, were largely left to live their lives as they wished, so that the Kings ruled in their own right and organized their own local defences against raiders in those far-flung rural areas where Rome had no desire to penetrate. The responsibilities of the King of the Federation were many and varied, but in essence they boiled down to being present and available at all times to act as paramount Chief, final judge and arbitrator in legal disputes among members of the three clans. While it was the responsibility of each individual Chief to settle disputes and other matters pertaining to the law amicably within his own clan, there were invariably situations in which an outside, clearly unbiased judgment was required in order to reach final settlement. Those judgments fell to the ruling King, or, when a King had died and no replacement had yet been selected, to the seven men who served on the Council of Chiefs.

Over the centuries, the Pendragon clan, thanks to the prowess of its warriors and the wealth accumulated by its thrifty traders, grew to be more powerful than the others, despite the fact that there were but two Pendragon clans as opposed to three Llewellyn, and for five generations past Pendragon had provided all the men selected in the Choosing as best qualified for Kingship, the greatest of those being Ullic Pendragon, father of the dead King Uric. The five successive Pendragon Kings had all been good men and good kings—good enough to have their name adopted as the Federation's own.

The home of the Pendragon was located on the southern side of the great estuary of the river that flowed by Glevum, nigh on a hundred miles to the north. There had once been a Roman garrison posted nearby, but it had never been a major or important posting, and the stone buildings erected there had soon fallen into neglect once the Province of Britain had been welcomed into the *Pax Romana,* the vaunted "Roman Peace" that had subjugated the entire civilized world for a thousand years and ensured the Imperial welfare. Much more important than the small Roman fort, however, was the ancient hill fort that overlooked it, which had survived there, according to local legend, for nigh on six hundred years. Its name was Tir Manha, meaning the Place of Strength, and it was as

serviceable as it had ever been. When the Romans left their tiny
buildings, the Pendragons moved back into Tir Manha, and over the
ensuing decades and centuries it proved to be a perfect place from
which to govern the diverse peoples and territories of the Federation. The mainland of Cambria, with its former Roman administrative centre of Caerdyff, lay less than an hour's journey by boat
across the estuary, and the rest of the Pendragon lands lay to the
south and east, with the great Tor of Glastonbury rising up out of
the extensive sea marshes directly to the southeast, and the other
ancient hill fort—the one that became Camulod—some five
leagues, or fifteen Roman miles, to the south and east of that again.

Now, Daris knew, at least one man would like to see the end of
the Pendragons' predominance. Meradoc, the strongest of the
Llewellyn Chiefs, lusted for the King's seat and had been pleading
his cause with the other Chiefs for months strongly enough, Daris
feared, that he might win. The Chief Druid's eyes widened as this
thought occurred to him, for until then, Daris had been unaware that
he actually feared it. He sucked in a great breath and blew it out
noisily, thrusting that thought away, too, as his eyes scanned the
scene laid out before him.

King Uric had been dead now for almost two months. But the
Federation was at war, and Daris had been forced to withhold the
summons until a lull developed in the fighting. Now they had
begun to assemble. Meradoc had been the first of them to arrive,
six days ago, and four of the seven were now present, with their
retinues, in the smaller of the encampments below. Three of those
were the Llewellyn Chiefs, Meradoc, Cunbelyn and Hod the
Strong, and the fourth was young Huw Strongarm, Chief of the
northern Pendragon yet no more than a boy. Three yet remained to
come, and two of those were the eldest of elders, Cativelaunus of
Carmarthen and Brynn of Y Gaer, Chiefs of the Griffyd clan.
Those two would arrive within the hour, for they were travelling
together and their party had been seen that morning crossing the
river ten miles to the north.

The only Chief now missing, with no word of his whereabouts,
was the remaining Pendragon, young Uther, son of the dead King

Uric, and it was he who was causing most of Daris's anxiety, for despite his being the only Chief not actively involved in the war in Cambria, Uther was the one who must stand against Meradoc Llewellyn, and Daris had serious doubts that he would—or should—do so. He sighed and muttered a curse beneath his breath. It was already too late for Uther to arrive in time. The odds were piled too high against him now. *Accept it and be glad,* he told himself. *You're far too old a fool to be wasting time in wishful thinking.*

The Choosing would take place tomorrow when the sun god rode highest in the summer sky, his benevolent influence at its greatest peak. The law was sacrosanct, backed by a thousand years of history, established long before this Federation ever gathered to choose Kings of its own. No man could interfere with it and none might force a cancellation or postponement of the solemn rites. The Chiefs would choose at noon.

Far away to the east, where the road met the forest's edge, Daris saw signs of movement where none had been before, and he watched for a while as a body of travellers came slowly into view. He felt his heartbeat surge at his first sight of them, but even as he began to hope, he recognized that this was the double retinue of the two Chiefs whose coming had been announced earlier. Daris sighed and swallowed his disappointment, then turned to make his way down from the wall. As Chief Druid, he should be present to welcome the two senior Chiefs when they arrived.

Moving slowly, he made his way out through the passageway formed by the overlapping ends of the protective wall, turning to his right as he emerged and pacing steadily towards the distant encampment that housed the Chiefs. He felt no need to hurry: he had no wish to reach the Chiefs' camp ahead of the newcomers. If he did, he might be accosted as he waited, and entreated or enticed to take some kind of stance concerning the upcoming Choosing. Daris had no need of that and no intention of allowing it.

It was Uther Pendragon's uncaring irresponsibility that grated on the Chief Druid. Daris himself had always been responsible, aware of his calling even as a child. Many of the boys with whom he had been apprenticed to the Druidic brotherhood had been there because they were placed there, committed by their families for any of a hundred reasons, from dire poverty to some bright, attractive talent noted and remarked upon by one of the Grey Brotherhood, as the Druids were called among the people.

That was not the case with Daris. He had been born to the Brotherhood. His idolized grandfather was one of the greatest Druids the people had known, and he had never, throughout his entire life, considered any other way of life. He studied hard at every task to which he was set, absorbing the arcane mysteries and knowledge of the priesthood as eagerly as he learned the great songs and sagas that were in the Brotherhood's safekeeping as guardians of the history of the people. Daris had long since lost count of the number of these sagas he had committed to memory, but he never ceased to be grateful for his own capacity to store them in his mind and recall them at will. Retention of the tales, and absolute fidelity to the ancient form and content of them, was but one of his responsibilities. Daris knew duty and fidelity to duty, what it was and what it entailed. And in his eyes, Uther Pendragon did not.

Meradoc would be a less than perfect King, Daris was sure. Outwardly he was upright and straightforward, if somewhat too loud and aggressive, and no one could deny his prowess as both warrior and strategist in war. In peace, he applied himself judiciously to being amiable and wholesome, despite the difficulties caused for him by his own disposition. He was not an easy man to like, lacking both in humour and in patience for the weaknesses of other, lesser men. And it quickly became evident to anyone who looked that Meradoc perceived all men as lesser men, despite the pains he took attempting to hide and disguise that fact. He had wealth of many kinds, and he showed no scruples over using it blatantly to buy the good opinion of his men. He failed, however, save in the most lurid ways, to purchase the opinions of their women. Women did not like Meradoc; they distrusted him instinctively. Daris did not know why with any certitude, since women, in the main, would not confide in him, a Druid, but the knowledge added to his misgivings about the Llewellyn Chief.

One more thing bothered Daris greatly. Meradoc kept a small crew of men about him who dwelt in fear-shrouded shadows, part of, yet apart from, his household forces. These men, newcomers all, were seldom seen, yet they were dreaded by the people. Informally known as the Chief's bodyguard, they were forbidding, solitary men who kept themselves apart from all contact, save when they accompanied their Chief on his travels. But they were rumoured to deal out sudden and secretive death to any, it was said, who failed to please their leader or sought to obstruct his designs. Daris had seen them and spoken briefly to a few of them—a series of wordless grunts on their part in response to his words. He disliked them and what they represented in their sullen surliness, but he did not know how much of what was said of them was true, and lacking proof of any crimes, he could not but ignore the hearsay in his assessment of Meradoc as a potential King.

Nevertheless, Daris was convinced that Meradoc was filled with *wrongness*. The Chief Druid had no other word to apply to what he perceived in the Llewellyn Chief. And yet, despite all that, he knew that Meradoc, as King, would *rule* his people, and he would do so here in Cambria, and that was more than could be said for the Pendragon. Uther, Daris felt, had been too long absent—in his person and in his heart.

Thinking about that now as he walked towards the others, Daris found himself almost glad that Uther had not come. For if Uther were somehow to emerge as the Chosen King, then, Daris believed, the destruction of the Federation would begin. Uther, despite any protestations he might make at the Choosing, would surely find himself drawn back to the comforts of Camulod and the life it offered. Then Cambria would be without a King, although its King remained alive, and there would be a jealous, angry and ambitious rival left at home to stir up anarchy and civil war.

"That is the fifth time I've seen Meradoc smile since we arrived here, and it's been what, an hour? Less than that."

Daris turned to smile at his old friend Cativelaunus of Carmarthen, amused as always by the elder man's acerbity. "He does seem to be trying very hard to be pleasant."

"Aye, but five smiles in an hour from that one tells me we all ought to be looking about us. Something's in the wind, and if it pleases him, I know I'll retch when I snout it . . . So, there's been no word of Uther?"

"Not a sound. Nothing at all. I think I'm relieved, too—at least, part of me is."

The old Chief looked at the High Priest sideways, one white, bushy eyebrow raised high in scorn. "What part of you is that? Can't be your reason—it's plain that's gone. You're glad the Pendragon's not here? When did this madness take you?"

"Shush!" Daris glanced towards the others, thinking some of them might have overheard what Cativelaunus said. They were all watching Meradoc, however, seeming to hang on his words, and the hectic flush on the Llewellyn Chief's wide-cheeked face showed that he was enjoying being the centre of attention. Cativelaunus blinked with surprise at being told to shush and started to draw himself up defiantly, but then he hesitated and nodded, dropping his voice and slouching his shoulders.

"What, too loud? Well, I'll tell you, my old friend, if this one comes to be the King, we'll all be whispering from that moment forth. Step outside with me. I need clean air."

As Cativelaunus spoke, Brynn of Y Gaer, the other Griffyd Chief and second only to his friend in age, walked up and spoke almost into his ear. "Clean air?" he said mildly. "I'll come, too."

"No, that you'll not," Cativelaunus said, without even turning to look at him. "You'll stay here and keep their thoughts away from what we're up to. If all three of us walk out, we'll be followed. If you stay here without me and make yourself seen and heard, they might not even notice I'm not here. Talk to them about the Choosing and find out how they all stand, as if we didn't know. I need to speak with Daris."

Brynn pursed his lips, ducked his head in a gesture that clearly said, "Very well, I'll try," and sauntered away again, headed directly to the group surrounding Meradoc, where he shouldered his way gently into the press. Someone spoke to him, asking him a question, and as he began to respond Cativelaunus caught Daris's eye and nodded his head slightly towards the open half-door of the stone-walled hut. The two moved slowly out the door into bright sunshine and walked away until a good twenty paces lay between them and the doorway.

The stone hut they had just left was the only permanent building in the smaller encampment known as the Chiefs' Camp, and it had been built in the distant past for private meetings of assembled Chiefs. Its doors were never guarded, for there was no need. For generations past, the hut had been the Chiefs' precinct alone, and no others ever approached it without being summoned.

There were people moving about in the bright afternoon, but none of them paid any attention to the Druid and his white-headed companion. Cativelaunus stopped and looked about him.

"This is far enough. I don't care if they see us speaking, so be that they can't hear us. High Priest and Chief, we two can talk all we want, but if Brynn joined us, those idiots would smell a plot . . . Tell me, then, what are we to do tomorrow noon without Uther? Withhold our votes? Meradoc would take that ill. Might as well stick out our necks for sacrifice. Or should we simply vote for him and accept that, at the end, our lives and our beliefs and all the things we've ever stood for or represented have been worth nothing and we have chosen a bad King through fear alone?"

Daris frowned as he listened. He had known that Cativelaunus had no great love for Meradoc, but this was more than he had expected. The old man's eyes were hard and grim, and his questions were delivered as a verdict rather than a query. Daris shook his head, searching for words.

"I don't think it will be that bad, old friend. He'll not be perfect, I'll grant you, but what King ever is? I've thought long and hard on this, and have decided—unwillingly—that he's the lesser of the two evils—"

"Lesser of the two—? Daris, you *are* mad! How could you even *begin* to believe that? Pendragon is—"

"Pendragon is *absent*, 'Launus. And that is by his own choice. Uther wants no part of being King. That is obvious. Had he felt otherwise, he would be here today."

"He's been delayed! Something has kept him back."

"No, I will not accept that! His father has been dead these past weeks, 'Launus. The summons went out to you and all the others a fortnight past. And it is four days, at most, from Camulod to here. Uther Pendragon is not here because he does not want to be here."

"Then why has our messenger not come back to tell us that? Knowing what must happen now, he would be bound to let us know as soon as he knew."

Daris shrugged. "The only thing I know is that Uther Pendragon has not come, and now he is too late."

"He's *not* too late. The Choosing won't begin until tomorrow noon. He could be here come morning."

"Aye, and what would he achieve? Which of the Chiefs would choose him now?"

"I would!"

"I know that. You would vote for him, and so would Brynn. What then?"

"Young Huw Strongarm would vote for him. He's Pendragon."

"Aye, that he is, and his vote, with Uther's, would give you four of seven, beyond doubt or dispute . . . but I doubt now that Huw would vote for Uther. My gut tells me he might not."

Cativelaunus was outraged and made no attempt to hide it. A man of ancient honour and tradition, he found it inconceivable that blood would not speak out for blood. In words that dripped scorn, he poured abuse on his High Priest for daring to suggest that young Huw Pendragon might be seduced away from the strict path of honour.

Daris stood listening until the old Chief ran out of words, and then he nodded. "Tell me," he asked mildly, "what is the sworn duty of each Chief on the day of the Choosing?"

"To pick the best man present to fill the King's seat." The answer was immediate, without the slightest hesitation.

"And how do you—you personally, I mean—decide whom to vote for?"

Cativelaunus hesitated now, scowling. "I . . . I judge each candidate, and then I pick the one I've decided is best."

"The very best, or the best present?"

"Damn you, Daris, you know as well as I do. The very best might be a thousand times better than the next in line, but if he's not there for the Choosing, then he might as well be dead. The Chiefs assembled are constrained to choose the best man *there*. That's why I'm so angry at Uther."

"Forget Uther, for the moment, 'Launus. Think about young Huw Strongarm. His duty is the same as yours: to judge the man he believes best suited for the kingship from among those present. Family loyalty can play no role in the Choosing. It never has before; it should not now. Huw, just like you, must make a choice and vote on it according to the prompting of his honour. I believe he has done so and that his choice has fallen upon Meradoc. Huw is young and headstrong and impressionable, but he's no fool. He sees strength in Meradoc. And I believe he sees weakness in Uther."

"How can you say that?"

Daris shrugged. "I have heard Huw speak on this matter, and he professed grave doubts about Uther's suitability as a King."

"Pshaw! And what about Meradoc's lacks? The gods all know there are enough of those."

"The criteria Huw was applying to his measurement of Uther were ably answered in Meradoc. Huw was concerned mainly about Uther's constant absences and about his lack of responsibility for his own duties even now. He wondered how such things would affect Uther if he were King."

"Hah! That's just Huw's youth—that and the lack of having Uther here. There is no weakness in Uther Pendragon. He is his father's son and Ullic's grandson."

"And he stays far away from their kingdom! Huw Strongarm, Pendragon though he is, can see that fault in Uther, and I believe he has decided against Uther because of it. I admire him for that. It is you who really surprise me. Do you really believe Uther would be a better King than Meradoc?" Daris could see from the old man's fierce eyes that he was not going to deign to answer, so he pressed on.

"Understand me clearly, 'Launus, for I am not disputing that Uther might be the better man, but this concerns kingship and the welfare of this land and its people. And so I ask you whether—despite the man's long record of ignoring everything that happens here, and despite his full-time residence in this Roman place called Camulod—whether you would really vote for him over Meradoc, who, despite *his* faults, is always here, doing his duty as he sees it?"

"Aye, I would, without a moment's thought."

"That is what I fear most . . . your lack of thought." Seeing that he had offended his old friend, Daris quickly held up his hand. "Forgive me, 'Launs. I know you've thought about this long and hard but—" He broke off in mid-thought, then resumed without changing expression. "We're being watched by one of Meradoc's bodyguard."

"Let him look, then." Cativelaunus made no move to turn his head. "Where is he?"

"In the doorway behind us. He's doing nothing, just watching us . . . Now he's coming over."

Cativelaunus turned then to watch the man approach, but neither he nor Daris made any move to welcome or rebuff the newcomer. He was an unprepossessing character, tall and dark-haired, with a clean-shaven, scowling face and a small, lipless slash of a mouth framed between deep-lined, sunken cheeks. A short cloak was looped over his shoulders and beneath that he wore a cuirass of unpolished leather, bossed with iron studs. Heavy boots covered his legs to just below the knees, and beneath his tunic his thighs were covered by some kind of knitted leggings. A wide, thick sword-belt girdled his waist, supporting a heavy-looking short-sword with a riveted, wire-bound wooden grip and a long, one-edged stabbing dirk.

The man came to a halt a good two paces in front of them and then stood for several moments looking at the old Chief and ignoring the Druid completely. Finally he nodded slowly in an acknowledgment of Cativelaunus that was an insult in itself, and raised one hand to his waist, hooking his thumb around the hilt of his sword.

"Meradoc wants you to join him."

Daris drew in his breath to speak, but Cativelaunus waved him to silence. "Does he now?" he answered, his voice quiet and calm. "And who are you to call a Chief of Griffyd to your master?"

The other glared at him, clearly disconcerted, but said nothing. Cativelaunus spoke again.

"I asked you who you are. You have a name, I'd wager on that. When I know what it is, I might speak with you. Until then, I'll speak *to* you when I wish, and you will not speak to me until I ask you to. Come, Daris."

He turned to look at the High Priest, and the stranger spoke, his face flushed with anger.

"Petifax. Men call me Petifax."

Cativelaunus turned back and looked him up and down from head to foot, and then he nodded very gently. "Petifax. Good. Well, Petifax, tell Meradoc we'll be along when I've finished talking with the Chief Druid."

"He wants you now."

Cativelaunus ignored the man and turned to walk away, stretching his arm out to take hold of Daris's arm, but the stranger's hand was faster. He swooped forward and gripped the Chief by the wrist.

"I said *now*, old man!"

For half a heartbeat, Daris could not absorb what was happening. He saw Petifax's right hand, his sword hand, fasten on the Chief's left wrist, jerking it downward and back towards him. And then Cativelaunus was moving far more quickly than Daris could credit, spinning quickly inward, towards Daris and then past him. He heard a lightning-quick metallic slither as the old man's Roman short-sword hissed from its sheath, and then came the sound of an impact and the grating sound of a wide blade sinking deep into flesh. Cativelaunus took a long step backward, tugging his left wrist free of the other man's suddenly impotent grasp, and then he braced himself and leaned forward again, twisted his wrist hard and jerked his blade back sharply, with the confident strength of a man three decades younger.

Horror-stricken, Daris swung around to see Meradoc's man stagger forward, pulled by the sword blade, and then stop, hunched over and teetering for balance, his eyes gazing incredulously at the blood that was pulsing, spewing from the hole beneath his breastbone. The sword had passed clean through the leather of his breastplate, and the turn of the old Chief's wrist had spread the edges of the leather, letting the blood escape. Slowly, the man cupped his hands together in front of his breast, as though he were trying to catch or staunch the flow, and he raised his eyes, wide-staring, to look at Cativelaunus. His lips moved and his mouth worked, but no sound emerged. Cativelaunus stood watching him, balanced on the balls of his feet, his sword arm cocked as though for another blow.

"Aye, fool," he growled in a voice that seemed to lack all anger, "you're finished. He sent you out to fetch the old man, didn't he? And you, like all your witless kind, thought you could have some sport with someone who could not fight back. I am a Chief of clan Griffyd, you mindless animal. That means I am not as old and done as other old men are."

The dying man's eyes filled up with hate, and he fell to his knees, but even in the falling he gathered his spittle, blood-flecked on his lips, to spit his defiance. Cativelaunus struck first, however. The flat of his blade clanged solidly above the kneeling man's ear and Petifax toppled slowly sideways to sprawl in the dirt with the ungainliness that always distinguishes a corpse from a living man. The old Chief bent over and wiped his blade on the other's short cloak.

"Petifax. What kind of name is that? The place is full of heathens and Outlanders nowadays. You'd think someone would warn them of the penalties for laying hands upon a Chief, wouldn't you?" He looked up at Daris. "Are you going to puke?"

Daris swallowed hard and shook his head, gathering his wits. "No, no, I'm not. You know me better than that. It was . . . It just happened very suddenly. I had not expected it."

He looked around, feeling his heart hammering and expecting an uproar. There were people watching, standing motionless all around them, their attention attracted by the short, sharp scuffle, but no one made any move to interfere or to question what had happened. The fallen man was a stranger to all of them, and as such, he held no great interest.

"Why should you have expected it? You're a priest. You don't deal in such things—not at first-hand, anyway. But you see what I meant earlier by what I was saying."

Daris frowned, looking back to the dead man. "I don't follow you."

"This filth." Cativelaunus spurned the corpse with his boot. "He was no kin of ours, and there's too many of his kind about our would-be King. This is what we can all expect if Meradoc is chosen. 'Come here, now! Do this! Do that! Be here when I command! Come kiss my Kingly arse!' There'll be no life for any of us here, Daris, and little peace in years to come if he is chosen, because I, for one, won't suffer him or any man to dictate my comings and goings. And neither will any of the others. Cunbelyn and Hod might think now that they'll love having a Llewellyn in the King's seat, but they'll be marching to another drummer within months, you mark my words. We choose that one, we'll be at war within the year, and it won't be with Cornwall or any other Outlander. Our wars will be among ourselves."

Daris was staring at his friend now, appalled, recognizing the truth as he heard it. "That was the single strongest reason for my fears over Pendragon," he said finally. "I had it reasoned out that if Uther were King, and then went off to Camulod for any time, Meradoc would foment civil war."

"And so he would. You're right. But he'll do it anyway even as King, and if he's King, he'll be stronger than ever. So we have to decide what to do if Uther stays away."

"What *can* we do?"

"We can declare an interregnum."

Daris's jaw dropped. "How can we do that? We have a candidate."

"Aye, but he could be dead by this time tomorrow. That wouldn't surprise me at all. Men die all the time. Look at poor Petifax here." The old Chief grinned suddenly. "Shut your mouth, Daris, before something flies into it. I was but jesting. You don't think I'd mention it to you, the Chief Druid, if I was serious, do you?"

Daris turned his face away to cover his confusion, and then he stiffened. "Another one. Now the trouble begins."

"What trouble? He attacked me."

Cativelaunus turned and looked to where another man had emerged from the doorway of the hut and now stood staring at them, his eyes moving from the two standing men to the body sprawled at their feet. They both saw his eyes focus low down on Cativelaunus, and the old man bent forward to look down at himself. "Damnation, I've got blood all over my leg. Didn't jump back fast enough." He looked back up to where the newcomer stood watching, unmoving, but then the other man turned and walked away without a backward look.

"*There's* interesting, now. Who was that fellow? Another of Meradoc's animals?"

"Aye, but I know him. He's a Northerner. Owain of the Caves, they call him."

"Another foreigner. They're all foreigners. I wonder why he walked away like that? You'd think he'd be curious about his friend here, not to mention the excuse to raise a few voices. And where did he come from? He wasn't in there earlier."

Before Daris could answer, Brynn of Y Gaer emerged from the doorway and stood blinking in the sun. He saw them quickly, and they saw the shock on his face as he noticed the dead man. He glanced once over his shoulder to the door behind him, and then moved directly towards them.

"Watch this old rogue," Cativelaunus murmured. "Did you see how his jaw fell when he saw sweet Petifax here? Watch you now, by the time he reaches us, he'll have us believing he sees dead men lying at my feet every day." He raised his voice. "Have you been sent to fetch me too?"

Brynn reached them and sniffed gently, glancing casually towards Petifax's body. "Not if it means sharing that one's bed tonight. What happened?"

"He laid hands on me. Thought I wasn't being quick enough to please him or his master."

"Hmm. Well, his master's pleased enough right now. He just announced that he'll be King tomorrow. Uther won't be coming. He offered to take wagers on it."

"Did he, by the gods? What happened?"

"I don't know. Some fellow walked in and stood against the wall and—"

"Was it that fellow yonder? The one walking away, over there in the green?"

Brynn turned and peered in the direction of Cativelaunus's pointing finger, squinting against the sun's brightness. "Aye, that's the one. Who is he? Do you know?"

"That's not important. What did he say?"

Brynn shrugged his shoulders, dipping his head to one side as he did so. "Nothing, didn't say a word. He simply walked in and leaned against the wall for a space, then went out again as soon as Meradoc had finished speaking. I happened to be looking towards the door as he came in, else I might not have noticed him. Didn't pay much attention to him, either, except to wonder who he was that he could simply stroll into the Chief's hut like a Chief himself. Then I realized he must be one of Meradoc's crew . . . his special ones. So I turned back to Meradoc, and that's when he saw the fellow too. He stopped in the middle of what he was saying . . . something about Lot of Cornwall . . . and next thing I know, he's announcing that Uther Pendragon will not be coming for the Choosing. The word had come to him this morning, he said, that Uther remains in Camulod and has no interest in being King in Cambria. I tell you, it was strange."

"What was strange, Brynn?"

Brynn of Y Gaer turned to look at Daris. "Everything, Daris, everything. He said he'd received word this morning, but it seemed to me that he was making an announcement of something he had just learned. You know, the way he spoke, blurting it out like that when a moment earlier he'd been talking about something else altogether. It didn't make sense."

"Ah, but by the gods it did!" Cativelaunus's voice was low, angry and filled with tension. "The message was delivered when that other whoreson walked in through the doorway. He didn't have to speak, I'll wager. If he had been sent to get rid of Uther Pendragon, then all he had to do was show his face to announce it done. Whoreson!"

Cativelaunus began to walk, moving quickly, his jaw set. Daris reached out and caught him by the sleeve.

"'Launus, wait! Where are you going? You can't just walk in there angry and confront Meradoc with your suspicions. He has his men about him, and you don't. They'd cut you down before you could say anything."

"You take me for a fool? I don't want to breathe the air that whoreson breathes. I'm going to find some of my own men, and then we're going to find that other whoreson—what did you call him?"

"Owain. Owain of the Caves."

"Aye, him, and once we have him, we'll have what he knows, because he doesn't have the balls to stand the kind of pain I'm going to put him through without spilling his guts. And once we have his story on Uther's death, then Meradoc's dead too, and we have inter-regnum. Come on, Brynn."

Daris stood and watched the two old men sweep away towards their own section of the camp, moving with a speed and determination that belied their age.

SEVENTEEN

Meradoc was aware that Cativelaunus had not come at his summons, but for the time being he cared little. The other old fool, Brynn, had wandered outside to join his friend, so by now he would have told Cativelaunus the news about Pendragon, and it really made no difference whether the old Chief came or not. His good opinion was no longer anything for Meradoc to fret over. It was already too late for anyone—even the oldest, most respected Chiefs—to alter tomorrow's outcome. Meradoc would be chosen with his majority of four votes. The votes of the two old Griffyds were now worth no more than gusts of hot air.

Meradoc turned away from the others, moving towards the cask of ale that sat against the wall behind him and leaving Chief Cunbelyn talking to himself and blinking his bulging eyes as he accepted the fact that Meradoc had snubbed him once again. Meradoc was unconscious of the insult he had given. In his eyes, Cunbelyn had always been a fool and always would be, and Meradoc avoided him, except for those times when he needed the man's support as a Llewellyn Chief. Now he had more important things than Cunbelyn's witless prattle to think about. Tomorrow Cunbelyn would cast his vote in favour of Meradoc, and after that he would be expendable again, practically useless.

Meradoc had not known how concerned he was over Uther Pendragon until Owain of the Caves had walked through that door and sidled sideways to lean his back against the wall. No smile, no recognition, no acknowledgment, no hint of satisfaction—merely the simple fact of his being there. That was Owain, blunt to the point of absolute silence. "I'm here," his presence said. "Make your own judgment on the how and why of it."

Meradoc had made his judgment immediately, surprised to feel his heart bounding beneath his ribs in profound relief. He had been talking at the time, he recalled, but no longer had any idea what he had been saying. Whatever it was, it had lost all significance beside the import of the Cave Man's appearance. He had stopped, he knew, in mid-word, but then he had resumed almost immediately, making the transition smoothly, he believed, as though catching up with his own thoughts. He had mentioned only casually that he had been informed earlier in the day that Uther Pendragon should no longer be considered in contention for the King's seat. Uther had announced his decision not merely to absent himself from the Choosing, but to remain as far away from the Pendragon lands as he could. His home, now and forever, would be Camulod. Meradoc had been casual in his announcement, almost offhand, he reminded himself now, amazed at his own reticence when he had wanted to leap into the air and scream in triumph, trumpeting the Pendragon's death to the world.

Now he could take time to savour the satisfaction, and in the act of pouring a mug of beer, Meradoc suddenly realized that he was ravenous. He gulped at the foaming beer, then put it down again and ripped a wedge of bread from the large loaf on the table in front of him, digging a hole in the soft centre with his fingers and stuffing it with several of the small, crisp-skinned, strongly smoked fish he had loved ever since early boyhood, feeling the saliva spurting beneath his tongue as their strong, salty odour filled his nostrils. Clamping the folded wedge of bread tightly, he raised it to his mouth, but before he bit into it he caught sight of Janus, his most trusted man, watching him from his position against the far wall of the room. Meradoc paused, anticipating the bite he was about to take, and beckoned the man over with a toss of his head. Janus was beside him in two strides.

"I sent Petifax to fetch the old man, Cativelaunus. He hasn't come back. Find him and send him to me. Then find Owain. Tell him I want to see him within the hour in my tent. But find Petifax first."

As Meradoc was speaking, a shadow darkened the doorway as Daris, the High Priest, paused awkwardly on the threshold. Meradoc watched him step inside, silent, wondering what had made the Druid stop the way he had. Daris had seen him and was looking at him strangely.

"He is dead," the Druid said.

Meradoc blinked, uncomprehending, wondering if by some freak chance Daris had heard about Uther's murder.

"Who is?" he asked, aware that he still held the bread up in front of his mouth.

"Your man, Petifax."

"What?" Meradoc had heard the words, but their meaning had not yet penetrated.

"Petifax is dead. Cativelaunus killed him."

"Cative—?" Meradoc stood staring, his thoughts tumbling over each other. All sound in the room had died and he knew that everyone was listening, waiting for his reaction, but for long moments he had no words with which to respond. Finally he jerked his head in a short, sharp negative. "That can't be. I sent him to bring the old man to me."

"I know, and he tried too hard. He laid hold of 'Launus and tried to drag him here. 'Launus killed him where he stood."

"By the swarming gods! Where is he?"

Daris raised an eyebrow. "Who, 'Launus or Petifax? 'Launus is gone, I don't know where, but your man Petifax is lying out in front of the hut."

Meradoc threw his untasted bread onto the table and strode to the door, shouldering Daris aside as he passed, aware of the others crowding behind him. He saw the sprawled body immediately from the doorway and stopped short, so that someone following too close behind bumped into him, pushing him forward through the exit. Ignoring the jostling, Meradoc gathered himself, taking a firm grip on his shock, and made himself walk forward slowly, ignoring the others as his eyes swept the space ahead of him.

There were several people standing around gaping, but the body lay in a space of its own and was very obviously lifeless. Meradoc kept moving, more and more slowly, until he was within touching distance of the dead man. Someone else passed by him and stopped even closer to the corpse. Because he was looking down at Petifax, Meradoc could only see the other's lower legs, but he knew it was young Huw Strongarm.

"He's dead, no doubt of that." The young Chief's voice was very mild.

"Aye," Meradoc muttered, his voice choked with fury. "And I'll be—"

"And so he should be, the fool."

Meradoc glanced up, his eyes wide with disbelief. "What do you mean?"

The Pendragon glanced quickly at him, and then his eyes returned to the body at their feet. "What kind of fool lays unwelcome hands on a ruling Chief? A soon-to-be-dead fool! This idiot obviously thought he was dealing with an impotent old man. Hah!" The bark of laughter was savage, belying the age of the boy from whom it issued. "Old 'Launus, impotent? I'll wager Petifax didn't even see the stroke that killed him. He was lucky. Cativelaunus could have had him flayed alive, as an example to others. I once watched my father chop the hands off a drunkard who attacked him on a dark night, not even knowing he was a Chief. It's the one law that no one ever is allowed to break: lay hands on a Chief and die."

Meradoc was staring wide-eyed at the younger man, gritting his teeth and forcing himself to quell his anger. Huw Strongarm's conviction was absolute, and Meradoc knew that he himself, despite his fury, was going to have to accept the younger man's judgment as the verdict of all other thinking men. What Huw had said was true, and had the dead man not been one of Meradoc's own closest and most trusted confederates, then Meradoc himself would have been the first to condemn him and swear that Petifax had earned the death that claimed him. But Petifax had been *his* man! And so this killing was a challenge to his strength and should be—*must* be—punished. But there were politics involved, matters of great delicacy, so this was not the time to rant and rave.

The Llewellyn inhaled deeply, straightening his spine, stretching his head high and turning his eyes towards the others who now surrounded them, being careful to keep his face calm and empty of expression. Vengeance he would have, he swore to himself; Cativelaunus would die for this, but later, and in secret. In the meantime, he had spent too much time courting and cultivating Huw Strongarm's good regard to jeopardize it now. Even the thought of risking the young man's vote chilled him as it occurred to him. An abstention by Huw Strongarm, combined with the antipathy of the two old fools from the northeast, would make three votes against his three Llewellyn votes and give the final Choosing vote to the High Priest. The thought of that was not pleasant, for Meradoc knew in his deepest soul that even without Uther Pendragon's competition, Daris, given the chance, would cast a vote for interregnum before he would back Meradoc. He let out his breath slowly, then reached out one foot and slid his toe beneath the dead man's wrist before pushing the lifeless arm to lie closer to the body.

"Aye," he said quietly. "Petifax was hotheaded, and sometimes foolish because of it. He was ever . . . obedient, nonetheless, and I had sent him to bring 'Launus to speak with me. I meant, of course, that he should *ask* the Chief to join me, but I might not have made that clear enough. Who would have thought I'd need to? But Petifax was not of our people, and so I sent the poor fool to his death . . ." He stopped, then shook his head sorrowfully for the benefit of those around him.

"Farewell, then, Petifax. I prized you for your loyalty, but never for your brains."

No one else spoke, and Meradoc looked over to where some of the loiterers stood watching the gathering of Chiefs. He pointed to the largest of them.

"You there, the big fellow. Pick out a couple of your friends to help you take this body and dispose of it. Bury him deep, and then report to me for the reward you will have earned. And mind you treat him well—he was a faithful follower of mine. Handle his body with respect and bring his weapons safely back to me. I'll pay you well." He swung back to the others. "Come, my friends," he said, his voice filled with sadness. "There's naught more we can do for Petifax, except remember him. He fell foul of the law and died for it. Come you and drink with me to Petifax's death and to the life he led."

As the group filed back into the stone hut, Janus sidled close to his Chief.

"You still want me to find Owain, Master?"

"I do, but I will meet him later, now that this has happened. Tell him to come to me after the evening meal."

The drinking to the memory of Petifax grew into an evening-long carousal, and Daris left early, knowing he had a hundred things to do before the fall of night.

Some time after the Druid's departure, Janus returned with word for Meradoc that Owain of the Caves was nowhere to be found and had evidently left the encampment. Meradoc was angry at first, but he soon convinced himself that he should be tolerant of his servant's laxity. The man had done good work, and he had been gone in the doing of it for a month. He deserved a night to himself . . .

Cativelaunus of Carmarthen and Brynn of Y Gaer remained absent and unregretted at the festivities.

Meradoc struggled awake and pushed himself up onto one elbow, blinking at the shadowy shape that towered over him in the grey light. Then, recognizing the Cave Man, he shook his head in an attempt to clear his mind and winced at the hammer blow of pain the movement caused. Cursing and groaning, he struggled to sit up, spitting to clear his mouth. Owain of the Caves made no sound but simply stood there, slightly hunched, beneath the sloping roof, staring down at him.

The sound of heavy rain battering at the leather of the tent above Owain's head set the Chief's teeth on edge. Through the partially open flaps he could see shimmering puddles of rainwater being whipped by the force of the downpour. He squinted and spat again, then pulled his knees up until he could sit straight-backed.

"How long has it been raining?"

"Most of the night."

"By the swarming gods, I must have drunk the entire cask last night. Where were you?"

The big Northerner shrugged. "I had things to tend to. I thought you'd have no need of me, and I'd been long without a woman."

"Hmm. What hour is it?"

"Just after dawn. I thought you'd want to be astir early today. I brought water, in case you need to wash the sleep out of your face before going out."

Meradoc looked to where Owain was pointing and nodded his head, seeing the leather bucket that hung from the pegged frame at the foot of his cot. "Good. Where's Janus?"

"He was here when I arrived. Don't know where he is now, but he probably went looking for food. There are no cook fires this morning. I'll be outside when you're ready."

Meradoc watched the tall man leave, stooping to clear the flaps as he went, and then he dragged himself free of his sleeping skins, stood up and stretched. His head felt awful and he reeled, staggering sideways for half a step until he regained his balance. Mumbling curses to himself, he scratched at his groin, aware that it was past time for another delousing, and then he stooped to fling cold water on his face, scrubbing at his eyes and then rinsing his mouth. Shivering from the shock of the water and the dampness of the morning, he dried his hands and face on a sour-smelling piece of rag and then dug into a chest of clothes, pulling out a warmer tunic than the one in which he had slept. He pulled the soiled tunic over his head, noticing the stink of stale beer that clung to it, and shrugged into the heavier one, tugging and pulling at it until it hung comfortably, then strapping his sword belt over it. When he had finished, he glanced up again at the roof of the tent, noting the shiny wetness of the saturated leather, then peered blearily about him, searching for his campaign cloak. It lay in a heap on the floor in the corner where he had dropped it several days earlier. Moments later, safely muffled in the heavy garment, he thrust aside the tent flaps and stepped out into the torrential rain.

There were upwards of half a score of men standing about, all evidently waiting for him to emerge, and he blinked at them, failing to recognize them immediately since they were all swathed in protective, heavy-weather cloaks of wax-scraped wool. Owain of the Caves he recognized, since he had seen him mere moments earlier, and Huw Strongarm was there too, his beardless face setting him apart. He recognized Cunbelyn next by his elaborate cloak, despite the fact that its bright colours were rain-sodden almost to the point of blackness. He recognized the other Llewellyn Chief too, his own cousin, Hod, by the width of his enormous shoulders. Then another of the watchers raised his hand and pulled his hood back from his face, revealing himself as Cativelaunus, which meant that the smaller man behind him must be Brynn of Y Gaer.

"What's going on?" Meradoc demanded, his face flushing in a frown as he looked from face to face. "Where's my man Janus?"

"Trying to find a pool that's still enough to let him see which of his two faces is redder," someone said, joking about the two-headed Roman god who could see past and future at the same time. But no one laughed. "In the meantime, we came to help you welcome the Choosing day."

Meradoc turned to face the man who had spoken, knowing that something was badly wrong. "Garreth? Garreth Whistler, is that you?"

"Aye, it is, wishing a good day to you, Meradoc."

"How came you here today?"

"He came with me."

The voice was deep, its tone emotionless, and its owner, a tall, broad-shouldered man who had been standing farthest away at the very rear of the crowd stepped forward as he spoke, throwing the hood back from his head. Meradoc felt his heart freeze as he recognized Uther Pendragon. And beside Uther, Owain of the Caves stood motionless, staring at Meradoc with his arms crossed over his chest, hands tucked beneath his armpits for warmth, his face expressionless. Owain wore no cloak, and the shoulders of his tunic were sodden. Meradoc gaped from Uther to Owain and back to Uther. Uther did not wait for him to find his tongue.

"We arrived late last night, long after everyone had gone to bed, so we made no noise, wishing to disturb no one. Are you not glad to see me, Meradoc? I almost missed the Choosing. That would have been shameful, would it not?" He waited for the space of three heartbeats and then spoke again. "What, have you nothing to say?"

Meradoc made to speak, then coughed to clear his throat, determined to brazen this out despite the fact that he had no idea what had gone wrong. "Well," he grunted, "I'll not pretend I'm glad to see you, Pendragon, for I'm not. We had received word that you would not be coming."

"No, Llewellyn, not so. Word that I was dead is what you had, and you believed it. Because when Owain here came back yesterday, you assumed he had done what you sent him to do, which was to kill me, in much the same way you had my father killed." The pause that followed was very slight, but Meradoc felt the world crash down around him then at the flat, truthful accusation in the Pendragon's words.

"Except, of course," Uther continued, "Owain's arrow would not have been tipped with venom. Owain does not deal in poisoned arrows—has no need to."

Meradoc tried to swallow, to clear his mouth, but his throat was swollen with panic, and the beat of his heart was hammering loudly in his ears. He tried to conjure a way to win back the initiative as Uther continued speaking, but the words hit him hard, falling like hailstones about his unprepared ears.

"But the gods permitted me to save Owain's life, and so, being a man of honour, he made no attempt on mine. He knew you'd have him killed for that, though, and he was prepared to leave Cambria in order to save his life. Until I offered him a place with me. He liked that, because he knows he'll be in less peril with me . . . I do my own killing, unlike you."

"You're mad, Pendragon." Meradoc's fingers closed around the hilt of his sword beneath his cloak.

"No, Llewellyn, that I am not. You suborned some of my father's guards, and they allowed the Cornish bowman to sneak through our lines and kill their King, my father. Then you killed the guards before they could be questioned and condemn you."

Meradoc had no way of knowing that Uther Pendragon was merely provoking him, quoting what he had been told without a feather's weight of proof, for what he had said was the complete truth. And so Meradoc moved, leaping towards the Pendragon,

screaming denial and whipping his sword from its sheath, thrusting
the folds of his cloak back over his shoulder to free his arm. But he
was far too late. As his weapon swept up and down in the killing
stroke, Uther's sword arm emerged from beneath his cloak to block
the blow, his long cavalry sword already bare, and the blades
clashed and then slid together loudly as they met. Each man leaned
into his blow, absorbing the strength of the other's strike, so that
they strained together for long moments, face to face and chest to
chest. Then Uther spun sideways and away, leaving Meradoc to
sprawl forward onto his hands and knees while he himself sprang
backwards, shrugging his loosened cloak so that it fell behind him,
leaving him unencumbered. He stepped carefully away from the
wet, discarded cloak, leaving it well clear of his feet, and then began
to circle, half crouched, as he watched Meradoc struggle to his feet
and divest himself of his own cloak.

Uther was in no hurry. He was quite content to give Meradoc
all the time he needed to collect himself and prepare to die. The
others moved to form a wide ring about the two, and as they did
so the rain stopped falling, so suddenly that the absence of its
noise seemed louder than the noise had been, and the sound of
squelching feet was loud.

Meradoc hefted his sword in his right hand and pulled his long,
one-edged dirk with his left, then began circling too, his narrowed
eyes fixed on Uther's. Both men were renowned warriors, both
champions, and none of the watchers made any attempt to wager on
the outcome of this fight.

Meradoc made the first move, darting forward and swinging his
sword upwards in a backhanded, lethal slash that Uther blocked
easily. But in the moment of the block Meradoc changed his thrust,
pulling his sword away and twisting his body to the right as he
brought the dirk in his left hand up in an underhand thrust that
should have disembowelled the Pendragon. Uther, however, had
been waiting for him to do precisely that. He had seen Meradoc
fight before, and as the wicked, stabbing thrust arched towards him,
Uther rose to tiptoe and bent sharply at the waist, twisting away and
sucking in his gut so that the blade slid by him, catching its point in

his tunic. His left hand dropped to catch Llewellyn's left wrist and he pulled sharply, swinging his weight and dragging the other man across in front of him, then smashing him savagely on the back of the head with the pommel of his sword as he passed by.

The Llewellyn Chief went to his knees again, his hands in the mud, his grip on the dirk lost as he fell, and Uther moved quickly, stepping sideways again until he stood alongside Meradoc's left shoulder. The desire for this man's blood, the blood of his father's murderer, was a hammering urgency that threatened to overwhelm him, and he came close to ending it then and there, raising his long sword to plunge its point between the other's shoulder blades and into his heart. But that would have been too easy, too swift. He screamed his hatred and kicked Meradoc hard in the side of the head instead, knocking him over onto his side in the mud, and then he stepped away again, grounding his sword, and waited for him to get up.

Behind his back, someone in the circle muttered something indistinct, and suddenly Uther was facing the onlookers, ignoring Meradoc as he searched their faces in the strengthening morning light, his sword point weaving in front of him as he silently challenged any of them, all of them, to come against him. But no one moved, and nothing else was said, and so he turned back towards his enemy. The Llewellyn was up on his knees again, shaking his head, trying to clear it. He had lost his sword as well as his dagger. Uther saw both weapons, the dagger lying close to his own feet. He stooped and picked it up with his left hand, then threw it gently so that it landed with a clank across the blade of the sword. When he spoke, his voice was calm and quiet, betraying no hint of the rage in him, and because of that his words were more chilling than they might otherwise have seemed.

"Two weapons, Meradoc. There they are. Yours to use on me, although from the way you keep losing them, I begin to think you've lost the knack of how to employ them. Too many others have been doing your killing for you recently. Pick them up, whoreson, and clean them, so they won't slip in your grasp. Take your time and get your wind. I want you to be well aware of what is happening when I kill you. My father's blood demands more punishment than a swift stab in the back. Get up and fight, for you have no other choice. Owain of the Caves now stands with me, and all your other creatures are dead, so there's no hope of further treachery saving you."

The taunts brought Meradoc to his feet, where he stood swaying, blood and spittle drooling from his broken mouth. He wiped his face roughly with a sleeve and then bent slowly to retrieve his weapons, never taking his eyes off Uther, expecting to be attacked when he was most vulnerable. But Uther merely stood waiting, making no attempt to close the distance between them. Meradoc cleaned the hilts of both weapons on his outer tunic, then grasped them firmly, hefting them, testing their weight and breathing deeply until he had regained his wind. Then, crouched and silent, he moved forward.

The fight went savagely after that, neither man taking the slightest risk of losing his footing on the treacherous ground. The sound of clanging blades seemed to go on forever as they dodged and weaved, each seeking the advantage and neither seeming able to gain sufficient momentum for a clean killing stroke. The watchers made no sound, aware that they were witnessing an epic struggle, their eyes constantly shifting from one to the other of the two superb fighters. Meradoc was grim-faced, frowning in concentration, calling up every vestige of his renowned skills in what he knew was his only opportunity to salvage anything of honour, or even life. He cursed monotonously under his breath as he sought, time after time, to win the advantage promised to him by having two blades against Uther's one. Uther, on the other hand, showed no emotion at all. His face was impassive, the planes of his cheekbones and forehead almost polished in their smoothness. Only his tight, seemingly lipless mouth and glittering eyes betrayed the implacable anger that consumed him. He moved on his toes, with the confidence and strength of the great red dragon that was his emblem, his every movement precise and dangerous, wary and murderous.

And then, after one breathtaking display of stroke and counterstroke, Uther jumped back, blood streaming from his left arm, where the edge of his opponent's blade had nicked him deeply above the elbow.

He held his arm up, showing the blood to all of them but speaking to the Llewellyn. "Feast your eyes on it, whoreson. It is the last Pendragon blood you will ever see."

He leaped forward and the angry clangour of iron began again. This time, however, it ended quickly when Uther's scything blade struck Meradoc's sword arm, cleaving it above the wrist and almost severing the hand completely. With a strangled cry, Meradoc dropped his other weapon and clutched at the upraised stump that was already jetting bright life blood, and as he strained there, mouth agape, Uther stepped in and stabbed hard, thrusting with his entire weight, his blade plunging into the soft flesh beneath the other's sternum. The Llewellyn Chief screamed, choking, and Uther raised one foot high, placed it on Meradoc's chest, pulled his weapon free and then stepped back. Meradoc hung there, gaping and gasping, unable to utter a sound, then fell to his knees, head down, staring at the hole in his chest.

Calmly, his face expressionless, Uther stepped forward again and took a position by the kneeling man's side. His sword swept up once more, high over his head, then hissed down with all his strength behind it. The blade sliced cleanly through the Llewellyn's outstretched neck, severing his head, and a fierce jet of blood gouted three times before the headless body fell to earth.

Uther had turned away before the corpse collapsed, crossing directly to where the other Llewellyn chiefs, Cunbelyn and Hod, stood stunned by the swiftness of their kinsman's death. The Pendragon came close to them, facing them directly, his right arm extended slightly to hold the tip of his red-dripping blade above the wet earth, not threatening anyone directly but visibly in evidence. More blood dripped from his other arm, this his own, but he ignored it completely.

"Cunbelyn," he said, "Hod, do I yet have living enemies among Llewellyn? Does either you feel any need to avenge your kinsman's death as I have avenged my father's?"

Cunbelyn merely shook his head, unable to find words, but Hod the Strong lived up to his name. He drew himself erect and looked the Pendragon Chief straight in the eye. "No," he growled. "I see no need to fight with you. You challenged him on what you had been told. He drew his blade on you and we all witnessed it. The fight was fair, and more than fair. You won. And if the information that you threw at him was true, he deserved what befell him."

"It was true. And he made no attempt to deny it, because he knew whence it came."

"Aye." Hod the Strong turned his head slightly to look at Owain of the Caves, who stared back at him, his face expressionless. "But we'll never know for sure, will we?" He glanced back at Uther. "Very well, then. I'll tell my people what occurred, and I'll make no attempt to stir them against you, but I can't speak for Cunbelyn."

The other, hearing his name, held up his hand palm outward and shook his head. "Nor I," he said. "Nor I."

"So be it." Uther turned away from the two Chiefs back towards the other witnesses, who were now standing in a quiet group.

"Have someone clean that up," he said to no one in particular, nodding in the general direction of the headless corpse, and then he stalked away, still carrying his bloody sword, followed by Garreth Whistler and Owain of the Caves. He had taken no more than four steps, however, before he stopped and looked back over his shoulder to where young Huw Strongarm stood watching him. For a short while he stood there, staring deliberately at the younger man, and then he dipped his head in the tiniest of nods.

"You'll yet have some questions to ask me, I think, eh, Cousin? More than had occurred to you when we spoke earlier, no? Come then, if you like, and I'll try to answer them for you."

Young Strongarm nodded in return, then threw his cloak backwards, over his shoulders, drew a deep breath and stepped forward to accompany the trio.

Cativelaunus watched them leave and then threw off his hood and shook out his long white hair before turning to Brynn of Y Gaer.

"So," he said. "There's an end to uncertainty! No interregnum. Daris will be happy. Let's go and tell him." He snapped his fingers to attract the attention of one of his own minor chieftains, then waved towards the body of Meradoc.

"Throw this in a hole with the others—a deep hole. Three bodies, four heads. Make sure you plant them well, too, because we don't want to be snouting them later." He stopped short, staring at the man to whom he had been speaking, then leaned slightly forward and repeated himself more slowly. "Three bodies, I said— four heads. Count them if you don't believe me. Meradoc, Petifax and Janus the two-faced Roman!"

EIGHTEEN

Huw Strongarm felt very strange. He would be hit with an over-powering urge to laugh, shout and leap around, and then within the space of a few heartbeats, he would want instead to weep like a child—although his dignity as a warrior and a Chief would never have permitted any possibility of his being able to do either. Nonetheless, his breast felt filled to bursting with tumultuous feelings, all of them demanding some kind of violent, demonstrative, physical outlet. Rather than give in to any of them, however, Huw forced himself to walk stiff-legged, taking great strides, chin pulled in to his chest, fists clenched, arms pumping, his eyes fixed on the path ahead of him, following the tracked footprints in the mud.

Huw Strongarm, Chief of the northern Pendragon clans, was not yet seventeen years old, a boy in all but size and rank. But no one who knew the youth had ever doubted his natural leadership. Even in childhood, he had outstripped his cradle-mates at every stage of growth and development, being the first among them to crawl, and then to walk, to talk and even to reason coherently and with logic. By the time he was eleven, approaching twelve, his voice had begun to break, and long before his thirteenth birthday he had acquired a coarse body hair. But even so, no one, himself included, had been pre-pared for the incredible growth that he experienced in the two years that followed. Almost overnight, it seemed, between one season and the next, the boy exploded in size, outstripping his own friends almost visibly day by day, until he towered even over his father's chieftains, some of whom were the largest men in the Federation.

Encouraged by all the wonders that were happening to him so quickly, he might easily have become a bully or a loud-mouthed, unpopular, opinionated lout. But Huw did neither. By the time his beloved father drowned, just prior to his son's sixteenth birthday, Huw had completely endeared himself to all his people simply by being himself—modest yet confident, admirable and unmatchable in everything he did. He had undergone the Manhood Rites at the age of fourteen, a full year ahead of his birth-year brethren, going alone into the forest to subsist by his own wits for two long weeks, and then returning with the skins and pelts of creatures he had hunted and killed during that time. Among those had been the pelt of a black wolf and the tail and knife-edged tusks of a wild boar. Few men in living memory had returned with two such trophies from a single foray, and only one boy entering manhood had ever equalled either kill in size, by bringing back the skin of a large bear.

Huw knew that there were some who sniggered behind his back at the enormous spurt of growth that had shot his body into a man's size, and who claimed that his mind had been weakened accordingly by deprivation, but most of the time he was able to ignore such things completely, being clever enough to understand that the disdain of his detractors was born of jealousy. They called him a freak, envious of his size and strength, and some of them even whispered that his shocking growth had been magical, achieved through sorcery. For many months now, however, no one had dared say or even whisper such things within range of his ears . . . not since the day he had been pushed too far and had thrashed two of his own cousins, breaking bones, blackening eyes and drawing blood from both, despite the fact that they were both half a decade older than he was.

As he walked now, Huw smiled, remembering that occasion. People thought he had lost his temper that day—the first time in years that anyone could remember Huw Pendragon having done so—but Huw himself knew differently. What he had done was deliberate, carefully considered and planned in advance, and then carried out with precision and dispatch. He had even manipulated the circumstances, staging the event so carefully and completely that not even the principals, two bullying louts from another branch of his clan, had suspected that they were being used. Huw had contrived matters so that his cousins had ended up taunting and challenging him in a public place, raucously belittling his unseemly size. The punishment he had then meted out was swift, thorough and well-deserved, and a clear warning to others to respect the matter, and the manner, of the differences that set him apart.

In the aftermath, while they were still dazed and uncomprehending, he was deeply solicitous, apologizing for his loss of temper as he saw to the tending of their injuries.

Since that day, there had been no challenges of any kind issued to Huw in any way. Upon the death of his father earlier in the year, the elders of his clan had ratified Huw's succession to the Chief's chair, ignoring his extreme youth and honouring instead his physical prowess, his natural sagacity, astounding in one so young, and his unfailing goodwill.

Now, Huw's conflicting moods were born of the knowledge that he would be one of the six men personally responsible for raising Uther Pendragon to the kingship. Part of him—the better, more realistic part, Huw knew—was convinced that he would be doing the right thing and that Uther would make a fine, perhaps even a magnificent King—a natural champion of truth and honour, seeking and achieving nothing but the best for the people who were his responsibility.

Another part of Huw, however, was less than convinced of that. That jaundiced, less trusting and more cynical part of him lay deep down, hidden at the very bottom of his mind, sullied and stained by the impressions of the trampling, careless feet of those who had disappointed and disillusioned the young man during his boyhood—ambitious men to whom truth and honour were worthless things, sacrificed early in the struggle to realize their own designs. That such men were everywhere, and that they were not always easy to identify, Huw was acutely aware. One of them, Meradoc, lay newly dead, and until a short time before his death, Huw had been completely in his thrall, convinced that the Llewellyn Chief was the man who should be the chosen King and that Uther Pendragon was an enemy to the good of the Federation.

Huw was forced to admit to himself that he had permitted Meradoc to treat him as a foolish boy, easily gulled. By following Meradoc's suggestions uncritically, Huw had unwittingly condoned the man's treatment of him, making himself appear foolish and justifying Meradoc's outrageous belief in his own rightness.

It was only when the young Chief had stopped short, gazing wide-eyed at the bloodied corpse of Meradoc, that he had felt the truth of that.

Huw was now making his way back to his own tent, his mood still swinging wildly from elation to consternation each time he remembered an important question he should have asked Uther but had forgotten. He felt the weight of responsibility that came with his vote, and a new feeling that one could never be certain about any man while the course of his life and the tests of his character still lay ahead of him.

He did not see the young woman who stood waiting for him until he had drawn level with her and heard her call his name, but then he swung towards her and his face broke into a great grin of welcome.

"Glynda! What are you doing out here? I thought this was your day to work with Balin, slaving over accounts and reckonings?"

"It is—I mean, it was—but he didn't want me there today. They're all too excited about the Choosing, so Lord Balin let me go free."

"You mean Balin admitted that there are some things more important than teaching my little sister to read and write? I find that difficult to believe."

"No you do not, you beast! You are simply being nasty because you have a mean and vicious nature and you cannot resist being deliberately cruel and unpleasant when you find someone who cannot stand up to you."

His sister's laughing eyes belied the apparent harshness of her words as she swung towards him, linking her arm with his and then pulling him into a spinning, dance-like turn that threatened harm to his dignity. For the space of two heartbeats Huw tried to resist, and then he threw back his head and laughed, taking her hands in his own and dancing with her, throwing himself into the spin and leaning back against the pull of her weight as he swung her around, hard. Five, six, seven times he swung her in a circle, faster and faster each time around, until her toes seemed barely to touch the wet ground and she was in as much danger of flying off her feet as he was of slipping on the treacherous wet earth. Huw nonetheless continued to swing her at hurtling speed for four more turns before slowing down gradually until he could safely release her. As soon as he did so, both of them checked themselves and laughingly attempted to stand erect, but dizziness sent them staggering helplessly until they fell to the muddy, rain-soaked grass and sobered rapidly with the shock of the cold earth.

"Huw, you oaf!" Glynda shrieked. "Help me up, quickly!"

Huw, however, was incapable of helping her. Twice he tried to struggle to his feet, only to fall back each time, laughing helplessly and spreading his hands to indicate his powerlessness to help his sister, whose disgust seemed to increase from moment to moment. He referred to her constantly as his "little" sister, but Glynda was, in fact, older, a half-sister, born to another of their father's wives, who had also borne a stillborn son a year and a half later, mere weeks before Huw's arrival. The two children, although born eighteen months apart to different mothers, had grown up together, because their mothers had become close friends during the common time of their pregnancy and that friendship had endured, with Huw's mother supporting Glynda's after the loss of her stillborn child and sharing her own newborn, Huw, with the other woman, easing her loss. As a result, the two children grew to be in each other's company almost constantly and to develop much closer bonds to each other than most of their true siblings had. Two members of an enormous number of the Chief's offspring, with Huw the eldest son, they had also benefited from the fact that their numerous siblings were grouped apart from them in age. Many of the girls were far older than "the two close ones," as their father called them, and a few brothers and sisters were much younger, born to their father Caerliss's last and youngest wife. Caerliss himself, half-brother to the mighty Ullic, War Chief and King of the Pendragon Federation, had been Ullic's youngest sibling and a potent, productive Chief of his own clan, fathering no fewer than twenty-seven children upon five wives.

Before Huw could catch his breath, Glynda was back on her feet, brushing at her clothing while she pretended to be angry.

"Look at me, I'm soaked through to the skin, and you're no better, Huw Pendragon! Have you no sense at all, knocking me off my feet like that to land in a puddle?"

Huw's mouth gaped. "Knocked you off—? I didn't knock you off your feet, you fleering little devil. You fell down with no help from me. You were the one who set about me, pulling me into your wild dance, and me with a Chief's matters to attend to." He pulled himself up to his full height, crossing his arms on his chest and thrusting his chin into the air. "Now behave yourself, woman, and guard your tongue."

She blinked at him. "Guard my tongue? Against what?"

"Against arrest. If you keep this up, you will force me to summon my guards and have you locked away where your nagging won't deeve me . . ."

Quite suddenly, however, the bantering mood had passed, and now Glynda was looking down at herself in dismay. "Look at me, Huw! Now I'll have to go and change everything before I can go to the Choosing. These clothes are destroyed."

"No, they are not. They're fine—they'll dry out directly and you'll never be able to see they were wet."

She looked at him as if he were demented. "I can't be seen looking like this! What will people think?"

Huw was half laughing, looking slightly bewildered. "They'll think what they want to think, and who among us cares? If you do, it'll be for the first time ever. If anyone asks you what happened and how you got your back all wet, tell them it might have happened one of two ways: either you were rutting in the rain with a stranger, or you were dancing on the wet grass with your brother and you slipped. They think we're both mad enough, anyway, and they all love to be able to shudder in outrage at the antics of me, who should be a sober Chief always."

Glynda was standing almost on tiptoe now, pulling at the cold, wet material of her bodice where it clung to the shape of her waist and belly.

"What's he like, Huw? Is he lovely?"

"What's who like?" For a moment Huw had no idea what she was talking about.

"Uther! Uther Pendragon. He's to be King, after the Choosing, isn't he?"

"I can't tell you that, can I? The Choosing hasn't happened yet. The voting hasn't taken place."

"Phah!" The noise his sister generated between pursed lips was extremely vulgar. "There's a nonsense . . . Meradoc is dead, is he not? And Uther killed him. There were only two of them eligible for the Choosing, apart from you, and you are too young for it. Now there's only one of them eligible, so why do you even need to vote? A blind man could see that Uther will be the new King. But what is he like? That's what I want to know."

"Well, I still say I can't tell you that."

"*Dia*, and why not? You've been with him all morning! There must be *something* you can tell me."

"Something like what? Is he lovely? That's what you asked me, is it not? Men are not *lovely*, Glynda, not to other men, at least." He paused, hesitantly, then continued, grinning slightly. "Well, he is certainly not unpleasant to look at. Anyway, he is much too old and far too important to have time for you, dear Sister, so you'll have to wonder in vain."

"Oh!" Glynda swiped at his shoulder with an open hand. "You are a beast, Huw Pendragon, and when it comes my turn to wed I shall make life miserable for you, mark my words."

Huw threw up his hands in surrender. "Very well, as you will it! He is a man, and thus he has two eyes and ears—two of almost everything in fact, except one nose and one head. And he speaks normally, shouting seldom. He smiles from time to time, and he might even laugh, though not too often, I should think, after slaying someone a short time earlier—" He broke off, raising his eyebrows dramatically. "Or do you mean how does he appear, in physical terms, in terms of what young women wish to see? Well, let's see . . . I suppose he is fair to look upon. He stands tall, as tall as me—and that's unusual—perhaps even slightly more, for I fancy I had to look up into his eyes, and I am not accustomed to doing that. Oh, and his eyes are bright blue. I mean they are *really* bright . . . the colour of them jumps right out at you."

"Like periwinkles," his sister supplied. "I've heard tell of his blue eyes. They are the blue of periwinkles."

"Good, then, if you say so. His hair is black, almost blue in the sunlight in fact, so dark is it, and he wears it long, down to his shoulders, which marks him, even among his short-cropped horse troopers, as one of us, despite all his Roman trappings. And it is clean. His hair, I mean. It is so clean that you can see each single hair shining—no matting, no tangles. He must wash it regularly."

"Aye, *some* of us do things like that. The people in Camulod certainly do. It makes you smell better. You should try it, Brother." Glynda saw that Huw was preoccupied with some thought that had occurred to him and had not even noticed her jibe, and so she continued. "And? What more can you tell me? Surely you can do better than that!"

The young Chief shot his sister a sidewise glance and looked impatient for a moment, as though he might take issue with her over such silly questions.

"Very well, he is strong and well-made, his arms and legs as sound and solid as my own. He is huge across the shoulders and deep through the chest. He has a cleft chin, and a long, straight nose, and he keeps his face clean-shaven, in the Roman style, save for a moustache framing his mouth."

"His teeth?"

Huw grinned. "As white, clean and regular as yours, and he has all of them. Now, tell me, because the question just occurred to me a moment ago. Who was it told you about his periwinkle eyes?"

His sister flushed immediately, a tide of rosy colour sweeping upwards from her neck to stain her face. "That is none of your affair, Brother," she snapped, clearly disconcerted by what had been an obviously unexpected question. Then, suddenly, she was turning to leave. "I have work to attend to now. Fare thee well."

Huw stood gaping in astonishment as his mercurial sister turned her back on him abruptly and flounced away to disappear quickly in the direction of the encampment. Then he remembered where he was and what he was about, and he made his own way towards his preparations for the day's ceremonies.

The Choosing flowed smoothly and without incident, despite the fears of those who had expected the untimely death of the Llewellyn Chief to provoke his followers to violence. No such thing occurred, and it quickly became apparent that Cativelaunus's opinion had been right: Meradoc had been less loved than he himself believed, and his death had plunged no one into inconsolable grief.

The ceremony itself was solemn and impressive. The ruling Chiefs, now six in number, were led in procession into the sacred precincts of the temple by an escort of Druids to the accompaniment of a throbbing rhythm of massed drums that resembled the pulse-beat of a human heart and quickly took on a numbing, hypnotic resonance. No other sound marred the silence of the occasion, and the watching crowd stood motionless. No one stirred or spoke or sang, and there was no sound of movement, for all the participants in the procession walked barefoot in ancient tradition and none carried weapons on this sacred occasion.

Daris, dressed in his finest ceremonial robes and surrounded by his most senior priests, stood high above everything at the outset, gazing down on the procession from the top of the ramped earthen wall that protected the inner temple. From where he stood, a pathway six paces wide lay open, stepped with temporary stairs for the occasion down to the temple floor, and on either side of this aisle, packing the ramped sides of the high wall on either side so that they circled the temple completely, the common people of the Federation served as witnesses to the day's events.

Daris watched the procession circle the temple, weaving in and out among the pillars and pausing each time the vanguard reached one of the Chiefs' chairs set between alternating pairs of the standing stones. There, on each occasion, the Chief whose chair this was would step out of the procession to be flanked by a pair of red-robed priests who led him to his seat and then stood behind him, one by each shoulder, once he was seated. When all six surviving Chiefs were finally seated, the two remaining chairs sat conspicuously vacant. One of them would be filled within the week by Meradoc's chosen successor, since the dead man had had no son of his own old enough to inherit his position. The other, largest of all, would soon hold the new King.

Daris raised his staff in a signal, then slowly turned his back on the temple below as a series of horns began to sound, their differing, brazen tones blending into a fiery, somehow majestic crescendo that announced to all the world that something signal was about to take place within these precincts. Daris luxuriated in the sound of the horns, allowing its reverberating potency to wash over him and raise the skin of his arms up in gooseflesh. He stood motionless, facing directly east, his head thrown back to welcome the sun and his eyes closed against its blinding brightness. Three times the swelling crescendo of the horns was repeated, and then, as the sequence began again for the fourth and penultimate time, the High Priest turned towards the temple again and began to make his way down the narrow stairs. It was a sequence he had practised many times, and his timing was sure enough that as the crescendo gave way once more to the fifth and last repetition, he reached the ground and walked slowly and with conscious dignity towards the centre of the sacred circle, followed by his twelve senior priests, pacing himself to arrive just as the soaring notes reached their final climax. As the trumpets fell silent, the last echoes fading away into stillness, Daris came to a halt in the exact centre of the temple.

There, in his strongest oratorical voice, he asked the assembled Chiefs why they had come to this place on this day, and with that question and its shouted response, "To choose the King," the Choosing ceremony began. It was brief and solemn, and by the time it was over, less than half an hour from the outset, Uther Pendragon had been selected by the unanimous choice of the Chiefs as High King of the Pendragon Federation.

It was Daris's last duty to make the formal announcement of the result to the assembled witnesses, and he did so four times, from the exact centre of the temple floor, turning to all compass points, confident that the acoustical excellence of the temple would carry his voice easily to every listening ear. The crowd, knowing the protocols involved, waited for him to finish the fourth repetition before reacting, but when they did, there could be no doubting the overwhelming approval in their cheers, which seemed to grow even louder as Daris and the five remaining Chiefs led the new King to the King's seat before bowing deeply to show their commitment to his kingship.

Remaining seated, Uther received the oath of support and loyalty from the five individual Chiefs, taking each man's hand and clasping it between both of his own as the other undertook to assist the King in the legal governance of the land and its people. That done, he then rose and bowed deeply towards Daris, paying his own homage to the gods in the person of the High Priest, after which he continued to stand bareheaded in front of the King's seat, listening to the roars of approval. Finally he turned again to Daris, pitching his voice to carry to the Druid's ears over the noise of the sustained cheering.

"High Priest, the central spot from which you spoke, may I use it to speak to the people?"

"Use it?" Daris knew he was being dull, could hear it in his own voice.

The King pressed on. "May I speak to the people from your spot in the middle of the temple? Is there any law that says I would profane the temple by so doing?"

"No, no, none at all."

"Good."

Uther was already moving to the central spot, and when he arrived there he held up his hands, supplicating the crowd for silence. It took some time to come, but when it did, it was absolute. The new King cleared his throat, then spoke out strongly, turning himself casually from side to side as he spoke, so that his voice rang out clearly around the arena formed by the banked walls. He wasted no time attempting to thank or to flatter the crowd but cut directly to the meat of what he wanted to say.

"You know me, all of you, by repute if in no other way. I am Uther, son of Uric, son of Ullic Pendragon, and I stand here as chosen King in their name and in yours . . ." His voice faded away and none sought to break the silence that followed. He allowed his listeners to absorb what he had said and then he spoke again.

"From this day hence, my home is here among these mountains with you, my people. When I leave these hills, it will be because you, the people of our Federation, need me to go, to safeguard our well-being."

Again he stopped speaking, unhurried, allowing what he had said to sink home to his listeners, and as he waited he turned slowly in a complete circle, looking up into the throngs that packed the ramped walls. Finally, when he gauged that they had absorbed what he had said and were on the point of starting to discuss it among themselves, he spoke again, his voice loud and confident, carrying clearly in the silence.

"I have gained knowledge and learning from my time in Camulod, and the lessons I have learned I will put to work here in our lands. Like every whole man here, I am a warrior. But unlike most of you, I have learned to fight as the Romans fought, and then, in Camulod, I have learned to fight as the Romans never thought to fight—from horseback. I have learned crafts and skills in fighting that we here, among our mountains, have never known, and I have not learned those skills and crafts alone. I had companions with me there in Camulod, lest you forget . . . Pendragon companions from among your ranks, who learned the same lessons with me, by my side, and who are now possessed of knowledge their forefathers never had. Knowledge of horses and of saddles with stirrups and of the use of them in war. Knowledge of ways of waging war never known in Britain until now, because they never existed until the warriors of Camulod brought them into being. This new knowledge, all of it, will keep our Federation safe and strengthen it against those who would seek to harm us."

He spun quickly around so that he was suddenly facing the crowd that had been at his back, raising his voice as he turned, so that he could still be heard by everyone.

"My men are here among you today and will remain here, and some of them are Camulodian. Talk to them, speak with them, question them on anything that interests you. You will find them still to be much like yourselves, I promise you . . . Many of you gathered here today have been in Camulod, at some time in the past few years, and you know the people there are all our friends. We have had dealings with them in true and open friendship since the days of my Grandfather Ullic.

"There might be some among you, however, who condemn them still for not being Pendragon, as though that marks them as somehow inferior to us. Well, I will admit that they are not Pendragon, which means that they are *different*, but what of that? They are the next best thing to being Pendragon! They are *friends* of Pendragon, and have demonstrated that for almost three entire decades now. And far from being inferior in any way, they have shown themselves, time and again, to be our equals in a host of ways that we cannot begin to emulate—allies, proven in the fires of war against the invaders, whether those be Saxon Outlanders or Hibernian pirates or Cornish boars.

"The Camulodian people stand with us against our enemies. There is nothing *Roman* about Camulod. The people there were all born and bred here in Britain.

"I wear the armour of Camulod for but one single reason—I wear it because it *works!* There is no stronger, tougher or more effective armour in the world. It will turn any blade, deflect any missile, save for a well-shot Pendragon long shaft. It is the finest armour ever devised by man, and I trust in its strength and its utility. I wear it not because it makes me feel better than you or different in any way from any of you. I wear it because it makes me feel safe to know that if anyone wishes to kill me, they are going to have to face me, eye to eye, and carve or hack their way through my fine armour before they can succeed." Again he paused, looking around him, then continued.

"We have a war to wage, as you all know, against Cornwall. The leader there, a pestilence called Gulrhys Lot, is a human serpent. He sent his murderers, bearing poisoned arrows, to shoot down your King, my father, Uric. He did the same in Camulod, where his creatures used the selfsame venom-bearing weapons to bring about the death of Picus Britannicus, the Legate Commander of Camulod and son of its founder, Caius Cornelius Britannicus. This Gulrhys Lot is an evil man and a craven one. He will send others to do what he dare not attempt himself, and he is afraid to show his face to any of us in the light of day, but he will strive to destroy us all, to serve his monstrous lusts. This is a creature of darkest night, and he is hungry for this land of ours . . .

"I swear to you . . . I *swear* to you . . . he will have none of it! His armies might come swarming to our shores, but we will meet them and destroy them as they come. And as we meet them, Camulod will guard our back, its cavalry, invincible in war, committed to our use when we have need of it, as our longbows will be committed, too, to their defence. Together, we will stamp out Gulrhys Lot and sear the name and memory of him from people's minds. Cornwall will regret the day he moved against Pendragon."

Someone at the back of the huge crowd, high up on the ramped walls, called out Uther's name, repeating it in approval, and scores, then hundreds of voices added their weight to his, so that the thunder of the chant soon became overwhelming. Uther raised both hands in acknowledgment and turned slowly in a circle, mouthing his thanks and keeping his hands extended, as though in a blessing, until he had completed his turn and stood facing the front once again. And as he turned, his eyes scanned the crowd constantly, so that each person there felt that, at least once, he had made eye contact with the new King and that the King had been speaking directly to him or her at that time, offering his thanks.

At least one of those people, Huw Pendragon's sister Glynda, sat entranced, wide-eyed with adoration. And when Uther had stopped speaking and the assembly was dismissed, she turned to her companions with sparkling eyes.

"Isn't he wonderful? Mairidh, would you not love to meet him and to know him? You could, you know, I am quite sure of that. Lord Balin here is an important man, an ambassador. I am sure you could arrange to meet King Uther easily."

Her listeners exchanged knowing glances as she was speaking, and now Mairidh smiled gently at her young companion, seeing the innocence in the girl's young eyes. "Child," she said, "we already know Uther very well, and have known him for years. Our friendship with his family reaches far, far back, before you were born."

Glynda went slack-mouthed with surprise. She turned her gaze from Mairidh to Balin, seeking reassurance. "Is that true, Lord Balin?"

She was completely unaware of casting a slur of any kind on Mairidh's veracity, and the old man smiled and shrugged. "Aye, child, as far as the friendship goes, I have known Uther's grandfather, Ullic Pendragon, for many, many years—in fact I have been privileged to know all of his grandparents, save one. His Pendragon grandmother, Ullic's wife, was long dead ere I even met Ullic, but Publius and Luceiia Varrus of Camulod, the parents of Uther's mother Veronica, have been friends of ours for many years. But then, I am an old man and I tend to dwell in the past, as all old people do. The friendship with young Uther, to which Mairidh refers, was more hers than my own, but it has lasted—how long now, Mairidh? Ten years?"

"At least that long, my love." Mairidh smiled again at Glynda. "He saved my life once, did you not know that?" Glynda's eyes became enormous with wonder and Mairidh nodded in confirmation. "It's true. I was abducted by a raiding party and Uther happened to see it. He followed us and saved me heroically while my abductors slept. He is your King now, but he was my saviour then, and no more than a mere boy at the time, almost a child, perhaps younger than you are now."

"How? Oh, my lady, do tell me about it, please."

Mairidh shook her head at the anguished urgency in the young woman's voice. "Ah, my dear, it was a long time ago, and it is a very long tale. Perhaps later tonight, after dinner. We shall see."

And so it was left, with Glynda fretfully wondering whether she would ever get to hear the story, and Mairidh reflecting yet again upon how she had really met Uther Pendragon for the first time. She would never, could never, forget any detail of that first meeting, or of any of the many that followed it, but she felt no tiniest portion of guilt at having deceived her young friend, however gently, regarding the details.

As she and her party joined the departing throng and began making their way towards the exit from the temple, the woman called Mairidh walked with her head down, ignoring everyone around her and allowing her memory to drift back across the years.

NINETEEN

July was supposed to be a month of blue skies and summer breezes, but this year it had been more like late November, with dull, leaden skies, heavy with rain-filled clouds, and cold, howling winds that could cut through the warmest clothing and chill a body right down to the bone. The current storm, the latest in a series, had begun the day before, buffeting Nemo with cold, blustery winds and torrential rain. She had been drenched and chilled within an hour, the thickly woven, waxed wool of her heavy, hooded campaign cloak soaked through, so that it became an added burden to be borne, dragging at her with its sodden weight. And she was still a full day's ride from Camulod.

A year had passed since the Choosing, and nine months since Uther had driven Lot's forces back to Cornwall, and the time had been swallowed by the crises and small miseries of everyday life. A harsh winter had hit them hard in Tir Manha, diminishing their stores of corn and provender with frightening speed, and now summer was bringing little relief, its sullen, rainy malevolence threatening the harvest yet to come.

For hours she rode though the trees, away from the deserted road, hoping to find shelter of some kind, but there was nothing, not a cave or even a large animal burrow into which she might crawl. An enormous fire had burned the entire forest several years earlier, and nothing had had time to grow again to any decent size. The solitary ruined hut she found in a narrow ravine on a hillside that had somehow escaped the blaze had been completely useless to her, abandoned for decades, its roof long vanished and its decayed walls incapable of sheltering her from the howling wind.

She struck out directly for the only place she knew of that would offer her at least a rudimentary roof over her head: a ruined stone cattle shed, abandoned countless years earlier, but which still retained a remnant of a once good, thick roof of sod laid over rotted logs. If the remaining portion of the roof had not collapsed since the previous winter, it would offer her at least the opportunity to try to build a fire.

It had been dark for more than an hour by the time she finally crossed the ten or twelve miles and reached the crossroads close to where the shed lay. It took her another hour after that, working in the windblown darkness, to locate the ruined building—the roof, such as it was, was still in place—and then to find a spot within its walls where, by tenting her soaked cloak as a barrier against the gusting wind, she could create sufficient shelter to strike sparks into tinder and finally kindle a tiny flame strong enough to feed with twigs, huddling over it constantly to protect it from the cold, questing breath of the destructive wind.

Only when the tiny fire was burning briskly did she reach into her scrip for the thick tallow candle she always carried, and she lit it carefully with a flaming twig. Then, carefully guarding the candle flame in the hollow of her arm beneath her upraised cloak, she was able to move sufficiently far away from the fire to see and reach the supply of old, sun-dried wood, whitened with age, that lay against one of the walls, used and replenished by travellers like herself. Cautiously then, prepared to react at any moment to threats from the wind, Nemo set about building a real fire, feeding the dried-out lengths of wood one at a time to the hungry, growing flames. Her mood improved from moment to moment as they began to leap and dance vigorously, filling the angle between the ruined walls with flickering shadows and yellow brightness, and at last defying the wind to do its worst.

Nemo stood up and removed her sodden cloak, then reached behind her back with her left hand and grasped the naked blade that hung there, flipping it strongly, straight upwards, with an easy, accustomed movement that allowed her other hand the purchase to draw the long cavalry sword that hung through an iron ring between her shoulder blades, its hilt projecting high above her right ear. As soon as the sword was free, she reversed her grip on it and thrust the blade into the dirt floor. The sound of its point grating into the soil pleased her, and she gazed at the long, deadly weapon swaying there within her reach before she reached down and picked up her shield, a wooden disk covered with iron-studded leather. Slowly then, taking pains to position everything correctly, she lowered the loops at the back of the shield down over the hilt of the sword so that it hung securely, anchored to the pommel and the boss of the hilt by its own weight against the tension of the straps. Then, satisfied, she gathered up her cloak again and hung it carefully over the framework she had formed, where it could be dried by the fire's heat. She checked it to be sure that the cloak would not fall down, and then she moved away reluctantly, loosening her short-sword in its sheath, and went to look after her horse.

Strictly speaking, as a cavalry trooper, she knew she should have attended to the horse's needs before her own, but she was chilled and exhausted, close to the end of her resources, whereas the horse was still in good condition—cold and weary, perhaps, but yet far better able to withstand the ravages of the weather for another hour than she was. There was no place to stable him, for the broken roof that sheltered her was barely large enough to cover her and her fire, but she led her mount into the lee of the building's wall, out of the worst of the wind.

Working quickly, she first removed her precious saddlebags and the iron flail that she carried so proudly, hanging from a hook beside her saddle horn exactly as Uther's hung from his. Then she took off the animal's saddle and its thick saddle blanket, the latter amazingly warm and dry where the heavy saddle had sheltered it. The big gelding tossed his head and snorted his relief, flexed his back muscles and turned his hindquarters directly into the wind, lowering his head in search of grazing. She knew he would not move away before she returned.

She draped the blanket and saddlebags over the saddle and hitched it up until it rode on her left hip. Then, picking up the flail in her free hand, she carried everything over to the fire, where she positioned the saddle with care and spread the blanket out over it to dry out. From the saddlebags she removed the equipment she carried for the horse: a cylindrical leather nosebag, folded flat, a set of leg hobbles, a wide, stiff-bristled grooming brush and a leather bag of oats, sealed by a drawstring, that was about one-quarter full. From the other bag she produced a tightly folded and bound one-man blanket, woven of thick wool yarn that had been brushed and coated lightly with a scraping of wax. She also removed her most precious possession, a leather boiling bag, given to her years earlier by Uther. Its edges had been carefully stretched and sewn over the rim of the wide iron ring that formed its top, and she checked carefully, as she always did, to make sure that no damage had been done to it in her travels. She laid the bag aside, along with the long, slender, hand-crafted legs of the collapsible iron tripod on which it was made to rest. Within the leather of the boiling bag itself reposed another, smaller bag, this one containing a spoon and a cup, both made of horn, the cup itself containing a measure of salt wrapped in a twist of cloth, and several individually wrapped plants and herbs: small onions, cloves of garlic and dried mushrooms. Nemo ignored the cooking items for the time being, taking out only the horn cup and replacing everything else where it had been, except for the folded and tied blanket, which she stowed carefully for safekeeping beneath the curve of the saddle by the fire.

She filled the nosebag with oats, then scooped up her metal helmet and removed its leather liner. A steady stream of rainwater poured from one end of the sagging remnant of roof, and Nemo moved towards it, holding her helmet upside down to catch the falling water. When it was almost completely filled, she held it carefully in the crook of her elbow and bent to pick up the nosebag, and then she made her way around the sagging wall to the rear of the building.

The horse was used to being hobbled and made no attempt to move away as Nemo knelt awkwardly, fighting the stiffness of her armour as she fastened the restraints around his forelegs; he knew that as soon as she had finished with the hobbling, she would stand up and remove the bridle and the hated bit from his mouth. Moments later, his head was free and he was slurping noisily from the water in the helmet. He was not very thirsty, however, and he soon tossed his head to show that he had had enough. Muttering softly to him, allowing him to hear the comforting sound of her voice rather than any kind of sensible words, Nemo strapped on his nosebag and left him to eat. He tossed his head gently and stomped about a little until he had himself placed the way he wanted, rump firmly presented to the unfriendly wind, and then he lowered his head and its hanging bag to the ground and settled down to eat his oats. Nemo watched him for a moment or two and then collected her helmet and left him there.

Back by the fireside, Nemo sat on the saddle and undid the fastenings of her armoured coat, then spread it wide, throwing it open to allow the heat to penetrate her damp, quilted tunic. She reached beneath her right arm to pull out the thick leather wallet that she carried there for safety, protected, like her heart itself, by the thick armour of her fighting coat. The wallet contained the dispatches that Uther had entrusted to her care for delivery to Merlyn, and she peered down at it closely to make sure that it was still securely closed. Then she tugged hard on the strap that crossed her chest and held the wallet firmly in its place, testing it, too, before thrusting the wallet back into place beneath her arm. She used the blanket from her saddlebag then to dry her face and neck as well as she could, towelling her short-cropped, wet hair. Stripping completely to dry herself properly would have meant stripping off her armour, and when it was cold, wet and stiff, removing armour became a formidable task. Putting it back on quickly would have been simply impossible, and there was something too intimidating about exposing herself naked to anything that might be out there watching in the night, seeing her barely sheltered by broken walls and a sagging fragment of roof, and lit up by the fitful, flickering firelight, with the darkness pressing in upon her from every side.

When she was as dry as she could be, she propped the damp blanket up beside the fire, one end of it weighted and secured on the ground by a few large stones, and the other raised towards the fire on two long sticks stuck into the dirt. She sat beneath its shelter then and fed herself slowly, cutting pieces of smoke-cured, salted venison from the supply she carried in one of the pockets of the deep leather scrip that hung by her side. She chewed each piece slowly, savouring the deep, smoky tang of the meat and feeling the warmth of the fire slowly begin to penetrate the quilted thickness of her tunic. After attending to her horse again, she finally lay down beneath the blanket lean-to and slept fitfully, waking every now and then to feed the fire, prompted by fears of what she would have to go through to light it again if she allowed it to die out completely.

In the morning, she was still cold to the bone, shivering in her wet clothes and heavy, chafing armour. The daylight, uninspiring as it was, nevertheless encouraged her to take thought for herself and her welfare, and she swallowed her misery and went back out into the rain to gather more armloads of firewood to replace what she was using. She then built the fire up into a roaring blaze and stripped naked in its warmth, towelling heat and life back into her body with the warm blanket. She warmed most of her cloth garments close by the fire while she sat huddled nearby, wrapped in her blanket, planning how she would handle the day ahead of her. As she did so, she ate a dry breakfast of roast grains, shelled hazelnuts and chopped, sun-dried fruit. After leaving the shelter briefly to relieve herself, she squatted naked for a while in front of the flames, holding her blanket wide open and allowing the radiant warmth to wash over her until every bit of her felt stretched and tingling with the heat. Then, precisely at the moment when she felt she could absorb no more without burning up, she turned away and pulled dry, light under-clothing from her saddlebag. After that, she slung her precious dispatch wallet across her chest and tucked it beneath her arm again before pulling on her damp, heavy tunic and leggings, her heavy woollen socks and iron-studded boots, and dashing out quickly to bring her horse into the building itself. Beneath the roof and out of the rain, she rubbed him down as well as she could, leaning heavily on the stiff-bristled grooming brush and taking plenty of time as she squeezed and combed the night's moisture out of his heavy coat, taking particular care with the broad expanse of his back, where the chafing weight of the heavy cavalry saddle, imperfectly placed, could quickly make the animal's discomfort intolerable.

After she had saddled her mount, she laid her main armour—a heavy leather coat and wide, trousered leggings of the same leather, all sewn with thousands of tiny, overlapping metal rings—across the saddle and lashed together her shield, helmet, cuirass and thigh guards, using their own leather straps and buckles to join them to each other, before laying them over the ring-mail and covering them with her heavy woollen cloak.

A wide, strongly made sword belt supported a sheathed Roman-style short-sword that hung by her right side, its handle projecting just behind the large leather scrip that also hung there, and a matching dagger rode by her left hip. Attached to the sword belt in two places, ahead of and behind the dagger on her left side, another belt of the same weight and thickness rose diagonally between her breasts and crossed her right shoulder. Fastened to the back of it, between her shoulder blades, hung the wide iron ring that supported her sword. Nemo pulled the long cavalry sword from where it had stood in the floor all night supporting her cloak and used both her hands to guide it into place. Satisfied with the feel of it then, she took hold of the horse's bridle and led it out into the weather, where she turned her face in the direction of Camulod. She decided to walk, to keep herself warm and conserve the animal's strength, since she herself was unencumbered by armour and therefore able to move more quickly and easily.

Almost six hours later, Nemo was beyond weariness. Her entire attention was focused solely upon reaching Camulod and its hot baths as quickly as she could. The rain had stopped more than an hour earlier, and encouraged by a break in the clouds and a flash of blue sky that she had seen off to her right, she had stopped in an empty cattle byre and dressed herself again in full armour, prepared to ride into Camulod properly attired. But no sooner had she pulled herself back up into the saddle after that than the rain began again, heavier than ever. Her final reserves of patience vanished almost immediately, although now she could almost see the topmost towers of the rear walls of Camulod as she spurred her horse to scramble up the steep slope at the back of the hill. The walls were very close, but they were almost completely obscured by a billowing, low-lying cloud that shrouded the entire hilltop, it's sullen weight spewing rain.

Cursing and muttering to herself, Nemo urged her horse forward along the path that was now growing rapidly less steep. As she looked up into the slanting rain, she heard a sentry's challenge and the blowing of a trumpet to summon the guard commander.

"Who goes there?"

Nemo cocked her head, hoping to identify the voice, but it was unrecognizable.

"Nemo," she shouted back. "Decurion. Uther's Dragons. From King Uther, with word for Merlyn Britannicus. Nemo."

There was silence for a spell, and then a new voice, one she knew well, came down to her.

"Nemo? Is that you? What did you do last time when you came back from Glevum?"

"Chain duty. Four months you gave me, Centurion Dedalus. You know it's me. Let me in."

The heavy gate swung open and Nemo spurred her horse forward, passing through the entrance and the narrow new curtain passageway that had been built inside it after Lot's first, near fatal assault. She glanced up at the faces of the guards looking down at her from the high walls, recognizing a few of them and seeing for the first time how effective this winding passage was. Anyone attacking through this door in future would have to fight their way through a narrow, high-walled tunnel lined with defenders above them at every step.

"Hey, Hard-Nose, you look as though you've been out in the rain!"

Nemo ignored the taunt and all the others like it as she made her way through to the end of the curtainway. There, in a wider but still confined courtyard, she was met by Dedalus and a trooper who stepped forward to take her horse. She raised her hand to wave the trooper away, but Dedalus forestalled her.

"Let him take the horse, Nemo. You look as though you'll have enough to do taking care of yourself. My advice would be to stop at the bathhouse before you go anywhere or do anything else. It should be quiet there at this time of day."

Nemo hesitated, looking at him with a scowl, and then she shrugged her broad shoulders and reached for her saddlebags, slinging them over one shoulder and relinquishing the horse to the trooper with a surly nod.

"Merlyn Britannicus?"

Dedalus knew what she meant. "He's out on patrol, but not a long one. He'll be back later this afternoon. They're getting ready to leave on an expedition to the other side of the country, Verulamium, to attend a meeting of churchmen."

Nemo was not interested in churchmen. "I have messages for him from King Uther."

"I know, I heard you. He should be back by the time you have thawed out. Do you have any dry clothing with you? No? Then go ahead and warm yourself back to humanity. You can eat later, once you feel better. In the meantime, I'll send someone to the laundry to find you some clean clothing. He'll bring it to you in the bathhouse. I'll tell him to shout out your name and leave the new clothing in the dressing rooms. Leave your armour there for him, too, he'll pick that up at the same time and take it to one of the smithies to dry out near the forges before it can start to rust."

"It won't rust. The rings are bronze."

Dedalus twisted up his face and shook his head as though in pity. "Nemo, do you really think I didn't know that? Go now. Away with you." He paused, eyeing her as she turned to go, and called her back. "No, wait you, Nemo . . . Before you go to the bathhouse, you might feel better to know that your dispatches for Commander Merlyn are safe. Where are they?"

Nemo glowered at him, then reached across with her left hand and patted her armour on the right side. "They're safe."

Dedalus grinned. "Aye, safe now, but will you take them into the hot pool with you?" He watched her blink, then start to frown, her scowl deepening by the moment, and he took pity on her. "What you need to do, Nemo, is find someone that you can trust . . . and if there's no one *you* can trust, then find someone you know Uther would trust. Were I you, I'd take my dispatches into the administration building and leave them with one of the senior legates there before I went to bathe. Titus or Flavius, doesn't matter which. They are equally trustworthy."

Nemo looked at him narrowly and then looked down at the arm still stretched across her breast. She hovered indecisively for several moments, and then nodded once and made directly for the administrative building.

An hour later, having made her progress through the intermediate baths, Nemo was luxuriating in the *calidarium*, the deep hot pool, and deliberating with herself whether or not she would make the effort to climb out and make her way into the curtained-off *sudarium*, the steam room, where the tiled walls and hanging leather curtains contained the roiling clouds of vapour that belched out of floor-level vents, heated to boiling by the furnace below the bathhouse. She decided to remain where she was, thinking that she could never have enough of this magnificent hot water and remembering, too, how she had believed, only short hours before, that she might never again be warm.

There were only two others in the bathhouse with her, and two more had been leaving when she arrived. All of them had known and recognized her, and had acknowledged her with nods. None of them had attempted to speak to her, and none had paid any attention to her sex, elaborately ignoring her nakedness as though it were as unremarkable as their own. Nemo had barely noticed. She had settled all of that kind of nonsense very emphatically long years before.

Apart from the most basic and obvious evidence of her femininity, her appearance was very masculine. She had always been short and squat of stature as a child, with immense strength for her size and age, and by the time she had volunteered for Uther's cavalry force, her arms, chest, back and shoulders were massive and dense with muscle. Her breasts and pectorals were less feminine than many a man's, except that they were hairless and tipped with large and obviously female nipples. Her hips and buttocks, belly and thighs, were lean and hard. Only the black-haired cleft at her centre ruined the illusion of swarthy, virile strength and male vitality.

And yet, there had been some among the troopers of Camulod who had insisted upon seeing only the woman in her, purely from the perspective of male rut. Her female body, unused, was an insult to their manhood. Many ventured to deal with her as they thought appropriate, singly and in groups. And all of them failed, humiliatingly and publicly, because, brutal and debased as they might have been, they could not conceive of, let alone match, Nemo's implacably savage response to their assaults. Where they had sought to bully and conquer her as a woman, she had responded as a threatened man, maiming and disabling, so that invariably they went reeling and limping, broken and bleeding, in every direction. Two of these died, killed in the struggle when a group of six of them jumped her here in this very bathhouse. One of those deaths came from a straight-armed smash with Nemo's open hand, the heel of which drove one attacker's nose bone into his brain. The second was caused when another assailant slipped and fell, trying to dodge a flying kick that would have unmanned him. He landed strangely and crushed his skull between the corner edges of the deep pool. Two more of the surviving four had been grievously injured, one with a broken leg and the other with shattered ribs, before the other two fled, unsatisfied.

The official inquiry into the matter exonerated Nemo. She had acted in self-defence, it was said, and therefore legitimately. Merlyn Britannicus had raised a questioning eyebrow on more than one occasion as the inquiry progressed, but he had invariably bowed to the judgment of his cousin Uther, who stood staunchly behind his subordinate and insisted that she be treated as a trooper, first and foremost, and as a woman only incidentally and under protest. And whenever one or another of the Roman-trained officers of Camulod questioned the propriety of having women in the ranks, as several of them did, Uther withered them with scorn, citing the names of Boudicca and a dozen other notable Celtic women, all of them renowned as warriors, and several among them Pendragon chieftains. He rattled off their names with impressive speed, proclaiming them unimpeachable examples of how the women of Celtic Britain had always fought as equals with their men.

After that, the realization had sunk home to everyone that Nemo was not to be trifled with. If you had to fight her as you would a man in order to possess her, the common wisdom of the day held, then she was a man—and what did that say about you? Thereafter, she mingled freely with the other troopers, going naked among them in the bathhouse, and only newcomers took notice of her—and then only for a short time, until they could be taken aside and warned.

Later, dressed from the skin out in fresh, clean clothes and wearing only the light, dress armour of the Camulodian garrison troopers, Nemo stepped out of the bathhouse to discover that the storm had passed while she was indoors and the entire world about her had changed. The sky over her head was bright blue and cloudless, and the air was clean-scented and warm with the appropriate warmth of July. Even the muddy cobblestone street was drying rapidly.

A pair of troopers came towards her, evidently headed for the bathhouse, and she saw at first glance that they had just returned from a patrol of some kind, for their cloaks were wet and travel-stained. She held up one hand to attract their attention and asked them if they knew whether Merlyn had returned. They both nodded and one of them waved his hand in the general direction of the administrative building.

Nemo strode past the guards and through the doors directly to the desk of the Officer of the Day, where the Legate Titus was deep in conversation with another travel-weary newcomer. Titus saw her approach from the corner of his eye and without interrupting his conversation reached sideways beneath his table to pick up the wallet she had left in his care, then held it up above his head for her to take from him in passing. She collected it and moved straight on past the desk towards the door that was Merlyn's day-room, where she stopped on the threshold and knocked.

"Come!"

Inside, Merlyn Britannicus slouched in a high-backed, armless chair by a long work table in front of a high, double-arched window. He was reading something, a document of some kind, holding the cylindrical scroll up to the light with both hands and frowning as he whispered the words to himself. He paid no attention to Nemo until he had finished, and he allowed the scroll to spring shut before throwing it onto the tabletop.

"Damnation," he muttered, looking up to see who had come into the room. When he saw Nemo, he frowned and cocked his head to one side in a gesture that said plainly that he ought to know the person he was seeing but could not put a name to him. Then he stood up, quickly, the frown on his face deepening.

"You're one of Uther's people, are you not? The one called Nemo . . . That's right . . . Is your master here? In Camulod?"

Nemo held herself at attention but shook her head, unwilling as always to speak aloud. Instead, she held out the leather document case and stepped quickly forward. Merlyn moved to take it, slowly, his eyes searching her face, but as soon as his hands had closed over the case she relinquished it, took one step back and snapped into a cavalry salute before spinning on her heel and beginning to march out.

"Wait!"

Nemo stopped dead. Turned around.

Merlyn was still frowning at her, his expression speculative. "Is Uther well?"

Nemo nodded again, and Merlyn's frown grew deeper. "What's the matter, can't you speak?"

Nemo cleared her throat. "Aye, sir . . . Commander. King Uther is well." Her voice sounded rusty and unused.

"Good. And he is still in Tir Manha?"

"Aye, sir."

"And how goes his kingdom nowadays? Is all well? It has been what, a year, since he was chosen? As King? Aye, it must be, and nine months since he threw Lot's crew out of Cambria and chased them screaming back to Cornwall. Has he no plans to visit us here soon?"

Strange thoughts were passing through Nemo's mind. There was something in the tone of Merlyn's voice as he spoke to her that set her instincts aquiver. Looking into his eyes, she felt that Merlyn meant the opposite of what he was saying, and that he would be perfectly happy never to see his cousin Uther again. It made no sense to her, and she could see no reason for it, but she knew that Merlyn Britannicus had no wish for Uther ever to return to Camulod.

She said nothing but only stood staring at him, holding herself upright and at attention, her helmet clutched in her bent left arm. Nothing of what she was thinking showed on her face. Her expression remained unchanged, her close-set black eyes unreadable beneath the frowning, unbroken bar of her thick brows.

"Well? Does my cousin plan to visit us?"

Nemo blinked, aware of a need to answer. She nodded her head. "Don't know, sir. Doesn't speak to me. Not of plans."

"Hmm. Very well. My thanks for bringing these." He held up the leather wallet. "Are you instructed to wait for a response?"

"No, sir."

"Good. You may go."

Nemo saluted smartly and spun on her heel, then marched away as though she were on parade, feeling his eyes on her until she had marched out of the building and into the sunlight again. She turned right, and then as soon as she was out of sight of the administrative building, she broke step and put her helmet on, tapping it firmly down over her brows with the flat of one hand. Then she fastened her chinstrap and adjusted her cheek-flaps before walking on normally, her mind seething with unaccustomed, troublesome thoughts of Caius Merlyn Britannicus.

She had known Merlyn for years, ever since his boyhood, but he had never come to know her at all, and she and Uther had both preferred to keep it that way for their own reasons. Now she sensed instinctually a very real menace emanating from Merlyn Britannicus and directed towards Uther.

Merlyn had changed. His attitude to Uther had changed. He no longer bubbled with that warm, open, pleasure-filled joy of companionship and brotherhood that had always made her feel jealous and left out when the two were together. Merlyn no longer loved Uther. That made her blink. Did she truly believe that? She was unsure. But Merlyn no longer laughed with joy at the thought of seeing Uther, and she would happily swear to the truth of that.

For the space of half a heartbeat, she wondered which way to

go, and then she turned sharply right, simply because Merlyn and
the administrative building lay to her left. She took one quick step
and collided immediately with a woman who had been walking
towards her. The frail figure practically bounced off the solid bulk
of her body and fell backwards, a flailing bundle of blue-clad
limbs. Nemo hurled herself forward instantly, her arms scooping
in front of her, and managed to catch the reeling woman before she
hit the ground. The woman's eyes were wide with shock and
incomprehension, and the cowl that had covered her head and
concealed her face had fallen away to reveal long, once-black
hair, heavily shot through with grey, and wide, startlingly blue
eyes. Nemo recognized her, and her heart leaped with fright at the
thought that she had almost killed Uther's grandmother, Luceiia
Varrus.

Luceiia made it clear that she was uninjured and would like to
be allowed to regain her feet, and Nemo released her awkwardly,
helping her to stand up before doing so. Then the old woman
nodded and brushed herself down, absently patting the arm of
another, younger woman who was her companion, reassuring her
that she was uninjured. Now Luceiia composed herself and turned
back to Nemo, nodding her head and looking up into her eyes.

"Thank you, young man," she said. "I know not how you
managed to move so quickly, but I am very glad you did. I find that
I am very slightly out of breath, but otherwise none the worse for
wear. Hitting you was rather like hitting a wall, I believe, although
I never have hit a wall quite that hard." She stopped and looked
around, aware for the first time of the crowd of onlookers who had
stopped to gawk at her. "Thank you all," she said in a tone that was
eloquently dismissive. "I am quite well now and have suffered no
harm, thanks to the quick-wittedness of this young man. Please go
about your affairs now." She stood and watched the people hesitate
and then move on, and then she turned back to Nemo, cocking her
head to one side. "That is the uniform of the Pendragon Guards, is
it not? The Dragons?" Nemo cleared her throat but could only nod.
The old woman blinked at her. "I thought so. I should know my own
grandson's emblem. And your name is?"

Again Nemo cleared her throat, and then she spoke in her deepest voice, keenly aware that Luceiia thought she was a man. The words resonated inside her helmet, sounding distorted to her own ears. "Geddius, Milady. I'm Geddius." The lie was out before she knew it was there, but it was born of an irrational fear that Luceiia might complain to her grandson that she had been jostled by one of his men. Had this been anyone else in the world, Nemo would have been contemptuous, but she was well aware of the incomprehensible awe and love that Uther held for his aged grandmother.

Luceiia was peering sharply at her, trying to make out the features beneath the full face-guards of Nemo's huge trooper's helmet, but Nemo knew that the old woman could see little more than the gleam of her eyes.

"Have you brought messages from Uther?"

Another nod. "Yes, Milady. Dispatches for Lord Merlyn."

"I see. Well, I trust we shall find out what my grandson has to say before the morning's done. For the time being, once again, I thank you, young man. But perhaps in future you might pay more attention to your surroundings as you make your way. Good day to you. Come, Deirdre."

Nemo stepped back, watching with awe as the old woman began to move away, and only at the last moment did her eyes move to the younger woman whom Luceiia Varrus had called Deirdre. She found the woman gazing back at her, the tiniest frown marring the smooth skin between her brows, and something about the sight of her brought Nemo snapping back to awareness. She knew this woman, but she had no idea from where. Then, as Luceiia Varrus took the other's arm and they began to move away, she saw the huge swelling of a late-term pregnancy showing unmistakably beneath Deirdre's gown.

Nemo stood in the middle of the roadway and watched the two women head towards the entrance of the administrative building, seeing the almost reverential way in which the ordinary people looked at them in passing. A trio of off-duty garrison troopers standing talking near the doors stopped their conversation and held themselves at respectful attention as the women passed by them, and only resumed talking after Luceiia and her companion had disappeared inside.

Nemo wandered over to where they stood, schooling her face to appear no more than casually interested. The troopers paused as she drew near them, and one of them nodded courteously. Nemo nodded back and used her "man's" voice.

"Just got in from Cambria. Who's the woman with the Lady Luceiia?"

The man who had nodded to her grinned. "That's the Lady Deirdre, Commander Merlyn's wife."

"Hmm." Nemo jerked her head in a nod of thanks and farewell and walked away, her head spinning with speculation.

TWENTY

"That's the Lady Deirdre, Commander Merlyn's wife."

The words echoed in Nemo's head as she walked away, following the slight, naturally declining gradient of the hilltop until she found herself approaching the main gates of the fortress. They were wide open at this time of the day, and she noticed that the guards on duty, none of whom she recognized, were having an easy time, lounging indolently as they supervised the few vehicles that came and went while keeping a wary eye alert for approaching officers.

She had almost drawn level with the gates when she became aware that someone behind her was calling her name repeatedly, and she turned her head to see who was shouting at her. When she saw the waving hand and its owner's grinning face, with its artificially enhanced colouring and enormous, flashing eyes, she grew angry at herself immediately for even looking, and for not recognizing that distinctive voice immediately. It belonged to Nennius, one of the masseurs who worked in the bathhouse. Sexuality of any kind was immaterial to Nemo, whose interest in such things was virtually nil, so she had no difficulty with the knowledge that Nennius's preference was for boys and men, but the fellow was an inveterate talker who was incapable of keeping quiet and had an unquenchable thirst for other people's business, and his incessant chatter always threatened to drive her mad.

Nennius, however, had been indefatigable in pursuing Nemo's friendship ever since the earliest days of her arrival in Camulod and he had steadfastly refused to take offence or to be discouraged by her continuous and ill-mannered hostility towards him. How could he take offence, he had asked her repeatedly, when he understood too well the pain with which she had to live incessantly, day in and day out? They were two of a kind, he assured her, but of different aspects, like the two faces of a coin. Nemo was a man cursed by some malign fate to live his life inside a woman's body, whereas Nennius was a woman walled up inside the body of a man. So brazen had Nennius been in his pursuit of Nemo, and so unfailingly charming and attentive to her, that even Nemo's immeasurable fund of ill nature had eventually been exhausted, and she had begun to develop a tolerance for his attentions, accepting and eventually even coming to enjoy his therapeutic ministrations in the massage room after she had bathed and sweated the soreness out of hard-used muscles, nevertheless insisting upon what was, for Nennius, an almost unbearable degree of silence.

Today, Nemo had neither time nor patience to spare for Nennius, and she waved him away with a deep scowl that even Nennius, thick-skinned as he was, had no choice but to accept. He held up both hands in a gesture of apology and then stood there watching Nemo as she strode away through the gates.

Merlyn Britannicus had taken a wife, and he had said nothing about it—had sent no notice, either before or after the event—to Uther Pendragon. The insult was unforgivable. Nothing on earth, Nemo knew, would have kept Uther from attending his cousin's nuptial feast had he known of it. Nemo felt the unmistakable stirring of nausea in her guts and sucked air in deeply, holding it hard and willing her insides to settle down, but her head felt light and giddy and there was a high-pitched whining in her ears. No matter what she thought of Merlyn Britannicus personally—and she had held many different feelings for him in the years that she had known him, ranging from admiration to dislike, from envy to indifference and even to blind jealousy—he was one of the underlying constants of her life. His life, in many ways, defined hers. His behaviour had always had a beneficent influence on his more volatile cousin, and Nemo had benefited directly from that. In consequence, the information she had just received, deepening her conviction that something had gone seriously wrong in Merlyn's dealings with Uther, was devastating.

And this was all because of a woman. That information taunted her, spinning slowly in the air slightly beyond her grasp. An unknown woman was threatening all that Nemo held to be of value. A complete stranger, a creature who had sprung out of nowhere and was completely unknown to Uther Pendragon, whose world she was about to destroy by depriving him, for her own selfish reasons, of his lifelong friend and closest companion. By destroying Merlyn's trust in Uther, which she had evidently begun to do already, this woman would surely demolish Uther's ability to trust anyone else in future. By stealing Merlyn's friendship away from Uther, with neither reason nor provocation, this woman had demonstrated that, whoever she might be, she was a self-centred and remorseless thief.

Nemo had spent her entire adult life among rough and violent troopers, and she had heard all of them talk at one time or another, some with cynical amusement and others with angry scorn, about how a woman—any woman—could divide and alienate the best and oldest of friends and set brothers at each other's throats, all because of that terrifying thing called love. A hundred times and more she must have heard those tales, and she had always doubted them, taking them, as men say, with a grain of salt to help her swallow them.

Now, however, she had no choice other than to face this reality, and so she began to plan. She had never been in a similar situation before, but she was not completely without direction on how to proceed, for one of the first and best-learned lessons she had absorbed from Garreth Whistler, while he was teaching it to Uther Pendragon, was that no one, no commander of any rank or stature, should ever commit his resources to a fight or a struggle without first finding out everything there was to know about the forces against which the fight would be waged.

"*Know your enemy.*" As soon as Nemo remembered the instruction, she immediately began to wonder where she might start digging for information on this Lady Deirdre. No sooner had she asked it of herself, however, than she answered it with a response that surprised her with its simplicity. Nennius the masseur would know everything there was to know about Merlyn Britannicus's new wife, simply because that kind of information was precisely what Nennius thrived upon. The woman was young, pregnant and newly, suddenly arrived. Nemo was sure of that, because there had been no sign of anyone resembling a Lady Deirdre the last time she had been here bearing dispatches from Uther to Camulod, and that had been less than four months earlier. So, this Deirdre had sprung out of nowhere and captured the love of Merlyn Britannicus. Where could she have come from? And when could he have met her? Nemo knew that Nennius would have done everything in his power to satisfy his insatiable curiosity on such important points.

Moments later, she was striding towards the bathhouse again, her fingers fumbling with the clasp of her cloak as she prepared to throw it off, along with the rest of her clothing and her boots, and to pass as quickly as she could through the intermediate pools to the rear room that held the stone-built plinths of the masseurs. As she shed her clothing she made her way to the steam room, calling for Nennius to alert him that she would have need of his talents.

It turned out to be more difficult that she had thought it would be to simply lie there quietly, saying nothing while Nennius kneaded and belaboured her like a large lump of dough, talking all the time as though his tongue and his breathing were irreversibly interconnected. Several times, Nemo had to restrain herself forcibly from turning on him to rend him with her tongue for fear that this time he might take offence and refuse to speak to her again. She was burning with the need to talk to him about what troubled her, but she knew that would be the worst thing she could do because, Nennius being who and what he was, she could afford to give him no slightest inkling of a suspicion that she was even remotely interested in Merlyn Britannicus's new wife. Accordingly, she gritted her teeth and tried to shut out what he was saying to her. Occasionally, she grunted with pain for, kindred spirit or no, Nennius was being anything but gentle with her. Nemo recognized that he was punishing her, albeit very slightly, for her earlier discourtesy.

On arriving, she had grunted an apology to him, muttering that she had had important matters on her mind. Nennius had waved that aside as being of no importance, and had then launched into his normal chronicle of news and information from all over Britain, collected from every conceivable and available source to which he had access. Nennius was very proud of what he called "my people," the network of informants who kept him supplied with information, and he liked to convey the impression that if he did not quite know anyone and everyone who was worth knowing, he at least knew someone else who did.

It had been no accident that she had apologized for her rudeness by asserting that she had important matters on her mind. Nennius was well aware that Nemo was King Uther's most trusted personal messenger, and that every time Nemo came alone to Camulod, it was to deliver dispatches from Uther to Merlyn. He had never been able to gain the tiniest insight from Nemo in the past regarding what she carried or what her dispatches might portend, but Nennius was a creature who lived in hope, and this was the first time he had ever seen or suspected Nemo to be disgruntled with any aspect of her tasks. Finally, and with what he imagined to be great subtlety, Nennius manoeuvred the conversation to the point where he could ask, with the disdainful tones of utter disinterest, what it was that had upset Nemo so visibly earlier that afternoon.

Nemo grunted and turned her head to look up at him, raising an eyebrow, openly intimating that the question was impertinent.

Nennius then shrugged and went on to point out that he had no interest in the specifics of anything, but was merely curious as to why his friend Nemo should have been so put out that she could then be rude to a perfectly inoffensive friend who merely happened to be passing by and waved to say hello.

Nemo nodded at that, muttering that Nennius was right and that there had been no call for her to be so rude. She had been angry, she said, because she had gone to call upon Commander Merlyn at the administrative building and had been kept waiting for the longest time because the Commander was closeted with some young woman— some woman on the verge of having a child. She would not normally have minded being kept waiting, Nemo said, but she had arrived only a short time earlier and had gone directly to deliver her dispatches, which she had been told were urgent. What that urgency might imply, she had no idea, but King Uther had been specific in his instructions. Nemo had been told to waste not a moment in delivering the wallet containing the King's messages into the hands of Merlyn Britannicus. And she had found it galling that, after riding day and night through foul weather to carry out his orders, she should then be forced to stand around and wait for such a length of time while Commander Merlyn took his pleasure with some young wench.

Nennius listened to this open-mouthed, his huge, lustrous eyes glistening and gleaming above the lines of black kohl painted on their lower lids. He made no attempt to interrupt Nemo, but as soon as the other had finished speaking, he waved a hand expressively and nodded deeply, saying he could understand perfectly why Nemo should have been so upset. But really, he added then, his eyes gleaming wickedly, it was not really accurate to speak of the young woman as "some young wench." Her name was Deirdre, and she was the Commander's new wife.

Pretending to be startled, Nemo raised herself up on one elbow, her face, as much as she could make it, a picture of astonishment. The Commander's *wife?* Commander Merlyn was *married?* When had that happened, and how? Ten days before, Nennius said, smiling still at the effect of his announcement . . . No, Nemo had heard absolutely nothing, had known nothing. If word had gone to Cambria, to King Uther in Tir Manha, then it had clearly passed Nemo on the road. Ten days since the wedding? But the woman was big . . . about to give birth. Where had she sprung from? Where had Merlyn Britannicus been hiding her?

Nennius threw up his hands and shook his head before slapping Nemo on the bare flank to indicate that their session was at an end. The birth was far from imminent, he said, despite appearances. From what he had been told, there yet remained at least two months of carrying time before the Lady Deirdre's burden would be dropped. But then, as Nemo sat upright on the edge of the stone plinth, tucking the large towel into place about her hips, Nennius admitted that, to his great frustration, he had been unable to unearth any information from anywhere about the woman's former whereabouts. She was from Eire, the daughter of some heathen Eirish King, that much he could affirm, for she had turned out to be the sister of the Eirish Prince Donuil, the big fellow Merlyn had taken as a hostage two years earlier during Lot of Cornwall's first attack on Camulod. She could not have come directly to Camulod from Eire, however, gravid as she was, not without dire sorcery of some kind being involved, for Merlyn had not been away from Camulod for longer than two or three days at a time in more than a year.

Whence, then, had come the pregnancy? As far as Nennius had been able to discover, and as plain logic dictated, the Lady Deirdre must have been living somewhere nearby throughout the entire year, at least. Yet no one in Camulod—no one anywhere, for that matter—had ever seen her before the day she had ridden into the fortress, close on a month earlier, blooming with health and beauty and yet nonetheless as ethereal as a mountain sprite, riding on a light cart and accompanied by Caius Merlyn and his great-aunt, Luceiia Varrus.

Nemo expressed surprise then, in her usual surly manner, that Nennius had not been able to worm some kind of information about the young woman from some of her servants or associates. She must have said something in the course of a month to indicate where she had been and where she had come from . . . unless she was mute.

But she *was* mute, Nennius replied, and Nemo felt as though every vestige of air in her lungs had been kicked out as her mind made a sickening series of connections and a number of things all fell into place at the same time.

The Cassandra woman! No wonder the Lady Deirdre had looked so familiar at first sight—though the well-dressed, high-born lady with the hugely swollen belly bore but little resemblance to the pallid, emaciated waif Nemo had found kneeling in the forest so many months before. How long ago had that been? Nemo thought back quickly and realized that nigh on three whole years had passed since then.

They had found the girl, an insipid, lacklustre little thing, while on a routine perimeter patrol of the Colony, and she had ridden back to Camulod behind Uther's saddle, with her arms clutching him around the waist. In time they had discovered that she was mute, and they had called her Cassandra. Three years ago!

Realizing that she had stiffened into immobility and that Nennius was watching her closely, his head tilted to one side with the force of his concentration, Nemo made an enormous effort to relax her body and breathe normally while she simultaneously fought to school her face into betraying nothing of her shock. She muttered something barely audible about mute people, and then, suddenly inspired, she looked Nennius in the eye and asked him if mute people could hear anything. His eyes flew wide and he spread his hands, suggesting that he did not know, and Nemo nodded her head sagely and walked away slowly while he was still confused, offering her thanks as she left. Then, highly pleased with her own unusually glib performance, she dressed quickly and left the bath-house, her mind teeming with thoughts of the Cassandra woman.

Cassandra . . . the very name twisted Nemo's guts, because it struck directly to the root of the trouble between Uther and Merlyn. She remembered that night . . . in the private quarters Uther and Merlyn once referred to as their games room. Nemo had never been able to discover precisely what had occurred, because only Uther and Merlyn were present at the time and neither of them spoke of it afterwards. The waif Cassandra had been there too, however, along with a small number of other women, all of whom disappeared from public sight the following day, permanently, leaving Camulod in a covered cart.

Nemo had witnessed only a few important scenes of the drama: Cassandra bursting from the games room, apparently running for her life. Merlyn appearing at the door a few moments later, unclothed, but ducking back inside and closing the door when he saw the guard watching him. Uther storming out, clearly in a fury. She discovered later that Uther, accompanied by a small group of his Dragons, rode out of Camulod then and returned home to Cambria. The girl Cassandra had been abducted that same night and dragged or carried into a barn, where she had been beaten, ravaged and brutalized, and then abandoned by her attacker, who had clearly thought her dead, and whose identity was never established.

Cassandra had been discovered the following morning, barely alive, and Germanus, the senior military physician in Camulod, had worked hard for hours to save her life while Merlyn Britannicus, as Officer in Command during his father's absence on a patrol, fearing for the young woman's safety, arranged to have her placed under heavy, constant guard. And then, in the middle of the following night, the woman called Cassandra had disappeared without a trace, evidently by sorcery, from a building that was heavily guarded inside and out.

Rumours had flown in all directions for a long time after that, including one that Merlyn had foreseen Cassandra's disappearance in a dream. That rumour formed the basis for the other whisperings that Merlyn was a sorcerer of some kind. Nemo had also heard a rumour, believed by some, that Uther had been responsible for beating the girl, but that was clearly so foolish and so contradictory to the facts that Nemo merely shook her head and disregarded it completely.

One thing she did know, however, and it came from no rumour. The lifelong bond between Merlyn Britannicus and Uther Pen-dragon was broken that night of the fight in the games room. From then onward, the two men, who had been inseparable for so long, were seldom in each other's company again.

Nemo had never dared come out openly and ask Uther what had happened between them that night, and he had never offered to tell her, but she had been convinced then, and was still convinced, that the woman Cassandra was at the bottom of it. Before Cassandra had been found in the forest, Uther and Merlyn had been closer than brothers for five and twenty years, but then, within three days of her appearance in their lives, that bond had been severed.

It had taken no great leap of imagination at that time for Nemo to connect Cassandra with all the kitchen tales of witchcraft and malice that she had absorbed during her miserable childhood among the Druid's people, and she had quickly come to perceive her as a witch, sent to destroy the bonds between the two magnificent young men who had become known throughout the countryside as the Princes of Camulod. How else could she have escaped, unseen, from a guarded room? Once convinced, Nemo had then spent months looking for the woman, determined to force the creature, somehow, to undo the damage she had done, or failing that, to ensure that she would no longer pose a threat to Uther Pendragon. But Cassandra, it seemed, had indeed vanished, swallowed up and absorbed by the darkness of night.

After a year had elapsed without further sight or sound of her, Nemo had eventually forgotten her. More accurately, she had ceased to think of Cassandra as a real, living person, but she remained aware of the damage the witch had done.

And now, after three years, Cassandra had returned, carrying Merlyn's child. How it had been made was a mysterious matter, and Nemo's blood chilled as she thought of the old women's tales she had heard in her childhood, tales of enchantment and witchcraft, sorcery and the seldom mentioned magic, the arcane, terrifying, secret lore that was named for the learned men who practised it, the magi. She had heard the tales about Merlyn, too, since her arrival in Camulod, tales that whispered that he was a magus, a practitioner of the dark arts, and Nemo was not one to dismiss such a possibility out of hand.

Nemo was convinced that Cassandra, or Deirdre as she apparently called herself now, was a witch, returned as a different person to ensnare Merlyn with the lure of her young body. And that she had clearly been able to do so, in utmost secrecy, was fundamental proof to Nemo that she was right in her suspicions. Merlyn had fallen to the witch's lure, and because of Merlyn's weakness, Uther's peace of mind would soon begin to crumble, and with that her own life would crash in ruin once the word of what the witch had wrought was carried home to Tir Manha.

Nemo knew she had but little time remaining in which to counteract Cassandra's evil, and so she bent her mind to recalling what she could of the kitchen lore she had heard years before regarding the killing of witches. She remembered some fat old woman from her childhood bending over a bubbling pot of stew that steamed deliciously, sprinkling a handful of chopped herbs into the pot and declaring to all the world that there were only two means of inflicting death upon witches without taking the risk of their returning to drag you, screaming, to the fiery underworld. One was fire, the old woman had said, tugging at a burning log and causing an explosion of fierce heat and whirling sparks and embers. A witch burned was a witch destroyed. The other means involved the use of iron, but Nemo could not recall what the old fool had said about it or how it was supposed to be used. The only other thing she could remember from the old woman's ranting was that the iron used to kill a witch could never again be used by human hand. That made no sense to her, now that she came to think of it again, because the iron weapon of any man's choice would be a sword . . . sometimes a spear, perhaps, or an axe, but in most cases it would be a sword. And what fool would risk attempting to kill a witch, knowing that if he were successful he would lose his most valuable weapon? But the task of grappling with that thought was too taxing for her, and so Nemo stopped thinking about it. Either way, she decided, using fire or iron, she would find a way to defeat the witch's designs. She would watch carefully and wait, and then take any option offered to her.

Two days later, Merlyn Britannicus left Camulod at the head of a large body of troops made up of four cavalry squadrons, each forty troopers strong, plus all the support equipment and personnel required to keep such a force in the field for a month or longer, including commissary wagons, a water wagon and extra horses. There were one hundred and seventy-five fighting men in the group, including officers and exclusive of the commissary staff and herd boys, who brought the overall number up to just over two hundred. The expedition made a fine and imposing spectacle as the troopers rode out through the main gates of Camulod and down the winding roadway to the plain beneath, but they were not riding to war. They were headed for the distant town of Verulamium to attend a debate between Christian bishops that would supposedly decide on great and important matters having to do with the gods and how the workings of men's minds in that regard would be judged in times to come. Nemo had had it explained to her by several people, but it all sounded to her like wasted time and effort, and it made her glad she was no Christian. But thanks to all of that, Merlyn had gone from Camulod, leaving his wife behind.

Witnessing the departure that day, Nemo turned her face to where Cassandra, the Lady Deirdre, watched her husband ride away and

waved to him each time he turned back to look at her, and her guts
burned with loathing, as though she had eaten something indigestible.

She found it surprisingly easy to remain in Camulod unnoticed
for the week that followed Merlyn's departure. Nemo was under no
great pressure to return to Tir Manha, and so she had no reason to
concern herself over being late in reporting there. Her face and
uniform had become sufficiently familiar within Camulod to enable
her to remain hidden there in the fortress in plain sight simply by
drawing no attention to herself and taking great care to remain out
of the path of anyone in authority who might wonder why she was
lingering so long after she had delivered her dispatches and fulfilled
the tasks allotted to her. She simply left the fortress each night and
camped, either on the hillside beyond the walls or in the woods by
the edge of the training ground below, and it quickly became apparent that as long as she changed her campsite every night, never
remaining in the same place twice, she could remain completely
unnoticed. She re-entered the fortress each day through the main
gates, but revolving duty guaranteed that the guards were never the
same from day to day. Her daily visits to the bathhouse were the
only part of her routine during that week that had consistency, and
they were noticed only by Nennius, who, if he thought at all about
the length of Nemo's stay on this occasion, made no mention of it.

For the entire week during the daylight hours, she charged
herself with watching the house of Luceiia Varrus, waiting for the
Lady Deirdre to emerge and then following wherever she led. The
witch seldom ventured out alone, but she came out at least once a
day, either with the Lady Luceiia or with one or other of the women
of the Varrus household. Even when she did move abroad alone,
however, she kept to the busiest public thoroughfares, and Nemo
never had the slightest chance of approaching her.

But then, at the end of the week, something different occurred,
and watching it unfold, Nemo realized she was watching something that had been planned, and her heart began to race with
excitement. The witch, dressed in a gaudy robe of brilliantly bright
yellow, rode out of Camulod alone, mounted on a small, light cart
with high, narrow wheels, pulled by a single horse. Nemo watched

from a distance as a procession of servitors from the Varrus kitchens loaded the cart at mid-morning with a variety of foodstuffs and provisions—clothing and blankets and bedding—and she estimated that the cart contained enough resources to last two people comfortably for perhaps a week. But no second person emerged to join her, and Nemo finally began to hope that this would be her opportunity. Then, sure enough, as noon approached, Luceiia Varrus herself emerged from the house and embraced the other woman, then stood watching and waving as Cassandra rode away alone, handling the reins herself and making a leisurely progress through and beyond the main gates, where she proceeded down the hill.

Nemo followed on foot as far as the gates and watched the cart as it turned onto the eastward road towards the great Roman high road that ran north and south the length of Britain. Then she went directly to the stables and saddled her own mount. After that, it took only a few moments to collect her kit from where she had left it in care of the stableman, and she was soon on her own way, occasioning neither notice nor comment as she walked her horse out of the gates and down the hill. Only when she had reached the bottom of the hill did she kick her big bay gelding into a canter and then to a full gallop, allowing the animal to stretch its muscles while it devoured the distance separating its rider from her quarry in the light cart ahead of them.

Moving at full speed, Nemo missed the place where Cassandra had swung off the east road and headed southward, to her right. Fortunately a brief glimpse of startling yellow attracted her attention as she galloped past. She then hauled hard on the reins, bringing her horse to a skidding halt, and stood up, first in her stirrups and then climbing up onto her saddle, to see better over the bushes that intervened between her and the spot where Cassandra, still moving at the same leisurely pace, was disappearing into a grove of trees, headed towards the low hills.

Aware that she would never have seen where Cassandra had gone had it not been for the brightness of the other woman's clothing, Nemo realized that she had best take care that nothing about her costume betray her in the same way. It was a summer afternoon, and her armour, cuirass and helmet were of burnished metal. A flash of reflected sunlight could easily indicate her presence. Moving quickly then, Nemo removed her helmet and hung it from her saddle horn by its chin-strap. She then unrolled her long, thick riding cloak and wrapped it about herself, covering the shiny parts of her armour completely. She wrapped one end of the cloak around the dangling helmet, covering it and tucking the material between the helmet and her saddle. That done, she struck away from the road again, pushing her horse hard towards the spot where she had last seen Cassandra.

For two hours she followed Cassandra high into the hills, far from any path, noticing how faint and indistinct were the signs that even narrow, iron-tired cartwheels left in the hard ground. Unwilling to trust in Cassandra's supposed deafness, Nemo rode quietly throughout her pursuit, as careful to make no sound as she was to remain unseen, and kept far away from her quarry. But then Cassandra vanished, and Nemo thanked the gods that she had been watching when it occurred. Had she not, she might have fled in superstitious terror when her quarry vanished between one heartbeat and the next. What she saw was Cassandra and her cart apparently sinking into the earth, turning backwards as they did so. Frightened, Nemo nevertheless gathered her reserves of strength and crept forward, using extreme caution and preparing herself to flee at every step, to investigate what she had seen, and when she reached the point where Cassandra had vanished, she sat high in her saddle, looking down at the entrance to a steep path that doubled back on itself, shrouded on either side by dense bushes, and descended rapidly into a declivity impossible to detect from more than ten paces distant. She pulled on her reins and raised herself until she stood fully upright in her stirrups and gazed around her, her head tilted backwards in an attempt to gauge, from the height and density of the bushes and trees in front of her, just how large and deep this fold in the earth might be.

She sat for a few moments, her eyes unfocused, gazing into the middle distance, and then, afraid to hesitate any longer, she breathed in deeply through her nostrils, gritted her teeth and then used both hands to draw the long sword from between her shoulders, reaching back with her left to push the blade upwards behind her back and then drawing it down and forward over her shoulder with her right. She hefted the weapon for a moment, feeling its balance, and then she kicked her horse forward slowly down the steeply sloping path.

Within moments she was completely shut in by the growth around her, as the bushes on either side of the narrow track shot straight up and then arched beneath their own weight to meet over her head. Summer leaves filtered out and almost quenched the afternoon sunlight, so that Nemo and her mount moved downward through a thickening, green-tinctured gloom. She moved her head constantly from side to side, her nerves stretched tighter than she could ever recall, but there was nothing untoward to see. The ground rose steeply on one side of her and fell away at the same angle on the other, and the dense growth of long, rank clumps of grass, spindly saplings and springy undergrowth seemed to creep towards her from both directions.

She could see that the track she followed now had once been wider, but its edges had been swallowed by the encroaching grass and twiggy bushes, so that in many places the narrow wheels of Cassandra's coach had straddled the pathway completely, leaving tracks in the long grass on either side and sometimes even stripping the bark from fragile saplings. Nemo reached out with her sword, and half of its blade was among the bushes before her arm was fully extended. She knew immediately that she had drawn the wrong weapon and that her sword was useless here, its blade too long for such thick growth and cramped quarters. She reined her horse to a halt and replaced the long blade carefully in its harness, trying to move without making a sound and grateful that she was wearing the long cloak to muffle the grating sounds of iron upon iron as the sword slid down into the ring between her shoulders. When it was safely lodged in place, Nemo bent forward slowly and gathered up the heavy iron flail that hung from a strong hook set into the frame of her saddle close by her right knee. It was an invention of Uther's, a treasured gift to her. She had even painted it a dull, deep red to match his exactly. She slipped her right hand through the leather strap and grasped the weapon's thick wooden shaft, clasping it close

to the bottom end, where the iron ring that anchored the short chain
was riveted to the wood. Holding it thus, she could feel the weight
of the heavy iron ball at the end of the chain, dangling at the level
of her right stirrup, pulling her arm straight down by her side. She
felt better holding the flail than she had felt with the sword. She
kicked her horse forward again and rounded the next narrow bend
in the track with less trepidation than she had felt before.

After negotiating several more bends and the steepest part of the
incline—a straight, plunging slope of at least forty paces that turned
back on itself and stretched as far again without relief—she eventually arrived at the bottom and moved slowly forward until she
could look through a screen of trees into a small and very pleasant
valley, whose existence she would never have suspected or believed.

It was neither very long nor very wide, probably less than sixty
paces at its longest axis, she estimated, and perhaps as long again on
its widest, but it was deep and well hidden, steep-sided and secure
and filled with trees, mainly birch and willow, as far as she could see.
The centre of the place was taken up by a tiny jewel of a lake that
seemed to be fed by a sliding fall of water that ran almost soundlessly
down the full length of the steep rock face that formed the far side of
the depression. From the plunging angle of the rock face's descent,
Nemo could guess that the lake, while small, was very deep and
probably extremely cold even in summer. A narrow shelf or ledge of
beach ran along the water's edge closest to where she sat on her
horse, and in the distance, almost completely screened by the trees
that flanked it, someone had built a tiny stone hut. The scene was
idyllic, and her first sight of it banished any doubts Nemo had held
about where Merlyn had hidden Cassandra for so long.

As the thought occurred to her, the door in the stone hut opened
and Cassandra herself emerged, holding a basket of some kind that
she carried towards a spot that was marked by fire-blackened stones.
Kneeling down carefully, she set out very conscientiously to build
a fire, and Nemo watched her, fascinated, as a spark instantly—
perhaps magically—leaped to flame, reminding her of why she was
there. Her chest filled up with fear again. Nemo believed, with all
her being, that she was about to die, here in this hidden place, but

she was determined that she would die as Nemo the Dragon and that she would take the witch with her into the other world.

Now she lowered her helmet over her head and hooked together the cheek-flaps that would protect her face. Then she hefted the dangling ball of her flail and kicked her horse forward, out of concealment, rowelling the beast savagely with her spurs. Startled, the animal stomped and snorted, leaping sideways and attempting to rear up in protest, but Nemo reined it in brutally, pulling its head hard down and forcing it forward.

The woman in the distance looked up and froze for a moment, attracted by either the noise or the horse's movements, Nemo neither knew nor cared which; she knew only that she had been seen and that her life was now in dire peril. Digging her spurs deep, she launched herself towards the woman at the far end of the beach.

Cassandra watched her coming for what seemed an age, and then she turned and began running as quickly as she could in her swollen condition towards the cart, where the horse yet stood between the shafts. Nemo spurred harder, believing somehow that if Cassandra reached the cart before she reached Cassandra, then her life would be over and Uther's would be forfeit. As she thundered up to the cart, she hauled herself up in her stirrups and swung the heavy flail over her head, whirling it twice and then smashing it down in the killing stroke.

As the lethal ball came whistling towards her, Cassandra lost her footing and fell on one knee. The ball missed her, hissing over her right shoulder and striking the side of the cart, where it tore one of the thick oak side panels loose from its mountings, splintering the wood and twisting the iron bar that secured the panel in place. Whimpering with terror, Cassandra turned and stooped lower, scrambling beneath the belly of the enormous horse that reared above her. She threw herself sideways, to her right, as Nemo's horse reared and turned in the opposite direction. She turned again, this time to her left, and ran away from the water towards the trees.

Nemo's blood pounded in her ears and a wild cry rose from her throat as her horse, with a thunderous hammering of hooves, struck the witch's right shoulder, throwing her forward and off balance.

Nemo's heavy, hard-swung iron ball caught her beneath the right collarbone with massive, crushing force and lifted her into the air, throwing her as though she were weightless back towards the water's edge. She went spinning through the air until she hit a willow tree by the waterside and fell sideways across a low branch, to hang there like a sagging, swollen sack from which blood poured to the ground in thick, ropy runnels.

Cassandra was dead with that first fearsome blow, but Nemo took no chance of failure. She wrenched her horse around and brought it up again onto its hind legs, where she could brace herself in the stirrups and create sufficient momentum to deliver a full swing, and this time the killing ball crashed into and through the swollen lump of belly that contained Cassandra's unborn child. The force of this terrible blow knocked the body into the shallow waters at the lake's edge.

Then, her vision blurred and her heart banging against her ribs with terror, Nemo clambered down from the saddle and fell to her knees, where she swayed for long moments before falling forward to lie full length, face down upon the grass, shuddering and shaking.

Later, much later, when she had convinced herself that she was still alive and had won the battle with the witch, Nemo began to wonder at the ease with which she had achieved her victory. She had expected unearthly powers to come against her from the underworld. She had expected to be faced with fire-breathing furies and the powers of the damned. She had expected to be exhausted by the effort required to fight, let alone kill, a witch. And she had expected, most of all, to die herself in her quest for victory. But none of those things had happened. She was still alive and still breathing, and slowly, frighteningly, she was beginning to regret the lack of all of the things she had expected . . . beginning to wish she had felt even one of them. Any one of them.

At one point, before she could clench her jaws and close her mind and thrust the disturbing thought aside, it occurred to her that her victory could hardly have been easier had the dead witch been an ordinary, pregnant, helpless woman.

And once that thought had entered her mind, it refused to leave again, and she had to force herself to go and examine the dead witch.

Nemo knelt above the shattered body and gazed at the destruction she had wreaked. She tried to tell herself that this was Cassandra's witchcraft, that she could bend people's minds and make them believe that what they saw was different from what it actually was. This woman, had she been allowed to live, would have been a danger and a threat to Uther, and so to all that Nemo held to be of value. But gazing at the dead woman, who lay on her back in the shallow waters of the lake's edge, her face above the surface, eyes closed and skin unmarred in any way, she found herself amazed at its beauty and at the serenity stamped on it, despite the awful fury of her death. The dead face bore no trace of pain or fear, as though someone had come along and soothed her terror at the moment of her passing. Nemo found herself staring at the gentleness of that face, afraid to think of what she was thinking. She forced herself to stand upright and walk away, and as she went, the flail that still hung from her wrist by its leather loop dragged behind her through the water and then bumped on the narrow strip of sandy grass that formed the beach.

Two ways to kill a witch: fire and iron. But the iron used may never again be used by human hand.

Nemo spread her feet, slipped her hand free of the leather loop and swung the iron flail over her head until she could hear it hissing through the air and doubted that she could swing it any harder. Then, at the top of her swing, she opened her hand and released the weapon, knowing that it would soar and fall into the centre of the little lake and be lost in its depths. But she had misjudged her throw. The weapon, released, flew for more than twenty paces, but to her right rather than forward, so that it struck the water quite close to the bank, yet sufficiently far from the body of the woman to escape detection.

She walked over in that direction to see if she could see anything, but there was nothing visible. The flail had landed in a bed of reeds and had plunged deep into the muddy bottom. It was no great loss, other than in the fact that it was the first such weapon ever made. Since then, however, it had become quite common to see troopers riding with them hanging from their saddles. Once Uther and Merlyn had begun to use them, others had rushed to copy their design, because the things were far less difficult to make than a good sword. Nemo would quickly find a new one.

She turned and walked back to where the body of the witch Cassandra lay sprawled in a shapeless, sodden tumble of bloodied limbs. The edges of her clothing drifted and eddied in the shallows and the surrounding water had turned pink with blood, so that the skin of the dry, upturned face was creamy white by contrast. Fascinated, Nemo stared down at it for a long time, reminding herself of all that had occurred. Finally she nodded, satisfied that what she had done was right, and as she did so, she caught a movement from the corner of her eye. It was completely unexpected and her startled reaction was out of all proportion to what she had seen.

It was Cassandra's horse tossing its head, and now Nemo wondered what to do about it. It was still tethered between the shafts of the wagon, and she knew it would be cruel merely to leave it behind that way. And yet if she were to release it or even leave it harnessed to the cart, the animal would eventually make its way directly home to Camulod, where its arrival would set alarums clanging and precipitate the discovery of the witch's death. She heaved a deep sigh, knowing she had no options, and crossed to where the beast stood waiting for her, twisting its head to see her as she drew close to it.

The long cavalry sword made a slithering sound as it cleared the iron carrying ring at her back, and she held it out at arm's length, aiming it at the downward sloping column of the horse's neck. But then she thought about the bones and muscles in that massive neck and changed her mind, deciding to use her wickedly sharp double-edged dagger instead. She bent forward slightly, reaching completely beneath the horse's neck, and then plunged the pointed blade upwards into the animal's jugular on the other side with all her strength. Then, gripping the hilt strongly with both hands, she pulled the long blade back strongly towards her, slashing and slicing hard and deep. The horse barely made a sound, beyond an initial grunt of pain, and its leap of surprise was stillborn. Blood sprayed everywhere and the animal fell immediately to its knees and died quickly, still between the shafts.

Nemo stepped away from it and looked down at herself, shaking her head in disgust. Her entire lower half was drenched in blood. She found a length of white cloth in the back of the cart and carried it to the water's edge, well clear of the spot where the dead witch lay. There she soaked it and used it to clean the worst of the blood from her armour, scrubbing at the tiny bronze rings that covered the heavy leather leggings of her armoured trousers.

When she was finished, she dropped the cloth in the water and left it there. She then took one last look around the lovely little valley, noticing that the mid-afternoon sun had already started bending the shadows slightly towards the east. She glanced once more time towards the body in the water, wondering how long it would be before someone found it, and then she sighed and spat loudly before crossing to her horse and pulling herself up into the saddle. She had decided not to return to Camulod for the evening meal, as she had originally planned, but to strike out immediately for Cambria and home instead, pitching her camp that night wherever sunset found her. Within three days she would be in Tir Manha again with Uther, secure in the knowledge that the threat to him had been removed and that he and his cousin Merlyn could be friends again.

TWENTY-ONE

Within an hour of Nemo's departure from Camulod in pursuit of Cassandra, Uther himself rode into the Colony from the west, accompanied by a small group of hand-picked companions. It was obvious from their appearance that he and his party had been riding hard and taking little or no time to rest, because their horses were lathered and caked with dust and sweat and their riders looked little better. Uther rode through the main gates at a fast trot, barely nodding an acknowledgment to the guards on duty, and made his way directly to the administrative building, where he strode to the Duty Officer's station and demanded to see Merlyn Britannicus immediately. The Duty Officer that day was Jacobus, a junior decurion, an officer trainee, which was not unusual, since there was seldom any need for seniority in making the kinds of decisions that were called for in the middle of a normal working day in the administrative building.

From the way Uther phrased his demand to see Merlyn, Jacobus knew that his response was not going to be well received. Snapping to attention and saluting Uther, he spun and clicked his fingers to attract the attention of one of the runners on duty, knowing as he did so that the gesture was unnecessary. The runner was already standing by his side, gawking from him to Uther and back, waiting for an explosion. Jacobus sent the fellow running to bring the Legate Titus, the Commander of Camulod in Merlyn's absence, then cleared his throat and informed Uther that Merlyn had left Camulod several days earlier to ride eastward into the Saxon-occupied area of Britain known as the Saxon Shores in order to attend a debate among Christian churchmen in the old Roman town of Verulamium, approximately thirty miles northwest of Londinium, the former administrative centre of Roman Britain. Jacobus awaited the explosion, but it did not come. Uther drew in his breath sharply, making a tiny, sucking sound of annoyance between his teeth, and then nodded abruptly.

"I'll wait for Titus. Where should I wait?"

Jacobus indicated the *cubiculum* against the outer wall of the building that contained the commanding officer's table and chair and was illuminated by a long, low, shuttered window. Uther nodded his thanks and asked the young man for his name before he made his way inside to wait.

Moments later, Titus himself swept in from the courtyard outside and joined him, closing the door behind himself and leaning back against it, slightly out of breath.

"Titus." Uther nodded, smiling at his old friend. "You look well, but you sound a little puffed."

"Age, Uther, age. I don't have the resilience I once had."

Titus straightened and crossed to embrace Uther with both arms. Then he stepped back and held the younger man by the shoulders to peer up at him. "It will hit you, too, one of these days, no matter how immortal you believe yourself to be. Before you know it, the masseurs will be plucking grey hairs out of your head, and your joints will be starting to feel stiff on cold mornings."

"They already do, my friend. How long do you expect Merlyn to be gone?"

"At least a month. Why, what's wrong?"

Uther's face had darkened, his anger, always sudden, ignited by this unexpected complication.

"Everything. Everything's wrong, damnation! Can we send after him, bring him back?"

"Not easily. We don't know with certainty what route he'll follow. He is on his way to Verulamium for a debate with a party of two hundred . . . more of an ambassadorial journey than anything else, really. His mission is to demonstrate Camulod's strength to whoever might turn up for this debate among the bishops."

"What debate? And what in the name of all the gods at once is Merlyn doing among bishops?"

"I'll tell you in a moment, but first tell me what's going on and why you're here. I understood you had no plans to leave Tir Manha this year. What changed your mind?"

Uther moved around behind the table, punching one hand into the open palm of the other. "Gulrhys Lot, what else? Nemo had barely left with my last dispatches for Merlyn when I received word that Cornwall is seething with armed men again. Where is Nemo, by the way? Is she still here in Camulod?"

Titus shrugged. "I have no idea, but I doubt it. She delivered the dispatches a week ago."

"Word came in to Tir Manha that Lot might be making a nuisance of himself again, that Cornwall is an armed camp. My first reaction was to ignore it. It didn't seem to me that Lot could have raised another army in so short a time after the thrashing we gave him less than a year ago. But then I remembered the nature of the beast, and so I sent out scouts. Didn't waste any time. I sent them on the run, the same day the report came in, with orders to examine anything unusual that they could find down there and then bring the information back to me as quickly as they could. I sent two scouting expeditions, one by sea and the other overland. The overland group was a squad of my own Dragons, some of my very best.

"The seagoing party, two galleys, came back first, within a week. They had barely crossed the river estuary before they saw action, and they didn't even begin to approach the open sea. They were fortunate to escape capture as it was. According to the two captains, the entire northern coast of the peninsula down there is alive with shipping, so it's a safe wager the south coast will be, too. They told me there are vessels arriving from every direction every day, filling up every little bay along the shoreline and unloading men, then setting off again, presumably to transport more.

"That was all I needed to hear. I know Lot inherited his father's love of assembling mercenaries from beyond the seas, so I decided to ride over here myself and get our joint preparations underway without any waste of time. But even before we could leave to come here, the other scouting party came back, too . . . or what was left of it. They had set out to ride directly southwest into Cornwall, travelling cautiously and hoping to attract no unwelcome attention, holding to the west of Isca where the land is bleak and barren. But they were less than sixty miles into Lot's territories when they were found and challenged and forced to turn back. By that time, fortunately, they had seen all they needed to see, but they had to fight every mile of the way home, and they lost more than half their number.

"Lot has a large army gathering down there, Titus, and there's only one way for him to bring it out, as you and I both know. I don't think we have any time at all to waste sitting around talking. But I haven't even mentioned the most important information we uncovered with our overland expedition. The army my people found down there—the southern army, I've been calling it—is only half the story. According to the prisoners taken and questioned by my men, the call has gone out for an enormous assembly of men, all under Lot's banner, to take place to the northeast of here close by Aquae Sulis. When they are all together, they will start a systematic devastation of the towns in this region, beginning with Aquae itself and Glevum."

"What? But that's insane! There's nothing left in Aquae Sulis to plunder, nor in Glevum. Twenty years ago, even ten years ago, there might have been some point to that, but the towns are empty shells nowadays. Lot must know that."

Uther nodded, his face expressionless. "He probably does, but it won't make any difference to him. He is selling the idea of plunder for the taking. The picture of fat towns waiting to be sacked and looted is what he's using to raise his army, and you can be sure the rabble he's attracting have no idea his promises are empty. When they find out the truth, they'll be murderous, but Lot will be back in Cornwall by then, and we'll be the ones left to deal with it, on top of everything else."

"Hmm." Titus's face was still, his eyes narrowed. "What do your people tell you about Lot's preparations? Are they far advanced? And are any of his forces trained?"

"If any of them are, they'll be units who have fought together before now, on the continent, for the Romans, and they'll be in a

minority. The vast majority of his people, as always, will be
savages. Fearsome enough in hand-to-hand fighting, but totally
lacking in any kind of co-ordinated skills. As for how close they are
to being ready to move, your guess would be as good as mine. But
simple prudence would dictate that we take no chances and incur no
risks by being complacent."

Titus nodded. "Look, we can't rely on catching up with Merlyn
and bringing him back here. He has been gone too long. My people
would not even know where to begin searching for him. We know
that he headed east originally, by way of Sorviodunum and Venta,
but that is really all we know. He intended to improvise from then
on, depending upon what he discovered along the way, and there is
no certainty that he would even stay on the main roads if he encountered trouble at any point. So you and I had best decide on a campaign of our own, lacking his involvement."

Uther grimaced. "So be it. I don't like it but there seems to be
no other choice. Tell me about this gathering in Verulamium . . .
what did you call it, a debate?"

"Aye, that's what it is . . ." Titus launched into a brief description of the issues at stake among the Christian community in
Britain, reminding him of the visiting monastic priests who a few
years earlier had threatened all the people of Camulod with excom-
munication and damnation if they did not immediately renounce all
their former beliefs and do as they were bidden for the salvation of
their souls. Merlyn's father, Picus Britannicus, had refused to be
bullied or browbeaten by the zealots and had expelled them from the
Colony, declaring publicly in Council that he would make no decisions regarding the safety and welfare of his people's immortal
souls until he had heard the reasoning underlying such sweeping
changes clearly defined by a source possessing more authority and
dignitas than a herd of unwashed, intolerant, wandering priests.

A debate to address this question was to take place within the
following month in the great Roman theatre of Verulamium, and
Merlyn had decided to attend the gathering, as his father would
have, in order to keep track of what was happening within the
Church's teachings and equally to ensure that the bishops making

these decisions should be aware that there was a strong Christian centre of influence in Camulod, far to the southwest.

Uther himself had never been more than nominally Christian, seeing no more appeal in the Christian god than he found in any of the other, older gods of Cambria and Britain, or even Rome. He had been baptized a Christian years earlier, but that had been to please his grandmother. It had nothing to do with any feeling of personal conviction. Now he looked at Titus, his arms crossed tightly over his chest, frustration stamped on his features.

"You believe this journey of his—this expedition all the way into foreign, hostile territory—is worthwhile, even though it calls him away when he is needed here by his own people? This is not merely grandiose nonsense?"

Titus shrugged. "What should I know of such things? Is it not enough that Merlyn thinks so?"

For a few moments, Uther looked as though he would answer that with an angry negative, but then he sighed and accepted the inevitable.

"Yes, well, I suppose we will leave him to get on with it, then, for lack of any real alternative, and we will make our own plans for how we defend ourselves during his absence." Uther dragged a hand wearily down his face, closing his eyes as though to banish his frustration and focus his thoughts, "We should be combining our forces, Camulod and Pendragon Cambria, more than we have ever done before, melding bowmen and infantry in an army group consisting of two or possibly three compact, self-sufficient armies, just as Picus Britannicus described to us a thousand times. Each army will be self-reliant and will have set battle tactics, but all three will function as a solid legion whenever the need arises. And surrounding and protecting them, heavy cavalry strike formations, mobile and hard-hitting, radiating in all directions, but always launching from the central hub formed by the army. What think you?"

Titus smiled. "I think Picus Britannicus taught you well. And you know I would never disagree with a style of warfare I was taught to fight in boyhood. Fortunately, we have already begun training more of our people to fight together, combining their different skills, after last year's events. I see no great difficulty facing us there, other than the obvious lack of time to prepare. Let me send for Flavius. I have the feeling we're going to need his input right from the outset."

Uther remained in Camulod for three days on that occasion and slept on each of the three nights in the home of his grandmother. From Luceiia, during one long evening's talk, he learned the story of Deirdre's pregnancy and Merlyn's marriage, and if he felt any pain over his evident exclusion from his cousin's nuptials, he said nothing of it, remembering the suspicions Merlyn had harboured over the night Deirdre, who at that time had still been called Cassandra, had been attacked and brutally raped. He also heard from his grandmother the strange story of how Deirdre's real name was discovered when she was reunited with her brother Donuil after years of separation.

The remainder of Uther's time in Camulod was spent in conference with the interim Joint Commanders Titus and Flavius and the senior staff officers of the armies and garrison of Camulod, drawing up plans to deal with the invasion they all believed would come from Cornwall and trying to cover as many contingencies as they could envision. By the time he left to return to Tir Manha on the fourth morning after his arrival, it had been decided that Uther would command an entire brigade of heavy cavalry, one thousand strong, during the coming campaign. In the meantime, he must return to Cambria and raise as many Pendragon bowmen as he could within the month, bringing them back to Camulod to train with the infantry for as long as circumstances would permit.

Before Uther had even departed from the fortress, the hard-core training of both infantry and cavalry had begun, and the great plain at the base of the hill of Camulod was once more obscured by clouds of dust from dawn until dusk each day.

As soon as he returned to Tir Manha, Uther rode out again, this time to raise warriors from the westernmost territories of the Griffyd clans, where another young Chief called Dergyll ap Griffyd, who was not much older than Huw Strongarm, had succeeded Cative-launus of Carmarthen. The old man had fallen into an icy mountain stream swollen with melting snow at the end of the previous winter and died. Uther and Dergyll had known each other very briefly during one boyhood summer long before and had formed a mutual liking and admiration at that time, so it was easy for them to get along with each other again after a gap of many years. The expedition was a great success, and Uther returned to Tir Manha accompanied by Dergyll himself and a large company of several hundred warriors.

He arrived, however, to discover that fresh word had come from Camulod and that his mother, Veronica, wished to speak with him immediately. Intrigued, he went directly to his mother's house, and she told him about how Merlyn's young wife Deirdre and the babe she had been carrying had been murdered. A courier had arrived from Camulod three days before, bearing a letter from Luceiia Britannicus in which she described the little that she knew about what had happened. She had known where Deirdre was, and in fact had planned the expedition with the girl, who had been pining for the solitude she had loved while living in her secluded valley for months, and so a week and more had passed without Luceiia being unduly worried. But when the younger woman had failed to return as promised during the second week, Luceiia had grown concerned and asked Daffyd, Merlyn's Druid friend, to visit the young woman and make sure that she was well.

Daffyd found a scene of carnage: Merlyn's young wife slaughtered, her unborn babe destroyed with her, her decomposing body floating in the lake, bloated and ravaged beyond recognition. By Daffyd's initial estimate, later confirmed by other findings, Deirdre had been dead for at least a week, perhaps longer, by the time he found her, and the cause of her death had been a brutal battering, administered by someone of great strength. Daffyd discounted a sexually motivated attack from the moment of his first objective assessment of the crime, judging by the fact that the corpse was still fully clothed, even to her loincloth and other undergarments. And yet robbery could not have been the reason, either, as nothing had been taken from the wagon.

Daffyd judged then that it would be best for everyone—he was thinking most particularly of Luceiia's sensibilities—if he were simply to bury the sad remains of both mother and unborn child as close as possible to where he had found them and to recommend them to the gods as creatures worthy of respect and kindness. Having laid them to rest beside the lake beneath the sacred trees— all trees were sacred in the eyes of Druids—he then searched the entire locality thoroughly and painstakingly, looking for signs or traces of the unknown assailant. He found nothing, however, apart from an area of scuffed and trampled earth that might have been torn up by the hooves of an attacker's horse or, equally likely, by Deirdre's own cart horse, which lay close by, dead in its harness.

He stood vigil by the young woman's grave that night, praying over her, and then, convinced that there was nothing further to be learned at the scene, he returned to Camulod bearing his tragic news.

Luceiia withdrew to her rooms, where she remained in mourning for two days, greatly distressed by the knowledge that word could not reach Merlyn in Verulamium in time to bring him home ahead of his scheduled return. By the time the messengers crossed the entire country to reach him, if they survived the journey at all, it would already be nigh on the time for him to set out for home on his return journey.

Uther sat listening in silence as his mother told him the story and read to him from his grandmother's letter. When she had finished, he rose to his feet and stood over her for a while, gripping her shoulder tightly with one hand, incapable of speech. Then he turned away and walked from the room.

Concerned by the look of him as he walked away, Veronica rose quickly and followed him, watching as he left the house and made his way directly to the cluster of long buildings that had been erected several years before as stables for his cavalry mounts. The sullen trooper Veronica disliked, the woman-man called Nemo, had been standing outside the house, waiting for him to come out, but he waved her off impatiently, and she instantly fell back and walked away, plainly knowing her superior well enough to gauge his mood and know she was not welcome for the present.

Veronica stayed back and waited and watched until her son emerged again from the stables a short time later, riding his huge chestnut gelding, and as he disappeared towards the main gates of

Tir Manha, looking neither to right nor left, she turned and signalled to a passing trooper, bidding him find Garreth Whistler and bring him to her house immediately.

"Are you ever going to speak again?"

Uther turned his head very slowly and threw Garreth Whistler a long, considering look, then turned back and kicked his horse forward, down the sloping bank to where the narrow river bustled through its gorge.

Garreth dipped his head in a private gesture that said, *Well, I tried*, and followed horse and rider down the steep incline. He had caught up to Uther easily, within five miles of Tir Manha, because Uther had been making no attempt to move quickly, but he had made no effort thereafter to impose himself upon the King, content simply to ride along half a length behind him and wait to be noticed. Uther, however, had paid him no attention, apart from a swift glance to determine who it was that had followed him, and more than an hour had elapsed since then. Garreth could tell, however, that Uther was not displeased by his presence.

They had been sitting side by side for almost half of the past half hour, simply gazing down at the torrent in the gully below, and now Uther was approaching the edge of the fast-flowing stream and rising in his stirrups prior to dismounting. Garreth waited until he had dismounted completely and moved to sit on the trunk of a fallen tree by the riverside, and then he swung down from his horse, too, and dug into one of his saddlebags. From it he withdrew a cloth containing a cold fowl, a loaf of bread and a small, stoppered horn filled with salt, all provided by Uther's mother. He carried the bundle to where Uther sat on the tree trunk and perched beside him, placing the cloth between them and untying its knot.

"Here, eat. Your mother told me what happened. She also told me you must be starved."

Uther glanced down at the food and shook his head, still apparently not ready to speak.

Garreth shrugged and ripped a leg off the bird, then sprinkled it profligately with salt and bit off a succulent mouthful. He chewed with relish for a while, then stuffed the meat into one cheek and spoke around it. "You're acting as though this was personal to you . . . as though you had known the woman herself . . . What was her name? Deirdre?"

Finally, Uther spoke. "Deirdre, yes, but she was Cassandra before that. You never knew about the fight we had, Merlyn and I, the night Cassandra was attacked, did you?"

"No, not really. All I know is that after a lifetime of seldom being more than an arm's length apart, you two spent nigh on a year without seeing each other."

Uther shook his head and heaved a great sigh. "Do you know, Garreth, that to this day I regret that night. But even at the height of it, while Merlyn and I were almost at each other's throats, I had no notion of how great the rift would grow to be between us . . ."

Garreth's voice, when next he spoke, was pitched low. "The two of you were at each other's throats?"

"Aye, almost, or I was at his. I was in a foul frame of mind that night, spoiling for a fight."

Garreth said nothing, made no move that might interrupt the mood as Uther continued, speaking as though to himself.

"That was the night Cassandra was attacked—raped and beaten so badly that she almost died, and for days everyone thought she would. You were in Tir Manha when that happened, not in Camulod. I can remember how glad I was to see you when I rode home. I was still angry, still bitter, still seeking to find blame in others for what I myself had done."

"That sounds ominous. What had you done?"

"Everything that I ought not to have done. I vented my anger on a little girl, for one thing. That was my first wrong step."

"I don't follow you."

"Cassandra, the girl. I abused her, treated her abominably, tried to thrash her. That's when Merlyn and I first locked horns. He knocked me down and pinned me there until the girl could run away to safety."

Garreth made no response to that, other than to raise his eyebrows in a silent, cynical query.

"On my life, Garreth, it is no jest."

"Hmm. Then I think you had better tell me about it. What did you do to the girl?"

"Ahh . . . well, it was . . . You know the kind of thing. Merlyn and I were in the games room with a few willing girls, and everything was . . . as usual. But then I noticed . . . I noticed Cassandra's mouth. She was there in the room with us. Watching us, watching everything." His voice tailed away into a long silence. "I noticed her mouth, and once I had noticed it I could not rid myself of the thought of how it would feel . . ."

"Sucking you."

"Yes."

"And how did it feel?"

"I don't know. She wouldn't do it. Set her teeth and refused to open them and I began to get angry and to force it . . . and she bit me."

"Ayee! Hard?"

"Hard enough. I was in a foul frame of mind and that bite set me off on a rampage. You know what my temper can be like. This was me at my worst."

"So you hit her, and Merlyn knocked you down, and she ran."

"Yes."

"And that was it? That was all that happened? Did you and Merlyn continue fighting after the girl had run?"

Uther shrugged. "No. Merlyn let me up, and I left. I walked out of there and went directly to the stables, picking up a few of my own Dragons on the way—no one in particular, just troopers unfortunate enough to cross my path while I was in that mood. I dragged all of them with me and rode back to Tir Manha, as I told you."

"And because of that, that wrestling bout, you would like me to believe that you and Merlyn didn't speak to each other for a whole year?" He waited, but Uther made no attempt to respond.

"That makes no sense, Uther. I mean, it's not as if Merlyn had never seen you lose your temper before, and all the gods know you two have knocked lumps and pieces off each other since you were both old enough to swing your arms and call each other names. And I will not believe it arose out of jealousy because Merlyn resented your approaching a wench in whom he had an interest—you two have been sharing your women since you learned what to do with them. So there's something you are not telling me. What is it?"

Uther pushed himself up to his feet and stepped away from the tree trunk, turning back to face Garreth Whistler. "Well, there are a few details that I failed to mention to you. I told you the fight was all that happened, and that was the truth. What I did not tell you was what was *said*."

"Said? Said by whom? You have lost me, Uther."

"Said by me, Garreth, said by me. I swore I would kill her." His face twisted into an expression of self-loathing. "A man should never utter meaningless threats. That was one of the first lessons Grandfather Varrus ever taught Merlyn and me. Never utter meaningless threats, because they will confound and defeat you."

Garreth shrugged his shoulders. "So you were angry and you overreacted. She had just tried to bite off your cock, hadn't she?"

Uther gazed into Garreth's eyes for the space of five heartbeats and then nodded an affirmative. "I threatened to kill her, Garreth, and then I stormed out of there and rode out of Camulod without a word to anyone. And that same night, some time after I left that room, someone *did* try to kill Cassandra, and almost succeeded. Now, had you been Merlyn Britannicus, what might you have thought about that?"

"Ahh . . ." The sound that escaped Garreth's mouth was more breath than anything else. He was completely bereft of words, and his eyes reflected consternation as the import of what Uther had said continued to sink home to him.

"Bear in mind, Garreth, that the girl was deaf and mute. She could not talk about who had attacked her. She could tell no one. All she could hope to do—all anyone could hope she would do—was point a finger when and if she ever recognized her assailant. But that meant that her life was in danger every moment, since the unknown attacker would have to kill her in order to protect himself. And so Cousin Merlyn arranged somehow—and I have no idea how he achieved it—to have Cassandra vanish from a heavily guarded building. He's a clever lad, our Merlyn."

"But—wait a moment, Uther, wait a moment . . . If Merlyn believed you were the one who had done this, why would he go to such lengths to protect the girl? He knew you were gone far from Camulod, so how then could she have been in danger? Why didn't he simply denounce you?"

Now Uther smiled for the first time, a narrow, bitter smile. "Because, aside from being a clever lad, our Merlyn is also a just one. He was not completely convinced of my guilt. He was very close to being convinced, but he did acknowledge that there could be some doubt, and so he took the steps he did."

"He never accused you of anything?"

"No, he did not, not publicly. Merlyn would never make a public spectacle of his suspicions without proof to back them up. He confronted me about it later. He had smuggled Cassandra away to protect her, he told me, for fear the killer might be someone else, but as soon as she was well enough to withstand the shock of confrontation, he intended to bring her face to face with me again."

"And that would have vindicated you, would it not?"

"Yes, it would, Garreth, but that had never cost me a moment's thought. I knew I had done nothing to harm the girl beyond that first explosion of bad temper. What hurt me more than I would ever have believed anything could hurt was that my Cousin Merlyn could suspect me of such a thing, such depravity. Even as angry as I was, did he think I could do something so deeply, foully evil?" Uther's guts churned then, remembering that those who knew his rage had always feared a darkness in him.

"Shit!" The expletive reflected the depth of Garreth Whistler's frustration and was the last word spoken by either man for some time, but then Whistler shook his head and rubbed his nose with the palm of his hand. "There's still something missing . . . some part of this I am failing to understand. You said you had been in a foul mood. Well, then, what was it that made you angry enough and unhappy enough to dig yourself into the hole you created that day?"

Uther looked at Garreth again and grinned, shaking his head. "Something I don't want to talk about, old friend."

"Now that's very sad, Uther, because you are my King, and had

I but a pinch of pity in my breast I would bleed for you. So speak to me, share the burden. Get this pus-filled sickness out of your mind and let your conscience breathe again. What is it, this enormous secret of yours, this thing that has caused you so much ill feeling?"

"This place."

"This place?" Garreth looked around him, frowning.

"No, not here. Cambria, and Tir Manha. It's not my kingdom, Garreth, although I am its King. It is not my home—not my true home, the home of my heart."

"That's Camulod."

"Yes, it is."

Uther reached behind his back with one hand and closed his thumb and fingertips on either side of the blade of the long cavalry sword that hung there, thrusting it upwards hard, so that it almost slid out of the ring between his shoulders, and as it fell forward he grasped it by the hilt, twirled it around and jammed its point into the ground, where it stood swaying gently. Garreth looked at it and said nothing.

"That was the start of it, right there."

"What was, a sword?"

"A cavalry sword, a long sword. Cavalry has always been my first thought of Camulod, Garreth. Every time I hear the name, I think of cavalry—tall men riding tall horses, all of them in armour. There could be no Camulod without cavalry, and without cavalry there would be no long swords like this.

"What I am trying to say, Garreth, is that Camulod and Cambria are like light and darkness to me. My memories of Camulod—all my memories of Camulod—are filled with light and laughter and enjoyment. The people there enjoy their lives! Here, on the other hand, we seem to live most of our days in darkness. Smiles are few and far between in Tir Manha, or anywhere else in Cambria. It is as though our people have no natural feeling for enjoyment. We seem to see it as a sign of weakness. We have no laughter in our souls, or if we have, we save it all inside us until we can laugh at someone else's misfortune, jeering at their pain. Our elders are stern, humourless and unforgiving; our women are dark-faced and lowering. Not always, not always . . . I'll grant that. But more often than otherwise.

"That year my mother had been sick, of some kind of fever, and had been confined to bed for weeks. My Grandmother Varrus was concerned for her. She had received word from my father that he, too, was worried. Anyway, my grandmother had suggested that I might want to return home to be with my mother, at least until she grew well enough to be up and about again, at which time she might like to return to Camulod with me for the remainder of the summer. Well, I resented being told what to do, especially by an old woman, even if she was my grandmother, and even more than that, I resented the implication that I did not know where my duty lay. I had decided that it would be impossible for me to return home; I was far too necessary to the welfare of the Colony simply to take a leave of absence and disappear for some indeterminate period of time. Anything might happen while I was away, and I was determined that no one would be able to say I had neglected either my duty or my military responsibilities.

"Of course, the truth was that I simply did not want to come home again to Tir Manha. My father's elders were outspoken in their disapproval of my lengthy absences—they saw it as misconduct. For my part, I dreaded the thought of being stuck here for any length of time . . .

"On the last night of our patrol, the night before the incident with Cassandra, I had a dream in which I saw my mother lying dead in her bed in Tir Manha while I was enjoying myself in Camulod. It was a terrible dream. I sprang awake bathed in cold sweat, not knowing where I was, forgetting I was on patrol and that we were miles from anywhere, surrounded by forest. I found it impossible to go back to sleep again, and finally, I gave up and rolled out of my blankets well before dawn, then went to inspect the perimeter guards. They must have thought I was insane, but all I was worried about was that they might have heard me crying out in my sleep.

"That dream, the memory of it, stayed in my mind all that day and was still there late that night while I was lying in the games room with those women, making a pig of myself. I was coupling with one of them, and a vision of my mother, lying sick and perhaps dying, sprang into my mind. I couldn't think about that and continue with the woman, so I started looking around for something to take my mind off what was troubling me. And that's when I saw Cassandra and noticed her mouth. That, effectively, is how the entire incident began.

"And now it has ended with her brutalization and death at the hands of persons unknown . . . again. Poor woman, it would seem she was fated to die by violence. And what do you think is the most ironic part of all of it?"

"I don't know, Uther, tell me."

Uther looked Garreth Whistler in the eye and smiled. "I was there again, Garreth. If what Daffyd the Druid suspects is true, then Cassandra—Deirdre, as they call her now—died on the first day of her visit to this secret place she shared with Merlyn, and I was there in Camulod the day she left. She had gone by the time I arrived, less than an hour before, as it transpired. But I was there in Camulod when Deirdre met her death. I wonder what my Cousin Merlyn will make of that?"

Garreth sat blinking at Uther for a long time, saying nothing, and then he looked down at his right hand, which still held the clean-picked bone of the fowl. He blinked his eyes, as though awakening from a dream, and then flipped the bone into the river, wiping his hand on his tunic as he stood up.

"What *should* he make of it?" he asked. "There's nothing to be made. You weren't alone in Camulod, were you? The only person in the fortress?"

"No, of course not."

"Well, then, there will be people there who saw you and who can attest to your presence all that day and for how many more?"

"Three more."

"Aye, and what did you do during those three days?"

"Discussed strategy and tactics with the military staff."

"Good, so you could not have been doing that and riding off into the countryside to some unknown place to slaughter a young woman at the same time, could you? So now that we have settled that, may you and I return to Tir Manha and discuss strategy and tactics with our *own* military staff? We have a campaign to plan, and if I may remind you, you are supposed to be leaving to return to Camulod again within the week. By that time, all our arrangements must be firmly in place here, with Huw Strongarm, Dergyll, Owain and everyone else, including me, fully aware of who holds what duties and who is answerable to whom. Do we have time for that?"

Uther smiled. "Yes. We have time for that."

Garreth rewrapped the uneaten fowl and they remounted. He put his horse to the slope and Uther's followed, so that the conversation continued in a series of shouts.

"I am not the one you have to talk to, Uther . . . Merlyn, I think . . . needs to hear all that you have said to me today . . . most particularly . . . now that he has lost his wife." They gained the level surface again and were able to lower their voices and ride side by side.

"And you need to tell it to him, looking him in the eye as you do so. He'll need his friend back, and he will feel great guilt over what he suspected about you, I think, so it will be up to you to see that he forgives himself. Can you do that, think you?"

"Aye, I believe I can . . . What happens after that is entirely in the hands of the gods." He glanced up at the sky. "It's going to rain. Let's ride!"

Men make plans, but the gods decree the outcome, and Uther was never to enjoy the chance of commiserating with his cousin over the death of Deirdre. A month after his discussion with Garreth, Uther saw Merlyn again most unexpectedly. Uther had been working for days to bring about a confrontation with a large party of Lot's forces, harrying them constantly and eventually chasing them up into the Mendip Hills, where he had painstakingly set up an ambush for them. He never dreamed that Merlyn and his party returning home from Verulamium might ride into the middle of it and spring the trap. Spring it they did, however, and in the opening moments of the fighting that followed, Merlyn's party absorbed heavy casualties before Uther could come riding to their rescue. Thereafter, the cousins fought side by side in the grim conflict until, in the fury of the fighting, Uther saw Merlyn unhorsed and struck down by a killing blow from his own flail, swung by an enemy who had not known with whom he was engaged. The battle, little more than a skirmish, savage though it was, was won shortly after Merlyn's fall, and Uther then carried the unconscious, almost lifeless body of Merlyn Britannicus home to Camulod. There he lay for months, tied to his bed, his head immobilized while the surgeon Lucanus drilled a hole into his skull and saved his life. His life, but not his mind. From that day forward, Merlyn Britannicus won slowly back to life, but even when he had apparently recovered fully, in that he could talk and move and function normally in every way, his mind was destroyed, his memory erased as though no knowledge had ever existed in its depths.

BOOK FIVE

Cornwall

Greetings, dear Mother, I hope this finds you well.

I know it has been less than a month since I last wrote to you, so I hope you will not be alarmed to receive this, another missive from me, in so short a time. I am very well, but I have tidings that might affect Uther, and since I have no way of knowing whether or not he remains in Camulod, I decided to send them through you.

You might remember my telling you several years ago of a woman called Mairidh who lived with us here in Tir Manha for some months. Her husband, Balin, was in the service of Duke Emrys of Cornwall at that time, although he and our dear Ullic were friendly for many years. Mairidh and I, too, became good friends, and she has written to me on several occasions since she and Balin were summoned home. I have recently received another letter from her, and the tenor of her message has prompted me to write this to you.

Mairidh and Balin have been living quietly in retirement since the death of Duke Emrys, but it seems that Gulrhys Lot recalled Balin more than a month ago and charged him with the kind of task he performed so well and for so long on behalf of the old Duke. Lot, benighted creature that he appears to be, initially attempted to coerce Balin to his will by proposing to keep Mairidh in his custody as a hostage against Balin's good behaviour in the performance of his task, which was to be a special envoy to Eire. He misjudged the temper of his man, however, for Balin, knowing how important his participation in this venture would be, defied Lot openly, citing his own advanced age and the necessity of having his dear wife accompany him to tend to his health and well-being. Lot relented, seeing that he had no other choice, and permitted Mairidh to accompany her husband.

Lot's foolishness has perhaps worked to our advantage, since it prompted Mairidh to sit down and write to me, telling me about Balin's new task and her disgust with the creature Lot and his inept attempt to control her husband. Briefly, Lot formed an alliance some time ago with the King of the Hibernian Scots in Eire. The result of that alliance was the Erse invasion of Camulod in which Merlyn captured and held hostage the Erse prince, Donuil. Since then, the Scots of Eire have made no hostile incursions into this land, and nothing further has come of the alliance.

That might now be changing. According to Mairidh, Lot has visions of using the sea power of the Erse King Athol Mac Iain, who apparently owns great fleets of galleys, and he has sent Balin into Eire to negotiate a renewal of the alliance, which is still nominally in place. Should he be successful, Lot could, at a blow, acquire vast resources of shipping and enable himself to move large numbers of men and weaponry along the coast, thereby threatening both Cambria and Camulod. I believe it is imperative that Uther know of this immediately. Please send word to him as quickly and directly as you can.

In another portion of her letter, Mairidh wrote of how Lot has set about systematically to vilify Uther in the eyes of the people of Cornwall by spreading monstrous lies and rumours about him. She knows, of course, that none of what is being said is true, but she wished me and Uther to be aware of what is being said of him. Rumours are being spread of atrocities and outrages being committed by

*Uther and his army. They speak of rapine and mass slaugh-
ters being carried out on ordinary villages and hamlets,
with children and old men being hanged and killed out of
hand, while women, young and old, are being violated,
mutilated and debauched, most of them by Uther himself.
So successfully has this campaign of lies been carried out,
Mairidh told me, that women in Cornwall now threaten
their errant children with the name of Uther Pendragon,
frightening them into obedience.*

*Not all of this is new to me, for we heard rumours of
it in the past from travellers. I even mentioned it to Uther
half a year ago, but he merely laughed at my outrage and
passed it off as some kind of tribute. Only people who
inspire fear and constitute a real threat to the status quo at
any time are ever honoured with such malignant attention,
he told me. The fact that Lot of Cornwall goes to such
lengths to denigrate the name of Uther is merely a testament to how greatly Lot fears Uther.*

*At the time, I was calmed by his amusement, despite
my fears, but now I wonder again. The reputation that he
now has in Cornwall might help his campaign there by
spreading terror, but I cannot see how such a thing can
benefit his future memory.*

*Give Uther my love, if he is still with you in Camulod,
and write back to me soon.*

                              Your loving daughter, V.

TWENTY-TWO

Lagan Longhead spread his right hand and twisted it sideways to lay his rigid fingers delicately against the iron of his axehead, fanning the tips so that they lay almost exactly along the edge of the blade. The heavy iron head lay on his left hand, resting on an oily cloth, and its shaft lay beneath his right forearm, reaching right to the elbow. His fingers left clear impressions in the thin film of linseed oil he had just added to protect the metal against rusting. *Shit!* he thought, and reached to wipe the marks away with an end of the rag draped across his other hand. Then he laid the axe gently on the top of the low tree stump beside him. That done, he wiped his hands conscientiously with a clean rag, finishing the job by scrubbing his palms and fingers against the rough hide of the sheepskin leggings that enclosed his thighs, fleece inward. Only then did he take hold of the axe shaft, hefting it so that the clean-lined muscles of his forearm rippled and flexed. He ignored the leather thong looped through a hole in the handle's end, allowing it to dangle. Only in battle would he loop the thong around his wrist.

The axe was magnificent, his favourite weapon and his dearest possession. Its broad, heavy head gleamed dully, surmounted by a wicked, tapering, thumb-thick spike, and the tempered edge of its chopping blade was keen enough to cleave cleanly through metal and bone. Its shaft was perfectly cylindrical, of thick, close-grained wood, and its entire surface was engraved with intricate designs of twining brambles, thick with thorns and delicately picked-out leaves, stained to a rich, dark brown and polished by decades of care and handling. Lagan had no idea how old the weapon was, but he knew it had belonged to his grandfather, who had taken it in a fight against some invading Outlanders.

He swung it up again and caught the shaft near the head in the cradle of his extended left hand, sighting along the line of the spike towards another, tall and much-scarred tree stump some fifteen paces from where he stood. As he did so, he heard the sound of his son's voice, shouting as he ran towards the house. Lagan cocked his head to listen, his arms still extended. Even though the house stood between him and Cardoc, he could gauge the boy's excitement by the tone of his voice and the speed with which it approached. He heard his wife, Lydda, call out then, telling their son his father was at the back, and then he returned to his sighting, His right arm flew out and back, and he hurled the axe just as his son rounded the end of the building behind him. The weapon flew end over end, its shape a whirling blur, then smacked against the tree and clattered to the ground. The boy almost skidded to a halt, his eyes wide. He seldom saw his father miss a throw.

Lagan turned his head and looked at his son, keeping his face expressionless. "Bring that thing over here."

The boy brought the fallen axe, and Lagan nodded. "Stand back."

As Cardoc obeyed, Lagan swung again, this time pivoting completely and throwing round-armed when all his weight had shifted to his left foot. The axe whirled again and thumped hard into the wood of the tree, its edge biting so deeply that Lagan had no thought of asking his son to retrieve it. He walked forward himself and levered strongly upward on the shaft, prising the deeply buried edge free before turning back to his son.

"You look guilty, lad. What have you been doing?"

Young Cardoc shook his head, his face flushed. "Nothing, but I distracted you when I ran around the corner."

His father shook his head, dropping the butt end of his axe handle into the metal loop on the belt at his waist so that the head rested against his left hip. "No, you did not. I heard you coming long before that. I misjudged my throw, that's all."

The boy was grave-faced. "You don't often miss."

"No, I don't, not when I have a stationary target. But even so, it's really a stupid thing to throw an axe. An axe is for swinging, not for throwing. As soon as it leaves your hand, you're weaponless, and a living target won't stand still waiting to be killed. If you can miss a dead tree, think how much easier it would be to miss a running man . . . And if he's running *at* you to kill you, you're dead." He wiped his hands again on his leggings, then rubbed the palms together briskly. "I heard you shouting as you came to the front of the house, but I couldn't hear what you were saying. What was it?"

"Uh, the King is looking for you, and no one knew where you were. Master Lestrun sent people to search for you. One of them saw me and sent me here to see if you were at home. Lestrun says you are to come immediately."

Lagan sighed and bent to pick up his rags and a pot of linseed oil, placing them on the small, roofed shelf against the back wall of the solid log-and-clay house that was his home. "Well, when the King commands, we must obey." He cocked his head at his son. "I don't suppose you could have any idea what this is about?"

The boy shook his head, wide-eyed and mute, and his father nodded and began to walk around to the front of the house, the boy trailing behind him.

Lydda was waiting by the open door, Lagan's long travelling cloak folded over her arm.

"You might need this."

Lagan eyed it distastefully, shrugging his shoulders beneath the thick, warm tunic of fleece that already encased him from neck to mid-thigh. "I doubt it. If I do, I'll come back for it. Lot may be the King and his affairs important, but I am not leaving on any journey in mid-morning without bidding a proper farewell to my family simply to keep him in a pleasant good humour at having his own way immediately."

Lydda smiled at her husband. "So you say, old Gruffy, but you know you do everything he asks you to, exactly when he wishes it to be done."

Lydda was a tall and stately woman, but her husband placed his arm about her shoulders and drew her easily beneath his own. She fitted against his side with the ease and compliance of long custom, and he dipped his face to kiss the top of her head. "I had better see what he wants. It might be urgent. But let's hope it doesn't involve a journey. If it does, I'll come back home before I leave." He squeezed her against him and she raised her mouth to his kiss. Then she leaned in the doorway, still clutching the spurned cloak, to watch him until he disappeared from sight.

Cardoc sat on the doorstep, watching his father and saying nothing.

Lydda reached down and tousled his hair. "What are you up to today?"

The boy turned to look up at her, teeth flashing in his shy smile. "Oh, nothing much. I was playing with Tomas and Ewan. I think I'll go back."

"Away you go, then." She watched him vanish, too, then moved back into the house, leaving the door ajar, wondering as she went what it was that had Gulrhys Lot so excited this time. She liked the King well enough, she supposed, having known him for many years, and his friendship with her husband had broadened to include her, too, but she would not have been prepared to take a blood oath that she trusted him entirely. Lagan, on the other hand, was utterly loyal to him. "The King's true man," she had heard others call him on several occasions, and the tone in which the words were said invariably left her wondering whether or not she had imagined resentment or sarcasm or even sneering condescension in the utterance.

The two men had been bosom companions since early boyhood, and their friendship had grown and strengthened. Since Cardoc's birth, however, Lot's visits had become far less frequent.

Lagan would hear no ill of "Gully," though the gods knew well that there was enough ill being spoken of the King to deafen all the underworld. The tales of atrocities committed by Gulrhys Lot and in his name by others—most particularly by those loathsome Outland creatures of his, Caspar and Memnon—were harrowing and plentiful. Lydda suppressed a shudder, remembering the King's hideous Egyptian sorcerers, long since vanished from Cornwall and unmourned by any. Rumour—violently and vehemently denied by Lot himself—had it that they had died in Camulod among the godless savages up there. If so, Lydda, thought, the world was a better place.

As for the tales and rumours of the horrors that went on in the King's name, Lagan had never seen the slightest evidence to support their truth, and so he gave them no credence. Lydda knew how much of Lagan's value to the King lay in his innocence and integrity. She suspected that Gully would go to great, even extreme lengths to hide his less pleasant doings from her husband's eyes and ears. And that suspicion troubled her deeply, for it suggested that her fine and noble husband could be gulled and thought a fool, and she knew he was no such thing. Innocent, honest, trusting, loyal and open-minded, yes, he was all of those, and prepared at all times to extend the benefit of doubt until faced with irrefutable evidence of fault or guilt. Once faced with such proof, however, her husband was implacable. That same sense of perfect probity which led him to expect the best and the finest, noblest behaviour also enabled him, when necessary, to be the harshest in securing justice and prosecuting the guilty.

She stopped by the window, arrested by that thought, and stood staring out into the bright morning light, seeing nothing.

Did Gully see Lagan as a fool—gullible, trusting and capable of being swayed? Could Gully be that evil, that manipulative? Lydda blinked and shook her head, thrusting the thought aside, assuring herself that she was being silly. She looked about her, trying to remember what she had been doing before, and then went back to her household work.

As Lagan crossed from the shade between the houses fronting the King's residence and stepped into the bright, morning sunlight, he sensed, rather than saw, the King's guards stiffening to attention at his approach. Lagan Longhead had never liked the guards, even before the death of old Duke Emrys, whose fear of being murdered had led to their posting. Emrys was long since dead, murdered by time and ill health, and his guards had been helpless to forestall either of those stealthy marauders. But the guards remained, their presence now surrounding and supposedly sustaining Emrys's son and heir, Gulrhys Lot, self-appointed King of Cornwall.

As he strode through the main portals into the elaborate compound, Lagan felt the eyes of the guards still upon him, and he kept his gaze fixed straight ahead. Three men stood on either side of the main gate, and he knew they had a superior nearby within the walls. They would not stop Lagan, for they knew him as the King's closest friend—some malicious whisperers said his *only* friend—and knew that Lagan Longhead's access to the King was unlimited, a fact that set him above and apart from all others.

Inside the portal lay a narrow yard, a catchment area some fifteen paces long and six wide, with a guard hut for the duty sergeant directly to the right of the entrance. At the far end, facing Lagan and bristling protectively at his approach, two more guards watched him, unsmiling, their eyes scanning him from head to toe until he had passed between them through a massive pair of hand-hewn, iron-studded doors and into the coolness of the large hall beyond.

Eight men, Lagan was thinking as he blinked in the sudden darkness of the hall. Eight armed Outlander mercenaries to guard the King in his own hall from the advances of his own people. There was something fundamentally wrong in that.

Pausing just inside the door, Lagan allowed his eyes to adjust. A heavy, sour stink of old woodsmoke hung in the air, and thin, eddying wisps of it drifted from the ashes in the massive fireplace in the single stone wall opposite the door. The King's hounds, eight huge, rough-haired beasts the size of small ponies, lay sprawled in the rushes that covered the earthen floor, and only one of them lifted its head to gaze, tongue lolling, at the newcomer. Apart from two more armed guards flanking another doorway in the wall to Lagan's left, the animals were the enormous room's only occupants.

Lagan coughed, his lungs protesting against the reek of the foul, smoky air, and made his way towards the guards as soon as he could see his way between the heavy tables and benches that strewed the floor. When he was within two paces, one of the guards swept his sword from its sheath with a slither and brought the point up threat-

eningly, its tip angled at Lagan's throat. Lagan stopped dead, tilting
his chin downward to stare at the sword's tip, then looked into the
guard's eyes.

The man was a stranger. Keeping his face utterly expressionless,
Lagan moved his eyes slowly to the other guard's face. This one he
knew. No one spoke for a space of heartbeats, and then the second
man brought up his hand and placed the back of his fingers against
his companion's blade, growling something in their own tongue.
The first man grunted and remained motionless for a count of four,
then straightened slowly and put up his sword, sneering very
slightly, his eyes warning Lagan wordlessly that this time he had
been lucky, and that the guard would readily have spilled his blood.
Lagan made no response. He simply stepped past the fellow as
though nothing had happened and reached down for the iron handle
to push the door open.

Lot was leaning through an open window, peering out into the
yard beyond, and he turned when he heard Lagan enter.

"Ah, there you are," he roared.

Gulrhys Lot came bounding across the room and tried to catch
Lagan in a headlock that quickly turned into a mighty hug. Lagan
clasped his own arms about the King's shoulders, marvelling, as he
did every time, that he had finally grown accustomed to this highly
unusual form of greeting. The King was the only man Lagan knew
who indulged in this very intimate, personal gesture, a mannerism
he had picked up somewhere in Gaul in his boyhood, and the
majority of his men, with the exception of his Gaulish mercenaries, were extremely uncomfortable in receiving, let alone returning,
the affectionate embrace. To the dour, Celtic mind, such overt
demonstrations of friendship smacked of emotional excess, and
Lagan had seen many a fearless chieftain and warrior flush with the
embarrassment of it.

Now Lot thrust him away and held him at arm's length, gripping
his upper arms tightly and peering into Lagan's eyes. His own eyes
narrowed. "You're angry about something. What is it?"

Lagan tossed his head, jerking his thumb back towards the
doorway behind him. "I'm not angry, Gully, not really, simply

annoyed. One of your tame killers out there drew a sword on me when I sought to come in here."

Lot's face darkened immediately. "What? Against you? He threatened you? I'll have the whoreson's head!" He was already moving towards the door, but Lagan grasped him by the sleeve and turned him around.

"For what, Gully? He's new, and he didn't know me. The man on duty with him pulled him off. Besides, the fellow was only doing what he's supposed to do."

"And what's that? Threaten my friends?"

"No, protect your kingly arse against imaginary dangers. I'm dying of thirst. Have you anything to drink here?"

Lot barked a harsh, abrupt laugh and moved immediately towards a table that held several clay pitchers, each covered with a cloth and an array of cups. This room was his personal domain, and he permitted no servants to intrude upon his privacy. The Keeper of the Household had prescribed hours during which his staff could clean and maintain the room, but when the King was present, their absence was ordained.

The walls were of plain stone, but they were hung with weavings of undyed, thick, heavy wool, which Lot's father had believed helped to keep out the winter's chill. The eastern wall was pierced by a Roman-style window, with two arches separated by a central pillar, that opened upon the interior courtyard where the boys trained. Two sets of shutters, exterior and interior, enabled the King to shut out the cold and the outside world whenever he wished. Flanking the window and vented to the courtyard, an open fireplace held a brazier basket made of heavy iron strips, and the floor, save for the area closest to the brazier, was strewn with clean, dried rushes that were changed regularly and often.

The room was sparsely furnished, yet comfortably appointed to Lot's own needs. It contained one deep, stuffed and padded armchair made of softly tanned leather and another, less luxurious but still comfortable chair with a padded, upright back in the form of a classic Roman *stella* for a guest. These two chairs faced the fireplace, one on either side. Three other plain, armless wooden chairs were spaced against the walls around the room, and there were two tables, the small one Lot was using now, which always held jugs of mead and wine, and another, longer work table, much larger than its companion, which was set against the rear wall of the room, accompanied by a plain, three-legged stool. That table was where the King spent most of his working day, for Gulrhys Lot took pride in telling everyone that he *worked* at being King. That was true, Lagan knew, and no exaggeration. But he also knew that Lot enjoyed the sense of power that accrued to him because of his literacy in a time and place where very few could read or write.

Lot read well and wrote a clear, flowing script that always surprised Lagan in its neat and methodical firmness, for it was cleaner and more legible than Lagan's own. The two had learned together as children, their teacher an elderly, crippled Roman scribe who had undertaken to educate both Duke Emrys and his son in return for a roof over his head and the protection that entailed. Lot, stubborn and wilful even then, had refused to learn unless his friend could learn with him, and so Lagan Longhead had been set apart from all his fellows by being taught to read and write.

Glancing at the work table now with all its paraphernalia —quill pens and styluses, ink pots, parchments and papyrus— Lagan noted a scattering of scrolls, several of them rolled but two unfurled and held open by heavy weights. Gulrhys Lot had quickly seen all the advantages of literacy, and nowadays he insisted that his primary advisers knew how to read and write also. Lagan often smiled at that thought, for he believed that there were several among those primary advisers who were as literate as tree stumps, but they were all clever enough to keep more learned men about them, and thus they were able to survive, serving the King and preserving their own privilege.

As Lot was bringing Gaulish wine for both of them, a howl of boyish outrage drifted in through the window, and Lagan crossed to look out to where a cluster of six boys was grouped around a seventh, this one holding his arms tightly clasped around his head and keening at the top of his voice. One of the smaller boys hung back, clutching a heavy dowel of ash wood and looking apprehensive. Off to one side, an elderly, dour-looking warrior stood silently watching, scowling in disapproval. Lagan grunted, smothering a laugh.

"Looks like young Twoey got in a good one on Owen. Is this what you were watching when I came in?" He took the drink the King was holding out to him.

Lot nodded. "Aye. They improve daily, learning the disciplines of fighting intelligently, in spite of their dislike of each other."

"Or perhaps because of it. They are a fractious crew, aren't they?"

Lot did not respond other than to turn away, looking out into the small exercise yard. Lagan winced to himself, thinking that he might have offended the King. Gully was unpredictable when his sons were the subject of discussion. He could criticize them; others could not. This time, however, Lot took no offence.

"Six of them," he grunted. "You would think at least two of them could get along."

"Perhaps it's their mothers' fault," Lagan answered quietly, half turning to where the King stood gazing out and down.

"Perhaps? That's a foolish observation. There's more jealousy among those six bitches than among all my chieftains combined. I ought to banish all of them."

Lagan allowed himself a smile. This, too, was a common theme between them. "You chose them, Sir King," he drawled.

"Chose them be damned. They chose themselves, through pregnancy. They are a herd of cows!"

"The regal concubines . . ."

Lot's head jerked around. "There is sometimes too much of the Roman in you, my friend. You are impertinent, with too much Latin."

"I learned it by your side, Lord Lot, from your own teachers."

"Aye, you did, better than me!" He grunted a laugh and swallowed a mouthful of wine, then looked out into the courtyard again.

Lagan took a sip from his own drink. "You sent for me. What do you need?"

Without looking at him, Lot turned and moved away from the window, crossing directly to the table, where he put down his cup and picked up a rolled scroll and a tubular dispatch case made of toughened hide. He slipped the scroll into the cylinder and then turned and offered it to Lagan.

"I need you to go to Herliss today. Give him this and bring me back his answer as quickly as you can."

Lagan pursed his lips and took the container from the King's hand, hefting the weight of it in his own. "Is my father expecting this? Will he be surprised?"

"No, he is not expecting it . . . not immediately, at any rate. But no, he will not be surprised. Inconvenienced, perhaps, but he is my steward, and this relates to his duties."

Lagan merely nodded. "And why so sudden, Gully? You made no mention of this when we spoke together yesterday."

"There was no thought of it in my head yesterday."

"Am I allowed to ask what it concerns?"

"Aye, of course you are. Sit down, man, sit down. Since when have you needed to stand in my presence?"

Lagan never had, but he knew better than to spoil the mood of the moment by saying so. Gully had little ways about him, and this was one of them: by reminding Lagan that he had no *need* to stand, he intimated that he had the power to *make* him stand.

Lagan sank into the chair the King had indicated, and Lot hooked another forward with his foot, settling into it and leaning close.

"There are two matters of great import that your father holds in his stewardship, and both of them are dealt with in this missive. I could not exaggerate their importance, Lagan, even were I so inclined. Suffice to say that only you could carry it for me. There is no one else I could or would trust with such a mission, and you will see why when I tell you that the first of them is treasure. Your father holds great stores in my name. Gold, jewels and weaponry, but chiefly weaponry. I need it now. I believe he has it scattered for safe-keeping throughout his strongholds on the coast."

Lagan nodded in agreement. His father had four coastal strong-holds, each of them guarding a harbour for Lot's marauding pirate fleets. In return for safe anchorage, the pirates paid him tribute in Lot's name—one full half of the booty they brought back from every voyage. Herliss collected all of it and held in safekeeping for the King.

"Lagan, I believe Uther Pendragon will be back here again with the spring weather, hammering at our gates. The winter has been mild, so spring is almost here." The King was being his most appealing self, his voice deep and low and filled with trusting confidentiality. Lagan waited, saying nothing.

There came a thump at the door behind them, and one half of it swung open, held by the arm of a guard, to admit Lestrun, Lot's most senior adviser. The old man ducked under the extended arm as he shuffled in, then nodded to Lagan, offered the same gesture, perhaps somewhat more deeply, to his King, and proffered a pair of tightly rolled scrolls from beneath his right arm. Lot looked at them contemptuously, and for a moment Lagan thought he would savage the elderly Lestrun for interrupting them, but then he nodded curtly, jerking his head towards the long work table.

"Put them over there with the others."

Lestrun bowed his head but remained where he was, facing the King. "I will, as you say, Lord Lot," he said quietly, almost hissing in the sibilant, lilting tones that were so unmistakably from the northwest of Cambria. "But not before you promise me that you will read them as soon as you are alone. Both are highly important, and a decision must be made today on one of them, at least, if you are to achieve what you have told me must be done."

As the other spoke, the King's face went white with sudden fury. "Curse you, man! Will you have me do your bidding like a threatened boy? Put them down and get out!"

The old man nodded calmly, unimpressed. "I will do so, but not before I have your word. It is your own designs, your own intent, that are at risk, here. Rail at me all you wish, but if I fail to have you do what must be done, you will have my head off in any case."

Lot's nostrils flared, and Lagan wondered, as he had many times before, at the old councillor's utter lack of fear in defying a man who was so notoriously ill to cross. And then, to his astonishment, the King's choler disappeared abruptly and he barked a laugh that might have been admiring.

"By the gods, Lestrun, one of these days you will push me too far, and I will regret having killed you after it is done . . . Very well, I promise I will read the blasted things as soon as I am alone again, and I will make my decision immediately upon having done so. Now get out."

The old man bowed, then nodded to Lagan, his face expressionless, before turning to withdraw, and again an unseen guard held the door ajar until he had gone. The sight of a disembodied arm clad in leather armour, stretched across the open doorway, suddenly incensed Lagan intolerably. When the door closed again, he looked at Lot.

"Why do you have these people, Gully? It's hardly as if you need them."

"Who, my advisers?" This was said with a half smile.

"No, damnation, these guards. You don't need guards. To guard against what, your own folk? I had to pass by ten of them between the main entrance and your quarters. Six outside, two in the yard and two right here outside your chamber. Are you expecting to be attacked?"

The King's small smile remained in place, but he did not answer immediately, and the thought occurred to Lagan, not for the first time, that the well-known half-smile concealed far more than it illumined.

"Do you believe I'm expecting to be attacked here in my own house? No, Lagan, no." The smile was full-blown now, the voice that spoke the words mellifluous and confiding. "It is not the man who needs the guards. It is the rank, the title."

Lagan blinked, his brow furrowing. "I don't follow you."

"It's quite simple. I am a King, Lagan. Kings require guards, not to protect them—at least not all the time—but to *define* them."

"Define them as what, Gully? And to whom? You are as clearly defined in my eyes today as you were when first we became friends two decades and more ago."

"Aye, in your eyes, my friend. In your eyes, I have not changed, and in the name of all the gods at once I swear I have not. But in the eyes of others . . ." A rising intonation made the statement a rhetorical question. "I have changed my station. I am a King, today . . ." He turned suddenly and walked away to perch on the edge of the table that held the drink flagons, his left leg extended and his right knee bent and supported by a foot on the seat of the wooden chair by the table's side. "Sit down there, where I can see your face."

Lagan moved silently and sat facing Lot, squinting slightly against the brightness of the late-winter sunlight that now fell across his face. Lot waited until he was settled, cup in hand, and then continued, leaning forward slightly to rest his elbow on his knee.

"When my father became clan Chief, and as both his fame and his influence grew, he was able to travel beyond these shores, into Gaul at first, and then southward all the way into Iberia. On those journeys—for not all of them were warlike—he encountered Kings among the upstart Burgundians of southern and central Gaul, and even among the incoming Franks, whose holdings lie further afield. And he took note of how such men behaved: how they dressed; how they conducted their lives; and how they governed their peoples.

"It was after he came home from one such voyage, victorious and rich with booty, that he took for himself the title *dux*, or duke, of Cornwall, and he set out thereafter to live in ducal style. The Romans, who set great store upon such things, were far from stupid. They knew that people see what they are shown. Show people a humble man in rags, and they will treat him as a nothing. Show them that same man dressed up in furs and leather, with warriors at his back, and tell them he is a duke, and they will bow to him and grovel for his favour, though they know not a duke from a cook . . .

"As Duke Emrys, my father demanded and received far more respect and obedience than he had ever known formerly. The duke became much stronger and far more powerful than the man. The duke became a symbol . . . a symbol of his people, of his clan, of his possessions." Lot stopped and gazed down at his right hand, one finger of which wore the heavy ring he used to seal letters and documents. He wiggled his fingers, so that the heavy ring flickered in the light from the window. "This seal is such a symbol. Its boar's head is my mark, my identity. The presence of its imprint on the wax seal of a document is the visible proof to all men that I have approved and authorized the contents." He removed the ring and held up his hand, splaying his fingers. "Take it away from me, however, smash it with a hammer, and until I have another made to replace it, you have deprived me of the ability to express my authority to distant people. Surely you see that?"

Lagan nodded slowly before taking another deliberate sip from his cup.

"Good. Well, a King is another, similar symbol, and a King is greater, stronger, richer than a duke. Duke Emrys, my father, brought prosperity to Cornwall and it flourished under his leadership. Upon his death, I swore to increase my father's successes in every area, and I did so. I renegotiated with the mercenaries he had hired and extended their range of operations. I increased his wealth, and I increased his holdings. Overall, I increased his power—my power. My task now is to preserve and defend that power, that prosperity and that leadership, for those who depend on it."

Lot paused, watching his listener keenly.

"Lagan, let me put it plainly and bluntly. Cornwall is now a kingdom, and I am at its head. In all my dealings with others beyond our lands, I must be seen to be a King and to have the strengths and resources of a King. So, when visitors come to our doors, they will be met by guards, whose solemn duty is the guarding of the King. There is no more to it than that." He broke off, frowning. "Now what's wrong?"

Lagan was shaking his head, pursing his lips. "No visitors come here," he said flatly, and for a moment he thought Lot was going to fly into one of his rages. But then the King burst into laughter.

"By the gods, Lagan, you vex me sometimes, but I'm grateful for your thick-headed common sense, nonetheless. You're right, of course. No one comes here to visit . . . not yet, at least. But they will, Lagan, they will, and soon. They will come in swelling numbers to beseech the favours and the mercy of Cornwall."

"The siege engines."

"Aye . . . the siege engines. It's time for Cornwall to grow."

"Hmm. And what about Camulod? That could stunt your growth. Now that Merlyn Britannicus no longer commands in Camulod, Uther Pendragon seems to have the running of its armies, as well as his own. And Pendragon's a hard man, from all I hear of him, and a bad enemy. Harder than his cousin Merlyn ever was.

He'll do everything in his power to make sure you won't grow much beyond Cornwall as long as he's alive."

Lot's eyes filled with fury. "Then that whoreson will not live long! I have designs for him and his maggot breed. When your father brings the wagons from the south, you'll see some changes here. Our men will be better armed than the enemy, and they'll be trained to use those weapons."

Lagan had heard enough, and he had no wish to revisit this debate on weaponry. In his eyes, from all that he had gathered and from the small amount of fighting he had experienced directly in this war, the disciplined cavalry forces marshalled by Camulod were outstripped only by the long, deadly bows and arm-long arrows of Uther Pendragon's Cambrian warriors. Those longbows, Lagan was convinced, were the most dangerous weapons in existence, and Cornwall possessed no effective counter to their deadly threat. He moved back to the window only to find that the boys were gone, set free by their tutor, who was alone in the yard now, piling their mock weapons neatly beneath the lean-to where they were stored. He spoke again, hoping to steer Lot away from the discussion of weaponry.

"You said there were two topics in this message. What's the other one?"

"My wife, Ygraine."

Lagan half turned towards the King, looking at him over his shoulder. "What of her? I saw her when I was at my father's place last time, and I thought she was looking well. I told you that, did I not?"

"Did you, by the gods? I don't recall it. And did she send her love to me?"

" I had no opportunity to speak to her. I saw her from afar." He turned completely now, his back to the outer courtyard, and noticed the expression on the King's face for the first time. "What's wrong, Gully?"

Lot sniffed angrily and threw a lock of hair back from his forehead with a toss of his head. "Nothing is wrong, but my wife—my Queen—needs to come back here. *I* need her to come back here, where I can keep an eye on her."

Lagan was puzzled. "How so, keep an eye on her? What has she been doing?"

"Nothing . . ." Lot's hesitation was short-lived. "It's not her I need to watch, it's her family." Lot almost smiled. "We were speaking of symbols a moment ago. Well, Ygraine is another symbol, the symbol of the alliance between me and her family in Eire."

Lagan nodded, frowning slightly. "As I recall, it wasn't much of a success, that alliance, was it?"

"No, it was not, but I need to keep it alive, now more than ever. You may recall that Ygraine's father, King Athol Mac Iain he calls himself, sent an army against Camulod when first I marched north against them. It was a fiasco. They fell foul of that swine Merlyn, who caught them on the march and butchered them, then sent them home with their tails between their legs. And since then, they have refused to renew hostilities against Camulod, claiming some prince of theirs is held as hostage to their blood oath."

"So why do you think it's worth keeping your alliance alive?"

Lot looked at Lagan and then let his gaze slide beyond him towards the window at Lagan's back.

"Because Athol Mac Iain controls two large fleets of galleys. Transportation that I am going to need one of these days."

"I see. But how has Ygraine suddenly become so important?"

"I—" Lot stopped short, then began again. "Your Uncle Balin is in Eire. Did you know that?" Lagan merely shook his head. He had heard nothing of his father's brother in many months, and they had barely spoken at all since Balin's return to Cornwall. "Well, he is. I sent him there more than a month ago to maintain contact with old Athol. Now he has sent word to me—it came last night—that the old man is taken with a desire to see his daughter and so may visit us this summer."

"Ah, and so you need the Lady Ygraine here, comfortably installed and living as your Queen before he comes. Well, that's understandable."

The King's face was a flinty mask, showing no trace of humour or tolerance. "It pleases me to hear you say so, but the understanding of others matters nothing to me. I find it politic that she should come here now to be with me, so that her overfond father, old and doddering as he may be, will have no reason to withdraw from this alliance on the grounds that I have mistreated his daughter."

Lagan looked his friend squarely in the eye. "But you have, Gully. You can scarcely deny it. Perhaps mistreated is too harsh a word, but you have neglected her." He ignored the cold blankness of Lot's eyes and pressed on. "You may think I'm being too bold, but I believe you have to ask yourself if you really believe you can undo the damage already done to the lady's pride. She must already be resentful, hidden away where she is. She probably feels she has been slighted and ignored for all these months." He paused, meeting the King's angry stare without blinking, speaking eye to eye, friend to friend. "I have never understood why you sent her to live with my father out there in isolation on the coast."

Now Lot smiled, but the effort it cost him was obvious, and the result was more of a grimace than anything else.

"She is a shrew, Lagan, worse than all the other six combined. There can be no peace with her and me beneath the same roof tree. Besides, I have sons enough. She was a price I had to pay to form this alliance— an evil-tempered wife unfit to wield a besom. Now, however, things have changed . . . my needs paramount among them. I will bring her back into my household now for the sake of my kingdom, above all. I will honour her publicly as my Queen and perhaps I'll even sire a get on her . . ." His eyes drifted off again, fixed on some inner space, and then he snapped back to attention. "And speaking of sons, how is yours, the warlike young Cardoc?"

Lagan's face lit up. "Apart from Lydda, he is the greatest delight of my life. Every time I come back home, even if I've only been away for a matter of days, he seems to have grown another hand's breadth taller."

"Aye, and that reminds me, you almost did not come back at all last time, and I had to wait for days to learn of it."

Lagan looked uncomfortable for a few moments, and then smiled and shrugged. "It was not worth mentioning. It was over and done with, and no harm incurred."

The King made a tutting noise between his teeth. "You really must take people with you when you ride away, Lagan. For a man with the name of Longhead, you can be remarkably stupid and stubborn sometimes. I heard about the escapade, but there were no details. What happened?"

Lagan shook his head and shrugged his wide, strong shoulders. "Nothing much, but I was lucky that Docca and his fellows came along when they did. I rode too close to a band of louts who were braver and more numerous than I at first suspected. We were exchanging . . . opinions, when Docca arrived."

"Aye. Docca *opined* that you had killed three of them by the time he reached you."

"Four, but I was glad to see him. I didn't know he was there until one fellow fell away from me with an arrow in his eye. The tussle didn't last long after that. It's amazing how shortened odds can sap some strong men's courage." Lagan turned away and reached for his sword belt and cloak. "I was careless that time, it's true, but it taught me a lesson. Still, I prefer to travel alone, and most of the time I have no trouble." He thrust one arm completely through the loop of his sword belt and allowed the sheathed weapon to dangle while he swung the cape up and over his head to settle comfortably over his shoulders. "And now I should go home and tell my wife I'm going away again. Do you really want me to leave today?"

Lot nodded, his half-smile back in place. "Aye, I do. We have little time now, it appears, and every hour might be precious. Were it not so, I would otherwise leave you to take your own time in going and returning."

"Aye. Well, my father will doubtless have to gather your weapons from his various castles before he can send anything back here, so there will be a wait involved. Will you want me to remain and come back with the wagons, or should I return immediately with word of how long it will take?"

"Well, we must leave that to your father and you, to a degree, at least." The King made a display of deliberating, drumming his fingers reflectively against the back of his chair before continuing. "But if it looks like being less than, say, ten days, then you might wish to remain there to oversee the proceedings and then ride back here with the train. If it looks like taking any longer than that, though, I think you should come back at your earliest opportunity and advise us as to the length of time we will have to wait before the material is in our possession."

"Good, so be it." Lagan quickly buckled his belt about his waist before picking up his cup and draining it, smacking his lips. "I will take my leave of you, then, and go and kiss my wife and son before I take to the road." He swung away and then stopped, clearly considering some idea that had newly occurred to him. "D'you know, I think I might take Cardoc with me. It would do him good to see his grandfather, and the journey will be a relatively safe one, crossing our own territories. Besides, I had promised to take him fishing."

The King's hesitation was so minute that it almost did not happen at all. "Then take him, my friend . . . and the lovely Lydda, too. She will enjoy that as much as the boy. So be it you are sure they will not slow you down. If I need you for anything, it will be unimportant enough to wait another day. Go and take pleasure in your family, but bear in mind that this task on which you ride has a large degree of urgency and import."

The smile faded from Lagan Longhead's face. "Aye," he said. "You're right, as ever. Perhaps it would not be a good idea, after all."

"There will be other times, then. Take them when you return, and you will have as much time as you want, if Camulod has not come round our ears."

"Aye, I'll do that. Farewell, then."

As the door closed behind Lagan Longhead, the smile faded slowly from the King's face to be replaced with a look of pouting, heavy-eyed displeasure. He plucked moodily at his heavy lower lip, frowning thoughtfully at the solid oaken door, and then he rose and made his way slowly to the window, where he placed one hand on the central pillar of the window and leaned through to look out into the empty courtyard. Thunder rumbled far away, and he leaned further forward to look upward, twisting his head and craning his neck to see that the blue sky had vanished, replaced by a thick canopy of dark grey cloud. Gulrhys Lot grunted deep inside his chest, and then turned away, moving directly towards the long work table where Lestrun had placed the two scrolls.

Lagan was deep in thought as he strode from the King's residence, ignoring the guards completely. He was not totally lacking in cynical awareness of the King's ways and moods, and the final little piece of manipulation had not escaped his recognition. He had known even as he spoke the words that he was making a mistake in announcing his desire to take his son with him, but the impulse had been overwhelming, and once begun, he had no way of unsaying it. In consequence, he had known before he finished speaking that he would not be allowed to take the boy. Better to have held his tongue and simply taken the lad, than to have mentioned the possibility of doing so to Lot, because Lot's demands on one's loyalty, as everyone knew, were absolute. He would brook no weakness, no distraction, under any circumstances. He insisted ruthlessly that he be the centre and the only focus of attention, and many a warrior had learned to his cost that he could not marry while the King had need of him. Lagan kicked at a pebble in his path, cursing himself for his enthusiasm and wishing he had kept his mouth tightly closed.

Despite the urgency of Lot's demands and the willingness of everyone involved to fulfill them, it was no small matter for Herliss to amass everything he had been asked to supply and then prepare it for safe delivery. The siege engines, in particular, presented a problem in transportation that almost proved insuperable until one bright fellow had the idea of stripping the wheels and axles from the heavy wagons and attaching them directly to the massive timbers of the devices themselves.

The huge Roman siege engines had never been designed to travel great distances. They were massive, cumbersome affairs constructed for strength, stability and endurance, built with solid wheels to provide them with a degree of mobility but intended in that respect purely for positioning each apparatus and, in the case of the artillery pieces, for altering the field of fire they commanded during battle. They were meant to be manhandled but had never been intended for overland travel.

Duke Emrys had acquired them somehow at the time of the Roman withdrawals from Britain, and knowing their worth, he had taken them into his custody and guarded them against a future need. They had been dismantled carefully, the component pieces clearly marked and numbered for reassembly, but they had been in storage for decades since then, split up for safety among Herliss's four coastal forts. In the intervening years the enormous wagons originally used to transport them had been used for other purposes, scattered and eventually lost. In consequence, Herliss faced an enormous task, and he dared not take the risk of mixing or misplacing the component parts of each device, be it ballista, catapult or storming tower, for the men who would transport and reassemble them had had no training in such things.

The time flew by, so that Lagan quickly found himself on the wrong side of Lot's ten-day division, with yet another two weeks' work to go, according to his father, before all the individual pieces would be ready for moving. He had spent all of his time on the south coast moving among the four forts, and by the time he realized that he would have to return with the unwelcome word of delay to Lot, he had not yet found time to visit Queen Ygraine in his father's home fort of Tir Gwyn some twenty to thirty miles inland.

Reluctantly, without having seen or spoken to the Queen, he bade his father farewell and set out again for Lot's stronghold of Golant, bearing the news that Herliss would be ready to move northwards with his treasures in no less than two weeks. Lot, Lagan knew, would not be happy with the tidings. But then, he reflected, Ygraine the Queen was likely to be even less happy at the prospect of being reunited with her husband. According to Herliss, Queen Ygraine did not hold Gully in high regard.

So busy was Herliss that he barely noticed his son's departure. His mind was too full of logistical concerns to leave time for family matters. He was content, knowing that he would follow Lagan within weeks and would finally be rid of the wearying responsibility for all Lot's stored goods.

As for the Queen, Ygraine, she remained unaware for days that her husband had taken note of her again and summoned her to Golant, or even that Lagan had been in the south. The word of her imminent journey came to her eventually from Herliss, whom she had grown to regard almost as a father. Ygraine listened to what he had to say but made no complaint. She understood all too well that Herliss had no choice but to deliver her upon Lot's instructions, and so she accepted the inevitable. But she could find little in his tidings to look forward to, and so filled was her mind with the unwelcome prospect of being reunited with her estranged spouse that it would never have occurred to her to wonder about her own safety on the journey from Herliss's stronghold to Lot's.

TWENTY-THREE

The ambush, swift, terrible and thorough, was rendered all the more terrifying by the small amount of blood actually shed. And in the duration of it, within the space of moments, Ygraine's status changed from Queen to hostage. Caught completely unprepared, her escort, strong though it was, had no chance of counterattacking. One moment they were marching in good order through a wide, shallow valley under bright, early-spring sunlight, and the next they were caught squarely between two parallel masses of alien warriors, grim-faced and silent, terrifyingly different from any she had known before. They had literally sprung from the ground on either side of the narrow road, already grouped in attack formations and aiming hundreds of great longbows in massed ranks.

She was amazed, however, at how clearly she was able to see what happened in the momentary chaos that followed. Her escort had already begun to surge into a disciplined but already useless attempt to rally some kind of defensive formation, and in the middle of the protective swirling of her own personal bodyguard, at the time when the first hail of arrows should have been wreaking ruin and havoc amongst her protectors, Ygraine, Queen of Cornwall, daughter of Athol Mac Iain of Eire, perceived clearly and unmistakably that someone, for some unknown reason, was withholding death and mass destruction.

Only one group of warriors, under the personal command of Gylmer, her husband's most faithful and hotheaded captain, succeeded in forming a shield phalanx and moving forward to engage the enemy on the sloping hillside above. They had barely left the road, Gylmer on his mountain pony riding in their centre, rallying them, when they were slaughtered, all twenty of them obliterated instantly by a lethal rain of long, deadly arrows, fired with appalling accuracy from the other hillside, *behind* them. Ygraine heard the missiles hissing overhead, moving from right to left, and spun to look, thus avoiding the actual sight of the death that fell upon her quickest men so suddenly, and she was stunned to see that none but the farthest ranks on the right of the hill behind her had fired, in response to some hidden, but deadly signal. They were already stringing new arrows when she swung back to see what they had done. Not a man of the twenty remained standing. And no single bowman in the ranks facing the slaughtered men seemed to have loosed a shot.

The warning was not lost on anyone, including Herliss, the grizzled veteran commander entrusted by her husband with the task of shepherding his Queen and a valuable train of goods and provisions between two of the royal strongholds that dotted his territory. As Ygraine caught sight of Herliss now, his yet-unhelmed head flung back in outrage and his right hand raised above his head, fist clenched, to rally his forces, she recognized the fury and hopelessness that swept across his face as he slowly lowered his hand.

Herliss, the only remaining mounted man in the train, was stunned by the swiftness of this defeat, by its totality and by his own helplessness. They had sprung from the ground like devils, pouring up out of holes and trenches dug in the soft hillsides on either side of the narrow, rutted road, the only warning of their coming the sudden, shocking sight of rectangular sections of grass-covered ground being lifted up and thrown aside to give them passage. And as they came, they had drawn their bows, arrows already nocked, forming themselves with daunting speed into solid blocks of death: tight, disciplined, inexorable; ranks spaced far enough apart to enable each to fire over the heads of those beneath them; drawn weapons pointed grimly down towards the long train reeling in disorder and panic below. Young Gylmer, as usual, had been the first man to react, kicking his pony forward with a shout and attracting the attention of his men before panic could overwhelm them. But Gylmer had died for his decisiveness, and his men had been struck down with him, destroyed by a response so quick and so complete that every man who saw it knew it had been planned for just such a move.

Now Herliss looked about him, assessing his ruin. Men hung in impossible postures of indecision everywhere he looked, as though frozen in place in the blink of some mad god's eye. Among them, in the very centre of the roadway, the Queen's group of women eddied, as yet too stunned to have begun screaming. Behind him, he could hear wails of panic rising from among the wagon-drivers. Only the Queen's personal bodyguard of Ersemen seemed prepared to match the threat of the massed ranks above. They had formed a circle, their shields a solid wall behind which they now crouched, grim-faced and prepared to die about their lady.

A stillness fell over everything. The voices behind Herliss died away, and in the silence, the men up on the hillside lowered their threatening bows, relaxing the tension in their arms. It was then that Herliss became aware of a truly frightening truth: only half of them had been aiming. As the bows were lowered, the other half were raised, extending the promise of death, and yet withholding its delivery. And still nothing moved on the valley floor.

Herliss drew a deep breath, aware of the Queen's eyes staring at him. He was the King's Commander. Gulrhys Lot would hang and disembowel him for what had already occurred. His sole alternative was to meet death on terms he chose himself, no matter how one-sided. He straightened his back and drew his heavy, bronze-bladed sword, bringing up his arm again, as slowly as he had lowered it, expecting to be shot down at every moment.

"No, Herliss! No! I forbid it!" The Queen's voice cut through the silence. "Everyone, hear me! Lay down your weapons."

A few turned their heads towards her, including Herliss.

She spoke again, her voice ringing. "Are you all mad? Can you not see? They have no wish to kill us. If they did, we would be dead! Lay down your weapons." She could see that some of them wanted to believe her, but no one moved to comply with her command.

"The woman's right, Herliss!"

The words came booming from the chest of a giant man who stood some thirty paces away on the hill behind her, and she spun to face him, as did all the others. He wore no helmet, and he had thick, black hair and a full, close-cropped beard that masked his features almost entirely. He was also one of the few on the hillside who carried no bow. His hands were empty, crossed over his chest, the index finger of each one hooked into the armholes of his breastplate, the other fingers spread on the swelling muscles of each arm. He looked completely at his ease. A mustard-yellow, ground-length cloak was thrown back over his shoulders, and his armour was of toughened, layered bullhide, studded with lozenges of black iron. Even from afar, separated from him by the protective circle of her bodyguard, Ygraine could see his bright blue eyes blazing, flashing with either humour or scorn, she could not tell which. As her eyes found him, he spoke again, directly to Herliss, who sat staring from his horse's back, the hand holding his sword still partly raised.

"The women's presence is the only reason you remain alive. Our lord does not make war on women. Throw down your weapons, and you'll live. Otherwise die here, and die quickly."

Herliss rallied himself quickly, finding his voice again and filling it with truculence. "Your lord? These are King Lot's lands. Who is this *lord* of yours?"

"One far more powerful than yours." The black-haired spokesman's voice betrayed no hint of anything other than arrogant surety. "You have two hundred men trapped here, ten women and a score of puny little bows. We have four hundred longbows pointing down at you. Therefore our lord has more power than yours. Throw down or die. My patience is not endless."

Ygraine felt fingers clutch at her elbow from behind and knew it was her cousin Alasdair Mac Iain, the captain of her bodyguard, but she had eyes only for Herliss now, and she shrugged the fingers away, only to feel them grasp again at her sleeve immediately.

"Herliss, hear me in this," she called, pitching her voice to keep her words from the men above. "You will be of no use to me or to anyone else if you are dead. Do what he says, and what I command. Tell your men to lay down their arms." She watched Herliss debate with himself for long moments, then saw his shoulders slump and knew she had won, but she waited until she saw him pass the order to surrender before she swung back to face her own captain.

"Lady Ygraine—" he began, but she cut him short, hissing with urgency before he could begin his protest.

"Alasdair, be quiet. I know what you will say and I refuse to listen. My father charged you with my life. He will not thank you if you endanger it in this." She forestalled his anguished reaction, silencing him with a stabbing jab of her flattened hand. "They *have* us, man! What would you do? Fight to protect me and be killed, leaving me prisoner?"

"But we *must* fight, Ygraine, we have no option! We—"

"You have *two* options!" Ygraine spat the words at him, trampling his protest underfoot with her own imperatives. "Fight and die, or yield and live. No more! Think what you're saying, man! If we conduct ourselves correctly, we may yet win something here."

The captain gaped at her, his lack of understanding written plain upon his face, so that she made herself speak more slowly, softening her voice against her will but articulating each word precisely. "You heard what that man said, Alasdair. His lord, whoever he may be, does not make war on women. Have you ever heard the like? Perhaps he has a weakness for women's beauty, like my own lord. If he does, we'll use it, and we'll win free of him alive, all of us. These men are disciplined. Ours are warriors, not soldiers. So please, I want you to avoid confrontations with me or with them. Trust me in this. We will not be harmed."

Alasdair Mac Iain sucked in a mighty breath and held it as he glared eye to eye with his headstrong cousin. Then he capitulated and swung away towards his men, sheathing his sword and nodding at them to sheathe theirs and lower their shields. They did so with obvious reluctance, glaring defiantly at the enemy who surrounded them on the hillsides.

"Stand down," their captain warned them. "But show these animals no fear. We'll fight another day. For the time being, heed the words of the Lady Ygraine, but hold your positions and be prepared to die defending Athol's honour should these heathens prove false."

As her bodyguard obeyed Mac Iain's orders, Ygraine turned to the woman closest to her, a beautiful, tall woman in her mid-twenties, with long, blond tresses spilling from a silken cowl.

"Morgas, call out to Herliss, but quietly. Tell him to dismount and come here, but not to come to me. Call him to *you*. Then tell that fellow up there on the hill that it is over, though I can see he knows that. Do it now."

The woman called Morgas did not obey immediately. She levelled her lovely blue eyes at the Queen. "Why me, Ygraine?"

Ygraine smiled. "Because, my dear, you are the fairest of my flock, and you shall be the Queen for now, until I have had the opportunity to weigh and judge what has happened here. This lord of theirs might have a sweet tooth for women, who knows? And if he has, he might be malleable thereby. If so, he will delight in you, and should he be the half part noble, so might you in him. Why are you frowning? Do as I say."

"But . . . they already know *you* are the Queen. They heard you order Herliss not to fight."

The Queen's faced hardened. "No, they heard a woman's voice begging for life. Most of them would have no idea which woman. The shield wall stands between us and Herliss, and he and his group between the wall and the enemy, whose eyes were on the shield wall and the men forming it. If they have looked at us at all since then, they have seen but female shapes, and the promise of lechery to come. We are not yet *people* to them. Now do my bidding."

Morgas inclined her head, her eyes veiled, and turned to obey.

Ygraine stayed among her women to watch, and as soon as Morgas had carried out her wishes, she saw the black-bearded man raise a horn from his waist and blow two distinct signals at no great volume. In response, his men began to move, half of them slinging their bows across their backs and moving down towards the road, the other half spreading themselves about to cover any eventuality, their vigilance, if anything, increased. Herliss had bidden his own men yield, and now, having thrown down their weapons, they moved together sullenly, forming separate groups, their hands free of weapons, their eyes shifting fearfully as they watched the enemy descending towards them.

The black-bearded giant moved down directly to the Queen and her ladies, passing between two of the warriors of her bodyguard who now stood weaponless. As he approached, Ygraine saw that he was even more impressive than from afar, towering over Alasdair, the tallest of her bodyguard. Herliss had already arrived and been informed of Ygraine's wishes, and now he stood sullenly to Morgas's right, glaring at his conqueror. Watching the big stranger approach, Ygraine was impressed by his comeliness, obscured even as it was by the black beard and by his surprising youth. She estimated his age to be no more than twenty-one or twenty-two; younger than herself or any of her women.

"Which of you is the Queen?" The voice was a deep but strangely gentle growl, the words uttered in a Celtic language strange to Ygraine's Erse ear, but understandable. He ignored the men completely, his eyes moving from face to face among the women. When his gaze met hers, quickening with evident intent to speak to her, she lowered her eyes demurely and turned away, hoping to disarm him. She was surprised at herself: at the strange sensations that were coursing through her; at the heat she could feel rising in her cheeks; and at the compulsion she felt to look back frankly into his blue eyes and speak to him, an unknown stranger and a proven enemy, a brigand and a thief. She closed her eyes, gripping her elbows in her hands, steeling herself, and then, aware somehow that he was no longer looking at her, she opened them again and glanced towards him, noting that every woman in her group was watching him watching Morgas. Ygraine breathed again, feeling relief sweep over her. It was no surprise that he had fastened upon Morgas, but it was gratifying to know that her judgment had been sound. He had dismissed Ygraine, drawn to the brighter blossom.

As he moved towards them, approaching very close to where they stood, Ygraine moved closer to Morgas, almost interposing herself between the two, inclining her head slightly, with an air of submission towards the blond woman. The man loomed over her.

"Lady," he growled, "are you the Queen among these people?"

"I am." Morgas's voice was cold, with no hint of graciousness.

The big man bowed to her, almost brushing Ygraine's breast with his shoulder. Her nostrils flared in anticipation of the smell of him, but instead of the rank odour she had expected, she caught nothing but the mild hint of warm, clean sweat.

"Lady—" He broke off, straightening himself up. "Your pardon. What should I call you?"

"That will suffice." The voice dripped icy disdain.

He nodded. "I am Huw, called Huw Strongarm, captain to Uther, King of Pendragon."

Ygraine felt her spirits falter. Uther Pendragon, the Cambrian King himself, already here in Cornwall and the snow not a week gone! Her people's hopes had all been pinned upon his late arrival after a long, hard winter, but he was here already. Then she frowned, looking anew at the young giant who called himself Huw. He seemed like an unlikely captain for the fabled Pendragon hordes. She had heard many stories, they all had, of the savagery of the Pendragon warriors, and many more of Uther, the chimera they called their King, with his lusts for rapine and slaughter and the torture of innocents. It was common knowledge that the friends he owned equalled the number of the enemies he had met: none lived in either case. His name was anathema to all decent folk, and he and her husband had been fell enemies since boyhood. Gulrhys, she knew, detested him to the bottom of his soul.

Faced with a stony silence, and clearly at a loss because of it, the big man cleared his throat. "My lord has been delayed. He should have come this morning, since he knew that you would pass this way today—"

"How could he know that?" The question, uttered in clipped, sterile tones, came from Morgas.

Huw looked at her and almost, Ygraine thought, began to smile. Instead he frowned and shrugged. "He knew. But we must wait close by here, up in the hills, until he comes. In the meantime there is work to do. We must unload these wagons and distribute their contents among our men."

"God save your sorry wit! You would *carry* their cargo? On your backs? That bespeaks little brain inside your brawn."

Huw gazed at Morgas for the space of three heartbeats, then raised one eyebrow. "We used our brawn to dig these pits on either side . . . but it was our brains that told us we might do it. Wagons leave broad tracks, lady. Footprints are less obvious and more difficult to follow."

He glanced away from Morgas, looking directly into Ygraine's eyes for a moment, and she lowered her eyes immediately, but not before noticing that again he almost smiled before returning his attention to Morgas. "We built the trap, milady. You entered it."

Morgas bit her lip, bereft of a suitable response.

"Which wagon holds your tents? I'll have my men unload them and your people may bring them separately, so that you will have comforts while you await the King."

"Uther Pendragon is no King, not here in Cornwall! Here, Gulrhys Lot is lord." Morgas was flushed, with a hectic colour in her cheeks, and her eyes were glittering. She held her head high, attempting to wither this man with her scorn. Ygraine saw her glance briefly in her direction before returning her attention to the big man who stood so close to her. Then Morgas raised her voice, its tone still tight with a tension masked as anger. "Derwyn!"

The man called Derwyn turned to her immediately, and Morgas pointed to him, speaking icily to Huw.

"Derwyn is our steward. He knows where everything is and his people will unload our wagons. He will not require your assistance."

Huw nodded. "No, milady. But I will require my men to assist him, despite that, to watch your people." He looked to Derwyn. "Come."

When the two men were out of hearing and she had looked about to see that they were free from the attention of other strangers, Ygraine addressed those who remained about her.

"Good. That went well. Now, move about and find something to do. The gods know there's enough to be done. But remember, all of you, Morgas is Queen until I say otherwise, so bring her my chair and bring her chair for me." She turned to Morgas. "Walk with me,

Morgas, but ahead of me, and mind you keep us clear of these people. I have no wish to be overheard. Dillys, walk beside me, behind Morgas."

No one seemed to pay any attention to them as they began to walk, although it was mere moments before Ygraine became aware that their movements were being mirrored by a trio of men on the hillside above, each of whom carried a casually slung bow. These men's eyes remained fixed on the three women, and their duty was obviously to watch and to guard against any attempt at flight. Ygraine ignored them and looked around her to where her own men were being herded into groups and guarded by squads of dour-faced bowmen who stood above them on the flanks of the hill, each squad focused upon one group of disarmed Cornishmen. Her own bodyguard stood closest to where they walked, huddled dejectedly and yet somehow defiantly in a single group, stripped of all weaponry. Ygraine nodded silently to Alasdair as she passed them, and then she waited until she and Morgas had gained an open stretch of road before speaking.

"You find that Huw attractive. Keep your wits about you. You're my bait, but for the monster Uther, not his lackey."

Morgas swung to look at her, wide-eyed. "What are you talking about? The man's a pig."

Ygraine jerked up one hand to forestall her companion's response. "Please, Morgas! The man's attractive—no denying that—but he is unimportant. Just remember who you are supposed to be, for now at least, and why. We have a bigger prize than Huw Strongarm.

"At best we might be held for ransom. Only our presence, if we can believe what we are told, has saved our men from being slaughtered as quickly as were Gylmer and his group. Their lord does not make war on women. Faugh! Uther Pendragon, the man whose name is used to frighten children? Better to be tortured by the alien Saxons than well treated by such as these, Morgas. These are our deadly enemies. They come to kill us all! They come in war, to rape and steal and kill and burn and devastate our homes, to hang and mutilate our children!"

Morgas, however, was no longer listening. Her eyes, which had been fixed on Ygraine's lips when she began to speak, had filled with anger and then swung away, across the Queen's shoulder. But there they had focused and grown keen. Ygraine frowned, and then turned to see what had distracted her.

A party of nine men had ridden into view over the brow of the hill above and were now descending towards the activity in the valley below. All were mounted on huge horses, but four of these men looked enormous, almost godlike, their apparent height increased by the great, crested helmets that they wore. The remaining five were less impressive, bare-headed and wearing no armour, but nonetheless richly dressed in heavy, beautifully coloured clothing that proclaimed wealth and privilege. Their route took them diagonally across the view of the three women, oblivious to their presence, and the women watched them ride by, noting the heavy armour that the warriors wore and the metal greaves that clád their legs above their booted feet, thrust into long stirrups, which the women had never seen or heard of before.

Morgas was round-eyed. "Romans," she whispered, gazing at their backs.

"No, I think not, not Romans." The Queen's voice was filled with scorn, but her companion did not notice.

"Aren't they huge! I thought the other one, Huw, was big, but these are giants."

"No, they're big, but their armour makes them seem bigger."

"Not the leader. He's bigger than all of them." Morgas turned to look at Ygraine, belatedly aware of the Queen's strange tone. "What are they, then, if they're not Romans? Those are Roman helmets."

"Aye, but those swine are Celts, like us. There have been no Romans in Britain since before we were born. Those are Pendragon, Morgas, and the leader, the one in the red cloak with the golden dragon and the gilded armour, is Uther, their King, or I miss my guess." Ygraine turned to look at Morgas, straight-faced. "Our captor. Your new lover . . . if he's human, which I doubt. Come, we had best be getting back."

TWENTY-FOUR

Huw Strongarm heard the silence that fell as Uther Pendragon came into view over the crest of the hill. Huw had been talking to two of his senior captains, instructing them on their duties as guardians and captors of the Queen and her train of women, and as soon as the noise above him on the hillside diminished suddenly, then began to die away completely, he knew the cause and dismissed his officers with an abrupt nod. Watching them walk away then and seeing how they glanced up over their shoulders to where Uther would be approaching, Huw allowed himself a smile, finding himself moved yet again to wonder at the respectful awe Uther Pendragon unfailingly inspired in his fierce followers.

Huw had once thought, briefly, that this widespread fascination, close to reverence, was based upon fear, but for years now he had known better. The plain truth was that Uther Pendragon was heroic, a larger-than-life figure of epic energies, courage and enthusiasm, and his warriors revered him as something they themselves could never be. Exactly what that something was, however, Huw had found more than difficult to define. He had tried to identify it many times, only to give up at last and simply accept it as part of the enigma that was Uther, his friend and commander, Chief and King.

Huw continued to stand with his back to the newcomers, determined not to turn around while knowing that he might well be the only person there who did not. He allowed himself one last look around the scene of his recent success. Two enormous piles of weapons lay to his right, where they had been discarded by the men disarming the captured Cornish warriors. They had been thrown haphazardly, tossed aside disdainfully by the men who stripped them from their former owners before herding those owners away like cattle to be held under close guard. Now, each pile of weapons was being sorted by a detachment of Huw's Cambrians. The best of the pickings would be kept as spoils of war, the remainder taken away, buried and left to rust.

Even the men who had been sorting through the weapons now stood motionless, watching their leader approach from above, and Huw's eyes moved beyond them to where a smaller group of prisoners also stood staring up the hill: the Cornish leader, Herliss, and his twelve senior officers, with Herliss himself standing as far apart from the others as his guards would allow. Huw smiled again as he realized how far removed these men were from anything that Uther's Camulod-trained Cambrians would recognize as an officer. He looked then towards the women of the Queen's party, noting that the Queen herself and the two companions with whom she had walked apart were now returning to join the others. A glance up the hill in front of him revealed that Owain of the Caves had been keeping pace with the Queen, as Huw's instructions had specified.

Satisfied that all was as it should be, Huw finally allowed himself to turn around and look to where Uther was approaching, close enough now for the sounds of the horses' hooves and creaking saddlery to be audible. He took two steps forward and stood erect, facing his commander directly and waiting to be recognized.

Uther headed straight towards Huw until he towered over him, looking down from his tall horse and reining it to a halt.

"Huw," he said, nodding, so that the plume on his high helmet dipped visibly. "Everything appears to be well in hand. You had no trouble?"

"No, Commander, everything went as planned. One flight of arrows finished it. When they saw what had happened to their best and swiftest—all cut down and dead within one breath—they lost any thoughts they might have held of resistance. They saw what our bows can do, and they believed."

"How many prisoners?"

"One hundred seventy, all told."

"By the Christian Christ, Huw! What are we supposed to do with two hundred prisoners? That's the last thing I needed." Uther turned his head very slightly to the left and gazed towards the huddle of women without making it apparent that he was looking at them. "Tell me about the women. There was nothing of women in our report."

Huw frowned and shrugged his shoulders. "A last moment addition, from what I can gather. They were all under cover in the wagons, sheltering from the rain, so we had no idea they were there until we showed ourselves. None of them was harmed."

"I can see that, but who are they?"

"One of them is Lot's Queen. The others are her ladies."

Even beneath the coverings of heavy cloak and armour, Huw saw Uther's entire body stiffen in shock, and it was several moments before the King spoke again.

"Lot's *Queen*? Ygraine? No, that can't be right."

"I don't know her name, but she's the Queen." Huw's voice was resolute. "I spoke with her. I asked which of them was the Queen, and she answered me."

Uther reached up and flipped his helmet's cheek-guards up so that they framed his helmet's cask like wings or horns, allowing him to peer down at Huw. "But how did *you* know? You didn't know there were women with the train, so how could you have known one of them was the Queen?"

Huw nodded, his face solemn. "They made it obvious, the moment we launched our attack. The common soldiery, Lot's men, were caught flat-footed, as we expected, but the others—the group over there, behind my right shoulder—showed themselves to be of a different mettle altogether. They threw a defensive ring around the women instantly, a wall of shields. They were ready to die, then and there, protecting those women . . . or one of them. As soon as I saw them move and form up, and the way they held themselves, I knew they were either an honour guard or a blood guard of some kind." He shrugged. "I don't know who they are or where they came from, but they're fighters, and not one of them wears the crest or the trappings of Gulrhys Lot. My guess is they're all mercenaries, garrison troopers from the private army of some powerful warlord. The others, all of them, wear Lot's dung-coloured trappings."

Uther scratched his nose gently with the tip of his middle finger, his cupped palm masking his mouth as though to cover a smile. "And which one is the Queen? Don't look at them!"

Huw checked himself, on the point of turning to indicate the woman. "The tall, fair one in the yellow robe."

Uther lowered his cheek-flaps back into place again, enclosing his face. "How is her temper?"

"Icy, but what would you expect? She has no love of Pendragon, especially you. She looks on you, above all, with less than favour."

Uther cocked his head, his helmet's crest dipping noticeably to one side. "Are you being insubordinate, young Strongarm?"

"Me, Commander? How could you even think such a thing?" Even beneath the covering flaps of the war helm, Huw thought he could discern Uther's teeth flashing in a grin, but he schooled his face to remain blank. "Her eyes almost fell from her head when she heard your name, Commander, and I thought she might puke."

Now Uther did laugh, a short, deep bark. "Aye, she had probably been told I would not arrive here in Cornwall until next month at the soonest. But you allowed her to walk apart unguarded. Why?"

"Not so." Huw's head shake was barely visible. "She's been under constant guard. Owain of the Caves has been watching her every move, from up there on the hill. Had she tried anything, he would have stopped her quickly enough. Shall I bring her to you?"

"No, not yet. You did well here, Strongarm. Are there any signs of other military activity in the area?"

"None. I've had scouts out ranging for twenty miles in every direction since we arrived here yesterday. Nothing moving anywhere, except this group."

"Good." Uther braced himself, straight-armed, in the saddle, one hand on the front and the other on the rear, lifting his armoured body clear of the seat and turning himself from side to side to look about him again. Then, satisfied that he had seen everything there was to see, he lowered himself back into the saddle and smiled once more at Huw. "Now tell me about the train. What's in the wagons?"

"I have no idea, Commander. Haven't had time to look. We only took them less than an hour ago, and since then we've been organizing the prisoners. As soon as that was done, I had thought to have the wagons unloaded and then burned. No point in leaving them for Lot to reclaim."

"Good. How many wagons?"

"Twenty-four, not counting the four that held the women and their goods. A rich haul."

Uther dipped his head sideways. "A large one, at least. Whether it's rich or not is something we'll find out later." He straightened his legs again and gripped the saddle horn, pulling himself upright so that he stood in his stirrups, then reached up to grip the metal housing of the high red horsehair crest that surmounted his helmet and used it to press the heavy cask down onto his head. When he was satisfied with the way it felt, he turned his head and looked about him one more time. The three officers and five unarmoured men who had accompanied him all sat their horses quietly, waiting patiently. Huw saw no sign of Uther's gaze pausing or taking note of the Cornish leadership, but when the King's eyes returned to his own, Huw was unsurprised at the first question.

"What's his name, the leader over there?"

"Herliss. That's all I know."

"Herliss! Is it, by all the gods? Then we have won a prize, whether the woman be Lot's Queen or no. I know this Herliss, or I know some relatives of his at least, and I've heard much about him. He is one of Lot's best . . . certainly one of his most experienced, since he served the old Duke Emrys before Lot's time. Herliss is a real warrior, unlike his King. But then, I'd expect no less of the man set to guard Lot's Queen, if that is who she is. I fear his master will be less than pleased with his success. Have one of your men bring him over here, Huw, but not yet. Now, the other group of prisoners on the left there, the Queen's guard, who commands them? Have you isolated him?"

"No, Commander, I have not. As long as we hold the Queen close, they should give us no trouble, and if we split them, we might regret it. And so I left them with their leader. Was I wrong?"

"I don't know, Huw. That might depend upon how good a leader he is. But if you were wrong I have no doubt we'll hear of it. Very well, then, let's move on. I think I might best remain mounted for the time being, looking down on lesser mortals from up here. Have someone bring Herliss to me, and start your men unloading the wagons." Uther turned in his saddle to one of the well-dressed civilians behind him. "Samson, you read and write. Organize the unloading and make some kind of list of what we have here. I have no need of accurate amounts for now, but I would like to know the substance of what we will all be carrying up into the hills. We may wish to bury some of it somewhere and return for it later. See to it, would you?"

The man called Samson nodded and swung himself down from his saddle immediately, where he detached a leather satchel that hung from his saddle horn. Then, grasping the bag tightly, he nodded to Huw and fell in behind him as the big Celt walked away. Uther watched them go and then turned to the man closest to him on his right.

"There's no work for you here, Quinto, and I confess that concerns me. What am I to do with two hundred prisoners? I expected at least *some* of them to fight . . . and therefore die. And you would think that, with their Queen among them, they'd have made some effort to defend her life, if not her honour."

The man to whom Uther spoke was Mucius Quinto, a veteran surgeon in the forces of the Colony of Camulod, trained in the Roman Army Corps of Surgeons, and one of the small group of surviving officers who had served in Rome's legions with the Legate Picus Britannicus. Second in rank to his friend Lucanus, Mucius Quinto held the responsibility for the medical welfare of Camulod's entire populace, military and civil. For this campaign in Cornwall, Quinto had been seconded to accompany Uther's army and see to the physical and medical welfare of its personnel.

Now Quinto nodded towards the score of corpses laid out neatly in a row alongside the road.

"Some of them did attempt to fight, but apparently they spilt no blood other than their own."

"Aye, but not enough, Mucius, not enough of either: too few corpses, too little blood." Uther's gaze moved from the small pile of dead men towards the press of prisoners. "What in the name of all the gods are we to do with all these people? Can't simply kill them all out of hand, can we? That would really give the people around here a tale to frighten their children with. Uther the man-eater . . . I can hear the outraged screams already. What would Cousin Merlyn do now, think you, if he were here?"

"Probably much the same as you will do," Mucius Quinto replied, permitting himself a small smile. "Disarm them, tie them together like chains of slaves, keep them terrified for a time in the sure expectation of death, then leave them behind, somewhere distant, to free themselves."

Uther Pendragon sucked air through his teeth and quieted his horse, which had shied nervously at a fly bite. "Free themselves to do what, return home? To face Lot's mercy after having lost his wife? Would you go home to that?"

Quinto's negation was slow and measured, a deliberate head shake. "No, Commander Uther, I would not, if even half of the things we hear of Lot's nature are true. But then, I am from Camulod, and I'm no warrior." He turned to glance towards the group of mounted men at their backs, four of whom were members of his medical staff. None of them appeared to be paying any attention to what he and Uther were saying. Mucius Quinto shrugged and turned back to Uther. "From these people, you need fear nothing more. Away from Lot, they'll not carry arms against Camulod or Cambria again."

"That's true, we might have cut Lot's forces here permanently by two hundred men. Now, look me straight in the eye, Mucius, and you others, pay attention." He waited briefly until he was sure all of his small, mounted party was listening to him. "I want none of you to look at him, but there is a man approaching us now who has reason to know how merciful *King* Lot can be when he is dis-pleased. Don't look at him if you value my friendship. We don't want him to think we find him worthy of our notice, for if he does, he will surely start to act as though he were. Now here is what I wish you to hear, so listen carefully.

"I have no idea of what this man and I might say to each other, but he is a man of power, and close to Gulrhys Lot. If I should find that I have things to say to him for his ears only, I will raise my right hand, like this . . . The moment I do so, I want you all to turn and ride away, leaving us alone to talk without fear of being overheard." He turned his head quickly, catching the eye of one of the two remaining uniformed officers beside him. "Believe me, Philip, I will be in no danger. Now, watch me closely. Everything will depend on how I feel in my gut about this man."

Herliss approached the command group slowly, flanked by two guards with drawn swords, and he held his head high as he glowered up at the mounted newcomers. He had watched them arrive and had seen the fellow Huw receive his orders, after which, summoning two of his troopers, the big warrior had come straight to where Herliss stood. He had paused along the way only long enough to issue orders of his own to one of his subordinates, who had then moved away immediately, evidently full of purpose, thrusting his head and one shoulder through his long, strung bow so that the stave hung down his back, summoning others as he went. Already Herliss could see a gathering process among and around his train of wagons.

Huw had said nothing to Herliss when he reached him. He had merely stood silently as his men flanked the enemy commander, one on either side, and indicated that he should accompany them. They had not laid hands on Herliss, but one of them, waving his drawn sword gently towards the distant group of horsemen, had made it plain that they wanted him to start moving in that direction. Herliss had not allowed his face to betray any hint of what he was thinking or how he felt. He had merely begun walking, holding his head high and resisting the urge to look down at the rough, uneven ground beneath his feet. Better to trip on a tussock of grass and fall, he thought, than to walk with a bent head and appear dejected and beaten.

Herliss kept his unbroken gaze fastened on the big leader mounted on the enormous horse. This must be Uther Pendragon, he knew. He had seen the man's eye light upon him once, briefly, and then move on, ignoring him. He had thought that the fellow had said something to the fat, older man sitting the horse next to his, but the big man's face was shadowed in the recesses of the ornate Roman helmet he wore, and so Herliss could not be sure, and none of the men in the mounted group even glanced in his direction as he approached.

Only when Herliss had come to a halt and was gazing up defiantly at Uther did the Pendragon leader turn his head to look down at him, and then he brought his great horse around, sidestepping delicately, until he was gazing down at the Cornishman from directly over the animal's head between its ears. Thereafter, he sat motionless for a time, his face shadowed in the recesses of his helmet, but his eyes gleaming as he stared down at the enemy leader.

Herliss was an enormous man, although lacking the commanding height of Uther Pendragon. His wide, heavily muscled shoulders were more than three times as broad as the width of his head, and the tight-skinned planes of his face looked as though they had been shaped from slabs of clay. His great, pale-brown eyes were almost feminine in their size, but there was no hint of femininity or weakness in the way they blazed from the deep recesses beneath the massive height and breadth of his forehead. A thick band of rich yellow cloth, woven with gold wire, encircled his brow, and above it his hair was light brown and thick, with only a hint of silvering, in spite of his nearly sixty years. Two long braids hung over his shoulders and down onto his breast, interwoven and tied with ribbons of the same gold-laced cloth that bound his brow. The nose that dominated his craggy, rugged face was wide and cruel-looking, broken at some time in the far distant past. A full moustache, but no beard, finished the face off, emphasizing the deep-channelled grooves that swept down from the broad nose to bracket his wide, tight-lipped mouth on either side.

Uther had no illusions about the calibre of the man who faced him. The fierce face would have proclaimed its owner a nobleman and a warrior, but his clothing, too, drew attention to the man's singularity. His garments were rich, with the lushness that bespoke wealth, privilege and ease of access to the far-from-ordinary. Lacking only a helmet, Herliss wore armour that was almost as Roman-looking as Uther's own, consisting of a breastplate made from overlapping layers of heavy, toughened bullhide and studded with metal lozenges, and a skirt of overlapping straps of the same thick leather that hung from his waist and protected his groin and thighs, its panels also strengthened with the same kind of metal plates, pierced at the corners and sewn to the leather straps with iron wire. Thick, heavy greaves, shaped to the length and contours of his lower legs, completed his armour and fitted snugly over the tops of heavy, Roman military boots. A thick cloak of equally rich, deep-red wool, edged with deep-piled fur, hung down his back from his shoulders, secured across his chest by a chain of wide, heavy silver links and held back by his bound arms.

Uther waited in silence until he was sure that his adversary would say nothing before being addressed, and then, just ahead of the point at which the silence might have become a battle of wills, he nodded his head once and spoke in Latin, knowing well from his long talks with Balin that his brother Herliss was proficient in the tongue.

"Herliss, I have heard much about you. I wish we had met under better conditions."

Herliss said nothing, but his nostrils flared and he raised one eyebrow high in disdain. Uther ignored the look.

"I am Uther Pendragon."

"I know who you are." The voice was a deep, leonine growl, the Latin flawless and fluent. "The Trickster."

Uther frowned, then blinked, his body inclining slightly forward. "The what? What did you call me?"

"The Trickster. Why not? It is your name. You would deny it?"

"You have me confused with someone else. I am no trickster, nor am I known as such."

Herliss sucked in his cheeks as though he might spit, but then he merely swallowed what was in his mouth.

"Why lie about it when the whole world knows you for what you are? Do not treat me as you would one of your own fools. Did you not spirit a woman out of a locked and guarded room, and was it not witnessed by a multitude?"

Uther had stiffened in anger as Herliss began this response, but before it was done he had slumped back in his saddle, and now he threw back his head and laughed aloud, tugging his horse's head down with one hand, so that the great beast snuffled and stamped in protest.

"Ah, Herliss, now I understand your error, even though you do not. Time and distance can warp even the truth of truth, it seems. It was my cousin, Merlyn Britannicus of Camulod, who dreamed up that escapade and made it happen, earning the reputation you now attribute to me. Merlyn's your Trickster, not I. And he became the Trickster simply by being cleverer by far than anyone and everyone else who dealt with him, including myself."

Uther drew himself up until he was sitting arrow-straight, and at the same time he raised his hand in the prearranged signal. Behind him, immediately, he heard the sounds of movement as his people began to pull away, leaving him alone with Herliss in a circle of men who watched, but were too far away to hear what was being said. He watched Herliss's eyes narrow as the Cornish leader tried to understand what was happening, and then recaptured the veteran's attention with a question.

"Where did you learn to speak the Roman tongue? You speak it very well."

"I should. I learned it among the Romans years ago." Herliss was frowning, plainly wondering about the sudden, unexpected departure of Uther's escorting party. "Where are they going and why?"

"They moved away because I told them I might want to talk to you without being overheard. You saw me give the signal. They obeyed it. There's no trickery involved."

"Mayhap not, but you are a trickster, nonetheless. You won this victory here by trickery."

"Aye, perhaps I did, but trickery is legitimate in warfare, and I know you know that well. From what I have heard, you have been famed for your own deceits at times. Besides, your point is moot. All I did in this instance was set a trap. You were the one who walked into it in the full light of day. No trickery involved there, Herliss. Carelessness, perhaps. Negligence ... one might perhaps propose an argument in favour of such a thing. But trickery? No, not on my part. Had your scouts paid attention and scouted properly, they would have found us, or at worst found signs of our preparations. We had hundreds of men concealed in these pits, Herliss . . . impossible to hide so many without trace. But your people found nothing, and that was mainly because they did not look closely, or closely enough."

Faced with such incontrovertible logic, Herliss could make no response, but Uther spoke right on through the silence that ensued.

"I know your brother, Balin, and his wife, Mairidh. We have been friends for years, the three of us. I like them both immensely." He waited briefly for a response and received none.

"Your son, Lagan," he continued. "Is he yet well? I never met him, but years ago your brother used the story of Lagan, his favourite nephew, to convince me that my overwhelming hatred of all things Cornish was foolish and ill advised, and so I have grown to manhood with the strange feeling that I have a friend whom I have never met among your people." He paused, his eyes fixed on his enemy, and then continued.

"I can see you are confused and taken aback by hearing things you might never have expected to hear, so I'll ask no more of you for now than this: try to contain yourself in patience for a while and to accept the restraints I will put upon you as my prisoner. Were I to set you free now and alone, your life would not continue long once Lot had heard of your survival at the cost of his Queen's freedom. In holding you, therefore, I merely hold your life in safekeeping. If your Queen is to continue living, be it in freedom or in servitude, then she will need someone—some man, strong and used to authority—in whom she can confide and in whom she can place her trust with confidence. You will be that man. So be it you offer no trouble to the men I set to guarding you, your conditions of confinement shall be light and in no way onerous. I promise you this, however: cross me in this, and I will have you trussed like a captive cockerel bound for the stewpot." He stopped and gazed at the older man. "Will you consent to this?"

Herliss pursed his lips and nodded briefly. "Aye, I will, so be it you do not ill-treat my men."

"Their treatment depends upon their own behaviour. Good will beget good, ill, ill." Uther glanced towards the senior of the two men who had brought up the prisoner and waved him forward. "Take the Lord Herliss back to the others, but when we stop tonight to make camp, keep him apart and see to it that he is well fed and well quartered."

He glanced once more at Herliss and nodded in dismissal before hauling on his horse's reins and straightening his back, standing up in his stirrups again to look about him. He saw immediately that Huw Strongarm was returning, walking quickly and intently. Uther sat silent and waited for Huw to reach him, knowing that the only thing that could have caused such a precipitate return on Huw's part was the nature of the wagons' contents. When Huw arrived, he paused for a moment to gather his breath, and Uther forestalled him.

"What have we captured? Weapons?"

Huw jerked his head in a nod. "Aye," he said. "Weapons of a kind, anyway. Great balks of timber, grey and well seasoned, huge wheel sections and miles of hempen rope. You had better come and look, see for yourself."

Less than an hour later, his inspections of the wagons complete, Uther, still mounted, sat waiting once again for Herliss to be brought to him, but this time, when the veteran commander arrived, Uther wasted no time on pleasantries and gave the grizzled Cornishman no chance to speak until he had spoken his mind.

"Siege engines," he began, an edge of incredulity in his voice. "You are carrying siege engines? Where would Gulrhys Lot find such things? And why would he want them? No one has had any use for those things here in Britain since the Romans left almost thirty years ago, and even *they* used no siege engines in Britain for a hundred years before that." He did not wait for Herliss to respond. "But if Lot is moving them, taking the trouble to shift them, then he is thinking of employing them, so where? He can't have need of them here in Cornwall. The fortifications here are primitive—hill forts, all of them, even his own Golant. Excellent strongholds and highly defensible, but steep slopes and deep ditches, Herliss. No stone walls or towers. Hill forts can be invested, encircled and cut off and then starved out over time, but they cannot be taken by artillery or siege engines. Primitive they may be, but they're also nigh on impregnable and impervious to every weapon except time, thirst and starvation." He paused and looked hard at Herliss. "The only exception that I know about in all this land of Cornwall is your own place, Tir Gwyn, the White Fort. Balin told me it is strongly fortified, high on a defensible ridge with great, glistening walls of snow-white, glassy stone that blazes in the sun, visible for miles. Lot could besiege your Tir Gwyn and probably take it from you if he lusted for it. But why, then, would you be taking him the means to do that to you? That makes no sense at all . . .

"The only thing that does make any kind of sense to me is that your lord is dreaming of attacking us again in Camulod, carrying the war into our bourne yet again, hoping to force us to recall our armies from Cornwall and keep them immured thereafter in our own lands, away from his and yours. But who would undertake that task? Not Lot himself, that much is certain. He hasn't got the guts or the balls to try a thing like that, where he might get hurt. Twice now, he has sent armies up to our lands in treachery, killing, looting and marauding without any provocation, and on each occasion his people died swearing that he was there with them. When it was over, however, and the remnants of his armies had been sent running for their sorry lives, it transpired each time that the mighty monarch, King in Cornwall, had elected not to accompany his armies after all and had remained safe at home."

Herliss stood silent, making no attempt to speak.

"Those two incursions into our lands have cost me dearly. Gulrhys Lot will someday pay the price to me in person, and he will pay in blood. The first attack, led by two foul, sorcerous creatures, both of whom lie dead in Camulod, cost me a favourite uncle and a lifetime friend, dead by envenomed arrows. The second, less than a year ago as you well know, cost me my dear cousin, Merlyn Britannicus, still alive in body but dead inside, his wits driven from him by a blow to the head.

"I learned long ago that Lot has no stomach at all for fighting personally. He would never dare come into Camulod in person. He would far rather send a warring group of underlings to squabble endlessly and achieve nothing, as they did the last time, than put himself in any danger. And that, Herliss, is why I am here in Cornwall. I have no interest in laying your land waste, but I will tear the heavens and all of earth apart to reach that foul toad's guts and rip them out of his stinking carcass while he still has eyes to watch me do it."

Now he swung his eyes to meet Herliss's gaze head on. "So, if he plans to march on Camulod again, with siege engines this time, he will send an underling. But it must be an underling who understands the principles of siege warfare. You?"

Herliss shrugged his enormous shoulders. "Not I, not now. Besides, I know nothing about fighting that way. I fight with my hands."

"Yes, quite. Who, then? Would you tell me if you knew?"

"No. Is it important?"

Uther grinned—a small, tight, ferocious snarl—and shook his head. "No, it is not. Not now and not ever, now that I have the engines. Where did they come from?"

"From my own holdings. I had them stored in several of my places along the south coast. They belonged to Lot's father, the Duke Emrys, and he obtained them openly years and years ago from the Roman garrisons along the Saxon Shore in the far southeast, while the coastal routes were still open. On the death of the old Duke, they passed into the nominal possession of King Lot under my continuing guardianship. He has always known they were there, and recently he asked me about them and made arrangements to have me bring them to him. He made no mention of where he would use them, and none of my being put in charge of them after they were in his hands."

"Just as well, because he'll never use them now." Uther turned to a mounted trooper who sat close behind his right shoulder, and then he stopped, plainly on the point of issuing an order. Instead, he turned slowly back towards Herliss. "Wait you, though. You were on your way to Lot to deliver the siege engines, is that not so?"

Herliss nodded, plainly considering the answer obvious.

"Then whence came Lot's Queen? Was she with you in the south?"

Herliss felt his face flush red, but all he could do was curse himself for a fool and nod abruptly in an attempt to brush this off as unimportant. Already, however, he knew his face had betrayed him.

"Aye," he growled. "She was staying with me, as my guest in Tir Gwyn."

"Your . . . guest."

"Aye, my guest. You find that strange? My youngest wife and she are good friends, close."

"I see. And how long had she been there? I promise you I shall find out the truth, so don't start lying to me now, Herliss."

The other man shrugged and looked away, mumbling an inaudible response.

"Your pardon, I missed that. What did you say?"

"I said she had been with us for some months."

"I see. Then she must be pining for her husband, and he for her by this time."

"Aye, mayhap she must."

Uther turned back to the trooper. "Nemo, go straight to Huw. Tell him to burn everything in the wagons except food and any portable equipment we can use easily. Tell him to burn the wagons, too, and not to fret about the smoke being seen. If anyone comes looking for the source of all the smoke, we'll give them far more to worry about than a mere fire. Go."

As the trooper wheeled away, Uther nodded again to Herliss. "My thanks for being honest, although there was nothing else you might have done. You may return to your men."

He glanced at Herliss's escort and waved them on with a tiny gesture of his fingers. And then, as they moved away, he tapped the pad of his index finger against his pursed lips, making small, sibilant kissing noises as he thought about what had happened and what remained to be done. Finally he reined his horse around and kicked it into motion.

Uther rode until he reached a blazing cook fire, where several of his party had dismounted and tethered their horses as they waited to be fed. Uther climbed down for the first time since mounting his horse that morning, some six hours earlier, and moved to pick up a broken loaf of hard-crusted bread, ripping off a large piece and taking a great bite of it. By the time he had chewed it for long enough to moisten it, Huw Strongarm had reached his side again, and Uther looked at him with one eyebrow raised.

"Is there something amiss?"

"No, everything's in hand. I simply wanted a drink of water."

"Good. Drink, and take something to eat. Then, as soon as the fires are blazing too fiercely to be put out, let's get everyone on the move and up into the safety of the hills. You know what to do—have the prisoners' wrists tied behind them, then string them all together by the neck in single file like slaves. Let them think they're all going to die, but don't let any of our people abuse them unnecessarily. We'll let them go eventually, once Lot and his people know exactly where and who we are. By that time, they'll no longer be a threat to us, since everyone will know our whereabouts. In the meantime, keep them under close guard. Who did you leave in charge of firing the wagons?"

Huw grunted and spoke around a mouthful of half-chewed bread. "Hard-Nose."

"Good." Uther took off his heavy helmet and placed it carefully beside him before he lowered himself and stretched out full length on the ground close to where the horses were tethered. "Half an hour. Wake me when we're almost ready to go."

He was asleep in moments.

TWENTY-FIVE

Ygraine had no words to describe what she saw among the enemy forces that day. She watched with horror as the Camulodians, with organized efficiency, set fire to the wagons and their contents and then quit the scene of the ambush, with its blazing beacons and towering pillars of black, roiling smoke. They wasted no time in clearing the area, their mounted troopers serving as guards for the long lines of prisoners who were strung together, neck to neck, twenty-five men to a file, and then almost literally dragged behind trotting horses.

Untroubled by any responsibility for the prisoners, the long-legged bowmen moved away quickly too, in large, tightly organized groups, travelling on foot and maintaining regular formations. From where she sat watching them, Ygraine marvelled at how quickly they swept upwards and away, in connected bodies, rank and file, until from a distance they appeared to move across the hillsides like cloud shadows, their bows and quivers slung across their shoulders to leave their hands free for climbing. It was clear to her that they were moving well away in anticipation of reprisals and pursuit, but she could have told them that they had no reason for concern. There was no body of Cornish troops close enough even to see the enormous towers of smoke that marked the place, and it would be many days before Lot took the time to notice that Herliss was late in arriving. But of course, she said nothing.

Ygraine and her women, each riding behind one of their captors and constrained to clasp him around the waist for fear of falling from the horse's rump, travelled fast and hard for more than three hours, pausing only briefly, from time to time, to give their horses time to rest. And the bowmen, to Ygraine's great surprise, kept pace with them.

Eventually they arrived in another valley, a pleasant, shallow place with an ample stream running through it and a large, well-established encampment already in place. Heavy commissary wagons were set around a broad, open area that was scattered with blackened fire circles, all surrounded by logs for seating, and beyond that lay acres of cleanly laid-out horse lines and tent sites. Ygraine was astonished to realize that there were more horses and horse troopers camped there than there had been bowmen in the ambush that had captured her. Uther's force was a raiding party, she could see, but it was a large one and well equipped. She and her party attracted great curiosity among the troopers close enough to see that they were women, but they were lowered from their horses courteously enough, and then grouped together and loosely guarded while their captors transformed their end of the peaceful valley into a hive of activity, adding their own dimensions to the layout of the camp and setting up their own bivouacs.

A short time later, a trooper, whom she identified from his armour as some kind of officer, approached the women, leading a ten-man squad and a heavy wagon pulled by four heavy horses. He scanned the ground around them and then chose a spot halfway between where the women were standing and the edge of the river. He then began issuing orders and indicating where and how he wanted certain things done, and his troopers moved quickly to do his bidding.

None of the other women paid much attention to what was happening at the outset—there were far too many other interesting sights to attract their attention—but Ygraine was fascinated to see the straight-faced concentration shown by the troopers toiling in and around the big wagon. She walked closer to where they worked, unnoticed by any of them or by anyone else, and leaned against the gnarled trunk of an ancient hawthorn as she waited to see what they would do. And there for two hours she remained as they unloaded from the wagon a bewildering number of poles of various sizes, bale after bale of leather, bundles of metal pins or pegs and wooden pulleys and what seemed like miles of rope. Out of all that chaos, the troopers created a soaring edifice of roped leather sheets, the sight of which was breathtaking. It was a tent unlike any other that Ygraine had ever seen, larger, more spacious and more carefully crafted. She guessed that it might be a Roman command tent, but only because she had heard of such things and had listened skeptically as others had sought to describe their virtues and dimensions. The panels were of the finest, hand-tanned leather, sewn with double seams and then carefully waxed for weatherproofing, increased durability and extended use. She noted that the sides, and even some of the roof panels, were vented with hanging, overlapping flaps that could be opened to the weather in clement times, either rolled up and tied in place or propped open on long, thin sticks that slotted into pockets sewn to receive them. She knew that her husband would have shrivelled with envy to see such a thing.

Ygraine counted twelve tall structural poles around the outer perimeter of the tent, each of them an arm's length longer than the height of a tall, helmeted man, and there was an additional, inner square of four more, each of those thicker than the exterior poles and set four full paces from its neighbours. These raised the roof fully half as high again, and then finally, in the very centre of the edifice, was one enormously tall, strong pole that was almost as thick as her waist through its base. This central pillar was constructed to break down into manageable lengths, so that it could be quickly assembled or dismantled and carried in a single large wagon. When it was erected, a suspended, circular collar of some kind ringed the top of this pole, and to that were attached the leather panels that formed the highest sections of the roof. Everything, it seemed—all the stretched skins of the walls and roof and all the poles themselves—was secured with ropes wound through pulleys and attached to heavy iron pegs hammered deep into the ground.

Ygraine assumed, quite naturally, that the tent was being erected for the King, Uther Pendragon, so she was more than surprised when Huw Strongarm advised Morgas that he was placing it at the disposal of her women. At first Ygraine thought he was mocking them, and so, to her credit, did Morgas. But it quickly became plain that he was not, and so Ygraine said nothing, merely gazing at Morgas and nodding her head almost imperceptibly to indicate that she should accept the concession as graciously as she could.

Now night was falling quickly, and the women were gathered together in the centre of the tent, grouped around the brazier that had been carried in by two of Huw Strongarm's troopers and placed beneath a wide, open roof flap that allowed the smoke to escape. Lamps had been lit and torches guttered in iron baskets on poles stuck in the ground. Morgas was the only one seated, and the others were all grouped about her. Ygraine, standing close behind the taller woman, had undone the lengths of Morgas's hair and was preparing to brush it. Over by the main entrance, one woman stood alone, peering out into the gathering night. Suddenly the watcher tensed.

"There's someone coming. I think it's the Cambrian!"

The group of women went still as soon as she spoke, and in the sudden hush, the guttering of the flames in the lighted lamps around the large space could be heard quite clearly. Morgas, the tallest of them all, turned completely around and glanced up, wide-eyed, at Ygraine. But the real Queen had already taken charge, turning towards the woman who had spoken and motioning to her to step away from the doorway.

"Remember, all of you," she said, her voice low-pitched and calm. "No one looks at me. Morgas is the Queen." She stepped back immediately, away from Morgas, at the same time waving for another of the women to step forward. The one called Dyllis took her place, holding a hairbrush, and immediately began brushing Morgas's hair.

She had barely begun when the leather flaps of the tent were pulled open and the first of two men entered, stooped over and holding up one arm as if to keep the tent's roof from falling on his head. His face was completely concealed by the bulk of an enormous bronze helmet that was surmounted by a high crest of red-dyed horsehair, but the size of him and something in the way he moved made it clear to her that this was the man called Huw Strongarm. Behind him, an even larger man followed, this one Uther, King of Pendragon. This was the first time any of the women had seen him up close, and every pair of eyes in the gathering was fixed upon him, although he was so completely muffled in clothing and armour that there was little of the actual man to see.

The men moved towards the centre of the tent, where Uther stood quietly, making no attempt to speak but simply looking at Morgas and her satellite women. While he looked at Morgas, Ygraine looked at him, absorbing the imposing height of him, emphasized by the bulk of his clothing and armour and the giant shadow he threw on the wall of the high tent.

The tent had seemed enormous until then, but the looming presence of these two tall, cloaked men, in their bulky armour and high-crested helmets, made the space seem suddenly smaller and crowded, and that, in turn, made the men seem even bigger, darker and more menacing. The walls were alive with leaping, flickering shadows, and the heavy cheek-flaps of Uther's helmet made it practically impossible to see his face. Ygraine immediately decided she did not enjoy that at all. She wanted to be able to watch his eyes, to see what he was thinking. And then she experienced the distinct feeling that she herself was being watched, and her gaze moved immediately to Huw Strongarm. Sure enough, his eyes were fixed upon her face, and as he saw her look at him, he nodded. He was standing at a different angle to her than was Uther, and so as he smiled she saw his teeth reflect the light. She ignored him and moved her gaze away quickly, allowing her eyes to wander over the faces of the other women in her party. They were all staring at Uther Pendragon, transfixed.

The silence grew and stretched and no one moved until, finally, Uther bent forward slightly, exaggerating the movement deliberately until it was almost a stoop, and peered down sideways to where Dyllis, the smallest of all Ygraine's women, stood, still clutching her hairbrush. Of all the Queen's women, Dyllis was the most innocent and the most easily shocked, and Uther's elaborate interest in her brought the high colour of embarrassment flooding up into her face. The King held out his hand, one finger extended, in an unmistakable invitation for the young woman to take it. Completely flustered now, she looked rapidly from side to side for guidance from her companions, but none of them would look at her, and

Ygraine felt herself grow tense with the anticipation that Dyllis might appeal to her directly. Finally, however, Dyllis reached up and took hold of Uther's hand. Keeping his arm stretched high, he led her gently out from where she stood and took her sideways across the floor of the tent towards one of the four central supports. He held her quietly in place with one upraised hand and then looked directly at Ygraine, who was now standing closest to Dyllis, and beckoned to her with his other hand, bidding her approach.

Frowning slightly, Ygraine moved slowly to obey, wondering what he was about. When she reached him, he positioned her beside Dyllis, on the other woman's right. Thereafter, one at a time, he brought all of the women except Morgas over until he had them all standing in a straight line facing him. Morgas, meanwhile, seeing herself being gradually isolated, sat watching all of this with a frown. Uther ignored her completely. When she realized that he would not look at her, Morgas turned her head angrily towards Huw Strongarm, but he was watching his King and had no eyes for her.

Uther went and stood directly in front of little Dyllis.

"Your name?" he asked her, his voice gentle.

"Dyllis." Her reply was almost a bleat, so breathless and frightened was she.

"Dyllis. A good name." He moved to stand in front of Ygraine. "And you are?"

"Deirdre." Ygraine had been ready for him and gave the name of one of her sisters, dead for many years. Her voice, as she pronounced the name, was cold and formal, her pronunciation clipped and terse.

"Deirdre?" He repeated it slowly. "Deirdre . . . Now that is an unusual name here in Britain. Forgive me . . ." He reached out and grasped her gently by the chin. She heard Dyllis gasp beside her, and for a moment she was afraid that the girl would betray her simply by her indignation. Uther tilted her head slightly to the side, towards the closest lamp. She wanted to resist, but then thought better of it and allowed him to move her face closer to the light. But his next words made her jerk her head free of his grasp and set the room spinning about her.

"You are not Deirdre of the Violet Eyes, however . . . I can see that."

By the time she could recapture her breath and brace herself for whatever he might say next, he had lost interest in her and moved on to the woman on her left, a voluptuous young beauty, only slightly overweight, called Amaryllis. Then she watched him, gradually mastering the fear that had flared in her, as he moved down the line, asking each woman her name.

When he had spoken to each one of them except Morgas, he stepped back and addressed them all, and against her will Ygraine found herself thinking that his voice was attractive, deep and resonant and mellifluous.

"I have ill tidings for you now, I fear, ladies. We will be remaining here in this valley for the next ten days, at least."

All along the line of twelve women, there were mutterings and outright gasps of consternation. Uther stemmed all of them by raising his hand.

"I regret the necessity of confining you here, but we have little choice . . . we can hardly release you to report our presence or our whereabouts, can we? It pains me, however, that we had not expected the company of women, and so we had no time to make arrangements for your presence. I can only hope that you will be comfortable with what we have been able to provide, lacking any warning.

"As you know, this tent will be yours while you are here with us, and you will be safe here as long as you remain discreetly inside and do not go wandering through the encampment. I'm sure I have no need to remind you that the men all around you are soldiers, and enemy soldiers at that. They are unused to having women close by while they are on campaign, and they tend to think of women— when they think of them at all, which is constantly—as part of the plunder. There is nothing I can do at this late stage to reeducate them quickly on that matter. However, they are not bad men, and for the most part they are disciplined and well behaved. They are far from being wild animals, no matter what you may have been told to the contrary. The guards I have assigned to you can contain them and will protect you from them should the need arise, but only if you co-operate, and certainly not if you provoke the men's lusts by bringing yourselves to their attention. Simply by making yourselves visible, you will generate more than enough provocation to violence. Have I made myself clear on that?"

"Perfectly." The word, dripping with disdain, came from Morgas. "And now that you have absolved yourself of responsibility for our eventual ravishment and death by placing the blame squarely upon us in advance, what else have you in store for us?"

Uther had stopped moving as soon as she began to speak, and he held himself motionless until she finished. Only then did he straighten his shoulders and turn his head slowly towards her.

"I will have words for you later, lady. For now, I have none." He turned back to the women. "My men are digging private latrines for you as I speak, working by torchlight. When they are finished, they will fence off a pathway between the entrance to this tent and the site of the latrines, which lie to your left. It will be safe for you to use, and it will be private. On the other side, to the right of the main entrance, we will build a temporary bathhouse for your needs. It will be a Roman-style, military bathhouse, but very basic, lacking a furnace and steam room. The water might not be very hot, but neither will it be completely cold, and the sides will be screened for your safety.

"We will feed you from one of our commissary wagons, and while we are encamped you will have a hot meal, with fresh-cooked meat, every night. For the rest of the time, you will eat what our men eat and when they eat." He looked about him again. "There are twelve of you. Twelve cots will be delivered here within the hour. There should be ample room for everyone."

Morgas spoke again. "There are thirteen of us, not twelve."

Uther turned and looked at her again, then raised a hand to Huw, who stepped aside and went to the doorway, where he spoke to one of the guards outside. A moment later, two more men entered the tent, ordinary troopers identically dressed. Uther stood motionless as the two crossed to stand one on either side of Morgas, who remained seated, a picture of icy detachment. Despite herself, Ygraine felt a flicker of admiration for her deputy and for the performance she was delivering.

Uther moved to stand in front of Morgas, looking down at her.

"You may take the chair with you if you so wish, lady, and if you insist, we will even carry you while you yet sit upon it, but you are not staying here with your women. You are going where I can keep my eye on you." He raised a hand to quell the instant surge of protest that arose from the women and spoke over the noise. "Your Queen will be safe enough, I promise you. Bear in mind, this woman has been wed to Gulrhys Lot. After such misfortune as that, I can promise all of you that she will come to no harm at my hands. I take her from you only because I cannot believe the gods have rendered Gulrhys Lot's Queen into my care, and I do not intend to lose her to any cause or condition." He glanced back to Morgas. "So, milady, I hope you do not snore, for only the wall of a tent will keep the sound of it from me. I, of course, do not snore."

He jerked his head to the guards and turned back again to face the row of women as Morgas rose to her feet and left with the two guards, accepting the soft woollen cloak that Huw held out to her as she walked past him. All twelve women were watching Uther, quiet and wide-eyed, and none of them as much as glanced at Morgas.

He looked at them and nodded. "You will all be safe here, believe me. Sleep well." Then he bowed and moved to the flapped doorway, where he ducked his head and disappeared, closely followed by Huw Strongarm.

Ygraine stood frowning, wondering what had happened here. She had prepared Morgas to seduce Uther, but neither of them had been prepared for him simply to abduct her. And yet, a voice inside her head was telling her, Uther could scarcely have done anything more suitable to her own designs, for in removing Morgas from the company of the other women, he had preserved Ygraine against her greatest fear: that over time, in such constrained quarters and under the constant vigilance of guards, one or another of the women must betray by act or word or gesture, or even through simple deference, that it was she who was the Queen and not Morgas.

She turned to her women, who were beginning to find their voices, whispering among themselves. But before she could even begin speaking to any of them, a raised voice from outside the tent announced that their cots and bedding had arrived. And shortly after that, while they were setting up their sleeping arrangements, another message came that their latrines had been finished and were in working order.

It was long after dark and the lamps were guttering low before the women got to bed that night, and before she fell asleep, Ygraine wondered what was happening to Morgas.

Even as the thought occurred to Ygraine, Morgas was alone in Uther's impressive campaign tent. Uther had conducted her there personally, accompanied by two guards carrying torches, and as one of the guards went about lighting a number of oil lamps, he had shown her how the space within the tent was divided by a T-shaped partition of leather walls so as to create three chambers, the front one twice the size of the two at the rear. The main partition, made of thin, supple, lightly oiled leather and reaching head high, stretched across the entire width of the tent between two poles, save for a space at each end that permitted access to the sleeping cubicles behind. The two rear compartments were barely separated from each other by a second, similar screen, strung between two more poles in the ground, that divided the space equally, the pole at one end almost touching the rear wall of the tent, while the other reached close to the lateral partition, leaving sufficient space for a body to pass from one cubicle to the other without having to go all the way around to the other entrance. Each compartment contained a simple military cot and footlocker, and a collapsible washstand that held a jug and a basin made of fired clay. The larger space at the front of the tent held a plain, large table and a smaller one that served as a washstand, with a basin and a ewer of water and a wooden rail mounted on one side from which hung a strip of towel. Then there were a wooden chair with arms, a three-legged stool, two more footlockers and a device of crossed poles fashioned to accommodate armour and clothing that was not in use. Uther led her directly into the sleeping chamber on the right and waved his thumb towards the cot.

"You will sleep here. I will be there, on the other side of the wall."

Her lip curled in scorn. "You will be there, will you? And for how long will you remain there? Do you expect me to sleep in peace, lulled by your solemn word alone that I will not be molested? How big a fool do you think I am, sir?"

One of his eyebrows rose, but for a long time he made no response other than a small, sardonic twitch of his lips that might have been the beginning of a pitying smile. Finally his head moved very slightly in the negative and the smile grew slightly larger. "Lady, I have no expectations of you at all, and your foolishness is already demonstrated by your marriage to the self-styled King of Cornwall. Have no fears for your chastity, for had I wished to have you in my bed, that is where you would now be. Bear in mind you are my prisoner. And on that same point, do not attempt to leave this tent. There will be guards outside at all times with orders to restrain you if necessary, and if that means you have to spend most of your nights gagged and trussed up with ropes, so be it. The choice is yours." He nodded in dismissal to the two waiting guards and they saluted and withdrew. Uther looked over to her. "Do you have any questions?"

She threw back her head defiantly, presenting her heavy, proud breasts for his inspection. "You say you have no interest in despoiling me. Why, then . . . by what right do you separate me from my women?"

"By my own right as your captor." He did not deign to cast as much as a glance towards her breasts but kept his eyes fixed on hers. "You will be permitted to spend some time with your women each day. Three or four may come at a time, but no more than that, to visit you here. They may stay with you for a maximum of two hours each time. None of them, however, will have any access to your bodyguard or to any male member of your retinue or escort. Be warned on that, and make sure you discourage them from attempting to defy that rule. It will be hard on anyone caught trying to communicate with your people outside.

"Nemo is the name of the commander of your guards. He is a decurion in my personal guard, and I trust him implicitly." He smiled again, a tight, wintry little smile containing little amusement. "Your . . . virtue . . . will be safe from him, as well, as his will be from you and any wiles you might think to deploy against him. I warn you, Nemo is not seducible, so do not even think about suborning him. But then, if you feel that you simply must make the attempt in order to demonstrate how irresistible you are . . . well, remember that I warned you."

He looked around the tent, noting that the lamps were all burning brightly and steadily. Satisfied, he looked back at her and nodded.

"They should be bringing you some food soon, and I will make sure that someone brings you a jug of hot water before you retire. Sleep well."

Then, before she could think of a single thing to say to arrest him or to put him in his place, he spun on his heel and walked away, out of the tent, leaving her fuming and decidedly out of sorts.

Morgas was not accustomed to having men ignore her physical attractions. Since the days when womanhood first began to emerge in her, she had been blessed not only with a winsome, lovely face and soft, wide, sensual lips, but with high, heavy breasts and a narrow back and waist that swelled out to lushly rounded hips above long, clean-lined legs. All males lusted after her at one time or another, she knew, and most of them did it all the time, devouring her with hungry eyes. That was something she had come to take for granted over the years, and now she expected no less. Even the King, Gulrhys Lot, had fallen under her spell after only a very short time, and no man to whom she herself had felt attracted had ever refused her, let alone ignored her, as had this upstart Cambrian. She consoled herself by planning exactly how she would behave at their next encounter and what she would say to him, how she would spurn his approach and shrivel him with disdain.

What she was completely unprepared for, however, was that it would be three entire days and nights before she saw him again.

On the morning after Morgas's "abduction" by Uther, the women were surprised to receive a visit from the senior surgeon of the Camulod raiding party, who introduced himself to them as Mucius Quinto and explained his position within Uther's group before offering them his assistance, should any of them have need of his medical services. His visit set off a buzz of scandalized discussion among the women, none of whom had ever heard of professionally trained and educated surgeons or physicians. In their kingdom, all illnesses and medical conditions were treated by those Druids who specialized in herbal knowledge and medicaments. Ygraine held herself aloof from all their talk, thinking instead about Morgas and Uther and wondering what had happened between them.

A short time later, when one of the guards brought word that three women might go and visit "the Queen" in her quarters, Ygraine stood immediately as one of the three. Her eyes never stopped moving, seeing and cataloguing everything there was to see as she and two others were escorted from the command tent to the smaller tent that was Uther's own. Morgas's prison—the King's Tent, as it was called—lay under heavy guard some hundred paces along the riverside on a stony bank above the water in a glade that was surrounded on three sides by thick-growing willows.

Ygraine was more than surprised to find, in answer to her first question, that Uther had not entered the tent at all the previous night, apart from having delivered Morgas there. How could it be that Uther Pendragon, whose monstrous behavior and rapacious sexual appetites were legendary, could have disdained the obvious and available lushness of Morgas's body? She began racking her brains to uncover a potential explanation for such uncharacteristic behaviour from the Pendragon King.

It did not even occur to Ygraine that Uther might simply have left the camp again that same night so soon after arriving. They did not discover that until much later in the day when they discovered, too, that Huw Strongarm had ridden out this time with Uther and the cavalry that Uther called his Dragons, leaving the camp in the charge of a subordinate commander, and Morgas, as Uther had promised, in the charge of the decurion called Nemo. And so for three days, the women established a pattern of waiting and being bored.

When the rumours reached Morgas that Uther had returned, she commanded one of her guards to take a message from her to the King, demanding that he come to speak with her. The man gazed at her in silence for a time, offered a derisive "humph" and returned stolidly to his post, leaving her to fume impotently and eventually to compose herself and wait in patience for her captor to return. This was his tent, she told herself. His belongings were here, as was his bed, and she believed that, having spent the last three nights on the ground beneath the open sky, he might wish to sleep in his cot for a change. She was determined to be ready for him when he did.

She dressed with particular care that day, taking pains to make herself look as alluring and as seductively attractive as she possibly could. The results were spectacular, drawing and holding the eyes and the stares even of her regular guards, who had all been selected, she had begun to believe, for their ability to remain undistracted by her charms. She wore a flowing, voluminous gown of material so fine as to be almost translucent, with nothing else between its draperies and her skin, so that the garment revealed breathtaking glimpses of her curves and swooping, fleetingly outlined silhouettes of breast and belly, hip and thigh as she passed between men's eyes and the bright light of the sun—which she contrived to do as often as possible, the better to gauge and evaluate the effect of such sightings. Overall she was encouraged by the slack-mouthed awe of her observers, who stood watching her, rather than pacing their posts as usual. So successful was she, in fact, that the sheer freedom of her unconfined body beneath the gown began to affect her erotically as her skin, and particularly her nipples, became sensitized to the gentle friction of the garment's fabric. But as her erotic tension increased, the afternoon drew towards evening, night fell, and her evening meal was served without any sighting of Uther Pendragon. Eventually she retired to her own cot, where she tossed and turned for a long time before finally falling asleep, angry and distempered.

She awoke some time later; perhaps hours later or perhaps only a fraction of that time, she had no idea. She knew only that she had been awakened by a heavy, muffled noise close by, and when she opened her eyes, startled and disoriented, she had no memory of where she was. It was dark and quiet, but there was a yellow effulgence on one side of her, a dim radiance that lit one side of the enclosure in which she found herself. Rigid, she lay wide-eyed, fighting down panic, and as her heartbeat fell back towards its normal pace, she began to think coherently again. She remembered where she was, and she remembered, too, that just beyond the walls of the tent wherein she lay at least two guards stood vigilantly, not merely guarding her, but guarding against any attempt she might make to flee.

Then came the noise again. This time she heard it clearly, and she saw an accompanying movement of shadows against the backlit leather wall close by her cot. Uther Pendragon had returned to his tent and was now in the act of removing his armour, evidently attempting to do so quietly without disturbing her. Then she heard a muffled voice speaking very quietly and saw the massive shadow on the wall split into two human shapes, one moving off to the right, where she could no longer see it, while the other remained in place. A picture sprang into her mind immediately of the cruciform wooden rack that was made to hold a full set of armour—cuirass and sword belt, helmet and kilt of armoured straps—and she knew that Uther was being assisted by a trooper, who had carried his discarded armour to hang it upon the device while his master looked to his own comfort.

A moment later the remaining shadow, which she presumed to be Uther's, also moved out of sight, looming first to engulf the entire wall and then disappearing completely, so that she knew he had now moved beyond the light, leaving it between him and her. She heard a quiet splashing as water was poured from a jug into a bowl, and then a muttered farewell as the trooper left the tent, evidently taking a light away with him, since the brightness on the far side of the wall decreased sharply as soon as he left.

Morgas lay quietly for some time after that, holding her breath for long stretches and straining her ears to make out every sound of movement from beyond the partition, but she heard only the sound of softly splashing water and occasionally the sound of breathing from the man on the other side. She heard a sudden, muffled grunt and then a sharp intake of breath, and then another silence stretched out, during which she heard nothing at all. A renewed sound of gently pouring water and a soft, scrubbing sound, and a vision formed in her mind to accompany the sounds to which she listened, a vision that excited her and brought a swelling of her heartbeat and a shortness of breath as she envisioned the man close by her, naked in the dim light of a taper, washing himself completely in the almost-dark. Before she knew what she was doing, she had risen from her bed and moved soundlessly to where she could see into the other part of the tent.

There, sure enough, she saw him naked at his ablutions, washed in the gentle radiance of a single candle so that much of him shone golden in the light while the rest of him was shrouded in darkness. So tall was he and so broad across his back and shoulders that he appeared gigantic, his bulk amplified and enhanced by the giant black shadow thrown now by the candle onto the wall opposite her. His slightest movement caused the flame to flicker and sent the shadow leaping to engulf fully half of the tent wall beyond him and the roof of the tent above him.

Aware but uncaring of her own nudity, knowing that he could not see into the blackness that contained her, Morgas approached the opening in the partition cautiously, making sure that she remained clear of the wedge of pale light spilling into her sleeping area from his candle. Moving slowly through the pitch blackness, she felt her heart begin to hammer in her chest as she allowed her lust to stir and stretch itself.

His chest was broad and deep, coated with crisp, curling black hair that tapered downward to his loins and blended with the dark, impenetrable shadows on the front of him. Behind, the golden candlelight limned the edges of his arms and torso and threw liquid light to outline the edge of his left buttock and the strong sweeping column of his thigh and rounded calf. As she watched, he raised one foot and placed it upon a low stool while he soaked the cloth he held in one hand and used it to wash his crotch, stooping and reaching backwards as he scrubbed and cleansed himself thoroughly. She could not see much in detail, but her imagination served her requirements admirably, and when he dropped the cloth into the bowl and reached for a length of towel behind him, she was delighted when he failed to reach it easily and had to take a small half-step towards it, turning towards the light to pick it up, so that she saw him completely. Then, standing thus, his every movement sensuous and redolent of lazy pleasure, he dried himself at leisure and turned back finally to the basin, where he took himself in hand and pissed, in an arcing stream, into the water wherein he had washed. That done, he took up the basin carefully in both hands and carried it to the doorway of the tent, where he shouldered his way through the flaps and flung the contents of the basin out onto the ground. He returned immediately, emptied the remaining water from the jug into the bowl, swirled it around and took it outside again, repeating the procedure. Returning again, he dried his hands once more with the towel and threw it into the bowl before turning quickly and picking up the candle, cupping his hand around the flame to keep it from guttering.

So directly and unexpectedly did he move in doing this that he caught Morgas completely by surprise, giving her no time to react or even to attempt to regain her cot. She froze, holding her breath, and watched the light move quickly across the front of the tent until its glow appeared behind the panel of the partition between the sleeping chambers. But then, just as she was about to move back to where she ought to be, it reversed direction and came swiftly and silently back towards her. Uther had obviously decided to check up on her before going to sleep, and she backed away hurriedly from the opening in the partition until she could go no farther, blocked by the rear corner of the tent. Less than three steps brought him to the gap opposite where she stood in the dark, but he did not see her as quickly as she saw him. He had not quite entered the sleeping chamber but had paused just outside it, bending forward and peering around the edge of the thin leather wall to where her cot lay empty. She heard the surprised hiss as he saw that she was not there, and then he straightened up immediately, moving quickly, and swept his candle into the chamber, until the light fell across the paleness of her naked form.

In another man, at another time, Morgas might have laughed at the evident play of his thoughts as they swept across his face. She saw surprise, doubt, incomprehension and finally a kind of wide-eyed wonder as his initial alarm subsided and he realized not only that she was safe and had not escaped, but that she was awake and out of bed and beautifully bared to his gaze. In another place, at another time, she herself might well have responded far differently than she did, but this time and place were all she had, and she found her own mind filled with contradictions. She had been instantly prepared to lash out in scorn, in words dripping with irony, to give him the lie for his former protestations of disinterest. But the words died on her lips unspoken as she watched his eyes take note of her. She had immediately formed the intent, too, to stalk across the chamber and snatch up a blanket, throwing it across her to mask herself from his gaze, but she found her feet unable or unwilling to move as his eyes moved slowly down and then back up the length of her body. She knew she should do something, scream for assistance or attempt to run from him, but instead she remained motionless, her heart fluttering harder in her chest as his gaze moved from one breast to the other, then down to her navel. And she knew, as the last possible moment when she might have done so died and was forever lost, that she should have said something, anything, should have protested and complained, but now it was far, far too late. So she stood silent, staring at the man, saying nothing, aware of his increasing arousal and of her own, less obvious but no less powerful.

Finally, it was he who broke the silence, swallowing audibly, and then opening his mouth with a dry, sucking sound, to speak in a quiet tone that, while not quite breathless and not quite a whisper, suggested nonetheless that he was surprised, and moved, and aware of others close by.

"By the gods, lady . . . I did not expect this."

Morgas believed him—the truth of it was stamped plainly on his face—but even more than that, she knew exactly how he was feeling, because experience had taught her that the kind of excitement she was feeling at that moment was never ever one-sided. On the contrary, she knew that it was born of acute and mutual anticipation, and she knew, too, that it would not be denied. She began to speak, then stopped, simply staring at him, feeling her insides turn hot and then melt, flowing downward to her centre.

"What did you expect?" she asked, whispering too, aware that she had to say something. He shook his head, gazing at her breasts again and running the tip of his tongue across his lips, and she continued. "You said you would not take . . . what you were expected to take . . ."

He shook his head again, drawing in a great, deep breath and letting it out with a shudder as he fought to master himself. "True," he said at length. "I did."

"And . . . and will you now?"

Again a head shake, this time stronger, more determined. "No."

"Not even be it freely offered?"

"What . . . ?"

She allowed the silence to hang there, vibrating in the air between them as he thought about what she had said last, and then she brought up her hands, moving slowly, and cupped them beneath her breasts. "Freely offered," she whispered.

Slowly, not taking his eyes away from hers for a moment, he half knelt and placed the candle sconce on the ground. Then he straightened up again and stepped slowly towards her. He stopped when he was almost but not quite touching her, gazing into her eyes, and she moved closer so that her belly came into contact with his hardness and he flinched, jerking away involuntarily. And then he took her shoulders in his hands and pulled her gently to him, stooping his mouth to hers as his arm dropped down about her waist and he brought her up to meet his kiss. She let herself be gathered and went limp, filling his arms with the weight of her inert body, anticipating that the unexpectedness of it would pull him forward and off balance. Instead, however, he caught her close with the arm that encircled her and swept his other arm up behind her knees, lifting her as effortlessly as he might a child. Then he carried her directly to the cot in the corner, where he knelt and lowered her down softly as she wrapped her arms about his neck and pulled him to her.

TWENTY-SIX

For more than a week Uther kept his distance from Ygraine and the other women, although he kept himself precisely informed of their well-being and their morale through his intermediaries. The only woman who saw him in all that time was Morgas, because he came to her bed each night. He made no attempt to speak to her about any of his plans, however, nor did he respond in any way to her questions of him. He came only to rut with her, and he rutted magnificently, which pleased Morgas immensely, since her lustful appetites matched his own. When he was sated, however, as he eventually was each night, he would rise and seek his own cot, and on the two occasions when Morgas sought to follow him and question him, he left the tent and went to sleep elsewhere instead. Morgas was angry at first, but then she accepted the situation. All things change, she knew, and she was confident that, given time, Uther would come to confide in her. She informed Ygraine that Uther was entwined in her clutches, but remained vague about what they discussed in bed.

Then, on the tenth day after the capture, came word that threw the King into a towering rage, a fury so overpowering that he knew he would have to leave the camp in order to rid himself of the temptation to do violence to the Queen and her women. Owain of the Caves had brought him the ill tidings that a party of envoys sent to Gulrhys Lot on the first day of the Queen's captivity had been received by Lot and then butchered out of hand as soon as they had delivered their message. Owain and a squadron of bowmen had accompanied the envoys—a mounted squad of Dragons under the command of a gifted young decurion called Lodder—but had remained nearby, securely hidden, when Lodder and his men rode forward openly to attract Lot's attention.

The "messengers from Camulod," as they were being called, had been received courteously and permitted to keep their weapons. Lot had been unable to meet with them immediately upon their arrival, having other duties and responsibilities that demanded his attention, but had invited them to present their case to him later that night at a banquet to be attended by his Chiefs and senior allies.

Lodder had delivered his King's message that night, explaining that the Queen, Ygraine, was Uther's captive, and then going on to outline Uther's terms of ransom, and when he had finished making his presentation, Lot had questioned him closely on the specifics, asking about the Queen and her escort, and about the ambush in which they had been captured. When questioned about the actual details of the skirmish, however, including its location, Lodder demurred, and Lot flew into a short-lived but highly spectacular fury. By the end of it, Lodder and his ten men were dead, hacked to pieces by the other diners.

After the slaughter that he had incited in his own Hall, Lot made a jest of the dead men and their mission, and then confiscated their horses and equipment, appropriating them for his own use. He drank a health to his hapless and unfortunate Queen, publicly swearing to do all in his power to win her back from Uther's clutches, but in his own way, and not at Uther's invitation or upon Uther's terms. His last words on the topic were a scathing and scornful condemnation, delivered in front of all his drunken, blood-stained crew, of what he called the inept and cowardly role played by the Lord Herliss in the loss of the King's wife, and in order to rectify that, he appointed Herliss's son, Lagan Longhead, to lead an expedition immediately to locate and rescue Queen Ygraine and her women. In the doing of that, Lagan was also to rescue and then arrest his father, Herliss, and bring him home to Herliss's own fortress of Tir Gwyn, there to stand trial for traitorous conduct and cowardice. In order to ensure that father and son would both return to Tir Gwyn, Lot then took Lagan's wife and son into what he chose to refer to as "protective custody," although everyone hearing him knew they would be held as prisoner-hostages against Lagan's return.

It had taken Owain four days to piece together the details of what took place that night, for he had had to prise the information with great care from a variety of sources and informants, permitting none of them to see or even suspect that he was being inquisitive. Now, he could report that Lagan Longhead was out scouring the hills to the south and far west of Uther's current position with a large army of mercenaries. He had already been gone for two days by the time Owain got the word, and he had begun his search by striking down into the far southwest corner of Cornwall's territories, since that was the region wherein his father held the largest tracts of land and property.

Uther listened to all of this in silence, although the fury growing in him was plain to be seen in his eyes and on his whitened face and in the spastic clutching of his hands as he held himself otherwise motionless. When Owain had finished and sat staring at him, the King opened his mouth to speak, but then snapped it shut again as though afraid of what might emerge. Finally, after a long, long period of utter silence, he raised one hand and pointed a commanding finger at Owain.

"Say nothing. Nothing . . . of any of this. To anyone. Before I return." With that, he turned on his heel, moving as if in a dream, and stalked away.

Owain followed him at a distance and watched the King saddle his horse and prepare to leave, and then he turned away to find his longbow and quiver, prepared to follow him wherever he might go. As he bent to pick up his arrows, however, he heard Uther's voice from above and behind him.

"Stay here, Owain, and don't try to follow me. I'll be riding hard and far to let the wind blow through my mind, and I'll come to no harm. I just need to be alone." With that, Uther swung his horse around and rode out.

By the time he had returned to camp, having spent long, solitary hours among the hills digesting all that he had been told, night had long since darkened the encampment. Heedless of the hour,

Uther went directly to Huw Strongarm's tent and summoned Owain, Garreth Whistler and Huw himself to join him there.

Speaking in terse, clipped sentences, Uther told them everything that Owain had told him earlier. It was evident, he said, that Lot had no fear of Uther's wrath. He had demonstrated that by his almost casual execution of the envoys, although it might be argued that his flamboyant cruelty was merely the token gesture of a braggart, since he had called them "Camulodian messengers," indicating that he might not know with whom he was really dealing. Either way, Uther had decided, the cost of that crime would be the loss of Lot's own skin, flayed from his living body on the day he became Uther's prisoner.

Equally clearly, Uther continued, Lot cared nothing about what became of his Queen, Ygraine, and the women unfortunate enough to have been in her company when she was taken. Had it been otherwise, he would have handled everything differently. The Queen was a mere woman and a chattel, bestowed upon him in a marriage of convenient alliance with a King who now lacked importance or significance. So he was careless of her fate, and that was unsurprising and expected in a man like Gulrhys Lot. What was far more significant, however, was that he should be so uncaring about the other twelve captured women. Certainly, he had sworn a public oath to find and rescue all of them, including Ygraine, and had dispatched an army to do that, but that had been no more than a token gesture of hand-wringing hypocrisy. The army he had dispatched was a rabble of mercenaries, and its leadership was questionable at best—a son forced into service against his own father by a threat against his wife and child. Ten of the Queen's women, he pointed out, were Cornish, the other two having come from Eire with their lady. But those ten Cornish women were all daughters of Lot's supporters, the wealthiest and most powerful of Cornwall's Chiefs and warlords, and some, if not all of them, must have value in their fathers' eyes. What, then, did this blatant unconcern say about Lot's dealings with his own most senior and powerful people? How could he afford to be so openly uncaring of what they thought?

The three men, the closest of all his followers, sat gazing at him without speaking, thinking over all that they had been told and trying to make sense out of any part of it. It was Garreth Whistler who eventually broke the silence.

"Uther," he said, "there's something very wrong here, something I can't grasp . . . And that leaves me thinking Lot must be insane. Could that be true? This hostage nonsense, taking this fellow Lagan's wife and son in order to make sure he goes against his own father . . ."

Uther was leaning forward, his eyes narrowed to slits. "What you are really wondering is whether or not the man is far enough gone in his mind to have taken hostages from everyone about him to ensure the ongoing loyalty of all of them. Am I right?"

"Aye, you are. Could he do such a thing? I've never heard the like."

"Nor have I, my friend, but it would not be impossible . . . given that you were insane enough to accept that everyone around you must hate and fear you." Uther looked from Garreth to the other two. "Owain, would you know aught of the like?"

Owain of the Caves shrugged his shoulders and managed to nod his head simultaneously. "I would. I lived with it for a while." He turned his gaze on Garreth. "That's what it was growing to be like with Meradoc. He was drunk with power and felt the stronger to have people go in fear of him. But it was going to his head, none'less, and he was getting worse . . . He would never have held hostages, though. That would have been too much work. He'd have had to feed them and keep them healthy. He had us, instead. We put the fear of dying into everyone around him. Didn't have to do anything most of the time. It was simply enough to be there, and to be seen and feared." He stopped short and looked quickly at Uther. "Think you that's what Lot is doing?"

"Aye, Owain, I do. I think he has surrounded himself with a force of mercenaries strong enough to carry out his every wish without compunction, and their strength guards his strength."

"Then he's a fool, as well as mad!" This was Huw Strongarm. "They are but hired men, with no loyalty to him."

"Aye, perhaps. But never doubt a mercenary's loyalty to the hand that holds the drawstring of the purse that pays him, Huw. As long as Lot can keep them paid—be it in booty, gold, food, drink or women—they'll do his bidding and fulfill his purposes. And if those purposes entail keeping his entire people terrified and on their toes, awaiting death, so be it."

"So where does that leave us?" asked Garreth Whistler.

"Well, it leaves us with a task regarding this army that's out looking for us. We know they're down in the far southwest, or they were a few days ago. What we must do is keep them there, where they won't interfere with us or our plans."

"And how will we do that?" Garreth asked.

"You will do it, Garreth, by leading our Dragons down there and finding Lagan Longhead, then taking vengeance for Lodder and his ten men. Lot's rabble will be as sheep against wolves, face to face with our Dragons, especially when you tell our troopers what befell their friends who went to talk with Lot and his carrion-eaters. But your task will be to harry them, Garreth, not to fight battles. Hit them hard and outrun them on horseback, then turn about and hit them hard again. Give them no rest, no satisfaction and no mercy. Set them reeling, then keep them staggering. Keep them in the field and in the far southwest, away from here."

"Aye, I'll do that. When d'you want me to leave?"

"I'm not sure yet, but it will be very soon. Probably tomorrow."

"Fine. And while I'm away, what are you going to do with all these blasted women, now we know their King won't buy them back?"

"I'm going to use them, Garreth, against Lot. And I'm going to use them very cleverly, I think. In fact, I have been thinking greatly on that this past week and have evolved a stratagem that might work . . . if I can charm their Queen."

Owain coughed loudly into his sleeve, unsuccessfully smothering a guffaw.

Uther looked at him, one eyebrow rising slowly in query. "Owain?"

"Your pardon," he said, smiling openly now. "But . . . you've bedded her, why shouldn't you charm her, too?"

Uther gazed at the big Northerner, his face betraying nothing of his thoughts, and then looked in turn at Huw and at Garreth, both of whom sat blank-faced, staring at him. When he had searched their eyes, all three of them, he nodded slowly.

"What would you say if I informed you that the one I am bedding is not the Queen?"

"Not the—" Huw Strongarm sat straighter, and his right hand dropped unconsciously to the hilt of his dagger. "But of course she is the Queen!"

"Ah yes, Huw." Uther laughed aloud. "She told you so, did she not? I had forgotten. You asked her if she was the Queen and she answered you that she was."

"Yes, she did."

"And did it never occur to you that it might not have been to the Queen's advantage to be known? Or that the one you asked might lie and all the others, too, to protect the true Queen's identity and person?"

"Well, I . . ." Huw's voice died away and he sat silent.

"Which one is the real Queen, then?" Garreth asked, and Uther grinned at him.

"You ought to know, Garreth. You have met her sister, or at least seen her, twice that I know of. And her brother, too."

Garreth looked incredulous. "Her brother? I have met her brother? How would I know the brother of a Cornish Queen?"

"Because she is not Cornish, nor yet from Britain at all. Think, man, think! Do you remember my Cousin Merlyn's adjutant, Donuil? Well, he had a sister . . ."

"Aye, you told me. Cassandra, the girl you found in the woods. Except her name turned out to be . . ."

"Deirdre, the red-haired one. Now, here's what I have in mind."

"Wait you, Uther, before you go farther." Owain sounded perplexed. "Before you go any farther, answer me this . . . How do you expect to charm the real Queen while you be yet tupping the false one?"

"I have already stopped tupping the false one."

"Have you, by all the gods? And when was that?"

"Last night. No, in truth it was this afternoon when I began to think this through. That is when I decided to stop."

"And d'you think she will take kindly to that? She'll be angry."

"Wherefore? At being deceived? I think not. Remember, she pretends to be the Queen, thereby deceiving me. Now listen closely. We will say nothing of this failed approach to Lot in any of our dealings with the women, but I want to separate them all from the true Queen, so here is what we'll do . . ."

In the brightness of mid-morning the following day, Dyllis was isolated by four guards and taken away from her companions without explanation, two of the guards accompanying and leading her, gently enough and without force, one on either side, while the other two used their spears as barriers to prevent any of her companions from attempting to aid her.

Bewildered rather than frightened by the suddenness of her abduction, Dyllis had barely begun to make sense of what was happening to her when her guards came to a halt and she found herself in front of another tent, this one far smaller than the King's Tent in which Morgas was confined. A wooden table stood in front of it, with two folding wood-and-leather chairs, and on her right, its reins loosely tethered to a hawthorn tree, an enormous brown horse, bridled and saddled, stood so close to her that she could hear the ripping sound of grass being cropped between its grazing lips.

"Sit, lady." One of her guards pointed towards a chair, and Dyllis moved timidly to obey him. As soon as she was seated, both guards stepped back from her in unison and stood with their spear butts grounded by their right feet, their left hands behind their backs as though their thumbs were hooked into their belts, and their eyes fixed upon some point far distant above her head.

Moments later, the flaps of the tent were pulled back and the giant form of Uther Pendragon emerged, wearing full armour, but carrying his heavy, ornate helmet in the crook of his left arm. He stepped forward until he loomed over her, forcing her to tilt her head back in order to see him, and then he smiled and nodded, placing his helmet on the table between them and sitting down carefully in the other chair.

"Lady Dyllis. I hope my men did not mistreat you?"

Dyllis opened her mouth to respond, but nothing emerged so completely surprised was she. She had heard terrible things about this man, this scourge of all things decent and familial, but his face was open and smiling, unlined and unblemished, even by a frown. It was a youthful face, with a long, straight nose, humorous and clean-shaven, apart from a full moustache that stretched down to his chin. She saw strength and confidence, but none of the cruelty, arrogance and disdain she had thought to see. And she realized that she was sitting gaping like a fool. She swallowed hard, coughed slightly to clear her throat, then tried to speak again, this time with more success, although all that came out was a frightened, wordless squeak.

Uther smiled again and spoke right on as though he had heard her perfectly and had understood every word she had meant to say.

"I sent for you because I have something important to do . . . a decision I must make, regarding you and your companions and the Queen . . . and it seemed to me that you would probably be the best person to ask."

Dyllis found her voice at that, frowning with disapproval at his presumption. "Why would you think that, Sir King?" She saw his eyebrow rise up on his forehead, but before he could interrupt, she swept on, finding the words now without difficulty. "On matters regarding my lady the Queen, she herself must be the best person to ask. I have no right to speak in her stead. Since you are an abductor of women and therefore without honour, you have no right to ask me anything at all, but most certainly you have no right to ask me for my opinion concerning what the Queen might think or say or do." She stopped then, having frightened herself with her forth-rightness, but Uther was nodding his head.

"I have no quarrel with that, lady . . . though I take exception to your remarks about honour. I will say no more than this. My honour lies in my own recognizance, and to this point I have done nothing to demean it with regard to you, your Queen or the rest of her women.

"Beyond that, however, on the matter of the Queen, I grant that what you say is true, and I have no justification for expecting you to speak on her behalf on any matter. But that is not what I would ask of you. My urgency lies elsewhere. Your Queen is in my hands, and as a hostage she is more than simply valuable: she is beyond price. And yet, if I do the wrong thing, or if I proceed less than judiciously, I could lose every advantage in negotiating with Lot for her release. I will release her, and unharmed—I can give you my assurance on that, so believe as you will—but we are at a crucial interval here, and I require your help in the form of an answer to this question: which one, of all the Queen's women, would be the best possible choice for me to send to Lot with word of his wife's capture?"

He stopped talking then, watching her eyes closely, and precisely when he saw her begin to gather her breath to speak, he held up a peremptory hand.

"Before you answer that, let me add something else for you to consider: the woman whom I send must have authority among you and must command respect in all your eyes, for only then will she achieve standing in Lot's eyes, I believe. But she must also be fluent and strong in argument, and she must enjoy the confidence of the Queen herself. Do you take my meaning?"

Dyllis nodded. "I do."

"And do you have such a woman among your number?"

Dyllis nodded. "Yes, but only one. The woman you require is called Deirdre. She has everything you seek, and she, above all others, has the power to convince King Lot of what he must do to safeguard and win back his wife, Ygraine the Queen."

Uther frowned. "You intrigue me. She, above all others, has the power to convince Lot? Are you saying—is this Deirdre then Lot's mistress? For if she is, she would be the worst person I could send, since it would be to her advantage to leave her Queen right here with me, rotting in bondage."

Dyllis coloured prettily and raised her head high. "Believe me, the Lady Deirdre is no mistress to King Lot. Nor need you fear her motives. Nothing would be more to Lady Deirdre's liking than to have Queen Ygraine safe home again as quickly as may be, and safe from your captivity."

Uther stared at her for long moments, his brows drawn slightly together, then nodded decisively. "So be it. I shall use your Lady

Deirdre as my messenger. She will be my interlocutor in dealing
with Lot."

"But—but you cannot . . ." the Lady Dyllis looked scandalized.
"You cannot, surely, think to send the Lady Deirdre out alone to do
your bidding? Surely you will grant her at least one companion?"

"One companion? She will have an armed escort. She will come
to no harm."

"An armed escort? That will be well enough for her protection
while travelling, but she will require a companion, someone with
whom she may be herself. She needs more than an escort of drunken
soldiery. Think you your base-born troopers could be fit company
for any high-born lady?"

Uther appeared to think about that for a time, then nodded in
agreement. "Very well, we will permit her a companion. Will you
accompany her?"

Dyllis sat blinking at him, her eyes awash with tears as she realized what was being asked of her, and then she nodded wordlessly.

Uther grinned and stood up. "My thanks, Lady Dyllis, you have
relieved my mind. Now please inform your friends that they will
soon be removed again, with your Queen, this time to a place of
safety, with clean, pleasant and private accommodations away from
the close proximity of common, base-born soldiery. They will all be
lodged there in comfort until this treaty is completed and they can
return home. And in the meantime, I can wage my war while the
Lady Deirdre sues with Lot for your deliverance." He paused, evidently thinking, and then resumed. "Your guards will take you back
now, but will you ask your Lady Deirdre to return here with them,
and tell her, if you please, that she will not be harmed in doing so?"
He saw her nod and returned the gesture as he stood up. "My thanks
for this." He beckoned to one of the guards. "Return the lady to her
friends and bring back the woman Deirdre."

Ygraine approached the meeting with Uther with misgivings, her
mind still full of the terrifying comment he had made to her concerning Deirdre of the Violet Eyes. His mention of that name had
shattered what small degree of equanimity had been left to Ygraine,

because the impossibility of his knowing it had been, to her sure knowledge, complete and unequivocal. Uther Pendragon could not ever, under any conceivable circumstances, have heard anything of Deirdre of the Violet Eyes, because Deirdre of the Violet Eyes had died as a mere child and had been dead for many years, and during the brief span of her life she had never left her home in Eire, beyond the sea and far beyond the knowledge of an untutored savage from the mountains of Cambria.

Now, summoned into Uther's presence, she walked slowly. Dyllis had informed her about every aspect of her own conversation with the Pendragon King, but still Ygraine wondered what might be coming. The guards, somewhat to her surprise, made no attempt to hurry her along, but merely walked beside her, adjusting their pace to hers. Abruptly aware of that, she stopped moving altogether, simply to see what they would do, and they stopped with her, standing in silence, waiting for her to start walking again.

They arrived soon after that at the tent that Dyllis had described to her, where the large, saddled horse still stood grazing beneath the hawthorn tree. There was no sign of Uther Pendragon, and when one of her guards bade her be seated, Ygraine obeyed the instruction and sat in one of the two chairs.

A short time later, Uther approached through the trees, surprising her because she had assumed he was in the tent. He came striding towards her, removing his helmet and drying perspiration from his forehead with the crook of his elbow, and when he reached the table in front of her he stopped and inclined his head in an informal salute.

"I am glad you agreed to speak with me," he said. "And grateful."

She looked directly up at him, keeping her face free of expression. "Grateful? You mean I could have chosen not to come?"

"Of course."

"And had I so chosen, what then?"

"Then my guards would have brought you anyway, but not so gently."

"I see. Well, now that we both understand the terms of my presence here, what would you have of me? I have no wish to remain any longer than I must."

"Lady," the big man said with a rueful grin, "I was jesting. In truth, had you chosen not to come, I would have come to you, instead." He looked over to where the two guards stood at attention and nodded to one of them. "I no longer need you. I'll look after the lady myself now. Dismiss." He stood watching the two troopers as they marched away in lockstep, then turned back to where Ygraine sat watching him. "I will not keep you long. I imagine that the Lady Dyllis has already informed you as to what I want of you?"

"You mean regarding the Queen and her ransom."

"Yes." He placed his helmet carefully on the tabletop, then reached out and took hold of the other chair, pulling it towards him. When it was positioned properly, he swept his cloak out from behind him and slung it across his arm to keep it out of the way before he sat down across from her with the table between them. When he was securely seated, he released the folds of his cloak, draping them across his knees, and then looked her directly in the eye.

"Would you be willing to serve as liaison between myself and Gulrhys Lot in this matter of the Queen and your captivity?"

"To what end?"

He frowned, a quick drawing together of his brows that briefly registered surprise that she would ask such a thing. "Why . . . to the end of gaining your Queen's release. What other end could there be?"

Ygraine tilted her head to one side and made no effort to disguise the depth of her cynicism. "Well, let me see . . . You are a man like Gulrhys Lot, so that means there could be ancillary ends . . . pressing, even self-serving reasons for your concern over the Queen. I say that with no wish to offend you, but surely you must see how someone might judge your concern for her welfare as springing from reasons more concerned with your good than with hers. You might, for example, hope to gain some military or even monetary advantage over King Lot from your possession of her person."

He gazed at her, straight-faced, but she fancied she saw a hint of humour in his eyes. "No, never! How could you even think such a thing might be possible? That I, or anyone, might seek personal gain from such a circumstance?"

"Laugh at me if you wish, Sir King, and hope as highly as you may. Your hopes will be soon dashed."

He gazed at her for several moments after that before he responded. "How so?"

She pursed her lips, then spoke quietly. "Why, because you will be basing false hope upon Gulrhys Lot's sense of honour and his regard for his wife, the Queen."

Uther smiled a small, chilly smile. "Lady, I would never be fool enough to suspect Lot of knowing what honour is, so how then could I base any hope upon his having any? But are you telling me he has no regard for his Queen?"

"No, I am not. I am telling you that Gulrhys Lot is not sufficiently weak as to allow consideration for any woman, be it his wife or even his mother, to interfere with what he believes to be his destiny. You may send anyone you please to talk with him and to create some set of terms by which he may obtain the Queen's freedom, but he will gull you at the end and use your silly honour to gut you when you least expect it."

"Would he do that if it cost him his Queen's life? I doubt that, lady. Not even Gulrhys Lot would be so careless of the fate of his lady wife."

Ygraine smiled, but without humour. "Doubt all you wish, it matters not to me."

"So you will not go to Lot, to deal with him on behalf of the Queen?"

She made no response, but looked over to where the horse had stopped cropping and now stood with his head erect, his ears twitching from side to side as he took note of the noises around him.

"Lady? I require an answer of you, if you will. Are you telling me you will not go to Gulrhys Lot bearing my message? I have arranged that you will not go alone. The other woman, Dyllis, will accompany you."

"She told me that already. And I will go if you yet wish to send me, but I can tell you now, before we proceed farther, that should I go, Lot will not permit me to return. There would be no advantage to him in so doing."

"Of course there would. He would regain his Queen."

"Aye, but at what cost? Besides, Ygraine is no Queen. Boudicca of the Iceni was a Queen; she ruled her people truly, but men killed her four hundred years and more ago. Ygraine is a King's wife, no more than that—not even a companion, and less than a concubine. She is a dowered wife bestowed upon Lot by her father to seal a bargain made between two men. Her value may be accurately gauged in terms of weapons, warriors, and gold and silver bars, and Lot already has all those in his possession. Those things subtracted, Ygraine the so-called Queen is merely another woman, and no King ever lacks for women . . . did you not know that? By simply keeping Dyllis and me, Lot could undo all you think to have gained at this time. You would have deprived him of a woman who was but a wife, but in so doing, you would have presented him with two replacements, potential concubines to be used without commitment."

Uther was staring at Ygraine now with widened eyes. "By the gods, lady," he murmured. "You have no great love for your King, do you?"

"Love? I said nothing of love. But I have no great regard for Kings. Indeed, I have but little love for men in general, and when men and matters of governance are mixed, I have found that women always fare badly. Gulrhys Lot is a man and so are you, and both of you take pride in being Kings. Between the two of you, you possess all the wealth and all the weapons you require to wage your wars, and that makes us, as women, insignificant."

"Hmm." Uther sat staring at her, pinching his lower lip between finger and thumb. Finally he sighed and stood up. "What makes a person or an event insignificant? I do not expect you to answer that, Lady Deirdre, but it occurs to me that there is something I should tell you now, so that you can pass the information to your Queen before she hears a different version elsewhere." He paused and scratched his chin. "There has been one occurrence here within recent days that might seem more significant than it really is, if it were reported wrongly. Five days ago, a party of my men marched out of here, escorting some six score of men captured in the raid in which we also took you prisoner. All of these six score men were common soldiery, wearing the shoulder insignia of Herliss. Today, my men returned, but they brought no prisoners back with them. Now, what think you about that?"

She was staring at him, appalled. "You killed them? No, you could not do that." It was almost a question, and he could see from her expression that she believed he could indeed do exactly that. He said nothing, gazing at her in silence until she blurted, "You murdered *all* of them? Six score of them?"

"Aye," he said, sighing. "That's what I thought you would think—the first thing that sprang into your head. No, lady, I did not murder them, nor did I have my men murder them on my behalf. I gave them back their weapons and some food and set all of them free on the high moors, miles from anywhere."

"Hah! You expect me to believe that? That you would free men to return home and rearm themselves to come against you again? I would have to be a fool to think so!"

He shrugged his wide shoulders, looking her in the eyes and seeing how desperately she would have liked to believe him. "Perhaps you are, then. You would know that better than I. I think, though, that you would certainly be a fool to think that any of those men would dare go back again to Lot, expecting forgiveness for having lost his wagons and his siege engines, as well as his wife and all her ladies . . . but most particularly his siege engines. I doubt if I would be that brave or that foolish . . .

"I set them free, lady, certain that they all knew that Lot would never have done the same. None of those men will ever come against me again, and that is no more than the simple truth."

She gazed into his eyes, recognizing that it was as he said, and she felt something, something that had been hard and sharp-edged, break loose and fall away inside her.

He reached out and touched her shoulder, turning her gently to face the direction from which she had arrived.

"Come, lady, let me walk back with you." He left his helmet lying on the tabletop as he turned and moved away slowly, deep in thought and making no attempt to touch her again, so that she followed him,

walking quickly until she had gained his side. He spoke to her as they
went, his tone conversational.

"Tomorrow, the Queen and her other women will leave here and
travel northward, back to Camulod. We have a wagon for them, so
they will not have to walk. There they will be lodged in comfort and
in far more safety than I can offer them in the middle of a raiding
campaign until Gulrhys Lot has come to terms with me. Should he
turn out to be the man you have described to me, then . . . I know
not what I might do. That's a bridge I won't cross till I need to, as
they say. But that's it. I have made up my mind. So please tell the
other women what I intend to do and that they need to be ready. And
some time later, you and the Lady Dyllis will leave in search of Lot,
to acquaint him with my terms for the Queen's return. When he and
I have agreed upon those terms, the Queen and all her women will
be freed to return home. Ah, there they all are. They must have been
concerned for you. I'll stop here."

He did so immediately, and Ygraine, on the point of hurrying
forward to where the other women awaited her, turned suddenly and
raised one hand to prevent him from leaving immediately. He
paused, one eyebrow raised as he waited for her question, but she
had to cast about before she could find the words with which to
phrase it.

"My wom—, the women, my friends, and the Queen . . . should
Gulrhys Lot refuse to discuss . . . what did you call it, terms for
them? Should that occur, would you . . . will you . . . kill them?"

Uther Pendragon looked at her solemnly and then drew himself
erect, heaving a huge sigh. "Barbarian," he said. "Is that the kindest
word you might have for me, perhaps? No, lady, I would not kill your
friends, nor would I feed them to my dogs or even give them to my
men for sport. I would not even keep them prisoners, adding a further
insult to their own King's disregard for them. Now, were you to tell
that to Gulrhys Lot, then he would certainly refuse to treat with me
on their behalf, but you yourself would be betraying your Queen and
your friends in the telling, so dwell upon that if you will. And now
farewell, lady, until I send for you again." He bowed and walked
away, back towards his horse, leaving her staring after him.

Ygraine did not sleep well that night, because the word she took back to the women's tent regarding their impending move northward to Camulod set off a storm of fearful speculation among them that not even her authority could have quelled, and it did not die down until long after the lights had been lit and supper had been brought to them.

What would the Cambrian King's reaction be when he discovered how he had been duped? Ygraine told them of his promise, but surely, if he was the ogre he was said to be, his anger would be boundless and unrestrained. Would any of their lives be safe from his fury? They began to whisper stories and dimly remembered rumours of the savagery of the Camulodian raiders who had first penetrated Cornwall several years earlier, and the atrocities they had reportedly committed against peaceful Cornish farmers and residents, and there was little sleep in the command tent that night.

There was little sleep in Uther's tent, either, for the King lay awake for hours, fretting in spite of his own admonitions to himself. It had been important to him that day, far more important than he had known at the time, to assure Ygraine of his good intentions and to dispel the image of the fearsome villain that Gulrhys Lot had hung about his neck. He tossed and turned incessantly, fighting that lifelong war within himself, the struggle between who and what he was and who and what he ought to be, brandishing a torch against the darkness he felt inside, trying to banish the ogre that raged inside him. He had seen fear in her eyes. And in the darkness of his tent he recalled, though he tried not to, the fears of his mother, who would not bear another child lest it be branded with the hatreds of the Pendragon clan. And so he lay awake until the morning light crept in to chase the shadows away.

TWENTY-SEVEN

Come morning, the guards were everywhere, under the unsmiling eye of the surly one called Nemo, shepherding the women as they gathered up all their belongings and made shift to decamp northward. Bemused, Ygraine watched all of their preparations, amazed at how, after mere days in strictly confined seclusion, such a small number of women could have gathered and dispersed so great an array of clothing and belongings. After little more than an hour of chaos, however, everything had been gathered up and packed, and a stream of troopers had carried the cases from the enormous command tent to the equally gigantic commissary wagon that had been placed at the disposal of the women for their journey.

Six matched horses, all of them larger than any horse Ygraine had ever seen before, were tethered in the traces of the huge wagon, which sat upon shaped layers of leafed, iron springs fastened to its axles and rode on four vast wheels bound with broad, thick tires of solid iron greater in width than the entire span of her hand. So massive was this vehicle and so high its bed above the ground that the women had to use a ladder to climb up into it.

Ygraine and Dyllis embraced each of the women in turn as they climbed up into the high wagon, and Ygraine was one of the few who remained dry-eyed at the parting, although she attributed most of the flowing tears to her companions' natural and understandable fears rather than to any grief over leaving her and Dyllis behind. Then, as the teamster gathered the reins together in one huge hand and cracked his whip over the beasts' heads for the first time, she stepped back and away, holding her hand high in a gesture of farewell but watching the straining muscles of the enormous animals as they threw their weight into the traces and pulled the heavy wagon into rumbling motion. She stood there motionless for some time after that, aware of Dyllis's closeness and watching the receding wagon until it turned and was lost to sight behind a bank of trees.

Over by the King's Tent, she knew, guards would be loading Morgas and the other women, along with their possessions, into the cart. Ygraine wished she had been able to speak with her before their separation, but she had had no opportunity even to approach the other woman since learning that they were to be moved. She had, however, sent one of the others, Fyrgas, as her messenger, with advice and instructions for Morgas on how to behave in her role as Queen.

Shaking her head slightly at the thought that the headstrong Morgas was now beyond her control, Ygraine hooked her arm through Dyllis's and began to walk back towards the now empty command tent. Nemo, the captain of the guard, stood waiting for them beside two troopers, whose arms were filled with the few possessions she and Dyllis had retained. As soon as the women came into view, Nemo turned quickly and led the two men away, plainly expecting her to follow.

Ygraine fell into step behind them, moving at her own pace. But when she saw where they were leading her, she stopped dead in her tracks. Nemo turned and came back to where she stood, staring, then took her none too gently by the upper arm and propelled her firmly the rest of the way to the King's Tent. The two tall, helmeted and uniformly cloaked and armoured guards who flanked the entrance paid her not the slightest glance of interest or attention as Nemo pushed her roughly between them and through the doorway.

"Wait here." She was pushed again, this time towards a chair, and she sat obediently, sensing that she would end up tied to it if she offered any resistance. Nemo gazed at her for a moment with eyes so empty that the sight of them made her suppress a shudder, then turned away to beckon to the two men carrying their belongings. They each moved directly into one of the two sleeping cubicles and laid down their burdens, then came out and saluted Nemo, who waved them away. Turning back to the women, Nemo ignored Dyllis and swept Ygraine from head to toe with a look that was neither interested nor curious.

"Wait here. Don't move." Nemo marched out of the tent, leaving them alone again.

Ygraine turned to Dyllis and asked her to go into her sleeping cubicle so that she could be alone. With her companion gone, Ygraine sat quietly for a while, adjusting to her new situation, letting her eyes drift around the tent with its sparse furnishings.

It was exactly as she had seen it on her earlier visits to Morgas: bare, functional and showing no sign at all of human occupancy. The poles of the frame for holding armour were bare; the footlockers were closed. She crossed to the washstand and lifted the jug, noting that the surface beneath it was dry.

"It's empty."

The words came from close behind her and she almost dropped the ewer in her shock and surprise. She swung around immediately, anger and resentment welling up in her, only to discover that the Cambrian had not, as she had assumed, crept up on her while her back was turned. He stood framed in the tent's entrance, balancing his weight lazily on one straight leg, with the other knee bent and one hand gripping the hanging flap. The sun at his back turned him into a looming silhouette.

"Shall I send for water for you, lady?" Now she saw that he was almost smiling.

"No." She shook her head and crossed quickly back to her chair. "Do you intend to keep me here now, a prisoner like—?"

"Queen Ygraine?" He shrugged his shoulders and moved into the tent. "What other choice have I? You can hardly remain all alone in the big tent, can you?" He glanced around him. "You are alone, though. Where is the other woman, Dyllis?"

"She is here, behind the partition."

He nodded. "Good. So you will stay here. You will be comfortable, and it should not be for long."

"Too long, I think. This is your tent. Where will you be sleeping?"

He raised a mocking eyebrow. "As you say, lady, it is my tent. I had thought to place my cot in here in the front. Would you rather have me sleep outside upon the ground?"

"Lacking another alternative, yes, I would. But I would have thought you might sleep in the tent that you were using yesterday."

"That tent belongs to my subordinate commander, Huw Strongarm. He sleeps there."

Ygraine tossed her head. "There should be ample room for both of you. Besides, I venture to think *he* might be safer sharing a tent with you than any woman—or any two women—would be."

"Tut, lady, you have a jagged tongue—" he dipped his head in a gesture of acknowledgment, his lips twisted in a rueful little grin "—but little consideration for junior commanders. I will not dispossess young Huw to please your whim, no matter how well he might adjust to it. That's not my way. But I will do as you request and sleep outside, not on the ground, but on my cot. So you may rest easy."

"Did my lady the Queen rest easy here?"

Uther made a face and spread his hands in a shrug. "She did not suffer, to my knowledge. Did she complain to you?"

When Ygraine made no reply, Uther looked around him again and raised his voice slightly. "Lady Dyllis?"

Dyllis poked her head out from behind the partition. "Yes?"

"Look to your lady here." He turned back to Ygraine, smiling. "I must leave for a day or two to scout out the lie of the land and make sure there are no unsuspected threats out there, but I shall return. In the meantime, Nemo will look after you and provide you with anything you require."

He saluted quickly and walked out, leaving Ygraine to turn to Dyllis, open-mouthed.

"'Look to your lady,' is that what he said?" Dyllis nodded, unable to respond, and Ygraine shook her head in a frowning, troubled negative. "We must have misunderstood him."

Uther was as good as his word and returned two days later to find Ygraine and Dyllis sitting outside in the spring sunlight, their guards close by, deeply involved in repairing some of their outer clothing that was the worse for wear. He paid no attention to what they were doing and insisted that they come into the tent with him immediately. Discovering that there was no place to sit, he strode back outside to fetch the chairs they had been using, and when they were seated, he picked up one of the two low footlockers set against the partition and placed it atop the other, then sat on both.

"Have you been well treated while I was away?" They acknowledged that they had and he nodded, evidently having expected nothing less. "Well, it's time I let you in on more of the details of your situation. You should know now that when I first captured you, I sent off envoys to Gulrhys Lot with the authority to discuss terms for your release."

"And . . . ?"

He shrugged. "And I thought at that time that if all went well, I might expect to hear something from them within two weeks . . . by today or tomorrow at the latest."

"And . . . ?" This time he made no response, merely raising an eyebrow, and Ygraine continued. "What if all did not go well? What if Lot has killed your envoys or holds them prisoner? He is capable of that. He has his mercenaries, and he has no fear of consequences."

"Aye, I have no doubt he's capable of it. But would he do such a thing in this instance, d'you think, knowing that his Queen and her women would bear the brunt of such behaviour? Is he that low?"

Ygraine allowed her face to betray nothing. Instead, she answered him in measured, level tones. "He is a man and a King. You are a man and a King. Ask yourself that question, therefore, not me. Would you do such a thing?"

Uther's face grew dark so suddenly that the sight of it chilled her. "No, lady, I would not," he hissed, almost snarling with anger.

He stood up then, sudden and forceful, and moved angrily about the tent, looking at neither woman. He braced himself in the doorway with a white-knuckled grip on the leather flaps and gazed fiercely out into the bright afternoon light. The women looked at each other and exchanged glances of baffled wonderment, but neither made any attempt to speak. Finally Uther sighed, deep and hard, and turned back to face them, looking at Ygraine.

"I would never consider such a thing, lady. But Gulrhys Lot did. He killed my messengers, all of them, when they were guarded by his oath of protection and safe passage. And for that, I promise you, I will have his foul guts stretched and dried to string my men's longbows. You must be fell proud of your husband, lady."

"*What?*" Ygraine felt the blood drain from her face. "What did you say?"

Uther looked at her and sucked in a mighty breath, then held it long before he let it go again. "I said 'your husband,' Gulrhys Lot, the man to whom you stand condemned to wife—"

He stopped abruptly as she jumped to her feet, the colour draining from her face, and his scowl deepened as he saw what he took to be fear filling her wide eyes.

"What?" he growled, exasperated. "Are you to scream now? Think you I'm going to flog you for being your husband's wife? You scoffed when Huw Strongarm told you I do not war on women, but he spoke the truth. Gulrhys Lot does enough of that for both of us. It is his nature, part of what sets him apart from ordinary, human folk. I hold no blame over you for the actions of that man, and none, either, for having wedded him. I know your story, and it leaves you blameless."

She took one hand in the other and squeezed with all her strength, digging her nails into the side of her palm and forcing herself to be calm and to think clearly. He knew her, there was no avoiding or gainsaying that . . . but that was unimportant. What was important was . . . She swallowed hard, fighting down panic. What was important was that Lot had killed his messengers, slaughtered them under promise of safe conduct.

"When did you discover this . . . treachery?"

"Several days ago, lady. I heard the tidings several days ago."

"And why have you said nothing until now? Why this mummery of sending me with messages to Lot? You knew then that would be worse than useless."

"Aye, lady, I did."

"And did you know then who I am?"

"Aye, that, too."

"And when did you discover that?"

"The first time I set eyes on you by the roadside, after the ambush in which Huw Strongarm captured you and your train."

"Then what of Morgas, who was supposed to be the Queen? Why did you permit that pretence?"

"Because it suited my purpose. It did me no harm to have you think your secret was secure."

"But you were bedding her!"

He shrugged. "I was bedding a woman, not a Queen. That was no hardship, for her or for me. We both enjoyed it, I think."

"But . . . but then, why send her away and keep me here?"

"Because I had to separate you from the rest of the women. Once I heard that Lot had scorned his chance to gain you back, they became an encumbrance, and you took on a new importance."

She cocked her head to one side. "Even though you knew he would not treat for me?"

"Most particularly so."

Ygraine shook her head in denial. "You say you knew me when you first set eyes on me, but that is simply not possible. It means that you must have seen me somewhere before. But I have never been beyond Cornwall since first I set foot in Britain."

He shook his head. "I did not say I had seen you before. I simply recognized you for who you are. That's why I mentioned Deirdre of the Violet Eyes."

So astounded was she at hearing him use the name a second time that she could not even think to protest. "Explain that," she whispered.

He glanced quickly from her to Dyllis and then back to Ygraine.

"Deirdre was your sister, who suffered a strange childhood illness and died many years ago, is that not correct?"

She nodded, too stunned to speak.

"Aye, well, she did not die when your family thought she had. She survived for many years, though she was deaf and mute, and she travelled eventually to Britain, where she met and wed my beloved cousin, Merlyn Britannicus of Camulod. He and I found her alone and lost one day in the woods while we were on patrol—actually, I found her, or Nemo did, to be strictly truthful—and we took her back with us to Camulod. She had your face, unmistakably."

"She *had* my face . . ."

"Aye, she did. She is dead now, killed, murdered, almost a year ago, and we never discovered who did it. She died carrying my cousin Merlyn's child."

"But—"Ygraine looked away, trying to find words. Her head was reeling, her shock overwhelming her ability to deal with all the information that had come at her so swiftly. She shook her head, hard, and forced herself to think clearly, grasping at the one incongruous thought that had occurred to her in listening to what he had said. "But wait . . . she was deaf and mute from childhood. Her world was one of silence. How, then, could she have told you who she was?"

"She did not tell us. It was your brother Donuil who told Merlyn her real name, when the two, brother and sister, met again in Camulod—Lady!"

Strange noises had been buzzing in Ygraine's head for what seemed to be a long time, but when she heard her brother's name on this man's lips, suddenly everything about her began to spin. And then she felt as though she were flying through the air, weightless and without substance, with only a roaring in her ears, filling her head.

With a red haze fading quickly from in front of her eyes, she regained her senses moments later to find Uther Pendragon's face close to her own, his brows knitted in a ferocious scowl, while from above his shoulder Dyllis peered down at her, wide-eyed. Somewhat frantically, Ygraine struggled to sit upright, realizing only as she did so that the man's arm was completely encircling her, supporting her weight as though he had been carrying her. She realized then that she had fainted, and that he must have caught her as she fell, then borne her to the cot on which she now reclined with his support. Her heart fluttering, close to the edge of panic, she sat bolt upright and swung her feet around and down until they were solidly on the ground, pushing him away from her as she did so, protesting that she was perfectly well and required no assistance.

Uther stood upright immediately and took a long pace backwards, and she concentrated hard upon not looking at him as she brought herself back to order and decorum. Finally, when she felt that she was in command of herself again, she nodded once, curtly, in tacit acknowledgment of his assistance and courtesy.

"Lady, I said too much, too soon. You will have much to think about now. I will leave you to the questions that must be bubbling in your mind, and I will come back later. At least then I might be able to answer some of your questions. When I do come back, let there be no more talk between us two of Gulrhys Lot. His crime is committed, his foulness demonstrated, and neither you nor I can hold the other one responsible for his degeneracy. So let his name lie cursed and unspoken from this time between you and me." He raised his clenched fist to his breast in salute, then bowed stiffly from the waist and turned. Just before he left, however, he hesitated and half turned back to speak over his shoulder. "Forgive me, lady, if my bluntness has angered you. I had not intended saying all I said, and I had not considered how it might offend you to learn of it so suddenly and unexpectedly. In truth, I did not think at all . . . So now I, too, must spend some time alone, considering all the many complex strangenesses that are involved in this."

They watched him leave the tent, dipping his head as he passed through the doorway, and then Dyllis turned, her eyes filled with wonder, and opened her mouth to speak, but Ygraine cut her short.

"Leave me alone now, Dyllis, if you would. Go you and find you something to keep you occupied. As our jailer said, I have many questions calling to be answered, and I don't even know how to ask most of them. I have to think, and the last thing I need is to have you hovering there, gazing at me wide-eyed."

As soon as the other woman had gone, Ygraine adjusted her girdle until it was slack, arranged her gown loosely about her for comfort and lay down on her cot, closing her eyes against the light. Her mind was buzzing with long-repressed memories of her childhood in Eire and the swarm of siblings and cousins and relatives among whom she had grown up. Some of their names and faces had been lost to her for years. Even Deirdre, her younger sister, whose name she had borrowed in her vain attempt to deceive the Cambrian, had remained walled up until now in some vault in her memory; she had chosen the name simply because it was one she thought to be safe and beyond any random association with her own. Now, however, she allowed her thoughts to drift to the terror she and all her kin had felt when the child had suffered for so long and then survived the terrifying illness that had stricken her, an illness that resembled no other sickness known to anyone, not even the eldest and most learned Druids in her father's lands.

Deirdre had clung stubbornly to life and in the end had survived, but at a terrible cost. The magnificent violet eyes that had given her her name had been faded and permanently dimmed, leached of their colour in some frightening manner by the severity of the fevers that had consumed her tiny body, so that they were pale grey forever after. Even her rich, chestnut hair had lost its lustrous colour. She had lost her voice, too, in that illness, and her hearing, and thinking back on it again, Ygraine shuddered afresh, thinking it was no wonder that the people of her father's kingdom had eyed the child uneasily thereafter and whispered among themselves of witchcraft and the interference of the dark gods of night and death.

Several years after that illness, little Deirdre fell ill again, and this time she wandered away unnoticed from their father's encampment one night in the grip of a high fever and was never seen again. Everyone mourned her then as dead, for it had been inconceivable that the child—she was a mere twelve years old, even then—might survive a second time, unable to hear or speak or to fend for herself in the wild forest that surrounded their home.

And now this upstart Cambrian Outlander brought word that Deirdre had not only survived but had married his cousin, Merlyn Britannicus of Camulod. It was inconceivable! For years now, since the days before she had come to Britain to be bride to Gulrhys Lot, she had been imbued with the tales of Uther Pendragon's savagery, his sullen, violent malevolence, and his furious lusts for blood and conquest. And hand in glove with those tales, she had heard much about the cowardly behaviour of his cousin, Merlyn of Camulod, a bird of the same plumage, fed on the same seeds of depravity since childhood, but less brave, although no less malicious, than his kinsman. And now she was being asked to believe that her own sister had married this same Merlyn Britannicus, and that her brother Donuil also lived in Camulod on friendly terms with these people? It was a ridiculous thing to suggest.

Ygraine found that she was frowning, even though her eyes were closed, and grinding her teeth as she dug deep to find and bolster the hatred that had always lain within her breast for Uther Pendragon. She could remember Gulrhys Lot describing to her father all the reasons why it was necessary for the two Kings and their two peoples to form a strong and enduring alliance. United, they would be able to withstand the advances and thwart the ambitions of this brash, hybrid tribe who called themselves Camulodians and who had but recently emerged from an alliance between the Pendragon clans of Cambria and the upstart dregs, deserters and leavings of the Roman armies that had fled Britain. Uther Pendragon and Merlyn of Camulod had always been among her greatest personal foes, the avowed enemies of the people of Cornwall.

Why then, she found herself wondering now, could she not summon up the anger and hatred that she knew was there inside her? She found herself shaking, as though she was in a fever, and she suddenly realized that she was shaking with fury, and that her rage was not directed at her captors. She sat completely upright, her eyes staring blankly at the wall, and shouted for Dyllis.

The flaps at the front of the tent were ripped open and two guards sprang in, bare blades already raised and ready to strike. Seeing her alone on her cot, sitting upright, they paused, frozen in mid-step.

"Lady?" growled one of the guards, while the other, Nemo, looked all around the tent. Ygraine shook her head, swallowing to free her voice.

"A dream," she said, huskily. "It frightened me. I was asleep. A dream, no more. My thanks."

The guards retreated slowly and went back outside, sheathing their swords and looking all about them, not yet convinced that all was well. Dyllis stood by the gap in the partition, her troubled gaze on Ygraine's face.

"Don't be concerned, Dyllis. Come over here and sit with me. I need to talk with you."

Ygraine turned sideways on her cot so that she could place her feet on the floor of the tent, which was no more than the grassy surface of the meadow surrounding them. She slipped her hands beneath her legs, palms downward between her thighs and the cot, and leaned forward to gaze directly into Dyllis's eyes.

"You are from Cornwall, Dyllis," she said. "Tell me, then, about Gulrhys Lot, my husband. But tell me as you would a friend, not as you would his wife or his Queen."

"My lady?" Dyllis's head was tilted slightly in confusion. Ygraine tried again.

"Dyllis, listen to me carefully, my dear . . . We have been together now for, what, three years? In all that time, I have never heard you or any of my women say anything about my lord and husband that might be taken as defamatory or treasonous or malicious. Or even honest, for that matter. Have I?" She shook her head and closed her eyes to shut out Dyllis's agonized look. "And yet I know that Morgas has been Gulrhys Lot's mistress since before I wed him, and so remains, from time to time. And I know, too, that this husband of mine has possessed every other one of my women, including you, since he wedded me. I know, in fact, that of all of us thirteen women, I am one of the least frequently blessed by his lustful potency." She heard a whimper from the other woman and opened her eyes quickly to see the pitiful expression on her face, a mixture of grief, fear and pain. "No, Dyllis, no, I am not angry. By all the gods, I swear I am happy for this, because—" She stopped short and drew a deep breath, conscious of the enormity of what she was about to say next and anticipating the pleasure she would gain from saying it.

"Because, Dyllis," she continued, "I, Ygraine Mac Athol of Eire, loathe and detest and hate my so-called lord and master, Gulrhys Lot of Cornwall. He is a foul and repulsive toad of a creature, for all his false, gentle smiles and winning ways. He is an evil, treacherous and overweening blot upon the earth. And it has taken me three years to acknowledge it. Since I have come to Cornwall, my ignoble lord has lain with me a total of five times. The first time, I was ecstatic, virginal, excited and afraid, and filled with wonder—and he brutalized me. The second time, more than a month later, I was no longer virgin, but even more afraid, and he tied me down and beat me and abused me, left me whimpering and terrified and sick . . . On the last three of those times I lay beneath him like a rotted log, my soul writhing in disgust and shame at what I had to do in being his wife.

"Two times, Dyllis. That was all he needed to convert his wife from a trembling novice into a disdainful, dutiful vessel into which he might relieve himself at his leisure. I have thanked all the gods in silence ever since then—the gods of Cambria and Eire and of everywhere else that gods might lurk—that there are many women willing to appease a King's lusts at any time. And I thanked the same gods doubly that he chose to send me off to live in exile with our friend Herliss in his white fortress of Tir Gwyn. There, away from his lusts and his bestiality, I have found a kind of happiness."

Ygraine sat silent then for several moments before withdrawing both her hands and holding them out impulsively towards Dyllis. The smaller woman took both of them in hers and leaned closer to her mistress, although she was still manifestly unwilling to speak, perhaps unsure of what to say.

"And yet," the Queen continued, "I have been at pains . . . have gone to extreme lengths . . . to maintain an outward show of loyalty and duty to this—*thing* that was my husband. Why? Can you tell me that Dyllis? Can you tell me why I should strive so hard to do that when the creature has debauched every one of my women, overcoming any loyalty they might have had to me by striking terror into them, if not for themselves, then for their families and loved ones? Or can you tell me why I have remained silent for as long as I have, knowing in my heart that my friends and their families were being abused and betrayed and terrorized by his outrageous and inhuman behaviour? Dyllis, I have spent years now wed to a creature beside whom a serpent would seem admirable and upright. Can you tell me how and why I have permitted that to be?" She squeezed the other woman's hands. "Fear not, my dear, I do not expect an answer . . . I am but talking aloud to myself at last, with open eyes and without fear.

"But listen carefully now. I would like you to number for me, if you will, every single instance you have seen or heard of the famous savagery and brutal depravity of this King Uther Pendragon. Point out to me, if you will, how and when and where he has abused us, any of us or any of our Cornish people, since we fell into his hands." She made a gesture with open hands, inviting comment, then fell silent, waiting.

Dyllis sat blinking at her for a long time before she, too, nodded and spread her hands.

"My lady, I cannot."

"No, you cannot. Nor can I, Dyllis, nor can I. And there is something else I cannot do, something of far greater import: I cannot remember ever having heard a single report of Uther Pendragon's foulness that did not come, in one way or another, from Gulrhys Lot."

She rose to her feet and crossed to the front of the tent where she pulled open the flaps and called for the guard. A moment later, Nemo pulled back the flaps and looked at her inquiringly. Ygraine nodded and spoke quietly and with courtesy.

"Your King said he would return here later to talk with me. Would you inform him that I would like to speak with him, if he has time?"

Nemo blinked once, glanced incuriously towards the other woman, then turned and left without a word.

A very short time later, Uther's voice sounded from the front of the tent, asking if he might come in. When Ygraine invited him to enter, he did so, stooping automatically to clear the lintel even though he wore no helmet and there was ample room above his head. Once inside, he stopped and looked from Ygraine to Dyllis, then back to Ygraine.

"You wish to speak to me?"

"Yes. I want to ask you some questions. Will you sit?"

The two footlockers still sat as he had arranged them earlier, one atop the other, and he moved to sit on them again. Ygraine remained standing, watching him as he moved. When he was settled, she moved closer to him, holding her hands clasped behind her back.

"Tell me how my brother Donuil came to be in Camulod."

Uther gazed calmly at her, then nodded. "Merlyn captured him three years ago when your people attacked us from the north as Lot attacked from the south. Merlyn captured, then released, almost two thousand of your folk and kept Donuil as hostage against your father's promise to remain uninvolved. It was to be for five years, but Merlyn and Donuil became friends, and Merlyn freed him from his oath as a hostage a year later. Donuil chose to stay in Camulod after his release to work with Merlyn."

"He *chose* to stay?"

Uther shrugged. "Aye, he did. Wanted to become Merlyn's adjutant. I thought they were both mad and told Merlyn so, but he paid no attention."

"What is an add—?"

"An adjutant. It is a Roman rank, administrative . . . an army officer."

"An army officer. A *Roman* army officer. My brother. Why do I find that difficult to credit?"

He shook his head. "No more so for you than it was for me, lady. But then, there are no Romans in Britain today. Your brother is in the army of Camulod, and as I said, he and Merlyn are friends."

"And what about Deirdre? Tell me of her."

"I have already told you almost all I know. Much of what happened occurred while I was in Cambria, not in Camulod."

"Tell me again, if you would."

Briefly, Uther retold all that he knew of the story, ending with the discovery of Deirdre's body in her hidden valley. As he was speaking, Ygraine finally sat down in one of the two chairs, listening closely, and when he had finished, she sat silent for a few moments more.

"And Merlyn of Camulod, what has he done to solve the mystery of her murder and avenge her death?"

Uther drew a deep breath. "It was right at that time that Lot launched his invasion of our territories—Cambria by sea and Camulod by land. Merlyn had been away for some time on Camulod's affairs and knew nothing about that until he was on his way home. He rode into an ambush in the Mendip hills, near Camulod, and was almost killed.

"I was close by there at the time with my cavalry, chasing a group of Lot's German mercenaries, cavalry troops that he had found somewhere in Gaul. I knew that this was the biggest danger facing us in the invasion, because having cavalry of any kind offered Lot an opportunity to equal our potential, and I had listened all my life to tales my grandfather told of the magnificent German light cavalry used by the Caesars in ancient times. I did not think he was aware of what he had there . . . not yet . . . but I knew that if those people were to win a single victory of any substance, Lot would turn the world upside down to find more of them and we, in Cambria and Camulod, would be in danger of being swamped and stamped out.

"So we were there. We had been chasing these mounted mercenaries halfway across Britain for weeks, trying to herd them into a place where we could trap them and wipe them out, and we were getting ready to bring them to battle finally when Merlyn and his party blundered across their path. Thank the gods we were as close as we were, for Merlyn's people were hugely outnumbered and caught in a death trap, and if we hadn't been there none of them would have survived. We smashed the German cavalry and managed to save the lives of most of Merlyn's men." Uther paused, realizing then that he and the captive Queen both had grief and loss to share between them. "Merlyn himself took a heavy blow on the head and hasn't recovered from it yet. Probably never will. He has no memory of who he was. Doesn't know me or anyone else. Doesn't remember who his wife was or even that he had a wife. He is alive, but he is not . . . He's not my Cousin Merlyn any more."

Ygraine stood up and moved slowly to the door of the tent, where she opened the flaps and stood looking out into the late-afternoon sunlight for a while, as Uther had done earlier in the day. Finally she straightened slightly and turned again to face him.

"Tell me exactly what took place when your envoys went to meet with Gulrhys Lot."

"Aye. One of my best scouts, a man called Owain, went right into Lot's encampment and lived there for days until he had found out everything there was to know about what happened in Lot's hall that night." He told the story swiftly and succinctly, omitting nothing and including the information about Lagan Longhead's mission to find and arrest his father Herliss.

When the sorry tale was done, Ygraine shook her head as though in disbelief.

"I know Lagan," she murmured, but when she spoke again it was with furious conviction. "This is iniquitous. Damnable. Lot has—Lot *had*—no followers more faithful or loyal than Herliss and his son, Lagan Longhead. And now he holds the man's wife and son, threatened with death, to ensure Lagan's continuing friendship. He is insane."

She was quiet again for a long time, then asked, "Tell me now honestly, if it pleases you, what was in your mind when you decided to keep me here and send my women away?"

He sat staring at her after that, his lips pursed and his eyes wrinkled at the corners as he mulled over her question. She stared back at him, her face expressionless, and made no attempt to speak again, content to wait. Across from her, Dyllis fidgeted slightly, then sat straight-backed, tucking in her chin and staring off into the distance.

"I'm tempted to answer your question with a question, to ask you what you thought was in my mind. But neither of us would be happy with that. So I will tell you the truth, even though it might make me look foolish in your eyes. It was in my mind that you might be . . . more valuable to me as a hostage to your father in Eire than you could ever be in any dealings I might have with Lot."

"Valuable . . . in what way?"

Uther shrugged his wide shoulders, shaking his head slightly at the same time. "It was a foolish, passing thought, and short-lived, although I fancy something might have come of it in time. But it had occurred to me that your father, on being convinced of how Lot had left you thus to your fate in enemy hands, might be sufficiently angered to withdraw his friendship and support from Lot as the price of your safe return to his hall. We have a precedent, in Donuil's case, and it seemed to me that your father might be willing to deal once again with Camulod, knowing we deal more honestly than does his current ally."

"Does he know that? Does my father know that Donuil chose to remain in Camulod after being freed?"

Uther blinked at her, plainly at a loss for a response, and then he nodded, although uncertainly. "I think so. Yes, he must."

"Must he? He thinks his son is bound for five years, you said. Are those five years complete?"

"No." Uther did a quick calculation. "It has been three years, but Donuil has been free for two of those."

"Yes, but my father might not know that, and that would make your logic faulty when it comes to your dealings with him on my behalf."

Uther nodded, his gaze reflective. "Aye, you might be right. But I could always send Donuil to him as my envoy and Merlyn's friend. That much is feasible."

"Aye, and my father would be much impressed." Ygraine paused. " You said I might think you foolish over this. I do not."

He smiled. "No, the foolish part was when I allowed myself to think that he might be persuaded to reverse his alliance and throw his weight into this war on our side. And yet, even with your presence here, I suspect he might be reluctant to commit again to Lot."

"So you would sell me back to my own father?"

"Aye, I would, but not for coin. It would be advantageous to my cause were he to withhold aid to Cornwall." He raised an eyebrow. "Would that displease you, to return home to Eire?"

"No."

"Good. Your bodyguard would be freed to go with you, of course, for I presume they are all your father's men and not Lot's?"

"They are. But what of poor Herliss? He is an old man now and would not come to Eire. I think he would have little love for starting a new life in a new land at his age. And he could not stay here in Cornwall, for as you say, Lot has already marked him for death. What might you have in mind for him? He has done wrong to no man, neither you nor Lot, and ill deserves to die for simply guarding me."

Uther shook his head. "I have nothing in mind for Herliss."

"Then you should have, Sir King. *I* have. Would you be willing to listen to a woman's thoughts on that matter?"

"Happily, if the woman should have some thoughts worth listening to."

"One more question, then. Why are you here in Cornwall with your army?"

He sat back as though she had swung a slap at him, but his expression was good-humoured. "Is that a real question, one that you expect me to answer honestly?"

"Of course it is."

"Of course it is. Well, then, let me answer it briefly and truthfully. I could say I am come here to rid the world of a foul pestilence, but I need not be so grand, since the truth is far stronger. I am here to prevent Gulrhys Lot from leading, or sending anyone else to lead, any more invasions into my territories and killing any more of my people. I am here to ensure that he will never again send armies to invade my cousin's territory of Camulod and slaughter any more of its people. I am here to make sure that he will never again cause the death of any member of my family or, incidentally, of yours, since your brother Donuil now rides with us. That is why I am here in Cambria with my army, and the moment Gulrhys Lot lies dead by my hand or through my efforts, I will withdraw, taking my army with me, and never venture here again."

"You are speaking of the man to whom I am wed."

"I know that, lady. Would you have preferred it had I lied?"

"No. You could not have given me an answer that would please me better than the one you gave." She saw his brows go taut with surprise as his eyes widened, and she spoke into his startlement. "If I were a man, a King, feeling about a wife as I, a simple wife, think now about my husband, I should send her away, divorce her and set her aside. I am no King, but I am a Queen, and thus I choose to divorce Gulrhys Lot. In my eyes, he is dead, part of my life no more. So be it." She ignored the Pendragon King's open-mouthed stare and continued speaking. "I have a stratagem concerning Herliss that I think might succeed, even for you, and me and my father's men. And for Dyllis here and the rest of my women, of course. It is still largely unformed, but it is there, in my mind. Let me think on it tonight, and I will lay it out for you tomorrow morning."

Uther rose to his feet, grinning openly now, his eyes filled with admiration and wry amusement, and he bowed deeply to her, his clenched fist at his breast in a salute.

"Lady," he said, "I wish you may sleep well and thoughtfully. I will come by in the morning." He turned then to Dyllis, bowing to her, too. "And you, Lady Dyllis. Sleep well."

When he had gone, Ygraine sat straight upright and looked intently at Dyllis.

"It will be dark soon, and we have changed sides, and I have renounced an unfit husband. Are you hungry, child? I could eat King Uther's large horse."

TWENTY-EIGHT

The following morning they were awakened by the noise of great comings and goings beyond the walls of their tent. It was evident that large numbers of men were either arriving at camp or leaving it, but try as they would, they could see nothing beyond the looming shoulders of the guards who flanked the entrance to their tent and who would not deign answer their questions. Uther arrived soon after that, however, asking if they were astir, and although they assured him that they were, they refused him entry, holding him at bay until they had had time to perform their morning ablutions and make themselves fit to be seen.

The King finally strode into their tent bare-headed and smiling, followed by a trooper carrying a wooden bucket that was covered with a length of cloth. He loosened the ornate clasp fastening his great war cloak and removed the garment, folding it carelessly before dropping it on the floor of the tent, and then he moved to take the bucket from the trooper, dismissing the man with a nod of thanks. He carried the bucket across the tent and busied himself at the table in the corner, keeping his back to the two women to mask what he was doing.

Ygraine watched him, noticing the way his hair curled on the nape of his neck and how his great, wide shoulders stretched the fabric of his white woollen tunic. This was the first time, she realized, that she had seen this man completely unarmoured, and a little voice within her head whispered that it was, in fact, the first time she had seen this man at ease in her company. There was little of the warrior King about

Uther Pendragon this morning, apart from his massive Celtic torc, the collar of solid, hand-worked gold that circled the thick column of his neck. Although she had never seen a living Roman, she had an image in her mind of what they must look like, and what she saw in Uther suited that image. He wore a simple but rich tunic of heavy, snow-white wool, with a square-cut neck and elbow-length sleeves, and the edges—bottom hem, neck line and cuffs—were all worked with a Greek key design in blood red. A wide leather belt cinched the tunic at his waist and held a short, sheathed dagger, his only weapon, and under the tunic he wore some kind of tight-fitting trousers of the same white wool that encased his legs to just above the ankle, where they were tied with plaited woollen strings. On his feet, he wore thick, knitted socks that she could see between the broad straps of his heavy sandalled boots, military boots, with massive soles of layered leather studded with hobnails that left dents in the ground as he walked.

She lowered her eyes quickly when he finally turned around, holding two earthenware cups, and offered one to each of them. Ygraine looked into the bowl of her cup, which was startlingly cold, and saw that the liquid inside looked black and viscous.

"What is it?"

Uther smiled. He had picked up a cup for himself and now held it up at eye level. "Taste it and see." He sipped his own, delicately for such a large man, and his smile returned, wider than before. "Go on, try it."

Ygraine sipped, and Dyllis followed her example, and then both women were gazing at him, delighted. Dyllis identified the drink first.

"Brambles! It's bramble juice."

"Aye, it is, but there's more . . . there's honey in it, too," Ygraine added.

Uther's smile was enormous now. "Right, both of you, bramble juice and honey and a little water. Just enough to dilute the juice and the honey very slightly."

"But how can it be so cold?"

"A trick we learned from the Romans, lady. We brought it down from Cambria, packed in snow and ice from our Cambrian mountains."

"Snow? But it is almost high summer—"

"Aye, it is, but there are hills in Cambria to the north of our territories where the snow remains on the hilltops all the year round. We do not go there often, but when we do have need to go, we always take the time to cut large blocks of ice and transport them home to Tir Manha—my home base—in wagons that we take with us for that purpose. We wrap up the individual blocks in straw, then stack them together and cover them tightly. That keeps them cold and stops them from melting too quickly. The Romans also taught us that chipped ice, mixed with sawdust and some ordinary salt, grows somehow even colder, and liquids packed in such a mixture will stay cold for great lengths of time, so be it they are kept sealed and the vessels holding them intact."

He sipped again before continuing. "You heard the commotion this morning? Well, my main army—my infantry—has arrived from Cambria. They brought this with them in their commissary train, and I thought you might enjoy some of it. We rarely have such luxuries, and there is little of it, but enough, I thought, to be shared with you. Now, may we sit?"

A short time later, when he had finished his drink, he placed the empty cup on the floor by his feet.

"Last night you asked for time to think about a stratagem that might save Herliss's life and serve my ends as well. It sounds impossible to me, and I fail to see why I should even care, but I stand prepared to be amazed. Are you ready to share it with me?"

Ygraine nodded and came straight to the point that had been circling in her brain all night. "He must escape. Herliss must escape."

"Escape . . . How, and to what, lady? Lot will have him hanged as soon as he sees him, if Herliss survives long enough to be taken back that far. Don't forget he has already been outlawed and named a traitor. Anyone who sees him now is free to strike him down on sight."

"That will not happen, not if he is with me and my guards. No one would dare approach us then, and Lot would be powerless to act against us, if we were to win home free."

"Ah! You are to escape, then, too, and your Erse bodyguard. Forgive me, I missed seeing that." Uther covered the entire lower part of his face with his hand, but he could not conceal the mirth in his dancing eyes.

Ygraine ignored his sarcastic tone completely. She frowned. "You disbelieve me?"

"No, no, lady, truly, I believe you." He waved his hand in denial. "I believe you absolutely . . ." He paused, struggling against his own amusement. "What . . . forgive me . . . what I fail to understand, though, is how you can expect me to accept what you are saying, because if I understand you correctly, you are suggesting that I should simply permit you and all your people to ride off from here, unhampered and unharmed."

"You distrust me, then."

He blinked once, slowly and deliberately, and then shook his head. "It is not a matter of trust, lady. It is common sense. Why should I do such a thing as to allow you to escape? You are my prisoner. My only hostage. I would be mad to let you simply walk away."

"Of course you would be, were there no advantage to you in doing so." There was no trace of humour in the Queen's face or bearing.

"Ah! Then you believe it would be to my advantage to permit this . . . escape?"

"Of course it would. If, of course, you believe me and trust me."

"I see. Well, let me think on that for a moment or two . . . you must see that it is a novel adventure for me to consider placing either trust or belief in anyone or anything having anything to do, however remotely, with Lot of Cornwall . . . And what about your women, on the road to Camulod since yesterday? Are they to be abandoned, or are they to escape, too, while on the road?"

"Yes—"

"Of course they are. I could see that coming. But how? How are they to escape? And then where will you all go once you have won free? To Eire?"

"No, I have already said Herliss is too old to leave his homeland. We will return to Lot, wherever he may be now."

"To Lot? You will return to Lot. Despite everything you said last night about divorcing him?"

"No, I will return to Lot *because* of everything I said last night about divorcing him."

Uther's his eyes flicked from Ygraine to Dyllis and then back again. "Explain that, if you would."

Ygraine stood up quickly, her face flushed suddenly with anger. "Gods, man! Can you not see? I should not have to explain something so obvious—" She stopped as suddenly as she had begun and stood glaring at him, clenching and unclenching her fists and breathing deeply through pinched nostrils. Then she spun to look at Dyllis, who was staring at her, her eyes wide with awe and something else that might have been consternation. "How many men are guarding this tent right now?" Her back was to Uther, but there was no doubt that she was speaking to him.

"Two. And their captain, Nemo, is close by."

"Then will you send them away? Ask them to escort Dyllis while she takes a walk for half an hour. You and I must talk alone."

Plainly mystified, Uther rose to his feet and crossed to the flap of the tent, where he stuck his head out and ordered one of the guards to bring Nemo to him immediately. Nemo could have been no more than ten paces distant for she was there almost before Uther had swung his head back into the tent, and she stepped directly inside and snapped to attention. Uther kept his gaze steadily on Ygraine as he ordered the captain to take the Lady Dyllis and her two guards and to conduct all three on a long walk that would keep them clear of the tent for at least an hour.

When they had all gone, he perched himself on top of the two footlockers again and sat gazing at Ygraine, who stared directly back at him, making no attempt to speak. The silence between them stretched and grew until it began to approach the point at which it would become a challenge and a matter of stubbornness, but before it did so, Uther grinned wryly and nodded, as though conceding victory.

"Well, lady? You wanted to talk . . ."

"How well do you know my brother, Donuil?"

"Not well. I barely know him at all. He is my cousin Merlyn's friend."

"A friend, you say. But is he a true friend? Or is he a coddled favourite, a pampered pet? What are you smiling at? Do you find me amusing?"

He held up a hand as though to fend her off. "No, lady, I do not, but by the gods you are prickly. What was amusing me was the thought of your enormous brother bowing his head meekly to be petted like a puppy." He shook his head, all sign of humour vanishing. "No, lady, they are friends and I can tell you positively that your brother Donuil must have earned that ranking and the privilege that goes with it. The trust between the two of them is solid and deep-rooted. That I know."

When Ygraine responded to that, her voice sounded slightly mollified, but she was still plainly unconvinced. "You *know*, you say. But how much do you know, in truth? How well do you really know this cousin of yours, this Merlyn?"

Now Uther was sombre. "Better than any other person in the world. We were raised almost as twins. There is no man in the world more dear to me than he is."

"And he feels the same way towards you?"

There was no mistaking the pain that underlay the long hesitation that stretched between that question and its answer; she saw it in his eyes and heard it in his voice when he finally responded. "He—he used to . . . It is my hope that he still does."

"Why would you doubt it?"

"I . . . I told you yesterday, he is not himself . . ."

"But there is something else that makes you hesitate . . ."

He shrugged again, dismissing the thought. "It was long ago, and he suspected me of a misdeed—one that was evil, worthy of punishment . . . But I doubt that I would have judged the event as harshly as Merlyn did. He could be very narrow-minded in his judgments. In my case, I was innocent of the crime. I took more pain from thinking he could believe I might do such a thing than from anything he ever did or said to me concerning it."

"Very well, then." She sat gazing at him, clearly thinking about what she would say next. "You obviously admire your cousin greatly, so I must ask you this: why does Lot call him a coward?"

To her astonishment, Uther Pendragon threw back his head and laughed, a great, booming shout of enjoyment. "A coward! Caius Merlyn Britannicus, a coward? Ah, lady, Lot calls Merlyn a coward because he cannot suffer people to suspect the simple truth: that Merlyn Britannicus is everything that Gulrhys Lot can never hope to be. Lot would shit himself with fear if ever he found himself within a mile of coming face to face with Merlyn of Camulod. He hates Merlyn, not simply for being a formidable enemy and an upstanding man, but for being the person that he *is*. Oh, he fears him, too, but mainly he hates him, because Merlyn stood by and witnessed Lot's first downfall at my hands, when he and I were twelve years old and Lot was fourteen or fifteen, bigger than both of us."

"What are you talking about? Did you know Lot that long ago?"

Uther sat straight up and looked away from her as he came to grips with what he had just heard. She watched him closely, seeing the puzzled frown on his brow, and then the way his face lightened as he turned back to her.

"Yes, my cousin Merlyn and I first met Lot that long ago, and that is what?—twelve years? thirteen? It was no meeting of like minds, I promise you. He came to Camulod with his father, the old Duke Emrys, and he was loathsome from the outset, trying to dominate and bully Merlyn and me. He was not simply nasty, he was . . ." Uther paused, groping for words. "He was intolerably *foul*: foul-mouthed and foul-natured; loathsome in all he said and did—and then, on top of and in addition to all of that, he was a braggart and a bully. Well, Merlyn and I had never met a bully we couldn't thrash together, so we were not abashed by this lout from Cornwall. But then he insulted my mother, viciously and inexcusably and in such a way that I could not ignore it, and we fought. He left Camulod right after that, as soon as he grew well enough."

"Did you thrash him that badly?"

"Thrash him? No, lady, I didn't thrash him. We fought with Roman swords. I stabbed him, but unfortunately for everyone, I didn't do the job properly—we were interrupted and stopped by my father before I could finish it."

Ygraine's eyes had grown round. "You would have killed him?"

"I *should* have killed him. Now there are hundreds dead who might have lived, had I done so." He checked himself, seeing her expression. "What is wrong? Lady?"

She shook her head, a terse, dismissive little gesture. "Nothing is wrong, I think. But much has been wrong, including my own foolish, willful blindness." Her eyes drifted away from him and she sat staring into the middle distance, looking at nothing and seeing only what was in her mind. After a while, she breathed in deeply through her nostrils and sat up straighter. "I have been cursing you and everyone in Camulod for three years now, in utter ignorance that my own brother and sister were living happily there with you and your family while I suffered shame and outrage and indignities here, from my own husband." She paused again, frowning, and then turned her frown on him. "You are . . . you are nothing like the monster I was told you were."

Uther held her gaze, his features softened now, and let out a small sigh. When he spoke next, his voice was easy and quiet. "You said we two needed to talk, and so I sent the guards away with Lady Dyllis. What, then, did you want to talk about?"

"Just this: Lot will not negotiate to gain me back. He will not, because I mean nothing to him and he has no need of me, so he will count himself fortunate to be thus rid of me, without blame to him. But that also makes me an encumbrance to you—something for which he will be grateful. The only option you can see facing you is to send me back home to my father in Eire in the hope that he will withdraw his support from Lot. Well, that might serve you, but no more than slightly, for my father's few people could hardly be considered a major contribution to Lot's forces. Returning me to Lot, however, is another very real option, one that is potentially invaluable."

"What? I don't follow you."

"Then hear me plainly. I would now return to Lot as a willing spy, on your behalf. In doing so, I could save the life of Herliss—a dear friend for whom I feel responsible—and bring about the downfall of this loathsome man to whom I have been wed. It is a choice easily made, and made already. I see no disloyalty involved in it. In order to command loyalty, one must understand what it is and return it openly in like measure. Gulrhys Lot has never shown a trace of loyalty to anyone that I know of—not to me, not to any of his most faithful followers and most certainly not to any of those over whom he claims kingship. His people live in terror of him and his sick fancies, afraid that some imagined slight of theirs will bring his mercenaries down about their ears, dealing death and destruction to their families, their homes and their few, pathetic possessions."

She had been almost talking to herself, but now she moved her head and looked into Uther's eyes. "These are not idle fears, you must understand that. Lot and this pestilence he has inspired have blighted all of Cornwall. He has surrounded himself with a living wall of mercenary killers who have no regard for anything or anyone, and whose atrocities do not simply go unpunished, but originate, more often than not, with the man who employs them." Again she paused and looked directly at him, her eyes flashing.

"You perhaps believe that my conversion to your viewpoint has been too facile. I can do nothing to alter that or influence your thinking. But until yesterday . . . until now, today . . . I have been able to conceive of no way to make things better. Not only am I a woman, weak enough at the best of times, but I am a woman with no vestige of power or influence. I have been a prisoner for two years now, since long before you captured me. My prison was Herliss's White Fort, to which I had been banished by my husband, and until mere days before we moved into your path I was comfortable there, and thankful to be removed from all my consort's evil. In Tir Gwyn, I was able to avoid my own conscience. There I was able to close my eyes willfully to what was going on in this bright and lovely land in which I now live. I was able to pretend, in truth, that I was in no wise associated with the man who called himself my husband." She stopped abruptly, and a single tear broke from her lashes and cascaded down her right cheek. Angrily she dashed it away.

"And so, Sir King of Cambria, I am now come to the point where I will gladly and willingly make pact with you to end this man's . . . dominion. His tyranny. Gladly and willingly. But if we

are to make the most of this opportunity, then it had best be soon."
She stopped and peered at him again, her head tilted to one side as
though challenging him to take issue with her logic. "Cornwall is
not that big a place, and if Lagan is out there as you claim, scouring the country for his father in order to protect his wife and son, he
is bound to find you here sooner or later."

Uther nodded. "But I have my cavalry out there harassing him,
keeping him away from here."

"I know you have, but how long will they be able to contain him?
How large is Lagan's army? Do you know? And how much does he
know of your own strength? Does he believe that your entire force is
attacking him? Surrounding him? Or might he think, perhaps, that
you but play with him to keep him captive wherever he is?"

Uther screwed up his face and shrugged. "I cannot answer that,
not yet, although I expect to have that information soon."

Ygraine nodded. "And what about this army of your own that
has just arrived, how big is it?"

"Three thousand men."

"You will never keep that secret. Three thousand mouths
consume a deal of food."

Uther nodded sombrely. "Aye, they do . . . So, go on with your
stratagem. If you escape, what then, and how could it save
Herliss?"

"We would seek to avoid Lagan and win back to Lot's stronghold before Lagan can come to grips with you. We could then
pretend that Herliss came up with the plan himself and brought
Alasdair, the captain of my bodyguard, into it. That way, when Alasdair backs him with no prospect of gain for his own ends, no one
could gainsay Herliss's heroism, and Lot would be forced to
readmit Herliss to his favour . . .

"Besides, I think Lot would not dare take the risk of offending
Lagan any more deeply at this time. Lagan and Herliss have both
power and influence, and between them they have many friends. If
Lot has taken Lydda and Cardoc, Lagan's wife and son, as
hostages, he will not have harmed either one of them, and being
Lot, he'll still believe that he is capable of convincing Lagan that

it was all a misunderstanding, once Herliss has been restored to favour. The man's monstrous arrogance is not to be believed."

Uther twisted his face up into an exaggerated expression of doubt. "Well, I think you might be wrong there—about Lot's reception of Herliss after the escape. And how could Herliss manage such a coup without it being perceived as obviously false?"

"By using the tools Lot uses all the time: bribery, corruption and treachery. We could say that he suborned some of your guards, offering them large rewards for their assistance."

"But Herliss is a prisoner, and even Lot would not believe my men fools enough to deal in future promises. If they are to be bribed, they'll want their hot hands on the bribe as soon as it is offered . . . immediately. So where would Herliss have found these large rewards?"

"Among the chests belonging to me and my women . . . jewels and fine clothing and other precious items."

Uther sat back, his eyes wide with surprise. "And do you have such things?"

"Of course we have such things. No one deprived us of them after our capture."

"Aye, well, that may be, but now they are on their way to Camulod with their owners."

"Of course they are, but we are making up a tale, King Cambria! We are discussing subterfuge . . . a false bribing."

"Aye, you're right." Uther broke into a grin. "I had forgotten that already. But—" His face grew sober again as a new thought occurred to him. "But can you then trust your own women and your guards not to reveal the deception? Bear in mind the women will be returned from Camulod with all their jewels intact."

"The women . . . some of them I would trust. Others I would not. But they are on the road to Camulod, as you say, and may remain there in comfort for some time. If you and I agree, they will be well looked after and may come home safely later. My bodyguard, on the other hand, I trust implicitly. They are my kinsmen, sworn to my father for my protection and well-being. And yet they are but men, and men will talk in drink. There must be a way to safeguard against that . . ."

"There is, but Herliss would have to be let in on our plan."

She looked at him in surprise. "How so? What mean you?"

"Well, if Herliss were to agree, then we could arrange matters so that he would conduct the escape as though it were genuine, without anyone else having to be involved. That way your bodyguard need never know the truth and could go back to Gulrhys Lot's domain with their heads held high and boast thereafter to their hearts' content, when they are in their cups, of how they won free of the Cambrians."

"And what if Herliss refuses?"

"Then he must remain here, unfortunately. Herliss is a man of honour, by your own assessment, and honour, once entrenched, is massive difficult to unseat or change."

"Aye, but true honour is ever open wide to ethical challenge." She turned and looked at him, her face a picture of wonder and amused excitement. "Do you not agree?"

He grimaced and shrugged. "Lady, it matters not what I might think. The decision of what to do lies firm within the options open to Herliss."

"Will you send him here to me and keep the guards away?"

"I will, right now."

"No!"

Uther stopped on the point of rising, his face blank with surprise at her vehemence, and she felt a tide of colour begin to surge in her cheeks. She moderated her tone, speaking more quietly. "No, not right now. Not yet. First you and I must strike an agreement."

He began to move again, rising slowly to his feet. "Aye, and what would that be, lady?"

"That we two be allies from this moment forth, trusting in and relying upon each other, and that we will work together henceforth to remove Gulrhys Lot from the ruling of Cornwall."

"That will mean killing him, lady."

"So be it, if it must. And you will call me by my name, Ygraine, or Lady Ygraine, if you prefer, so be it you no longer call me 'lady' alone."

He nodded slowly, his face breaking into a broad smile that she watched grow with distinct feelings of pleasure. "So be it, Lady

Ygraine," he murmured. "Will you shake hands with me to seal our pact?"

Ygraine extended her hand and felt it enveloped in his, not as a man might grasp another's hand, but as a large, warm blanket that enwrapped her slowly and gently, almost caressing the skin of her wrist, so that involuntarily, all the tiny hairs along her arm stood up on end. He raised his hand then, carrying her captive hand gently towards his mouth, where he held it short of his face yet close enough for her to feel the soft warmth of his breath against her fingers. Then, slowly, his other hand came up to grasp her forearm, its touch, too, a caress, and her heart began to pound in her chest. He stooped his head slightly towards her, keeping his eye fixed on hers, and then released her.

"I will bring Herliss to you now. Don't go away."

She made no response but watched him closely as he collected his great cloak and shook out its folds before swirling it up and letting it fall across his shoulders. He fastened its clasp, then bowed slightly to her from the waist and left her standing alone, watching him vanish from sight.

Uther found Herliss in the small compound in which he was being held and waited patiently while he shrugged his way into his tunic and swept his cloak over his shoulders. They had barely left the enclosure when the veteran warrior found his voice.

"Where are you taking me?"

"To the Lady Ygraine."

"The Queen left yesterday with her women." Herliss's voice was a low growl.

"You are well informed for a prisoner, but aye, you're right . . . that one did, at least. But this is the real one. Through there." Uther pointed and stepped aside, then followed Herliss as the other dipped his head and shouldered his way through a screen of hanging willow branches that opened on to the grassy clearing in front of the King's Tent. Herliss noticed the lack of guards immediately and hesitated, looking back over his shoulder at Uther.

"Aye, no guards, I know. No witnesses. Don't worry, Herliss, did I wish to kill you, you would now be dead. I am no Gulrhys Lot.

Your Queen is in there, waiting for you. I'll wait out here until you call for me, and I will not be listening, so call loudly."

Uther turned and walked away without another glance, aware that the older man was standing stupefied, staring at his retreating back. Then, just at the far range of his hearing, he heard Ygraine's voice calling Herliss's name from inside the tent.

Uther half smiled to himself and kept moving until he reached a short, thick log that lay beside a shallow firepit, about twenty paces from the entrance to the tent, and lowered himself to sit on it, aware that the only sounds he could hear were made by soldiery somewhere behind him and to his right. No slightest sound reached him from the direction of the King's Tent where Ygraine and Herliss were in the earliest stages of what was bound to be a most important conversation.

Swallowing his impatience and aware that he was ill at ease simply sitting still with nothing in particular to do, Uther looked about him, searching for something, anything, that might hold his interest while he awaited the outcome of what was going on between his two prisoners. For a while he fought the nagging urge to rise and move about, but then he gave in and stood up abruptly, moving away through the fringe of willows to stand by the river's edge. He stood gazing down into the water, thinking that he should be able to see trout moving down there, until he remembered that he had brought upwards of a hundred men here only weeks before, many of whom had been fishing along the entire length of this stream at every spare moment since they arrived. He grinned and shook his head, then sat on a mossy stone on the riverbank, where he undid the leather thongs that fastened his heavy boots and kicked the cumbersome footwear off. Moments later he had removed his thick socks, too, and pulled up the legs of his woollen trousers until they were above his knees, so that he could plunge his bare feet into the cold waters of the river, flinching against the sudden shock and immediately relaxing and remembering with pleasure doing exactly the same thing as a boy.

That memory prompted him to wonder when he had last done such a mundane thing for the simple pleasure of doing it, and he winced to recall that it had been more than ten years. He eased himself forward off the bank, balancing precariously, and stood up in the stream bed. The water surged once above his knees, wetting the lower extremities of his pulled-up trouser legs, then settled back to flow steadily by the tops of his shins. Awkwardly, almost teetering as he did so, he unfastened his cloak and swung it quickly up and over his head, whirling it around to twist it upon itself before he threw it to land on the grassy bank. He had not been quick enough, however, and the hem of the garment scattered an arc of water drops as it swung upwards, and as he turned to watch it spin towards the bank, his foot stuck in the sandy bottom of the stream bed, he almost overbalanced, swaying dangerously and waving his arms as he fought to retain equilibrium. He managed to save himself from falling, although barely, and as he straightened up, splay-footed and tentative, he found himself wondering what Ygraine might have thought had she seen him swaying there so ludicrously on the point of toppling headlong into the water.

Carefully then, moving slowly and deliberately on the treacherously muddy slope of the riverbank, he clambered back up onto the grass, where he sat down again and dangled his feet in the water to wash the mud of the river's edge from between his toes. When he was satisfied that they were clean, he dried them roughly with an edge of his cloak before pulling down the wet lower legs of his trousers and retying them, allowing his thoughts to drift to this Lady Ygraine, who had fallen into his hands without his volition.

At first glance, beside the golden, long-haired beauty of the tall and voluptuous Morgas, Ygraine's beauty had been barely noticeable: quiet and restrained, understated and gently but effectively concealed almost completely beneath an air of modesty and shyness. Once he had adjusted to the fact that her role in his camp dictated such an attitude and air, however, Uther had looked beyond and seen the woman herself, finding her to be surprisingly spectacular in her own way. Her hair was a deep, dark, chestnut red with golden highlights that shone when she moved in bright light. Her face, small and oval, was fair-skinned and placid, yet surmounted by green eyes that could blaze and flicker when her temper was aroused—and that the woman had a temper was a matter that he never held in doubt, once he had seen beyond her air of quiet reserve. She had a wide, mobile mouth that smiled and laughed easily, although he had seen her do so only from a distance, and her teeth were white and regular, free of blemish or weakness. Her nose was neither straight nor hooked, but clean-edged in profile, with pleasing, smoothly flaring nostrils. Her eyes, perfectly spaced above high, wide cheekbones that looked as though they had been chiselled from smooth stone, were surmounted by smooth brows of a lighter red than her thick tresses. All in all, he thought, a woman of fine beauty, worthy to be wife to a King. And he angrily pushed that thought from his mind.

Much had changed since Lot's Queen had first become his prisoner, so that now he had left her alone and unsupervised with one of her own men . . . potentially the most dangerous of all the enemies he held confined here in his camp. She was Cambria's ally now, Camulod's and his. He blinked, thinking about that, and visualized her as she had looked when he left her to bring Herliss to meet with her. She was pleasant to visualize, even in the plain, unadorned brown gown that she had been wearing that morning. Unrelieved by highlight or by jewelled brooch or belt, it had simply clung to her, hanging in drapes and flowing folds that brushed the grass at her feet and revealed every curve and every hollow in her shape.

Feeling himself begin to respond physically to his thoughts, he abruptly sat upright and coughed, clearing his throat and his mind simultaneously, and reached for the socks he had discarded. He pulled them on, stretching them over the ends of his trouser legs, and then pulled on his heavy boots again, tying the lacing thongs tightly and then standing up and stamping his feet until they felt comfortable. No sooner had he done so than he heard Herliss calling his name. He scooped up his cloak and settled it about his shoulders, then made his way back to where the older man stood outside the tent, waiting for him.

As Uther emerged from the screen of willows, Herliss saw him and began striding towards him, holding up a peremptory hand so that Uther stopped in surprise and waited for the other man to reach him.

"What's wrong?"

Herliss was glowering at him. "Nothing, but you and I have to talk, alone. I need to know, where do we go from here?"

Uther grinned in satisfaction. "You mean you are in favour?"

"Do you take me for a complete fool? Of course I am in favour, and not merely because mine is the first life that will be saved." The old man looked about him. "I need a drink of something, something cold. Do you people drink beer?"

"Come."

Uther turned immediately and led the way along the riverside towards the main body of the camp. They came to a fallen tree, shorn of its limbs, that stretched across the stream, and crossed it in single file. When they reached the commissary tents, Uther went directly to the second one in line and called for beer, and moments later turned back to Herliss, a large flagon topped with foam in each hand.

"Here. Cambria's best."

They drank, and Herliss swallowed enormously, draining half his flagon, then nodded judiciously and belched loudly.

Close by them, in front of one of the commissary tents, was a trestle table flanked by a long bench on either side. Uther nodded towards the benches and moved to sit on one of them. Herliss sat opposite him and placed his tankard on the tabletop.

"Good beer. Now let's talk about how to proceed from here."

"You made your mind up quickly."

Herliss's response to that was swift and keen-eyed. "You think I'm gulling you?" Uther kept his face expressionless and made no attempt to speak, and finally the other man grunted and growled in his deep, rough voice, "Either that, or you think me an idiot and a facile coat-changer."

He waited, cocking one eyebrow in defiance, but when Uther again failed to respond, he continued. "I spent most of my life being loyal and obedient to Lot's father, and, in the old Duke's memory, I have been loyal to his son. Not always obedient, though, and not recently. Loyalty, however, I've given. Too much. It is a strange word, loyalty. Loyalty is honour, or it was where I was raised . . . and when I was raised . . .

"Where loyalty and honour and even obedience are passionately involved, people can go blind and deaf from time to time, and things can happen that don't get looked at too closely. But loyalty makes demands of its own. It has to be two-way, otherwise it can't live long. It's a give-and-take thing, and there's no getting around that. And if people don't get loyalty in return for their own loyalty, sooner or later they stop being loyal. And then they start to see things they didn't see before, and to hear things they never heard, and they start to pay attention to what's going on around them . . . Things like having their own sons sent out to bring them back in chains and being forced to do that under the threat of danger to their families. Lot is holding my grandson's life over my head as a threat . . . Ach!" He spun away and spat. "But why should I be surprised? He's been doing the same thing for years to almost everyone I know. That is how he ensures their loyalty."

Herliss picked up his tankard again and emptied it. "Tell me, what are your plans for Cornwall?"

Uther gazed at him blank-faced for a long count and then shook his head. "For Cornwall? I have no plans for Cornwall, other than to kill this creature who kings it and then get back to my own home as quickly as I can. I have hundreds of plans for Cambria, for my own home, all of them urgent, but I can tend to none of them since every time I turn around this rabid animal who calls himself your King is sneaking and snarling at my back. I want him dead. Dead and dismembered. I want his loathsome hide nailed to a wall for everyone to see and spit upon. I want him gone from this world, never to harm another living soul, his maggot-eaten skull impaled before my tent, a grinning warning to all men who would be like him. What I want, in the end, is the opportunity to live my life among my own, in peace and comfort. I want a wife of my own, and sons to bear my name, and I want them to live contentedly in Tir Manha in Cambria."

Herliss had sat gazing at Uther throughout this declaration, his eyebrows rising slightly as the outpouring increased in fervour and in vehemence, and when it was done, he sat with pouting lips for a count of five heartbeats. Then he nodded.

"Fine. We both want the same thing: Lot dead and you gone back to Cambria or Camulod or wherever you want to be, so that

Cornwall can recover from the chaos and the damage he has caused. Lot is a rabid animal and must be treated as one, struck down swiftly, immediately and lethally. To do that, though, we'll have to be close to him and in a position of trust. Closeness we can achieve, but that last is near impossible. He trusts no one. This nonsense with Lagan and my grandson proves the truth of that."

"But if you win free from here and take the Queen back with you in a spectacular escape, then he will have to welcome you for the sake of appearances. Is that not so?"

"Aye, it is . . . at least it would be so, were he a normal man. But I believe he's crazed, and growing more so all the time. So what will actually happen once we do win back is in the hands of the gods. But if we succeed without disaster blasting us, what then? Will the Queen start sending you intelligence of what Lot intends to do? Will you need me to do that, too?"

"Aye, but only as and when you learn, or the Queen learns, of developments in Lot's planning. And we must take great care as to how we go about such things. If we are to rid ourselves of this monster, then we need to work closely together and yet take as few risks as possible, for you and your people will be unable to trust or depend upon any of Lot's mercenaries."

"Agreed. So how will we go about this?"

"You will start by bribing my people, immediately and lavishly, so that they will arrange for you to visit the Queen's bodyguard. Once there, you will tell Alasdair, their captain, that the Queen has provided you with treasures from her and her women in order that you might suborn our troopers and arrange a mass escape. It will be obvious that you have made a successful start on your planning. I'll provide the people to be bribed, and they will be my best and most trusted. They will go along with everything, and your own troops will be none the wiser. You'll achieve your escape and return to Lot, avoiding any encounter with your own son on the way, and once you are safely reinstalled in your own home and your own responsibilities, I will find a way of coming to you and we can work out ways and means of remaining in touch with each other."

"Good. I'll wager that Lagan will be our main liaison."

Uther smiled and nodded. "I hope you are right. I would enjoy meeting him. And we have a mutual friend in Cambria, the Lady Mairidh."

"Lydda's sister. Aye. She is married to my brother, Balin."

Uther called for two more tankards of beer before turning to smile at the grizzled Cornish veteran. "We have agreed on mighty things here, you and I. Our world will not remain the same, I think, in the aftermath of what has occurred today."

Their beer came quickly, and as they tipped an offering onto the ground to appease and thank the gods, Herliss nodded, his eyes on the foam atop his tankard.

"Aye . . . Uther, Ygraine and Herliss. A strange mix, I think. I wonder, will anyone take note of it in times to come?"

TWENTY-NINE

Until the moment he found himself kissing her, Uther had had no conscious intention of bedding Ygraine of Cornwall. She was a hostage for one thing, and his honour as her captor and her value as a commodity both dictated that he treat her with care, consideration and courtesy, returning her undamaged at the end of her captivity. That her husband had refused to trade for her was a setback, but Uther had almost expected Lot's indifference and had been thinking, from the moment of the woman's capture, that he could surely trade her with advantage back to her father, Athol Mac Iain, King of the Hibernian Scots in Eire. For that reason alone, therefore, Uther would have regarded any contemplation of Ygraine in a sexual light as a foolish, irresponsible and reprehensible waste of time. Besides, he was fresh from the bed of the magnificent Morgas, who, if she lacked many of the attributes of the ideal wife, lacked none of the requirements of the ideal mistress.

There was one other factor, however, over and above all others that would have prevented him from ever making advances to Ygraine of Cornwall, and that was his own sense of culpability over what had happened to her unfortunate sister Deirdre. Even now, years removed from the tragic events that had estranged him from his cousin Merlyn, the memory of what took place that night in the games room at Camulod still had the power to make Uther writhe and cringe within his own mind.

Uther Pendragon had little experience of guilt in his life; it was an alien emotion to him and one that he was ill-equipped to handle.

He could be awe-inspiring in his rages and utterly implacable in his anger, but he seldom had cause to regret or to reconsider the consequences of his actions at such times. He had not fought in anger since the incident with Nemo's three assailants. Instead, he had learned to give his rage full rein, vociferously, concealing his displeasure from no one, but once his initial anger had spent itself, he would then act calmly, dealing out redress dispassionately for the wrongs he had suffered. He had no truck with guilt, and no need to bear it.

Shame, however, was an entirely different matter, and sufficiently close to guilt to be indistinguishable from it in Uther's mind. His sense of shame was highly developed, despite the fact that he had never consciously recognized its overriding presence in his life, and it was shame and not guilt that made him squirm and brought him his worst mental anguish. He would struggle awake at night sometimes, drenched in sweat and writhing with half-remembered sensations of the aftermath of follies he had committed as a boy, in his hare-brained, determined and unnecessary attempts to perform wonderful deeds that would earn his Grandfather Ullic's approval. His grandfather and his father had been men of great probity, and he could well remember their stern disapproval of people who brought shame of any kind close to them or theirs. What had happened that night in the games room—his precipitation of the ensuing events—appalled Uther and was his darkest, most shameful secret.

He had ridden away from Camulod that night in the blackest of foul moods, spurring his horse savagely and plunging the few men he had conscripted into reckless, careering danger, leading them blindly through a stormy night that was as black as his own despair, a swirling, wind-churned chaos of cold, rainy squalls. And as he rode, rowelling his unfortunate horse and driving it far more savagely than his needs dictated, he raved and cursed silently in his head, damning and condemning the girl for daring to bite him, for scorning him, for rejecting him. As his first unsustainable rage ebbed away, he realized, from the pain in his chilled, clenched hand, that he was brandishing his sword for no reason, behaving like a madman, and the shame began to well up in him.

The child had done no wrong. She had merely defended herself in the only way open to her. She was a frightened, threatened little animal—mute, deaf and defenceless. He, in willful arrogance, had thrust his penis into her unwilling mouth, and when she had bitten him deservedly, he had been swept up by an insensate fury and attempted to thrash her. Only Merlyn had stopped him. Uther shuddered with revulsion at his own behaviour and flushed with burning shame, despite the chilling, wind-swept rain.

Thereafter, he rode his mount more gently and thought more penetratingly than he had thought in many a year, stripping himself of false protestations and facing the unpalatable truth. His mother lay sick, perhaps dying, and he had been avoiding his obligation to return home to her, vainly seeking to convince himself that his true duty lay in Camulod. To that end, he had sought diversion in the games room that night with willing women . . . willing but ineffectual in distracting his mind from the knowledge that he was behaving abominably, betraying himself with his fear of returning to bleak, inhospitable Cambria and Tir Manha, the home he resented and the people he despised for their dour, bleak lack of tolerance and compassion. Recognizing the truth now that he had faced it, he was horrified by the knowledge that his own vain, indefensible dislikes should have deprived his mother of his presence in a time of need, and he wondered, not for the first time, at the deep-buried, bitter harshness in him that had the power to make him behave as he sometimes did, against all the urgings and concerns of his better nature.

It was a long, miserable journey to Tir Manha, and he would never forget the aching relief he felt on arriving to discover that his mother had recovered from her sickness. His shame, however, did not abate. On the contrary, many weeks later, when he discovered the whole truth of what had happened in Camulod after he left, it grew enormously, for he knew beyond dispute that had he, in his rage, not driven the terrified girl out into the night, she would never have met the man, or men, who had savaged her, leaving her for dead, battered and bleeding, ravished and sodomized, so that she survived only by some miracle. So great was his self-loathing then that he was incapable of defending himself in the face of Merlyn's suspicions that he had been responsible. In Uther's own mind, he *had* been responsible for the girl's flight. But it pained him and saddened him more than he would have thought possible that Merlyn could suspect him of such foul baseness as had been perpetrated under the cover of darkness upon the poor little waif. That pain would remain with him for the rest of his life, and because of it, he would never have imposed himself knowingly upon another member of Cassandra's family. Whatever lusts he had, however intense, he would direct them elsewhere.

Ygraine, on the other hand, had no such scruples. But neither had she any sexual appetites—or so she believed. She would have ridiculed the notion that she might ever indulge in sexual pleasure with anyone, let alone her Cambrian captor. Ygraine of Cornwall had known no man in almost three years and believed that she had purged herself forever of the need to know another. Her few physical encounters with her own husband had been terrifying and depraved, and they had appalled and disgusted her, frightening her and scarring her deeply. She had come to believe, deep within her being, that no man could possibly be attracted to her after the defilements her husband had heaped upon her, and at the same time she had convinced herself that all men were as he was, and that no man would ever again have occasion or opportunity to defile her as he had.

The two of them were destined to rut, nevertheless, and months later they would agree that the die was cast for both of them at some point on that first afternoon when they had admitted Herliss to their newly hatched plan to save his life. The huddled, conspiratorial intimacy brought them close enough to each other mentally and physically to ignite their awareness of each other, and it was like the explosive combustion that engulfs and consumes a moth that has fluttered too close to a candle flame—a completely unexpected turn of events that took both of them unawares and swept them irresistibly up and out of themselves as it hurled them into each other's arms with the inevitability of death.

Uther was vibrant with excitement over their plan, and at one point he reached out spontaneously and squeezed her forearm, easing the pressure of his grip almost immediately but making no attempt to remove his hand as he spoke earnestly to her, gazing directly into her eyes. That was when she first felt the awareness— *the lusty thing*, as she thought of it afterwards—stirring in her belly.

"This is going to work. Herliss has agreed to take part. Now we have to plan, all of us . . . and carefully. The worst thing that could happen here is for anyone but we three to find out what's afoot."

Ygraine sat staring at him as he went on to outline their next moves, but she barely absorbed half of what he said, for she had been thunderstruck, instantly dizzied, her whole being plunged into turmoil by the sudden, physical awareness of his hand upon her arm. All the reactions that she would have thought of as normal had been instantly routed by the incredible, undreamed-of sensations that the touch of his hand, even through the fabric of her sleeve, sent rushing and flushing through her entire body. Her skin rose up in tingling gooseflesh, her nipples hardened, her throat constricted, threatening her ability to breathe, and her head filled up with a roaring, rushing sound that made her feel nauseated.

She was appalled by her own body's tumultuous reactions, and she was excruciatingly aware of the hot flush that had suffused her face and neck. Had they seen? Was it possible they had not noticed? But Uther and Herliss were intent on their discussions, and as time passed, her pulse rate slowed down, her breathing gradually settled to an approximation of normal, and she felt the hectic colour subside slowly from her face and neck until she eventually reached the stage at which she knew they might look at her and see nothing beyond the normal.

Inside herself, however, Ygraine felt far from normal. Never before in her life had she been so unexpectedly overcome with lust, and the experience had shaken her, rattling her confidence and making her doubt her own perceptions. Since her escape to Herliss's White Fort, Ygraine had been celibate. But now she was convinced by the furious tide of sensations that had assailed her that she had but little true knowledge of her own body and its dictates. She heaved a deep breath, fighting to keep it silent, and then, struggling to appear natural and casual, she allowed herself to look again at her two companions.

They were deeply involved in the logistics of the escape, attempting to reconcile their needs and requirements with the realities facing them. They had to arrange the disappearance, silent and unnoticed, of approximately fifty people, almost all of whom would be afoot. Only Herliss, the Queen and Dyllis would ride horses in their flight. The others, mainly Ygraine's bodyguard, would march out as they always did. Ironically, however, all the normal difficulties of escape would be reversed in this instance. None of the obvious problems of organizing a large-scale breakout would cause the slightest difficulty here, since this was an engineered escape. The real difficulty, verging upon an impossibility, lay in the need to keep its true nature secret from the very people who would be escaping.

"We can't afford to overlook Popilius Cirro in all of this," Uther was saying to Herliss when Ygraine began to listen again.

"Who? You mean the fellow who came in this morning with your army?"

"Aye. Popilius is a good man—none better—but he's not really one of mine, and he is of the old ways, the old Roman ways."

"What do you mean?"

"Popilius is the senior soldier of Camulod, the highest-ranking soldier—as opposed to a trained staff officer—in all their army. In the Roman legions he would have been called the *primus pilus*, the First Spear, and to tell the truth, that's what they call him in Camulod to this day. He actually served in the legions as a boy, in Asia Minor with my uncle Picus Britannicus, when Picus was senior cavalry legate to Stilicho—" He broke off, seeing the expression on Herliss's face. "You've heard of Stilicho, haven't you?"

"Aye, I think so, a long time ago. Wasn't he the Emperor?"

"Almost. He was imperial regent for the Emperor Honorius."

"Blabbety-blah-blah . . . what does that mean?"

"Imperial regent? It means a temporary ruler, governing in the name of an emperor too young to govern by or for himself. Stilicho did that after the death of Theodosius while the old man's son, Honorius, was still a little boy. Much good it did him, though. As soon as Honorius was old enough to stand on his own, he wiped out all his former friends and supporters—had Stilicho murdered with the rest of them. He would have killed Uncle Picus, too, as part of the same sweep, but Picus managed to escape and made his way back here to Britain. Merlyn and I were seven years old when he got back. He brought a small group of friends with him, and Popilius Cirro was the youngest of them, hardly more than a boy. But boy or not, he had saved Picus's life and stood by him throughout their flight, and so Picus trained him personally after that once he himself had taken over as Commander in Chief of Camulod. Now Popilius is answerable only to the Legate Commander of Camulod. And Popilius is so trustworthy that it makes him a danger to us . . ."

"How so?" It was the first time Ygraine had spoken and she was surprised that her voice betrayed no hint of a tremor.

Uther turned to her. "Because of you, lady. He has no idea who you really are, and I think we would be foolish to tell him."

"Why is that?"

"Well, to begin with, he might, and probably would, refuse to set you free, no matter how I tried to convince him otherwise. Consider this from his viewpoint. I am his ally in this war, but my priorities and his—Cambrian and Camulodian—might not be the same. You are a prize beyond value, the spouse of the enemy's Commander in Chief. Popilius would see it as culpable folly to release you, and he would judge me insane and perhaps even treacherous to be considering this plan of ours. But even if he were to go along with our designs and do all that we asked of him, he would still be duty bound to make report on his return to Camulod on what I had done. And once that report was lodged, our secret would be out. That kind of knowledge cannot be contained once it has been released, and Lot has spies and informers everywhere, even in Camulod, for we can't keep our gates closed against the world, and the place is always full of strangers coming and going. Mark my words, Lot would hear of it within days, one way or another, so I say we should tell Popilius nothing. We have already sent one Queen to Camulod. Let him believe she is the real one.

"Within the week, I'll ride with Popilius to raid the southern coast, as we had planned. By that time, your arrangements should be made. All of your dealings in this matter will be with my men alone, my Cambrian Dragons. While we are gone, leaving only a small holding force here, you and your people will make your escape and head northwestward, avoiding Lagan completely. Popilius will hear nothing of escape or flight, and if he asks where our female prisoners have gone, I'll tell him that I sent them home. I do not wage war on women. Popilius knows that."

My lord does not wage war on women. Ygraine remembered the scorn with which she had greeted Huw Strongarm's utterance of those words and was swept by a shudder.

Uther glanced sideways at her. "Are you cold, Lady Ygraine? You're shivering."

"No." She straightened up and shook her head vigorously, denying the possibility.

"Good. Well, are we done here?" Uther turned directly back to Herliss. "You know what to do from this point onward?" Herliss growled in affirmation, and Uther continued. "Excellent. I'll take you back to your own quarters now, and I'll talk to my people this afternoon. Nemo will be the one with whom you will have all your dealings—the most loyal and trustworthy trooper I have. Been with me for years, Nemo, ever since we were brats together. So be it. I've things to think about. I'll have Nemo assign two guards to look after you day and night. Their names will be Cadwyn and Lohal, and one of them will be with you at all times from now on. But think of them as hand-picked messengers, not guards. They are completely trustworthy. They'll carry word to you and from you, acting as go-betweens for myself and the Queen . . . and you, of course. To everyone but us, it will seem that you've been placed under heavy guard for some transgression or other, so you'd better come up with a good reason for it, because you're sure to be asked why you've been so suddenly upgraded . . ."

Shortly after the two men left, Dyllis returned from her long walk, almost breathless with excitement over the number of men now in the camp. Ygraine had heard Uther himself say that Popilius Cirro had brought a thousand men with him, but she had never seen a thousand men assembled in one place and could not begin to visualize what such a gathering would look like. Her own father, Athol Mac Iain, she had often been told, could assemble a thousand warriors from his own clansmen and put them into the field within three days, but Ygraine had never known him do so. And her husband, Lot, who dealt, she knew, in thousands of men, assembling armies of mercenaries time after time, had never dared to have that large a host, potentially hostile and uncontrollable, assemble anywhere close to him at any time.

Dyllis told her that behind their tent and facing down into the river valley, row upon row of infantry tents, each of them large enough to accommodate four men sleeping side by side, were laid out in grids and blocks, covering the hillside entirely on the south side of the river and filling up the valley. These tents had been rigorously paced out so that no tent was closer to or farther away from its neighbours than any other, and between these regular blocks of tents were much wider divisions that served as streets, broad enough to accommodate columns of men marching ten abreast or mounted troopers riding four abreast.

The two regular day guards had accompanied Dyllis, Cavan and the older Derek Split-Eye, named for the spectacular scar that bisected the left side of his face, a knife slash that had opened him from above the eyebrow down to the edge of his mouth. Somehow, savage as the blow had been, it had been shallow enough to miss the eyeball, merely slicing through the lid above and below the eye itself. It had deadened that side of Derek's face, however, paralysing the cheek and leaving patches of grey hair in his eyebrow and moustache. Derek Split-Eye was a veteran, one of Uther's original Dragons. Cavan, on the other hand, was much younger and far more comely, smooth-faced and bright-eyed, with teeth that were still white and sound. His shoulders were broad, his hands and arms almost hairless and strongly muscled. Cavan had never spoken to Dyllis before that day, but both women had known that he was strongly attracted to her, barely able from the first day of his assignment to keep his eyes off her as she went about her business. She and Ygraine had even laughed about it. Now it became plain to Ygraine that Dyllis had hardly been impervious to his charms, either.

Ygraine stood erect in the corner by the washtable, her back to Dyllis, who continued to chatter, oblivious to the fact that her mistress was no longer listening. Instead, the Queen was thinking of Uther Pendragon, bare-headed and smiling with that upward-curling lip that came so close to sneering yet did nothing of the kind.

"*Lady?*" she heard him say, smiling with his voice, and a rush of gooseflesh swept across her skin. She remembered how he had reached out one hand to her, saw the long, strong fingers with their square, blunt nails and the tiny black hairs that curled over the knuckles. She shuddered deliciously, feeling the now familiar sensation of breathlessness swelling in her chest. And then she inhaled sharply and deeply, willing herself to think of other things. Uther, she knew, harboured no such thoughts of her. She had long since learned to detect the slightest signs of attraction in the men around her, and how to ignore and discourage them. In Uther Pendragon's case, she had seen and felt nothing, not the slightest intimation of interest in her as a woman.

"Ygraine, my lady?"

She returned to her senses quickly, aware that Dyllis had been speaking to her, and swung back to face the other woman, banishing her dangerous thoughts. But she could not listen to Dyllis's rhapsodies about young Cavan—not if she wanted to keep her wits about her. The air suddenly seemed hot and humid, and Ygraine felt constrained and confined in the command tent. She wanted to be outside walking in the fresh air. Uncaring whether she might be bruising her friends' feelings, she sent the younger woman to her sleeping quarters with orders to mend a shawl that Ygraine had torn earlier, and then she crossed to the entrance of the tent, where she called to Cavan and asked him to take her to Uther.

Uther was not in his tent when she arrived there, and no guards stood outside it, but she knew he would not be far away, and so she decided to wait for him. She dismissed Cavan and sent him back to his post, although it was plain to see that he was not happy about leaving her there outside the King's Tent, unguarded. She smiled and asked him what he thought she might steal if left alone, or whether he thought, with so many troopers about, that she was planning to escape in broad daylight. Cavan nodded and left, flushed and flustered by her humour.

Left alone, Ygraine crossed her arms on her breast and looked about her. There was no place to sit down, but the air was cooler here outside the tent, for the site was pleasantly sheltered by the thick leaves of the surrounding trees, and so she lingered, looking up to the western sky. A heavy thundercloud had rolled in and now towered upwards for miles, flickering with lightning, an ominous tower of dark blue, black and purple, shot with malevolent highlights of yellowish brown. She stared up at it for a long time, trying to discern the direction of its drift, wondering if it would blow by or sweep closer to them and unleash its burden on their heads. She was still standing there with her head raised and her eyes closed, breathing deeply and slowly, when Uther arrived. She heard his approaching footsteps and opened her eyes just in time to experience one of those moments that are remembered forever by those who witness them. He was less than four paces from her by then, his surprised pleasure evident in his eyes, and seeing her look at him, he began to raise his hand to greet her or to question her, but then the world turned white in a blinding flash that seemed to explode directly between them with a solid, yet somehow silent concussion, like the mute crack of a mighty whip. They both felt the force of the explosion physically, and it left them stunned and badly frightened, their nostrils filled with a strange, almost salty smell, as though the very air had been singed. And then, before either of them could even begin to recover, a solid deluge of ice-cold rain hit them, soaking them instantly and depriving them of what little breath had been left to them.

Uther was the first to recover. He stepped towards her, scooped her up into his arms as though she were weightless and carried her into his tent in three long strides. He lowered her feet to the ground as soon as they were safely inside the tent and made to step back, but Ygraine clung to him, whimpering in her throat and quivering with what he took to be terror. In fact, she was shaking with an instantaneous resurgence of the same raging lust that had assailed her earlier, and it had consumed her so thoroughly that she shuddered with the strength of it.

Uther held her awkwardly in his arms, peering over her head into the dimness of the tent, highly aware of the soft pliancy of her body beneath the thin stuff of her gown and of the way her thighs pressed against his own, and debating foolishly with himself on what he ought to do. His eyes had still not recovered from the blinding white flash of the thunderbolt that had struck so close to them, and what remained of his hearing was overwhelmed by the drumming roar of the heavy rain on the leather roof panels above their heads. Ygraine moved again, almost writhing against him, and he distinctly felt the changing shape of the soft flesh of her thighs. He coughed, clearing his throat with embarrassment, and tried a second time to push himself away from her, but she clung more tightly to him than before, and he stopped, wishing that he had had the foresight to wear his armour, or at least a leather cuirass and studded loin guard that would have stopped the shape and softness of the woman from impressing itself against his body. For the first time since capturing her, he had become acutely conscious of her femaleness, and he raised one arm, cupping the back of her head in his open palm and holding her face gently against his shoulder. As he did so, however, she pulled her head back and looked up at him, her eyes enormous and her mouth open as though to speak. He dipped his head towards her and waited to hear what she would say, but she said nothing and simply continued to stare at him with those huge eyes. And as he gazed back at her, he felt her lean back further against his encircling arm, the movement, deliberate and unmistakable, pushing the lower half of her body against him, enflaming and engorging him, and he knew he had to get away from her. He reached up with his free hand to disengage her arms from about his neck, but as he did so, she rose up on the tips of her toes and grasped his head in both hands, pulling him down to where she could kiss him, her mouth closing over his and her tongue thrusting against his lips.

His surprise was a fleeting thing, real and startling and huge, but vanquished instantly by the urgency and reality of what was happening. He was lost within heartbeats, all his resolve and all his fine, noble intentions swept into nothingness by the unexpectedness of what had occurred and by the moist, living heat of her lips and mouth. Ygraine, for her part, had passed beyond any possibility of self-restraint the moment Uther had swept her up into his arms out in the rain, and in the searing, starving beauty of that first kiss she had, for a single evanescent moment, consciously sneered at herself for ever having thought that she could live without what she was feeling. Giving herself up completely to the storm inside her, she wrapped both arms around his neck and let herself go limp, her dead weight pulling him forward and off balance. On the point of falling, however, Uther rallied himself and looked around the tent, and then he half pulled, half carried her to the sturdy table that held the wash basin and ewer. He swept the tabletop clear and leaned her back against the edge of it, his hands on her waist and his mouth seeking hers again, and within moments her clothing seemed to have dissolved and her legs closed around his waist as he took her to him.

Their coupling was short and furious, to the accompaniment of drumming rain and heralded at the climax by a continuous chorus of thunderclaps, and when he had finished he remained standing in front of her, quivering all over, his body bent forward from the waist, his forehead between her breasts, while she lay back beneath him, her head dangling from the end of the table as she stroked the damp hair at the back of his neck and kneaded his hips gently and rhythmically between her knees.

Finally he sighed and braced himself up on one arm, reaching out with the other hand to cradle the back of her head.

"Lady," he said, his breathing still uneven, "I did not know that was going to happen."

"I know you didn't. I didn't either, until today."

He cocked his head on one side. "Today? When?"

"Earlier, when you gripped my arm."

"When I . . . I don't remember gripping your arm. Oh, yes, I do now. What was so special about that?"

She smiled at him. "It was . . . significant, and I'll say no more. Ah—!" The last sound was a tiny bleat of complaint at the unheralded withdrawal of his flaccid phallus. He grunted and moved his pelvis closer as though to reinsert himself despite the immediate impossibility of doing so, and she stirred against him.

"More," she murmured. "I want more of that."

He nodded, pretending to be serious. "That should be possible in a little while."

"And then I'll want more again after that."

He smiled and shook his head. "But I have things to do, lady, concerning your own plans. You charged me with certain duties, and I've not had time to do them yet. I still have not spoken to Popilius Cirro . . ." He paused, reflecting. "Still, I could talk to him tonight in the refectory when we go to eat . . ."

"No." She heaved her body lasciviously beneath him. "Go now, talk quickly and briefly, do whatever else you must do, and then come back here to me."

He cocked his head again, grinning down at her. "I thought you wanted to be alone tonight?"

"I did and I still do, you blind man. I want to be alone with you."

"Do you, indeed? That is wonderful. It's almost incredible, in truth, but I'm delighted to hear you say it. Now one more kiss, and I'll go and put old Cirro's mind to rest. After that, there's nothing else for me to do other than to tell Nemo that I mustn't be disturbed, and as soon as I've done that, I'll be back here."

"Good, then kiss me and go. Wait! What's that down there? Oh, that was quick . . ."

"Aye it was, wasn't it? Should I take it with me, or shall I leave it here?"

"Hmm. Leave it here with me, but swear me an oath that you'll come back for it."

"Oh, lady, I'll come back, I swear to you. Within the hour. Should I bring some food from the commissary wagons? Will you be hungry later?"

"No, you need bring no food. I might be hungry later, but only for you and the . . . gifts you bring to me . . . Now go, and come back soon. I shall go to bed and wait for you."

"No need for that, I'll carry you to bed. Here, hold me around the neck."

She interlaced her fingers behind his neck and moaned very gently as he entered her, and then he hooked one elbow behind each of her knees and lifted her effortlessly from the table. He hitched her slightly higher then, stretching the length of his arms along her thighs, and carried her, impaled, to his narrow cot, where he left her eventually to await his return.

THIRTY

That night with Ygraine, long and intensely pleasurable as it was, beginning and ending in full daylight, was the first of only four occasions on which the two of them would be able to lie together, and the last of those four times would not occur until after the birth of their son, Arthur.

In the morning, Uther left her alone and unguarded very briefly, as he had arranged to meet again with Popilius Cirro, and he knew that if he did not appear, Popilius would seek him out. And so he swallowed his resentment at having to get up and leave her alone in bed, acknowledging, as he always did, that his duty took precedence over all other things. When he stepped into Cirro's tent a short time later, he was the embodiment of a Camulodian cavalry commander, clad in gleaming, polished armour from head to foot.

He confirmed to Popilius Cirro that there was nothing at all to prevent them from setting out within thirty-six hours to execute the deep penetration raid that they had planned more than a month earlier in Camulod. His party had been camped here in this valley for more than a week, ever since capturing the Queen and her party, and yet his mounted scouts had seen no sign in all that time of any activity from Lot's people anywhere within a day's journey on horseback, which was the equivalent of almost two days' marching.

Popilius was surprised but well pleased to hear that and made no effort to conceal his relief. His thousand men created an enormous presence, almost impossibly difficult to conceal, and he had been greatly concerned by the need to insert them deeply into this hostile territory without being detected. For that reason, he had led them overland in night marches ever since quitting the great road west of Isca, and those harsh, punitive exercises were pleasurable to no one, particularly on moonless nights when the darkness was unrelieved and every minor dip in the ground could result in painful accidents and injuries to feet and ankles. He had brought his men through without being detected, however, and to reward them he had relieved them all of duty for the entire day, warning them that they would be back at the daily grind on the following morning, parading at dawn and drilling hard in preparation for the expedition they would undertake on the day after.

By the time Uther left him, they had agreed not only upon the drills and exercises their combined forces would undertake the following day, with Uther's cavalry and bowmen combining forces in an assault upon Cirro's two cohorts, but also upon the order of march for the day after that. Half of Uther's Dragons would form an advance guard and ride ahead of the main body of the infantry. The other half would ride as a rear guard, and Uther's Pendragon bowmen would range on either side of the main marching column, so that their line of march would be direct and no less than two hundred paces wide at any point.

He was satisfied that he had thought of everything long before he reached the tent where Ygraine awaited him, and thankful that he had dismissed her guards earlier that day. He was already tugging at the buckles on the straps of his armour as he entered, but he stopped short just inside the entrance, taken completely by surprise.

The interior of the large, leather-walled tent, after the brightness of the late-afternoon sun, was dark and yet paradoxically brilliant in places with blinding light. Bright shafts of solid light streamed through three flaps propped open in the roof panels, making the rest of the enclosed space seem much darker than it was. Then, while his sight was still blurred and hampered by the strange effect, he saw the bed that had been made in the centre of the front area of the tent. Squinting and blinking, trying to clear his vision, he saw that Ygraine had spread a heavy leather groundsheet beneath another of woven straw, and on that, side by side, she had laid the two thin palliasses from the cots in either sleeping area. On top of the straw mattresses she had then piled campaign sleeping skins, most of them taken from the tent's four footlockers.

All this he managed to see in the instant before he raised his eyes to look at the Queen, sitting motionless in one of the two chairs beyond the bed. A brilliant column of light at her back threw her almost completely into silhouette, transforming her into a phantasm of light-limned shadows. He could not see what she was wearing, but he could see that she was completely covered, the curves of her body broken up and angled by the drapes of a garment of some kind. She made no move to stand and she said nothing, merely looking at him. He straightened up to his full height, and when he had removed his helmet, he bowed slightly to her, inclining his head at the same time.

"Are you a goddess or a Queen? And if you are a Queen, who made the bed?"

She stood up, and he saw that she was wearing a single loose sheet of some fine fabric, covering her arms and shoulders and falling to the ground behind her. Now that she was standing, the light at her back revealed her fine figure in shadow.

"I made the bed," she said quietly. "And I am neither Queen nor goddess. I am a woman, and those cots are far too narrow."

She released the corners of the material and the sheet dropped away, falling to the ground without a sound and allowing the light from behind her to spill onto the curves of her hips, shoulders and neck.

Uther's eyes were adjusting rapidly to the light by that time and his heart began to race as he looked at her, seeing her clearly perhaps for the first time. In the utter silence of the tent he tried to swallow and found that his mouth had gone completely dry. He tried again, more successfully this time, and then sucked air audibly through his nostrils, holding it in for a count of five before expelling it explosively. He moved to step towards her then, and everything he was wearing seemed to creak loudly, except for the hilt of his short-sword, which clanked against the bottom of his cuirass. He stopped abruptly, clutching at the matched sheaths of his short-sword and dagger to keep them from rattling, realizing that he was ill-prepared to handle her nakedness. She read his expression and smiled, raising her hands and spreading her fingers to cover her breasts.

"I have been waiting for you and thinking of this moment and how I would greet you . . ." Her smile grew wider. "But everything I imagined was completely wrong. Who would have thought you would come back in armour? Do you believe you are in danger here, King Uther? I promise, I will not attack you." She covered both breasts then with one forearm and dropped her other hand to conceal the dark triangle at her centre, shaking her head. "At least, I will not while you are wearing that cold, metal breastplate and all those weapons and belts and buckles."

It seemed to him in the moments that followed that he had forgotten everything he had ever learned about removing armour quickly and efficiently, and he knew even as he was doing it that he would have drawn long spells on punishment duty during his early training for the careless and impatient way he now threw each single piece aside as it came loose. He had never behaved that way before, but then he had never before had such a prize in front of him, taunting him for his slowness.

Freed of his clothing at last, he stepped towards her, for she had made no move to approach him or to help him divest himself of weapons or armour, preferring to stand watching him as he stripped himself down. He felt the slippery, warm pelt of one of the bedskins beneath his bare foot as he moved to her, and then his confidence evaporated all at once, and he stopped short again, abashed and suddenly awkward, his gaze fixed on her eyes.

She stared back at him, her face a picture of serene, slightly amused dignity. "What is it, King Uther?" Her voice was barely louder than a whisper. "Does your kingship stop short of what it desires? Reach out, sir, and take what is yours."

Slowly, gently, he placed his hands on her waist and pulled her towards him, stooping to her mouth and banishing the image of Merlyn Britannicus and his wife, Deirdre, that sprang instantly into his mind. Her arms came up behind his head, and everything but her mouth was forgotten as the moist warmth of her lips closed over his and she went limp again, simply dropping her dead weight into his arms as she had before. This time, however, he yielded to the slump, allowing the weight of her to pull him down to the bed.

He left her reluctantly before the sun had reached its zenith, making sure that she was escorted discreetly to her own tent.

Much as it pained him, he was obliged to spend some time with his subordinate commanders, infantry, cavalry and bowmen, ensuring that they were all prepared for the following day's march and the campaign it would launch. He met briefly again at the end of the afternoon with Ygraine and Herliss in the King's Tent, Dyllis having been dispatched with young Cavan to find their own amusements, and so comfortable were he and she in their new-found intimacy that they had no trouble at all in concealing it from the veteran Cornish commander.

They discussed the latest developments in their escape plan, and Uther explained to the others exactly what he had told his trooper Nemo. When the main strike force left the following day, Nemo would remain behind in camp with a small holding force of Dragons, to guard the remaining prisoners, the Queen's bodyguard and keep them safe pending Uther's return. Then, within the following few days, Nemo would make a move, along with four hand-picked companions, all five of them apparently suborned by Herliss and rewarded with gold and jewels. They would all five draw night guard duty, and after nightfall, when most of their companions had fallen asleep, they would attack and immobilize the others who stood guard with them. That done, they would next overpower and bind their sleeping comrades one at a time, before freeing Herliss and the Queen's bodyguard.

Uther assured them again that the escape would be smooth, since none of his men would offer any resistance when the time came for them to be "overcome." Alasdair Mac Iain and the Queen's bodyguard would know nothing of that, of course. They would see only the result. Nemo and the other four would flee with the escapees, and as soon as they were safely out of sight, the "bound" guards would free themselves and resume their duties as caretakers of the base camp. Nemo and the four men would later strike out from the escaping party on their own as they approached the coast, where they would say they hoped to find access to a ship that would take them over to Gaul. Once on their own, however, they would immediately make their way back to the camp.

Herliss nodded throughout all of this, plainly impressed with Uther's thoroughness and untroubled by any detail of what he was hearing.

When everything had been discussed, Uther excused himself to Herliss and Ygraine and made his way directly to the commissary, where he spoke with the head cook and obtained a heavy, lidded kitchen basket filled with fresh-cooked meat, both venison and fowl, a large loaf of new bread, a round of goat cheese and a small, cloth-wrapped bundle of apples that had been sliced and then dried in the sun. A jug of beer, sealed with a waxed covering, and two earthen mugs gave the basket a fine, substantial heft.

By the time Uther returned to the King's Tent, Herliss had gone and Ygraine was waiting for him. They ate slowly and without interruption, enjoying the meal and the beer, and when they were finished, Uther got up and carefully fastened the leather flaps that formed the doorway. Then, moving almost formally and being careful not to touch each other, they remade their bed together slowly, enjoying the deliberate and titillating build-up of anticipation. When the bed was ready and he would have kissed her, Ygraine held him off even longer, motioning him away from her as she began to remove her clothing, licking her lips lasciviously and motioning to him to take his clothes off, too. They watched each other hungrily, then collapsed slowly on to the bed-skins and made love continuously, with only minor intermissions when they recouped and talked in whispers, until darkness fell more than three hours later.

They had more sleep that second night, but not much. Twice in the night Ygraine woke him with lips and questing fingers, and twice more he wakened her by penetrating her gently as she slept and drawing her slowly to the surface of sleep with his caresses.

He was astir before dawn, however, bathing himself in water from the ewer on the washtable and refusing to allow her to come near him while he did so, since they both knew the dangers of her being too close to him when he was naked. She helped him to buckle on his armour, however, and she slipped the long-bladed cavalry sword through the iron ring that hung at his back, then held his helmet while he swirled the great red war cloak with the gold-embroidered dragon over his head and let it settle comfortably across his shoulders before fastening the clasps that held it securely in place. When he was ready, he stood in front of her bare-headed, holding his heavy helmet in the crook of his left arm, its rim propped against his hip beneath his cloak. She came close to him and wrapped her arms around his waist, sliding the right one between the helmet and his cuirass under the heavy cloak and shrugging the heavy, thick material over her shoulders to hang down her back. She was bare-skinned and smelled deliciously of their lovemaking. He pecked her with a gentle kiss and peered down at her.

"Well, lady, shall we meet again?"

She tilted her head back and looked at him. "If you do your part properly and well, and soon, ridding Cornwall of Gulrhys Lot, then yes, my lord, we will."

"Ridding *Britain* of Gulrhys Lot, you mean. He pollutes far more than Cornwall. Have no fear, lady, I will do my part."

"And I'll do mine. I know not how, but I will send you word by some trusted messenger whenever I hear anything that you might use to confound him and his foul ambitions . . . I find myself wishing now, for the first time in my life, that I could read and write, for I could then sit down and write to you all that is in my mind. But I never learned in Eire. Writing must be a Roman trick."

Uther snorted. "Aye, it is that. I learned it myself, but only barely. I read, but I never write, although I could, if I were forced. Merlyn's the scribe in our family."

"So I shall have to be content with sending messages by mouth and memory."

"My memories of your mouth will sustain me as I wait, lady."

"Aye . . ." She did not smile, her brow creased in thought. "As I told you, I cannot say when it might be, Uther, or who might be my messenger, but I will reach you somehow. And if ever you come close to where I am at any time, I will find a way to come to you or have you brought to me."

He grinned. "Then we would spend all our time in bed, lady, and little of it talking."

She smiled now, too. "What better way can time be spent? Time enough for talking when we grow old. Look at that little man of yours. There's nothing old about him, is there? Young and upstanding, yet he is stiff-backed and not nearly as hard-headed as he first appears. Over all, though, he communicates his meaning excellently well, considering he spoke not a single word in the entire two nights of our dealings with one other. He is a very clever and talented little fellow and I have grown to like him very much, so see you, King Uther Pendragon, keep him safe for me."

"Aye, lady, you can rely upon me for that," he replied, smiling. He stooped and kissed her, long and deeply, and then raised his head high, gazing into nothingness. "I have to go now. I don't want to, but I'm already late. Fare thee well, sweet Lady Ygraine, until we meet again. The day after tomorrow, you will be free again."

"And on my way back to my wondrous husband. Gods! I think I would rather die. But I will go, and I will tell him what he wants to hear . . . tales of your depravity and wanton cruelty. I will pretend I do not know that he refused to rescue me and set my very life at risk by killing peaceful envoys, and I'll scream at him for vengeance upon you. And then I will listen carefully at every moment, and whatever I may hear, you will hear shortly afterwards. When will you return to Cambria?"

"In October, if the weather holds. Everything in war depends upon the weather. As long as I can move my troops around without their freezing on me, I'll stay here."

"What if I have tidings for you in the meantime, how will my messenger find you, and where?"

"In Cambria, in my stronghold of Tir Manha in the southwest. I stay there during the winter, without moving much, unless I have to go and visit one of the other clans in the Federation. I am never absent long, however, and your messenger will find no hardship in waiting for me for a few days. Otherwise, if I am not expected to return soon, I might be in Camulod, four days distant."

"And will my messenger be safe searching for you?"

He looked back into her eyes now, his own eyes narrowing, and then he removed a ring from the smallest finger of his right hand. The ring was of solid gold, the main body of it carved into the likeness of a dragon with its wings folded and its tail coiled, tiny jewels set into its head as glittering, brilliant, blood-red eyes. He pressed it into her hand, closing her fist over it.

"My colours, gold and red. This ring was my father's and his father's before that. I'll pass the word among my people that anyone carrying this ring must be brought to me immediately, no matter where I am. Don't lose it."

She raised both eyebrows. "But I always lose things! Everything! I lost my heart and my chastity to you, did I not? Now kiss me and be gone, before I drag you back to bed."

He did so, thoroughly and well, and then turned and left her before he could be tempted to do it again.

The raid that Uther led out that morning with Ygraine's scent still clinging to his skin was spectacularly successful, for they had struck directly southwestward, avoiding detection almost until they had penetrated to the very end of the long finger of Cornwall that thrust out into the sea. There, on both sides of the spur of land, lay a profusion of bays and inlets, many of them with narrow beaches and high, protective cliffs that Lot's people used to great advantage, landing their mercenary troops in sheltered coves and beaching their seagoing vessels.

Like his father before him, Gulrhys Lot offered safe harbour and anchorage to anyone wishing to use the deep coves of Cornwall for shelter. He made no moral judgments, betrayed no interest in the activities of his visitors and made no demands on them other than one. In return for their safety, security and the right to come and go at will, the raiders must pay him a bounty of half their booty in the form of *specie*—coins and vessels and ornaments of gold, silver, copper and bronze, and any jewels that they might acquire. Coinage was seldom used anywhere nowadays. Now everything was barter, and once-precious metals were largely worthless. What point in having silver and gold coins if you couldn't use them to buy anything? And so Lot's coffers were always full of coinage, and the pirates were well pleased with the bargain.

What few of them knew, however, was that Lot melted the coins and pieces down into bullion. Thick, heavy bars of solid gold, silver and copper were always sure to stir the hearts and minds of greedy men wealthy enough to hunger for more. Few such men lived in Britain nowadays, but there were still enough of them in Gaul and throughout the other provinces on the mainland to provide a lucrative market for his endeavours. Thus Lot could transform his bullion into ships and men and weapons, and ensure an unending supply of mercenaries for his wars.

On the cliffs above the largest and most important of these inlets, those dedicated to the protection of the pirate fleets that earned him his bullion, Lot had constructed fortifications on the landward side. Many of these were little more than barricades: heaps of logs piled high upon each other and reinforced with sand, with perhaps a stepped ditch behind the crest where bowmen could stand in defence of the entrance to the narrow pathway to and from the beach below. Several, however, more than a score in all, were sophisticated enough to qualify as crude but real forts, fit to be manned most of the time, and a few of them were garrisoned full time.

Uther's raiding force fell upon these outposts like thunderbolts, striking terror into the defenders, since none of them had ever really expected to be attacked by hostile forces from within their own lands. It was beyond the power of their imaginations to envision an invading force strong enough to strike downward clean through the heart of Cornwall and reach the southwestern coast unbloodied. Their incredulity worked well on Uther's behalf, and he took full advantage of it, striking savagely and ruthlessly and driving the demoralized enemy out of their holes and back down onto the beaches, where they scattered and made their individual escapes as best they could. It frequently took his troopers longer to destroy the fortifications than it had to capture them.

Only one fort did Uther avoid on that expedition, and that was Tir Gwyn, Herliss's own White Fort, a massive construction that looked not only impregnable but inviolable since it was built entirely of a local, snow-white quartz. Uther halted his raiders on a nearby hill and allowed them to admire the castle from afar, blazing in the sunshine like a beacon of purity, but then he swung them around and put many miles between them and Tir Gwyn before night fell.

That raid marked the beginning of a season of warfare in which Uther's Dragons went from success to success and earned themselves a reputation among Lot's forces that often resulted in the Cornishmen throwing down their weapons and running away without attempting to strike a blow. Only the hardest of Lot's mercenaries stopped the year from becoming a complete rout for the Dragons. Several groups and divisions of those, mainly Germanic tribesmen who had trained and fought as imperial mercenaries, combined forces under a pair of talented generals called Cerdic and Tewdric and for a time came close to halting Uther's free-ranging progress.

The two armies met late one afternoon across a narrow valley with steep sides, and Uther knew that his were not the only guts squirming with fear and apprehension that day. But as the opposing forces eyed each other, waiting for the dispositions that their commanders would decree, a storm broke over them, battering both armies with terrifying power. Both hosts sat still, absorbing the blasts, waiting for them to blow over, but time passed and the tempest showed no sign of abating. The rain was icy, mixed with hail, and the temperature plummeted. The men were soaked, and then grew chilled, then frozen, and still the storm flared about them, with lightning bolts that shattered trees and scattered men. Night fell, and the world was a quagmire. Day came and the hillside opposite Uther's position was bare of men.

There were no crushing reversals for Uther's Dragons, no battles lost or defeats sustained by his forces, and most of the talk about the campaign, among the allies from Cambria and Camulod, continued to focus on the undeniable success of Uther's ideas about combining infantry with bowmen and cavalry in carefully planned manoeuvres against enemy forces that ought to have been overwhelmingly victorious simply by virtue of their numbers. Apart from that, however, things were going annoyingly wrong for Uther in other areas—piddling, insignificant little areas—and he became increasingly unable to understand why. It seemed to amount to no more than trivial annoyances at first, gadfly occurrences that demanded to be scratched: spies and scouts being caught and killed when they ought to have been safe and free from threat; messages and messengers going astray and never arriving at their destinations; shipments of supplies arriving from Camulod partially spoiled and in one instance totally unusable.

Hand in hand with that kind of thing, indications of incompetence and mismanagement among his own forces began to come to his notice. In the space of a single month, he received four separate reports of inaccurate information being provided to troop commanders and then acted upon without any attempt to obtain verification, resulting in time and effort wasted and men endangered without valid cause. On the worst of those occasions, a ten-man troop had been dispatched to scout a pathway through a dense growth of forest in the northernmost part of Cornwall, assured by their chief scout that the terrain between their departure point and the edge of the forest was wide open and free of hostile forces. It was not, on either count. Reconstructing the scene afterward, the troop commander had found clear indications that the troop had been ambushed by a party of not less than a hundred men who had left ample evidence to establish beyond doubt that they had been living openly and for some time in caverns among a jumble of large rocks close by the road the troopers used. All ten troopers had been killed and their horses stolen.

Incompetence and mismanagement, deplorable though they may be, are remediable, and Uther made it his prime urgency to put a stop to it. The remedy involved close scrutiny of several of his individual commanders, the execution of his chief scout, who was proved to have lied in order to cover his own laziness, and two swift demotions of intermediate commanders to the ranks, where they fared badly at the hands of their former subordinates. That not only clipped the pinions of the officers involved, it also served notice to everyone that high rank, forfeited, entailed a long, hard fall.

Against what most people called sheer misfortune and plain bad luck, however, Uther, like everyone else, was impotent: a scouting troop of twelve mounted men, caught unexpectedly in a narrow valley by a large band of Lot's mercenaries who ought not to have been there, broke and ran down the valley to the eastward in the reasonable hope that their horses' speed would carry them to safety. Instead, it led them into a dry, brush-choked ravine in which they all died when the enemy fired the brush with burning arrows. In another incident, an entire squadron of cavalry, thirty-six strong and operating independently of other support, found itself wiped out when one of the horses came down with some unknown kind of fever and infected all the others. The pestilence spread through the horse lines in the space of two days, and twenty-eight of a total of fifty horses died. The remaining twenty-two animals had all shown symptoms of the illness but had recovered by the end of the fifth day. The squadron commander, a young man called Rollo who had been born and raised around the stables of Camulod, had not dared assume the risk of taking potentially lethal animals back into the healthy herds remaining in Uther's base camp. Upon his own initiative, he ordered that every one of the surviving animals be slaughtered, and he and his men walked back twenty-three miles to rejoin the army, carrying their saddles and equipment.

It gradually became apparent to Uther and to those around him who enjoyed his confidence that something fundamental had changed within his army during the course of the year's campaigning. Had anyone chosen to consider such things prior to the start of that campaign, they might have said that Uther's was a lucky army; everyone had taken that for granted. During the latter part of that summer, however, that perception changed radically, and "Uther's Luck," as it came to be known, was regularly talked about around his army's campfires. The rate at which his best intentions and most careful planning went wrong soon began to generate a plainly noticeable kind of superstitious awe among his followers, and Uther himself eventually reached the stage where he could not blame his people for what they were thinking. He could not charge them openly with disloyalty, either, for the truth was that he, too, suspected some malign, supernatural intervention in his affairs.

From that first night with Ygraine, it seemed to him later, nothing that he planned had ever come to full fruition in quite the way he had envisioned, and he convinced himself eventually that lying with Ygraine had been the very worst thing he could have done. He was incapable of forgetting that Ygraine was sister to Deirdre, who had been Merlyn's wife and was now dead, and that before all that, Deirdre had been Cassandra. Forgetting the pleasure of their coupling, he could not banish the shame of having used his captive for his own desires, in contradiction of everything he had been taught about honourable conduct, acting in the basest possible way, giving full rein to the darkness in him. He felt sure he was being punished for this transgression with the falseness of those around him. And deep in his soul, it sometimes rankled when he gave way to his despair and remembered how he had renounced all his boyhood ties to Cambria—even to being Pendragon—because of his loyalty to Merlyn and to Camulod. A sacrifice that big, made in the name of loyalty, he told himself on the few occasions when he allowed himself to wallow in self-pity, should protect anyone against disloyalty in others . . .

Most of the time, however, Uther would have nothing to do with such thoughts. He had little patience for those who were forever looking back over their shoulders. Only at night would the shadows overtake him, subjecting him to superstitious fears and reminding him of the darkness he acknowledged in himself. It was hardly surprising, therefore, that he seldom permitted himself to dwell on such things, forcing himself instead to remain in the bright light of the approval of his people.

THIRTY-ONE

In the autumn of the year, towards the end of the campaigning season, an unknown warrior on a tall red horse rode into Uther's camp one evening and demanded to speak with King Uther Pendragon. He was detained but not disarmed, while Nemo, who was decurion of the guard that night, set out to find Uther. But Uther had seen the man arrive and had already come himself to find out who would dare to ride so boldly into his camp alone and on such a magnificent mount.

The King strode quickly towards the group clustered about the newcomer, and the stranger began to step forward to meet him, only to be seized and forced to his knees by the zealous guards. Uther barked an order, bidding them step away and allow the stranger to rise. The man then rose to his feet, squaring his shoulders and holding his head high, glaring around defiantly at his captors.

Uther walked right by him, ignoring him completely, and went to examine his horse, instead. He inspected the animal's teeth and ran his hand expertly over its withers, then turned to its master.

"A fine horse. Unusual for us to see horseflesh as good as our own in this part of the world. I'm Uther Pendragon. Who are you?"

Instead of answering, the stranger reached out and unfolded his left hand, palm upward, revealing Uther's own ring, worn facing inward, on his little finger. The King gazed at it in silence for a count of several heartbeats, his lips pursed, then turned to lay a hand on the arm of one of the guards.

"Marek, go you to the commissary if you will, and bring some cups and a jug of ale to my tent . . . a large jug, I think. Our friend here looks thirsty." He turned back to the newcomer and inclined his head. "Come with me. Your horse will be looked after while we talk." He glanced at Nemo, who stood glowering at the stranger. "See to it, Nemo, will you?" Then he strode away towards his tent without a backward glance, and the visitor walked close behind him, leaving the guards looking at each other in mute wonder, unable to decipher what had just happened.

Darkness had already begun to fall, and lamps and smoky, pitch-dipped torches were being lit everywhere. In the King's Tent, they found a trooper busily lighting the high, tallow candles that augmented Uther's dim, smoky campaign lamps. Uther waved the man to a chair and then leaned with his buttocks against the single table, his arms folded across his chest, waiting until the trooper had left the tent.

As soon as they were alone, he spoke. "The Lady Ygraine is well, I hope?"

"Aye, she is. And nearby, too. She bade me bring you to her, if you can make the time to visit her."

Uther was staring at the stranger, assessing him as he had been doing since first he set eyes on him. The man was no ordinary warrior, nor was he a servant of any kind. Quite apart from the magnificent horse he rode, his speech and his clothing proclaimed him high-born to some degree.

"Who are you?"

"My name is Lagan. They call me Lagan Longhead."

The King smiled. "Of course, Herliss's son. I see the resemblance now. Is your father well? I have heard nothing of him since I saw him last."

Lagan inclined his head solemnly. "He is well and safely back in Tir Gwyn where he belongs. I am grateful to you for releasing him and for the way in which you did it. You saved his life, and perhaps my own and those of my wife and son. My entire clan is in your debt."

Uther smiled and shook his head. "No need for that, Lagan Longhead. I did what I did for my own benefit, believe me. I needed allies in the war against Lot, and your father and the Queen needed someone who could help them win back some portion of their lives. We all benefited equally."

He was interrupted by the arrival of the trooper Marek, bearing a jug of ale and two mugs. Uther took them from him and thanked the man, then poured. Lagan raised his mug immediately and drank down half of the contents in a single long swallow. Uther watched him, smiling faintly, then picked up the jug and refilled Lagan's before sipping his own. He made no move to sit in the other chair, content instead to remain lounging against the edge of the table, looking down at his seated guest.

"I thought you had the look of a thirsty man about you. How far from here is the Queen?"

Lagan wiped his mouth with the back of his hand and belched quietly, showing no awareness that Uther was looking down on him. "A three-hour ride—four in the dark, but there's a harvest moon tonight. She is in the Crag Fort, one of my father's smaller strongholds, the smallest of them, in fact, but warm and habitable. If you are able, we can leave immediately, for the Queen will be impatient. Tomorrow, she must be back in Tir Gwyn where her husband, our greatly beloved King, will join her. And while Lot is in Tir Gwyn during the next few days, less than a day's journey from where the Queen will lie tonight, my father hopes that you will burn the Crag Fort."

Uther frowned. "And why would I do that? Is your father so wealthy that he can afford to lose a castle for a gesture?"

"He may be. More to the point, however, he can't afford not to. Lot is beginning to wonder why so few of my father's holdings have been attacked this year."

"So few? You mean some of them have been attacked?"

"Aye, two."

"I did not know that."

"Aye, and for that we thank the gods. When every other castle in the land is being attacked, it becomes very noteworthy when those belonging to one single, powerful man sit safe and unthreatened. You attacked two of my father's castles recently, within a month of each other, and one of them you mauled quite badly, stealing all its stored grain and burning the empty granaries. That was just enough, and beautifully timed, to lull Lot's suspicions. Now another month has elapsed, and the complete destruction and loss of a third castle belonging to the noble Herliss should tip the balance—to Lot's eyes at least—back in the direction of uneasy trust."

"Hmm." Uther was bracing himself with one straight leg, holding his mug in one hand and drumming on the rim of it with the nails of his other hand, his head tilted slightly as though he listened to the rhythm of his fingers. Finally he jerked his head in a tight little nod. "So be it. If you will wait here for me, I have some people to talk to and some minor arrangements to put in place to cover my absence. I'll instruct my grooms to have your horse brushed down and prepared for a return journey, and I'll rejoin you here as quickly as I can. We'll leave immediately after that. Should I bring an escort of some kind?"

"Not unless you absolutely want to draw attention to yourself. But if you feel you must have an escort, then bring one."

Uther looked the other man straight in the eye, remembering what he had been told about him years earlier. The two of them were close in age, Lagan perhaps a couple of years older, and if his long-time friend the Lady Mairidh were to be believed, they were close in temperament as well. Lagan stared right back at him, one eyebrow slightly quirked, almost but not quite arrogant, and certainly not lacking in self-assurance.

Uther grinned. "No, I don't think so. No escort. Wait, I won't be long."

He turned quickly to leave, but before he could take a step, the other man stopped him with a word, bidding him wait. Uther turned back and looked at him curiously.

"What? What is it?"

Lagan looked him up and down and back again, head to foot, then motioned with his hand. "Appearances," he said quietly. "You might as well bring the escort if you're going to wear that."

"Wear what?"

"King Uther Pendragon's armour. I recognized you as soon as I saw you coming—bright-red and gold cloak, gold dragon, bronze armour with red enamelling, crimson horsehair crest on the helmet. It's hardly unobtrusive, is it? I simply thought you might want to bring a trumpeter with you, too, so that we can alert anyone who doesn't see you at first glance . . ."

Uther stood glaring at the man's effrontery, and then his face broke into a slow grin and he nodded. "You do have a point. Let me see what else I can find to wear. There are not too many men my size among our forces but there are a few. Wait for me. I'll be back as quickly as may be."

Lagan sat still for a moment, then looked down into his mug and drank deeply again before rising and moving to help himself from the jug. Armed with another brimming mug, he went back and sat in the chair, placed the mug carefully on the ground beside him and then stretched his muscles hugely, arms, back and legs, groaning softly with the pleasure of it.

When Uther returned some time later, dressed now in a plain black woollen cloak with a hood and a mixture of nondescript pieces of armour, he found his visitor asleep with his chin on his breast, his long legs stretched out in front of him and his body slouched deeply in the chair. The mug on the ground beside him was still full.

Uther learned more about Gulrhys Lot that night than he had previously been able to accumulate over a lifetime. Thinking back on it later, he would have no clear idea when during their journey the tenor of their talk had changed, but eventually everything Lagan Longhead had held tightly restrained inside him concerning Lot— all the anger, frustration, disillusioned bitterness and pain—had poured out of him in some kind of cleansing catharsis.

Within the first few moments of their beginning to speak to each other once they were free of the camp, Uther felt a kind of bond between himself and Lagan, undefined and accepted without question or comment, that tacitly permitted them to speak openly without fear. It was a phenomenon that Uther had never encountered before, because it was not in his nature either to be garrulous among friends or to confide easily in strangers, but he merely accepted it and shrugged his shoulders mentally, while Lagan gave him no sign that he was even aware of anything unusual.

Uther started talking about Merlyn, and somehow the topic drifted naturally to his loyalty to his cousin, and then to Camulod and to his own Dragons. Always, however, it swung back to Merlyn, and loyalty and, at length, to betrayal by disbelief, with Uther even broaching the subject of his own doubts and uncertainties. And before long Lagan Longhead began laying bare his own soul in return, talking about his own experiences with loyalty and betrayal, and about his decades-long friendship with Gulrhys Lot.

"Gods, man!" Uther interrupted. "You sound as though you think you lost something of value!"

"I did lose something of value." Lagan glanced sideways and saw the disbelief on Uther's face, and he grinned and shook his head. "But we all see value differently at different times. You never knew Lot as I once did. He has a marvellous sense of the ridiculous, and we have had some wonderful times together, he and I . . . happy times, laughing ourselves sick, weeping tears of mirth until we fell on the floor clutching our ribs."

"Gulrhys Lot? Are you talking about Lot of *Cornwall?* You can't mean that."

"Oh yes I can, and why not? I stand against him now, but I was his true and devoted friend for nigh on twenty years, and that was not, I promise you, because he was a miserable, treacherous, inhumane bully. He could be all of those things and more when he wished to be, but he never was to me. Never. I never saw that side of him.

"I know people thought me foolish and blind and stupid—even Lydda, my own wife, thought so. She tried to warn me about it many times, but of course, I never listened. I was a man and she merely a woman, so I tried to be patient with her foolishness, told her that she was wrong. Well, she wasn't, and I was the one who proved to be the fool."

He stopped and rode without speaking for a while, and Uther held his peace, knowing that he had not finished.

"You would like him, Uther. You would like him mightily, whether you choose to believe me or not. You would respond to him instantly and enjoy him thoroughly—until you saw through and beyond the living mask he had put on for his dealings with you. He wears a different mask for everyone. Even for me. And he deluded me so well, so damned completely, that for most of my life I would not believe he wore a mask at all, no matter who told me otherwise."

Uther turned himself in the saddle to face Lagan. "How could he be that way with you for so long and not thus with everyone else? And how could you not see beyond it?"

"How indeed?" Lagan screwed up his face and nodded his head, affirming his own thoughts on the question. "When he took my wife and son as hostages against my good behaviour, he lost me forever, but he and I had been close friends as children, and we remained close throughout our growing up. The Lot I loved was the Lot of our boyhood."

Uther grunted his disgust. "I met him when he was a boy, and he was a loathsome pig. I tried to kill him."

"I know, Ygraine told me about that. I remember how sick he was when he came home that year. He was shut up for weeks before they'd let me see him, and I never did find out what really happened. But Lot was fourteen by then, at least fourteen. When I speak of our boyhood, I mean the days when we were children, seven, eight, nine and ten years old . . . the days when we were yet innocent of blood, or adulthood, or sexual corruption. Boyhood, Uther—you must remember boyhood? Surely you had one too?"

Uther smiled, then sobered quickly. "Aye, I had. But you and I were changed by all of those same things, Lagan, and yet you and I are not crazed madmen, pulling our whole world down around our ears."

"That's true. But no matter how low we might think he has sunk, Lot retains a bottomless well of attractiveness and warmth that he can draw from anytime he wishes. And when he finds someone who can be of use to him, or someone who is in a position to provide him with some new benefit, or even someone he wants to influence to his own ends for some specific purpose, there seems to be no limit to the efforts he will make to win them to his way of thinking." Lagan grimaced at the thought. "I've watched him doing it for years, and believe me, he can be incredibly seductive and alluring when it comes to making people do what he wants them to do. He could coax honey from a hungry bear. But you can guess at what must happen time and again: those people who found themselves basking in the warmth and enthusiasm of his attention and approval one week would find themselves abandoned and ignored the next, when his directions changed. And being suddenly removed from light and warmth, then thrown back into the cold shadows among which they had lived before, they felt the cold more keenly, and the dimness of their former lives now seemed like darkness. Do you wonder they became bitter?"

"No. And yet I was thinking that Lot must be too clever to allow that kind of thing to happen, to permit people to think of him that harshly when there's no need for it. It is bad leadership . . . bad kingship. It's bad policy, from every viewpoint." Uther thought about that for a moment, and then dismissed the subject offhandedly. "But then, he's Lot of Cornwall, and he's insane."

Lagan barked a laugh.

Full darkness had fallen on them suddenly, between one word and the next, and both men reined in their mounts and turned in their saddles to look up at the moon, which now lay behind them over their left shoulders. It had vanished behind the edge of a large, fast-moving cloud that blocked out the surrounding stars, but as they sat staring it emerged from its trailing skirts to bathe the world once again in light. Lagan turned away and was making tutting sounds between his teeth, scanning the skies to the northeast.

"Storm coming in. That cloud was moving very quickly, and it's only the first. Look over there, it's as black as Hades. Perhaps we should ride a little faster."

"How much farther do we have to go?"

"Five miles. An hour's ride, the way we were going. We'll be wet long before then."

"Then let's shorten that hour while the light's good."

They kicked their mounts into motion again and prodded them into a canter, riding in silence as they adjusted to the increased speed and the changing shadows. They were on the high moors, and there were no trees or bushes to impede their progress, but both of them knew that the ground under their horses' hooves could be treacherous, strewn with loose stones and pitted in places with the holes of burrowing animals. After about a quarter of an hour of this, the horses began to breathe more heavily and their riders slowed them again to a walk. The sky overhead was still clear, save for the occasional small, unthreatening cloud. The massed storm banks in the northeast seemed to be moving very slowly, despite the speed of the first cloud that had covered the moon.

Uther had been thinking about what Lagan said, and now there was one question remaining in his mind, one point on which he had to be certain.

"Would you still be his friend if he came back and asked you to?"

Lagan glanced quickly at Uther and then shook his head decisively. "No. It's gone far beyond redemption now."

"And does Lot know that?"

It took a long time for Lagan to answer that, but eventually he looked up and shook his head. "No. He has no idea that I feel the way I do."

"Are you sure about that?"

Now Lagan snapped his head round in scorn and his voice was a rebuke. "Of course I am sure of that! Were it otherwise, I would be dead, and so would my whole family, from my father to my youngest nieces." He stopped short, clenching his eyes tight shut and scratching at one eyebrow with a fingertip, and when he opened his eyes and spoke again his voice was under control once more.

"I am forced to live a lie, you see, in order to save lives. Not my own—I care nothing for that—but . . . others. I tell you, my friend, you can have no idea how much pleasure it would give me to march into his presence, among all his swarming guards, and tell him what I really think of him and his perverted ways. But do you know the most sickening part of all of this?" He glanced at Uther and then shook his head, answering his own question. "The worst of all of this is that, even as he was having me hunted down and killed with all my clan, he would be feeling hurt and ill-used. The thing you have to understand about Lot is the strange self-love he has. In Lot's own mind, he has no flaws; he can do nothing wrong. It's always the other people in his life who betray him, one way or another. There is never any possibility at all that he might be at fault—What was that? Did you hear something?"

Uther stopped dead, standing up in his stirrups and leaning forward to throw the lower edge of his cloak forward over the head of his horse, blinding it. The animal had been trained to stand quietly and make no sound when covered thus.

"Something," he said. "Sounded like a shout, cut short."

"That's what I thought, too. Can you see anything?"

"No. Shut up and listen."

For a long space of moments there was nothing, and then, from the far side of a slight rise ahead of them, came a clink of metal on metal, followed a short time later by another.

Both men dismounted quickly, Uther dropping his reins to the ground, knowing that would stop his well-trained horse from moving away. He then wrapped his borrowed black cloak around him and moved forward towards the top of the small rise that Lagan was already climbing, bending low and finally crawling forward on his belly to where he could see beyond the crest.

The ground fell away steeply on the other side of the little knoll, stretching down to the deep, dry bed of what must once have been a fair-sized stream, and the entire watercourse, as far as they could see on either side, was choked with heavily armed men, moving from north to south. Directly ahead of where the two watchers lay, between them and the traffic, one man sat apart, being aided by a couple of others, and it soon became obvious that he must have been the one who had shouted out, because one of his companions was holding the man's leg tightly while the other was binding up his ankle, ignoring the muttered litany of curses that poured from his lips. Seeing the fellow squatting there with his leg extended in front of him, Uther thought again about the burrowing animals that abounded on these moors, and how dangerous their excavations were to nighttime travellers.

Their binding finished, the two men hauled their comrade to his feet and then each took one of his arms across their shoulders and led him away, limping heavily between them. Neither of the watchers even glanced at the other, but Uther sensed Lagan's head coming close to his own, and he leaned closer to him to listen.

"Don't know who these people are, but they could be Lot's own mercenaries," Lagan mouthed, his lips almost touching Uther's ear. "They're headed due south, to Tir Gwyn. Lot is to be there tomorrow. But I don't know why they would be marching secretly at night, or so soundlessly. Unless, of course, Lot has sent them ahead to ensure that Herliss is not plotting to surprise his King when the great man arrives."

Uther spoke from the corner of his mouth, his voice as low as Lagan's. "Who else could they be, do you know? I mean, could they be other than Lot's people?"

"No, not unless they're yours. They must be Lot's. And they're going south, so they are headed for Tir Gwyn. The Crag Fort is to the east, directly ahead of us, so they can't be going there. We'll simply have to stay here and wait for them to pass, but we'd better move off a bit."

"Should you not make some attempt to warn your father that they're coming?"

"Aye, and I will when we reach the Crag Fort. He is there waiting for us."

Uther nodded and they withdrew, making their way backwards until they felt it was safe to stand upright again. Then they returned to their horses and sat down by their feet.

A short time after that, a single, heavy drop of rain landed on Uther's ear. He glanced up at the sky, which had turned completely black, stood up and thrust his heavy helmet back onto his head, then wrapped his cloak completely around himself. A moment later the skies opened and the thundering of heavy raindrops on the metal helmet shut out every other sound in the world.

There was no point in trying to go anywhere. They stood there like statues, two men and two horses, and the deluge inundated them completely, so that they could not have been seen from more than five paces away. In all, seven flares of lightning lit up the darkness and revealed the black, empty land, obscured by driven lines of pelting rain, and then the worst of the storm passed over and the strength of the downpour abated slowly. Gradually, almost imperceptibly, the darkness lightened until the two men could see each other again, albeit dimly, and still they stood, waiting patiently for time to pass and for the rain to end.

When they moved forward slowly again, the river of men had vanished, as though the storm and the night had obliterated them. Uther's jaw was sore with biting down to keep his teeth from chattering, and he shuddered.

"Never mind," said Lagan. "We've still got a mile to go, but when we get to the Crag Fort they'll have firelight and warmth, and ale and roasted meat."

"Could we reach it in less than a mile if we move quickly?"

Lagan grinned and wiped a raindrop from the end of his nose with the back of his hand. "We might . . . they say there's a first time for everything."

THIRTY-TWO

"So, Lot has his hounds out coursing for my downfall."

Herliss was sitting close to the roaring fire in the main hall of the fortified hamlet known as the Crag Fort, and above his head the sloping roof of the building rose up into smoke-filled blackness. Ygraine, Queen of Cornwall, sat on the other side of the stone fireplace, flanked by two of her ladies. Uther sat on Herliss's right, so that Herliss was between him and the fire, and Lagan stood beside him. Behind Lagan's back the huge room was dark, save for an arrangement of iron candelabra that illuminated a table against the wall farthest from the fire.

"That's what it looked like to Lagan," Uther responded. "He assumed immediately that they were on their way to your White Fort, although he could not understand why they would need to be so secretive—"

"Not until I had thought about it for at least half a heartbeat," Lagan interjected. "Then it became clear. They are our King's men, going about his lawful affairs." His voice was heavy with irony, but it provoked only a half-smile from Uther.

"Anyway," Uther continued, "I could not tell where they were going or why. All I knew was that they weren't my men. That left me to assume that they were Lot's . . . Cornish in name and allegiance. And so I kept my head down." He glanced at Lagan to see if he had anything to add, but the Cornishman stood slightly hunched, staring into the flames and oblivious to what was being said for the time being. His arms were crossed on his chest, and in one hand he held a pot of ale.

Uther then looked directly at Herliss, taking care to avoid Ygraine's eyes. He was highly aware that she was staring at him, and he was afraid of looking back at her lest his face betray his thoughts and feelings to the others in the room. One of the two women sitting slightly behind the Queen was the Lady Dyllis, but the other was a stranger.

He and Lagan had arrived in the Crag Fort an hour earlier, and Uther was impressed by the way they had been received. The fort was strongly guarded, encircled by two separate lines of vigilant sentinels, the farthest of these about a hundred paces out from the walls and made up of pairs of guards, each pair posted some twenty paces from its neighbours on either side. The walled fort itself was small, its rectangular enclosure no greater than seventy-five, perhaps eighty paces to a side, but it was a strongly built affair, made from local stone, and Uther had identified it at first glance as a military installation, built hundreds of years earlier by the Romans to house regular patrols, or perhaps even a permanent garrison of approximately one hundred and twenty men and officers, that being the number of men in a maniple, the tactical fighting unit of a cohort. A tight cluster of guards had been on duty by the heavy, wooden main gates, and it had been evident from the outset that Lagan was expected, because no one had sought to question either him or his companion as they unsaddled their horses and left them to Herliss's stablehands before crossing the guard lines and entering the main fort. Uther had felt, going in, that no one even glanced at his face, but he had not permitted himself to believe it. He had simply accepted that Herliss's people, at least, were alert and knew what they were about, well prepared to safeguard their own part of Cornwall.

Once safely within the walls, Lagan had led Uther directly to the main building, a log structure that had once served as the headquarters building of the Roman garrison. It was the largest building in the enclosure and was surrounded by some half a score of smaller buildings, all built of logs around four or six supporting posts. About half of these, long and low, were evidently barracks, and others were plainly used for storage and maintenance and other utilitarian purposes. Several of the remaining buildings looked like substantial dwellings, and Uther had seen three, at least, that were connected to each other by enclosed walkways.

They found Herliss waiting for them in the main hall, and as they greeted each other Uther's eyes went immediately to the far wall, where a few household servants were loading food onto a table that already groaned beneath the profusion of dishes—hot, cold, flesh, fowl, fish, fruit, vegetable and bread—that lay piled upon it. Herliss explained that the Queen and her women would join them soon and had already been informed of their arrival. None of them had yet eaten, he added, the Queen having decided to await the arrival of their expected guests, and in consequence, everyone was hungry and impatient.

Herliss summoned one of his guards, who had been waiting to lead Uther to the quarters that had been assigned to him. There, Herliss explained, he would find a hot brazier and a selection of clean, dry clothing. Uther had begun to thank the old man when, without warning, Ygraine walked into the hall.

He managed to greet the Queen somehow and pay his respects to her women without betraying his absolute confusion, and then excused himself, dripping rainwater, to scurry away with his head down, following the guard who had been waiting for him. Once there, however, safely ensconced and alone, Uther felt under no constraint to hurry and change his clothes before rushing back to the hall where the others awaited him. Instead, he changed slowly, drying himself at leisure and luxuriating in the glow of the brazier as he dressed himself again in the clean, warm clothing that had been laid out for his use. And while he was doing so, he permitted himself for the first time since the arrival of Lagan Longhead in his camp to consider all the chaotic thoughts that had been going through his mind.

His first thoughts upon hearing Lagan's unexpected invitation had been of ambush and treachery, but those had been short-lived. Lagan had been wearing Uther's own ring, as arranged between Uther himself and Ygraine, and Uther could think of no circumstances that might have induced Ygraine to give up that secret to anyone else. Not even Herliss had been privy to that arrangement. And so he had accepted Lagan's invitation at face value. From the moment of that decision, however, he had been forced to reflect upon the feelings that he held for Ygraine. It had been many months since he had last seen the Cornish Queen, and the bare truth was that it had been an equally long time since he had thought of her to any degree.

Only now, in the privacy of this strange chamber with its welcome brazier, did he admit to himself that he had been intrigued by the thought of seeing her again—and to be truthful, a voice in his mind said, of bedding her again. As the thought occurred to him, he turned his head and looked at the bed, a substantial affair that was raised high off the floor on solid legs and covered with a wealth of rich bedding. It was a sturdy, solid bed, made for everything a man could require of it, and he smiled to himself.

The simple sight of her, her welcoming smile, had blinded him. Her radiance and beauty had almost rocked him physically with the force of its impact. Stunned by the instantaneous awareness that he had been able to forget how beautiful she was, he had hesitated momentarily in mid-step as he moved to greet her, feeling his eyes go wide and knowing that he was betraying far more than was wise. He had been consumed instantly and utterly by the red, fire-lit glory of her hair seen from fifteen paces distant and by the forgotten brilliance of her great green eyes in the startling whiteness of her flawless face. And then the memory of her smooth, bare hip beneath his hand had caused an explosion in his chest, bringing his heart up into his throat and snatching the breath away from him. He remembered the weight of her, defenceless and abandoned in his arms, pulling him down as he lowered his head to kiss that generous, laughing mouth with its wide, full, soft lips.

When he had found himself face to face with her, gazing into her smiling eyes, he had thought he might never be able to find words with which to greet her properly, but words came to him and he had muttered something that aroused neither comment nor surprise from her or from anyone else. He had felt her fingers close warmly over his own and had known beyond doubt that she was even happier to see him than he was to see her, but he could think of nothing to say or do other than to bend forward, slip one arm around her pliant waist and sink his face into the silken warmth of her soft neck. And even as that thought filled his mind, he had imagined the gentle breeze of her warm breath in his ear, and his throat had closed completely with lust and embarrassment. Ygraine, however, had seemed to notice nothing amiss and looked away from him, still smiling, to say something to Herliss. Awkward and fumbling and tongue-tied, he had been grateful for the excuse to flee to his quarters, where he might find time and opportunity to overcome this unaccustomed panic. He had managed to be pleasant, he knew, to the Lady Dyllis and to her companion, whose name was Roman, Lydia, and he knew, too, that he had eventually managed to escape without making an utter fool of himself.

He recalled now hearing his Uncle Publius speaking years before about being thunderstruck—the awestruck love of an adolescent boy for a beautiful woman whom he has seen for the first time. But he was no adolescent youth, and this was no first-time encounter: he was Uther Pendragon, King of the Pendragon Federation of south Cambria, and he had lain with this woman months earlier. How, then, could he have been so dumbfounded at the sight of her? The truth was disconcerting and confusing, and by the time he had returned to the main hall he was still less than fully prepared to meet the Cornish Queen with equanimity, face to face, eye to eye.

Lagan was already there, and when Uther arrived they gathered around the dining table. There was no formality in the seating arrangements, save that the Queen's two women sat together at one end of the table and Ygraine herself sat at the head. Uther approached the table as eagerly as anyone, for he had eaten very little since the previous night and was sharp set with hunger.

Only when the edges had been chewed from their appetites did conversation begin, and then it was desultory, confined to mundane things, until Uther asked Herliss to tell him about how the Queen's party had managed their "escape" and their eventual homecoming.

It had been a simple matter, Herliss began. After Uther's departure with Popilius Cirro and the main body of the raiding party, the skeletal force left behind to guard the camp and look after the remaining prisoners had remained at high alert for twenty-four hours and had then relaxed. The night after that, the escape plan had been put into effect. Once the remaining guards had been "overcome" by Nemo's crew, the escapees had made their way out of the valley without difficulty and had managed to win safely back to Lot's main base at Golant within a matter of days. Nemo's group had remained with them for two days and had then left them close by the sea coast, in the professed hope of finding a ship that would carry them to Gaul. None of the Queen's party had thought the fleeing group would survive to reach foreign shores, but they had made no move to interfere with Nemo's intentions. What was far more important was that none of the Queen's bodyguard, including their leader, Alasdair Mac Iain, had thought to question any aspect of the affair, and all of them were convinced that they owed their safety and their lives to Herliss and his loyalty and ingenuity. They truly believed, the old man told Uther, that their captors would have killed them sooner or later rather than set them free. All of them had seen the other Cornish prisoners being marched away under guard, never to return.

Uther sniffed when he heard that. "Did any of the others ever return here?"

Herliss grunted. "Aye, well, the false Queen, Morgas, and the rest of the Queen's women were brought back quickly enough once your messengers had delivered your instructions to Camulod to set them free and return them to their homeland. They were here within a matter of two weeks, I would say. Some of your people from Camulod rode with them as escorts and then sent word to Lot that they could be collected from the edges of his land. By the time Lot's people arrived to meet the women, the Camulod troops had gone."

Uther nodded. "Good, that was as I instructed. But I was not speaking of the women. I was wondering about those other warriors of yours . . . the people we set free up on the moors?"

Old Herliss turned to him with a raised eyebrow. "You loosed nigh on a hundred and twenty men—six score, all of them mine. None of them was ever reported seen again."

Uther's forehead was creased in perplexity. "Are you saying they all vanished?"

"Apparently so. Lot pronounced them dead, telling the world they had been foully murdered by you while you held them prisoner, their deaths attested to by the members of the Queen's own body-guard. None of the missing men had any names, you see . . . at least none that were known and reported to Lot's people. Tragic loss . . . it could have created havoc among my own people here in the south, had not the gap they left been quickly filled. Six score newcomers came wandering into my lands about that time, can you believe that? They even set up house among my folk, adopting and consoling the widows and families of the men who had been killed in captivity."

"That was most amazingly fortunate."

"It was . . . Miraculous, if you really think about it . . ."

Uther glanced around the table and found that everyone was smiling, including the young woman Lydia. He found himself able to look straight at Ygraine now and direct his next question to her. "So tell me, lady, if you will, about your King's reception of the news that you yet lived and had escaped?"

Still smiling, Ygraine looked at Herliss, motioning for him to continue, and he spoke up immediately.

"He took it very well, considering all that he had done to prevent it. As I said at the outset, we went directly from your encampment to his stronghold at Golant, which was, in fact, much closer to where we were than was my own fort of Tir Gwyn, and when we arrived there we found Lot was expected to arrive the following day. That was surprising, for I had anticipated that he might be up on the north-ern coast, supervising the building of his new fortress at Rosnant."

"Rosnant?" Uther sat up straight. "Lot has a new fortress? When did this come into being?"

Herliss scratched at his beard. "Well, it didn't come into being—the place has always been there. Perhaps you've heard of it as Tin-tagel? The local people call it that." Seeing Uther's head shake, he glanced wide-eyed at his son, who said nothing. "Well," Herliss con-tinued, "it's a natural, impregnable fortress, completely safe from attack—sits on a spur of land attached to the mainland by only a tiny, impassable causeway that would give a goat trouble and could be defended by a single blind man. Can't be captured by a frontal attack, 'cause it can't be reached. Can't be invested and can't be starved out, because it's surrounded on all sides by the sea. And it can't be attacked from the sea, either, because the cliffs are too high. Supplies can be landed there and carried up the cliffs to feed the defenders, but no attacking force could ever climb up there. Impossible."

Lagan leaned forward and spoke for the first time. "I don't think you need to worry about Rosnant, Uther. It's a defensive place, a place for a last stand. Lot can't be touched there, true, but he can't touch you from there, either. And if he should try to escape by sea, he'll have to keep going until he reaches Gaul or some other land, for there will be no place for him to land here again. The people will back you against him. There is a sickness in our land and its name is Gulrhys Lot. People will go to any lengths to be cured of it, believe me."

"But what about the mercenaries? Seems to me there are more of those in Cornwall than there are Cornishmen."

Herliss spoke up again. "You might be right there, but they are Outlanders, and in the fight for our own lands, our folk will win. Of course, you will assist us."

"I will? When?"

"Wherever and whenever it is possible, I presume, since we both seek the same end."

Uther decided that he did not yet want to pursue that. "Tell me about this other place, his stronghold, Golant. It's north of here, is it not?"

"Well, more east than north, but aye, it lies above us some thirty miles along the coast. What do you want to know about it?"

"What kind of place it is . . . how strong. Is it takeable?"

"By siege, you mean? I doubt it. It's one of the old circular enclosures built before the Romans came. Two earth ramparts, one inside the other with a ditch between. Main entrance in the east. There the inner rampart remains circular, with a simple gate leading to the central enclosure, but the outer ring extends eastward and becomes more pointed, like an egg-shape, making a space, entirely surrounded by high ramparts, that can be used to amass forces for a raid outside the gates, or to contain and slaughter any enemies who might get by the first, outer gates."

"This outer gate, is it hinged?"

Herliss blinked for a moment in confusion, but then he realized what Uther was asking him and his face cleared. "You mean like a door might have hinges? No, it's not a gate in that sense. It has no doors. In order to understand that, you have to begin with the rampart, the outer wall. D'you know the Roman measurement they call a *pes?*"

"Aye, it's supposed to be the length of a tall man's foot. We don't use it but I know what it means."

Herliss grinned. "We use it all the time now. The old Duke started using it first. He said it made more sense than trying to describe every distance in terms of paces, and since I've become used to using it myself, I agree with him. A hundred paces for a man's a lot farther than the same hundred paces for a boy, but a foot's an understandable unit to both of them. Anyway, the outer rampart measures thirty-five to forty feet thick. It stands about six feet high, too, with a twelve-foot-deep ditch in front of it that measures another twenty-two feet from edge to edge. The gate, then, is a narrow passageway, walled with wood and no more than six feet across at its widest point. It runs the full width of the rampart wall—that makes it thirty-five to forty feet long—and the ramparts on both sides are built up like flanking towers, with bridges stretching over the passageway from side to side. Anyone entering the place has to come in through that passage, and for anyone unwelcome, it's a long way." He paused. "The only other possibility is to fight your way across the outer ditch and up the incline to the top of the rampart. If you get across that, you've another ditch and another rampart to go before you reach the enclosure, and may the gods of war and fortune be on your side, because you'll need them."

"Is the other ring, the inner one, the same size as the first?"

"Not quite. It's completely circular but slightly narrower—say, twenty-two feet thick. The same kind of passageway, however, lined with wood and overlooked by defenders on both sides and on bridges above. The inner circle, the living space inside the walls, is about two hundred and fifty feet from side to side, a good hundred paces no matter how you count it." He sat quietly then, gazing at

Uther and continuing to scratch at his beard with one fingertip. "Why are you so interested in Lot's defences? Are you thinking of attacking them?"

Uther laughed and shook his head. "No, not at all, but I like to know what I'm up against at all times. If we drive the man into hiding, I'd like to know the odds against keeping him there or winkling him out again." He looked back to where Lagan sat listening. "I ought to have asked you sooner . . . your wife and son are well?"

Lagan nodded, "Aye, they are, and safe at home again."

Uther was unable to hide his surprise. "You leave them at home? I would have thought you'd keep them within sight of you at all times now." He knew before the words had left his mouth that they were tactless, but it was too late to recall them. Lagan, however, took no offence, but merely shook his head.

"Here in Cornwall, things are not always what they seem. In fact it is safer for me to leave my family unprotected than to keep them close by me."

"What my son means," Herliss growled, "is that Lot's madness grows more and more extreme from day to day. But as long as Lagan can willingly leave his wife and child open to the threat of Lot's displeasure, then Lot will believe that Lagan cannot possibly be plotting against his King. The truth, of course, concealed in openness from Lot's blind eyes, is that Lydda and Cardoc are better protected at any time of the day or night than is Lot himself. At the first sign of a threat to either of them, Lot's world will come crashing down onto his shoulders and his cursed head will spin on the ground between his feet. In the meantime, however, Lagan is left free to do as he wills: to go and find you, for example, and bring you here to meet with us, because Lot could never dream that anyone might be sufficiently courageous or foolish to plot against him while his loved ones are vulnerable to his venom."

"Good," Uther grunted. "How then do we destroy this pestilence, and when?"

"We have a plan for that." This was Ygraine. "That is why I decided to send for you. Herliss, will you explain our strategy to King Uther?"

Uther held up his hand. "Wait!" He looked directly at the woman sitting beside Dyllis, the one called Lydia, and then turned his gaze back to the Queen. "Lady Ygraine," he said, "I trust that no one will be grossly offended here, but I enforce a policy among my own people that I have found to be sound. We never speak of future plans or secret things when there are ears around belonging to people we do not know well enough to trust." He pointed at the woman Lydia. "I do not know this young woman here, and until I feel far more at ease here in Lot's country, I will take no other person's word, not even yours or Lord Herliss's here, on her behalf or on behalf of any other stranger." He half turned towards the astounded Lydia and nodded to her. "Forgive me, lady, but every word I say might well win back to Gulrhys Lot."

The young woman rose to her feet, pale-faced, and bowed formally to the Queen and then to the rest of the group before turning and gliding from the hall. As she did so, Dyllis did the same, after asking the Queen's permission to retire and pointing out that there was no real need for her to remain. Ygraine nodded and watched as Dyllis hurried after her companion, and as soon as she was out of sight, the Queen turned to Uther.

"That seemed excessive, King Uther."

Herliss saved him the trouble of replying. "Nonsense, child, Uther's absolutely right." The old man's voice was the rumble of an aged bear newly wakened from his winter sleep. "When that whoreson can force my own son to come against his father in fear for his son's life, then nobody can trust a soul. The girl might weep because her feelings are hurt, but she'll get over it. If that's the greatest pain she ever has to suffer through, she'll live to see her grandchildren through several generations."

Uther was looking about him again. "How can you safeguard against betrayal here? There must be half a hundred people, counting all your guards. I assumed the place would be empty and abandoned, but you marched me into this place in plain view of all your men, and we have been surrounded by people ever since I first arrived. Any or all of them could be in Lot's pay."

Herliss had sat nodding as Uther spoke and now he smiled and shrugged.

"I am not so stupid as you would think me, nor am I as foolishly trustful." He waved one hand around, indicating their surroundings. "Everyone here, each living soul, has been betrayed and savaged by Lot's treachery. Some have lost loved ones, family and friends; others have been dispossessed and banished; many have been tortured and mutilated; while others have been merely robbed and beaten. But I will swear to you, there is not a person here who would ever consider betraying us, or anything heard or seen here, to Gulrhys Lot. I have staked all our lives on that."

Uther gazed at the older man for several moments and then nodded in acquiescence. "Very well, then, tell me about this plan of yours."

The plan, as dreamed up by Ygraine and laid out by Herliss, was simple and straightforward, and it was predicated upon the likelihood of Lot's continuing to import mercenaries from beyond the seas. There were thousands of mercenaries currently in Cornwall. Herliss could not name the number, but he said it was enormous, and he was insistent, calling on Lagan to agree with him, that there would be thousands more by the following year. Lot had no shortage of armed men, the veteran commander pointed out, and that meant that he had no real need to concern himself with the loyalty or the disposition of his native Cornish troops. He believed that the superior numbers of his imported minions nullified any threat that might arrive from his own people, and so he grew increasingly arrogant, offending all his own noblemen and warriors. But he seemed amazingly unaware that he sorely lacked good leaders, generals and strategists to employ all his imported mercenaries to advantage.

Lagan interjected at this point to explain that the reason for the lack of leaders was not hard to find, since Lot had routinely cut down and isolated any and every leader among his own Cornish people whom he had seen as a potential threat to his own rule.

He had a few able leaders in his camp, nonetheless, Herliss pointed out, and he named Cerdic and Tewdric, the two Germanic leaders with whom Uther had come face to face the day of the great storm, along with a pair of others called Issa and Loholt, who preferred to fight alone, commanding their own armies and beholden to no one other than their nominal commander, Gulrhys Lot. Apart from those four, there was no one else, unless one wished to include two Cornish generals called Cuneglas and Ralla, who were sufficiently useless to have avoided the King's jealousy and sufficiently spineless for him to believe that he could still rely upon their loyalty. Lot had no other able generals, and that was a truth that cried out to be exploited, because the jealousy among the six tied Lot's hands most of the time. All of them saw themselves as supreme commanders, and none was willing to be seen as subservient to any other.

Uther was frowning as he listened to that. How, he asked, did that benefit him or any of them in any practical way? Herliss's response was flat and brusque.

"Lot is planning to invade your territories early in the spring by sea and by land at the same time, in the hope of catching you before you can strike south and keeping you tied down where you are. The sea invasion will hit your lands in Cambria, and it will hit hard, beginning at Carmarthen, where there are beaches for landing men and wharves for landing supplies and provisions. From Carmarthen they'll strike eastward, following the main Roman road along the coast towards Caerdyff. They intend to use the road itself as a base line and to use the existing ruins of the old Roman marching forts, consolidating their advances as they go and then launching co-ordinated raids unto your northern territories as they progress eastward. This will be a large army . . . probably the biggest invading force ever to hit your shores. The generals Cerdic and Tewdric, the two co-operators, will lead that host and hold responsibility for Cambria."

Uther made no response to this. It was evident to him that he was listening to truth and he knew it would have been pointless to interrupt. Instead, he listened, absorbing every nuance of what Herliss was saying.

The old man paused, obviously considering the words he would say next. "About Lot's mercenary Outlanders . . . the countryside is crawling with the foreign filth, as you saw last night on your way in. They are everywhere, and no one's life is safe, since Lot believes no one in his beloved Cornwall really loves him, although I can't imagine where he would find grounds for believing that . . .

"The thing is, they believe they are invincible, these Outlanders, because they have never been challenged in Cornwall." He stopped and reconsidered that. "Well, they have been challenged by your people on several occasions, but never in real strength, and they have never been really thrashed . . . If you are interested, I could provide you with an opportunity to thrash them within the next few days."

Uther frowned. "What does that mean?"

"It means I'm offering you the opportunity to destroy an army immediately, at little risk to yourself. A large contingent of mercenaries, almost a thousand strong, will be leaving the far northwest to come down this way in three days' time, four at the very latest. Nominally, they will be under the command of Cuneglas, which means they'll be under no control at all and therefore easy to deal with. Their line of march will bring them very close to where your raiding force sits now, and it transpires that the place where you could meet them is perfectly fashioned for an entrapment using those long, lethal bows of yours. It's a killing ground. Interested?"

"Of course, but you want me to burn down your fort here within the next few days . . . I can't do both."

"No matter." The old man smiled. "I'll burn it myself and lay the blame on you. As long as you are interested, we will talk later, and by the time you leave tomorrow you'll know everything there is to know about the Outlanders, the route they'll take and the place where you can set your trap." Herliss paused then, frowning, and asked the next question in his mind. "What of your Cousin Merlyn? How is he?"

Uther fought to keep his face expressionless and his voice casual. "Merlyn? He is well enough. He was badly wounded last summer, and it left him incapacitated for long months, but he improves daily now and will be himself come the new year. Why do you ask?"

"Because that's not what Lot's spies have been telling him. They have brought word that Merlyn of Camulod has lost his mind . . . that he was struck down last year by a metal ball swung on a chain and has not been right in the head since then. They say his skull was broken and his memory dashed from his mind so that now he does not even know his own name. They say he'll never lead the armies of Camulod again, and that in fact he never leaves the fortress nowadays . . . and they say he cannot even remember the name of his own wife. How much of that is true, Uther?"

Uther sat straighter, looking from Herliss to Lagan and finally to Ygraine. Then he nodded his head, once, acknowledging the truth. "All of it," he said. "It's all true. But it is not as bad as it sounds. He could regain his memory at any time, and there's nothing wrong with him physically. He's as strong and as skilled as he ever was."

"Aye, but he is not himself, is that not so? And so who has taken his place as Commander of Camulod?"

"No one . . . or no one in particular. We have several excellent senior officers, any one of whom is capable of commanding all our forces at any time."

"Good. Are any of them as good as Merlyn was?"

Uther hesitated, unwilling to lie and mentally reviewing the list of candidates for the supreme leadership in Merlyn's place. Before he could respond, Herliss was speaking again.

"Aye . . . that's what I thought. Well, they're going to have to be, because those other two whoresons, Issa and Loholt, have convinced Lot to allow them to carry out a two-pronged attack on Camulod, from the south and the east. Now understand me clearly here. I'm not talking about a two-pronged attack by a split force, I am talking about two separate attack campaigns by two separate armies. Issa and Loholt are as jealous of each other as a pair of spitting whores, and each of them knows that the first army to enter Camulod will have not just the pick of the booty but all of it, so the competition to sack Camulod is going to be fierce. The only compromise those two have made to each other at this stage is to agree to spin a coin in order to decide which of them will have the southern attack and which the east. The southern route to Camulod is shorter, but the other army will leave a week ahead of the southern attackers. We'll see what happens."

"What happens if the earlier army steals the southern route? What then?"

"What then indeed? I wouldn't be surprised to see that happen, particularly if Issa wins the toss. There's not much to choose between those two, but I think I might take Loholt's word before I'd trust Issa's. Anyway, that is enough from me on that topic. You must have some questions."

Uther rose from his chair and began pacing the floor. "Aye, a hundred of them. You said you had a plan of some description, but all you've done is tell me that I won't be here at all next year, because I'll be too busy staving off catastrophe in Cambria and Camulod. I must be missing something."

"You're missing nothing except, as you said, the connections. You know now that these invasions are planned, and you know where they'll be coming from, particularly in your own lands in Cambria, so you have the entire winter to prepare some surprises for the invaders. Will that be long enough for you? Can you be ready in time, think you?"

"To defeat them in Cambria, aye. The terrain there is mine, and the advantage will be mine, but—" An image flashed into Uther's mind of Camulod and the huge, barren drilling plain that lay at the foot of its hill. He saw Herliss's expression sharpen as the old man noticed the expression on his face, and then he nodded. "Aye," he grunted, "and in Camulod, too, now that I think of it. I have an idea that might work well . . . and as you say, we have six months at least, perhaps seven, in which to make ready. We'll be prepared to welcome them with more than milk and honey when they come . . . So what are the connections that I'm missing?"

"Numbers, Uther. We spoke of four of Lot's good generals going into your lands. He has six, you may remember."

"Four good ones and two others, the two incompetents you mentioned earlier . . . Ralla, and I forget the name of the other one."

"Cuneglas. Neither of them is fit to be allowed to go to the latrine alone, but they will remain behind in Cornwall to organize the remaining holding army. Theirs will be the honour of keeping Cornwall safe for Gulrhys Lot."

"And?"

"And by the time you have drawn first blood from those invading you, and they begin to learn that all might not be quite as simple as they had foreseen, we—myself and my son here, with the able help of the decent men left in this country—will have taken control of the forces of Cornwall . . . the *real* forces of Cornwall. Most of the mercenaries will be in Cambria and Camulod, because none of them will want to stay behind when there's booty and plunder to be had. The forces that remain behind will be Cornish, with perhaps a strengthening core of Outlanders. We'll soon be rid of those, and of Ralla and Cuneglas. And if, with the blessings of the gods, Lot has remained in Cornwall, we'll rid ourselves of him at the same time, and most of our troubles will be over. I doubt, though, that our noble King will run the risk of staying here at home when all his mercenary allies are away. That might be too much to hope for.

"Then, my friend . . . then everything will depend on you, because if you do your part properly and break your attackers' teeth in the first charge, you should be able to have your forces ready to combine as soon as you've thrown back the invaders—in both places, Cambria and Camulod. If you've hit them hard enough, if you've taken enough advantage of your advance warning, you should have taken the wind out of their sails to a great extent, and when you finally send them limping home, they'll find their strongholds there are held by a determined enemy. You must follow hard on their heels then, harassing them with the biggest army you can muster. With us holding Lot's forts and denying them entry, and you and your cavalry and those wild bowmen of yours hacking and shooting at their backs, we should be able to smash them finally, and get rid of Gulrhys Lot. What say you?"

"What say I? I say I'd be a fool to say anything before thinking all of this through. Where does your information come from?"

Herliss shrugged slightly and shifted in his seat, opening one hand, palm upward, and then gesturing towards the Queen. Uther sat blinking, not having expected that, and Ygraine turned her eyes to meet his gaze directly, the slightest tinge of colour beginning to stain her cheeks.

Finally, after what seemed to him like an unconscionably long time, he was able to clear his throat and speak to her. "I, ah . . . Ph'hmmm . . . Are you so far . . . ?" He stopped short, feeling a great, threatening panic begin to well up deep inside him, and then he charged ahead, blurting out what was in his mind. "Are you then so far restored into your husband's favour, lady, that you enjoy his confidence again?"

Ygraine stared back at him without expression, her face filled with utter calm. "No, Sir King, not again. I never knew his confidence in times past. I have come to know it now since my return from your captivity. I do not enjoy it. But was that not the reason for my return in the first place?"

"What?" Uther caught himself frowning and knew he was treading upon dangerous ground, although he would have been hard put to say why that should be so. He coughed again, desperately trying to gain time, then decided openness might be the best policy here. "Your pardon, Lady Ygraine, but I fail to understand you. Was *what* not the reason for your return in the first place?"

"My husband's confidence. Did I not return in order that I might make myself privy to his secrets, and did not that entail that I must work to gain his confidence? For if it did not, sir, then I have sorely misunderstood my reasons for being here these past few months and I will not be happy, knowing that I need not have been here."

"Yes, lady, yes! I ask your pardon, I misunderstood . . . but—"

"But—what, sir?"

"I—" He raised a hand in surrender, shaking his head ruefully. "Now I really do ask that you pardon me, my lady, for only now have I begun to see what we have asked of you since your return to Cornwall. My own stupidity in failing to see the truth of it appalls me now and I—"

"King Uther!" Ygraine's voice, crackling like heaving ice, cut him short. "I knew what was involved from the beginning, and I did not think it worthy of mention then . . . I find it even less worthy now."

Uther fell into an abashed silence, chastened as he had seldom been, and for a space of moments no one spoke. But then, surprisingly,

Herliss heaved himself to his feet and gestured with his head for his son to join him.

"Come, you," he growled, "we need to talk, we two."

Uther sat gaping as the two Cornish warriors left the hall, and then he turned to the Queen, surprised to find her smiling at him. He knew his mouth was hanging open, but he could only wave one pointing finger towards the far door through which Herliss and Lagan had vanished.

"He knows? Herliss knows?"

"About you and me?" Ygraine's smile grew wider. "I think not, but I cannot be sure. Herliss is no fool, and he is older than you and I combined, so he outstrips us in experience. Besides, he knows I have no love for Lot, despite the matter of sharing his bed. Herliss is highly aware of my pretences there."

"But he . . . approves."

"No, he does not approve, Uther. He resents the need for it. Herliss is a noble and honourable man, and it angers him deeply that I should be forced to stoop to such measures. But he is unable to do anything other than accept the need for what I do, as do I myself. If what I endure leads to a quick end to Lot's rule in Cornwall and to all the evil that walks hand in hand with him, then I will do all that I can and more."

"May I ask you a question that might anger you?"

"Yes."

"Do you wish Lot dead?"

Ygraine sucked in her cheeks, tilting her head slightly to one side as she considered her response. "No," she said eventually, drawing the word out to far beyond its normal length, "I have no wish to see him dead. I believe he will die before all this is over, because he will cling tooth and nail to everything we seek to take from him, but I have no personal wish to deprive him of his life. My wish is to remove him from the King's place he abuses, to strip him of his power and wealth; without the one he will forfeit the other. I want to see Cornwall emptied of foreign mercenaries and ruled by men who understand honour and justice, so that its people can sleep quiet and safe in their beds night after night until they forget that there was a time when they could not. That is what I want and what I wish, and it involves removing Lot, deposing him. After that, I care not what he does or where he goes.

"He can be charming when it suits him." Her voice dripped with bitterness and quiet anger. "When Gulrhys Lot wishes to be pleasant, he is unmatchable . . . and he has been that way with me since my return. Invariably. Since the day I arrived back, he has been unfailingly gracious, concerned and attentive to my every need, even admitting me nightly to his bed as though I were his beloved wife and the crowning pride of his life . . .

"I discovered the reason for that change soon after my arrival. My brother Connor had come to visit Lot, asking after me, while I was your prisoner . . . shortly before I came back here, in fact. Lot has no wish to offend Connor, or my other brother, Brander." She was smiling very slightly as she said this. "My father's people live upon the seacoast, in large part. They are boat-builders, renowned throughout all Eire for the quality of their galleys. My father commands galleys—fleets of galleys. My brothers, Connor and Brander, are his admirals. Lot prides himself on being a commander of pirates, but he knows my brothers could sweep the sea clean of every craft he owns if he offended them.

"Before I returned from my captivity, my adventure with you, Connor came seeking me at Rosnant. I was not there, of course, but I know that what frightened Lot—and it really frightened him, for some reason—was the fact that he could not tell Connor where I was. He could not even lie about it, lest Connor insist on travelling to find me. I have no idea what was said between the two of them, but I know it must have made a deep impression upon Lot, for since the moment I appeared again, he has been lavishing me with attention, catering to my every wish and generally trying to be the most adoring and attentive of husbands."

"So you are sleeping with him . . ."

"Aye, I am." Her head came up high, her eyes flashing. "And even rutting with him, but not often . . . I told him I would kill him as he slept if he ever dared use me again the way he did when we two first were wed."

"What?" Uther sat straighter. "What did he do?"

"Nothing that you need know about, and he would never dare try it again. But here is something you *should* know about. I went into his bed without protest when I returned because I thought I might be with child by you. I was not, but I thought I might have been."

"But it was but two nights!"

"*One* time is enough, Uther Pendragon, if it is the destined time. Surely you are old enough to know the truth of that?"

"And . . ." He cleared his throat and tried again. "Were you . . . would you have been unhappy to find yourself with child?"

"I don't know, because I never really had to dwell upon the thought. My courses came in their due time and life went on. But in the meantime, Lot had been close enough to me to guarantee that if my belly did begin to swell, he could call himself the sire, and that suited me well. Little point in dying for something so fleeting as the time we two had together, don't you think?"

Uther frowned, unsure of how he ought to answer that, and as he wondered, he heard the sounds of Herliss and Lagan returning. Ygraine spoke quickly into the silence between them, lowering her voice.

"I've placed you in a room apart from everyone, but close enough to mine to be reachable. Does that please you?"

His heart leaped in his chest. "Yes, it does. How will I find your room, and when?"

"Be content. I'll come to you. I know the way and none will see or hear me. Now let's talk of other things."

Uther turned his head slightly and saw that Herliss and Lagan were bringing another person with them, this one a tall, robed figure carrying a harp of some description beneath one arm, a harp, Uther thought, that was smaller than any he had seen before.

"Look what we found," Herliss shouted. "Anrac is here! It's been more than six years since last he came and sang his songs for us, and here he is, appeared from nowhere, when we have dire need of a bard's songs and music."

In the bustle of greeting the tall Druid, the entire tenor of the gathering changed, and as the man was tuning his harp and preparing to

play for them, Ygraine sent a messenger to summon Dyllis and Lydia
to join them again and share in the entertainment. The fire was stoked
up, the candles and lamps renewed and replenished, the servants were
invited to come in and listen, and for the following few hours, the hall
rang with music.

THIRTY-THREE

Some time in the middle of the night, they woke each other up and made love for a fourth, or perhaps a fifth time. They were in no rush now, voluptuous in their enjoyment of each other, delighting mutually in the gradual and deliberate buildup of pleasure that would eventually become intolerable, but in the building was indescribable. They luxuriated in the warmth and softness of the bed and in the intimacy of their coupling, and when it was over, Ygraine moaned softly with contentment and rolled onto her back, snuggling her bottom into Uther's lap, the back of one thigh draped comfortably over his waist. He adjusted himself to her movement, rolling inwards voluptuously with a slow thrust of his pelvis towards her centre, scissoring one knee up along her left leg and bringing an arm around to hook his elbow behind her upraised right knee, clasping her thigh's heavy firmness tightly and pulling her knee up to his shoulder, unwilling to risk falling away from her embrace, and they lay together in companionable silence, each aware that the other was awake. Neither felt any urge to speak.

They had spoken for hours, earlier, first in the public forum of the discussions around the dinner table, around the fire after that, and then in private, face to face and mouth to mouth when she had first come to his bed some time far in advance of midnight. Now, lying together, they each had their own thoughts, and neither felt any compulsion to share them with the other, or to communicate in any way apart from the physical sensations that still joined them.

It was Uther who spoke first, running an open hand along her thigh. "I'm glad you sent for me, lady."

"Hmm, so am I . . ."

"But why did you? Send for me, I mean . . . If you had gone so far as to trust Lagan with this task, then you could easily have entrusted him with your tidings, too."

"I could have, but I wanted to tell them to you in person." She stirred slightly, then paused before asking, "Do you mean you had no thought that I might simply want to see you for yourself? For my own benefit?"

"No . . . I suppose I didn't think you would take such a risk for purely selfish reasons."

"What better reason could a woman have in summoning a man? In very truth, though, since you are so forthright in stating your opinions, I sent for you because . . ."

The silence was so long that he had to prompt her, impatient with waiting, not knowing whether he was being teased or not. "Because what?"

"Because I *could*. I was on my way, and it had taken me months to arrange to come here to the only place in this entire land where I could meet with you in safety without being afraid that we would be taken and you slaughtered."

"You would have been slaughtered too."

"I would have made the trade willingly enough." She hesitated, then resumed in a more sombre tone. "No, that's not true. Lot would not dare to kill me now, not after that last confrontation with my brother. It would mean an end to him, were I to disappear for any reason, and he's far too careful of himself to risk that."

"I see, but still you would gladly have taken the risk of dying, would you? Am I that wondrous?"

"Come here." She twisted her body backwards and down somehow, and he rose up to meet her and she kissed him deeply, the scent of her hair filling his awareness, overwhelming everything else. When she would have pulled away again, however, he held her to him and whispered into her ear, "So, what will you do now if we have made a child this time?"

"I'll cherish it and love it and raise it as a son of mine and yours."

"But you would not tell Lot."

"No, d'you take me for a complete fool? That kind of vengeance would be self-destructive. He would simply kill the child and be amply revenged on both of us, me and you . . . not because of jealousy, but simply because he does not want to hear such things."

She felt him stiffen slightly in the bed beside her. "Yes, well, *no* man would want to hear such things."

"Of course not, but in Lot's case, it is more than doubly true. I believe my husband is not capable of siring children, and I am glad of it from the bottom of my being. It makes me suspect that the Christians might be right, and that there is a wise, just and allknowing God who looks out for all people."

It was pitch-black where they lay, unrelieved by any speck of light, but she knew he had turned his head and was looking at her. "What do you mean when you say he cannot sire children? Didn't you say you lay with him to lull his suspicions in the first place?"

"Aye, I did. He is more than capable of rutting—goes at it like a stallion. But that does not mean that he's capable of getting sons."

"Oh, come, Ygraine, of course it does!"

"No, it does not!"

"Yes, it does! If he were unable to do it . . . if he could not . . . stand or perform, I might agree with you, but by your own admission he can do the deed."

"But that means nothing, Uther, nothing at all." He could hear the bewilderment in her voice as she continued. "Or is it—? Do you think—? Surely you do not believe that only women can be barren. Is that it? What about his other wives, then, the ones before me? He had three of them, you know, and they're all still alive. Do you believe that all three of them were barren? Do you?"

Uther lay silent, offering no contribution.

"Well, if you do think that, then you must also believe in strange coincidences, for the one begets the other, if you but stop to think on it. Two of those barren women have had children since leaving him."

Still Uther remained quiet, making no attempt to speak or to criticize.

"I have lain with him for months, and I was sick with fear, throughout much of that time, of getting with child by him. But it has not happened, and it has not been for lack of effort on his part. I think my brother must have convinced him that a son and heir would be looked upon with great favour in my father's lands in Eire. Be that as it may, however, he has achieved nothing in the way of quickening my womb, and so I have been speaking to the mothers of his six so-called sons. And what think you I have found?"

Uther's only response was to raise an eyebrow, but she was already answering her own question.

"Lot sired none of the brats, not one. And all the men who did sire them were killed, in one fashion or another, before their sons were born. Lot had no connection with the death of any of them, it seemed, and none of the men knew him personally, but he adopted all of their children, knowing that he could not have fathered them. He made sure, however, that in return for their continuing welfare and existence, the boys' mothers would remain silent about the true paternity of their children." She allowed that thought to hang between them for several moments before she spoke again.

"It is disgusting and pitiable, but Lot adopted those boys—and all their mothers agree with me in this—solely because he wants the world to think he sired them. And that can only mean that he himself suspects his own incapability of breeding sons. And yet he would never admit such a failing even to himself—particularly to himself, in fact. That is where the sanity of what he does breaks down and falls apart. He cannot bear to think of himself as being unable to breed an heir of his own, and he refuses to believe the evidence of his own experiences.

"He has no idea I know any of this, needless to say, and I would go to almost any lengths to stop him from suspecting that I do. But since I do know, I have been able to ask him some questions and to raise some points—all in seeming innocence—in conversation with him, and I have found the results to be most interesting. It galls him—no, it infuriates him, to be forced to consider, even indirectly, any suggestion that he might be, could be, incapable of getting himself an heir. He grows inflamed at the merest suggestion of such a thought and flies into the most frightening rages."

Uther hitched himself closer to her and increased the movement of his hands on her body, and soon a minor resurrection was achieved between the spread forks of their legs. He penetrated her almost without assistance and then lay lodged there, stirring only minutely.

"Did you really think you might be with child by me?"

They were lying almost at right angles to each other because of the way they were joined, their legs intertwined, and she reached out in the darkness and twined her fingers in his hair at arm's length. He reached up and clasped her wrist, running his fingers along her arm to her locked elbow, then dropped his hand straight down to her breasts, cupping and kneading the fullness of one of them, pinching the nipple between his thumb and forefinger. She stiffened against him and snorted with pleasure, pushing herself down onto the flesh that impaled her, and then twisted her fingers in his hair and wrenched his head sideways gently.

"The thought occurred to me, King Cambria, because I am a normal, healthy woman of child-bearing age, and I had been thoroughly serviced by a virile man during the space of two long, active and intensely satisfying nights. Have you fathered any children yet?"

He lay thinking for a moment and then shook his head in the darkness. "I don't think so . . . None that I know of, anyway."

"I would not be too sure of that, were I you. Do you remember Morgas?"

"Of course I remember Morgas. What about her?"

"She is no longer with me. Soon after her return from her captivity in Camulod, she left my household and returned to her home country to be wed, but I heard from another of my women that her monthly courses were already late by the time she left to return home."

Uther rose up to rest on one elbow. "Do you think there is any truth to it?"

"I have no idea, but it would not be impossible, would it? Would it concern you greatly, were it true?"

"No, I don't suppose it would—" his tone was reflective, "—but it would be nice to know."

"To what end? If Morgas is now wed, her husband will assume the child is his, so it were best you let it be."

"Aye, I suppose so."

"Now," she said, "empty your mind of thoughts of Morgas and her beauty." Ygraine lay smiling in the darkness.

"I confess," he said slowly, pushing his pelvis against her again, "that I am jealous, knowing that now you'll have to lie with Lot again, simply to stay ahead of his suspicions."

"Jealous? That would make you jealous?" He could hear the amusement in her voice.

"Yes, that would make me jealous."

"Well, then, you need not be, for what he claims of me is his by right of marriage, but what I choose to withhold from him is mine by right of possession. Besides, I'll have no need of going to him this time. I have been with him recently enough to render him incapable of suspicion. You, on the other hand, I simply wish to render incapable, eventually." She moved against him lasciviously, drawing him further into her, and all need or desire for conversation faded immediately.

They were all astir just after dawn, Uther and Ygraine managing, somehow, to appear as well rested and refreshed as any of the others. Over the course of a short breakfast of eggs, mixed on a hot skillet with chunks of smoked meat and served on thick slabs of bread fried in animal fat, Uther discussed ways and means of remaining in touch with Herliss and Lagan over the course of the coming winter. The device of using his ring had worked well, and none of them could see any need to change the procedure, and so Ygraine kept the ring in her possession for future use.

Now that he and Lagan had formed an amicable relationship based on mutual trust, however, Uther conceded that it should be easier for the two of them to meet in future, providing that they kept their actual meetings hidden from curious eyes and used a go-between in the final stages to set up the times and venues. Since either one might have to call such a meeting, Uther acquired a token from Lagan similar to the one he had given to Ygraine. Lagan's token was a thumb-tip-small, distinctive granite pebble. It appeared to have been painted in alternating stripes of black and orange, but the colours were natural layers in the stone, and the granite itself had been polished to a glass-smooth finish and drilled with a hole that permitted a leather thong to be looped through it. Uther took it and slipped the leather thong over his head, allowing the pebble to rest against his chest under his tunic.

Herliss had been sitting watching and listening to the two younger men, and now he leaned forward, swallowing the last mouthful of his breakfast. "So," he grunted, "the season is almost over, and Lot's people are already preparing for winter. They'll be launching no campaigns this late in the year, nor will you, I presume. When do you think you will be returning to Camulod?"

"To Camulod? I don't know. Popilius Cirro and his infantry will return there directly, once our work here in Cornwall is done, and that should be in a few weeks—a month at the very most, if winter holds off that long. But I have to return to my own place in Cambria and set my house in order there before I head for Camulod. Camulod has no shortage of able leaders and Roman-style administrators to keep things in order from year to year, but in Tir Manha we have no such luxuries. I alone am King, and I have been away from home for nigh on seven months. The gods alone can tell what I'll find waiting for my attention when I reach home again."

"So if we have to send for you or to you, it were best to seek you first in Cambria?"

"Aye, it would be wisest to do that . . . And when I do decide to go to Camulod, I'll send you word and let you know, too, how long I intend to remain there. What would be the best way to do that? With no direct meeting involved, there will be no need to use the stone for such an errand, will there?"

"No," Herliss grunted, shaking his head. "When the time comes, all you need do is send a messenger to me at Tir Gwyn. My White Fort's famous throughout Cornwall, so he will have no difficulty finding it. Tell him to ask for me and to present . . ." He broke off and thought quietly for a moment, then nodded. ". . . to present a wax seal imprinted with a cross of some description. That will identify him, since the Christian symbol is seldom used down here, and I have never known it used on a wax seal that sealed nothing. Can you remember that?"

"Aye, I will. A wax seal, marked with a cross and sealing nothing. Can you read or write Latin, Herliss?"

"Very badly, and I have not tried these thirty years, so I think the true answer is no. But Lagan can."

"Can you, by the gods?" Uther made no attempt to hide his surprise as he turned to Lagan Longhead. "Where did you learn that?"

Lagan smiled. "As a very young boy, I was a close friend to Lot when his father, Duke Emrys, decided that it would do his son no harm to be able to use the Roman tongue. Lot was headstrong even then, and he insisted that if he had to undergo the learning of Latin, then he should have company in his suffering. We had a wonderful teacher who imparted her own love of Latin to me. You know her as Mairidh, the wife of my Uncle Balin. She lived in your lands for a while."

"Aye, she did . . . right in Tir Manha, in fact. So were I to write to you, you would be able to read the letter and write back to me?"

"I would."

"Excellent. So be it."

Herliss coughed, clearing his throat. "Now, about your leaving today. Your helmet's plain enough and undistinguished, but roll up that black cloak you are wearing and cover it with a plain blanket, then tie it behind your saddle. It's too easy to see, too noticeable. We have nothing like it in Cornwall; all our cloaks are either brown or grey. We will lend you one of ours, in my colours, for riding out. You came in during darkness, but you're going out in daylight, and the countryside is swarming with Lot's people. Lagan will go with you, riding your horse—he is known for his love of large horses—and you'll go along as one of his escort, a hunting party of twelve men all riding plain garrons. You'll stop in the forest, to hunt, of course, and they'll ride back without you, later tonight. By that time, in the darkness, no one should notice that Lagan comes back riding a different horse from the one he rode away on." The old man stood up and stretched his arm across the table to Uther. "And to that end, may the gods ride with you, and may we, between us, be able to topple our enemy within the coming year. Farewell." He turned to bow briefly to the Queen, offered the same bend of the waist to Uther, and then left.

Uther was grinning as he watched Herliss depart, but when he turned to Ygraine, the grin faded swiftly. "Lady," he said, "I must thank you for your hospitality." He heard the sound of feet behind him and turned his head to see Lagan leaving the room, heading for the main entrance and according them, he presumed, a moment of privacy.

Ygraine moved to approach him, but Uther waved her back with a tiny, tight gesture of the hand at his belt. "No, lady," he murmured, pitching his voice so that none but she could possibly hear what he was saying. "Come no closer. I thank you again for your hospitality . . . all of it . . . and I shall carry the memory of your smile, your kiss, the scent of your hair and the touch of your skin with me until we meet again. Farewell." He bowed deeply to her, straightened himself to his full height, then spun on his heel and strode out of the hall, heading directly towards the main doors where he knew Lagan would be waiting for him.

The Cornishman was there and clasped hands with him briefly before giving him a few final instructions, pointing him towards the main gates and telling him about the group that would ride out with him. They were his own best men, Lagan said, chosen for this task because of their loyalty and their often demonstrated ability to follow his commands without question or debate. He had told them only that Uther was an important personal ally to his father and to him, and he assured Uther that none of them would speak to him or even pay him much attention. However, should any outsider seek to approach the party or to interfere with them in any way, including an outright attack, they would fight for him as they would fight for Lagan. He himself would follow them alone within the hour. He would catch up with Uther some time later that morning, a safe distance from the Crag Fort and from prying eyes belonging to any of Lot's spies who might be prowling about.

Moments later, Uther was outside the main gates and approaching the group of horsemen who sat there, already mounted, awaiting his arrival, holding the sturdy and unremarkable garron he would ride. They were an ill-matched group of varying sizes, and their weaponry was as diverse as their appearance. The only element they had in common was that they all wore long, grey cloaks like the one Uther himself had been given by Lagan.

One man sat slightly apart from the others, tall and upright on his garron's back, and his helmet, more ornate than any of his companions', marked him as the leader of the party. Uther ignored him and went directly to the main body of the group, nodding to them briefly in a general greeting and being careful to catch no one's eye. He took the reins of the extra horse from the man who held them out to him and vaulted cleanly onto the animal's low, broad back, holding the reins easily and gripping the stocky beast tightly with his knees, reflecting with some amusement that it had been many years since he had straddled a similar mount and thanking the gods that the Camulodian horses were all far bigger than the Celtic garrons, for his long legs almost touched the ground on either side. The garron raised its head, and its ears swivelled from side to side as it assessed the presence of the stranger on its back. It snorted and shook its head, preparing to question his authority further, but found itself quickly curbed and mastered, its head dragged downward and held there by the strength of the arm controlling the bit in its mouth. Uther glanced towards the man in command and nodded almost imperceptibly. The fellow nodded briefly and swung his mount around, kicking its barrel with his heels.

Their outward ride was uneventful and, as far as Uther could tell, unnoticed by anyone. As Lagan had promised, none of his companions made any attempt to speak to him, and in fact none of them seemed to pay him any attention at all, so that he was aware of only three of them who had glanced in his direction since they had moved away from the Crag Fort. Their route led them northwards at first, until they had crossed the humpback spine of the narrow peninsula that was little more than a score of miles wide at that point, the sea lying slightly more than ten miles ahead of them, northwest of the Crag Fort. As soon as they were beyond the ridge of high land, they headed downward into a tree-filled valley and waited there for Lagan to catch up to them. It took a little over an hour, and Uther spent the time making up for some of the sleep he had forfeited the previous night.

Once Lagan had arrived, however, they wasted no time on civilities. He dismounted and adjusted Uther's stirrups back to their proper length, which was clearly indicated by the deep-grooved buckle marks on the leather straps. Uther watched him, smiling but saying nothing, then swung himself up into his saddle and leaned down to clasp the other's hand one last time. A brief word of thanks and a wish to meet again soon, and he turned his horse around and headed northward, taking care to remain well below the skyline of the high land on his right, since on the other side of it, some score of miles again northeast of the Crag Fort and close to the seacoast, lay Gulrhys Lot's home stronghold of Golant.

Almost four hours later, two of which had been spent cursing uselessly at the bitter, gale-force wind that had sprung up from nowhere and had several times battered him with gusts strong enough to threaten to blow him off his horse, Uther caught sight of the long, transverse ridge that swept inland and upward from the estuary of the western river the local people called the Cam. The ridge concealed his own encampment from the southward, but nothing could have concealed the enormous, wind-torn clouds of black, heavy smoke that swept along the horizon. Fighting against the alarm that flared in his breast, he put the spurs to his horse and drove forward in a flat-out gallop, wondering what had gone wrong this time.

What had gone wrong was soon clear. A raiding party of seagoing marauders, Ersemen or perhaps Franks—Uther had no way of knowing what they were, other than Outlanders—had sailed up the small river estuary and landed looking for plunder. They had seen the cavalry encampment with a single double squadron in residence, and estimating their own strength against the party they could see, they had guessed that the wind blowing from their backs would give them a fine advantage and decrease the odds they would be fighting against. And so they had fired the long grass, thinking that the grazing horses would scatter in fright and be lost, and that they themselves could then charge right into the enemy encampment under cover of the smoke that would be blowing ahead of them. What they had failed to see was the second double squadron of Dragons riding back towards them from a patrol to the northwest, over their shoulders, and the camp of Popilius Cirro's thousand men in the bottom of a well-watered but narrow valley just beyond the cavalry encampment.

The fight had been short and sharp, and Uther, who was still some distance away and approaching rapidly, watched with approval as Garreth Whistler, in command of the returning cavalry, called off the chase that would have put an end to all of the surviving raiders. Uther doubted that they had enough men left to man their craft, and Garreth plainly had more urgent matters on his mind. The raging grass fire that the Outlanders had started was burning out of control, sparks and whirling embers blown everywhere by the wind so that the conflagration was spreading faster than a man could run. It had already crossed the flat plain of the ridge's top and swept down into the narrow valley behind, where the wind funnelled it and led it directly to the rows of infantry tents that lined the hillsides.

The fire lasted only moments, but the damage it did in that time was appalling. More than half of the infantry's leather tents, all ranged in perfect formation and clean lines, were destroyed, along with everything in them. And two of their four remaining commissary wagons had been badly burned, the bone-dry wooden bodies and wheel spokes catching fire instantly and blazing fiercely before the vehicles could be run out into the bed of the stream that wound through the valley bottom. Everything that they contained, all the provisions and supplies, was either destroyed completely or rendered unfit to eat.

It was one more example of Uther's Luck, and the only grounds Uther had for gratitude lay in the fact that their hospital tents and wagons had been laid out and drawn up on the flat, gravelly bottom-land of the bend on the far, north-facing bank of the stream. Four more large commissary wagons, long since emptied of provisions, had been turned over to hospital duties, and these were completely unharmed. There was little growth of any kind on the inhospitable ground there on the other side of the stream, for it was the flood lands of the little river, so although the storm of flying sparks and embers had swirled across the stream bed easily, the sparse grass that was there had been trodden down too thoroughly to burn fiercely.

Looking at the scene and visualizing the carnage that might have taken place had his wounded been trapped on the side of the stream nearest the fire, with its thick, dry grass, Uther sucked air sibilantly between tight lips and reminded himself that they were at the end of the campaigning season and due to go home soon anyway. Masking his disgust, he met with Popilius Cirro, Garreth Whistler, Huw Strongarm and the other officers and issued orders to break camp and form a column for one final march, to stamp out a crawling enemy column in passing, and then to head homeward to Camulod and a winter season of well-earned rest.

The march homeward was straightforward and presented them with no difficulties, despite the shortage of supplies caused by the fire. Even the enemy column, almost a thousand heavily armed men, caused them little trouble, for Herliss had been specific in his instructions, and his intelligence regarding the mercenary expedition was flawless. All of that, combined with the veteran Cornishman's comprehensive knowledge of the terrain over which the enemy would be moving, virtually guaranteed a victory for the Camulodians.

Uther set his trap in a long, narrow, steep-sided defile that provided the only easy route between two neighbouring valleys. The place was an obvious setting for an ambush, of course, and the enemy commander scouted it thoroughly before committing his troops to advance, but Uther had anticipated that and planned for it. His own scouts lay in slight depressions on the open ground above the defile on both sides, covered by nets woven with grass torn from neighbouring clumps. From more than twenty paces, they were invisible to the enemy scouts, who were looking only for large parties of warriors. They were invisible, too, to Uther's own advance guard on both sides of the defile, until they stood up and signalled that the enemy scouts had withdrawn, satisfied that the way was safe.

Uther's Pendragon bowmen then launched themselves at the run, quickly covering the half mile from where they had lain concealed while the scouting progressed. As they approached the lip of the defile on both sides, they dropped to their bellies and remained there, concealed from everyone in the narrow passageway below until the signal came to bring them to their feet. As the bowmen sprang into view of the enemy, Uther's cavalry charged both ends of the passageway, blocking advance and retreat, and the hapless mercenaries, most of whom were on foot, rapidly fell into a confused piled of maimed men and corpses under the hissing, deadly accurate rain of long Pendragon arrows, against which they had no defence.

When it was over, Uther was well satisfied. His men had ended the campaign on a high note, with a victory that would soon resonate from one end to the other of Lot's domain. He sent men to collect the enemy baggage-and-supply train—a rich and valuable haul—and to count the slain, and he was unsurprised that they brought back a tally in excess of seven hundred dead, not one of whom was Camulodian or Cambrian. Not all of the slain had died of arrow wounds, and many had been slaughtered out of hand upon surrendering. Uther knew that well, but he made no attempt to question the report. The hundreds of wounded now left alive, he knew, would be sorely injured and would provide no further threat to him or his. The less badly wounded, who might have been inspired to fight again some day, had all been inspired instead, by their captors, to succumb to their injuries. That was the way wars were fought. Neither side had time nor resources to handle large numbers of prisoners. Local warriors, native to the land in which they fought, might reasonably expect that they would be spared to return to their own homes. Not so mercenaries. Mercenaries understood their own risks when they hired themselves out.

After leaving the scene of the ambush, they encountered no other hostile activity along the way. They were able to keep hunting parties ranging ahead of them at all times, and to everyone's surprise and pleasure, the hunters were invariably successful. The marchers dined on venison almost every day, and in the early stages of their journey, in what appeared to be a reversal of their bad luck, they even found a burned-out farmstead with a pair of granaries that were almost full, one of them holding oats and the other wheat. They found them by accident, for the small buildings had been cunningly hidden in a dense copse more than a hundred paces from the farm buildings by a farmer clever enough to anticipate that it might be to his benefit to have a hoard that was not plainly visible. Unfortunately, it had done him and his family little good, for the marauders who came upon his farm had burned the place down about his ears anyway, evidently killing him and his whole family, without discovering the hoard of grain.

Eight days after that, fit and healthy, the returning raiders reached the point of their journey closest to Camulod, and the following morning Popilius Cirro and his thousand men split away from the Cambrian contingent and made their way without ceremony north by west for the last short stage of the journey home. Uther was sorely tempted to interrupt his own ride home in order to go with them, even for a brief visit, for the young boy in him still tended to think of Camulod, uneasily, from time to time, as his true home. He told himself that it was important that he visit the Legates Titus and Flavius, or whoever was in charge in Camulod nowadays, in order to pass on his news about the impending spring invasion, and for a time he almost yielded to the urge, but his common sense would not allow him to deceive himself that thoroughly, and so he grudgingly steeled himself against the lure of Camulod and its luxuries. Instead he spent an entire evening with Popilius Cirro, first outlining and then detailing and emphasizing the crucial instructions he wished the veteran commander to pass on to the authorities in Camulod.

Uther knew that his relationship with Ygraine, Herliss and Lagan Longhead was still a secret, and that Popilius Cirro knew and suspected nothing. He knew, too, that in order to safeguard that relationship, since the lives of his new friends depended upon it, he must be extremely careful in what he said about Lot's planned invasion the following spring and in the way he presented the idea, because he could not afford to provoke any curiosity about his advice or to suggest to anyone, even indirectly, that he might be in possession of secret or privileged information about Lot's plans. He could not even acknowledge the truth to his own people, simply from fear that any one of them might let the secret slip in a careless moment, not out of malice'but out of sheer human fallibility.

He decided that he would have to conceal his knowledge and present his convictions as a set of strongly worded reservations and suggestions based upon opinions and insights that he had gathered during his campaign in Cornwall. His task would lie in presenting them with sufficient authority to elicit an immediate and positive response from the Camulodian high command. If he could word it properly through Popilius, he knew that would suffice, for once the initial work was begun, he himself could add further details and substance to what was happening when he visited Camulod himself at a later date.

He spent hours talking to Popilius, and when he was convinced that he could not improve upon the other's understanding of the situation or increase his awareness of the urgency and strength of his convictions, Uther nodded, indicating his satisfaction. Then he asked the older man to pass along his love and filial affection to his grandmother, Luceiia Britannicus, and his promise to ride back and visit Camulod as soon as he could, in hopes of finding his Cousin Merlyn restored to full and active health. Only then did he allow the Camulodian detachment to strike out for home, carrying their few seriously wounded in their remaining wagons. Then, not even waiting to watch the infantry column until it was out of sight, he signalled to his trumpeter and set his own Dragons and his large contingent of bowmen back on the road for Cambria and Tir Manha.

Even in Tir Manha, however, Uther's Luck remained in force. They arrived back to find themselves the healthiest group in the entire countryside, and before they had been at home for three days, they themselves were beginning to succumb to the pestilence that had swept all of Cambria with the onset of autumn that year. It was not a fatal disease, whatever it was, but it was debilitating, frustrating and painful. Its symptoms were a high fever accompanied by vomiting and loose bowels, and a painful rash that itched unbearably as it began to heal—which it seemed to do after a period ranging from four to six days. The rash then scabbed over as the result of the scratching, and afterwards left small but permanent pits in the skin when the scabs had fallen away.

Uther himself was one of the first of his party to come down with the sickness several days before the Samhain equinox, and because he was the King, he had all the wisdom of the local Druids, and all of the lore they had garnered collectively about the sickness, directed towards his well-being. He was constantly reminded not to scratch the itch, unless he wished to disfigure himself and endanger his own kingship, since it was a matter of law that a King must be physically whole and completely unblemished. And so for the duration of his sickness Uther remained in his private quarters and submitted to the gentle baiting of Garreth Whistler, whose health was, for the time being, in flawless perfection, and to the gentler, more considerate ministrations of his mother and her women as they bathed him in a mixture of oatmeal and cold water to combat the unbearable itch that covered his arms, shoulders, back and torso.

Time passed, and so did the sickness, but the Samhain celebrations were poorly observed that year because their occurrence coincided with the worst of the outbreak, and even by the time the Roman holiday of Saturnalia came by, towards the end of December, Tir Manha still had not returned to normal.

That changed with the new year, and Uther found himself thankful that January arrived with a mildness that was most unusual. He had regained his strength by that time and was fit again, ready for the task that faced him, so that when Aelle of Carmarthen arrived at Tir Manha, Uther was pacing the floor impatiently, fretting to get to work.

Aelle was the closest thing the Pendragon Federation had to a seagoing warrior. His father had been a ship-builder, and Aelle himself had studied the art, but had soon discovered that he would far rather sail ships than build them. He had handed his interest in the shipyard over to his younger brother in return for a galley of his own, and had then assembled a crew and begun sailing up and down the coast, trading for whatever he could find. Because he and his crew had had to fight for what they held, Aelle of Carmarthen had earned himself a reputation over the years as a doughty fighter, and now he captained a trio of formidable galleys.

Uther took Aelle into his own chambers, where they would not be
disturbed, and told him openly all that he knew of Lot's invasion plans
for the months ahead. Which of the spots along the coast, he asked,
would be most suitable for landing an army and would also be most
likely to attract the eye of an invading general?

Aelle listened soberly and sat staring into middle distance as he
reviewed in his mind the possible sites. Finally, the seafarer sat up
and sucked in a great breath.

"I have five places, all within a day's march of here, north or
south—chosen out of a possible half score, mind you—but they're
all this side of the Severn. Think you the Cornish whoresons will
strike for you here in Tir Manha?"

The King shook his head. "I know not, Aelle. I've been told that
they'll hit Carmarthen, and while I would like to rely completely on
the truth of that, it's hearsay at this time and I can't be sure of it, so
your opinion would probably be better than mine on that."

"Aye, there's a pity, then. See you, it would be much easier if we
knew they'd come for you. Not knowing that, why, man, we have
ten leagues of northward-facing coast to look at on this side of the
river mouth itself, and the same on south-facing Cambria, across the
water from you here, with five hundred bays to every league . . .
bays, mind you, not beaches."

Uther knew it was the absolute truth. A Celtic league was a
distance somewhere between two and a half and three Roman
miles.

Aelle was making faces, screwing up his features and shaking his
head. "Look you, d'you need this answer from me now, today? Can
you give me three days or a week? I'd like to sail up and down and see
things through a raider's eyes, instead of my own. I've seen all the
bays a hundred times and more, but never once did I think to look at
them as if I might land an army there in any of them . . . d'you see my
meaning? Big difference there, King Uther. So I'd like to look, and
think, as I might well think of something different than e'er I thought
before, if ye take me."

Uther agreed, albeit reluctantly, and conceded that Aelle might
take as long as was needed.

The seafarer gazed at him with eyes that were mere slits from staring at horizons in all kinds of weather. "Look you," Aelle said gruffly, "I know what you have in mind here and what you have to do. You have massy decisions to make, for all of us, so I'm not going to waste your time. But how can time be wasted if it saves you time? Ask yourself that, King Uther. If I can come back to ye with word of where I'd land my army, were I looking to invade these lands, then you can take my word and make ready to fight off a landing there. If I can't choose between two or even three places, then you'll work on those. But if I tell you nothing or if you never send me out to look, then you'll know nothing more than you know now, and you might well end up with ten or a score of good places to try and choose from, and that would be a waste of time, if you take me."

Uther nodded, grinning. "You're right, Aelle, and I take your meaning perfectly. Go you and do what you must do, and I shall be the more happy to see you when you return."

The man was gone for a week and a day, but when he came back, his normally sombre face was wreathed with smiles, and Uther felt better simply looking at him. Aelle did not keep him waiting long for his tidings, but came right to the most important point ahead of all others: "Beer, King Uther . . . something long and cold and wet to cut a thirst, there's what I need, if you take me." The beer, still cold from the cellar, was served instantly, and Aelle drained his mug and refilled it and drank a quarter of it again before he even looked as though he might be ready to speak. Then he belched and leaned back in his chair.

"Three spots," he said. "I found three spots that I would use, each of them lovely. One of them's here on the southern coast and two are across the water on the Cambrian side. The one here's the only one that makes any kind of sense on this whole side, and it's four leagues farther up the coast, towards the river mouth. It's a clean beach, almost flat, in a well-sheltered bay behind a headland, so the men can leap overboard and wade in easily without having to struggle against great waves. Then, beyond the beach itself, there's a wide meadow of some kind, surrounded by a thick belt of trees. Land a whole Roman legion there, ye could, and lose them in the woods with no

one ever suspecting they was there. I went ashore myself, just to have
a look, and I'll wager mine was the first human foot to walk there in
a hundred years. An army could land there in comfort without fear
of being seen or attacked. It's far enough away from Tir Manha to
allow the landing fleet to arrive unseen, even from the fort up on the
headland there, and yet an army, once landed and organized, could
be here about your ears within half a day of reaching dry land. It's
perfect. The only place along the whole damn coast that a man with
a brain would choose for purposes of warfare, if you take me."

"What about the other two spots?"

"Neither one as good as the first one, but they'll do in a pinch.
But a leader, a what-you-call-it, a legate or a general, looking for a
place to fight you . . . no question in my mind he'd choose the first
one, here on the southern shore. Mind you, that all depends on what
he wants to gain or who he wants to hit, and whether or not he really
wants to fight. He might not be interested in prodding you at all. If
he wants to attack Caerdyff instead, he'll take the easternmost beach
and land three leagues to the north, and then march back south and
west. That could be done, too, without much trouble. But if he wants
to go against Carmarthen, as you said he might at the outset, then
he has no option but to choose the western beach, and that's a long
way from where you sit here. But again, it's a fine landing beach and
close enough to the town to land an army and then set it to encircling the town. That done, he could then come in by night and try
to seize the docks. But if he tries to land there, mind you, he'll have
all of Carmarthen down around his ears, and no way to escape other
than heading west again or east back towards Caerdyff. As I said, it
all depends on what he wants to achieve, this fellow in charge,
whoever he is."

Uther sat silent for a long time, mulling over all that Aelle had told
him, and then made his decision. Aelle himself was from Carmarthen,
so it was only natural that he should regard that as the strongest position in the Cambrian alliance, the place most naturally suited to
repelling any invasion in strength. Uther was more doubtful of that.
To his eyes, Carmarthen was looking more and more attractive by the
moment as a launching spot for Lot's latest mischief. Lagan and

Herliss had seemed absolutely sure that Cerdic and Tewdric, the German generals who were the joint leaders of the campaign, would launch their attack against Carmarthen, and the more Uther thought about that, the more convinced he became that his allies were right, for a number of reasons. A western invasion of Cambria would offer the invaders many advantages: it would force Uther, as King, to move far away from his own home base in order to conduct the campaign, and it could conceivably create friction between the allies of the Pendragon Federation, since the initial fighting would all take place in the deepest Griffyd territories, and the local chieftains there were likely to look with little favour on being commanded by someone who had not a drop of Griffyd blood in his veins, King of the Federation or not. Besides that, Uther's necessary presence in the region around Carmarthen during the invasion would keep him and his Dragons, and even more important, his bowmen, far away from Camulod and the other invasion—this one with two separate armies involved—that would be taking place there simultaneously. For all of those reasons, Uther was leaning more and more certainly towards Carmarthen as the site of the Cambrian strike.

He had three months of preparation time remaining to him, he estimated, and half of that would be sufficient once he knew the where and when, and providing that his information was as current as it could be. He decided to take Aelle's recommendations as presented, but to concentrate his own attention for the time being upon the Carmarthen landing place as the most likely target. He estimated that he could fortify the Carmarthen holdings with levies from Tir Manha and Caerdyff, while leaving both of those spots at half strength, but alert and on the defensive, which was better, he estimated, than being somnolent and unsuspecting at full strength. That way, even if the enemy commanders changed their plans, all would not be lost, and the force from Carmarthen could move quickly to relieve whichever of the two remaining spots was hit. In order to increase his advantage as far as was possible, however, he decided also to send a letter to Lagan, asking for any additional information that might now be or might become known. His decision made on those matters, he asked Aelle, then, if the seafarer would take him the following week to visit the site he had selected at Carmarthen. The seaman looked at him and nodded, then volunteered to do not only what Uther had asked, but to show him the other prime sites as well and explain why he had not chosen those. Well pleased, Uther thanked him and permitted him to return home for a few days' rest.

Uther spent a number of long, frustrating hours that evening with ink and paper, working far into the night by the light of a cluster of tapers as he struggled to find and then set down the words he wanted to address to Lagan Longhead. It was one of the most unpleasant and demanding tasks he had set himself in years, since it involved intense mental effort without physical release from the cramped constraints of writing, head down, for hours . . . everything, in fact, that he found least pleasing . . . but eventually it was done, and he had a fair copy, free of blemishes, of what he wished to say to his Cornish ally.

The following morning, he summoned Nemo and explained to her what he required of her. She was to ride to Lagan, carrying the stone about her neck to present to him, and once she had been received by him, she was to deliver Uther's letter and then return home to Tir Manha. Any response to the letter would be sent back by another messenger at a later date.

Nemo listened, nodded, saluted and left immediately to carry out her commission, and Uther, resigned, settled in to wait and to hold himself in patience.

THIRTY-FOUR

In late January a messenger arrived from Cornwall, bearing a letter from Lagan Longhead, its three pages dense with information. Uther greeted the messenger with grave courtesy and thanked him for his time and effort, then sent him off with Garreth Whistler to be made welcome in the kitchens.

As soon as he was alone and could expect to be undisturbed for a time, the King went into his own quarters and sat close by a burning brazier to read what Lagan had to say. He read slowly, concentrating fiercely on forming the sounds made by the block letters that Lagan had inscribed in a firm, bold hand, and listening internally to the music of the Latin words as he formed them, haltingly at first, and then more confidently once he began to catch the sense of what he was reading and saying aloud.

The Queen, Lagan reported, had worked hard to ingratiate herself with the two German generals, Cerdic and Tewdric, and had learned that their plans were well advanced—far beyond the initial stages. Their attack would be launched from Cornwall as close as possible to the middle of April, around the time of the Roman Ides, and the landing place would be Carmarthen, on the other side of the great estuary from Tir Manha. The reason for the mid-April timing was one of co-ordination. The other invasion, involving the twin armies of Issa and Loholt, neither of whom the Queen had been able to approach in any way, would begin moving northward, overland towards their attack points, some time in the first week of April, weather permitting. Their departures would be separated by a week in order to enable the first army, which had much farther to travel, to make the great, looping movement required to turn and attack Camulod from the east. In order to ensure that all three attacks combined should generate the greatest impact and preserve the element of surprise, Cerdic and Tewdric would contain their seaborne army in Cornwall for a full two weeks after the departure of the first of the two land armies. Only then, when both of those were close to being in position, would the naval invasion set sail.

The initial attack from the sea into Cambria would be a two-part thrust. The Cornish fleet would strike land initially in a large, shallow and sheltered bay with a gently sloping beach approximately three leagues to the west of Carmarthen, unloading its army during daylight, after which the newly landed force would move quickly against the town itself. They would spend the night on the hills behind the former Roman fort at Carmarthen and attack with the dawn, hoping to surprise the defenders and overwhelm them before they could organize any resistance.

According to Ygraine's report, Lagan wrote, the leaders of the planned assault were confident and self-assured. They had accurate information about the defences of Carmarthen itself and about the lie of the land in the immediate area surrounding the walls, and they had two contingency plans governing the outcome of their initial attack. If their surprise was as successful as they anticipated, they would simply take possession of the town and use its wharves and warehouses to unload and store their supplies. If, on the other hand, their initial surprise fell short of expectations, their vanguard would fall back in time to conceal the full strength of the attacking force and would then draw itself up in battle lines on the flat land outside the town walls, from where they would taunt the Carmarthen Griffyds until their warriors went out against them. As soon as that happened and the Griffyds were committed outside the walls, an arranged signal would be sent and half a score of Cornish galleys that had not unloaded their cargo of men with the rest of the invading fleet would swoop in and attack the wharves and docks along the waterfront, spilling sufficient warriors into the town from that side to attack and capture the town gates.

That was all Lagan had to report, but he promised to write again as soon as he came into possession of any other information. He ended his letter by mentioning that Gulrhys Lot had been seen smiling recently, since he had learned that his wife, Queen Ygraine, was with child and would give birth some time in June, just in time for his victory celebrations.

Uther sat gazing open-mouthed at the letter in his hand, his face gone blank, the colour draining from his cheeks, his awareness of the world around him suddenly suspended as he found himself reeling on the edge of an abyss called Fatherhood. He had joked about the possibility with Ygraine, but he had never really antici-pated for a single moment that it might be possible for such a thing to happen. Casual by-blows as the result of pleasurable but mean-ingless coupling occurred all the time, seldom drawing notice, but the fathering of an heir, fatherhood with responsibility . . . *paternity* as he remembered Merlyn calling it . . . was for other people— people who were *ready* for it. It was for men who sought it; men who had an eye to their mortality; men who were married and besot-ted with their wives. He was a King, still very young and untried, with grave responsibilities. He did not have time to be a father . . .

At that moment, he caught himself and remembered that this paternity would be no burden on him here, for Gulrhys Lot seemed happy to accept and acknowledge the child, if it should be a boy, as his future heir . . . his first-born legitimate son . . . But this would be Uther's first-born, not Lot's . . . most certainly *not* Lot's! And sud-denly he was deeply, viscerally angry that Gulrhys Lot should dare lay claim to a Pendragon child. Bad enough that he already had half a dozen sireless bastards all of whom he claimed were his, but that he should now seek to use a Pendragon, a blood descendant of Ullic and Uric, as a false crutch to prop up his sorry claims to manhood— it was too much!

"In the name of the lame god, what's wrong with you?"

The words brought Uther back to himself with a start and he turned to blink in surprise at Garreth Whistler, whom he had not heard entering the room. Owain of the Caves stood behind him, gazing calmly at the King over Garreth's shoulder. Uther gathered his wits and sat up straighter, responding to the unexpected question with false bluster.

"What d'you mean, what's wrong with me? There's nothing wrong with me. Good day to you, Owain."

Owain nodded wordlessly as Garreth Whistler grinned and held up his hands in mock surrender.

"Oh, then I'll ask your pardon. I simply happened to see the look on your face and the death grip you have on that parchment you're holding, crunched up into a ball . . . Lagan's news was good, then? I confess, from the look on your face I thought it might be disastrous."

Uther looked down at the crumpled missive in his hand and shook his head ruefully. "I . . . I was not aware of doing that. Here, sit yourselves down and listen and judge for yourselves whether or not I should be angry." He smoothed the letter out and then read it to them, leaving out only the mention of the Queen's pregnancy. When he had finished, Garreth sat quietly for a while, staring into the brazier, while Owain of the Caves sat gazing straight at Uther.

Finally Garreth spoke. "Where did that come from? It's specific. And it's not the kind of information given to the average grunt."

Uther nodded. "You're right, it's not. It came from my informant in Lot's camp."

"Your informant. I see. In Lot's camp. Of course, where else could it have come from? How long have you had one of those?"

Uther sighed and signalled to both of them to be seated, and when they were, he told them everything about his dealings with Herliss and Ygraine. They listened without interrupting until he had finished, and then Garreth Whistler asked, "Why did you not tell us sooner?"

"Because we didn't need to know about it." This was Owain, and his response, and the readiness of it, caused both men to look at him in surprise. "Well, it's the truth, isn't it? What we didn't know we couldn't let slip in our cups. Now, it's clear that you want us to know, so what happens next?"

"I'm not sure," Uther said. "That's why I'm asking for your advice." He glanced inquiringly at Garreth Whistler.

Garreth shrugged his broad shoulders and looked away, pursing his lips before responding. "I know we'll be able to make life rough for the seaborne invaders coming into Carmarthen," he said eventually, his eyes fixed on the glowing coals. "The terrain will work for us there and we'll have the advantage of surprise, so I'm confident we'll hammer them and throw them back to where they came from . . ." He turned and looked back at his protégé, the King. "But what can be done against the other two armies, the ones hitting Camulod? That's what I'm wondering . . . and I can see you are, too. There's no terrain advantage there for Camulod to use . . . nor us, either. A mile out of Camulod itself in any direction except straight along the high road, you're in deep forest, and deep forest works as much against you as it does for you. Can't use cavalry in there, and bowmen are useless most of the time. Too many trees and not enough space to shoot cleanly." He stopped and looked at Uther shrewdly. "Do you have anything at all in mind, or are you waiting for the Camulod people to work out their own salvation?"

"They *can't* work out their own salvation! Well, that's not true, I suppose they can—they're going to have to. But Merlyn's still not himself, and that's what frightens me most of all. He's the only one with balls enough to do what needs to be done. Titus and Flavius are good, but they're old now, both of them, and too set in their ways, having relied on Merlyn and his father, Picus, all their lives for strong leadership. Besides, they're cavalry officers above all else, Roman-trained and Roman-minded, and this fight that's looming has nothing Roman about it.

"Camulod will be relying heavily on us, and we won't be able to give them too much support, even if we slaughter the invaders at Carmarthen. By the time we march from there to Camulod, it could all be over. So I'm going to have to come up with some solution quickly. And what you say is right: knowing the terrain gives us no advantage at all in this instance. None at all . . ." He fell silent, staring into the brazier.

"The worst of it is, these two commanders, Issa and Loholt, are the best Lot has. They're probably among the best in Britain, because not only are they both Roman-trained, they're trained as independent mercenaries—guerrilla fighters accustomed to operating on their own without having to answer to a chain of command.

These fellows are fighters to reckon with. They were Rome's mercenaries long before they became Lot's. They hate each other's guts, too, from what I've heard, which means they won't be operating jointly, so I can't see any way of dealing with them as a single enemy force. Each of them will move in separately for the kill, with Camulod's wealth as the prize, and that means neither of them will waste any time in anything they do. And as you heard for yourself in the letter, each of their armies is the size of a full legion."

Uther looked from one to the other of his two listeners. "Two armies, each at legion strength . . . Even allowing for a huge exaggeration, that's at least three and perhaps four thousand men apiece. Greedy men, lusting for a prize, and all of them afraid they'll lose it if their allies reach it first. That could mean as many as eight thousand mercenaries, all of them unpredictable and all of them hungry, marching into Camulod from two different directions." He snorted, a bitter, self-deprecating sound. "The only clear idea in my mind is that we need a scourge, a sickness, like the one that hit us here recently, but far more fatal—and we need it now. It need not be a widespread pestilence, just a gods-sent little one that would kill Issa and his cohort Loholt. With those two gone, Lot's armies would not even march, because there's no one else who's capable of leading them."

"What about the other two we spoke of months ago, what were their names?"

"Cuneglas and Ralla, Lot's Cornishmen? They're incompetents. The German mercenaries probably wouldn't even march with them. But it would be a waste of time, I think, even to wish for anything like that. The gods have never taken the time to smile on me before, so the odds against one of them sending us a plague now, when I need one, are daunting. Issa and Loholt are healthy and itching to be on the road. They'll be massing for departure in six weeks. Which reminds me, is everything ready for our journey to Carmarthen tomorrow?"

Garreth nodded. "Aye, everything is in order. We'll be off at first light."

"Good. I want to be back here within ten days, and after that I'm going to ride down to Camulod for a brief visit just to see how things are progressing there. I'll be back here within the week after that, and by then it will be almost time to gird on our battle armour. So, Owain, where have you been? I haven't set eyes on you in months."

Owain of the Caves began telling Uther all that he had been up to since last they met, and as he listened, Uther's attention kept being distracted by a recurrent vision of Ygraine of Cornwall, sitting on a high-backed chair with a laughing child on her knee. It was a vision that was to remain with him constantly from that time onward, one that would catch him unawares at the most unexpected times and one that he quickly grew to love. On this occasion, however, all thoughts of Ygraine were suddenly banished when he realized that Owain of the Caves was asking an important question.

He had enjoyed working with Uther, Owain said, and he was grateful for the new life accorded to him here in Cambria among the Pendragon warriors, who had adopted him as one of their own. The fact that they had tutored him in the use and care of their magnificent longbow was more significant to him than any other recognition he had received from anyone in his entire life. Now, however, having learned that there was a life to be lived out there in the world that had no resemblance to the miserable existence he had known before joining Uther, something deep inside him was telling him to go and seize it before it became too late for him. He would fight in the coming war, he promised, but after that he would like to return to his place of origin, in the north of the country, simply to see if there was a life of any description up there that he might salvage.

Uther listened without comment until the big man was done, and then smiled, hiding the consternation he felt and putting the best face he could on what he was being asked to do. The taciturn Northerner had served him well, doing the few things required of him without demur or complaint, and Uther had come to depend upon the silent big man. He knew well that there was nothing to be gained in saying anything other than yes, but he felt it was important that he should not only accede to Owain's request, which was far from unreasonable, but also encourage the man to follow the demands of his heart. He finally stood and embraced Owain of the Caves, giving him his blessing and even urging the man to go as soon as he felt the need to go, knowing that a welcome awaited him back in Tir Manha should life in the north lands not turn out to be as he hoped.

Owain stood speechless after that, his eyes shining with what Uther assumed must be gratitude, and then he stooped and kissed Uther's hand before turning and striding quickly from the room. Uther glanced inquiringly at Garreth Whistler, who merely raised an eyebrow and shrugged before following Owain.

Alone again, Uther sat back down by the brazier and stared into the glowing coals for a long time, until the candles on the nearby table had burned down and begun to flicker and the fire itself was buried in glowing ash. Then, coming to awareness again, he rose to his feet and went to bed.

He slept very badly, plagued by formless dreams and imaginings, and when he got up the next morning, feeling as though he had not slept at all, Owain of the Caves was no longer in Tir Manha. He had left the previous night and had told no one where he was going. Uther said nothing when Garreth told him the news, but he felt abandoned, and he saw Owain's departure as an evil omen.

It was closer to fourteen days than to ten by the time Uther returned from his journey to Carmarthen, but he was well satisfied with what he had achieved there. The young Chief Dergyll ap Griffyd, whose home base Carmarthen was, had been made paramount Chief of all the Griffyd clans a year earlier and was quickly proving himself to be a superb warrior and leader. A handsome, broad-shouldered young man—Uther estimated his age at no more than twenty-three or twenty-four—of moderate height, strongly muscled and of slim, supple build, he was supremely confident in his own abilities, yet still blessed with an appealing sense of fun. His people looked up to him and admired everything about him, and from what Uther could gather, the man had no visible flaws and no discernible weaknesses. Uther and he had known and liked each other briefly in boyhood, but many years elapsed before each set eyes upon the other again, this time at the funeral of the veteran Chief Cativelaunus of Carmarthen. Uther had known that the old Chief had had a protégé called Dergyll, but it had never occurred to him that it might be the same Dergyll who had been his companion during one of the long summers of boyhood. He knew three other men called Dergyll, and had anyone asked him, he might have admitted to being prepared to dislike a fourth, simply for bearing the name of the three he knew.

As a fighter, Dergyll ap Griffyd had built himself a fearsome reputation, and he had the skills of a commander to match those of a warrior. Uther had left him in charge of the preparations on the ground above and surrounding the invasion beaches that Cerdic and Tewdric would use. He had left Huw Strongarm there, too, attached to Dergyll's command to back him up with a four hundred–strong contingent of Pendragon bowmen who, properly positioned exactly where Uther had ordained, would be able to decimate the invading troops who escaped Dergyll's first reception and might be foolish enough to seek to attack Carmarthen anyway. The position held by the Pendragon force, less than one-third of the way along the only route that led to Carmarthen from the landing beach, could not be avoided or evaded; any troops destined for Carmarthen would have to pass through the valley that Uther's bowmen had claimed as their killing ground.

Uther knew that the western invasion was well in hand. The enemy, anticipating no opposition, would land suspecting nothing, and no move would be made against them until they were all ashore. Only then, once they were disembarked and preparing to march eastwards to Carmarthen, would Dergyll's trap be sprung. They would be hit hard and continuously by a powerful army that had materialized, it would appear to them, from nowhere, and whose existence they could not have dreamed of. With Dergyll's Griffyds, Huw's Pendragon bowmen and the Llewellyn warriors who would be sent to reinforce them, the Federation's waiting army would number close to six thousand men, all of whom would be defending their homeland against an enemy taken by surprise and caught flat-footed with their backs to the sea.

Uther was far more worried about what would happen with the two armies destined to fall upon Camulod, one from the south and the other from the east. He felt consumed by the need to reach Camulod quickly to check on their defensive plans and progress there, for the war that Camulod would fight would be a demanding one. They would be lacking their natural leader, Caius Merlyn, and be sorely in need of greater assistance than Uther could offer them. Before he could leave for Camulod, however, he had affairs to tend to within his own Pendragon Federation.

He had summoned the Llewellyn Chiefs to join him in Tir Manha to discuss the final arrangements for their participation in the spring invasion, including the number and disposition of the warriors they would send to Carmarthen. The Chiefs were Cunbelyn and Hod the Strong, both of whom had voted in the Choosing of Uther as King of the Federation, and a younger man, Brochvael, who had succeeded the dead Meradoc as Chief of the largest Llewellyn clan after the Choosing ceremony. There was no love lost between Uther and any of the three Llewellyn Chiefs, thanks to the confrontation he had had with Meradoc, but neither was there any overt hostility between them. The Llewellyns had done whatever had been required of them since Uther had become King and had behaved themselves appropriately, and with that Uther could have no complaint.

In due time the Llewellyn Chiefs arrived, and Uther talked with them for a full day, outlining the exact dimensions of the threat the Federation faced and detailing the requirements he would have of their combined clansmen. There were a few questions raised in the opening stages, primarily by Hod the Strong, concerning the source of Uther's information and the reliability of his informants, but Hod was that kind of man, bluntly asking the questions that came into his mind and uncaring of the subtleties involved. He was prepared to accept that there were things Uther could not tell him, for fear of endangering his friends in Cornwall, and he professed to have no need of anything other than to be convinced that he could believe what he was being asked to believe. Apart from that, however, he wanted to be assured that he was not being asked to endanger his people needlessly. Uther addressed each of his questions openly, refusing to name names or to say anything that could be hazardous to his friends, but stating his reasons forthrightly each time he had to do so and otherwise concealing nothing.

In the end, they agreed that the combined Llewellyn clans would field a force of two thousand men to reinforce Dergyll ap Griffyd's four thousand and Huw Strongarm's four hundred–man force of Pendragon bowmen in Carmarthen. Brochvael, the young Chief, about whom Uther knew little, was displeased over what he perceived as the apparent lack of Pendragon commitment in the Carmarthen campaign, a mere four hundred bows as opposed to the Llewellyn thousands, but it was Hod himself who surprised Uther and laid those concerns to rest by pointing out that one Pendragon bowman, given a strong position with a decent field of fire and sufficient arrows for his longbow, was worth any ten, perhaps twenty warriors that he himself could put into the field. Four hundred such, he pointed out, strategically placed as Uther had described to them, would have the power to win an entire battle on their own without help from anyone else, providing a supporting force at the enemy's back could keep the enemy from running away from the long and deadly Pendragon arrows.

Brochvael seemed unconvinced, and Uther was on the point of showing his displeasure when it dawned on him that, astonishing as it might seem, Brochvael had never seen Pendragon longbows used in war. As soon as he realized that, he nullified the problem quickly by arranging a demonstration for the following day.

The weather was fine, cold and crisp, and the Pendragon bowmen treated the event as a celebration of their skills, taking delight in showing off for their visitors. Apart from individual displays of marksmanship that sometimes appeared magical and left the mouths of all three Chiefs hanging agape, the finale of the afternoon's demonstration was a display of massed archery, with four evenly spaced formations, each of a hundred men, loosing rapid-fire volleys at an array of one hundred standing logs, their sharpened ends thrust into the ground. Each squadron stood in two ranks of fifty men, the second line two paces behind the other, and the rank of bowmen closest to the standing logs was one hundred and fifty paces from the target. A space of twenty paces separated each squadron from the one behind it, so that the farthest rank stood some two hundred and twenty paces from the target stakes. On a given signal, the bowmen began to shoot, and at no time were there fewer than two volleys in the air, one rising to its zenith and the other falling on the target, each volley consisting of one hundred arrows. The entire exercise was completed in less time than a man in the front rank could have walked half the distance to the target area. Each man fired ten arrows, and on the shouted signal to cease fire, the target area was blanketed with four thousand arrows. Not one target log had been completely missed in the onslaught, and fewer than a hundred arrows had fallen short.

Uther watched his guests closely throughout the exercise and was amused to see that Hod the Strong stood grinning throughout, nudging his neighbours with delight, for he had seen the sight before, but Cunbelyn and Brochvael were stunned and speechless. Even then, however, Uther had no need to speak, for Hod was crowing with delight, jostling the still blank-faced Brochvael and demanding if he had ever seen the like before. Plainly, Uther could see, young Chief Brochvael had not even imagined such a thing, let alone seen it. He would raise no more objections, Uther knew, either then or in the time to come.

Four days after the departure of the Llewellyns in the pale, wintry sunlight of late afternoon, Uther was riding by one of Camulod's outlying boundary garrisons, and it was plain to see that the entire post had been greatly enlarged and strongly fortified very recently—the pointed wooden stakes topping the earth walls were still fresh from the axe blades that had formed them. Encouraged to see that some of his suggestions had been implemented, he approached and identified himself to the post commander and quickly inspected the installation.

Formerly little more than an outlying farmstead, the place was now a substantial stronghold, completely surrounded by a deep, sloping ditch, the sides and bottoms of which had been planted with angled, lethally pointed stakes. The earth removed in digging the ditch had been used to form a high defensive breastwork, backed with palisades of the heavy, sharp-ended logs he had first seen, and behind that was a defensive parapet from which the defenders could fight back. The place looked as though it could easily accommodate a garrison of several hundred men, and it had two entrances, each consisting of a narrow passageway, with gates at both ends, that pierced the breastwork. These were overlooked by bridges from which the defenders could attack anyone trying to pass through. A drawbridge of stout logs that could be raised by pulleys allowed passage from the fort across the ditch for offensive purposes, but denied incoming attacks. Uther was highly impressed, not merely by the obvious strength of the fortification but also by the speed with which it had been erected.

He was even more impressed, riding up to Camulod at the head of the First Squadron of his Dragons, by what he found on the huge plain that formed the drilling ground at the bottom of the hill. Popilius Cirro had once built a temporary fort down there, at the time of Lot's first treacherous attack on Camulod. It had served its purpose well, but it had been disassembled afterwards to permit the cavalry to use the training ground again. Now it was back in place and garrisoned again.

As always, news travelled with seemingly miraculous swiftness in Camulod, and long before he reached the huge gates at the top of the fortress hill, Uther could see that a reception party had turned out to welcome him. His heart leaped as he recognized his Cousin Merlyn among them, unmistakable by his size and the colour of his long, golden hair. Even from far away, Uther could see the white gleam of teeth that showed him his cousin was grinning, and he felt his stomach churn, hoping that Caius Merlyn might be himself again.

It seemed that he was, for as Uther approached the group in front of the gates, the golden-haired giant sprang out ahead of all the others and bounded to take hold of Uther's bridle.

"Tiddler," he shouted. "Late again, as usual, never where you are supposed to be at any time! We have been waiting for you now these three days past. Welcome home."

Ignoring all the others in his delight, Uther kicked free of his stirrups and swung his right leg up over his horse's head, dropping to the ground and throwing his arms around his cousin, hugging him close. Wordlessly then, he shifted his weight suddenly, grasped

Merlyn by the shoulders, hooked his right leg behind the other's knee and twisted. It was an incomplete movement, halted almost in the execution, but it was a trick from their boyhood, practised a thousand times and calling for a particular and specific response. Merlyn reacted immediately, countering in exactly the right way, intuitively and with consummate ease, and Uther's heart soared.

"Hah!" he roared. "How long since you've done that?" He leaned backwards and peered into Merlyn's eyes, gripping him by the upper arms. "I was speaking of that very move to Dergyll ap Griffyd only weeks ago." He thought he saw a flicker of uncertainty in the eyes that looked back at him, and he hurried on. "You remember Dergyll ap Griffyd. You threw him on his arse with that same move the first time we ever met him, when we were boys and my father took us up to Carmarthen for the first time. He remembered it well, for he spent months practising it himself thereafter. He asked to be remembered to you."

But even as he spoke, Uther felt his spirits sinking. It was plain that Merlyn held no memories of Dergyll or of the incident he was describing. The clear, golden eyes had gone blank and then filled up with something resembling panic that quickly faded to regret. Uther tried hard to give no indication of his overwhelming disappointment, but he lost the flow of words that had sprung so readily to his tongue. He stood there for a moment longer, gazing at his cousin and struggling against the grief that had suddenly swollen up in his throat. Nothing had changed, he finally admitted to himself. Merlyn was glad to see him and knew who he was, but only because he had learned. Although everything about the outside of the man proclaimed him to be Caius Merlyn Britannicus, the truth was, still, that he was not.

This was the Merlyn who had never known his own wife, Deirdre, or the expectant joys of impending fatherhood. That thought, springing from nowhere, almost confounded Uther, reminding him of the child that would soon be born to him and calling up pain-filled shame over the role he had played, however unwittingly, in the tribulations Merlyn had endured.

He fought down the sudden urge to weep, blinking his eyes rapidly and swallowing hard, and then forced himself to smile again before he reached up to tap the centre of his cousin's forehead with the knuckle of his index finger.

"It's good to see you again, Cay. Good to know that head of yours is as hard as it ever was." He drew a deep breath, then released his cousin and turned back to where the others who had come to meet him stood watching. "Gentlemen, well met again."

The Erse giant Donuil stood smiling there, close by Merlyn as always, and beside him the saturnine physician Lucanus, who dipped his head in silent greeting. Many of the other faces on the outskirts of the group were known to Uther, too, even if the names attached to them eluded him for the moment. The veteran legates, Titus and Flavius, stood in front, still wearing their old and proud imperial armour, and behind them towered the huge bulk of Popilius Cirro, the epitome, as always, of the dignified senior centurion. Before moving to meet them, Uther turned to where Nemo stood at attention, holding the reins of Uther's horse in one hand and her own in the other, and nodded a signal to dismiss the squadron. Only then did he move forward to embrace the two old legates and greet Popilius, who nodded courteously and bade him welcome, not quite smiling but plainly glad to see him.

As they moved into the fort, however, a thought occurred to Uther, and he turned again to Merlyn, who was close by his side.

"You called me Tiddler. I had forgotten that name. Haven't heard it in twenty years. How did you remember it?"

Merlyn smiled and shook his head. "Aunt Luceiia told me about it. She remembers everything about our boyhood."

Again Uther felt disappointment well up in him, and he turned to Titus and Flavius to mask it. "Where is my grandmother?" His tone reflected his sudden concern as he remembered now that he had expected Luceiia to come hurrying to greet him, not having seen him since the year before, and he became aware again of the bulk inside his tunic that was a heavy letter to her, written by his mother Veronica. "Is she not well?"

The Legate Titus answered him: "The Lady Luceiia is very well and will be disappointed to have missed your arrival."

Flavius completed the answer, making Uther smile as he realized again that these two men had been together for so long that they thought almost as one person. "She is down in the Villa with some of the women of her Council, but please don't ask us what she is doing. We seldom know, and we never inquire. Come inside and tell us about your journey. We have much to discuss, and perhaps we can deal with some of it—"

"Before your grandmother returns," Titus finished. "We have some excellent red wine, brought in from Gaul by a visiting bishop. Come you."

Once Uther had exchanged greetings with everyone and stowed his travelling gear in his allocated quarters, Titus, Flavius, Popilius and an assortment of dignitaries, including the governing committee of the Council of Camulod and several senior garrison staff, including his Cousin Merlyn, spent the next two hours bringing Uther up to date concerning the hurried arrangements they had made to forestall Lot's upcoming advance against the Colony.

All ten of the border guard posts protecting the outer limits of the Colony's lands had been refurbished and refortified, the resident garrisons of six of them increased to double standard. The remaining four, those guarding the southern and eastern approaches to Camulod, had been greatly enlarged to more than double their original size and garrisoned accordingly. It was one of those that Uther had passed by on his way in. A widening of the roadway down from the fortress gates to the plain beneath had already been in process when Popilius returned, in order to improve access and egress in time of need, and the reinstallation of the temporary fort on the drilling plain had been quickly achieved by setting upwards of more than a thousand people, including old men, women and boys, to the task of building it. It was a temporary erection, Cirro said, dirt and logs, ditch and ramparts, but it would endure as long as the need for it might last. In addition to that, artillery platforms had been built on Camulod's hillsides, overlooking the open spaces surrounding the fort below, and artillery machines—huge torsion-wound devices that could hurl rocks and missiles made from heavy tree trunks— had been built and set up on the platforms.

As the litany of preparations continued, Uther began to feel better and better about Camulod's prospects for surviving the attacks that were to come. It was the veteran Titus, however, who put into words what all of them were thinking: that all of these preparations were for a defensive war, with no contingency for going out to carry a cavalry battle, Camulod's single strongest advantage, to the enemy. Camulod, through its entire brief history, had never been involved in a defensive war. All things considered, however, it was clear to Uther that the situation was better than he had anticipated. The Colony could fight defensively, and effectively, for as long as it might have to. All the Colonists would be withdrawn into the safety of the walled fortress itself, and the place had its own water and was well enough supplied with other stores to endure a siege of six months or longer, should that much be necessary.

The informal meeting broke down into a general discussion of many things, and Uther soon excused himself, pleading road weariness and the need to find hot water in which to bathe. Titus and Flavius both accompanied him to the furnace-fired bathhouse against the rear wall of the fort and remained with him as he undressed himself and sank into the luxury of the hot pool. They left him then to complete his ablutions and dress to go and meet his grandmother.

Luceiia Britannicus Varrus was a constant source of amazement to her grandson. Luceiia had to be more than sixty years old, he knew, and that was an incredible age to him. He knew only one woman of comparable age in all of Cambria, and she was a wrinkled crone, twisted and warped with age and viewed with terror and superstitious awe by everyone, because she was widely believed to be a familiar of the dark gods who ruled the Cambrian night. How else could anyone explain such longevity in a land where the few women who lived to reach their fortieth year were old and withered?

Luceiia Varrus, however, bore her advanced age with dignity and retained the unmistakable characteristics of the magnificent beauty that she had been in her youth. Her back was long and straight, unbowed by time or tribulation, and her long hair fell in a heavy, silver mane, shot through with shimmering remnants of raven black. Her mouth, far from being sunken and toothless, was still full and generous. Granted, her lips were far less full than they once had been, and her teeth were more yellowish now than white, but she still had all of them, and her smile was a thing of beauty, filled with love and humour.

Greeting her again and hugging her gently to his chest, Uther wondered, as he always did, about the spirit that sustained her and kept her youthful. How could it be that she remained so vital, where others of her age were long dead and gone? But then another thought occurred to him fleetingly. Though there was no one like Luceiia in Cambria, there were other elderly women in Camulod, more than a mere few of them, and all of them were healthy, clean and well groomed despite their age. These were the women of her Council, primarily, the matriarchs of the founding families. They lived gentle lives, well cared for by their children and descendants, and they knew none of the hardships that ruled the lives of Cambria's women from day to day and year to year.

Luceiia's exuberant greeting pushed all other thoughts from his head. She was in fine fettle, as usual, and delighted to see her grandson. When she had finished fussing over his appearance, she took him by the hand and welcomed him into her home, insisting that he spend the night there. But he asked her indulgence and insisted in his turn upon remaining in the visitor's quarters assigned to him, since he might be awakened at any hour of the night now that the word was out that he was here, and only briefly. Luceiia accepted his demurral with no more than a tiny sniff of disappointment, and then demanded all his tidings, including his first impressions of Camulod on this visit.

He began by handing her the letter from her beloved daughter, but she made no move to open it and read it while he was there, preferring, he knew, to savour and anticipate the pleasure she would get from reading it when she could be alone to appreciate it. This time was for her grandson, and she listened closely as he told her all his tidings, smiling and frowning alternately. And when he had finished, she amazed him yet again.

"Tell me about those women you captured, the ones you sent here. The tall, beautiful one with the yellow hair like Cay's was striking, to say the least . . . She called herself Lot's wife, Ygraine, and for a while all the men here thought they had landed a prize of great value."

Uther smiled. "You knew, of course, that she was not."

"Well, not quite, not at first. I know the real Ygraine is sister to Donuil and to poor Deirdre, and I felt from the beginning that there was something far from right. I barely spoke to the woman at all, and I betrayed nothing. Call it a woman's intuition if you will. But I merely decided to wait for Donuil and wait upon his word . . .

"I knew he would be back the following day, for he had gone out hunting with Caius the day before, and so I watched for him and took him aside the moment he got back, before he had a chance to confront his 'sister.' Of course, one look was all that was required."

Uther was grinning widely now. "So what did you do then? Did you confront her?"

"No, Donuil and I decided to say nothing. We did not know what was happening, what was involved, but I decided it might be unwise to let her know we knew she was not who she said she was. I had mixed feelings about keeping her imposture a secret, but I decided to wait and see what would transpire. And then your messenger arrived a few days later with your written dispatch informing Titus and Flavius that she was not the Queen, but that they should say nothing about knowing the truth and simply release her and her women, under escort, back to the boundaries of Cornwall. So I have a question for you, grandson: how did you know she was not who she said she was? To the best of my knowledge, you knew nothing about the woman, and you barely knew her sister Deirdre or her brother Donuil."

Uther shook his head in admiration. "You are a clever old woman, Grandmother Luceiia."

"No, I am simply a woman. I have a mind that is not haltered by being masculine. So tell me, how did you find out who she was, or who she was not?"

"I knew, because the woman she pretended to be was there with her, pretending to be one of the Queen's attendants." And he proceeded to tell her the tale, starting from the beginning and omitting nothing except the intimate details of what had taken place between himself and Ygraine.

Luceiia sat silent throughout, eyeing him shrewdly, and when he had finished she pursed her lips and reached across in front of her to pick up a small silver bell from a low table. When a woman appeared in answer to her summons, she asked for wine for herself and her grandson and then sat silent again, staring into the brazier in the fireplace.

"I find that as I grow older, the cold becomes more sharp," she said, and then she lapsed into silence again, her mouth moving occasionally as she appeared to chew upon everything he had said. The serving woman returned with a tray bearing twin silver goblets and a beautiful silver ewer, misted with cold and beaded with drops of moisture. Uther thanked her with a nod and she placed the tray on the table and withdrew. Quietly, being careful not to distract his grandmother from her thoughts, he rose and filled the two cups with pale yellow wine, then placed one close by her elbow. Finally she looked up at him and nodded.

"So she is your source, Ygraine, and this Duke, Herliss. And the other woman, the blond one . . . Morgas . . . what of her? Does she know the truth?"

"Gods, no! Nor is she any longer in Cornwall. She returned to her home in the northlands to marry some local King there. I have not seen her since she left our camp to come here to Camulod."

"Good, that pleases me. She spoke of you, and I could tell she knew you, partially at least, but there was something about her that I could not warm to."

Uther felt momentarily uncomfortable, wondering how much the old lady knew or guessed, but he could see little profit to be gained in pursuing that, and so he let it pass.

Uther explained the thoughts he had entertained about how best to serve his mother in the coming fight, and how he had decided she would be safest at home in Tir Manha, where he hoped Luceiia would join her to wait out the spring campaign in safety. Luceiia, however, would have none of that. She herself was far too old and set in her ways now to leave her home in Camulod to seek some fleeting safety in another land. She would remain where she had lived for so many years, close to her memories and the graves of her husband and her brother.

On the matter of Merlyn, Luceiia had little to offer Uther in the way of hope for the future. Merlyn was physically well, she told him, alert and happy and in full possession of most of his faculties, apart from memory. But he had lost his aggressiveness and his love for fighting. Gone was his once brilliant and instinctive grasp of campaigning, strategy and tactical matters. He could still fight, she had been told, but it was as though he fought only for the pleasure of the exercise. Young Donuil was convinced that Merlyn had completely lost the propensity to kill, and in any real fight involving lethal weapons and ill feelings, Merlyn would be killed simply due to his own unwillingness to inflict harm on an opponent.

Luceiia laid her hand over Uther's. She had always loved Merlyn, she told him, but since his injury she had grown to love the *new* Merlyn Britannicus, with his gentleness and loving nature, even more than she would have believed possible. She would dearly love to have her great-nephew back, she said, but even were that to happen and Merlyn was suddenly restored to them as he had always been, she feared she might regret the loss of that new gentleness.

They were interrupted at that point by Luceiia's women bringing them an evening meal, and for hours after that they sat talking by the glowing brazier, discussing bygone days and precious memories of Caius Britannicus, his son Picus and Publius Varrus. Uther went to bed that night feeling a contentment he had not known in ages, and he slept well and soundly.

The following day Uther was up and into the kitchens before the cocks began to crow, and by sunrise, his belly pleasantly full and his heart at peace, he was meeting with Titus, Flavius, Donuil and Merlyn, and Popilius Cirro, arranging the final details of their plans as firmly as was possible, given the nature of the tasks ahead of them. He was finished by mid-morning and summoned Nemo to him, ordering his Dragons to be ready to leave by noon, and after that he took the time to say his farewells properly to everyone, including his grandmother.

He noticed something was amiss among his troops as he went to mount up in the main courtyard at noon, and he drew Nemo aside, out of their hearing.

"What's going on here? The men look angry."

Nemo blinked at him with her normal, vacuous look. "Some of them don't want to leave yet."

"Well, that's a pity, but I have to be back in Tir Manha quickly. There might be word from Cornwall." He began to move away, but then he hesitated and turned back. "And what's wrong with *you?*"

Nemo was gazing at the walls by the rear gate behind Uther's shoulder. She shrugged, her face still expressionless. "I like it here. We should come back and live here one day. It should be a Pendragon place."

Uther was surprised. Nemo seldom ventured an opinion on anything. He looked closely into the dull eyes that had been a part of his life for so many years, and there, under the customary stolid, vaguely sullen look, he thought he discerned, for the first time in as long as he could recall, the features of the lost child he and Garreth had saved rather than the hard-nosed, truculent Nemo. Inexplicably, he felt a lump come into his throat, and he coughed to hide his sudden embarrassment, turning to look at whatever she was gazing at so fixedly. He could see nothing but the high rear walls of the fort.

"Well," he said, turning back and speaking for her ears alone, "if the gods are good to us in this coming war, perhaps we will come back and live here some day, you and I." Then he stepped forward, seized the reins of his horse and swung himself up into his high saddle.

THIRTY-FIVE

Their journey back to Tir Manha was fast and uneventful, and they arrived less than three days after leaving Camulod, Uther having pushed the pace of their advance relentlessly. Tir Manha showed none of the building activity that had been evident around Camulod, but there were definite signs of preparation for war everywhere as they drew close to home. It seemed to Uther that every Pendragon warrior in the clans had come to Tir Manha, and there were groups and squadrons of bowmen practising everywhere he looked.

He dismounted quickly, throwing his reins to Nemo, and went looking for his mother, knowing that she would be wondering about her own mother and if he had brought an answer to her long and detailed letter. He had not, because there had been no time for his grandmother to compose a response, but he was able to tell her everything that he and Luceiia had discussed, and to tell her of Luceiia's promise to write back immediately and send the letter on to Tir Manha with one of her priests. Veronica insisted on feeding him while he was there, and he humoured her by sitting down to the quick meal of fresh bread and cold, salted meat with homemade beer that she laid out for him.

When he finally reached his own private quarters, which were attached to the King's Hall and separate from his mother's, he told the guard outside that he was not to be disturbed. One of the first things he had seen on entering the gates was a young woman, sitting on a low wall and suckling a hungry baby from a milk-swollen breast. The sight had hit him hard, filling his mind with

Ygraine and her expected child, and he had had no time since then to sit alone and allow the thoughts that teemed in his mind to settle down.

The afternoon was wearing on towards evening, and the small room in which he sat, dark on the brightest days, was filled with shadows that seemed almost solid. Kindling lay ready in the iron basket that filled the crude chimney in the far wall, and he used a twig to carry a flame from the open lamp on his table to the fireplace, cupping his hand to guard the flame and realizing that it would have been wiser to carry the lamp across the room and light the twig there. He stayed crouched in front of the basket until the flames were well established, then straightened up and went back to his table, where he lit three thick, stubby tallow candles from the smoky lamp. Then, enjoying the brightness of the growing, flickering light, he leaned back in his chair and closed his eyes, letting the saddle-weariness seep out of his bones.

He was dozing when he heard a footstep, and he jerked his head up as a looming shadow blocked the light from the doorway. Uther was surprised to see Owain of the Caves.

"Well," he said, "I'd wager you never expected to be told you're a pleasure to behold, but you are. I thought you had gone north. Sit down, man. What are you doing here?"

The big man shook his head. "Your guard didn't want to let me come in, but I convinced him. I didn't go north. I told you I'd fight this war with you."

"Then where have you been? It's been a month since you disappeared."

"I went to find this." Owain pulled something from his scrip and tossed it casually onto the table in front of Uther, where it landed with a soft thump.

Uther stared at it, a small, grimy bag of rough, poorly tanned leather, closed by a drawstring. Suspecting a hoax, he looked up at his visitor beneath raised eyebrows.

"What is it?"

"Open it and see. It's a gift."

Uther picked the bag up cautiously and tested the contents with his fingers. It was something flat, but not completely so, for there were bumps and irregularities that he could not define. Curious, he raised it to sniff at it.

"Don't put it to your nose, man! I want you to enjoy it, and you won't if you do that. It's a plague, but a tame one."

Utterly mystified now, and more than a little disconcerted, Uther inserted two fingers into the drawstring noose and gently pried the bag open, then shook its contents out onto the table. Two objects fell almost noiselessly onto the wood, and the sight of them sent Uther rearing back in shock, sucking in his breath with a startled hiss. He heard Owain's bark of laughter, but he could not withdraw his eyes to look at him yet. Lying on the table in front of him was a pair of human ears—a matched pair, judging by the tufts of black hair adorning each of them.

"Well, you like them?"

It took some time before Uther was able to respond. "Whose are they—were they?"

"Issa's."

"Who is Issa?"

"Issa, man! The one you wanted to get sick."

"You mean Issa, the . . . ?"

"Aye, Lot's general. They're his. Proof that he's gone. You'll have to take my word on the other whoreson, Loholt. I couldn't get close enough to him to take his ears, too many of his people around him. But I dropped the whoreson from two hundred paces with an arrow through the centre of his head, right above the ear. Best shot I ever made in my life. No one even saw me. They didn't know where the thing came from, because the force of it hitting him swung him around and threw him over backwards like a bird hit in mid-flight. By the time they thought to look farther than they thought could be possible, I was well clear. But I thought you might forgive me for not hanging around there to collect his ears."

The significance of this was slow to penetrate Uther's mind. The greatest threat to all that he held dear had apparently, and against all likelihood, been removed by this one man, this strange, solitary, friendless, enigmatic killer who had sought to take his life when they first met, and whom Uther had befriended almost without thought, on an unguided impulse. Uther sat staring at him, open-mouthed, unable to speak or to move.

"Alone," he managed to say, finally. "You killed them both, alone?"

"No other way. A man alone can go anywhere he wants, so be he doesn't act the fool. I had more trouble hiding my bow, coming and going, than I had with anything else."

Uther sat blinking at him, struggling to overcome his awe. "So how *did* you hide it?" he managed to ask eventually. He was finding it easier to speak by the moment, although his mind was in a turmoil with conflicting facts and possible consequences.

"Hid it in plain view. I used a trick the medics use in Camulod. Wrapped it lengthwise with twigs, the way they splint a broken leg, and then wrapped the ends in thin strips of plaited leather. Time I finished with it, it was nothing like a bow—just a long walking staff. No one even glanced at it. You should have seen the shot I made on that Loholt fellow, though. Two hundred paces if it was one. The other one was easy—Issa—I saw him head off hunting and followed him. Waited until he was alone, stalking a boar, then dropped him with one between the shoulder blades. He didn't even know he was dead. So, do you feel better now?"

Uther, finally in control of himself, rose to his feet and stared into Owain's eyes. "Aye, my friend, I think you have made me very well. I will never be able to repay you for this service, but I want you to know that anything I have is yours, and anything I can ever do for you will be as good as done the moment that you ask it. You may have saved ten thousand lives with just two arrows."

The Cave Man flushed a deep red, uncomfortable faced with praise, but Uther could see that he was pleased, nevertheless. He nodded once and then again, and then made a "harrumphing" noise in his throat.

"Aye, well, I'm glad. I'll go now and sleep a bit, I think." His eyes returned to the ears that still lay on the table. "D'you want me to take those away?"

Uther glanced back at them. "No," he murmured. "No . . . I

don't think so, not yet. I may have a use for them. Again, Owain, my thanks."

Many things happened very quickly after that, and time itself seemed to accelerate in the frenetic activity of the following months. Late on the evening of Owain's stunning revelation after hours of deep deliberation, Uther sat down and, with great difficulty and much muttering beneath his breath, wrote an important letter to his grandmother in Camulod. Luceiia, he knew, would grasp the situation immediately in its entirety and would see to it that things were done properly thereafter.

The unexpected deaths of his two senior minions would be a crippling blow to Lot's plans, he wrote, far more than any such disaster could ever be to Camulod, or even to himself in Cambria. Camulod had a disciplined army and well-trained deputies in place to step into the gap created by any single person's death, no matter how crippling that death might be. And even here in Cambria, were he struck low, his people were one people, and one or another of his own chieftains would soon step up to take his place in time of need. Not so with Lot. His own Cornish people lived in distrustful fear of him, and his only strength lay in his huge mercenary armies. Therein his major weakness also lay, however, for those mercenary armies had no underlying loyalty to Lot himself, other than that which he had already bought and paid for, and his control of them lay in the hands of powerful leaders like Issa and Loholt, who ruled their men by strength of will and personality, by the power bred from guts and strength and sheer experience, leading their armies to victory, plunder and conquest. Now, with those leaders gone, Lot had two armies of leaderless savages in his domain, and he would be hard put to deal with them. Cuneglas and Ralla, weak straws that they were, would be forever useless, and that left Lot now with no leaders of any stripe.

Based upon all of that and upon the chaos that seemed bound to follow in its wake, it seemed reasonable, he told his friends in Camulod, that there would be no springtime attack against them. But they could not depend on that completely. Lot had the armies, and he might still, by some chance, replace his fallen leaders with new blood. It was a possibility for which they must allow.

His recommendation was that Camulod not relax its vigilance. If, in the coming spring, no attack ensued, the governors of the Colony should be prepared to split their forces, keeping their garrisons in place, although at reduced strength, and dedicating the strongest army they could spare—mixed infantry and cavalry in far greater strength than the raiding force he had led the previous summer—to making a pre-emptive strike, as Balin called it, into the heart of Cornwall, where they might be joined and reinforced by Lot's own Cornish enemies. Uther himself would handle the attack in the west, which he was sure would come as planned, as swiftly and effectively as could be, and then he would bring the finest of his forces, including at least a thousand bows and twice that number of Cambrian clansmen from the Federation, to join the Camulod contingent. By striking swiftly and surely into the turmoil of Lot's anarchic chaos—those words were Balin's, too, but Uther endorsed them completely once he understood what they meant—they might finally be able to unseat the Cornish King and put an end to his rule of terror. He would await the Council's acceptance of his suggestion, he wrote, or their suggested alternatives to what he had proposed.

It was long after midnight by the time the letter was written to his satisfaction, for there was much important detail to be packed into it, and he was determined that nothing would be omitted that might be crucial at a later date. When it was done, he sealed it carefully before he went to sleep.

The following morning, he summoned Nemo to him before dawn and instructed her carefully in what he wanted her to do, then sent her off immediately to retrace his journey to Camulod and Luceiia Varrus.

Then, towards noon, an exhausted messenger arrived with a short letter from Lagan Longhead in Cornwall.

In haste: the country here is plunged in chaos. This may be no surprise to you. Issa and Loholt are both dead. Slain within three days, ten leagues apart. Issa first, Loholt after.

Killers escaped. Two single arm-long arrows used. Word
reached us in Tir Gwyn two days after the second death.
Uther, father said, as soon as he heard the news. He has cut
the heads off the snakes. No attack on Camulod now. No one
else to lead the armies. And then he said, Unless—

That was three days ago. G is insane with anger, turning
the countryside upside down, searching for the killers, but
they should be home by now. Father and I are set to disap-
pear for a time as soon as this is gone. At least until the
uproar dies away. Well done. Nothing likely to happen now
in your southeastern area, but the other attack, we think, will
go as planned. More word to come when anything changes.

That was all: no names attached, nothing hazarded beyond reason,
although Uther knew instantly that G was Gulrhys Lot. He showed
the letter to Garreth, and then he went off by himself again to try to
reason out what he must do next in the face of such developments.
By the end of the day, he had decided that his initial reactions had
been correct and all that remained was to maintain a close liaison
with Camulod while bringing his own clansmen to the peak of
readiness for the invasion of Cambria in April. It crossed his mind
then to be grateful for once that his mountain-bred people set no
great store by farming, for they would have no worries about fighting when they should be planting crops.

Mid-April passed with no sign of the invaders, but in the meantime
Uther had received a message from Ygraine in Cornwall, written
from her dictation by the same trusted priest who delivered it—the
first indication Uther had received that Queen Ygraine was a Christian. She was well, she told him, and in good health, her baby due
in early June, but the country was in dire condition and the people
lived in fear not just for their lives but for their children's future. The
murder of his generals had plunged Lot's kingdom into disorder of
a magnitude too great to describe. Bereft of their leaders—and it
appeared that Issa and Loholt had been revered by their fierce followers—the two armies had revolted and for a space of more than

a month had remained beyond Lot's control, burning the country-side and creating havoc among the local clans whose food and provisions they had plundered without hindrance.

Only thanks to the exerted strengths of Cerdic and Tewdric, his last two remaining generals, and by granting the mutineers great tracts of land of their own had Lot been able to establish order again and regain some semblance of authority. And even that had been greatly weakened by the fact that the land he gave to them had been land owned by his own people, so that he was dispossessing his clansmen of their own ancestral homelands to appease the greed of Outlanders whom he himself had brought into those lands. Lot would never recover from that treachery, she wrote, but for the time being he had the strength to override his people's anger and hatred.

There was talk now among the Outlanders of reorganizing their plans and carrying out their invasion of Camulod, but it was yet only talk, she said. New leaders were emerging among their warriors, but none of them had yet won undisputed leadership, and that was not likely to change in the near future. In the meantime, Lot roared and rampaged, black with suspicion and seeing treachery and disloyalty everywhere he looked. He was right in that, but for all the wrong reasons. Somehow, she wrote, in his demented logic, he yet perceived himself as being wronged and believed that all the world was conspiring to bring him down when all he tried to do was for the betterment of those he ruled. His suspicions extended even to her, she said, although she had done nothing, fearing for the child she bore, to incur either his displeasure or distrust, other than write this letter through a trusted friend. She begged Uther to make no attempt to contact her, since she was watched closely at all times and could not leave the walls of Lot's enclosure at Golant. Even her visiting priest had been stripped and searched before being allowed to see her.

She ended by telling him that the seaborne invasion, under Tewdric and Cerdic, was still planned, but that it had been enlarged by more than thirty galleys full of men. Herliss and Lagan had vanished into the hinterlands, she said, and Lot was raving about what he called their treachery and desertion. She had no idea how that would be resolved, nor did she know if either man had been in touch with Uther, but she was grateful that Lagan, at least, had taken his wife and son with him this time.

So, although the invaders were late, Uther knew they were coming, and in greater strength than previously planned. He worked his clansmen hard, going to extreme lengths of invention to keep them keen and on their toes, and prepared for a vicious, bitter fight.

Then, on a wind-wracked day close to the end of the month, out of a violent April gale, the ships were sighted. The invasion fleet sailed into the welcome shelter of the bay and spilled its cargo of men—hundreds of them wretchedly seasick—into Cambria.

The enemy loitered on the beach after landing, glad to be ashore. Perfectly confident that they had reached safety unobserved and unsuspected, their leaders took the time to form them up in regular divisions before they made any attempt to strike inland. The galleys that had brought the army, riding high in the water now that they were no longer laden, were in no hurry to strike out to the open, gale-swept seas again, and so they, too, loitered long after they should have dispersed and made away, clustered together in dangerous proximity to each other in the tranquil waters of the narrow bay.

Virtually unseen before they hit their first targets, volleys of flaming arrows began to rain down with deadly accuracy from the high, flanking cliffs onto the closely packed and tinder-dry ships below, each missile wrapped in burning cloths soaked in oily pitch. Within moments of the first attack, fire had broken out on a score of vessels, and as the rising screams of the panicked crewmen trapped out on the water began to reach the ears of the men assembling on the shore, the hissing cascade of accurately aimed destruction continued, and towering fires began to leap from ship to ship among the close-packed throng.

The army commanders on the beach reacted instantly. Horns and bugles began to signal the advance as the first heavy drops of rain began falling from stone-grey skies. The leading formations of the invaders struck straight into the belt of woods enclosing the beach, only to find themselves faced with an impossible and impenetrably dense forest that began no more than fifteen paces inside the leading fringe of trees. From that point on, the way was impassible, because

for months hundreds of Dergyll's Griffyd warriors, working in concealment, had laboured enormously within the woods to create an
appalling trap, digging large, deep, steep-sided, overlapping holes
among the growing trees, leaving no level ground on which to walk,
scooping the dirt out from among the exposed roots and studding the
sides and bottom of each hole with long, sharp, lethal stakes.

Initial dismay quickly gave way to mass confusion and then to
panic as the realization dawned on the invaders that they were
trapped and doomed, for the few ships that had escaped the rain of
fire behind them had already fled, and the surface of the sea was littered with charred debris and still-blazing galleys.

Uther watched it all unfold with grim satisfaction from a bare
knoll to the northeast of the woods that hemmed in the suddenly
unfriendly beach. On the landward side where the King stood, the
ground rose sharply, with only the merest trace of soil covering the
solid bedrock. The mass of Uther's army was drawn up on this bare
ground, looking down on the woods, but they made no attempt to
move, for the Pendragon bowmen who had set fire to the ships had
left their high positions now and hurried down to regroup in a long,
double line fronting their own army, facing the outer fringe of the
woods. From there, as the first of the men who had survived the
staked trap beneath the trees began to emerge, exhausted from their
passage, the bowmen shot them down remorselessly, so that a ring
of corpses soon marked the exit from the trees.

When he thought sufficient damage had been done, Uther signalled his bowmen to withdraw, and they clustered around the two
large wagons, laden with sheaves of fresh arrows, that sat off to his
right. There they refilled their empty quivers before returning again
to the high cliffs on either side of the bay on the far side of the belt
of trees. From those heights, overlooking the exposed beach, they
would set up a crossfire killing zone, taking advantage of the great
range of their longbows and making it impossible for any of the
Outlanders to return to the beach in search of safety.

In the meantime, as more and more of the enemy emerged cautiously from the trap among the trees, stepping over the arrow-
riddled corpses of their fallen fellows, they found themselves facing

rank upon rank of waiting warriors, fresh and unblooded, who stood calmly looking down on them, waiting for them to approach. More than a few turned and ran back into the woods, but there was nowhere for them to go, because the woods were choked with cursing, frightened men coming their way.

Uther found that he was clenching his jaw so hard that his muscles were beginning to ache. He sucked in a deep breath and made himself turn his head to look to his right and then his left. He knew what would happen from then on. His subordinates had been well instructed, and they would show the invading Outlanders no mercy. They had neither the time nor the facilities to accommodate prisoners. And the unforeseen destruction of the entire enemy fleet meant that there would be no salvation from the water for the Outlanders. The slaughter here today, he knew, would be appalling, but there was nothing he could do to obviate it. The Outlanders, were he to leave them alive, would show no gratitude. Indeed, they would interpret his mercy as a weakness, one in which they would never indulge. They would not then make their way humbly homeward, grateful for being spared. They would behave according to their natures and attack again, and so they must all be killed.

Below him, the destruction continued, and most of his army had not yet made a move towards the enemy. He turned to Dergyll ap Griffyd and nodded for him to take over, then swung his horse away and angled it uphill, back towards his own camp, hoping as he went that he had situated it far enough away from the battle to be beyond the range of his hearing.

Thanks to Uther's informants, the invasion was over almost before it had a chance to begin, providing him with a chilling lesson on the importance of secrecy, security and earning the loyalty of the people.

Uther was back on the road to Camulod again in early May, a full month ahead of what he would have considered possible only three months earlier, and at the head of a larger army than he could have anticipated—an army, moreover, that was strong in morale and confidence, its personnel still more than slightly drunk with the swiftness and totality of the victory they had won over Lot's invaders.

No move had yet been made against Camulod, and so Uther brought his mother, Veronica. Veronica and Luceiia would be able to look after each other, he knew, while he was gone, and he blessed the gods who had permitted everything to work out so well for him and his people, when they might easily have looked the other way. Perhaps, he dared to whisper to himself, his luck had turned at last.

Despite his gratitude for all his good fortune, however, Uther was sombre and uncommunicative, riding alone most of the time, closely followed by Nemo, who guarded him jealously and was never without an unsheathed weapon in one hand or the other. Garreth Whistler and Huw Strongarm both watched this, saying nothing to anyone but wondering independently of each other what could be bothering the King. He ought, by rights, to have been soaring high in the aftermath of his complete victory, but it seemed to them that nothing could be farther from the truth.

He was still in the same frame of mind when they reached Camulod, and as far as they could see, nothing had changed by the time he rode out with Titus and Flavius, Merlyn, Donuil and Lucanus to inspect the perimeter of the Colony's holdings and assess and examine the quality of the army Camulod had set aside for Uther's use.

Uther himself felt no burden upon him, other than the familiar one of responsibility and a novel, unaccustomed need to conduct himself with great caution and much forethought in the adventure he was about to undertake, for the political situation within the troubled land of Cornwall was not one that could be lightly dismissed by an advancing army from outside. He was about to launch a hostile incursion into that territory, and while it wouldn't be his first, he had never before faced such a dangerous Cornwall, teeming as it was with unsettled native Cornish troops—factions and private armies—whose loyalties were now highly unpredictable. When Lot fell, as he undoubtedly would in the near future, the fighting among the Cornish warlords would likely escalate into full and open war, depending upon who emerged from the ruck, fighting for dominance. That struggle in itself was dangerous enough to demand a cautious approach, but the risk of catastrophe was increased indescribably by the presence of the thousands of leaderless but highly volatile mercenary Outlanders who had formed the armies of Issa and Loholt. These might swing their support at any time to back any one of the contending warlords, depending upon who was able to negotiate most tellingly with them. Or instead they might produce new leaders from among their own ranks, as Ygraine had forewarned, and join forces to overrun Cornwall on their own behalf, crushing the local Cornish opposition.

Eclipsing even his preoccupation with the threat of war within war in Cornwall, however, Uther found himself haunted by the looming spectre of fatherhood. Ygraine would give birth to their son—it had never even occurred to him that the child might be a girl—in a matter of mere weeks, or perhaps even days, and it was not inconceivable that she might have already done so—which meant that he could already have a son and heir living in Cornwall. That, more than any other consideration, was what consistently gave him pause and had led to the unusual distance remarked on by his men.

Uther had been raised and schooled in the formerly Roman and traditionally Camulodian discipline of responsible leadership, where no commander ever lightly risked the lives and welfare of his men. His own life, however, had always been another matter altogether, barely meriting consideration. That it was invariably placed at the disposal of, and dedicated to the safety of, the men who relied on him for his leadership was a simple given, one of the facts of his life that was so much part of him as to be unremarkable. Now, however, for the first time in his life, Uther found himself considering his own vulnerability and mortality, visualizing himself as he truly was in battle: isolated at the head of his own formation, in front of all his men and presenting himself not only as their unmistakable leader, but also as the prime target of the enemy.

From the moment of his discovery that Ygraine was pregnant and Lot had acknowledged her child as his own, Uther had refused even to allow himself to consider that any relationship might ever develop between the child and Gulrhys Lot. He knew that Lot would soon die at his hands, and dead, Lot could make no claim to anyone's paternity. But then, more recently, a new thought had occurred to him: what would happen, he wondered, if he himself were killed, leaving the child an orphan—what then? The child would be as helpless as any other child must be—all of the children who were not his son and heir to Pendragon—for years at the mercy of all the ills that fate could shower upon a fatherless infant until it had grown to the point at which it could begin looking after its own interests.

He did not even attempt to delude himself that Ygraine might make do, left alone. She would be stuck in Cornwall, where being a woman meant being a slave, a chattel, with no more worth or value than her looks might earn for her on any one day. Certainly, a mother might look after a child's basic needs, but the strength and protection of a powerful and caring father was something no child should ever have to live without. It occurred to him that his own father's love for him had been uncommon, and that most of the other fathers he had known and observed had been very unlike Uric Pendragon, unwilling to show open love to their own sons or to anyone else. Be that as it may, he decided that he would be unstinting with his love to his own son. If he lived. If he stopped making a target of himself for eager enemies. If he survived to see his son grow up without the need to grow reliant upon his mother alone.

But if that were not to be, if he were killed in the fighting that loomed ahead in Cornwall, what could he do to ensure his son's welfare then? How could he arrange to have immediate and infallible assistance sent to Ygraine and her son, *his* son, immediately upon his death? No one knew the child was his except Ygraine herself. Sharing that knowledge with another, any other, meant increasing the risk of the word spreading, and if it spread too far too soon, then Lot would find out, and mother and son would die, long before Uther could reach them.

He could write a letter, a testament, and leave it in trust with his Grandmother Luceiia in Camulod when he rode off to war, with instructions that it was to be opened after his death in battle. He would acknowledge that the child born to Ygraine was his and would leave instructions for the rescue of the boy and his mother, and for their transportation to the sanctuary of Camulod, where they could both live in comfort and prosperity among family who would love them. After that, it would remain only for the rescuers to find the mother and child in the chaos of Lot's Cornwall.

And if that proved to be impossible? How long would it take until the boy outgrew the need for his mother's protection and became strong enough and clever enough to look out for himself? That would be at least fifteen years, he thought, feeling stirrings of panic in the pit of his stomach. But then he thought, well, twelve at least . . . twelve years for a boy to grow smart enough to run and hide, to save his skin. After all, even a tiny tyke like the seven-year-old Nemo could scuttle into hiding. Nevertheless, after seven years living as an orphan in Cornwall, how would the boy ever know that he was born of Pendragon?

Uther felt frustration and anger wash over him, and he knew that thoughts such as these could unnerve him completely. He threw himself into other activities, then, determined to lose himself in their urgencies. No matter what he did, however, the concern for his unborn son's welfare was there in the back of his mind, and the vision of Ygraine smiling at the infant on her knee was always close to the forefront.

By the time he returned to Camulod from his inspection tour of the perimeter defences, he had arrived at a concrete decision: his main priority upon entering Cornwall would be to find Ygraine and her child, separate them from Lot and his creatures and spirit them quickly and safely back to Camulod. Once that had been achieved, and he was sure of their safety in the custody of his mother and grandmother, he could settle in to the campaign properly and give it all the attention it required and deserved. He had able and loyal deputies who could stand in for him at the start of the campaign, until his first, main task—ensuring the welfare of his heir—was taken care of. After that, he would take the reins back into his own hands and, at the head of his cavalry—his own and Camulod's—he would sweep Gulrhys Lot, his presence, his treachery and his armies not merely out of Cornwall but out of the land of Britain.

He wrote his letter of testament slowly and with great care, reworking it several times until he was convinced that its meaning was clear and precise and that no one could possibly misconstrue what it said. Then he left it with his Grandmother Luceiia, with appropriate instructions as to how and when it was to be opened.

Foul weather caused Uther great concern and gave him much to fret over. With his allies and supplies all in place, his army had been assembled for more than two weeks, and his carefully prepared plans all indicated that he should already have been on the road for a full week, heading southwestward along the great Roman road to the ancient town of Isca, where they would swing west into the peninsula of Cornwall. But Uther had hung back, against what his mind was whispering might have been his better judgment, stubbornly hoping for a break in the weather and refusing to give the marching order until the last possible moment. He could see little sense in leading an army off to war if its personnel were already sniffling and miserable, cold and soaking wet before they even set out. Their morale, he maintained in the face of the little opposition and disagreement he encountered, would be non-existent before they even lost sight of the battlements of Camulod if they had to slog their way through pouring rain, chill winds and ankle-deep mud. And so he waited, living in hope from day to day that the abominable weather would finally break and that he could lead his men out in sunshine, dry for at least the beginning of their campaign.

It took eight days after their planned starting date for him to get his wish, but the break did come, and although it was not exactly a bright and clarion day of glowing sunlight, there were blue patches of sky visible between banks of clouds in the early morning, and the rain had died away during the second watch of the previous night. Encouraged by the early signs of brightening prospects, he had kept his men in readiness that morning, poised for departure while he waited until the strengthening sun could break through the cloud cover with something resembling authority. Then, when it eventually did, and as the strength of its warmth and light began to grow more and more apparent, he summoned Popilius Cirro to him, along with the senior cavalry commander from the Camulod garrison, and Garreth Whistler and Huw Strongarm from the Cambrian contingent. Telling them to mount up and ride behind him, he led them up to the reviewing stand by the edge of the great drilling ground at the bottom of Camulod's hill and sat there facing his army, waiting for his presence to bring silence.

This was a far smaller army than he had originally intended to command—a mere two thousand strong, as opposed to the six-thousand-man host he had visualized months earlier—but he was convinced that it would be more effective and more lethal than the larger host might have been. His deliberations on the condition of Cornwall after receiving Ygraine's letter had convinced Uther that the advantages he might gain from numbers would be more than offset by the difficulties of feeding and sustaining a large army in a ruined land, and his allies had finally come to agree with him. An army must sustain itself by feeding off the land through which it travelled, but Cornwall, as they had ascertained from the reports of scouting parties sent out for that purpose, was utterly devastated and incapable of feeding its own after the depredations of the leaderless mercenary Outlanders and the internecine wars of the various Cornish warlords. And wherever Herliss and Lagan might be now, the massed strength they had hoped to gather against Lot had evidently failed to materialize. Uther had heard from neither man since their disappearance after the deaths of Issa and Loholt. Against his own will, he had come to realize that leading a massive army into Cornwall would be folly under such circumstances, and so he had conferred with his allies, in both Camulod and his own Cambria, in an attempt to make the best of the unpalatable situation facing them. Lot's Cornwall must be invaded—they all knew that and there was no arguing against it—but the invasion Uther now proposed to lead would more resemble the thrust of a sword blade into the lines of cleavage in a lump of coal than it would the sweeping arc of a swung scythe. He would penetrate and cleave in a straight thrust, rather than surge on a broad front. And so the army waiting to depart now was composed of a mere two thousand men, half cavalry and half infantry, and included several hundred Pendragon bowmen. All of them, horse and foot, were hand picked, the best of the combined best of Camulod and Cambria, and as he waited for them to fall silent, Uther Pendragon felt proud of—and somewhat chastened by—the way they had competed among themselves to win a place in the ranks now facing him. He refused absolutely to allow himself to think he might be leading all of them to death, and he silently sucked in great, shuddering breaths to calm his voice before addressing them.

The army had been assembled in its divisions—infantry, cavalry and Cambrian clansmen—for hours, and complete stillness fell over the entire assembly as the men waited for Uther to speak. He took his time, savouring the anticipation in the air, theirs and his own. Then, when he judged the moment to be exactly right, he removed his helmet and slung it from the bow of his saddle before standing up in his stirrups and loosening the clasp of his great red cloak with its emblazoned golden dragon. He swung the garment up and off his shoulders, swirling it around in a great sweep of colour and then catching the folds of it in the crook of his left arm and draping it across his saddle in front of him. Only then did he begin to speak, using his command voice, and his words were clearly audible to every man there.

"Well, lads, the weather's breaking. It looks like a fine day to go to war."

The sound that greeted his opening words was a low rumble, like distant thunder, swelling rapidly, then dying away to silence again. Uther swept the assembled ranks deliberately with his eyes, moving his head slowly from left to right, his gaze taking in every element of the troops massed in front of him.

"We'll be in Cornwall three days from now, and you all know why. There is a pestilence in that country, and we are chosen to stamp it out. Think you we're up to it?"

"Aye, Uther, that we are!" It was a single voice, shouted from an unknown throat, but it brought a bark of laughter and a swelling chorus of agreement.

Uther shouted into the sound as it died away, "That man has won a jug of ale for himself and all his squad mates in camp tonight. Who was he?"

A stirring among the ranks then and a small commotion marked the source of the first shout, and the man, a Camulodian cavalry trooper, raised one hand above his head. Uther pointed him out to everyone who had not seen him.

"What's your name?"

"Cascady, King Uther."

"Well, Cascady, present yourself this night to the camp quartermaster and collect your prize, but you had better bring a friend to help you carry it and prevent you from drinking all of it yourself." This brought another shout of laughter, cheers and jeers, and Uther waited until it had died away completely before speaking again, his voice now sober and serious.

"We are two thousand strong, lads. Not the biggest force that Camulod has ever sent to war, but by all the gods, we might be the strongest and the most agile. We have horse and foot, both, and the finest bows and bowmen in the world. Camulod and Pendragon, side by side. Lot of Cornwall has nothing that can stand against us, but our dearest hope must be that he will try the truth of that. If he does—and he will—he'll rue the day he ever saw us coming. Are you ready for him?"

A great shout of "Aye!"

"Aye, we are, but hear me clearly. We are not marching into Cornwall to stand there and fight in enormous battles. We—you, every one of you—are a striking force. Our objective is to move quickly and constantly, striking hard and fast wherever we encounter hostiles. We are going raiding, lads, and even if we fail to find oily King Lot, we'll smash his mercenaries and we'll kill his confidence. Now, are you ready for him?"

"Aye!"

"Is *he* ready for *us*?"

"No!"

"Good! Then let's go and show him the damnable blunder he made when he invaded Camulod and Cambria. Move out!"

He stood up straight in his stirrups, drew his long sword and waved it above his head in the recognized signal, and as the cheering began to die away, the first signs of disciplined movement began among the individual columns of men and horses. Uther watched them for several more moments, then turned to his companions and nodded to each of them in turn before dismissing them to their individual duties. After that he rode back up the hill to the high vantage

point overlooking the campus, where his mother and his grandmother stood with Merlyn, Donuil, Titus, Flavius and several others
who had assembled to watch another Camulodian army start out on
a campaign.

From the centre of the assembly, in the middle of the vast campus,
a full score of enormous commissary wagons began to move, slowly
and ponderously, each of them hauled by a rough-matched team of
eight huge horses and commanded by an expert teamster, who sat up
high on the driver's seat, wielding the reins in one hand and a long,
leather whip in the other and rolling on his high, swaying perch like
a sailor in the mast lookout of a seagoing galley. Slowly and sedately
the wagons rolled forward and arranged themselves into pairs to
assume their place in the middle of the long column of Popilius
Cirro's infantry, where they would be safest from attack and depre-
dation. The commissary wagons were the soldiers' lifeline, representing food, drink and warmth, and no enemy would be permitted to
approach them casually. Watching these majestic vehicles lumber
slowly into motion, noting the size and number of them, their pon-
derous dignity and the enormous swarm of lesser cargo and supply
wagons that followed behind in support of them, Uther could appreciate more clearly than by any other example the scope and duration
of the adventure on which they—all of them, his Cambrian men and
Camulod's best and finest—were now being launched. By the time
they returned from this campaign, those among them who did return,
these mighty wagons would be empty of supplies and their ancillary
support vehicles long since emptied and set to service like the commissary wagons themselves as transportation for badly wounded
men. That would be many months in the future.

Uther had made all his farewells to everyone, and he had been
more aware than ever before that he might never see any of his
beloved friends and family again. Of them all, the leave-taking that
had pained him most was the parting from his Cousin Merlyn, who
had smiled and hugged him close and wished him well with
absolute conviction and sincerity—though the Caius Merlyn Britannicus with whom Uther had grown to manhood would have had
to be tied down to his bed and then locked up in a barred cell before

he would have permitted Uther Pendragon to ride off to war without him at the head of a Camulodian army.

As the main body of his infantry began wheeling and regrouping into their marching formations, Uther turned his head slightly and glanced again at his cousin. Merlyn was watching the troops closely, the expression in his eyes making it clear that he was enjoying the intricacy of their disciplined manoeuvres, but there was nothing there that reminded Uther of the Caius Merlyn of his younger days. He heaved a great sigh, filled with regret, then turned to his left and bent forward in his saddle, reaching out to where his Grandmother Luceiia sat beside his mother, close by him, in a light, one-horse cart that her husband Publius Varrus had built years earlier. Luceiia saw him lean towards her, reaching, and stretched her hand out to meet his. He kissed it, squeezed it gently, nodded to her one last time, blew a kiss to his mother, and then dug his spurs into his horse's flanks, kicking it down towards the departing army on the great plain.

THIRTY-SIX

Even before penetrating Cornwall, Uther had decided that he had no wish to waste time and manpower in besieging strongholds, so from the outset of his campaign he took evasive action every time his scouts identified a strongly held, fortified position. He preferred to send his army looping around the obstacle, rather than run the risk of being inveigled into a long, costly and unsatisfying siege that would tie up most of his resources. He took particular care, too, in not merely avoiding but staying far away from several of the largest and best-known strongholds, in particular Golant, Lot's own strongest holding and his most often used base, and Tir Gwyn, Herliss's White Fort. Herliss, he knew, was gone, and it would not have surprised him to learn that his stronghold had been seized by Gulrhys Lot. Until he knew one way or the other, Uther had decided he would be cautious and make no attempt to approach the place.

Passing it by on his first advance southward, however, he had dispatched Nemo alone on foot at the closest point of his approach to find out what she could about the situation in the White Fort. Nemo had gone willingly but slowly, in the guise of a homeless peasant and armed only with a heavy cudgel and a knife with a rusted but serviceable blade, and she had been clearly warned, however needlessly, about the potential dangers in penetrating an enemy stronghold.

Nemo was gone for nigh on three weeks, and then returned bearing mixed tidings. Tir Gwyn had been confiscated, as Uther had guessed it might be, forfeited by Herliss as punishment for his continuing absence from Lot's service, and it was now garrisoned by a

strong detachment of mercenary Outlanders. Nemo had entered the
fort easily enough, finding it full of rootless people whose only
common bond was that none of them was from Cornwall, and had
immediately begun blending into the place, attracting no attention,
but listening closely and waiting until she felt her face had become
familiar to the people around her. That had taken ten days, Nemo
estimated, and after that she had begun casually and indirectly
asking questions.

It was common knowledge that Lot's fury on learning of the
defection of Herliss and Lagan had been spectacular in its insanity:
he had slaughtered the entire party that brought him confirmation of
the disappearance, despite his full awareness that he himself had
sent them out specifically to discover and report the truth of the situation. He had apparently seen no irony in having them killed for
succeeding.

No one knew where Herliss and Lagan were hiding, Nemo
reported, but rumours abounded that they had been joined by
several other powerful Cornish Chiefs and leaders, and that they had
raised and were training an army of Cornish clansmen outside the
boundaries of Cornwall itself to invade their own homeland and
overthrow Gulrhys Lot. As a direct result of these rumours, Lot had
withdrawn most of his free-ranging mercenary forces and formed
them into armies again, keeping heavy concentrations of them
within the protecting walls of the score and more of hill forts, some
of them ancient and unused for hundreds of years, that were scattered the length and breadth of Cornwall.

Uther was prepared to accept Nemo's news with relief, since,
along with everyone else in his army, he had been finding it hard to
accept that they had spent more than four weeks in Cornwall,
marching openly from one end of the peninsula to the other and then
back again, without ever encountering an enemy force large enough
to fight. They had seen many small groups, but those were always
small enough and clever enough to disappear into the nearest hills
immediately upon catching sight of the Camulodian host.

Uther's Cambrian scouts, predominantly Pendragon bowmen,
ranged as far as three miles ahead of the main army at all times,

forming a moving, semicircular screen around the advancing troops, and they were the ones who monopolized such fighting as there was, surprising small, unsuspecting groups of enemy warriors, many of them hunting parties, and dispatching them swiftly and effectively from hundreds of paces away.

Despite the lack of a tangible, physical presence, however, it was plain to Uther's people that the enemy had been here recently, for the entire land lay ravaged in the aftermath of the Outlanders' revolt. Burned and ruined buildings lay everywhere they looked: huts, cottages, roundhouses and longhouses, many of them built of wood and recognizable now only by the shape of their charred remnants. They found larger settlements, too, where people had congregated in hamlets and permanent encampments, usually at a crossroads of some description, although the "roads" were frequently little more than well-worn tracks or livestock trails, and close to those settlements, all of them ruined and abandoned, the Camulodians could not fail to note, mainly because of the inescapable stench, the rotting corpses that hung from almost every tree.

Garreth Whistler brought it to Uther's attention that among the burned-out buildings, most of those that had been built of stone had had their walls pushed down after the fires, after the roof trees had fallen in, because the fallen stones of the walls invariably lay on top of the charred timbers and ashes of the thatched roofs. Plainly the damage had been more than a mere incidental by-product of war. These buildings had been demolished deliberately in order to deprive local people of shelter and living space.

Uther nodded and took careful note of the fact, filing the information away for retrieval later when he could think about it properly. For the time being, he had other matters on his mind, not the least of which concerned Ygraine's whereabouts. He had blindly expected her to contact him when he entered Cornwall. Now, after days of watching and waiting, he had to admit to himself that he had no idea where she might be and no way of discovering whether she was well or unwell, or whether she was free or being confined against her will in one of Lot's many scattered strongholds. The helpless frustration of not knowing dominated everything he tried to do.

Finally, sitting by his own small campfire on a cold night after a long and exhausting day spent ploutering about in fetlock-deep mud and pouring rain, Uther took Garreth Whistler into his full confidence and told him everything about what had happened between him and Ygraine. The King's Champion listened attentively, without attempting to interrupt the tale, and then sat staring silently into the fire after Uther had finished.

He had known, he said, that there was something going on in Uther's mind that was distracting much of his attention from the task at hand. Now that he knew what it was, he felt greatly relieved, particularly since he could tell that Uther was worrying needlessly. When Uther challenged him on that, surprised by such an offhand dismissal of his concern, Garreth merely shrugged and pointed out that the Queen was at the full term of her pregnancy, a cruel and demanding time for any woman, when her mind must be awash with fears and concerns over her own life and death, and with the entire spectrum of birth and survival and the health and welfare of both herself and her first-born child. Unrealistic, he grunted, for Uther to expect that she might make the time to sit down, empty her mind of her own concerns and write him a letter, even had she the freedom and a willing, trustworthy scribe to write for her.

He pointed out, too, that she had also told Uther openly in her last letter, by his own admission, that she was beset and surrounded by Lot's spies and was being closely watched, and that she had been able to write to him on that occasion thanks only to the god-sent, unexpected opportunity presented by the wandering priest who had visited her. Would she, then, be tempted to destroy herself and her child, the Champion asked, by entrusting any kind of message to the people surrounding her simply in the hope of soothing his troubled brow? Uther's fretting was pointless and illogical, since common sense could explain the Queen's silence. Besides, he growled, it was unworthy, womanish behaviour for a King at the head of an army that looked to him for manhood and leadership.

Uther's natural reaction to this was to bluster and object, but Garreth Whistler gave him no chance. Presumably, he continued, Ygraine had not yet come to the birthing stage. After all, had the birthing been successful and produced an heir born to his legitimate Queen, Lot would have had the tidings trumpeted from every dunghill in Cornwall. Had it been otherwise, had anything happened to Ygraine or to her child, be it male or female, that word would also be abroad in the land, whether Lot wished it or no. But word of neither event had been heard, so Garreth thought it safe to assume that there had been no birth yet.

Uther listened and was grateful, although he knew that nothing in Garreth's words spoke of Ygraine's welfare. The fate of the child's mother would mean less than nothing to Gulrhys Lot compared to the reality of having a son of his own. If there were the slightest question of choice, of the life and health of one over the other, Ygraine would die as soon as the question was defined. The birth of a daughter, on the other hand, would be unimportant to Lot, but it would remove both mother and child from danger.

Listening to the Whistler's words, Uther dismissed his anger and became convinced that he had been worrying needlessly and prematurely, for the hard-headed truths Garreth was uttering were exactly the kind of sensible, pragmatic direction and opinion he had come to expect from this extraordinary man. Garreth Whistler had now been Champion to three Pendragon Kings, having transferred his allegiance naturally and easily to King Uric upon the death of Ullic Pendragon, and Uther had been greatly pleased, when he himself had become King on his own father's death, that Garreth Whistler had agreed to serve as *his* Champion, in turn.

Uther was still thinking about the Whistler, smiling in appreciation of a loyal friend, as he lay down on his cot that night, and he slept better than he had in a long time.

Three days after that conversation, a letter arrived that changed everything, brought into camp at dusk by a messenger who carried Uther's own ring, the one he had left with the Queen, on a leather thong about his neck. The fellow carried Ygraine's letter securely bound at the small of his back, five large pages of fine papyrus covered in a strong but concise and clearly legible hand and folded lengthwise into a soft, narrow leather pouch.

Much news, little time to tell it. This must be completed and gone within the hour, a fleeting chance gained when least expected. I am speaking it aloud to Joseph, my priest and confessor, who has arrived at the perfect time to write this for me.

Your son is born and he is beautiful, the image of his father, save that he has shining, wondrous eyes of yellow gold, the like of which I have never seen. He came to us three weeks ago at the second hour of morning, and I have named him Arthur, since you were not here to advise me of any other name. He is glorious to behold, perfect in every detail.

May God defend us, for should this letter be found and read by unfriendly eyes, then we are dead, my babe and I. The man bringing it to you has been known to me all my life. He is Erse, his name is Calum, and he is one of my brother Connor's most trusted men, sent to me in secret, disguised as a mercenary, in order to find out if I am well. Connor wants to take me out of Cornwall, home to my father's Hall in Eire. Calum will return to my home when he leaves you, bearing the tale of my misery, although he knows naught of me and you, or of our son, and soon Connor will come to take me home.

In the meantime, I have my son. The Monster has not seen him and does not even know he lives, even after three long weeks of happiness for me. I am surrounded again by my own people, and have been so for several months, for which I thank God daily, and we have managed to achieve a miracle despite the presence of the Monster's creatures crowding around my doors. One of my serving women, Clara, had her child the night before I had mine, and we were able to conceal my birthing the following night. It was sudden and relatively silent, and the concealment was unplanned at first, until we found that no one outside my chambers had even been aware of the event. Now Clara suckles my child, although I do, too, when I can be unobserved. Another of my women has

sewn me a girdle containing a pillow large enough to
make me look as though my babe is still to come, and so
we have been able to pretend that nothing has yet
occurred. I know not how long we will be able to keep up
the deceit, but as long as we can, we will.

Here are some tidings that should be of note to you:
there is a heavy concentration of Saxon forces gathered in
the coastal region to the east, just beyond the borders of
Cornwall. The Monster's glowering minions have deemed
this to be a serious threat and he has sent an army to con-
front the Saxon interlopers and drive them back where they
came from. Need I tell you he did not go himself? The
army, ten thousand strong and under the command of a
new-found mercenary champion, a sullen, dark-faced lout
called Nabur, left weeks ago, just prior to your arrival. No
word of how they are prospering has come back to us.

And yet more tidings, far more doleful. You may already
know that Lot has seized Tir Gwyn and declared Herliss and
Lagan traitors, condemned to be killed on sight. That has
been so for several months now. The latest infamy, however,
is difficult to imagine, let alone to describe and set down in
words. It appears that some of Lot's creatures managed to
infiltrate Herliss's following and discovered where he was
encamped. Lagan was away when they made their attack,
but they captured Herliss, and Lagan's wife and son, Lydda
and Cardoc. Herliss they killed immediately, bringing back
his head to Lot in a cask of salt water, but they brought the
woman and her son alive, in chains, to face Lot's mercy.

By our dear Christus, I can barely speak of this, but if
ever proof were needed that my benighted spouse is insane
and needs to be killed, it is contained in what I must
describe next . Lot gave the woman Lydda over to his sol-
diers for their pleasure, and they used her until they even-
tually killed her. I know that in itself, although monstrous,
is not unheard of, but what followed is. He made the boy,
who was eleven years old, watch the atrocities that were

*being heaped upon his mother, telling him constantly as he
watched that his father, Lagan, was to blame for what was
happening. The poor boy was beside himself until his reason left him and he apparently fell silent, never to speak
again. Then, when Lydda was dead, Lot had her feet cut off
and sent them back, along with the child's hands, severed
from his body after his murder, to where Herliss and his
people had been camping when they were captured. This
was a reminder, he sent word to Lagan, of the penalties for
disloyalty to a friend.*

*I have no knowledge of Lagan's reaction, and I have
no wish to think about it, but the man must be demented
with grief.*

*And finally: at this time, Lot is hiding in the north, in
his northernmost stronghold, which is an ancient place with
no name other than "the Shelter." It is on the coast, some
twelve leagues north of the island fortress at Rosnant,
where there they are adding to the fortifications and building barracks, although there is not yet sufficient comfort in
the place for Lot's taste. He will stay in the Shelter, it seems,
until word reaches him of success in the southeast against
the Saxons. I have also heard a rumour, but not a solid one,
that he has gone there to await the arrival of a new fleet of
Erse galleys, nothing to do with me or mine. If that rumour
is true, then he might well be waiting for a fleet of galleys
belonging to our ancient enemies who call themselves the
Sons of Condran. If he is as terrified of my brother Connor
as I think he is, it would make a kind of twisted sense for
him to seek alliance with the Sons of Condran, and they
would be perfect for each other.*

*I think you may have a chance to deal with Lot once
and for all if you can take him while he is walled up in the
Shelter. They think of it as a coastal fort, but it is not quite
on the seacoast. My understanding is that it stands on a
headland overlooking the sea, but the cliffs are of soft stone
and subject to crumbling and collapse, and so the walls of*

the fort itself are set back some distance from the lip of the cliffs. I have been told, however, that you might be able to surround it completely and take it. You yourself will be the best judge of that when you see the place.

Those are all my tidings and my inky-fingered scribe has shown great patience with my stumbling and my changes. He assures me, however, that by the time he has recopied my words, you will see no sign of where the changes have occurred.

I have but one thing more to say to you, and it is this. We have never spoken of love, we two, and if truth be known, I have never really known what love is. Now, however, looking at our son, I know the feeling that threatens to consume me is love, and it is strangely like the feelings that have boiled here in my breast since last I saw your face. I know that when I gaze into your eyes again and see you hold our son in your strong arms, I will know love at last and forever. Farewell, and come to me safely. We will be moving soon to another of Lot's strongholds, since we have already been here for too long, and I will find a way of sending word to you when that occurs, so that you will be able to come and find us.

Farewell, and think of me sometimes.

Think of me sometimes. Uther smiled briefly upon reading that the first time. But then, slightly overwhelmed by the profusion of information in the letter, he left his quarters, saddled his horse and rode away to where he could be alone and free of interruptions. And there, on the bank of a fast-flowing stream, he sat down on a moss-covered tree stump and read Ygraine's words again several times aloud, allowing himself to be buffeted by the conflicting emotions they stirred up in him.

Among the first of these were pride and a sense of incredulous wonder. He had a son. That single piece of knowledge affected him more deeply than anything else he could remember. A son, Arthur Pendragon. He liked the name, sufficiently akin to his own to ring well in his ears when he spoke it aloud, as he did repeatedly. Arthur Pendragon. Uther Pendragon; Arthur Pendragon. And not merely a son, but an extraordinary one, beautiful and the image of his father, but with shining golden eyes the like of which his mother had never seen. He had heard of such eyes, however, among his own ancestry. Caius Britannicus, brother to his Grandmother Luceiia, had had such eyes—eagle's eyes, his grandmother had called them. And now they had resurfaced in his own son, the eyes of a golden eagle.

He sat silent for a long time after that, the letter loosely gripped in the hand that hung by his side as he sat gazing into nothingness, trying to imagine the boy and how he would grow up. But then other thoughts intruded and stole the warm glow from his eyes. Lagan Longhead had had a son, too, and had doted upon the boy. And now the lad was dead, his severed hands sent to Lagan, along with his mother's feet, in token of Lot's displeasure. *Displeasure!* Uther's stomach soured at the thought of what his friend must have endured on seeing those remains, and he had little difficulty in agreeing with Ygraine that Lagan must be well-nigh demented with grief and rage. But then the significance of Ygraine's news of Lot's present whereabouts came to him, and he sprang to his feet, determination swelling in his chest like a hard knot. He would find this Shelter and burn it about Lot's ears, and then he would send the whoreson's singed head to Lagan.

His mind resolved, and feeling more positive than at any time since entering Cornwall weeks earlier, he turned his attention to a new strategy, and as soon as he had regained his camp, Uther summoned his field commanders to discuss their imminent foray into the north to contain Lot in the bolt-hole called the Shelter.

Despite his wish to avoid prolonged sieges, Uther had nonetheless discussed the possibility of mounting a direct strike against a fortified position with his field commanders several times in the recent past, on the clearly defined understanding that they might be fortunate enough to gain absolute knowledge of Lot's whereabouts and be able to pin him in one place, unable to flee. That last point was arguable in this instance for a number of reasons, including their utter lack of knowledge about the place called the Shelter, and

Uther's senior commanders did not hesitate to raise their objections.
The report on which Uther was basing his proposed plan to march
northward against Lot was no more trustworthy, they suggested,
than an earlier report that had come to them about an army of Erse
warriors called *Galloglas* that was supposed to land on the north-
western coast of Cornwall some time within the following few days.
If that report was in any way true, they pointed out, then Uther
might well be leading his army into needless danger, and a costly
battle against a nameless enemy would do them little good when
their true quarry was Gulrhys Lot himself.

Uther did not accept that. The enemy army described as *Galloglas* in that report, which had come from a nameless sympathizer,
must, he believed, be the same Erse fleet mentioned in his report—
the fleet that Lot had marched north to await. Based on that belief,
he argued that the newcomers would sail directly to where Lot
awaited them in the fort known as the Shelter.

Some of his most senior commanders, including Mucius Quinto,
the military surgeon attached to the contingent from Camulod,
remained unconvinced that Uther's information was incontrovertibly
valid, despite Uther's fiery convictions, and their skepticism was
aggravated by his stubborn refusal to identify his informant, aware
as always of the need to protect Ygraine. Quinto's objections were
based upon the risk of useless slaughter. Slaughter was part and
parcel of warfare, Quinto knew, but needless slaughter was anathema
to him. The march Uther was proposing to undertake was foolhardy
under the circumstances, an unacceptable risk under any conditions
and one that directly flouted Uther's own rules governing the selection of military objectives and the responsible disposition of troops.

Agreeing with Quinto, Popilius Cirro went so far as to call
Uther's suggestion outrageously impulsive; it had to be considered
unjustifiable, until and unless they could obtain more concrete
information from at least one additional source about the supposed
threat posed by the Saxon army reported to be massed on Lot's
eastern borders. They had no proof that army was even there, Popilius maintained, and even less proof that Lot's main army had been
dispatched to deal with them. That lack of certainty, entailing the

very real possibility of a threat from their rear on a northward march, allied with this other unconfirmed report of an advancing army of Ersemen from the north, cried out to be resolved and settled before any major decisions could be made concerning troop movements and objectives.

Uther listened to all of them and then vetoed their disapproval, claiming that the existence of the written report he had received was proof enough. He even read the pertinent section of his letter aloud in an attempt to demonstrate his good faith, but his continuing refusal to put a name to his informant worked against the credibility of his information.

In the end, of course, Uther's will as King prevailed, but a degree of uncertainty over the outcome of his projected thrust remained, because none of his people had ever seen the fort Ygraine had described, and so they could not know how accessible the seacoast was from the fort's walls, or how wide the outer space around the fort, between the walls and the clifftop, might be. That information was vital, and Uther himself swore he wanted no part of attacking the position if Lot could simply escape by sea, leaving his mercenaries to defend his back. There was nothing they could really do to resolve that impasse, however, since they would not be able to answer the questions until they approached the place and saw it for themselves.

Once the decision to go there was made, however, Popilius and the rest of his commanders accepted his wishes, and the remainder of their planning fell quickly into place, although he reminded all of them, as always, about the standard observation and proviso governing all such planning. Uther had been taught by all his mentors and instructors that no battle plan, irrespective of how well or how painstakingly it might have been prepared, had ever been known to survive intact after the first real clash with the enemy. That was an accepted axiom of all warfare: to be effective and successful, a battle plan—and a commander's mind—must allow for an enormous amount of flexibility.

Uther and his commanders spent three days working on their strategy, and on the fourth day they set out for the northwest coast. They encountered no more opposition than they had in the previous

month, so they made excellent time, and the miles fell away at their
backs. Late in the afternoon of their fourth day's march, their
forward scouts sent back word that they had reached the coast and
were now within sight of the Shelter.

Uther called a halt and established camp immediately. Many of his
troops, he knew, would spend a sleepless night, as he would, anticipating the next day's battle, and all of them would be up and ready to
advance before dawn's hues first began to tinge the night sky.

All the sleepless nights, however, were wasted. As soon as
Uther came within sight of the stronghold called the Shelter and
stopped to take a long, evaluating look at it, he knew that their
journey had been but one more frustrating element in a campaign
already filled to overflowing with disappointment and inaction. The
thought had barely had the time to form in his mind, however,
before Garreth Whistler and Huw Strongarm rode up to put the lie
to it. They, too, had seen the hopelessness of the situation, but they
had seen beyond it, too, and sensed an advantage to be gained while
they were there in force.

The fort, a typical concentric ditch-and-dyke construction, had
been built on a headland, as his information had indicated, and its
walls were safely withdrawn from the edges of the cliffs of crumbling, friable rock, leaving a clear area surrounding the perimeter
that could conceivably accommodate an encircling force. Only an
idiot would have tried to put such a force there, however, for what
Uther's information had lacked was detail: the headland itself rose
steeply towards the sea, then ended in an abrupt, unscalable cliff,
and the fortification that had been established there over hundreds
of years had been adapted admirably by its builders to the steeply
sloping terrain. Many of the surfaces within the ramparts had been
raked so they were level, and the walls at the front of the fort, facing
the mainland, were more than twice as high as those at the rear.
Those walls showed Uther immediately that the place would not be
taken by direct assault; no besieging force could scale those enormous front slopes. Nor could any sustained attack be mounted
against the lesser walls at the back, for in order to reach the rear of
the fortification, any attacker would first have to circle the walls,

using the narrow strip of land between walls and clifftop as their only pathway. There was not a patch of cover anywhere. While the attackers would have to fight every pace of the way against the steep slope, the defenders on the ramparts high above them would be standing on artificially levelled ground. The entire area around the walls was a killing ground.

"Not what we thought, eh?" This was Huw Strongarm. Garreth Whistler said nothing at all, merely watching Uther with tightly pursed lips. "Still, it could be worse, from our point of view."

"Could it?" Uther asked. "How?"

Huw allowed his surprise to show fleetingly and then ploughed onward. "Well, Lot's in there, and he's stuck there as long as we stay."

"We have no way of knowing he's in there, Huw."

"Yes we have. He's there, I've just been told."

"By whom, and why have *I* not been told?"

Huw shrugged and dipped his head. "Because the word came to me through one of my own men no more than moments ago, and I'm telling you now. One of our scout patrols picked up two local farmers early this morning. They are no supporters of their King, and they didn't need much persuasion to tell everything they know about this place. They saw Lot's arrival here eight days ago, and he hasn't been seen since. So we have him, safely cooped up in there. There's no way out that I can see."

"You can't see the back view of the cliff, Huw. They could have flights of stairs leading all the way down to the beach there, for all we know. Lot could have left by sea days ago."

"Aye, he could have. It's possible, I'll grant you that. But I'll wager he didn't, and if he stayed, then he'll stay there now until we say he can leave. There *was* a way out at the back, for some of my fellows have been there, seen it and closed it off. You set me in charge of all the scouts, remember, and that means that all our scouts are now Pendragon. First thing I set them to do once they got here was to explore the seaward side of things. There's a way down to the sea from the back, certainly, but it's not man-made. There's a few flights of steps, but they're primitive, and the rest is as nature made it—steep and narrow and dangerous. About two-thirds of the way down from the top there's a chasm, as though the entire cliff fell sideways at some time. My fellows couldn't see the bottom of it, said it's just like a hole clear down through the earth. Anyway, the gap's about ten paces wide at its narrowest point, and crossed by a bridge. Or it was. My fellows chopped the bridge down."

"They chopped it down . . . Are you telling me it was unguarded?"

Huw grinned and shot a glance at Garreth Whistler. "Oh no, it was guarded. There's a guard tower above it and another below it, but they were built to guard against an attack coming up the path from the sea, and the people in them were not expecting Pendragon bowmen. No one was expecting our scouts and no one saw them arrive. They crept around the base of the cliffs under cover of night and then scaled them on either side of the path just after dawn. Then they flanked the guard towers and picked off all ten of the guards before the fools even knew they were under attack. After that, they chopped down the bridge. So no one will be leaving by that back route unless they sprout wings and fly across the chasm. And there will be no re-supply from the sea using that route, either."

By the time Huw had finished, Uther was shaking his head in admiration. But then Garreth Whistler spoke up. "Huw's people could be very important to us were we to leave them on the cliffs, Uther."

"How so?"

"Well, they're safe there from attack from above. No one can see them down there from the walls, let alone reach them. But then again they have the advantage of height and distance when the fleet that Lot's waiting for arrives—if it arrives. Lot's people in the fort up there will have no way of letting the newcomers know they're in danger. The fleet will sail in close, expecting to land safely at the base of the cliff, and my bowmen will use the same trick they used at home against the invasion fleet: fire arrows soaked in pitch. In the meantime, you can deploy your army right across the base of the headland there, and Lot's all trussed up like a fowl for roasting. Can't leave, can't escape."

"But then we'll be involved in a siege, and one we can't win. We have neither the time nor the resources."

"We don't need them. If Lot's Erse fleet comes when it's supposed to, we'll savage it and send it limping home. That'll be a victory, and we'll rub his nose in it, since he'll have to watch and do nothing. Then, with his fleet gone, we can hold him here by leaving a small force to keep him locked up while the rest of our army marches south again."

Uther sighed and then looked about him at the way his army spread across the landscape and at the way the old fortification on the headland reared above them. From where he sat, on a hill facing the rising headland, he could barely see the sea at all. The headland rearing up directly in front of him cut off most of the view, and he was left with no more than two small stretches of flat-horizoned seascape, one on either side of the promontory. Finally he nodded.

"Very well, we'll try it, but for no more than three days. I have no wish to sit around here growing old, waiting for a fleet that might not even be a reality. Make your dispositions then and convene a meeting of all officers in the command tent this afternoon an hour before dinner."

When the others had gone, Uther looked to where Nemo and a squad of Dragons were erecting the huge tent and estimated that it would be no less than half an hour before he could hope to move in and remove some of his heavy armour. Resigned, he swung his horse around and kicked it forward to where the individual units of his army were being dismissed by their commanders and were starting to lay out their encampment. He knew it would do no harm at all to spend the time he had riding among his troopers, letting them see his face and hear his voice as they sweated to lay out their barracks lines in a way that would not draw the wrath of their decurions. And while he was bantering with some of his own men from Tir Manha, a messenger came looking for him to tell him that there was a stranger bearing tidings and asking for him by name. Uther excused himself and made his way back with the messenger.

He recognized the newcomer immediately as one of Ygraine's servants. The man had been among her retinue at Herliss's Crag Fort.

Now, however, he looked very different. While he had once appeared
sleek and well-fed and unctuous, he now seemed haggard and frightened, his clothes torn and road-worn and his face and hands blackened with dirt. Uther's face closed into a thunderous frown and
remained that way until the fellow, whose name was Finn, had
assured him that the Queen was safe and that his own appearance
was due only to his difficulties in remaining hidden from the mercenaries who thronged the roads everywhere to the south. Mollified
upon hearing that, Uther called for ale and led the man into his tent,
which was just now fully prepared, and sat him down by a newly lit
brazier that soon began to throw out a comforting heat.

The Queen was well, Finn reported somewhat breathlessly after
he had drunk deeply from the flagon of ale that had been brought for
him, and so was her child, but they had recently been moved into a
stronghold less than twenty miles south of where the two men now
sat—much closer to Uther and his rescuing army than Ygraine could
ever have hoped for. Knowing that Uther would be a mere day or two
away from her, Ygraine had decided to send word to him immediately to come and get her and the child. She had been waiting for her
confessor, Joseph, to return from a journey so that he could write a
letter for her, but events had moved too quickly. Finn had been sent
out early with added urgency when she received unexpected word
from one of her informants that Lot's main army in the southwest,
having failed to bring the Saxons there to battle, had turned around
and was now marching back into Cambria, where it was to be reinforced and strengthened before joining with Lot's remaining forces
to exterminate the Camulodians. It was now known, Ygraine had
been told, that Uther's army numbered no more than two thousand
in all, and the army in the southwest, prior to being reinforced,
already outnumbered them by three to one.

Three undisciplined mercenaries were no match for one mounted
Camulodian trooper, the Queen knew, and were even less daunting
when matched against a Pendragon longbow, but she had wanted
Uther to know immediately of the threat at his back. Word had been
sent north by sea to Lot, she said, advising him of the change in plans
and the return of his army, and Ygraine had no idea what Lot's

reaction might be. She did not, however, believe that it would bode any good for Uther, and she wanted him to take nothing for granted.

The Lady Ygraine would be waiting for King Uther as soon as he could come to her, Finn concluded, and she was surrounded by a tight core of loyal followers, including her own bodyguard. The fort in which she was now held was a minor one, well removed from the normal paths of armies and battle, and it had little more than a skeleton garrison, since its present purpose was only to provide a quiet place for the Queen to bear her child, and no one expected any trouble. Her own bodyguard shared garrison duties there and was more than capable of overcoming the others and capturing the place. They would do so as soon as Uther sent her word that he was coming. In the meantime, he said, the lady was in no danger, but she was impatient for him to meet her son.

Uther listened to all Finn had to say, nodding from time to time as one point or another registered in his mind, and he soon found himself wishing that he had not been persuaded to besiege the Shelter. Lot's southern army might or might not be approaching him from the rear, but he had time to deal with that, should the problem materialize. What concerned him most now was his own impatience to see his living son.

He instructed Finn to return to the Queen and tell her that he would be coming for her within the week, but before he had even dismissed the man, he was interrupted by the arrival of yet another messenger, this one a Griffyd runner sent by the seaman, Aclle of Carmarthen, whose galley now lay along the coast less than a league south of Lot's present haven. Aelle, sailing northward and hugging the coastline two days earlier, had seen an entire fleet of Erse galleys unloading an army less than ten leagues—between thirty and forty Roman miles—to the north of Uther's current position. The discovery had been unplanned and unlooked for, and Aelle had been fortunate in being concealed from the seaward side by the land against his back. He had turned back southward as soon as he could safely do so, and knowing that Uther's force was headed north and west, he had begun dropping messengers ashore, a league apart from each other, to find and warn the King.

That information took the wind out of Uther's sails. He had guessed wrongly in interpreting the information brought to him earlier, and now he had one army sweeping towards him from the north and another possibly marching towards him from the south. Forcing himself to remain stone-faced and betray none of his thoughts, he thanked the Griffyd clansman and sent him to the commissariat to find food and drink. Then he thanked Finn and dismissed him, too, bidding him return to Ygraine immediately and instruct her to be ready to leave within three days, half the time he had originally named.

As soon as he was alone again, Uther sat down and reviewed his options, and no matter which way he assessed them, they all boiled down to flight: a withdrawal to ground of his own choosing, there to await an attack. He stood up then and went to call for one of his guards, but before he could send the man to look for Popilius Cirro, he found himself listening to a rapidly growing commotion. Curious, he brushed by the guard and stepped outside to where he could hear muffled shouts and see people straining on tiptoes, trying to see out towards the sea. He noticed one of Huw Strongarm's bowmen running away from the scene, passing close by him, and reached out to grasp the man's arm. The fellow tried to wrench his sleeve free, then stopped as he recognized the King.

"What's happening?" Uther asked.

"A fleet, lord. There's a fleet out there. Hundreds of galleys."

"Have you seen them?"

"Aye, with these." The man pointed at his own eyes.

"Where are you going, then, in such a rush?"

"To tell the Chief."

Uther knew he meant Huw Strongarm. "Good. Find him quickly and send him to me directly. Tell him I'll be here in the command tent. Now hurry. And if you see the Whistler, send him to me, too." He spun back to the guard, who had been standing listening. "Go and find Popilius Cirro for me quick as you can. Tell him I need him *now*." He turned then and went back into his tent, fighting the urge to run and gaze out to sea, counting the enemy ships like any of his rank and file. In the shadowed coolness of his tent,

Uther forced himself to think, refusing to say to himself that this could not be happening, not all at once, mere moments apart on the same day. An army in the south, an army in the north, landed from a fleet, and now a fleet off the coast. He could not remain here, that was clear. Even his men on the cliffs with their fire arrows were now at risk, because the *Galloglas* army coming from the north had been less than forty miles distant two days earlier and might now be just over the brow of the closest hill to the north. If they arrived before the Pendragon bowmen could be withdrawn from their cliff perches, then the bowmen would be lost, cut off and slaughtered or starved out. They had to be recalled immediately, and even that was going to take a deal of time to achieve, since the isolated bowmen would have to be contacted one by one.

Garreth Whistler arrived quickly, followed moments later by Popilius Cirro, then by Mucius Quinto and Huw Strongarm. A hurried conference generated a quick consensus, and no single person there thought to say a word about forewarnings or their earlier misgivings. The orders were for the army to retreat immediately in good order, and the senior commanders were dispersed to their various tasks.

Uther sent a runner to find Nemo, and when the trooper appeared in answer to the summons, removing her heavy helmet as she entered the tent, Uther waved her to a chair and handed her a large cup of honeyed mead. He had never done the like before, and Nemo accepted it wordlessly, watching closely as Uther sat down across from her on the other side of the brazier, where he lifted his cup in a salute and sipped a mouthful, preparing to say something but evidently not quite ready to speak.

Nemo waited in silence, as always.

Finally Uther smiled. "Do they still call you Hard-Nose?"

Nemo nodded.

"That's because they respect you. You know that, don't you?" Another nod. "Aye . . . and they all think of you as a man. That, my friend, is an astounding achievement. They all think you're a man. *Nemo*. And yet Nemo means No One. No Name. No Man. That's ironic, is it not? No Man. It's who you have become, and yet it's who you have always been . . . I know who you really are, because you and I have been friends that long. But I never did know your true name."

She frowned, bringing her brows together into a solid bar of black. "Jonet."

"What?"

"Jonet. My real name . . . Jonet. My mother was Naomi. I took her name when I ran away . . . when I met you. Then you called me Nemo. It was close, and I liked it."

"Jonet is your real name? I didn't know that. I prefer Nemo."

"Me too."

"Then Nemo you will remain forever, and Nemo only. I have a task for you, Nemo, a very difficult and dangerous task for one person acting alone. I would never consider asking it of anyone else. Will you undertake it?"

"Aye."

Uther stared at her. "That simply? You don't even know what it is."

Nemo merely blinked, her face unreadable. "I'll do it. What is it?"

"I need you to find a man and bring him to me. His name is Lagan."

"The Longhead."

"Ah, that's right, you know him from before, don't you? Yes, Lagan Longhead. Now, the difficulty lies in that I don't know where he is. He might even be dead."

"If he's alive, I'll find him. Why is it dangerous?"

Uther shrugged. "For several reasons. First, you'll be alone, and the countryside is swarming with Lot's mercenaries."

It was Nemo's turn to shrug massive shoulders, genuinely unimpressed.

Uther continued. "Another reason is that he might be mad, and therefore unpredictable. Have you heard about what happened to his wife and son?" Nemo shook her head and Uther outlined the story briefly. When he had finished, Nemo nodded, indicating that she understood.

."When do you want me to go, and what do you want me to tell him when I find him?"

Uther made a huffing noise through his nostrils and emptied his cup in a single gulp. "I want you to go as soon as you're ready, and when you find him, bring him back here to me. Tell him the Queen is safe, and that she and I need his counsel. Can you remember those exact words?"

"The Queen is safe and you and she need his counsel. I can remember that."

"You'll need these," Uther said, reaching into his scrip and pulling out two small items. "They are the tokens I arranged to use with Lagan. This one, the coloured pebble, is his own. It will prove to him that you come from me. The other, the wax seal marked with a cross, was to be my token to his father, Herliss, and to him. Keep them close and guard them well and never part with both of them at the same time. Always keep one of them in your possession. They are your guarantee of safe conduct through Lagan's army, wherever it might be."

Nemo closed her hand around the tokens and nodded. "Good. I'll go now." She stood up and gulped down the mead, then tucked the two small items securely beneath her tunic. Uther sat watching her.

"Tell me your message again, Nemo."

"The Queen is safe and you and she need his counsel."

Uther nodded, his face grave. "I won't try to offer you a reward for this, but when Lot is dead and we are safe back in Cambria, you can tell me what you want and you'll have it, if it lies within my power to grant it."

"I want to live in Camulod with you and the Dragons."

Uther was surprised and touched by the simplicity with which she said the words, so close to the dearest wish of his own heart. But he could not find it in him to tell her bluntly that he would never live in Camulod again. He knew, and she did, too, were she to think about it, that his life lay now in Cambria, among his own people as their King. He had sworn an oath to that effect. And so he said nothing of that, but grinned with pleasure at her request.

"Well, my old friend, none of us can know what will happen tomorrow, but if fortune smiles on us and all goes well down here in this wild land, we might all be able to fulfill our dreams. Now, we'll be leaving here today as quickly as we can arrange ourselves and make away without appearing to run off. Our line of march will be directly southward to Herliss's fort at Tir Gwyn. You've been there. When you find Lagan, you can intercept us anywhere along that route, or at Tir Gwyn itself if it takes that long. May all the gods of Cambria go with you, Nemo, and may we see each other again soon. Farewell."

He held out his hand and Nemo grasped it in friendship and loyalty, probably for the first time ever, then sniffed and turned her face away, vainly trying to conceal the tears that stood in her eyes. Uther drew himself upright and Nemo nodded, her eyes downcast now, and then turned and strode off, jamming her helmet onto her head. As she went out, another decurion passed her on the way in and saluted Uther.

"Your pardon, lord, but we have to strike your tent again. Have you finished in here?"

Uther looked around him with a sigh. Apart from sitting in a chair by the brazier and pouring two cups of mead from the flask, he had not touched a thing since the tent was erected hours earlier.

"Aye," he murmured. "Bring in your men. I'm done here."

Less than two hours later, two hours of intense, concentrated labour by everyone concerned in the preparations, Uther's army had reformed itself and turned backward to face south, the way it had come. A full screen of scouts already rode fanned out ahead of it as it advanced, and another, similar force would deploy behind it as it marched. Uther had called for volunteers for the rearguard, a hazardous post should the northern Ersemen be as close as he suspected they might be, and command of that contingent had gone to a young officer called Marcus Bassus, a gifted junior commander from Camulod who took great pride in being the fourth generation of his family to serve in the forces of the Colony.

As his men marched away, Uther Pendragon sat alone for a while, gazing up to the towering headland where his arch-enemy might be standing looking down at him. Then, when the last of his troopers had almost disappeared from sight, he spurred his horse and rode after them, leaving young Bassus to form up his mixed guard of bowmen and infantry and take their place far in the rear of the retreating army.

Late in the afternoon of the following day, his rear ranks were overtaken and attacked by a fast-moving body of highly disciplined troops, forcing Uther to make use of a formation seldom used in his training programs, since his forces had seldom had to fight on the defensive. In the process of throwing out a protective screen of heavy cavalry to shield the infantry while they regrouped, Uther had little time to think about what the attack meant in terms of Bassus and his rearguard or his screen of rear scouts other than to recognize that they must all be dead. The enemy had advanced and attacked with shocking speed. The swiftness of their approach had made it difficult for his people to number them accurately in the early stages of the attack, but Uther was prepared to accept an approximation of from seven hundred and fifty to a thousand men, split into three independently advancing groups, each with its own commander.

The newcomers were Germanic, not Ersemen. That was obvious from their discipline and their generally well-equipped condition, with ring-mail shirts and uniform, rectangular shields. Many of them carried heavy axes, Uther could see, but the remainder carried long, useful-looking spears. Uther had never seen real Roman soldiers, for the Romans had disappeared from Britain during his early childhood, but he knew instantly that his attackers were Roman-trained veterans, tough and hard and superbly disciplined, real soldiers rather than rough bandits, men who had served and fought together for years and would be easily and eagerly brought to fight, but not put to flight. Watching the way they moved to engage his forces, he could see that they were familiar with cavalry and showed no fear of the mounted troopers. They held their formations effortlessly and were magnificently well drilled, and that set him wondering immediately whether he might be able to use their discipline to his advantage. He spurred his horse into a dead run and, closely followed by Garreth Whistler, Huw Strongarm and a small group of senior officers of the Camulod contingent, galloped to the top of a low knoll nearby, where he could look down on the activities taking place on the level ground below him.

The officer commanding the cavalry sent to interpose themselves between the enemy and Uther's deploying infantry was a Camulodian called Nestor Strabo. He had formed his men into a wedge formation for his first attack, but even as they formed up and began to move forward to the attack, he had to give the signal to halt them again when two of the three independent enemy units began moving quickly towards each other, forming themselves into the famous Roman tortoise configuration, while the third unit wheeled and moved away from them.

The two units forming the tortoise, both of them on Uther's right, grouped themselves in the classic oval formations and covered themselves completely with overlapping shields, forming a pair of flawless, protective domes that rose from the grounded shields on all sides to form two impenetrable carapaces, each of them bristling with long spears projecting between shields all around the perimeter. The long spears held the cavalry at bay, and Nestor Strabo's force was effectively neutered and rendered impotent, for their swords were neither long enough nor heavy enough to do any damage, even could they have come within striking distance of the defensive shields, and the length of the spears projecting towards them ensured that they could not even ride between the two close-set formations.

Seeing this, Strabo issued new orders and swung his cavalry wedge around in a full gallop towards the third, most distant enemy phalanx, which had been moving quickly to outflank his group as they approached the two tortoises. Instantly, the third phalanx coalesced and formed a tortoise too, while the other two disintegrated fluidly and their men moved swiftly against Strabo's cavalry from the rear. Strabo saw the move and waved his followers aside, sweeping them out of their charge and across the face of the enemy, leading his horsemen back towards the original formations, which quickly regrouped at his approach. Strabo raised an arm and brought his men to a halt at his back, then stood erect in his stirrups, his head moving from side to side as he watched all three enemy formations. The situation was static, with both sides vying for advantage and neither able to do anything effective.

Uther was watching the activity too, but seeing the inability of Strabo's troopers to close with the enemy, an alarm flared in his mind and gave him an idea. He swung to face the Whistler, unhooking the heavy flail from his saddle as he did so and holding it out towards Garreth as though it weighed nothing at all, the thick shaft pointed at the other man and the heavy iron ball dangling at the end of the short length of chain that fixed it to the shaft.

"You have one of these?" he shouted.

"No, why?"

"How many of your men have them?"

"Almost all of them. It's your weapon, and they're your Dragons. They do what you do. Why?"

"Look at Strabo's people down there. They're useless. Those spears are no real danger to them. All the enemy can do is hold them out there to fend off the horses, but they can't thrust with them or spear anything. And yet Strabo's men are hamstrung, because their swords can't reach the enemy shields. Can't get past the spears. And even if they could, they couldn't penetrate the shield cover."

Uther brandished the flail, swinging it over his head. "Now, if I were down there swinging this, I'd wrap the chain around a spear shaft, sidewise, and rip the spear right out of the grip of whoever was holding it. Do it often enough, I'd rip out enough spears to allow me to move closer and smash the ball into one of the shields. I'd break the shield or batter it down. D'you believe me? Quickly, man, do you believe I could?"

"Yes."

"Good, and if I did it, if I knocked a hole in that tortoise's shell, do you think another ten or twenty men with me, all of them swinging flails, could do the same? Of course they could! But if I had another ten or twenty bowmen waiting nearby, watching and waiting until we had made those holes in the shell, they could then shoot arrows in through the holes we made."

Huw Pendragon's eyes were alight as he made the mental leap before Garreth Whistler could. "They could, Uther, and that would be the end of the tortoise, for we'd pour so many arrows through those holes that no one inside the shelter could survive and the shell would collapse."

Uther turned in his saddle to look at the officers around him. "Did you all hear that? Do you understand it? You see what's involved?" They were all nodding, some of them shouting in approval, and he grinned and held up the flail above his head. "Well, then, let's try it. Let's find out if I'm mad or not!" He pulled his horse backwards and around, tugging it into a rearing dance on its hind legs. "Garreth, we'll need three squadrons of cavalry, all Dragons and all with flails, and three more squadrons, without flails if need be, to back them up and add weight. Whichever way that works out, I want every trooper who has a flail to be involved in this attack. So, six squadrons in all. One double squadron to each tortoise.

"Huw, we'll need three squadrons of bowmen to work with them, waiting until the holes have been torn in the shells and then shooting into them. Mind you tell all of them to waste no arrows firing onto the top of the tortoise shell. Every arrow must go through a hole. Then, when the shells start to collapse, I'll want strong infantry formations waiting to move in and crush them. At that time, the bowmen will fall back and the cavalry will disengage and circle, looking for stragglers and escapees. Am I clear?"

From that moment forward, the entire impetus of the struggle changed, with the advantage shifting slowly but heavily in Uther's favour. The new tactics did not have any immediate or startling effect, simply because they were too new and therefore strange to Uther's troopers. For a long time they seemed to achieve nothing at all. But after several failures and several more ineffectual attacks, some of Uther's Dragons began to understand what was required and adjusted their movements, swinging their flails sideways, rather than vertically, and soon the protective spears, lashed by swinging iron balls and pulled by coils of heavy chains, began to break and to fall. And once that began to happen, then it gradually became easier for the flailing horsemen to come close enough to the enemy to smash down the shields and create holes into which the Pendragon bowmen could shoot.

The engagement was long-drawn-out and fluid, in spite of the static nature of the enemy defences, more a series of skirmishes than a set battle. Uther was not present to see the outcome of his newest strategy, for the fight lasted until late the following day, by which time, knowing his forces were winning, he had ridden off with a strong escort to find and rescue Ygraine.

In the end, as Uther had suspected in that first flash of insight, the German enemy was destroyed by its own perfect discipline and training, which proved too rigid to allow them to adapt their defences to meet the new style of attack being mounted against them. They fought well and ferociously, neither seeking nor showing mercy, and they fought off attack after attack, breaking away from time to time in good order and then moving decisively back to the attack, reforming and regrouping time after time until they were reduced to one under-manned formation incapable of forming the tortoise. When that happened, they finally drew themselves into a ring behind their shields, then stood there and fought until they died. But they took a large number of Uther's followers with them, and the broad path over which they fought their way for an entire day and a half was littered with dead and dying warriors, many of them Camulodian and Cambrian infantry, cavalry and bowmen.

When he arrived at the isolated stronghold that held Ygraine and her party, Uther found a scene of controlled chaos. The signs of heavy fighting were everywhere, with bodies strewn all around the entranceway and a heavy pall of smoke hanging over everything. He was expected, however, and he could see from the waving figures atop the first earthen rampart that Ygraine's bodyguard had been the winners of the struggle that had taken place.

The Queen herself, surrounded by a protective ring of her own guardsmen, was waiting for Uther when he reached the main gates, and she left the protective cordon and came to meet him as he entered and dismounted. Her face was radiant, her long hair hanging down her back, bound over her brows with a wide ribbon of some bright green fabric, and as she approached, not quite running, she held their child aloft in her hands.

Despite his haste and the many problems that swarmed in his mind, Uther was yet surprised to notice how small she was and to realize that he had been completely unaware of that in all the time he had known her. In his mind she had always seemed taller and more buxom than she looked now, despite the fact that her breasts were now swollen with milk and her waist was still thickened from her pregnancy.

No thought of secrecy or circumspection in her mind now, Ygraine came directly to him and handed him his son, her face wreathed in a smile of welcome, and as he took the child from her and held it up to where he could see it plainly, all awareness of pain, loss and battle-weariness faded immediately from his mind.

The boy was beautiful, even Uther could see that, despite his total ignorance of babies. He had thick, dark hair shot with streaks of pale brown, and enormous, shining eyes of a strange golden colour the like of which Uther had never seen. A great lump formed in his throat, closing off his breath, and for several moments he thought he might weep with the beauty of what was stirring in his breast. He was vaguely aware that everyone in the gateway and the courtyard beyond was looking at him, watching to see what he would do or say, but he had eyes only for the child, his son, Arthur, and he could feel Ygraine's wide eyes fixed on his face, gauging his reactions to what he was seeing.

He swallowed, hard, and drew a deep, shaking breath, holding it until he was sure he could speak without his voice trembling, and then he hefted the child gently as though measuring his weight. "Arthur, you said, that is his name? Arthur? There's little of the Cambrian in him." He saw her stiffen as though in shock and smiled at her, continuing to speak. "This one is Roman more than Cambrian, but British Roman. You made my son well, lady, complete with eagle's eyes.

"My grandmother has often told me of her brother, Caius Britannicus, who founded Camulod. He had eyes like this one here, bright, golden, eagle eyes. A soldier's eyes. A leader's eyes. A King's eyes, in truth. This one will be a King like none before him." He finally looked at Ygraine, smiling broadly and shifting the child into the crook of his right arm as he reached for her with his left, seeing the tears trembling in her eyes. "Now will you kiss me in front of all the world and be my wife and mother to my son for everyone to see and know?"

She swallowed a sob and moved quickly into the crook of his arm, lifting her face to him and kissing him deeply, and as they stood locked in their embrace, the child between them on one side, someone began to cheer, and the sound spread quickly, bringing him back quickly to awareness of where they were and what remained to be done.

"I can hardly wait until tonight," he said into her ear, hugging her close with the arm that encircled her and hoisting the child in his other arm. "We soon must make another one of these." He squeezed her even more tightly against him, already looking over her head and starting to take note of things beyond the gates in the interior of the stronghold. "But before then we have much to do. Is Lagan here?"

Ygraine shook her head and moved away from him, reaching for the child, and as he handed over his son she said, "No. I have no idea where he is, but they say he is tearing the land apart looking for Lot, with an army at his back, made up of clansmen from all over Cornwall. No one knows where he is, but the stories say he is everywhere. Where are your men?"

"Coming. At my back. We had some trouble with Germanic mercenaries. A strong force, far superior to Lot's usual filth. But things were well in hand when I left them, and my men should be close behind me. Are you ready to leave?"

"Aye, we are."

"How many people have you?"

"Fifty of my own guard under my cousin, Alasdair Mac Iain, another thirty of Herliss's clansmen and twelve of my women, with some other servants and attendants."

"Twelve *women?* Gods, Ygraine, we are at war! What am I to do with twelve women? I can barely look after my own men."

"What would you, Uther? I cannot simply leave them to Lot's mercy; he would kill them all. We have three wagons, each with a team of four horses. We will not hamper you."

"*You* could not hamper me, my love, not with my son in your arms . . . but twelve women . . . Well, we can but make the best of it. How quickly can you be prepared to leave?"

"We are ready now, and have been since last night. The fighting was all finished here by sunset. But we have just received word, a half hour before you came, that Lot is on his way here from the coast, a mere four leagues away."

"Damnation!" The news hit Uther hard. "That's no more than ten, twelve miles. How many are with him?"

"We don't know. The man who brought the news had not seen them, but he said he had been told it was an army . . . hundreds of men."

"Landed from the galleys that we saw earlier. Damn his foul, craven soul."

Ygraine was squinting up at him. "How did he escape you in the north?"

"He did not have to escape. There was nothing I could do to capture him. We had enemies approaching from all sides. We could not stay and wait for him to come to us and we could not attack him. I'll tell you all about it later. For now, we must be on our way, and quickly, and the only way open to us is to the south. Have you heard any more of this southern army?"

Ygraine shook her head. "No, only that they are on their way, moving north and living off the land, which means that they cannot be moving too quickly. But whether they are in the east or the west I know not, and I have no idea how close they are. I do know that my brother, Connor, is coming to find me, but he will land more than seven leagues to the southwest of here at the mouth of the river they call the Camel. That is close to where I *was*, but Connor does not know that I have been moved. Calum, the man I sent to you with my last letter, arranged for us—me and my guards, I mean—to meet him there. We know where it is, but it is a long way from where we are now. Connor will be there within the week, if our timing is right."

"Good, then we will head for the river mouth there, striking directly southwest, and hope we don't meet Lot's main army before we reach your meeting point." He began leading her towards the gates as he spoke, one arm about her shoulders. "I'll leave you there with sufficient men to keep you safe until your brother comes, and then I'll go and do what I have to do. We took severe punishment from the people we met yesterday. I didn't know Lot had units of that quality, and I hope he has no more of them. They savaged us, ripped us to pieces, and the fault was mine. I underestimated my enemy. Now, when we come face to face with Lot, I will be poorer by several hundred good men, and he already had us outnumbered by at least three to one. I only wish I could find Lagan and his army. There's no time to spare. So let's get your women loaded into those wagons and be on our way."

THIRTY-SEVEN

The addition of Ygraine's eighty men more than doubled the size of Uther's party, but they made good progress and intercepted the main Camulodian force without incident in less than two hours. That, however, was the last of Uther's designs that went as planned.

As soon as the two groups had reunited and even before the arrangements had been made to fit the extra wagons into the baggage-and-supply train, a messenger came from Popilius Cirro to summon Uther into a council of war. He went immediately, knowing that Cirro must have strong and convincing reasons for such a peremptory summons, but he was dismayed when the trooper sent to find him led him back towards the hospital wagons, where he discovered that Popilius had been twice wounded in the fighting earlier that day. The first injury, an arrow through the fleshy part of his upper arm, had knocked the veteran commander off his feet, and while he had lain on the ground, vainly trying to dislodge the barbed arrowhead from his flesh with his uninjured hand, he had been slashed in the left thigh by a running mercenary, who had himself been struck dead before he could raise his sword a second time.

The second injury, much more serious than the first, had severed the large muscles in Cirro's thigh, depriving him of the ability to walk and thus destroying his ability to command in the field. But the hardened old soldier had refused to yield to his pain and surrender himself to Mucius Quinto's medics before passing over his responsibilities formally to Uther and to his own second in command, the veteran Dedalus, who had terrorized Uther and Merlyn during their early training. Dedalus, while primarily a cavalryman, had nonetheless extensive experience as a commander of infantry and was above all a sound judge and leader of men. Uther had great respect for the man, remembering him as a stern and unforgiving, but absolutely just and impartial tutor. Despite that, however, Uther found it difficult to accept or even to envision Dedalus in the place of Cirro, and it took him long moments to overcome a sense of unreality about what he was seeing transpire.

Popilius Cirro, one of the last surviving veterans of the imperial legions left in Britain, was one of the few men in the world whom Uther Pendragon regarded with awe. Ever since Uther had been a snot-nosed boy, he had walked in fear of the big man, whom he had never seen in any condition other than impeccable, whether that referred to his uniform dress, his dignity or his conduct and deportment.

Now Uther found a Cirro he had never seen before, stripped of his polished armour and wearing only a white, knee-length tunic that was torn and heavily stained with blood. His hair, normally covered completely by his heavy, ornate helmet, was thick and completely white, matted and plastered to his scalp with sweat. The senior centurion was propped up stiffly in a camp chair, his back against the bole of an enormous oak tree, his face pale and haggard and his eyes sunken and feverish, the skin beneath them beaded with sweat. His entire left thigh was swathed in thick, blood-blackened bandages and his right arm was tightly bound and strapped against his chest to keep it immobile, but the steadfast old campaigner was deep in conference with the senior officer cadre of the army. The group surrounding him, gathered in a semicircle beneath the boughs of the oak tree, included Strongarm and Whistler, representing the Pendragon bowmen and Dragons respectively, and his own Camulodian cavalry and infantry commanders headed by Dedalus.

Most of the officers turned to look at Uther as he approached, then turned quickly back to Cirro, as though afraid to look away from him for too long, lest he expire between one breath and the next. Cirro himself was the only one who did not look away again

from Uther. He merely stared, solemn-faced, and nodded in greeting as the King approached.

Uther knew that everyone there was aware that he had brought
back women and a baby to join their party, and he knew, too, that
their curiosity about who these people were and why they should
have come with him must be immense. He himself had offered no
explanation to anyone and had warned his own people to keep
silent. Now he fully expected that Cirro, despite his obvious pain
and exhaustion, would demand to know what was going on, as was
his right as commander of the Camulod contingent of the army.

Uther marched directly up to the older man, laid a friendly hand
on his shoulder and asked him how he was feeling, knowing that the
question was stupid and yet unable to stop himself or to think of
anything more appropriate to say.

Cirro waved away Uther's concerns with a gesture of his left
hand and then surprised him by making no reference at all to Uther's
absence or to the newcomers he had brought back with him. He had
more important matters to communicate and discuss before relinquishing his command.

They had defeated the German mercenaries, he reported, speaking sibilantly through clenched teeth, but had lost more than a
hundred men in the encounter and almost as many again with
serious wounds. More than sixty of their casualties had been
infantry soldiers, but twenty of them had been Pendragon bowmen,
isolated and cut down by unexpected enemy manoeuvres. Another
half score and more had been cavalry brought down by arrows or,
in a few instances, by the axes and spears of the enemy. Almost
before the echoes of the fighting had died away, however, scouts
from the rear had come running to report the advance of another, far
larger host from the north, this one apparently composed entirely of
Erse *Galloglas*. The veteran German mercenaries who had caused
them so much trouble had numbered in the region of seven to eight
hundred men, according to Cirro's best estimate, but the new force
streaming towards them appeared to be almost twice as large as that.

Listening to the infantry commander's report and recognizing
the effort and the pain involved in making it, Uther sucked in his

breath and held it, realizing that he had committed a great error in judgment. He had assumed, when the German mercenaries attacked with so much strength and purpose, that this was the army he had been warned about, and that the earlier identification of it as an Erse force had been wrong. Now, faced with the reality of a second, larger host where he had anticipated only one, he was forced to reassess the odds he might be facing, and he was daunted by his own sudden uncertainty and his ignorance of what was really happening. This second army had to be the *Galloglas* enemy that Ygraine had named earlier, the Ersemen who called themselves the Sons of Condran, and they must have been landed, exactly as she had described, from a large fleet of Erse galleys somewhere to the northwest above the Shelter. Visualizing that, Uther felt the first, unfamiliar sensations of panic in his breast, stirrings that he grimly fought down, forcing himself to consider his revised options as dispassionately as he could. Turning his back on Cirro and the others, he reviewed the possibilities now swarming in his mind.

It now seemed highly unlikely to him that the mercenary force he had been fighting, which had come from the same northerly direction, could have been an advance unit of the *Galloglas* army. The temptation to accept it as such was strong, but when he looked squarely at the evidence, the combination of disciplined, battle-hardened imperial mercenaries and undisciplined Erse warriors in the same force was too alien to imagine. Besides, he told himself, he had been engaged with the mercenaries for a day and a half. Had the Ersemen been part of the same force, no matter how dilatory, undisciplined or unwilling, they would have caught up to an advance guard long before the end of that encounter.

Whence, then, had the Germans come, and where had they been going? And if Ygraine's report was accurate and yet another fleet had now landed Lot himself on the coast nearby, where had *it* originated? It hardly seemed possible that it could be part of the same Erse fleet. But then, if it was another fleet entirely, who commanded it, and how large a fighting force had it disgorged on his western flank?

Compressing his lips into a thin line, he swung back to face Cirro and the others, who had all been standing silent, waiting to see how he would react to the word of this new threat. Wasting no words, he told them that the women he had brought back with him were Lot's Queen, Ygraine—the real one this time—and her companions. In clipped tones that permitted neither interruption nor comment, he explained, to the astonishment of most, that his spy in Lot's camp had been the Queen herself, and that she was sister to Merlyn's Erse friend and former hostage Donuil, and also to Merlyn's own dead wife, Deirdre. She had a child with her, Lot's acknowledged heir, Uther said, declining for the time being, on a sudden impulse, to name the child as his own. He told them that Ygraine was to be picked up from the southwest coast by her brother Connor, who commanded the fleet of galleys owned by their father, King Athol Mac Iain of the Erse Scots, and that he, Uther, as commander in chief of the combined Camulodian and Cambrian armies, had undertaken to get the Queen to the meeting place safely, both in reward for her loyal and dangerous aid to this point and in order to keep the Erse King neutral in this war, and in recognition of the strength and the bargaining power Lot's legitimate heir would offer them as a hostage.

He also told them about Ygraine's latest report of the landing in the west, and that Lot himself was now bearing down upon the fort in which the Queen had been held, only a few miles from where the Camulodian army now stood.

He ended by telling them bluntly that, in his opinion, the combined odds stacked against them at this time were too great to defy, but he was surprised by the intensity of the relief he felt when all of them, Popilius Cirro included, agreed with him immediately, making no attempt to debate or deny his conclusions. The best thing they could do, based upon all the knowledge they now had, Cirro said in a greatly weakened voice, would be to withdraw immediately, as quickly and as discreetly as they could, heading directly southward as fast as they could travel until they were clear of any threat from Lot's newly landed fleet and its cargo of warriors on their westward side. After that, once they were safely out of the way of Lot's incursion from the west and ahead of the *Galloglas* behind them, they could change direction and make their way directly southwest towards the mouth of the River Camel, where they might fortify themselves for a while and await the arrival of the galleys Connor was sending to carry his sister home.

Uther listened now in silence, stifling his own doubts. He had no wish to see Ygraine sail off across the sea to Eire, carrying his son, but on the other hand, he was equally sure that he had no wish for her and the child to remain in Cornwall, in danger of being taken and killed out of hand by Gulrhys Lot. He said nothing of that, however, confining himself to agreeing with the general plan of evasion and hoping that Nemo would find them before they struck southwestward with news of Lagan Longhead, his whereabouts and the number of men in his command.

Uther ratified Dedalus's promotion to immediate, overall command of the infantry, satisfying Cirro, and then moved to see to his senior officer's comfort. Two of Cirro's own troopers lifted him gently onto a stretcher and carried him away to one of the hospital wagons, with the senior medical officer Mucius Quinto walking beside them, and as soon as they had gone, Uther turned his attention to the rest of his arrangements. The infantry, now approximately nine hundred strong but strengthened by the addition of Herliss's thirty clansmen and the Queen's fifty-man bodyguard, was to be dispatched within the hour to march south at maximum speed, escorting the baggage and supply train with its inclusion of the Queen's women, while the thousand cavalry, including Uther's Dragons and supported by Huw Strongarm's four hundred bowmen, would make its way more slowly behind their march, searching for a suitably open spot that they could use as a battleground on which to detain and deter the oncoming *Galloglas*.

Once he had found such a place, Uther explained, he intended to hold the enemy there long enough to permit the infantry and their charges to forge well ahead of pursuit. The Pendragon bowmen would do what they did best in any defensive situation, demoralizing and decimating the approaching enemy from a great distance until the *Galloglas* came close enough to be engaged by the cavalry. At that time, the bowmen would disperse and move ahead swiftly to follow and eventually rejoin the infantry, leaving the horsemen to savage the *Galloglas* in a holding action that Uther believed could be completely victorious. When this engagement was complete and the Ersemen demoralized, the cavalry would disengage and then catch up quickly with the remainder of his army, moving at three to five times the speed of the infantry column or of any *Galloglas* still functional enough to pursue them.

It was a good plan and it might have worked well, had the *Galloglas* behaved as Uther expected. Instead they hung back and refused to be drawn into a fight, melting away from sight of the Pendragon bowmen every time a force was sent against them. The lack of conclusive action was frustrating and time-consuming, and Uther found himself growing more and more aware that his men were tiring rapidly. He was still deep in hostile territory and highly vulnerable, separated from his woman and their child, under threat of attack from almost every direction and yet completely ignorant of where his main enemy was.

In the end, after another day of little progress, he dismissed his bowmen shortly after sunset to catch up with the infantry column, then posted doubled guards and rallied his troopers to be mounted before dawn and ready for anything.

Only one unexpected event occurred to add to his discomfiture as he waited in vain for the *Galloglas* to meet his expectations. Owain of the Caves came to him as he was sitting by his campfire, having just dismissed his bowmen. Uther was glad to see the taciturn Northerner, but Owain had not come to exchange pleasantries. He spoke, as he always did, directly and to the point.

"Why are you bothering with this Queen and her brat?"

Uther gazed up at him in surprise, but answered mildly enough. "Because I must. I made a promise and am honour bound to keep it."

"What promise? To see them safely out of your own power?"

"If you want to see it that way, yes, that's what I promised."

"Then you're a fool, Pendragon. More the fool than I would ever have thought you could be. They're Lot's creatures and they'll be the death of you. The brat's his flesh and blood. Better you slit their throats, all of them, and leave them here beside the road. That's what he would do to yours. You'll see no joy of this."

"Oh," Uther said, his voice still mild, "I think you might be wrong."

"Aye, well I know I'm not. They'll be the death of you. I said it and I mean it. Bear that in mind. As for me, I want no part of it. Give me the word and I'll kill them for you. Otherwise, I'm leaving."

"They are not to be harmed, Owain."

"So be it. Fare thee well, for as long as may be." The big Celt spun on his heel and stalked away.

Uther was sorely tempted to call him back and tell him the truth, but there were too many eager ears about, and he chose to say nothing for the time being, unaware that he would never see Owain of the Caves again.

The dawn came, and Uther led his cavalry on a surprise attack across a broad front that took the *Galloglas* completely by surprise and sent them reeling, scattered in every direction and apparently demoralized and terrorized by the co-ordinated force of the charging squadrons of horsemen, a phenomenon the like of which none of them had ever encountered. After the initial impact of the charge had shattered any semblance of resistance or cohesion among the Ersemen, Uther allowed his troopers to harry their fleeing foes for a while, and the reports of the slaughter they achieved were impressive, even allowing for the natural exaggerations of excited warriors in the heat of blood lust. He knew that the *Galloglas*, despite their vaunted savagery and courage, were no match for his cavalry under any circumstances. They could not even run away, since the horses chasing them were faster than they were, and their weapons were puny and useless against the mass, weight and height of the uniformly armoured troopers, most of whom fought with whirling iron flails that smashed men into nothingness.

When he judged that the rout had lasted long enough, Uther ordered the recall to be sounded and marshalled his men into their squadrons again. They had not lost a single trooper in the dawn attack. He swung them around and led them southward at a fast trot, determined to catch up quickly to the group ahead of them. It took him all of that day, but by the time night fell his army was reunited, and they seemed to have won free of any threat of immediate attack. He was able to spend the night, finally, sleeping with Ygraine in his arms while their son slept in a cot alongside theirs.

Uther was brought back harshly to reality, however, when the alarm went up some time before dawn and he came awake to the sound of clashing weapons and screaming men. He rolled out of bed before he even knew where he was, reaching for his sword belt and unsheathing his weapon even as he moved, and it took him several moments after that to become aware that he was as naked as the blade in his hand. By that time, he was already outside his tent, trying to see what was happening around him, and as he stood glaring into the darkness, seeing only indistinct moving forms and unable to distinguish friend from foe, someone came hurtling towards him, arm upraised to strike.

Uther instantly anticipated the downward slash of the weapon and stepped forward to his left, bending low to avoid the path of the blade that was hissing towards him, and then lunging on his right foot to stab with his long sword, feeling the point plunge home beneath his assailant's upraised arm. The man screamed as Uther twisted the blade before tearing it loose again to pivot completely on his left heel, sweeping his sword around in a full turn to bring the edge of the blade smashing down in a backhanded slash to the falling man's exposed neck. As the man fell away, Uther was already moving forward in a crouch, looking for another target, but then he heard his name being shouted and turned to see Garreth Whistler and four fully armoured troopers running towards him. Whistler seized him by the arm and pushed him back towards his tent, telling him to get dressed and that he and the others would guard the Queen's tent while Uther armed himself.

Uther emerged again a short time later, once more the King, fully dressed and armoured, but the attackers, whoever they had been, had already been beaten off. The entire camp was still in an uproar, and as Uther stepped out of his tent, sword in hand, Whistler was in the act of pulling himself up into his saddle. As soon as he saw Uther, he pointed to where another trooper held the King's mount, fully saddled and ready. Uther ran directly to the horse and heaved himself up into his own saddle, then stood upright in his stirrups, trying to make sense of everything he was seeing. Dawn was already flushing the eastern sky, and where he had been able to see only darkness and shadows mere moments earlier, he could now recognize individual men in the growing light. But nowhere could he see any enemies. He twisted in his saddle to look back at Whistler, who was moving up to his side.

"Who were they?" he shouted.

"Who knows? Whoever they were, they knew what they were about. They penetrated two rings of guards—one mounted and the other afoot—without letting a squeak out of any of them." Whistler's horse reared and he fought the animal down, grim-faced, "One thing's certain—two things, in fact: they were after the horses, and they must have friends out there close by. I can't imagine an unsupported group of under a hundred men attacking a force of this size otherwise, unless they were all crazed. They might be our *Galloglas* friends from yesterday, regrouped, but I doubt that. I don't think the Ersemen could have reorganized themselves that quickly after the treatment we dealt them. But the fact that they even tried this tells me there are others like them close by, and we might have them down on our heads at any moment. We're striking camp now."

"Good man." Uther pulled back on his reins, dancing his horse in a circle, his eyes taking in everything around him. "How many men did we lose, and who's chasing the raiders?"

"No one's chasing anyone—we don't know what's out there. As for the guards, I've sent one of my people to do the rounds of the sentry posts. My guess is that we lost at least ten, but it might have been twice that. How these people were able to approach mounted men and pull them down in silence is something I intend to find out. Apart from that, we lost a few men during the fighting here in camp. We could have lost you, too, the same way, leaping around bare-arsed in the open like some demented hermit. Ah, there's my man. I'll be back as soon as I have some answers."

Uther watched Whistler ride away and then dismounted and went quickly back into the tent, where he found Ygraine surrounded by her women, all of them involved in hurriedly repacking the sparse belongings they had unpacked the night before. The baby was still sleeping, unaware and uncaring of the commotion going on around him. Uther had a word with the Queen, caressed his son's cheek briefly and then went to supervise the activities outside, throwing his great red-and-gold cloak over his shoulders as he went.

They were on the move within the hour, before the sun had crested the horizon, headed due south in a condition of extreme vigilance, the cavalry moving in tight formations, circling the marching column constantly in a defensive screen. Strongarm's scouts, dispatched in the immediate aftermath of the aborted raid on the horse lines, had returned in an appallingly short time with reports of heavy enemy formations to the north, northeast and west of them, and even within the acknowledged limitations of distant views and round estimates of numbers, it was soon clear to Uther and his commanders that the three forces combined outnumbered his own army by at least half, three thousand to their two. Uther had no means of estimating the quality of the enemy troops, but his recent encounter with the German mercenaries had left him no room for optimism, and as he rode southward, scanning the horizon in all directions, he was more worried than he had ever been.

Behind him, he knew, the three separate enemy forces might well be coalescing into one solid mass, their differences abandoned in the heat of the chase, but three thousand rabble against his two thousand disciplined troopers was no great disadvantage, he knew—his mounted troopers alone were easily capable of routing twice as many again. What was looming huge in his mind was the fact of Lot's main army marching northward towards him. He would have given anything to know how far away they were and how great their numbers were, and because he did not know, he dared not turn again to savage the enemy at his heels. If he turned back to fight and the other army came up on him during the battle, then the three thousand pursuing him would become an anvil, and he and his people would be trapped between it and the hammer of Lot's main force. He could not permit himself to speculate on Longhead's army, or whether or not it might have intercepted Lot's main force.

He had no choice other than to keep moving south, hoping against hope that he would be able to swing southwestward and ensure the safety of Ygraine's party before the southern army came in sight. Tight-lipped, he issued strict orders that any fighting that occurred on the march must be purely defensive. On no account were any of his squadrons to be committed to an attack that would take them away from their defensive positions.

It galled Uther to appear so passive, and he had to fight down the black and bitter anger of his resentment lest it affect his own people. For the time being, however, there was no other responsible course open to him.

The first attacks, two of them coming simultaneously on the west and east flanks, hit them less than two hours into the first leg of their journey. They were jagged, undisciplined affairs, mere mobs of armed men rushing against the moving column with no visible order and obviously no central plan governing their movements. Each attack was stopped short and destroyed by co-ordinated cavalry charges. But that was only the beginning. Similar attacks followed, none of them posing any great threat to the security or good order of the moving column, but all of them cumulatively resulting in a general slowing of progress, since the speed of the column was governed by the need to keep the defending cavalry close to the main train. Dedalus's infantry were frustrated by the fact that all they could do was watch and keep moving forward, for their new commander allowed them no opportunity to become involved in the fighting. Huw Strongarm's bowmen fared little better; their orders were as rigid as those governing the foot soldiers. Uther kept them close, and they were forbidden to shoot at anything other than targets too close to miss. There were three wagons with the column that carried nothing but spare arrows, tightly bound and heaped together and then bound again like piles of firewood, but Uther knew he had to hoard those. He could see no benefit in squandering precious arrows on moving enemies who were too far away to hit.

Towards mid-morning they arrived at a river, and sitting on its high bank, staring down at the roiling waters below the edge,

Uther's frustration once again threatened to overwhelm him. The stream itself was not particularly deep—thigh-high at worst and no more than forty paces across—but it was fast-flowing, channelled by banks as high as a tall man on both sides, and its bed was littered with boulders that churned the waters into a powerful and treacherous torrent that could easily destroy his wagons. There was an island in the middle, but it was as boulder-strewn as the riverbed, and the sight of it offered him no comfort. In the normal course of things, he would have sent scouts along the bank in both directions, looking for a spot where he could ford the stream more easily, but the enemy was close on both sides of him now, and he knew that he could not afford to turn his people in either direction without inviting disaster. He called Dedalus to him and told him what he was thinking, and the taciturn infantry commander nodded and agreed, then made his dispositions without further comment, and the business of crossing the river was quickly organized and put into effect.

The infantry corps was split into three groups, each of approximately three hundred men, and two of those moved rapidly to form a defensive perimeter about the wagon train, forming a secondary line of defence should any attackers breach the cavalry curtain beyond them. The Pendragon bowmen were sent quickly across the river to set up another defensive half-circle on the far side, facing outward and vigilant against any hostile developments over there. In the meantime, the remaining three hundred infantry were set to creating a crossing place for the wagons. Fifty men set to work immediately with picks and shovels on each bank, tearing down the earth of the high riverbank to form a sloping path from the high ground to the water on both sides of the stream, while the remaining two hundred laboured to move the worst and biggest of the boulders to one side or another, in order to create a clear passageway for the wagons, a path that might permit them to cross without shattering wheels or axles.

It was a gargantuan task, and it was accompanied by the sustained cursing of the wet, cold men who struggled in waist-deep water to dislodge and roll the obdurate river rocks, which created new chaos as they incessantly changed the force and direction of the waters crashing against them. The job was accomplished in something under three hours, and by shortly after noon the wagons had all been safely manhandled to the opposite bank, each vehicle carefully harnessed by ropes to stop it from tipping or being overturned by the force of the water.

When it was done, Uther allowed his weary workers no respite but harangued them into motion again, regrouping them and marching them out while their clothing was still soaked. The delay had cost them dearly, for the enemy had made good use of the time and was now numerically far stronger and more concentrated than they had been before. Many of them had crossed the stream above or below Uther's crossing point and had circled inward in the hope of gaining an advantage by waiting on the far side. Only the arm-long arrows loosed by the Pendragon bows had kept them safely at a distance.

For the rest of that day, Uther kept his army moving at forced-march pace, hating the necessity of driving them so hard. The infantry had trained for this for years and, if anything, they bore the pace as well as the cavalry, who proceeded constantly at the walk and the trot, easy gaits for the horses to maintain. The sustained trotting, however, was punitive for the mounted troopers, whose bodies were continually jarred by the awkward rhythm of their jogging mounts, and there was loud muttering and cursing among the saddle-sore men each time they paused to rest the horses. It was the draught horses, pulling the heavy commissary wagons, that suffered most on the long haul, for their burdens were enormous and the constant demands of pulling them made serious inroads into their strength and stamina. But as the miles fell steadily behind the column, so too did the Erse enemy, who lacked the discipline necessary for such sustained effort.

Then, when they had travelled almost sixteen miles, they came to another wide stream, this one shallow and sandy-bottomed, offering them little difficulty in crossing. They had seen no signs of hostile activity for several hours by then, and their scouts had been searching actively for more than an hour for a suitable camping spot where the army could spend the coming night. The column was passing between the first two hills, which were low and covered with small trees, when the scouts brought back word that they had found a suitable spot, less than a mile ahead: an enormous, almost flat meadow, close to a mile in length and half as wide, at the base of a shallow bowl formed by the flanks of four hills.

Dedalus was riding at Uther's side, slightly ahead of the main command party, muttering darkly about how he hated hills and hated even more being on the low ground among them, when the narrow valley in which they were riding opened up to the southward and revealed the proposed camping ground. Uther sat up straight as soon as he saw the place, and his eyes went immediately to the flanks of the westernmost hill, which were bare of trees and broken by two long, strangely formed outcrops of craggy stone that arched outward from a common height and stretched all the way to the bottom of the hill on both sides, forming a pair of crude but protective walls that embraced the main width of the valley to the southwest and were at least a hundred paces apart at the base of the hill. Staring at the place, assessing its potential for defence, he saw the distinct line of a plateau of some kind less than a third of the way up the gently sloping hillside, just above the point where the stone outcrops emerged from a common fault. Above the plateau, the trees resumed again, covering the crest.

"There," he said, pointing it out to Dedalus. "If that level area up there is deep enough, we can command the field and fight here. Get the wagons up there somehow, and they'll be safe. It doesn't look too steep. Cavalry halfway up on both sides above those stone cliff outcrops, so they can cover the field wherever they're needed. Bowmen on the plateau there with a wide, clear field of fire. Infantry in front at the bottom, protected by the cliffs on either side."

Dedalus nodded. "Aye, if it's deep enough, as you say. But is it?"

"Looks deep enough from here. If it's as little as thirty paces, front to back, we can use it. If I'm right, then once we're installed there, anyone who wants us will have to come to us. We'll be able to see them coming and greet them properly, on our terms. Those cliff walls are widespread enough at the lower ends to let us attack outward, but they're high enough to stop us being outflanked or raided during the night as we were last night. We'll stand here and face these Ersemen when they reach us. I've done enough running for one campaign."

Dedalus dipped his head in agreement. "It's your decision."

"Aye, it is. Let's get our people up there. Send out your trumpeters to sound the recall and get everyone back here, the bowmen, too. Break off all engagements. We've held the Ersemen back long enough. Time for them to come to us. Do it now!" He swung around in his saddle and waved his arm in a circle, summoning the officers and commanders who rode with his party and barking out his orders even before they had crowded around him.

Uther had the impression that Dedalus had not moved at all when he turned back to him again. The infantry commander was still staring upward to the plateau on the side of the hill. Uther looked from him to the hillside and back again.

"What? You're still here? What's wrong?"

Dedalus did not even glance at him. "I sent out the trumpeters. They're on their way. But we can't take the wagons up there, Uther. It's too damn steep on the hillsides above those cliffs. They'd have to be manhandled all the way up, and we haven't got the time . . . And I don't even want to think about what might happen if we had to get them down again in a hurry. Besides, the horses are exhausted. It won't work."

The King's eyes flashed in irritation. "Don't tell me what we *can't* do, Ded! Find a way to do it."

Dedalus merely shrugged. "Bark as much as you want, but the truth's the truth. We'll be asking for grief if we try to get those wagons up there. Better to mass them, all the wagons, behind the infantry formations in the shelter there at the base of the hill. And we'll probably have the damned Ersemen about our necks before we can even begin to do that. They can't be far behind us."

Uther bit back another angry retort and looked towards the hillside again. He sniffed, and then spoke more temperately. "You're right. It's wishful thinking." He turned to where one of the cavalry commanders sat waiting for orders. "Philip. Take a squadron of your men and carry the women up on to that plateau on the hillside there. One woman to a horse, as many as you need. And one trustworthy man to carry the child they have with them, carefully, without injuring him. They'll need tents and bedding, too. See to it."

As Philip spurred his horse away, Dedalus was already issuing orders to marshall the wagons at the base of the hill and to send men to carry the King's tents up to the plateau.

Night fell slowly, the day's light lingering in the early-summer sky long after the sun had set. Uther spent the first two hours of the night making the rounds of the sentry outposts with Dedalus, exchanging at least a few words of comfort and encouragement with every man on duty. There had been no sign of the pursuing enemy.

Few of the army had much sleep that night, Uther among them, for they knew that, come the dawn, they would probably be facing death again. Uther sat by his fire for hours with Dedalus, Philip and several of his other senior officers, planning for the events that might come with the day, and then, when he was finally alone and all the others were asleep, he sought his own rest. Highly aware of the allure of the willing female body that lay inside his tent close to his son, he bit down on his desire and wrapped himself in his huge cloak, then stretched out on the ground by the fire outside, still in full armour.

In the morning, the Ersemen were back in sight. Uther's trumpets roused the army and sent them swarming into their formations.

"A mob. Look at them."

Dedalus sat his horse beside Uther on the lip of the plateau overlooking the scene beneath. The enemy hordes had come streaming from the valley between the two hills to the north and had then bunched there in a milling mass at the far end of the long meadow, obviously unwilling to come any closer to the area below the hill, where the tightly disciplined Camulodian infantry were now drawn up in order of battle.

Uther did not respond immediately, his attention focused upon the three Roman-style legionary formations of infantry below. Each of them was laid out cleanly and perfectly, rank and file, fifty men wide and four deep, with an additional hundred in reserve behind the fourth row of shields, waiting to fill the ranks of the fallen. The space between the files was the classic distance of two long paces, the first taken up by the infantry soldier with his long, grounded shield, and the other left as empty space, providing fighting room. Each soldier's duty was to protect the man on his right, making sure that no enemy could come close enough to strike his partner down. Behind the front rank, the other ranks were staggered, so that the men in the front line could fall back to rest and safety while the rank behind advanced to replace them. This technique, in use since before the days of the Caesars, had enabled the Roman legions to subjugate the world, and the founders of Camulod's small army had seen no reason to abandon it. Most of the foot soldiers who now stood facing the enemy, waiting for them to advance, had been born and raised in Camulod and had been drilled for years, since boyhood, in the stern discipline that gripped them now. They would stand there and fight until they had won or died, Uther knew, and he felt his heart swelling with pride for them.

Two of their formations faced the enemy to the north, the central one confronting the Ersemen squarely, the left angled obliquely backwards, looking towards the northwest lest the enemy try a flanking attack from that direction. The most westerly files in that formation stood protected by the outcropping spur of rock from the hill at their back. The third formation, on the right, stood at right angles to the centre, facing directly east towards the open meadow that, for the time being at least, seemed to offer no threat. Behind all three formations, close against the protective base of the hill on which Uther and his officers now stood, Dedalus had positioned his quartermasters' wagons, the hospital wagons and the extra, lighter wagons that had carried the women.

The wagons and the infantry were as safe as they could be, with the hill at their backs and their eastern and western flanks protected by the long ridges of rock and by vigilant cavalry massed in tightly dressed squadrons drawn up on the hillsides above them. Uther scanned the scene below one more time and accepted it as the best available to him, and then raised his eyes towards the mass of the enemy at the northern end of the plain. He did not bother to look at Dedalus as he responded to his observation.

"You're right, they are a mob. But a very large mob."

Dedalus hawked and spat. "Numbers count for nothing in a situation like this, Uther. I taught you that long ago. They outnumber us, but they don't like the prospect of attacking our lads. They can see that if they do, they'll be like water smashing against rocks."

Uther looked around him. He and Dedalus were at the centre of a small knot of twelve commanders, who would soon be moving down to join their individual units below, but upwards of two score more messengers, runners and riders both, were grouped in a wide semicircle behind them, and behind those, Ygraine's blood guard and the Cornish clansmen stood waiting to be used in reserve. At the rear of the plateau, the tents of the women and the King's party had been pitched, safely hidden from view from the valley beneath by the front edge of the escarpment. Above his head, rolling in from the west, great banks of lowering grey clouds were slowly blotting out the blue of the morning sky, skirts of rainfall trailing from their bellies.

"It's going to rain. Coming right towards us."

Dedalus glanced up at the clouds. "Showers, no more."

"Mayhap, but we don't need wet grass under our horses' hooves. Can you see any sign of anyone in charge over there?"

Dedalus leaned forward in his saddle, peering towards the enemy, his eyes shaded with one hand. "No, I can't, but that means nothing. Wait a moment, though. You see that group of bright colours on our left, on the hill above and behind them? That must be the commanders, whoever they are. Colour's a sign of rank among these Ersemen. The brighter the colours, the more important the man."

"I wonder what they're waiting for?"

"Guts. I told you, they're afraid to attack us. They have us outmanned, two or three, perhaps even four to one, but they know it's not enough."

"No!" Uther shook his head. "No, Ded, it's not that. They might not have our discipline, but they've no lack of guts. They're waiting for something."

"Runner coming in, sir, from the south. One of yours."

The shout came from behind him and the King turned to peer over his right shoulder. Sure enough, the returning scout was plainly visible, one of Uther's Pendragon bowmen, running through the long grass on the valley bottom, far to the south of where they stood, straight towards the ranks of the men drawn up closest to him. Uther watched him for a few moments, his lips drawn into a thin line. It was plain, even from this distance, that the runner was exhausted, for he was weaving as he ran, and at one point he stumbled and almost fell headlong.

"That man has important tidings," Uther said, almost to himself. "Were they less so, he would be kinder to himself. Let's hope he brings word of Lagan Longhead's coming." He turned to one of his aides. "Take an extra horse and go and meet him, then bring him here to me as quickly as you can. He won't want to ride, won't know how, but tie him into the saddle if you must."

Another shout came from behind him, but this one was more distant, coming down the hill from above, from the tree-covered summit at his back.

"Go now." Uther waved the aide away on his task and turned immediately to gaze up towards the hilltop. The trees up there were small and bushy, mainly hawthorn and hazel, but they provided very effective concealment from below. Uther scanned the entire hillside as far as he could see, but nothing seemed to be moving up there, despite the fact that there were a hundred of his own bowmen among the trees.

Then he saw a sudden flash of movement and a man came bounding down the hillside, leaping hugely and carrying his long Pendragon bow above his head in one hand while he clutched his arrow quiver tightly beneath his other arm. It was a man called Brock, whom Uther had known all his life. He reached the plateau and came running to where Uther and the others sat waiting for him, but there he had to pause for breath, gulping air into his lungs. Finally he shook his head and pulled himself erect, his voice unsteady with effort.

"We're being attacked up there, Uther. Hundreds strong, coming up the hillside from the back. We need more arrows."

Uther turned immediately to another of his aides. "See to it, Spartek, quickly. Two squads of men, each with two bundles of arrows. Get them up there immediately." He looked then to where

Huw Strongarm stood listening. "Huw, I need you to detach a hundred more of your bowmen to reinforce the men up there. Take fifty from each flank and move them up to the summit as quickly as you can. If there are hundreds attacking us up there, as Brock says, the people we sent up are sorely pressed."

Huw turned and moved quickly away, speaking hurriedly with his own deputy commander before they split up and headed down the hill, one to each side.

Uther spoke to Brock again. "Hundreds, you said?"

"Aye. Hundreds of them. Outlanders, they are, Uther. Real Outlanders. Black faces, some of them. And they've got bows, Wicked little things, strangely bent but strong."

"Where have they come from, do you know?"

"No, but I know where they're trying to get to, and that's the top of this hill. If they reach there, it'll be because we'll all be dead, and they'll be coming down about your ears, so I'd better be getting back."

Uther nodded. "Good man, and tell your mates up there another hundred bows are on their way to share the fight with them. Go now, and may the gods protect you. But send back word to me as soon as you can see how many are coming against you up there."

As Brock turned away, Uther spoke again to Dedalus. "Ded, form another unit of your men and get them up there, too, quick as you can. Take fifty from each of the three groups in reserve down below. We might not need them, but we've no way of knowing what the situation is on the other side of the summit. I don't know who these black-faced whoresons are or where they came from, but we can't afford to run the risk of losing the summit and having an enemy above us."

"Right." Dedalus summoned three runners and rapped out commands to all of them, sending them down the hill at the run. Then he turned and gazed up towards the summit above them, within easy bowshot. "How many armies does this gutter-spawned whoreson have, Uther?"

"Too many. What happened to that messenger from the south?"

Dedalus pointed with one raised arm. "Here he comes now." Together, he and Uther watched the newcomer approach them, wide-eyed with apprehension as he clung tightly to the horn of his tall mount's saddle. The fellow made no attempt to hide his relief on sliding down to the ground, where he nodded to Uther, almost but not quite making a gesture of acknowledgment and submission. Uther smiled slightly, a mere tugging at one corner of his mouth, and nodded.

"We saw you coming and guessed you had important tidings. Were we right?"

The man nodded. "Aye, King Uther, you were. Ill tidings, though. You won't like them."

"Let me be the judge of that. What have you?"

"An army, lord, coming up from the southeast, three, perhaps four hours distant."

"Whose army? We are expecting allies, an army of Cornish clansmen risen in revolt against Lot's tyranny. This might be them."

The man scowled, and Uther remembered his name was the same as the Whistler's, Garreth.

"I didn't see them myself, King Uther, but from what I was told by those who did see them, they're no Cornishmen. These are Outlanders, differently dressed and armoured than any clansmen from these parts. They march in formation, I was told, and they bear the banner of the Boar."

"Damnation!" The boar was Lot's own symbol, and Uther felt anger and frustration welling up in him. "How many are they, do you know?"

"Thousands strong is the word I heard. The man who brought it was almost dead from running. He said their strength was beyond counting, but that they had been found last night by the lights of their campfires, and they were on the march by dawn. Three leagues behind him, he said they were, and he was the sixth runner in the chain. I'm the seventh, and I left him almost a full league behind me."

"You ran a whole league? Three miles?"

"Aye, or most of it. Had to stop twice to rest. There should have been another man waiting halfway to take over from me, but I couldn't find him, so I waited as long as I could to catch my breath and then ran on."

"Good man!" Uther reached out, showing the man none of his anger, and gripped him by the shoulder. "Get you up on that horse again and go to the quartermaster's wagons below. Eat and drink. You've earned a rest."

He swung away then and lowered his voice to speak to Dedalus, whose face was blank, showing nothing of his thoughts.

"Four leagues. Twelve miles. They'll be here by noon."

"It's less than that. They've been moving since the first runner set out, so they've probably covered several miles already. Say they're nine, perhaps ten miles away. But if there are thousands of the whoresons they won't be moving very quickly, unless they send a faster moving force ahead of their main army. But why would they do that? They don't know we're here."

"We don't know that, not with certainty. I said just moments ago that those others down there, the Ersemen, were waiting for something. It could be that they've already made contact with these newcomers, probably the same way we have, using scouts and runners. If that's the case, we're in dire straits." Uther turned back to the messenger, who had refused to mount the horse again and was just beginning to move away on foot.

"Garreth! The route you took to come here, was it the only one you could have taken?"

The man frowned, thinking before he answered, then shook his head. "I think so. It's a long valley, straight and narrow, and I had to stick to the path along the centre. No other place to go. No gaps in the hills . . . none that would offer an easy crossing, anyway. Long straight lines of hills on both sides. So yes, I'd say I came the only way I could from where I was to here."

"My thanks. Go now."

"What are you thinking, Uther?" Dedalus's voice was low-pitched, close to Uther's shoulder.

"About what to do, what else? A long, narrow valley, he said, a league long, with no way out."

"Aye, but we can't block it, not with that Erse mob at our back."

"No, but we have three hours, perhaps four, and as you said, the Ersemen have little stomach for facing our cavalry. We could hit them now, the way we did before—scatter them and send them running north, their tails between their legs."

Dedalus looked dubious and turned to gaze at the distant enemy. "I think not, not this time. We scattered them the day before yesterday because we had them in the open with no place to hide. Look at them now. There's a narrow valley at their backs, so they won't try to escape through there. They might be Erse and stupid, but even they could see that would be suicide, jamming together in that narrow entranceway. My guess is if we attack them now, they'll scatter sure enough, but they'll scatter uphill, into the trees on both sides, where they can shoot down at us and our cavalry won't be able to reach them. What think you, Philip?"

The cavalry officer agreed with Dedalus, who nodded in acknowledgment and kept speaking. "Besides, if you're right and they've been in contact with this new rabble coming up from the southeast, they have no reason to run—hide in the trees, certainly, and wait until the others come, but run away? No, Uther. That makes no sense. I think we're better where we are, standing fast and waiting for them to come to us."

"And if they don't come to us? It doesn't look as though they will. And I don't like the thought of simply standing here and waiting for another army to come. Damnation! What's happening up there, and where are those reinforcements?"

A loud tumult of fighting had broken out on the hill crest above them, the sounds of clashing blades and raised voices carrying clearly down to where they stood, and Dedalus moved to look down into the valley. He spoke over his shoulder.

"Strongarm's bowmen are here now, on their way up on both sides. My lads had to be regrouped. They're just reaching the base of the hill now."

A glance confirmed that the reinforcements were on their way, but Uther was not convinced that they would be in place soon enough. He raised a hand and the leader of the Cornish clansmen moved towards him. Uther explained what was happening and asked the fellow if he would take his followers up above to help out, and the Cornishman nodded and wheeled, waving to his men, who were moving rapidly upwards into the trees mere moments later, evidently relishing the prospect of a fight. Uther barely paused to watch them go. His eyes had fixed upon the Queen's blood guard of Scots, and Dedalus seemed to read his mind.

"We ought to get those women out of here, Uther. Down the hill to the wagons or clean away, because there's no safety here with an enemy storming our rear. If anything spills over from the crest up there we'll be hard put to defend them."

Uther looked around at him, one eyebrow raised in a query. "Clean away? To where?"

"Southwest, over the flank of the hill and down into the valley that runs parallel to the one your scout used, behind the ridge of hills he said he couldn't cross. They have their own guards, and we can send an escort of our men with them for extra protection. But they'll have to move quickly if they're to escape without being seen."

The King nodded and dismounted, heading straight to his tent.

Uther found Ygraine waiting for him. He told her tersely what was developing, that he was beset on all fronts and facing a major battle, and that he was sending her out overland with her women, on foot and away from trodden paths, towards the coast to meet her brother. With her would go her own Erse guard, an escort of Camulodian troopers to carry their baggage and a strong party of Pendragon bowmen. The women must carry only minimal burdens, leaving most of their possessions here in his camp, and he would also send some of the Cornish clansmen with them to guide them safely to the River Camel and from there to the meeting place on the coast.

Ygraine was not at all pleased with the prospect of leaving him there, but she accepted the situation and made some suggestions of her own. She would meet Connor, she said, and embark on his vessel as planned, but she would then keep her brother there, riding offshore and safe from attack, for two days. When Uther had won his battle, he should come to her on the coast and either take her home with him to his own kingdom or bid a temporary farewell to her and his son and make arrangements for them to join him again at a later date, once his campaign in Cornwall was completed.

Uther promised to follow her as soon as he could, perhaps even overtaking her, if the gods were kind, before she reached the coast.

They were hugging each other closely in a last embrace when the woman Dyllis emerged from the rear of the tent, carrying the baby Arthur, and Uther straightened, staring at her and pushing Ygraine gently away to arm's length, turning her towards Dyllis, who stood staring back at him.

"You will have to change your clothing, Ygraine, you and all your women. Look at Dyllis. That yellow gown she is wearing would be visible for miles. Half a score of brightly dressed women like that would draw pursuers like flies to honey. Call all your women to you now. Tell them to remove everything bright and colourful and dress themselves in drab hues. They won't like that, I know, but if they want to live and get out of here safely, that's the price they'll have to pay. Now, my love, move quickly. Every moment is urgent. There's no time to lose. I'm going directly to speak to your cousin Alasdair. Your father charged him with your safety, and the time has come for him to see to it." He pulled her close and kissed her one more time, long and deep, then took his infant son from Dyllis and kissed him, too.

"I've never been a praying man, Ygraine, but I'll assail the heavens with cries for your safety until I see you again. Now hurry, and may the gods go with you."

The party that finally left the plateau on the hillside numbered close to a hundred, but they vanished quickly among the trees, unseen either from below or above. They would move along the hillside, well below the fighting on the summit, until they could safely strike upward and cross the crest of the long ridge of hills that stretched to the southeast, making their way down into the valley behind. Uther's heart was sore and his stomach sour as he watched Ygraine turn to cast one last look back at him before she disappeared from sight. Beside her, her cousin Alasdair, the captain of her guard, paused to wait for her. On his back, Alasdair carried his newest cousin, Uther's son Arthur, carefully swaddled and securely fastened in a leather satchel slung between his shoulders. Uther felt as though he were watching a vital part of himself being torn away as mother and son vanished beneath the canopy of leaves.

Another runner had arrived from the south, and Dedalus spoke into Uther's torment, informing him that the enemy army was now less than an hour's march away and coming on in good order. Uther ignored the news until all signs of Ygraine's party had vanished, and then he turned back to overlook the valley below him.

"In good order, eh? Well, I think we might put an end to that. We're as ready for them as we'll ever be, and we'll give them a fight to remember, those of them who are left alive. What I'm wondering, though, is what in Hades has happened to Nemo and Longhead."

THIRTY-EIGHT

Nemo, who was less than two miles from Uther and his army, might have considered Hades to be a very apt description of where she was, had she enjoyed either the wit or the time to wonder about it.

She had lost track of the days she had spent looking for Lagan Longhead, despite the fact that he was travelling with an army of men and ought to have been easily traced, but she had counted ten days of constant searching before simply resigning herself to the daily hunt. She discovered that, with the countryside swarming with Lot's mercenaries, Lagan had taken to keeping his forces in concealment in the deep woods during the daylight hours, and then moving to spread havoc by night, launching brilliant and ferocious attacks against any mercenary installations he could find. Nemo travelled the length of Cornwall searching for him, gleaning information on his movements from those few local clansmen who dared or were willing to speak to a stranger. But each time she went to a place where he had been, Lagan had already moved on.

She finally found him by accident when she was taken captive late one evening by a patrol of his scouts after she had made her camp for the night, and only the fact that she was unarmed and unarmoured saved her life—that, plus the fact that she carried his token, and it was recognized by one of her captors. They took her directly to their Chief, then, and Nemo found a man far different from the amiable Lagan Longhead she had met months earlier.

Nemo had heard about Lagan's recent losses from Uther and knew that his father, his wife and his only son had all been killed on

Lot's orders within a few short days of each other, but being Nemo, she had not thought about what that entailed and had made no effort at all to comprehend the effect the triple tragedy might have had on the man. Now, by his small campfire in the gathering dusk, she saw the evidence with her own eyes, and the changes penetrated even her indifference.

Lagan Longhead had always been a comely man, tall, strongly built and richly dressed, with open, wholesome, fine features and a ready smile that reflected his friendly, outgoing nature. But the Lagan Longhead facing her now was another person altogether. Still tall and strong, this man seemed stooped and older than his years, and much of the firm flesh and heavy muscle had withered from his frame, leaving him thin and ill-looking. But it was his face that showed the ravages of what had been done to him. He was hollow-cheeked and gaunt, his face deeply lined and heavily bearded where he had always been clean-shaven. His beard was dirty and untrimmed, too, as was his hair, and his eyes were deep-sunken, glittering beneath his frowning brows with a hectic but icy fire that whispered of madness.

He did not know Nemo at first, and he failed at first even to recognize the token that she brought to him from Uther. Eventually, however, he took it from her, unwillingly she thought, and clutched it tightly in his hand, sitting down on a stump close to the fire and gazing at his clenched fist for a long time before opening his fingers and staring down at what he held. It was a plain, waxen seal, marked with a cross, the same token she had brought to him and to his father on several occasions. He sighed and spoke, but his voice was so low that Nemo could barely hear. She tried to move closer to where he sat, but her guards, who had received no orders to release her, held her back.

"Lord," she said loudly enough to penetrate his trance, "Lord Lagan, read the words from Uther, the King."

He sucked in a breath and turned to look at her, then waved the guards back.

"Your name is Nemo."

"Aye, lord."

"I remember you. Uther Pendragon is your King. Lot was *my* King, and I served him well. What of *your* King?"

"He is in Cornwall, lord, at war with Lot, and he calls for you to join him."

"He calls for me. To join him. Why should I? None but a fool would ever trust a King."

Nemo did not know how to respond to that, and so she stood silent for a while.

"You say he is at war with Lot? You lie. I am at war with Lot from night to night, and I have seen no sign of your King."

Still Nemo said nothing. The letter she had given Lagan lay where he had dropped it, unread, by his feet. Finally she pointed to it.

"Read his words, Lord Lagan. He wrote them for you weeks ago. He was marching then to attack Lot in the north."

Lagan looked from Nemo to the letter at his feet, and back again. "Words," he said. "Words win no fights. My wife and son were killed in order to send words to me."

"Read them, lord. I have brought them a long way for your eyes."

Lagan sighed again, then pointed his foot towards another stump close to the one on which he sat. "Sit. Eat." He turned to one of his men. "Bring him food." Then he reached down and picked up the package at his feet, breaking the seal with his thumb and spreading the folded paper that lay inside the leather wrapping, and for a time he sat whispering to himself as he read the closely inscribed words. Shortly after that, without another word to Nemo, he issued orders to assemble his army and prepare to march north.

Nemo looked on in amazement as his army gathered in the darkness between the fires in almost complete silence. It was not a large force. She estimated it as being less than one-quarter the size of Uther's. But she was struck by the air of grim determination that radiated from the men. They were all heavily armoured in a featureless mixture of odds and ends and bits and pieces of equipment, and beneath this ill-assorted gear they wore plain, drab clothing, in some cases little more than poorly tanned animal skins, that showed no uniformity of any kind and bore nothing in the way of marks or colour patches to distinguish them even to each other. They were heavily armed, too, with weapons of every description, from spears to heavy clubs and long, thick staves, and the majority of them carried shields slung across their backs. She saw bowmen among them, and axemen, but most carried spears and a sword of some type.

They moved in a silence that seemed almost sullen, with no orders being issued and no signs of any predetermined formations. And she saw no signs of levity or humour anywhere among them, not even the black humour of bored and frightened warriors. She had been told they marched and fought at night, using the darkness itself as a weapon to spread fear and terror among their enemies, and now it seemed right to her that they should move in such grim silence.

Only as his men began to move away into the trees, leaving their small fires still smouldering, did Lagan Longhead turn to look at her again. He gave no indication that she should come with them, but she interpreted his look as an invitation and moved to walk behind him. He stopped walking immediately and looked her up and down from head to toe.

"You have no weapons, no armour?"

"No, lord, save this." She showed him the short, thick-bladed dagger concealed beneath her tunic. "King Uther warned me not to go armed. I was to find you and attract no attention until then from anyone. I could run away from any threat like this and not be thought worth following. If anyone did follow me, the dagger would have been enough."

Lagan stared at her and then turned to one of the group of men surrounding him.

"Noric, find him some armour and a sword."

The fellow he had spoken to jerked his head in a sign for Nemo to follow him, and he led her to what served as Longhead's quartermaster's stores, a small handcart piled high with an assortment of armour and weaponry, most of it heavily stained and crusted with old blood. She searched quickly and dressed herself in a battered metal breastplate with a thick leather back-protector, both pieces slightly too small for her, a dented helmet that fitted her tolerably well and an ancient Roman kirtle of armoured straps that protected her groin. She even found an old Roman short-sword with a scuffed sheath and a serviceable belt, and a heavy, ungainly shield, rectangular in shape, made from layers of hardened bullhide, studded with iron lozenges and reinforced in the back by latticed strips of wooden lath. By the time she and her guide caught up with Lagan again, she felt prepared to defend herself adequately in the event of a fight.

They marched all night, although marching was a word that no Camulodian would have applied to their progress. What they did was walk steadily and slowly, threading their way by moonlight, always northward, through endless groves of stunted trees separated by expanses of barren, rocky, heath-covered ground that was treacherous and dangerous underfoot. They kept going even after the moon went down, picking their way more slowly in pitch darkness but progressing steadily enough by the light of the stars to make her believe that these Cornishmen were somehow gifted with better eyes than other men.

And then, in the first dim greyness of dawn, when the dew on the ground had turned to mist that rose up to shroud them all in wet, ghostly wreaths, they walked straight into the path of another large force of men advancing eastward from their left.

Longhead's scouts had detected the advancing enemy, but not in time to permit any avoidance of the danger. Lagan's clansmen fell back as far as they could and went to ground immediately, lying motionless and hoping to stay concealed while the other group passed by, and they were almost successful, but one unit of the advancing enemy swung far to the right of their fellows, literally walked onto some of Longhead's men, and the die was cast.

The Cornishmen, prepared, made the most of the surprise their unsuspected presence caused, but they were outnumbered from the start, and the enemy were better equipped, many of them wearing shirts of ring-mail that could deflect the sharpest spear point. Slowly, the tide of the fight turned against the Cornishmen.

Nemo had lost sight of Lagan in the opening moments of the battle, and she suspected that he might be dead. She herself was isolated at one point, soon after she first smelled the smoke of burning grass, with a score or so of Cornishmen, and they formed a defensive knot, standing shoulder to shoulder and battling in grim near-silence with the endless stream of men who surged towards them out of the smoke-filled mist. And then Nemo was struck on the head and knocked to the ground, unconscious.

When she regained her senses some time later, she was choking in dense smoke, but she was fully aware of where she was and of the danger she was in, lying alone and defenceless on the ground. Her head was aching violently, and she had to vomit before she could struggle back to her feet, at which point she discovered that she had lost both her helmet and her shield. She still held her sword in her hand, however, her knuckles sore from clutching it, and as she stood weaving, fighting for balance and blinking her eyes until her vision cleared, she saw another sword lying close by. Her world stopped swaying moments later and she bent and snatched up the second weapon.

The knot of men with whom she had been fighting had been reduced to half their number while she lay unconscious, but they were still close by, and as soon as she saw them she ran to join them again, hacking and slashing at the exposed backs of the few enemies between her and her former companions, knowing that she would be safer in the group than she would be alone. Some time after that, fighting on the extreme edge of the dwindling knot of clansmen, she sensed a threat to her left and swung around just in time to take a spear thrust in her side. As her attacker ripped his spearhead free, she flew at him in a rage, feeling no pain from the wound, and slashed her short-sword across his throat, severing the arteries there so that he fell away in a spray of lifeblood. She fell then, too, on top of him, and the mixture of their blood must have made it appear that they were both dead, for no one leaped forward to finish her off.

She had been fighting for what seemed like hours, although she had no idea of how much time had actually passed, and she was growing weaker by the moment. Her arms were heavy with fatigue, her entire body slick with blood, much of it her own, and she had to contend with the ragged pain of the deep wound in her left side, where the spear point had penetrated beneath the edge of her ill-fitting body armour and then been ripped out again. Its barbed edges had torn through flesh and muscle, and even though she had barely felt it at the time, her attention focused tightly upon killing her assailant, the pain was now threatening to overwhelm her. She knew that if she did not rest soon and staunch the wound somehow, she would simply fall down and die, or be killed as she lay helpless. Even as the thought passed through her mind, her knees gave way and she fell heavily, almost losing consciousness in a blinding flash of agony. And yet her awareness of danger was so strong that she immediately began to struggle to her feet again, digging the point of the longer of her two swords into the ground and attempting to use it as a prop to pull herself back to her feet. But she could not rise. She managed to struggle up until she was kneeling on one knee, leaning heavily on the sword, but she could go no farther, and her eyes teared over with the effort.

Only then did she realize, hazily, kneeling and swaying weakly from side to side, that she was alone and the fighting had passed her by. The only sounds of conflict she could hear were distant now, muffled by the roaring of the flames in the nearby trees.

Someone moaned aloud close by her, but there was no threat in the sound, and she ignored it. Another man screamed repeatedly in long, sustained crescendos, but he, too, was far away, somewhere off to her right.

She lowered herself to all fours, retaining her grip on her shortsword, and began crawling slowly towards a huge beech tree, aware that the ground at its base was covered with thick, springy moss. When she reached it, she pushed herself up until her back rested against the bole and then set to work to remove the armoured breastplate that she had borrowed from Lagan Longhead's supplies. It had been made for a shorter body than hers, and that had left the gap found by the spear point that had almost killed her.

Weak as she was, her fingers could not cope with the blood-slick straps and buckles of the harness, and so she cut the leather, shrugged out of the armour and then pulled up her tunic, baring the wound. It was wide and deep, and strips of raw flesh hung in tatters where the barbs of the spear had been ripped free. Blood welled from the long trench and flowed down over her hip. She gritted her teeth and struggled to pull the leather scrip at her side around to where she could reach into it, and from it she pulled a thick wad of cloth, the pads and binding strips she carried to deal with the monthly flow of her menses. She untied the bundle, setting the long strips aside and wadding the larger pieces into one thick pad, and then she tore up a double handful of the sphagnum moss she was sitting on and packed it as tightly as she could into the raw wound, sucking in her breath and biting down hard against the pain. She held the moss in place until the sickening waves of fresh pain receded, and then she carefully placed the cloth pad over it and bound it tightly in place with six long strips of cloth, each of them wrapped twice around her waist and knotted as tightly as she could pull them.

The pain lessened immediately, and the dressing felt tight and strong as she pulled her tunic back down, then cinched her wide leather belt closely around her, pulling it until she could hardly breathe and then using the point of her small eating knife to pierce a new hole in the leather strap. After that, she laid her sword across her knees and leaned back against the tree, wiping the blood from her hands with another handful of moss and then reaching into her scrip again for a small package of dried, smoked venison. It was practically inedible, and she had no appetite, but she knew she needed the strength and sustenance it would provide. It tasted and felt like tree bark in her mouth at first, but she persevered, chewing doggedly until her saliva had softened the stuff and she could taste the rank, smoky flavour of it. It was a large piece of meat, and she forced herself to sit there and gnaw at it, mouthful after mouthful, until it was consumed, and she felt her eyes begin to close against her volition.

Nemo opened her eyes suddenly, surprised that she had dozed off, her heart flaring with panic. No one was near her. She was still sitting propped against the bole of the beech tree, and the pain in her side had diminished to a dull ache. She fumbled gently at the dressing on her side, testing it. Nemo checked her hand then for signs of fresh blood, but the bleeding seemed to have stopped.

Moments later, she again heard the sound that had snapped her from her doze. It was a sustained, agonized screeching, coming from a tortured throat, a demented, inhuman series of shrieks that set her teeth on edge and caused a formless, queasy stirring in her guts. She knew it was a man screaming and vaguely remembered having heard it earlier, but it seemed to her that the screaming had been more distant then. Now it was close by, and it sounded far worse than it had, and that frightened her, because she knew that such a thing could not be possible. No man who was wounded badly enough to produce such sounds could possibly move anywhere. Her entire skin rose up in a gooseflesh of superstitious horror as the thought came to her that the demonic sounds might not be coming from a man at all but from some hideous goblin, drawn from the blackness of the underworld by the smell of all the blood that had been spilled here in this place.

She was on her feet, holding her breath and clutching the hilt of her sword in both hands before she even knew she could move. Her head was filled with the ungodly screaming in the middle distance, and until the sound died away into silence she stood staring about her wildly, her back pressed against the trunk of the tree. Then she became aware of the stillness that surrounded her. The morning mists had evaporated and the winds had died away, and because of that the fires had died down so that the blackened trees on her right only smouldered now, angry smoke drifting silently upward on the edges of her sight, rising into lowering rain clouds. No bird sang and no breath of air disturbed the sullen calm. No sound of battle or movement anywhere. Nothing except the sound of her own heart pounding in her ears. Nemo looked about her at the carnage, unable to count the corpses that littered the ground, observing the way the bodies of her former companions all lay together where they had fallen, in a clear line that ended in a tangled knot of bodies, a long windrow of corpses showing the direction and distance of their slow advance into annihilation.

Suddenly the screaming came again, louder and more agonized than before, and this time she could tell where it was coming from, directly ahead of her when she turned slightly to her left. The ground there rose gently to a low ridge, and the sounds were coming from beyond that. And then, because it was the last thing in the world that she wanted to do, she sheathed her sword slowly and began to move towards the awful noise, biting down hard and pressing her left hand against the bulky dressing over the wound in her side as she placed one foot carefully ahead of the other, step after faltering step, surprised that she was even capable of movement. Slowly, painfully, she moved towards the low ridge, bending into the rising ground and leaning for support on everything and anything that came close to her and was big enough to bear her weight.

She saw the crown of the trees even before she breasted the ridge, and her throat closed up in terror as she recognized immediately what they represented: a Druidic circle of ancient oaks, towering over the scrub trees that surrounded them. But still she moved forward, until she reached the crest of the low ridge and could see them clearly, and she was appalled but unsurprised to hear that the unearthly screaming was issuing from there. Her eyes were filmed with tears from the effort of climbing the slight incline, but a huge image of her long-forgotten father's face, hated and feared throughout her childhood, interposed itself between her and the circle. He had come for her, she knew, and the screams were his—rage and anger, hatred and despair blended into one demanding, unforgiving summons. A chill shook her entire body, reminding her of the bowel-loosening terror she had known once before, when she had chased the witch, Cassandra, to her lair. But she had killed the witch. Perhaps, if the gods willed it, she could kill the ghost of Leir the Druid the same way, with black iron. Unsteadily, her head reeling, Nemo drew her sword again and moved down towards the ring of oaks.

She was unaware of time passing as she crossed the distance to the nearest tree in the circle, making her way slowly and painfully around and between the clumps of hawthorn and hazel that had grown up around the perimeter of the circle over countless years. All her attention was focused upon the screaming, which seemed to grow weaker and less strident as she approached. Finally she reached the first great tree and leaned against it, her face against the bark, her legs shaking with fear and her entire body drenched with clammy sweat as she tried to will herself to straighten up and move on. And as she leaned there, exhausted, a hand clamped on her shoulder.

Nemo shrieked, insane with fear, and spun around, thrusting blindly with her short-sword as years of military training took over. The thing she had imagined at her back was not a goblin but a man, however, and as the length of her blade stabbed into his unprotected neck, she recognized him. It was Noric, Lagan's man, the one who had taken her to find her armour the day before. She saw the shock on his face as he jerked his head, trying to look down at the sword that had killed him, and watched as the light of life faded immediately from his eyes. His body, unable to fall backwards, sagged forward against her, following the pull of her blade as she tried to withdraw it from his throat, and she brought the heel of her left hand up beneath his chin and thrust him away from her, jerking her blade free as he fell back. She turned back towards the circle of oaks immediately, aware that the violent effort of killing him had reopened the wound in her side.

The screaming had stopped again. Nemo looked down at the blade in her hand, still dripping with blood, then raised it and pushed herself away from the tree, lurching forward into the circle. She saw movement immediately, close by her beneath the closest tree on her right, but her sight was blurred and at first she could not define what she was seeing. She blinked, rubbing at her eyes with her sleeve, and then saw what it was: two men, one of them hauling the other up into the air by a rope around his chest and beneath his arms, the rope thrown over a low oak limb. The man being hanged was apparently dead, his clean-shaven face bloodlessly pale, and she saw that both his hands and his feet had been cut off. The other man, covered in blood and recognizable only by his size, was Lagan Longhead.

Nemo had no care for what Lagan was doing and no interest in the other man. She knew only that she had to bring Lagan to Uther. That had been the King's command, and nothing in the world had ever mattered more to her than obeying his wishes.

She tried to call Lagan's name, but all that issued from her mouth was a strangled grunt, and at the sound of it Longhead exploded into motion. Nemo saw the hanging body plummet to the ground as he released the rope and spun around, one hand whipping down to his belt while the other swung up to point at her. Then he turned completely on his heel and threw something at her. She barely had time to see that it was a whirling axe before it smashed into her forehead, killing her instantly.

Longhead barely glanced at her as he scurried to where she lay and ripped the axe out of her cloven skull, but even had he looked at her closely, Nemo was completely unrecognizable. The Cornish Chief remained in a crouch, brandishing the axe and hopping from foot to foot as he peered around, searching for other attackers, but when he was satisfied that there were none, he turned and scampered back in the same stooped run to his interrupted work, where he thrust the long handle of the axe into the belt at his waist.

The body lay where it had fallen, festooned with the coils of rope that had landed on top of it, and he stooped quickly to gather them up again, starting to loop them in one hand as he peered up at the bough above. But the large, richly brocaded bag securely fastened around the dead man's waist caught his eye and he stopped suddenly, crouching down even lower to look at it and finger its richness.

"Oh, Gully, Gully, Gully," he whispered, the words tripping over each other. "What have we here? This is perfect. Come here now, let's sit you up."

He grasped the corpse beneath the shoulders and struggled to drag it across the few intervening paces to where he could prop it up with its back against the bole of the oak tree. Then, when he was sure it was securely lodged upright and would not topple over, he stooped to undo the woven, brightly coloured belt that held the large bag about the dead man's waist.

"There," he grunted, holding the thing aloft and undoing its drawstring before spilling its few contents out onto the grass. "There, now we can do this properly, Gully. Can't send you off to meet the gods without your parts."

He turned and cast his eyes about the grass, then moved quickly, scuttling and spider-like, to snatch up the severed hands and feet that lay around him. When he had all four, holding them in the crook of his bent left arm, he went back and knelt in front of the corpse, arranging the severed extremities side by side in their pairs on the ground in front of him. That done, he twisted sideways and picked up the brocaded bag, tugging at it until the neck was wide open.

"Now," he whispered. "Feet first, that's the thing." The shattered ankles of the severed feet bristled with shards of jagged bone, showing plainly that they had not been easily removed from their natural place.

"Are you watching, Gully, can you see? Don't you go dying on me! Wait with me, we're almost done now. There. Two feet and two hands, one of them with two almost-missing fingers. Your own fault, that, Gully. You wouldn't keep still." The hand he held, which had been Gulrhys Lot's left hand, showed the clear signs of three distinct axe blows, one of which had almost severed two fingers, the smallest and the one beside that, and another, less heavily delivered, that had split the back of the hand, breaking the bones but not cutting completely through the flesh. The third had been a clean, heavy blow, cutting directly through the wrist and severing the hand. Longhead stuffed the hand into the bag and reached for the other.

The wrist of this dead and bloodless thing showed evidence of two hard, overlapping chops, and the index finger still bore the massive golden ring imprinted with the seal of the Boar, Lot's personal insignia. Longhead held it up to the corpse's eyes, as though the dead man might be able to see and appreciate it.

"And there's your seal. See you? Lucky this bag is big enough. Now, if we place this hand atop the other, the ring still up, the gods will know you when they see you, Gully. They'll see a King, just as you wanted. They'll know you for the stinking, festering pile of dung you are. There, now, my friend, my so-long-trusted friend."

He tied the ends of the belt together and looped them like a sling around the corpse's neck, and then stood up, collected the rope and coiled it carefully before throwing the loops up and over the bough above his head, catching the slack in his free hand as it fell back to him. Then, with not as much as another glance at the corpse, he bent his back to the task of hoisting the body into the tree and securing the rope around the thick and ancient bole. When he was finished, he stepped back and looked up at the dead man swaying above him.

"There, now. You're above and beyond everyone else again, as you always thought you ought to be. When the gods come looking for you, show them your mighty seal and tell them Lagan Longhead sent you." He grasped one dangling leg and swung it violently, setting the hanging body spinning, and then crashed to his knees, pressing the heels of his hands into his eyes and screaming his wife's name loudly enough to frighten himself. Snatching his hands away from his eyes again, he held them out at his sides as though preparing to take flight, and knelt there, hunched and quivering, for a long time, peering about him and tilting his head, listening. He leaped to his feet then and pulled the bloody axe from his belt before crouching to turn completely around again, his every move radiating menace. When nothing met his gaze he straightened, inhaling sharply, then ran off in a long, loping stride to disappear into the woods, leaving the Druids' circle to the silence again, disturbed only by the buzzing of the flies attracted to the fresh-spilled blood.

Two miles away from the Druids' circle, Uther, with no thought now of Lagan Longhead in his mind, was closer to despair than he had ever been. By his reckoning, it was shortly after noon, and below him on the valley floor his army was being slaughtered, overwhelmed by numbers that simply swamped their disciplined and normally impregnable formations. The enemy from the south had swept into view nigh on three hours earlier in numbers that appalled his eyes, marching in tight, disciplined phalanxes and spreading clear across the eastern floor of the valley before wheeling inexorably to attack the pitifully thin lines of his infantry. At the same time the masses from the north had swept down, cheering, to join them, completely surrounding Uther's now woefully inadequate force. But even above the tumult of the clash below, he had still been able to hear the noises from the skirmish above and behind him, where his bowmen and infantry were fighting what he feared would be a losing battle with the unknown forces swarming up the hill from the rear.

Three separate armies had combined in one engagement—ten thousand men, perhaps more, against his two thousand.

He himself had led the first successful cavalry charge against them an hour before, two hundred men at his back, hammering death down from the hillside and around his own beleaguered perimeter from right to left, cleaving a bloody and relentless path through the packed masses of the enemy, shattering them and sending them reeling. The Camulodian, Philip, had led a charge in similar strength from the opposite direction, sweeping down and around from left to right, passing Uther's force on the outside of his progress at the midpoint. The attack had worked miraculously well and had given the hard-pressed Camulodian infantry the chance to regroup and reform their ranks, but devastating as the double charge had been, it had been a mere swat at a swarm of bees, and the enemy had pressed in again as soon as the charging cavalry had passed.

What was worse, and heartbreakingly so, was that the manoeuvre had worked only once. By the time the second wave of cavalry had thundered down from above to repeat the assault, the enemy had prepared for them and met them with massed banks of spears, concealed until too late by the throngs in front of them. The spearmen had ignored the horsemen themselves and concentrated upon slaughtering their mounts, so that the surging masses of heavy horses crashed into ruin, unable to penetrate the densely packed formations that confronted them and foundering against an insurmountable barrier of their own dead. Uther had watched from above, raging but utterly helpless and unable to do anything to change the situation.

He heard his name being shouted and turned slowly to see Garreth Whistler coming towards him, accompanied by Dedalus, both men carrying bright, multicoloured bundles of the clothing that Ygraine's women had discarded before their escape.

"Uther! Get down! Come down here!"

Mystified, and giving way to his anger now that they had given him a focus, Uther leaped down from his horse.

"What in the name of all the gods are you two doing? Our army's being slaughtered down there, and you're collecting women's clothing?"

"Aye," Dedalus spat. "And we're being slaughtered up above, as well. We're finished, Uther. This battle is over, save for the dying.

All we can do now is salvage what we can, and try to live to fight again."

Uther stood staring, his mind refusing to work, and then he shook his head. "What are you saying, live to fight another day? Are you suggesting that we should run away? Flee the field? Damnation to that! If we are to die, then we're to die, so let's get to it!"

"No, Uther, we don't all have to die. Dedalus has found a way to cut our losses. With these." Garreth Whistler hoisted the bundle he held in his arms. "Tell him, Ded."

"With these—" Dedalus dropped his bundle and reached out to grasp Uther's red cloak "—and this. They all know this, those whoresons down there. They've seen you lead the charge and they know who you are. Now we have a chance to stop the killing, but you have to flee with the women."

"What women? You're mad. You think I'd flee like Lot? You've lost your mind."

"No, my plan will work. But even if it doesn't, at least it offers us a chance to do *something*." Dedalus paused, seeing that Uther had no idea what he was talking about. "Look, Uther. These clothes here are too bright to hide, you said so yourself. That's why the women had to take them off. They would have been visible from miles away. You would be, too. You *are*, already, with your red and gold. Now, if we mount men behind our riders, men dressed in these things, they'll look like women from down below. And if you ride off leading them, with the remainder of our cavalry and your standard-bearer riding ahead of you, and make your way along the flank of the hill here to the southwestward, everyone down there will see you going, and what do you think they'll do?"

"They'll laugh, as I should be laughing, had I the heart for it."

"Aye, they might laugh, Uther," Garreth Whistler said, "but they'll follow you, hungry to catch and kill a King and sate themselves on his women. Lot would reward them richly for bringing him your head. And if they follow you, if even *half* of them follow you, our lads below will have that much the better chance of living through this day. It's only numbers that have beaten them, not warriors or tactics."

Uther stood silent. Heartsick, he turned his head and looked around him, taking stock of what he saw. Then he nodded and reached up to loosen his cloak. "It might work. Here, have someone put this on, and this helmet, then put your plan to work quickly."

Dedalus shook his head. "That's no good, Uther. It can't be anyone else who goes. It has to be you. You're the King."

"That's right, I am the King, and I will not run away and leave my men to die."

"You have to, Uther." Garreth's voice was urgent. "You have to. You have no other sane choice. It would be a waste of everything you and all of us have fought for and believed in were you to die here, leaving Lot victorious when there's no need. Even if you do escape, you might still die out there somewhere, but at least you'll have a fighting chance to live and raise another army. No one else can do that, Uther. No one. Merlyn could have once, but not now. There is only you, now. *You* must live to fight again and put a final end to Lot, to avenge those who have died here today. And if you go now quickly, you will save more lives in departing than you ever could in staying."

Uther hesitated, still unwilling but almost convinced, and Dedalus added his voice to Garreth Whistler's.

"We'll stay here and hold the army together, what remains of it. Trust me, Uther. If you have ever believed me or admired me, trust me now. I know that when they see you leaving—and we'll make sure they see you plainly—those whoresons down there will think you're fleeing with your women, and they'll take after you like hounds after a stag. But they'll have to climb this hill to chase you, and you'll be mounted, and they will see only a small party leaving with you. We'll send out the rest of the cavalry unseen, ahead of you, by the same path the women took earlier. You'll cut up and around to join them on the other side of the hills once you're safely away from here, and when the whoresons catch up to you, if they ever do, they'll find you at the head of four, almost five hundred horsemen, and the 'women' they'll expect to slow you down will be your own Pendragon bowmen. What say you?"

Uther looked from Dedalus to Garreth Whistler. "Garreth, I can't believe I'm hearing this from you . . . that you're telling me to abandon my army and save my own skin. You are my oldest, closest friend . . . And so I charge you now to be truthful with me, to speak not as a friend, but as the King's Champion. Do you believe, in your heart, that this is the course I should take for the good of all?"

Garreth Whistler nodded slowly, looking his King squarely in the eye. "I do, Uther. I believe it absolutely. I believe it is your duty and your burden as the King to do this. And I know how badly it sits with you. But bear in mind your father's belief, and his father's before that: there comes a time when every King must bear the burden of being much more than a common man. That burden is called duty, and a King's duty lies in safeguarding his people."

Uther's eyes filled with tears and he turned away, sniffing angrily and staring off into the distance as he struggled with what the King's Champion had said. Finally, after a long, stiff silence, he turned back to his two friends and colleagues and spoke in a voice heavy with resignation and regret.

"So be it, then. I'll flee. See to your arrangements, and may the gods protect both of you."

"All of us, Uther. May they protect all of us, including our men left alive down there in the valley and your own son and his mother. If you ride quickly enough, you'll overtake them without much effort. They're afoot and have no road to follow, so I doubt they'll be making swift progress."

Dedalus turned away and began calling out commands, sending men running in all directions, while Garreth Whistler set about unfolding and laying out the bright, feminine garments that Uther's bowmen would wear as they rode behind the mounted troopers.

Even before they had travelled beyond sight of the remnants of his own army, making their way carefully along the high slopes of the hillside on the western flank of the valley that had brought the army from the south against him, Uther could see that Dedalus's ruse was working. A long-drawn, swelling roar had risen up from the swarming enemy in the valley below as men saw them and pointed, drawing the attention of others to their flight—the "women" in their bright and brilliant colours clinging to the backs of the troopers as they made their way slowly and precariously along the precipitous hillside behind Uther's enormous scarlet and gold banner. And slowly at first, but with a steadily increasing momentum, a surge of movement away from the fighting and towards the valley mouth had announced the beginnings of a hot pursuit, the visible prizes of a fleeing King and a crowd of high-born women having their predicted effect.

Uther took great care to remain in view and move slowly, exaggerating the difficulty of their route, until the floor of the narrow valley below them was jammed with running men, many of whom were already climbing the hill towards the mounted party. Once out of view of the battleground, he could not tell with any certainty how many of the enemy had followed him, but it soon became unmistakably clear that, once begun, the tide of pursuit had swollen to completion, with few of the enemy willing to forfeit such rich prizes to others who had simply moved sooner and more greedily. As he watched them swarming below him, Uther began to hope that the remnants of the battered army he had left behind might be able to regroup, consolidate their numbers and survive the catastrophe that had struck them. His despair at having abandoned them, however, was almost unbearable, and he rode in bitter, angry silence.

He maintained his slow progress along the flank of the hill for four miles and more, grimly holding his mount in check, yet easily outstripping those eager forerunners who sought to take him on the hill. Then, when he could see that the hillsides were alive with climbing men, he signalled his people to turn their mounts and set the spurs to them, climbing the hill until they crossed over to the other side and made their way down into the valley that lay there to join the far larger group, more than four hundred to Uther's forty, that awaited them.

Reunited with his men, he led them at a fast, sustainable canter that devoured the miles ahead of them, but he left scouts behind in sufficient numbers to be visible to the pursuing enemy and to create the illusion that they were almost within reach, and he dispatched relays to relieve them every half hour, so that there was a constant stream of troopers coming and going between his main force and the pursuing hordes.

They caught up with Ygraine's party in less than an hour after reaching the valley bottom, the women's progress having slowed almost to a crawl as the hardships of struggling on foot through a pathless wilderness exhausted them. Ygraine's guards, no doubt frustrated by their lack of progress, had heard his party approaching and were tightly grouped around the Queen and her women, prepared to die there, when Uther arrived.

Ygraine was delighted and surprised to see him so soon, for it had been less than six hours since they had parted, and she wanted to know immediately how he had fared in the battle, but he waved her to silence and wasted no time trying to explain what had happened. Instead, he deflected her questions by rapping out commands to have the women hoisted onto horseback behind fresh troopers while his bowmen dismounted, aching and sore from their long ride, and stretched their legs until they felt sound again. He hoisted Ygraine to his own horse, to ride in front of him, loving the feel of her waist in the bend of his arms in spite of his anger and frustration, and ordered the baby's carrying pack transferred to the back of one of his own troop leaders. Only then did he summon the leader of the Cornish guides who had accompanied the women.

"How far are we from the river now?"

The Cornishman shrugged and pointed towards the brook that ran along the valley bottom. "A league, perhaps another half. No more than that. All these streams feed into the Camel. And on our present course, we'll reach it about another league inland from the sea."

"Are you sure of that?"

"Aye, as sure as any man could be. I've lived in these hills all my life. They're growing smaller, the hills, and the trees are growing bigger as we move south. You can see that, can't you? That means we're closing on the Camel. By the time we reach it, you won't be able to see a hill in any direction until we reach the shoreline. There's cliffs there, to the south again."

"Good, then we'll keep moving. We can travel a league in less than an hour, even if the ground grows rougher than it is, so we should reach the coast before nightfall." He turned to speak into Ygraine's ear. "If your brother is on time, he should be there already. How far from the river's mouth will he be waiting?"

She pressed his arm against her breast. "There's a landing place, a bay with a steeply shelving beach below the third high headland to the south of the river's mouth. I've never seen it, but that's what Colum told me, and it's there that Connor will wait for us. Will you come with us?"

"No, I can't, not yet, but I'll see you safely delivered there before I leave you." He turned in the saddle and gave the signal to move on again, and as his men kicked their mounts into motion, moving in columns of four abreast, he saw a splash of yellow where one of them had tucked Dyllis's long, folded gown into the belt at his waist. A more careful look around then showed him that most of the other troopers had also kept the brightly coloured gowns after their "female" passengers had discarded them, safely distant from pursuit.

"We have your clothes with us, the gowns I made you leave behind this morning. We used them earlier to gull the enemy into thinking you were riding with us and wile them away from our army. I'll have them returned to you when we stop and you should give them back to your women to wear once you have reached the coast . . . but only then and not before."

Ygraine twisted in his arms to look up at him. "Why? You said they were too bright, and they are. You used them yourself for that very reason. Did the ruse succeed?"

"Aye, they followed us, and they're behind us now. That's why we have to keep moving quickly. But once on the coast, bright clothing, highly visible, will attract your friends. What was wrong inland will be right there."

Ygraine was still twisted in her seat, craning her neck to see his face.

"What happened this morning, Uther? You had no time to win a victory and then catch up to us."

Uther shook his head and avoided her eyes until she turned away, fatigued by the strain of peering up at him from such an awkward position, but after a while, as they rode on directly south, he began speaking quietly and bitterly into Ygraine's ear, telling her of his ignominious abandonment of his army. She listened intently, absorbing the depth of his shame, and made no attempt to interrupt his confession. Only when his voice had died away into silence did she speak, keeping her eyes fixed forward but pressing his free hand to the softness of her bosom.

"You have wise friends, King Cambria, and brave. You should be proud of them. Their advice was sound, and they were right. You did what you had to do, and the doing of it saved hundreds of lives that would have been wasted otherwise. Not merely these hundreds here with you, but all the others who remained alive after you left. You have no need for shame or guilt. Was Lot there?"

She barely heard his answer. "No, only his creatures in their thousands. Your spouse has little love of danger. And yet I thought he might be there to gloat . . ."

"Then he will be elsewhere on another day, and you will find him and destroy him."

"Aye, mayhap."

"Mayhap? There is no doubt in my mind, my love. You will."

"Aye, I will. I'll destroy him one day. But I doubt if even your Christian God could tell how I might find him. The man is swift and secret as a serpent."

As Uther said those words, a gust of wind caught Ygraine's long, loose hair and blew it up and back towards him, swirling about his face, tickling his cheeks. His shoulders stiffened at the contact and he sat more erect in his saddle, peering over her head, straight ahead into nothingness. Another gust buffeted him, and he drew rein, waiting. Moments later came another blast, stronger than those that had preceded it, and then the wind settled in to blow steadily from the south. Uther waited to see if it would die away, but if anything, it grew stronger.

A squadron of cavalry was leaving at that moment to ride back and relieve the rearguard still playing decoy to the pursuing enemy, and Uther waved to catch the attention of the squadron leader, a Celt called Declan, as he rode by. Declan hauled on his reins and turned his horse in a circle to bring it close to Uther's mount.

"Declan, can you make fire? Have you your firebox with you?"

"Aye, lord."

"Good, then I have new instructions for you. The gods have sent us this wind, and we should use it. Take your men up as you intended and relieve the rearguard, but on your way up, look closely at the spot where the valley broadens, less than half a mile behind us here. It is full of long, dry grass and bushes. Leave some of your men there to kindle a fire—small, but large enough to supply you with ample burning brands when you need them. Then go you and relieve the rearguard, and when they are safely gone, abandon the action there. Let the enemy see you fall back, and coax them if you can to follow you. Then put the spurs to your mounts, and when you reach the place where your men have the fire, set the grasses ablaze. *Ablaze*, you understand? Take the time to spread the fire wide, so there is no chance of its burning out. This wind from the south will do the rest and will funnel the smoke and flames back up the vale towards the enemy. Away with you now, and see to it."

The squadron leader smacked his forearm against his breast-plate in salute and wheeled his horse away, spurring it to a gallop.

Uther replaced his arm about Ygraine's waist. "That, if it goes well, might save us a deal of trouble. Now let's find the River Camel."

Some time later, just as the first of the returning rearguard were beginning to join them, they came to a place where the valley split into two, one branch leading off eastward to their left. Uther halted the advance and called again for the Cornish guide, who told him that the eastward valley led to a much-travelled route that crossed the entire peninsula of Cornwall and intersected one of the smaller roads built by the Romans. That road in turn led to the main Roman road running north and south by the abandoned town of Isca.

Uther thought about that information for a while and then lowered Ygraine gently to the ground while he rode back to meet Declan, returning from the north. The valley was ablaze, Declan reported, and the brisk wind had whipped it into an inferno that had

rushed up the northern valley like a river of fire. He had no knowledge of its effect on their pursuers, but he doubted that they would
be coming down about King Uther's neck anytime soon.

Uther thanked the man and turned back to where his officers sat
waiting for him. The senior cavalry commander with the group was
Philip, and Uther went directly to him and told him the decision that
had been taking shape in his mind since speaking to the Cornishman.
Philip was to take seven-eighths of their present force, approximately three hundred and sixty troopers and officers, and lead them
directly homeward, immediately. Uther would retain the remaining
troopers—a double squadron of his own Dragons comprising forty
men and five officers—to ride with him as escort to the Queen and
her women and to amplify the force of her own bodyguard and the
thirty Pendragon bowmen who had accompanied them. Combined,
the various elements of Uther's party would number in excess of one
hundred men, plus the women. Uther expected no trouble this far
south, he told Philip, but if he were wrong and trouble did develop,
he believed that his small force would be enough to handle it.

Philip was dubious as to the wisdom of splitting their forces, but
he wisely said nothing and merely asked the King how far he
thought he and the others might be behind them, once they had
delivered the Queen safely to her meeting place. Uther estimated
that he would be three days at the most before riding to overtake
Philip, but he was emphatic that Philip must not wait for him and
his party. He must get his own men home to Camulod in safety and
as quickly as possible.

Philip listened, nodded, offered no opinion pro or contra the
King's decision and promptly set about marshalling his forces for
the ride home. Uther and his party waited until the larger group had
disappeared from sight along the valley to the east, and then the
King gave the signal to resume their march south. Behind them, far
to the north and low on the horizon, the sky was obscured by a low,
dense pall of drifting smoke.

THIRTY-NINE

They reached the River Camel an hour before sunset, by which time the wind from the south had strengthened into a whipping, buffeting gale, although it brought no rain. Uther left a squad of cavalry behind as guards, posting them on the highest point of land to watch for unwelcome activity along the path his group had travelled. He did not believe there might still be danger threatening from there, but he would take no chances.

He had decided that they might be wise to camp for the night in some sheltered spot along the last league that separated them from the western sea. The river was placid, neither deep nor wide, although their Cornish guide told them that this was due only to the time of year, and that in winter and springtime the flood became impassable. Uther had already recognized that from the width of the broad, boulder-strewn expanse on either side of the stream bed and the fact that nothing green grew among the stones. There were drowned trees and bushes aplenty on both sides, all of them littered with masses of dead, trailing weeds, and he could see the high-water mark where the dried, dead grass and mosses clinging to the stones marked the height of the floodwaters. Beyond the flood spill and the banks on both sides, the forest was dense, although he could see few large trees.

Uther rode along the riverbank, scanning the growth on both sides with great care, but he saw nothing suspicious and felt no discomfort with his surroundings, and his resolve to camp somewhere inland for the night grew stronger. He had no wish to forge ahead and reach the coast in deep dusk, when he would be committed to making a camp hurriedly in some unexplored spot where they might find themselves trapped with the sea at their backs. All their fine leather tents and creature comforts had been left behind on the high hillside plateau overlooking the battlefield, so there would be little luxury in their camp that night. They would sleep on the ground, under the stars, wrapped in their cloaks—something to which all of them, except the Queen and her women, were inured by a lifetime of hardship. Better then, he thought, to sleep on the relatively soft earth of a dry mud riverbank than on the hard, pebbly surface of a sea beach.

They eventually found a secure camping spot on the far side of the river, midway between the point at which they had reached the Camel itself and the place where it spilled out into the sea, and as soon as Uther had examined the site to his own satisfaction, he gave the welcome signal to dismount. The spot was sheltered among a grove of enormous old evergreens and backed by a high stone cliff, with a spring of clear, fresh water that bubbled at its base and splashed down onto the rocks bordering the stream bed. As soon as they dismounted, some of the men left their horses to their mates and set about lighting fires and preparing the campsite, while others went foraging for an evening meal. Those who remained shared the task of unsaddling and grooming the mounts of the workers when they had finished looking after their own animals. The foragers did well; there were fish in the stream and deer in the forest, and so there was no shortage of fresh food that night for the King's weary party.

Later in the evening, but well before darkness fell, Uther stood by smiling while his infant son was bathed in warm water and made ready for sleep, and then, as the child suckled at his mother's breast until his strangely beautiful, gold-flecked eyes fluttered several times and finally closed, Uther stood close behind Ygraine with his hand resting lightly on her neck, while she leaned back against him for support. Around them, the camp was in that state of pleasant anticipation brought on by the end of the day's labours and the tantalizing smells of a meal in the final stages of preparation. The first watch of guards was in place, and nothing marred the stillness of the evening peace, but Uther felt a sudden, familiar prickling sensation on the nape of his neck and turned casually to see who was watching him.

No one was, as far as he could see, and he dismissed the feeling, shrugging it away and turning back towards his small, new family.

Ygraine stood up, holding the child securely, and went to place him in his leather sleeping bag, and Uther held the backpack open until she was satisfied that the baby was properly installed and sleeping comfortably. They left him then in the care of Dyllis and made their way slowly, arm in arm and talking fondly about the child's sweet temperament, towards the centre of the clearing, where the men who had cooked the various dishes were preparing to serve them. Uther cut each of them a thick slice of venison from the inside of a haunch, laying the meat on two thick slabs of heavy, wholesome bread that they had brought with them, baked the night before the battle to the north, then led Ygraine to a spot by the waterside close to the spring, where they settled down, listening to the birdsong that assured them there was nothing dangerous lurking among the trees.

Behind them, however, opposite the high cliff and high on the grassy slope of a small hill that rose above the trees to the west of them and overlooked the camp, they were indeed being watched. A man lay there, concealed behind a clump of grass. He lay almost motionless, gathering his strength and watching the activity below, and as he did so, he rubbed unconsciously at the stub of the single finger remaining on his left hand.

He and his companions had barely managed to escape the path of the growing fire that Uther's men had set in the narrow valley to the north, but they had clambered safely to the top of the western ridge and then swooped down to safety in the valley beyond, where they had stopped to rest and recover their breath before their leader decided what to do next.

They knew the enemy they were pursuing could not be far ahead, and they knew that the women in the fleeing party were slowing them down, making it possible for their hunters to catch up. But now they found themselves on the wrong side of the crest, and the hillsides on the other side were ablaze. Sooner or later, the leader knew, he and his men would have to cross over the ridge again to regain the valley they had so recently left. He had summoned the six fastest runners

among the four score who remained alive with him and sent them off
to the southward, bidding them run as far and fast as they could, until
they could scale the ridge again and find the enemy.

The runners had fallen away one at a time as exhaustion overtook them, but One-Finger, the last and strongest, had run on, his
long, wiry legs and effortless stride devouring distance. The lie of the
land itself and the thickness of the brush that choked the hillsides had
dictated the route he must take, and that route had pushed him farther
and farther west, away from the ridge on his left side as it sank lower
and lower, its summit angling steadily downwards towards sea level,
until he lost sight of it completely, separated from it by at least two
miles and hemmed in by an impenetrable press of stunted, thorny,
bushy trees that defied him to enter them and fight his way through.
Then, finally, just as he had been on the point of collapsing and
giving up, he had broken out of the high bushes that surrounded him
and found himself on the bank of a river. He had fallen on his knees
and drunk the river water, then rolled in the stream, cooling his
exhausted body. And afterwards he had climbed up onto the biggest
boulder he could find and looked about for a high vantage point. He
saw only one possible location, a solitary, low hill thrusting up from
the trees from which he had just emerged, about half a league east of
where he stood. He had headed directly towards it and had breasted
it just in time to see the arrival of Uther's party at their campsite.

Now as he lay watching, he felt excitement grow in him. If he
could find his friends quickly enough, he could bring them by the
route he had found to where it met the river. The enemy would pass
there early the following day, and he and his could be waiting for
them there in ambush. Carefully, keeping his head low and moving
with great caution, One-Finger crawled away until he was beyond
sight of the encampment below. Then he stood up, breathed deeply
several times until his lungs were full and set off northward at a
steady lope.

Uther and Ygraine had barely begun to eat when the alarm was
shouted and a lone rider came cantering towards the camp. Uther
stood up, his food forgotten as he heard someone shout Garreth

Whistler's name, and a great flood of dismay swept up from his belly. Despite the distance between them, he had recognized Garreth almost before he heard the distant shout naming him, for the King's Champion rode bare-headed, his long, white-golden hair catching the last of the sun's light. Ygraine, too, had come to her feet, and now she bent to place her food on the rock on which she had been sitting, and reached out to grasp Uther's wrist, her touch calming him and helping greatly to soothe his fears. He knew that Garreth's arrival could hardly bring good tidings, and a vision of a battlefield on which only ravens yet lived sprang into his mind. Forcing himself to remain outwardly calm, he, too, stooped slowly and laid down his food, then disengaged his wrist from Ygraine's hold and moved forward slowly to where Garreth could see him easily. Stone-faced, he watched as the approaching figure recognized him and angled directly towards him, keeping his horse at a steady lope until he had reached the spot where Uther stood. By that time, the King had seen the wide grin on his friend's face, but he ignored it, his own face a strictly schooled mask that showed nothing. The Commander's perception was the only one that counted here: this was a subordinate approaching who ought to be with his own men. Uther fought to keep his own imaginings under control.

Whistler brought his horse to a halt and swung his right leg forward easily over his horse's head, sliding effortlessly to the ground and striding forward to embrace his King. Uther halted him with an outstretched arm and spoke through stiff lips.

"What are you doing here, Garreth? I gave you clear instructions to stay with Dedalus."

Garreth Whistler stopped short, but his smile barely altered. "He didn't need me. He has everything in hand and more assistance than he needs. I thought your need of me might be greater than his."

"How so, when I told you what I required of you?"

Whistler looked from Uther's angry gaze to where Ygraine stood watching and bowed deeply. "My lady, I trust you are well?"

"We are, Garreth, all of us, as you can see. Thank you for asking."

"I'm waiting," Uther said, his voice soft and cold. "Make your report."

The other man looked back to him, his grin finally fading, and inclined his head. "Of course, my lord. Forgive me. I have to report that all is well with your army. Better than any of us could have expected earlier today. The plan proposed by Dedalus worked to perfection. The enemy went running after you in ever-growing numbers and left the field to us."

Uther blinked. "Left the—? You mean they *all* came after us?"

"Aye, lord, they did. Or most of them did. But not all at once. The first runners went after your party, seeing their chance for riches and hoping to catch you quickly. And then others realized what those first pursuers were doing, and they gave chase too, hoping to share in your capture—and especially in the capture and rape of the women they thought you had with you—your pardon, my lady." This last was to Ygraine, who merely nodded and said nothing. "Then, once things had reached that point, others joined in until the flow became a flood, and those who were then left behind, unsure of what to do, could see that Dedalus was strengthening his formations and making ready to fight again to the death. I think by that time they had had enough. Ded said all along they had little stomach for fighting our lads, and it was only their numbers that encouraged them. He was right. With what looked like more than half their army gone, chasing you, the others apparently thought it might be wise to follow them. Certainly none of them moved back to the attack. They simply melted away after that, many of them back towards the north. And as I said, they left the field to us."

"How many men did we lose altogether?"

"Too many. More than half. But when the enemy disengaged, we had a full five hundred still standing in formation, some of them slightly wounded, and more than a hundred mounted troopers regrouped on the hillside."

There was a long silence as Uther absorbed this. A silent ring of men had gathered around just within earshot, eager to hear the tidings Garreth had brought. He made no move to banish them, but when he spoke again he raised his voice slightly.

"You are describing a victory."

Garreth shrugged, his smile evident again, although it was a mere shadow of his former grin.

"Aye, Lord Uther, I am. When an army stands alone and unchallenged upon a battlefield after the fight, they have won a victory, no matter what."

Now a buzz of amazed speculation broke out among the listeners, and Uther let them talk while he motioned Garreth aside, all of his former anger dissipated.

"Come and eat, you must be hungry."

"Starved, lord."

"Aye, I have no doubt."

Uther turned to a nearby trooper and asked him to bring some bread and meat for Garreth, and then he led the Champion back to where he and Ygraine had been sitting. Garreth talked quietly to Ygraine for a few moments, asking about her son, and then seated himself gratefully on a smooth boulder. Uther, filled with thankfulness that his fears had been ill-founded, allowed his friend to rest quietly for a few moments before asking his next question.

"What happened then, after the enemy left?"

"We stood fast for more than an hour, lest any of them come back, and then we set about cleaning up the mess. Mucius Quinto organized his field hospital, tending to the wounded, and half of the men were assigned to burial duties and litter duties. The other half set up a defence perimeter, although there was little need. By that time, even the enemy wounded were aware that it was over and we had won, and they gave us no trouble. Quinto's people were attending to them, too. I asked him why, and he said that they had stopped being enemies and were now injured men."

"Aye, Quinto thinks that way, as does his friend Lucanus."

The trooper returned with Garreth's food, and after thanking the man Garreth dedicated himself to demolishing the succulent meat. Uther and Ygraine sat together side by side on neighbouring stones and watched him eat, neither of them making any move to resume their own interrupted meal but simply content to sit there quietly, close to each other. Finally, Garreth swallowed his last mouthful and drank from the flask at his side, and Uther spoke again.

"Did you see my guards on the way in?"

"You mean the squad you left behind to guard your back? Aye,

I did. Junius Lepo was in command. He and his men were bright and alert . . . half of them, anyway. The other half were asleep, the night watch."

"Good. So tell me now why you are here."

The King's Champion pursed his lips, looking speculatively at his friend. "Are you asking me as Uther, my friend and pupil, or as Uther Pendragon, my King and Commander?"

"Both."

Garreth sniffed. "I said before, I thought you might have more need of me than Dedalus did. He had most of his officers there . . . we lost relatively few, given what we had endured. He had already made all the arrangements to load his wounded into the wagons and was marshalling his remaining troops to march them homeward. He didn't need me. Besides, I knew what it had cost you to ride away as you did, and I thought you might be relieved to hear how everything had turned out. And so I bade farewell to Dedalus and came to find you, slipping away by the same valley you followed."

"Hmm. The thought of all the enemy forces between us didn't bother you?"

"No, not as long as I was travelling in the same direction they were. But do I look any older to you than I did when you last saw me?"

Now Uther smiled for the first time since his friend's arrival. "No, you do not. Should you?"

"Aye, I think so, for I must have aged ten years after you set that fire and sent the entire wasp's nest running back towards me. The wind from the south—and I suppose you must have thanked all the gods for it—turned that entire valley into a flue, and the flames blowing through it took everything, every tree and bush, every blade of grass, and the gods alone know how many of Lot's men. I tell you, I was really grateful that I had a horse, for if I hadn't, I would have been cooked like that deer meat I just ate. I saw the smoke belching up the valley towards me and guessed what it must mean, so I turned my horse and put the spurs to him without stopping to think, and I was able to get up onto the hill-sides close to the crest before the flames could catch up to me. It was a spectacle to behold, I'll take an oath on that. Never saw anything like it. Just like a bursting dam, it was, except that it was fire that spewed up, not water. A river of fire, moving faster than a horse could run." He paused, his gaze unfocused, and then made a deep "humphing" sound in his throat, remembering. Then he turned to Uther

"Where are the others? You had four hundred cavalry. Where are they?"

"I sent most of them home a few miles back where the valley forks." Uther briefly explained what he had been thinking at that time, and Garreth sat nodding as he listened, but Uther was more interested in the story of how Garreth had reached him.

"So, you were telling me about the fire, how well it worked. Go on."

Garreth shrugged and made a wry face. "Well, I managed to escape the flames, as you can see, but that damned fire still almost got me killed, for I wasn't the only one to seek safety up on the crest. I found myself among a large number of really unpleasant people up there. None of them seemed to know me for what I was. All too concerned with saving their own skins, I suppose, and getting their breath back. But after a while, one of them took a really good look at me, and then I had to ride hard downhill to get away. Could have come to a bad end there, too, because that horse was bouncing down the slope like a boulder, terrified, and staying on his feet only by magic. Don't know how we survived.

"And then, about half an hour later, damned if I didn't almost ride into a party of horsemen. By sheer luck, I was above them again and saw them before they saw me. They were riding through the trees down to my left, and I heard one of their horses screaming. It must have slipped and fallen on the slope. I couldn't count them accurately because of all the trees, but there must have been close to half a hundred of them. I had no idea who they were, but I knew they weren't ours, so I tried to keep well out of their way."

"You mean you failed? They saw you?"

"Aye, they saw me and came after me, but I managed to lose them."

Uther was frowning. "Who could they have been, these people? There were no horses among the army we fought."

"No, there weren't, so I guessed that whoever they were, they were no part of Lot's rabble. But I felt no temptation to ride down to them. I've heard that old nonsense about the enemy of my enemy being my friend, but you'll be an old man before you'll get me to believe it. And judging from the way they came after me, these were not friendly travellers."

"So how did you escape them?"

Garreth shrugged. "Around a hump in the hillside, a kind of shoulder in the rock. They were coming up hard to catch me on one side of the hump, so I went down the other side, passing them as they climbed. I went all the way to the bottom and then swung south again, following the road along the valley. It's not really a road, but on their way north earlier, Lot's army trampled it flat enough to resemble one. I made good time for about eight or nine miles, and when I knew I was far enough ahead to have lost any pursuit, I struck upward again across the crest and back down into the valley you were in. I was south of the fire by that time, close to the split in the valley where you say you turned the others loose. Come to think of it, I saw no signs of hundreds of horsemen having passed that way. How did you manage that?"

"The ground was hard there, that's all. Bare rock and little grass. Philip was aware of the need to leave no tracks for anyone to follow, and he made sure his men knew it, too." He coughed, clearing his throat. "So, you've seen no evidence of these other horsemen since you evaded them?"

"No, not a sign."

"Good. Then we had better get ourselves to sleep. It has been a long and wearying day, and this will be a short night with another long day tomorrow."

It had grown dark as they spoke, and the entire camp was almost silent, few of the tired men possessing the energy to sit up talking by the fires for an extra hour as they normally would. Uther slipped his arm around Ygraine, as Garreth Whistler vanished in search of his saddlebags and bedroll, and he led her close to one of the fires nearby. There he covered her with his great red cloak, draped his sleeping blanket over that and then lay down beside her in full armour, pulling the coverings over himself, too. They kissed a few times, each of them comforting the other, and then fell asleep in each other's arms.

Uther awoke before dawn in pitch darkness, brought to awareness by the sounds of banked fires being rekindled. He lay blinking up at the stars for several moments while he adjusted to where he was, and then he raised the coverings and rolled out of his ground-hard bed, lowering the covers back quickly over Ygraine before the night air could sweep in and chill her. It was cold, and everything was wet with a heavy dew, so he moved well away from his sleeping place before he began to stamp his feet, jarring the kinks out of his joints and swinging his arms to warm and loosen them, too. As soon as he felt that he could walk without creaking, he made his way downstream along the edge of the river until he was well clear of the camp, and there he relieved himself gratefully before washing his face in the icy stream.

By the time he returned, everyone was astir, even the Queen and her women, and he and Ygraine shared a quick breakfast by one of the fires, talking about her brother Connor and his expected arrival while they ate their normal morning travelling ration of lightly roasted grains and nuts mixed with chopped dried fruit, washing it down with fresh, cold water from the spring. Somewhere behind them, they could hear their son whimpering and fretting as one of the women changed his swaddling clothes, cleaning him and making him ready for the day's journey. After that, as the eastern sky was beginning to lighten with the first, faint promise of a new day, everyone shared the duty of cleaning up the campsite, the men rolling and tying their bedrolls and the women packing their few belongings, while the Cambrian bowmen readied themselves for the march, tending to their bows and bowstrings and wiping any moisture they could find from the blades of their other weapons. The troopers checked their harness and weapons and found their own mounts among the horse lines, saddling and bridling them and fastening bedrolls and saddlebags before pulling themselves up into the saddles. Controlled chaos became eddying confusion and then quickly gave way to order as the milling troopers formed themselves into disciplined units.

It was almost full daylight by then, and Uther, his head bare and his huge helmet cradled in the bend of his elbow, was waiting impatiently for everything to be in order, and as awareness of his disapproving frown spread among the men, that order was achieved, and a stillness fell. Uther nodded, satisfied, but just as he raised his clenched fist to give the signal to move out, a shout went up from the outer ring of guards and a mounted trooper came hammering towards them, shouting an alarm.

Uther rode out to meet the approaching man immediately, waving him down as he drew closer, but he already knew what the trooper, whose name was Curio, would tell him. Sure enough, he brought word of a large body of heavily armed and armoured horsemen approaching quickly, forty or fifty strong, coming down the valley from the north by the route that Uther had followed the day before. They had come with the first light of dawn, Curio said, and they had been moving slowly over the unfamiliar and nightshrouded ground, but fortunately young Telas, the man with the best eyes among the guards, had been on duty and alert for any signs of movement in the gathering light. He had seen the newcomers the moment they came into view and had raised the alarm.

Junius Lepo had sent Curio off immediately at full gallop to warn Uther, while he and his remaining ten troopers had gone into hiding, prepared to meet and engage the newcomers, hitting them by surprise. That had been less than half an hour earlier. Curio could not know how long Junius Lepo and his ten men might be able to fight off the strangers, or if they would be successful in holding them at all, but he had ridden at the gallop all the way, escaping unseen and sure that he was leaving his mates to their death.

Uther listened, resisting the urge to curse Garreth Whistler for his insubordination of the day before. It was by no means certain, he told himself, that the newcomers had followed the Whistler. They might have simply come south on their own initiative, looking for plunder of any kind. But even as he thought the words, he doubted them.

"Very well," he said to Curio. "Come with me and stay close by me, but keep your mouth shut. I'll do all the talking."

He wheeled his horse and spurred it back to where the others sat watching him and waiting, but he pulled up short of them, where none of them could easily hear him speaking quietly.

"Garreth," he called. "A word with you."

Garreth Whistler kneed his mount forward to where the King and Curio had drawn rein, some way from the rest of the party.

"Those riders you evaded yesterday, were they cavalry?"

The Champion's brow clouded. "No. They were mounted, but they had no formation and showed no signs of discipline. I wouldn't call them cavalry. Why?"

"Because they're coming down on us right now. Junius Lepo and his men are trying to hold them, but they're outnumbered. Call in the perimeter guards and have them form up with the others. Cato, over here!" Garreth moved away immediately, and when the junior cavalry commander presented himself, saluting smartly, Uther told him to send one of his best mounted men back along the track behind them to watch for the first signs of an approaching enemy and then bring word of how far away they were and how quickly they were coming.

Cato saluted again and turned away briskly, and Uther was already calling others to him: Alasdair Mac Iain, the Queen's captain; Ivor, the captain of the remaining Pendragon bowmen, no more than thirty of them left now; and Catt, their Cornish guide. Tersely, he told these three what was happening and ordered them to take their men and strike out immediately for the coast with Ygraine and the other women. They were sixty strong, he pointed out, and probably more than enough to fight off the newcomers, but the strangers were mounted and apparently well armoured, and that would give them an enormous advantage even against Pendragon bowmen in a running fight. For that reason, he and his troopers would remain behind to stop the oncoming horsemen, giving the foot party a chance to reach the coast where, if the gods were kind, Connor Mac Athol would be awaiting them with his own forces.

His listeners looked at each other, tight-lipped, but no one spoke. Finally Alasdair nodded. "So be it. Fight well, King Cambria."

Uther's eyes widened at the name that, as far as he had known, no one but Ygraine used. Then he nodded. "I need to say a word to the others to let them know what's afoot, and I need a few moments alone with your cousin and my son. As soon as I have done so, we will be gone and so will you. Waste no time on the road, my friend, even should it mean carrying some of the women."

He saluted the three men and then turned to face the remainder of his group, telling them succinctly what he had told their commanders. He wasted no words and made no attempt to lessen the impact of what he had to say. They listened grimly, and then the two groups, those on foot and those on horseback, began to move apart.

Uther shrugged out of his great red cloak and folded it twice across his arm before throwing it to one of his troopers. "Here, fold this tightly and then bind it behind my saddle here, if you would, with my bedroll."

He swung down from his seat then and went directly to Ygraine, who had turned to Dyllis and was now taking the baby's travelling pack from the smaller woman's arms. As Uther reached her side, the Queen turned to him, holding out the baby, who was snugly wrapped for travelling on such a chilly morning in the soft-tanned, pliant skin of a black bear that covered every part of him but his face.

"Your son, King Cambria. Arthur Pendragon. He wears the black bear emblem of your cousin Merlyn, but only against the morning chill. He is his father's son in every respect. Kiss him goodbye, and me, and wish us well. Then go and do what you must do and rejoin us soon. We will be waiting for you."

He kissed the child, sniffing deeply to inhale the clean, milky smell of him, and then embraced Ygraine.

"Uther, my love," she whispered into his ear, bringing his skin up in gooseflesh. "Be quick, and come back to me soon. I love you."

"And I you, lady. Your name will be in my mind and in my heart through all that happens. My love. My Ygraine. Go now, and take good care of my son." His eyes abruptly filled with tears and he swung away from her quickly, striding back towards his horse and almost leaping up into the saddle. "Away with you now," he shouted. "Farewell. And may all the gods of Cambria watch over you until we meet again." He pulled his horse up into a high, rearing turn and thrust his arm straight up and then out, back towards the direction from which they had come. He rowelled his horse's belly with the spurs and moved forward, hearing the creak and jingle of saddlery behind him as the column at his back surged into motion.

Uther led his men forward slowly, eastward along the riverbank, using the narrow strip of sand bordering the river between the boulder-strewn flood bed on his right and the dense growth of trees on the banks at his left. As he went he eyed the opposite bank closely, looking at the terrain there and preferring it to where he was. No more than two men could ride abreast here on the northern bank of the Camel, restricted as they were to where their horses could find footing, but the high cliff towering over the other side of the river had provided shelter for some large trees, and one large grove of enormous firs drew his attention. He turned to Garreth Whistler, who rode on his left.

"I hope Junius Lepo is still holding those whoresons, because we can't fight here, and I can think of no better spot between here and the valley mouth where we came out."

Garreth grunted. "No more can I, but it's no worse for us than it will be for them. We might have to fight them two against two if we meet them on this path, and if we do, then you and I must bear the brunt of it. D'you want to fall back and put someone else in front?"

Uther ignored the levity and shook his head.

"You're wrong, Garreth. You said it yourself, we're not going up against cavalry. When it comes to a fight, these people, whoever they are, will probably jump right down and fight on foot. That means they could fight among the trees. We can't. And we can't take the horses out onto the rocks on the riverbed, either. Those boulders are certain death for horses."

Garreth eyed the riverbed, a chaos of layer upon layer of smooth, rounded boulders of every conceivable size. "I've never seen so many stones. Where could they all have come from?"

"From the cliff there over thousands of years. Slide after slide, century after century, broken down and worn smooth by the river water."

He was interrupted by the drumming of approaching hooves, and the scout sent out by Cato came thundering towards them. The enemy was close behind him, he reported, no more than a mile. More than a score of horsemen.

"A score? That's less than half of what I saw." Garreth's eyes were wide.

Uther made a vexed, tutting sound through his teeth. "Damnation! That's why they're so close. You know what they've done, don't you? They left half their number behind to deal with Junius and his ten men while the rest of them came on. That means they know we're here, and they're clever and determined." He was standing in his stirrups, looking back across the river to where the fir trees towered along the base of the long, high cliff, and then he swung back to the scout.

"There's a spot somewhere behind you where the river narrows between high banks, and there's a huge dead tree lying clear across it from side to side. We had to detour through the forest yesterday to get around it. How far back is it?"

"Less than a quarter of a mile, Lord Uther, perhaps two-thirds of that. I had to go around it too, going and coming."

"Right. Here's what we're going to do, Garreth, but we haven't got much time. That tree will stop them as it stopped us. They'll have to dismount and lead their horses around it through the underbrush. We'll wait for them there in the forest. The river's shallow on this side of the fallen tree, but on the other side of it there's a great, deep hole, fed by a waterfall. They won't be able to approach us from that direction, even on foot, because the tree stretches all the way across and the water's too fast and deep.

"We'll send half of our men across the river on foot when we reach the tree, each of them leading two horses. They'll leave them there among those giant firs and come back to join us. We'll lie in wait for these whoresons in the forest, as I said, but then we'll fall back and form a line in the river, where they'll have to come to us.

But they won't be able to use their horses any more than we can use ours, and we'll be standing among the rocks as they clamber over them to reach us. It should work. Then, when the time is right, we'll fall away in front of them and mount up among the trees below the cliff there. They're enormous, and the ground beneath them will be free of growth. The enemy will follow us on foot, and we'll be mounted again, waiting for them. What think you?"

"Let's do it." Garreth's voice was decisive, and Uther stood up in his stirrups and backed his horse around to face the column at his back.

"Hear me now, all of you! We're going to fight close by here, by that big fallen tree we found yesterday. It's not the place I would have chosen, but it's the only place we have, and we'll make it work for us, so listen closely." He paused, giving them a chance to spread out slightly to where they could all see and hear him.

"We can't use our horses here. There's no footing in the stream bed and no room to move among the undergrowth up above, but that's to our advantage if we can be ready in time. So when we reach the tree, on my order, we'll dismount, and every second man will take two horses and lead them across to the other side of the river. Leave them there, out of sight, and then get back to this side quickly. In the meantime, every other man will come with me up into the trees. The others will follow us with Garreth, the King's Champion here, when they return. It's time for us to teach some Outlanders what being Cambrian means. We'll be fighting on foot at first, but then we'll fight our way back across the river to our mounts. So thank the trainers in Camulod now for all that infantry drill they put you through, then bring your favourite weapons and your shields. You've called yourselves Dragons for years, so here's your chance to live up to your name and bring death, fire and destruction to the Outlanders, standing on your own feet."

He looked to his standard-bearer, the man who had ridden by his side or just ahead of him for more than ten years now. "Gwyn, you will take my battle standard and carry it with you across the river, then hide it somewhere—somewhere you know you can find it easily later, when we want to show it to these whoresons coming against

us. Then come back and join me, but don't forget your horn." He
raised his voice again for all to hear.

"Listen for Gwyn's horn when you're fighting among the trees.
As soon as you hear it, disengage and make your way back down to
the river, then form a line on me, over there, about two-thirds of the
way across, where the water is less than knee-deep. You see the place?
Just beyond the deepest part of the stream. That's where we'll stand
and wait for them to come to us again, through deeper, faster water.
Then, on Gwyn's next signal or mine, we'll retreat again ahead of
them to where our horses are hidden among the fir trees. We'll mount
up there and finish them as they come out of the river." He scanned
the group, making sure that they had all heard him and understood.
Finally he nodded. "That's all, then. Fight well and fight hard. I know
you will, and I know you'll make me even prouder of you than I am
now. Now let's move on and wait for my order to dismount!"

Mere moments later, it seemed, they came to the fallen tree and
Uther gave the order to dismount. As the troopers swung down and
the process of gathering the horses began, Uther noticed that
Garreth's face was vacant of expression, his eyes fixed upon the
great, dead tree that bridged the river.

"What's on your mind? You look perplexed."

Garreth blinked. "An idea. Swimmers. I need ten men who can
swim. We'll come up into the woods with you to see what we're up
against, but then I'd like to pull them back here to the river and get
out of this armour. What I'm thinking of won't work if we're
weighed down in iron. We'll strip down and then, when we hear
your signal to fall back, we'll slip beneath the big tree and swim to
the bank on the other side. Once there, we'll be behind the enemy
and can hit them from there when they least expect it."

"You could be cut off and killed."

"So could you. But then again, we could succeed and pin the
enemy between our two groups."

"Aye, you could. Very well, find yourself some swimmers."

The fight in the woods was brutal from the outset, for Uther was right
and the enemy warriors simply abandoned their mounts at the first

sign of trouble, preferring to fight on foot and perfectly happy to be alone, each man for himself, among the trees and bushes. Uther's men, on the other hand, striving to maintain disciplined fighting units, were hampered by the encroaching undergrowth at every turn, unable to swing their weapons as they had been trained to do. Uther was reminded almost immediately of his father's lesson, taught to him in the long distant past, about the way in which all battle plans are rendered useless with the first clash of weapons and bodies.

He watched several of his own men go down to death after their shields were pierced by hard-flung spears. The heavy spears lodged in the shields and hung there, weighing them down unbearably and rapidly tiring the shield-bearers, whose arms could not sustain the dragging weight. And as the shields went down, the blades went in. Far sooner than he would have wished, Uther called to Gwyn for the signal to withdraw.

Uther's troops disengaged immediately, glad to be out of there, and ran back towards the river, hearing the wild shouts of triumph ringing out behind them. Uther had time to look quickly and see that there was no sign of Garreth Whistler and his volunteers, before all his attention was drawn to the loose, treacherous river stones beneath his flying feet. Only once did he land on a stone that began to shift, and he thought he was finished, but the movement stopped, checked by a more solid stone behind the first, and he was able to leap to a larger, safer foothold. He reached the shallow waters of the river and moved on, trying to hurry but forced to place each step with even greater care now that the rocks beneath him were wet and slippery with moss and algae. At the deepest part, the water surged above his knees, but he pressed on, using his long sword as a staff to probe his way, and he reached the shallows beyond, where there was almost no current. There he stopped and swung around, spreading his legs and finding a solid footing as his men formed up on either side of him, those of them who still had shields placing themselves between pairs of others who had none. He steadied them with a word and then focused his attention on the enemy on the far bank. They were milling around but making no attempt to venture out onto the river stones. And then Uther saw why, and his heart sank.

A group of the enemy, twelve or perhaps fifteen men, were bowmen, and they were in the process of settling down to shoot, clustered in a tight group on the right of the enemy line directly opposite where Uther's own thin line of approximately thirty men now stood as living, defenceless targets. Even as he saw them, the first arrow came hissing across the water and thumped heavily into a wooden shield, almost knocking its bearer off his feet.

Moments later it began to rain arrows, a lethal, hissing rain of death that dropped three men with the first volley, although two of the men staggered back to their feet soon afterwards, their breast-plates bruised and dented from the force of the missiles that had struck them. Uther himself made a prominent target, thanks to his huge size and bright armour, and two arrows pierced his shield while another glanced off the rounded dome of his helmet and several more hissed past him. Feeling the impact of the missiles striking his shield, Uther gave fervent thanks that the bows ranged against him were ordinary weapons and not the fearsome longbows of his own people. Pendragon shafts could strike right through armour and shields to penetrate the flesh behind them, the shock of their delivery alone enough to kill or completely disable a man.

And then Garreth Whistler burst from the woods behind the enemy, his long sword blade flashing and whirling above his head as he led ten naked, silent men straight for the bowmen, falling on them from behind and destroying them, savaging their unprotected backs before anyone could react to his attack and leaving not one of them alive. By the time the others swung about face this new and unexpected assault, Whistler and his fellows had already fled straight towards the river, leaping naked across the wide expanse of tumbled stones and splashing through the shallows, picking their legs up high as they went, judging their leaps from rock to rock and splashing water high around them as they ran in a series of antic leaps and bounds. Only one of them fell, misjudging a step, but he was up again immediately and bounding onward only slightly behind his companions. The line of men standing alongside Uther cheered themselves hoarse as their friends came running and staggering towards them, but Uther stepped forward and seized Garreth

Whistler by the wrist, steadying the Champion, whose chest was pumping like a bellows.

"Where did you leave your armour?"

"Behind you . . . in the trees."

"Get on, then, and get back into it. We'll hold them while you rearm."

As Garreth Whistler moved beyond him to obey his instructions, Uther's eye was drawn again to the opposite bank and to the mounted man who had emerged from the trees there and was now chivvying the men beneath them to attack across the stream. The fellow was enormous, tall and broad and heavily armoured in dull, battered equipment on which Uther could see the rust from where he stood looking. His face was completely hidden by a great, rusted helmet of iron with a rounded dome and full cheek-flaps, and he seemed to carry only one weapon, holding it with its butt resting on his thigh so that its long, curved blade jutted forward. It was a strange-looking device resembling a broad-bladed reaping hook with deep, serrated edges, mounted on a long kind of axe handle. Even disregarding the fact that he was the only man still mounted, it took Uther no great effort to perceive that this was the leader of the crew that faced him.

Under the prodding of their leader, who towered over all of them from the height of his enormous horse, the others began to move forward across the stream bed, advancing slowly and cautiously, their attention divided between the menace of Uther's line awaiting them and the dangers of the surface under their feet. But as they ventured out onto the stony plain, there came a surge of activity behind them and the remainder of their party came into view, ten or twelve men, moving quickly through the edges of the forest and thronging around the leader, whose urgent gestures left no doubt in Uther's mind that he was urging them onward into the water to attack. Several of them ran directly to the pile of bodies on the right and snatched up the bows belonging to the men whom Garreth's charge had destroyed, but they were obviously untrained in their use, and their inaccurately fired missiles sped harmlessly into the water for the most part, aimed too low. Still, Uther watched in horrified awe as one arrow landed flat against the surface of the river and was deflected upward, straight towards him. He barely had time to flinch before the missile slammed into his thigh, splitting the frontal muscles cleanly as it sliced vertically between their corded layers. It was not a serious wound, the arrow having had barely enough strength left to penetrate his skin, but it was a wound, and it bled freely. He reached down with his left hand and pulled the arrowhead free, hardly conscious of the pain, and then looked back to the slowly advancing enemy, their reluctance for this fight plain in the way their bodies were hunched in anticipation of the conflict facing them. Ignoring the wound in his thigh, he took a step forward and turned to face his men.

"Hold fast, lads. These newcomers are not fresh troops. They're only the remainder of the party we were expecting, the ones who stayed behind to deal with Junius Lepo and his men. I count twelve of them, but there must have been twice that many left behind, so Junius and his men sold their lives dearly. Look at these people, at the way they come. They're afraid of you, and so they should be. All we have to do is stand here looking at them straight-faced and wait. Let them come to us. That way, their fear will grow as they come closer."

"Who's the big fellow, Uther, do you know?"

Uther glanced at the Dragon who had asked the question and grinned. "No, I don't know who he is, Owen, but he's big enough to fall hard when he does fall, is he not?"

"Aye, he is. Almost as big as you are."

"Perhaps so, but I'm not going to fall. Right, no more talk. We wait in silence."

He turned back to watch the enemy advancing, but from time to time his eyes sought out their leader, who sat quietly on the opposite bank, seeming to stare back at him, although the bulk of the man's massive helmet deprived Uther of any way of knowing where his eyes were looking.

Then something happened that was utterly alien to Uther's experience, and the strangeness chilled him to the heart as a kind of fear he had seldom known swept through him, whirling him instantly back into childhood and the gruesome tales of goblins and night terrors that had sometimes terrified him as a boy, the grim tales told by men

purely to frighten and horrify their listeners. Everything faded to
silence around him; the screams and cheers of his men and the
advancing enemy dying away to be replaced by a silent, hissing
emptiness. The surrounding distractions between him and his view of
the enemy leader shrank and dwindled until he felt as though he were
seeing him at the end of a long, dark tunnel, but clearly, brilliantly, as
though framed and featured by a beam of sunlight. Fascinated and
strangely frightened, Uther watched as his opponent's huge horse
walked slowly forward to the edge of the riverbank and stepped out
among the stones, moving with excruciating, patient slowness,
placing each hoof slowly and deliberately, testing its purchase inexorably until it was clearly settled, and then moving forward relentlessly, one more step, time after time until all four of its feet were in
the water. And as the horse progressed, inevitable as some phantom,
inescapable dream, Uther was appalled by the dread that unexpectedly swept over him and threatened to consume his reason.

The approaching figure reeked of death, its emanations making
the very air about it waver as air did over a blazing fire, and Uther's
throat closed, watching it, so that he forgot to breathe. *Death, with his
reaping hook*, he thought, incapable of resisting the notion of the
ancient image that had sprung into his mind. He could see nothing of
the face beneath the heavy, rusted helmet, obscured by darkness and
shadow, but his mind supplied a sudden vision of a fleshless skull,
grinning teeth and empty, eyeless sockets hidden beneath the battered
dome. The King felt his entire skin rise up in horror and revulsion.

"*Uther!*" The urgency of the roar from behind him was slow to
penetrate his daze, but its repetition brought him back, jarring him
into reality again. The voice was Garreth Whistler's. "Uther! Fall
back and mount up. There's more of them on this side!"

Stunned and still enthralled by the vision that had transfixed
him, Uther shook his head as though trying to dislodge his own
thoughts. But then full awareness returned and he realized that they
were being threatened anew, and from behind. He spun around
again, almost losing his balance, all thoughts of the enemy across
the river abandoned for the time being.

"Back, lads," he roared. "Back to the horses now!"

He found mass confusion in the woods behind him, with troopers running everywhere, struggling to mount their beasts. His own horse was ready for him, held tightly in control by one of his Dragons, and nearby, Garreth Whistler was struggling to subdue his own rearing, prancing horse, curbing it tightly and pulling its head down as he danced it in tight circles until it lost its panicked fear and settled again to his restraint.

"What's happening?" Uther roared at Garreth as he pulled himself up into the saddle and fought down his own struggling horse.

"Damned if I know," he shouted back, "but there's scores of the whoresons over here coming in from the west, where we were camped last night. I don't know where they came from or who they are, but they're here, and they almost took us from behind."

"Damnation! Then let's root them out. Lead on. To me! To me, Pendragon!" He unsheathed his long sword again and swung it above his head, hearing the whistling sound of the keen-edged blade slicing through air as his troopers surged forward to surround him.

Thereafter, all was confusion: clashing weapons, spraying blood, screams of fear and rage and pain, and the heavy thudding of hooves as the Camulodian horses pounded the soft, needle-strewn earth beneath the soaring trees, plunging and kicking as they had been trained to do against the swarming bodies that surrounded them. Someone leaped up at Uther from his left, grasping him frantically and trying to pull him down from his horse, but he slashed downward viciously across his body, his sword held close, and the assailant screamed and fell away. As he fell, however, his grasping fingers closed on the shallow arrow wound in Uther's thigh, and a bolt of agony shot through the King's body. He reeled in the saddle, close to losing consciousness. Then someone below him shouted in triumph, the flat of a blade clanged harmlessly against Uther's chest, and he pulled his horse around to the right, hard, using its weight and impetus to smash down the men about him. Three men he saw, all glaring up at him, and he killed two of them with a double swing of his heavy sword, cleaving their skulls. The third man flung himself away, and for a moment Uther was free to look about him.

He was surprised to find himself close to the riverbank again, for he had been far to the west only moments earlier in the thick of the attacking throng of newcomers. Now he had a glimpse of the big rider from the other bank, who was still crossing the river, stark and silent and slow, but now waving his weapon high above his head. He had no more time to look than that and swung himself about immediately to face whatever dangers might be coming at his back. It crossed his mind that he would have to kill the man crossing the river, but the thought was a brief one, soon forgotten in the urgency of fighting for his life.

Then he saw Garreth Whistler fall.

The Champion had been hard beset, fighting with his usual invincible perfection, whirling his horse around with absolute mastery as he flailed about him with a crushing axe at the men surrounding him on the ground. But as he pulled his warhorse up in one mighty turn, freeing its front hooves to do the damage it was trained to do, one man leaped in beneath the flailing hooves and plunged a spear into the magnificent animal's chest, killing it almost instantly. Uther saw Garreth leap immediately, catlike, to the ground, kicking his feet free of the stirrups. But as he landed, his dying horse, whirling in its death throes, caught him with a lashing hoof high in the shoulder, and the Whistler spun away, tossed like an infant's toy, to crash face forward into the trunk of a nearby tree and then bounce back, his body twisting awkwardly to fall heavily, face down. His five remaining attackers were on him in a moment, swarming to destroy an enemy whose feet they were not fit to touch.

Black rage swelled up in Uther and he spurred his horse forward, digging bloody gouges in its side so that it crashed headlong into the press surrounding his fallen friend, hurling bodies in all directions. He had his feet free of the stirrups before the impact, and pushed himself from the saddle effortlessly, landing astride Garreth Whistler as lightly as a butterfly, his sword gripped in both hands. He killed one sprawling man before the fellow even knew Uther had come, striking his head cleanly off his shoulders with one solid, hissing slice, and then in quick succession he dispatched the other four, his whirling, slashing blade invincible and inescapable.

Finally, Uther was alone above his friend. He whirled to kneel and search for a pulse beneath Garreth's jaw, ignoring the tugging pain of the wound that still bled on his thigh. But there was no pulse. The King's Champion was dead, and Uther felt his heart swell up and break as hot, scalding tears flooded his eyes. Then, screaming aloud in his black and violent need for blood and vengeance, he grasped his sword hilt tightly in both fists and swung up and around again, looking for someone to kill. And there, less than ten paces distant, watching him from the back of a high horse and hefting his long, strange reaping-hook weapon in his hand, sat the giant in rusted armour who had come so slowly across the stream: the leader of this doom-laden band of alien horsemen.

As soon as he set eyes on the big man, Uther's frustrated rage flared up even higher and then immediately narrowed and condensed into a hard, cold, incandescent blade of tightly focused fury. A life-time of avoiding fighting in anger fell away from him and left him with nothing but the all-consuming need to destroy this enigmatic interloper who had brought destruction to his friends and compan-ions. He had no thoughts now that this might be Death himself. This was a man, dirty and travel-stained and fit to die for what he had brought to this cursed place. And yet Uther restrained himself from charging blindly forward to attack.

He knew he had to get into his saddle, that he was in dire peril afoot alone against the mounted man—any mounted man—for he had killed more than a score of men in the previous short space of time precisely because he was mounted while they were not. Steadily, grinding his teeth and keeping his sword raised high with both hands in front of him, he stepped backwards until his shoul-ders touched the tree beneath which he stood, and then he looked about him quickly. There were men aplenty around him, but none of them was his, and all of them stood motionless, staring at him and occasionally glancing towards their giant leader.

He saw his own horse from the corner of his eye, placidly crop-ping a patch of grass on the forest floor, but as far away from him in one direction as the threatening horseman was on the other side. The big man hefted his reaping-hook weapon again and urged his horse forward, and Uther quickly thrust his long sword into his belt, snatched up Garreth's fallen axe, turned sharply to his left and ran towards his horse, hearing the other surge heavily into motion behind him.

Reaching his horse on the dead run, he turned and spun to face the oncoming rider, swinging the heavy axe up behind his head, then throwing it with all his strength. The big man saw it coming and quickly lowered his head, tucking his chin towards his breast, and the whirling axehead struck the domed top of his helmet and glanced off. The shock of the deflected blow nevertheless threw him backwards, sending him reeling in the saddle and almost unhorsing him. Uther watched for the space of half a heartbeat, then spun away and seized his horse's reins, raising his left foot to the stirrup with surprising, painful difficulty and then leaning forward into the swing of his rising body. But his body would not rise and swing him up into the saddle. His left thigh was useless; the wounded muscles, strained beyond repair by the effort of running, had become incapable of bearing his weight. Disbelieving, he tried again, heaving desperately but vainly to lift his body from the ground. Behind him he heard the trampling of hooves as the big man regained control of his horse and moved again to the attack. Yet again Uther tried to mount, and this time a heavy blow landed across his armoured back, smashing him into the side of his horse, which had now begun to toss its head and sidle nervously, rolling its eyes, frightened by the indecisive nature of its master's movements.

Grimly, waiting for the next blow, Uther hooked the elbow of his sword arm over the horn of his saddle and fought to drag himself up into the saddle. The blow came, smashing him yet again, but he clung on doggedly, willing himself to rise up and find his seat. Once mounted, he could fight, leg or no leg, he knew. And then a third blow hit him, this one like a massive, booted foot crashing into the small of his back, and the pressure of its impact closed up his throat and took away his breath. He felt no pain as the wicked, serrated reaping-hook blade plunged deep into his flesh, penetrating far into his rib cage with its upward swing, beneath the edge of his cuirass, and he felt none as it ripped free again, tearing his back open

irreparably. But he was aware of the loosening, hot, debilitating
flow of pent-up blood gushing from his open back, and of the gathering darkness that was filling his eyes as his hands slipped from the
saddle horn. Slowly, his vision fading fast, he turned around to look
up at the giant figure looming above him, and when he opened his
mouth to speak, bright-red blood poured from between his lips and
splashed down onto his cuirass.

"Ygraine," Uther Pendragon said. "Ygraine." But no one heard
him.

The big man sat staring down at Uther's body and then spoke to one
of his companions. "Those other people, the newcomers. Bring me
their leader."

The man returned with the tall, gangling man called One-Finger,
who told his inquisitor that he had been dispatched by his Chief,
Othoc, with half of their party to make sure that this cavalry rearguard
were held at bay while Othoc and the others captured the women in
the first group. The big horseman sat straighter in his saddle.

"What women?"

One-Finger then told the story of the battle two days earlier and
the chase that followed it, and when he had done, the big man turned
again to his lieutenant.

"Get the men mounted right now and go after those women. See
that you find them before this Othoc lays hands on them." He looked
down again at the corpse in the bronze armour, and then at the
massive horse the dead man had owned. "I'll come after you as soon
as I've stripped this body and put his armour to good use. If these
people were from Camulod, and I think they might have been, then
all we've heard about that place is true, and we would do well to
avoid it. But this is the first set of decent armour in my size I've seen
in years. Go now, and take these others with you. Leave me two
men. That's all I'll need. When I'm done here, I'll follow you."

He watched until the others were on their way, and then he dismounted and went to kneel beside the man he had killed. Uther's open
eyes were vacant, uncaring of the robbery about to be perpetrated
upon his corpse. The kneeling man closed the staring eyes and then

went to work, stripping Uther's body. As he removed each piece of
equipment, he examined it to see if there was blood on it, and if there
was he handed it to one of his two companions to clean. Otherwise, he
laid each piece of the armour carefully aside, arrayed in order from top
to bottom. He had a difficult time with some of the blood-slick straps
and buckles, and at one point called on one of his two men to help him
turn Uther over onto his front, so that he could reach the fastenings
among the gore at the small of his back, but he did not mistreat the
corpse, and when he was done with it and the body was bare, he turned
away and began to remove his own battered, rusted equipment.

As he tugged at one of the straps holding his own much-dented
cuirass, he looked back several times at the dead man lying close by
him almost as though he expected to find the eyes open again, watching him. Finally he muttered an oath and turned to his two men.

"Each of you take an arm and haul this man away." He glanced
around him and saw a massive fir tree close by, its bole surrounded
by dead branches. "Lay him over there beside that tree."

Glancing at one another in surprise but saying nothing, the two
men stooped, each of them grasping Uther by one arm, and then
they tried to straighten up, lifting him. They failed, and the bigger
of the two turned to their leader.

"By the henge, Derek, this whoreson's as big and heavy as
you!"

"I know that. That's why I'm taking his armour. Now do as I
bade you and move him over by the tree. He deserves to lie in
dignity. Drag him if you have to, but lay him down carefully. Don't
abuse him. He was a fine, strong fighter and he died honourably.
'Twas not his fault that his leg would not hold him up."

As his men carried out his bidding, Derek of Ravenglass finished dressing himself in Uther's clothes and armour, placing the
great Roman helmet on his head last of all. Everything fitted him as
though made for him, save that he was very slightly smaller in the
head and thicker through the waist than the armour's former owner
had been. Nonetheless, Derek was delighted. He went next to the
dead man's horse, which still stood where it had been left, its reins
trailing on the ground. He saw the richness of the red roll of cloth

tied behind the saddle and unfastened the bindings, shaking out the huge red cloak and whistling at the sight of the golden dragon sewn into the cloth.

The two men had come back, having thrown Uther's body beneath the tree—Derek had not been watching in the end, and they had thrown the corpse asprawl onto the ground, as they would any other piece of offal, so that it lay awry, one bent knee hooked over a fallen branch. Now they stood wide-eyed, looking at the war cloak.

Derek of Ravenglass fingered the golden dragon. "I wonder who he was, this Chief."

The smaller of the two shook his head. "That's a King's cloak, Derek, and that helmet came straight from Rome. Could this be a Roman King?"

Derek snorted. "The Romans don't have Kings, man, they have *Emperors!*"

"Maybe it was Uther of Camulod," the other man said. "He's a King, isn't he?"

"Aye, that's what they say. Uther of Camulod's a King . . . a powerful King, like Lot of Cornwall. Think you then you'd find him in hole like this with only thirty men? His armies number in the thousands, man. No, this was no King, but perhaps a King's Champion. We'll never know. But at least the whoreson was big enough to bring me my new armour. Now let's go and find these women."

EPILOGUE

As Derek of Ravenglass spurred his newly acquired warhorse to overtake his men, a solitary figure, dressed all in black, with polished leather and burnished silver armour, an enormous, double-arched bow slung diagonally across his shoulders over his cloak, emerged from the valley less than two miles to the north of him and resolutely turned his mount westward along the riverbank towards the sea. Merlyn Britannicus, fully and painfully restored to conscious awareness after a two-year hiatus, had no knowledge of his exact location. He knew only that his cousin Uther was somewhere ahead of him, and that some time soon he would find him and confront him before taking vengeance for a murdered wife and child.

For more than a week now, Merlyn had been riding south and west through the war-ravaged peninsula of Cornwall, following the wide-trampled path of large bodies of men moving ahead of him. Who these men were, and whether or not the groups were large enough to constitute armies, he could not tell, but he knew beyond dispute that his cousin's original army had been harried and beset at every step of their journey. The bodies strewn along his present route, some of them charred beyond recognition as friends or enemies, bore eloquent testimony to the hard-fought progress Uther Pendragon had won.

Until he rode into the devastation of the battleground to the north two days before, however, Merlyn had believed in the myth of his invincible, implacable cousin. He had been completely unprepared for the story of Uther's ignominious flight from the battlefield, and the two reports he heard, from Mucius Quinto and Popilius Cirro, the two senior surviving officers among the battered remnants of the Camulodian army, were sufficiently similar, in one overriding respect, to close his mind to other disparities.

Both men described how Uther had fled the battlefield, accompanied by a party of captured, high-born women, one of them Ygraine, the wife of Gulrhys Lot himself.

Merlyn had been confounded and outraged to hear of this new evidence of his cousin's perfidy, for as soon as he heard Ygraine's name, he knew who she was: the sister of his own murdered wife, Deirdre, whose brutal death he was now riding to avenge, convinced that it had occurred at the hands of Uther. That Uther should now have abducted Ygraine, insult upon infamy, hardened Merlyn's heart completely against the man who had once, and for so long, been nearest and dearest to him. Had any doubts lingered in his mind about the rightness of his mission, these tidings of Ygraine had destroyed them.

It mattered nothing to Merlyn that Mucius Quinto had suggested, not unreasonably, that Uther, by his flight, had saved the lives of all the men yet living in the valley. Nor, by the same token, did it cross his mind to doubt the surgeon's accuracy when he told Merlyn that his cousin had ridden off at the head of a thousand mounted men, the entire cavalry complement of the force with which Uther had left Camulod. Merlyn had no interest in explaining, excusing or justifying his cousin's apparent cowardice. He wanted only to overtake the red-and-gold-clad King and bring him to justice. Every other consideration was superfluous beside that driving need. And so he had taken leave of the two veteran Camulodians and gone hunting once again for Uther, his armour and equipment clean and sparkling, unsullied by the dirt of either battle or long travel.

The following morning, he found the Cornish King, Gulrhys Lot himself, recognizable even over the gap of years since Merlyn had last set eyes upon him, hanging at the end of a rope thrown over the bough of a huge tree, but so great was his urgency to overtake Uther that he barely took time to examine the corpse or wonder who had hung it there. He was mildly mystified, certainly, by its mutilation and by the fact that its severed hands and feet had been stuffed into a large, richly brocaded bag that bore the crest of Pendragon on its face. Strangely, the King's great seal, a solid mass of gold, had been left intact upon the finger of one hand. He took it as proof of the man's death, but wasted no time being curious about the why or wherefore of the execution. Nor did he pay the slightest attention to the ruined, skull-cleft corpse that lay nearby at the edge of the clearing. Gulrhys Lot, he knew, had richly deserved to die a hideous death, and there must have been hundreds of men who would have been happy to provide one.

Turning to leave, however, he hesitated and then swung back to face the dangling corpse, suddenly filled with a swelling, angry resentment. This dead and bloodless hulk was the miscreant responsible for the war that had blighted and blasted southwestern Britain, but far worse than that, this corpse had been the dictator of countless deaths, among them the murder of Merlyn's own father, Picus Britannicus. That in itself demanded some form of vengeance, even *post mortem*. Merlyn kicked his horse forward, dismounted and began to build a pyre beneath the body, beginning with a tiny blaze and then feeding it until it roared so that he could scarcely approach it. There was no lack of dead wood lying close by, and so he soon had a huge conflagration blazing, the flames reaching as high as the corpse's waist, burning its clothing and licking at the rope across its chest. Merlyn sat his horse and waited until the rope gave way, dropping the body into the inferno, and then he turned and rode away, his mind fixed once again upon his cousin.

The riverbank pathway Merlyn now followed was narrow and dangerous in spots, but it was the only path available, and he could see plainly that it had been taken by scores of riders ahead of him. He rode forward attentively, keeping his horse tightly reined, and soon came to a place where an ancient, enormous tree had fallen clean across the river, bridging it from bank to bank, its ruined top blocking the path and forcing him to dismount and lead his horse around the obstacle.

There, within the screen of trees at the edge of the forest, he found more than a score of bodies, three of them wearing the dragon crest of Pendragon emblazoned on their Camulodian armour, and when he emerged on to the path again, he saw more corpses in the riverbed, some floating, face down and bloated, while others appeared frozen in position on the stones of the opposite bank, killed as they had tried to fight their way across. Numbed, however, and sick of the sight of so much death, Merlyn felt no compulsion to cross the stream bed to see what had happened over there, and so rode past, unknowing, within a hundred paces of his cousin's naked body.

A short time later, the pathway widened, allowing him to make swifter progress through a landscape littered with the remnants of battle. He noted in passing that the corpses he could recognize by their clothing and equipment seemed far fewer than those they had slain, and that one tight-knit group of dead had fought to the last man, falling as they had stood, in a compact, circular formation, their shields lying beside them. Having no knowledge of Ygraine's bloodguard of Eirish clansmen, he saw them merely as Outlanders who had sold their lives dearly against other Outlanders, and accepted the anomaly as one more of the inexplicable mysteries in what he thought of now as Uther's War. The direction of flight and fight, however, told him that Uther's party was still alive and still ahead of him, and so he rode ever faster, his horse's flanks beginning to show the marks of his pitiless spurs.

Only at one point did his resolute pursuit of his cousin falter. Resuming his journey after pausing by a brook to eat a hurried bite of food in the middle of the day, he emerged suddenly into a clearing where he found a burned and gutted farmstead and the slaughtered bodies of the family that had lived there. Only the mother remained alive, demented by grief, kneeling beside her murdered baby, staring dry-eyed into madness and horror. He had stopped and dismounted, thinking somehow to help her, but she attacked him with the savagery of a trapped animal, clawing and biting, ferociously protective of the tiny, pathetic body in front of her, and he withdrew hurriedly, flinging himself back into the saddle, sickened with anger and a great, helpless shame as he galloped away from the wretched scene.

Less than an hour after that, he reached the top of a cliff overlooking the sea and saw a broad trail of hoofprints stretching away along the shoreline below to his left, moving from west to east. Knowing that he was closing the distance between himself and his quarry, he set off again at a determined gallop down the hill and up onto the top of the next, where he was rewarded by the distant sight of his cousin's unmistakable red cloak, with its gold embroidered dragon.

Despite the legendary reputation for sorcery that would later accrue around his name and memory, Merlyn Britannicus was first and foremost a man, with all a man's limitations, including a tendency to short-sighted hubris and self-delusion. So intent was he upon his hunt and the long-delayed vengeance that lay ahead of him that his recognition of his cousin's presence was instantaneous and categorical. It would never have crossed his mind that what he saw was only Uther's clothing and colours. And so, his anger cold now, and focused, he set spurs to his horse again and thundered downward from his high viewpoint, using the animal cruelly as its hooves devoured the distance between him and the group ahead. He had accepted that his destiny involved confronting and then fighting his blood cousin, and he was prepared to accept the consequences, whether he lived or died in the struggle.

As he flogged his horse westward, parallel to the distant shoreline on his right and keeping to the firm footing of the ridge above the soft beach sand, he overhauled his quarry rapidly but remained far removed from the activities along the waterside. Thus, from a distance far enough to be confusing, he witnessed events that defied his understanding, for Uther, who was supposed to be escorting and protecting the Cornish Queen and her female attendants, now seemed to be chasing them, bent upon their capture, and even more mystifying, the women were being fiercely and successfully protected by a group of men wielding long, Pendragon bows that ought, by rights, to have been aligned with Uther's force.

By the time he realized that the large boat he could see drawn up above the high-water mark on the distant beach was to be the end of the long flight, Merlyn was too late to affect the outcome of the incomprehensible events across from him. His horse, tiring rapidly after its long run, scrambled down the slope towards the beach and then surged through fetlock deep sand that drained the last resources of its strength, and Merlyn watched in impotent horror as Uther's mounted men, still far beyond the reach of even Publius Varrus's great

African bow, reached the women clustered around the boat and plunged among them. The women's screams reached his ears as the mounted men, acting in concert, reached down and began hauling the women up to hold in front of them, using the female bodies as living shields against the lethal arrows of the bowmen, who had fallen back in formation and were wreaking destruction on the horsemen.

The tactic was successful, because, for long, fatal moments, the ranked bowmen hesitated, unwilling to shoot at or through the women, and by the time they rallied and began to shoot at the horses, instead of their riders, the enemy were on them and the bowmen broke ranks and scattered, to be hunted down and slaughtered.

By the time the last bowman had been killed, only Uther himself, two of the women and six other riders remained alive upon the bloodied beach, and as he continued to struggle towards the others, incapable of even raising a shout, Merlyn watched Uther pull one of the women down onto the sand to violate her, having stabbed her last surviving companion. Seeing it, he knew with sickening, heartbreaking certainty that all his suspicions about his cousin—about the darkness and the demonic fury that dwelled inside him—had been true, and yet they fell short of the evidence of depravity now unfolding before his eyes.

Some time later—a period that his intellect told him could have been no more than an hour, but which seemed to his exhausted body to have lasted much, much longer—Merlyn Britannicus stood peering outwards from the boat that he had first seen lying high and dry upon the beach while a skirmish seethed around it, mounted men attacking others on foot, male and female both, some of whom struggled uselessly to drag the vessel towards the waterline. Now the boat was afloat, and he was in it, drifting farther and farther away from the distant beach and its scattering of lifeless, bloody bodies.

A gust of cool wind came from nowhere, pressing his sodden tunic against his skin and raising gooseflesh. He shivered, glancing back to where his black ring-and-leather armour lay piled on the deck where he had thrown it, the planks beneath and around it soaked and water-stained. From there, his eyes moved again to the dry, black bundled bearskin that lay against the short mast in the middle of the deck. He shook his head as though in disbelief before crossing his arms over his chest and then turning away again, back to face the rapidly receding land.

He could see his horse standing there, still watching him alertly, its ears pricked high towards him, but now as he watched, it turned away, lowering its head and began to drift off in search of forage. On the sand, he could see the silver-and-black heap of his discarded war cloak, and he remembered throwing it down there across his huge double-arched bow. The bow was still strung, he realized, and he wondered how long it would last before the bowstring stretched or snapped. Then, realizing that he was allowing himself to be distracted, he grunted and pushed himself away from the boat's side to examine yet again the alien mass of gear, ropes and tackle that lay neatly arranged on all sides of him. He vaguely knew that all of it was required for manoeuvring the vessel, but Merlyn Britannicus had never been on a boat in his life and could barely begin to decipher the meaning of any of the meticulously laid out equipment. He recognized the oars, neatly piled in rows the length of the vessel on both sides, but they were all enormous, made for use by two or perhaps three men standing abreast. He knew, too, that the vast bundle of cloth hanging between two cross-shipped spars at the foot of the mast was a sail, and he could see the ropes and pulleys that had to be used to haul it up to where it would catch the wind. But the sail itself was dense and heavy, made from multiple layers of cloth, and the top spar to which it was attached had four thick ropes leading to it, each threaded through its own pulley block at the mast top. He knew that it would require at least one man hauling on each rope, all working simultaneously, to drag the heavy top spar and its burden up the thick stubby mast, so he felt no temptation to attempt anything so futile on his own. Besides, he thought, there was not a breath of wind.

But the boat was drifting helplessly, and he knew just enough about such things to know that a boat adrift was a boat in danger.

Frustrated, he flung himself around again to face the beach, only to find that the boat had swung about, and the land now lay behind

him to his right. Muttering a curse, he crossed the deck and leaned
on that side, where he discovered that the beach had changed into a
shoreline while his back was turned. His horse had disappeared
from view now, and even the strewn bodies that remained were
barely visible, shrunken to tiny coloured patches against the now
narrow, dun strip of sand.

Merlyn felt the boat tilt alarmingly beneath him, caught by a
wave, and his stomach heaved so that he had to fight off a surge of
nausea. He gazed mutely at the water stretching between him and
the land, noting the dark green of its depths and estimating the distance he had drifted. Even by the time he had first pulled off his
armour after climbing aboard, he had been too far from land to risk
swimming back, especially with a burden in his arms.

He turned and looked again towards the motionless black
bundle by the mast, and keeping his eyes fixed on the bearskin, he
shrugged out of his wet tunic and spread it over the rail of the boat.
Then, naked, enjoying the heat of the sun on his skin, he sank slowly
down to the deck, stretching out his legs and leaning back against
the sun-warmed wood of the sloping side and allowed himself to
think deliberately about what had happened that afternoon.

He had been ill prepared for the surprises that awaited him there
on that beach—less ready to face them than he had been to face anything in his life—and their arrivals had smashed him like a succession of hurled boulders.

First, the sight of Uther stripping away his armour to violate the
last surviving woman, inspiring in him a furious anger and a white-hot
lust for vengeance: vengeance for his own dead wife and for all the
other countless, screaming souls who had been so mindlessly slaughtered and condemned by Uther's lust for war and rapine. Incapable
even of raising his voice, Merlyn had put spurs to his exhausted horse
and begun to make his way laboriously forward through yielding,
shifting sand to where he could face and kill his treacherous cousin.

Uther's six surviving horsemen, surprised by Merlyn's unexpected appearance, had judged his intent easily and come cantering
towards him, intent on killing him. He was barely aware of them,
even as he stood in his stirrups with an icy fury and slaughtered

them one after the other with lethal, arm-long arrows from his enormously powerful African bow, according them only the time it took him to take aim, almost casually, before dispatching each of them with a single murderous missile.

Uther had seen him coming, finally, and he abandoned the woman on the ground, hauling himself hurriedly up into his own saddle and then swinging his mount awkwardly around to confront Merlyn, preparing to meet his death.

Even now, remembering, Merlyn's mind could not encompass the stunned incredulity that had made him reel in the saddle when he discovered that the man facing him, riding Uther's horse and wearing Uther's armour, was not Uther Pendragon, and that the running fight he had observed from the distant cliffs had been the opposite of what it had appeared to be. It seemed to him now that his mind, his entire awareness, had simply rebelled at the impossibility of everything and stopped functioning for a while, causing what he could only think of now as a featureless and frightening blankness within him—a strange and noise-filled emptiness that he could still recall but could not define.

When Merlyn's mind had begun to work again, the fellow facing him had still not moved. And yet something within Merlyn *had* moved within that time; something deep inside him had shifted and rearranged itself and changed him forever.

When the man removed Uther's huge helmet, Merlyn recognized him as an enemy he had once met and almost befriended, a giant of a fellow from the far northwest of Britain who called himself a King, Derek of Ravenglass. Merlyn stared in stupefaction, but no shock of recognition could combat the shock that had preceded it: the absence of Uther.

Dazed and still uncomprehending, Merlyn sat silent and emptyhearted as Ravenglass told the tale of how he had met and killed Uther, then robbed him of his armour, horse and weapons before hurrying to catch up with the fleeing group of women whom Uther had been protecting. The King's surprise at learning that the man he had killed was Uther Pendragon was too real to be doubted. He had seen only an enemy whose armour would fit his own giant frame.

Any interest that he might have had in the stranger's identity had been blotted out by the newly received tidings that he and his own men were within a short, hard ride of capturing a group of high-born women.

The northern King had no desire to fight Merlyn, for he believed him from past experience to be some kind of sorcerer. But he was prepared to fight and die then and there if the gods required it. And Merlyn, for his part, looking at the world through altered eyes, hardly knew whether or not his cousin deserved to be avenged. Sickened by all the violent death he had seen in the previous few days, he did not wish to add to it.

And so the two parted without fighting, Ravenglass riding off in Uther's armour and leaving Merlyn alone on the beach.

A heavy flail, still flaked with an ancient coat of dark-red paint, had been hanging from the saddle-bow of Uther's horse, and Merlyn asked Derek of Ravenglass to leave it with him. It was the flail he was once sure he had found close by the spot in which his wife, Deirdre, had been murdered. So how could it be here now, hanging from its former owner's saddle? Merlyn took the weapon and hung it from his own saddle to replace the one he himself had lost in the Mendip Hills on the day he lost his memory, driven from his head by his own flail.

The flail's existence here changed nothing, he told himself now. Uther could easily have made a new one after killing Deirdre and throwing away the murder weapon. But even as he thought that, he remembered what Mucius Quinto had told him on the battlefield that he had ridden through mere days before: Uther's fearsome weapon, easy to make, had been widely copied for years by his admiring soldiers, and then copied again by others. The things were commonplace today—brutal, uncomplicated instruments of death. A sudden vision of his father's face sprang into Merlyn's mind, and he heard again Picus Britannicus's words on granting the benefit of doubt as his beloved face gave way to a vision of Uther, gleaming teeth bared in a laugh of pure exuberant joy.

A sound over by the mast brought Merlyn's head up quickly, and he listened intently for several moments until he was sure that it would not come again.

Ygraine. The last surviving woman on the beach had been Deirdre's sister, Ygraine, and that recognition, too, had shaken Merlyn to the core of his being, showing him a ghostly image of the face of his beloved, long-lost wife one more agonizing time.

Merlyn had noticed only by accident that Ygraine was still alive, and he had gone to her assistance immediately, only to find that she was close to death. She had been trampled and kicked in the head by Derek's enormous warhorse as it had surged and stamped, fighting for balance and scrambling to accommodate the immense, ungainly weight of Derek's armoured bulk as he mounted.

Merlyn had cradled her in his arms, unable to do anything other than support her shattered head with his hand while she died, begging him frantically to look to her child, Uther's son, Arthur.

Mystified, Merlyn had assumed that she was raving, her mind unhinged with the pain of what had happened to her, for there was neither sight nor sign of any infant on the deserted beach. And then water from the incoming tide had swirled around his knees, and from the once-beached boat, now miraculously afloat and drifting out to sea, had come the wail of a child.

He clearly remembered splashing through the shallows and leaping out to clutch the side of the vessel, the ground already lost beneath his feet, knowing that if he lost his hold the dead weight of his armour would plunge him straight to the bottom. After hanging there for an age, feeling himself grow ever heavier, he had managed finally to twist his lower body upwards in one last, mighty effort and hook his right leg over the side of the boat, lodging his spur beneath the wood of the rail. He hung there quietly for a long time after that, collecting himself until he could rally his strength one more time and haul himself up and to safety.

Recalling what he had found after that, he focused his gaze on the black bearskin by the mast, and then stood up and moved towards it.

The child was awake, its strange, gold-flecked eyes gazing solemnly up at the shape that stooped over it. Cautiously, filled with awe, Merlyn knelt, then sat on the deck, supporting his weight with one hand while he reached out with the other to stroke the infant's

smooth, warm cheek with one bent, tentative knuckle. The golden
eyes, strangely ageless, shifted to gaze into his own. The child
would be . . . what, how old? Merlyn had no idea, but he knew that
it could be no more than a month or two. He felt his throat close up
unexpectedly, and his vision dissolved into a film of tears as his
breast filled with grief. He hooked his little finger, and the infant
seized it in its tiny hand, and he could tell that its sturdy little legs
were kicking beneath the bearskin covering. Tears ran down his face
and dripped from his chin, and he sat motionless, allowing all the
pain and the hurt inside him to well up into the light of day.

By the time he realized that he had stopped weeping for long
enough that the crusted salt of his tears felt stiff on his cheeks, much
of the burning pain he had felt was gone, but the infant still lay
staring up at him, its impossibly small hands now bunched at its
mouth.

"Well," he whispered hoarsely, swallowing to moisten his
aching throat. "We are well met, young Arthur Pendragon. But how
am I to get you off this cursed boat?" The child gazed back at him
as though listening. He nodded. "I'm your Cousin Merlyn . . .
Merlyn Britannicus . . . But I'm your Uncle Merlyn, too, because
your mother was my wife's sister. I knew your father all his life.
He's not here now, but he and I were . . . We were friends, the best
friends men can be . . . for a long time."

His throat swelled up again and he looked away, blinking fresh
tears from his eyes, and when he eventually spoke again, his eyes
remained fixed on some distant spot.

"We had our differences, he and I. And I was stupid . . . stupid
and . . ." He stopped, and then looked back at the child. "Arrogant.
That's what I was. Arrogant and unyielding. But that was then, and
this is now, and we have to get off this boat and back to Camulod. I
don't know how we're going to do it, but we will, because you have
a grandmother there, young man, who is going to love the sight of
you. You'll grow up there in Camulod, because I am going to see to
it." He paused, cocking his head to one side and gazed down at the
child with a tremulous but warm smile. The great, gold-flecked eyes
gazed back at him.

"You know, I was angry not too long ago when I found out that people were calling your father Uther of Camulod, because he really wasn't from Camulod at all. He lived in Cambria, and he was a King. But you, you will live in Camulod, and it will be your home, and by the time you grow to be a man, people might not remember that there ever was an Uther of Camulod—or even a Merlyn of Camulod." His smile grew wider, and he reached to touch the child's face again, caressing the smooth skin.

"But you, young eagle, with those golden eyes . . . I'll wager here and now that everyone will know and remember *Arthur* of Camulod."